The MX Book of New Sherlock Holmes Stories

Part XXX
More Christmas Adventures
(1897-1928)

First edition published in 2021
© Copyright 2021

The right of the individuals listed on the Copyright Information page to be identified as the authors of this work has been asserted by them in accordance with the Copyright, Designs, and Patents Act 1998.

All rights reserved. No reproduction, copy, or transmission of this publication may be made without express prior written permission. No paragraph of this publication may be reproduced, copied, or transmitted except with express prior written permission or in accordance with the provisions of the Copyright Act 1956 (as amended). Any person who commits any unauthorised act in relation to this publication may be liable to criminal prosecution and civil claims for damage.

All characters appearing in this work are fictitious or used fictitiously. Except for certain historical personages, any resemblance to real persons, living or dead, is purely coincidental. The opinions expressed herein are those of the authors and not of MX Publishing.

ISBN Hardback 978-1-78705-934-4
ISBN Paperback 978-1-78705-935-1
AUK ePub ISBN 978-1-78705-936-8
AUK PDF ISBN 978-1-78705-937-5

Published in the UK by
MX Publishing
335 Princess Park Manor, Royal Drive,
London, N11 3GX
www.mxpublishing.co.uk

David Marcum can be reached at:
thepapersofsherlockholmes@gmail.com

Cover design by Brian Belanger
www.belangerbooks.com and *www.redbubble.com/people/zhahadun*

CONTENTS

Forewords

Editor's Foreword: Never Enough Holmes Adventures – Even at Christmas! by David Marcum	1
Foreword by Nancy Holder	16
"It is the Season of Forgiveness" by Roger Johnson	18
An Ongoing Legacy for Sherlock Holmes by Steve Emecz	20
Undershaw: Eliminating the Impossible by Emma West	23
Baskerville Hall in Winter (*A Poem*) by Christopher James	33

Adventures

The Purloined Present by DJ Tyrer	35
The Case of the Cursory Curse by Andrew Bryant	48
The St. Giles Child Murders by Tim Gambrell	61
A Featureless Crime by Geri Schear	81
The Case of the Earnest Young Man by Paula Hammond	101

(Continued on the next page . . . .)

The Adventure of the Dextrous Doctor   118
    by Jayantika Ganguly

The Mystery of Maple Tree Lodge   134
    by Susan Knight

The Adventure of the Maligned Mineralogist   156
    by Arthur Hall

Christmas Magic   171
    by Kevin Thornton

The Adventure of the Christmas Threat   184
    by Arthur Hall

The Adventure of the Stolen Christmas Gift   210
    by Michael Mallory

The Colourful Skein of Life   226
    by Julie McKuras

The Adventure of the Chained Phantom   245
    by J.S. Rowlinson

Santa's Little Elves   269
    by Kevin Thornton

The Case of the Holly-Sprig Pudding   284
    by Naching T. Kassa

The Canterbury Manifesto   298
    by David Marcum

The Case of the Disappearing Beaune   336
    by J. Lawrence Matthews

(Continued on the next page . . . .)

A Price Above Rubies 　　by Jane Rubino	356
The Intrigue of the Red Christmas 　　by Shane Simmons	385
The Bitter Gravestones 　　by Chris Chan	402
The Midnight Mass Murder 　　by Paul Hiscock	423
About the Contributors	441

Editor's Foreword:
Never Enough Holmes Adventures – Even at Christmas!
by David Marcum

"It arrived upon Christmas morning . . . ."
Sherlock Holmes – "The Blue Carbuncle"

Dr. John H. Watson met Sherlock Holmes on January 1st, 1881, in a laboratory at St. Bartholomew's Hospital, where Holmes, not-quite twenty-seven years old, was taking advantage of the empty facilities to conduct medico-legal experiments related to blood identification. Watson, himself only twenty-eight, had been grievously wounded at the Battle of Maiwand just a little over five months before, and during his subsequent recovery, he'd nearly died from enteric fever, also known as typhoid. By the time he made the month-long journey back to England on the troopship *Orontes*, he was still just barely recovered, and his mood was certainly grim as he faced an uncertain future.

Watson wrote that he had *"neither kith nor kin in England"*, and though it isn't recorded, one can only imagine how bleak was the Christmas of 1880 for this poor veteran, living on his meagre wound pension, and getting through every long dull day in an unfriendly city while residing in a small unfriendly hotel off the Strand. Unexpectedly running into an old friend, Stamford, in the bar of the Criterion on New Year's Day, and then subsequently being swept along to a meeting at Barts with a potential future flatmate, must have been the most excitement that had intruded into Watson's life since his return.

Based on their initial discussion at Barts, Holmes and Watson met the next morning to look at rooms in Baker Street. Watson moved in later that day, and Holmes the day after. The argument could be made that this arrangement saved Watson's life. He went from the desolate daily existence he'd had for weeks, slowly living beyond his means and with no set promise for a better future, to good rooms, a motherly landlady who helped him regain his health, and the mental distraction of a most unusual new flatmate. Within just a few months, Watson would learn that Holmes was a *Consulting Detective* – the first – and Watson began participating in various investigations as his health allowed. This certainly contributed more to his recovery than simply sitting around a bleak hotel room would have ever done.

Holmes lived in Baker Street from 1881 until autumn 1903 – around nineteen years, not counting the three-year period from April 1891 to April 1894 when he was absent and presumed dead following his battle with Professor Moriarty atop the Reichenbach Falls. Watson knew him that entire time – again, with the exception of The Great Hiatus, and that period of time in the mid-1880's when Watson spent some time in the United States – though he actually shared the Baker Street rooms with Holmes for quite a bit less than that – cumulatively around fifteen. His time there was broken up by those occasions when he married and lived elsewhere, with residences and medical practices in Paddington, Kensington, and Queen Anne Street.

Throughout all of these years, both of Holmes and Watson were involved in a great many investigations of varying levels of importance. There are those who think that Holmes's entire career consisted only of those cases related in the pitifully few sixty stories of The Canon, along with the one-hundred-forty or so "Untold Cases" such as the Giant Rat or the Red Leech – and unbelievably some people don't even want to acknowledge the legitimacy of the entire Canonical Sixty. However, over the course of a career that lasted decades, Holmes certainly carried out many thousands of investigations. (In "The Final Problem", Holmes states that *"In over a thousand cases I am not aware that I have ever used my powers upon the wrong side"* – and that estimate from the spring of 1891 must have been drastically low. Those who want – who *need* – to picture Holmes sitting around in his dressing gown for day after day and week after week in the Baker Street sitting room doing nothing, filthy and depressed and drugged and broken, and only able to function through Watson's caretaking while waiting desperately for a rare client to engage him for just a sliver of his vastly empty time are mistaken. That is not The Great Detective.

In fact, Holmes and Watson's lives were crowded with adventures. These overlapped and twisted and twined through one another, and the excitement never let up. Could anyone like Sherlock Holmes have lived a life of any other sort? Certainly not. And Watson, the recovered soldier and man of action, needed such a life just as much. Their days and years were full – and this would have been true in late December during the Christmas season just as much as any other time of year.

1881, that first year the two shared rooms in Baker Street, was when they became friends, and as Watson's health returned and he joined Holmes's investigations more and more, his assistance would prove to be initially useful, and then indispensable. By Christmas of that year, Holmes's practice would have been well established in the Baker Street rooms (following his move a year earlier from Montague Street), and

Watson would have had a good understanding of both Holmes's methods and personality. When Christmas rolled around, they would have already been working well together as a team for a number of months, so Christmas-themed investigations would pose no more difficulties than what had already occurred through the previous year.

For those who simply wish to read Holmes's adventures as they find them, each of the stories in this collection will be very satisfying. But for those who delve a bit deeper, there will be some who notice that there is a bit of overlap. Several cases, for instance, occur around Christmases in the same year, and those paying closer attention might see that they even occur on the same day. Don't let that worry you – it can all be rationalized. This is not a contradiction or an error, meaning that one story has to be chosen as the other as the "legitimate" account of what really happened on that day, and the other is a mere fiction. As someone who has kept a massive and detailed Chronology of both Canon and traditional pastiche for decades, I can assure you that it all fits together quite neatly.

Holmes and Watson's adventures often overlapped, with a piece of one case possibly consisting of just a short conversation lasting a few minutes before the day's events shifted to a piece of another case, and then back again. When Watson wrote the stories, he carefully selected the relevant threads for each separate case from this tangled skein of many concurrent cases, *The Great Holmes Tapestry* as I call it, to construct a self-contained and straight-ahead narrative of just one adventure. He didn't necessarily include what else was happening at the same time in another cases to avoid confusion. Thus, when written from beginning to end, a story will tell just that single investigation without pulling in threads from some other side-by-side case which would spiral the story beyond its scope. Think how twisted and intertwined the events are in your normal everyday life. How much more convoluted, then, were the lives of Our Heroes? As a deep-dive Holmes Chronologicist for forty-five-plus years, I assure you that all of the pieces of the puzzle fit. I'm thankful that Watson has taken the time to separate these events into digestible and self-contained pieces.

That's how the fifty-seven Christmas stories in this new collection can fit within the more limited years of Holmes and Watson's experiences and fixed number of Christmases. Some of these cases occur in the days leading up to Christmas, some on the day, and some afterwards. Some of the stories are inextricably plotted with the trappings of Christmas. Others are set during late December, and even though they could have occurred at any time of the year, they are certainly influenced by the season that surrounds them. In some tales there is festivity, and in others tragedy.

Watson might be having a bad year in this one, and Holmes in that one – the same as each of us have both high and low Yuletide seasons.

Sometimes more than one case takes place on a certain Christmas day, but they are cleverly written so that when reading them, it seems as if they stand alone. *"It arrived upon Christmas morning . . ."* said Holmes to Watson in "The Blue Carbuncle". He was describing a goose – a most remarkable bird – that held a bonny and bright little blue jewel. But he might have been describing any of the many stories that came his and Watson's way on and around the various December Twenty-fifths . . . .

And it isn't just the brilliant fifty-seven Christmas adventures in these three volumes that have to be taken into account – for there are quite a few other narratives beyond the extent of this set of books that also tell what Holmes and Watson were also doing at Christmas. Below is a list of *still more* Holmes and Watson Christmas Adventures. I highly recommend that the true student of The Entire Lives of Our Heroes seek them out as well. Read them and enjoy them – and study them too. Make notes as you go, and you'll start to understand just how the entire *Great Holmes Tapestry* of both Canon and pastiche fits together so brilliantly . . . .

Short Stories

The MX Book of New Sherlock Holmes Stories – Part V: Christmas Adventures (2016 – 30 stories)
- "The Case of the Ruby Necklace" – Bob Byrne
- "The Jet Brooch" – Denis O. Smith
- "The Adventure of the Missing Irregular" – Amy Thomas
- "The Adventure of the Knighted Watchmaker" – Derrick Belanger
- "The Stolen Relic" – David Marcum
- "A Christmas Goose" – C. H. Dye
- "The Adventure of the Long-Lost Enemy" – Marcia Wilson
- "The Case of the Christmas Cracker" – John Hall
- "The Queen's Writing Table" – Julie McKuras
- "The Blue Carbuncle" – Sir Arthur Conan Doyle *(Dramatised for Radio by Bert Coules)*
- "The Man Who Believed in Nothing" – Jim French
- "The Case of the Christmas Star" – S.F. Bennett
- "The Christmas Card Mystery" – Narrelle M. Harris
- "The Question of the Death Bed Conversion" – William Patrick Maynard

- "The Adventure of the Christmas Surprise" – Vincent W. Wright
- "A Bauble in Scandinavia" – James Lovegrove
- "The Adventure of Marcus Davery" – Arthur Hall
- "The Adventure of the Purple Poet" – Nicholas Utechin
- "The Adventure of the Empty Manger" – Tracy J. Revels
- "The Adventure of the Vanishing Man" – Mike Chinn
- "A Perpetrator in a Pear Tree" – Roger Riccard
- "The Case of the Christmas Trifle" – Wendy C. Fries
- "The Adventure of the Christmas Stocking" – Paul D. Gilbert
- "The Case of the Reformed Sinner" – S. Subramanian
- "The Adventure of the Golden Hunter" – Jan Edwards
- "The Curious Case of the Well-Connected Criminal" – Molly Carr
- "The Adventure of the Handsome Ogre" – Matthew J. Elliott
- "The Adventure of the Improbable Intruder" – Peter K. Andersson
- "The Adventure of the Deceased Doctor" – Hugh Ashton
- "The Mile End Mynah Bird" – Mark Mower

Holmes for the Holidays (1996)
- The Watch Night Bell – Anne Perry
- The Sleuth of Christmas Past – Barbara Paul
- A Scandal In Winter – Gillian Linscott
- The Adventure in Border Country – Gwen Moffat
- The Three Ghosts – Loren D. Estleman
- The Canine Ventriloquist – Jon L. Breen
- The Man Who Never Laughed – J.N. Williamson
- The Yuletide Affair – John Stoessel
- The Christmas Tree – William L. DeAndrea

- The Christmas Ghosts – Bill Crider
- The Thief of Twelfth Night – Carole Nelson Douglas
- The Italian Sherlock Holmes – Reginald Hill
- The Christmas Client – Edward D. Hoch
- The Angel's Trumpet – Carol Wheat

More Holmes for the Holidays (1999)
- The Christmas Gift – Anne Perry
- The Four Wise Men – Peter Lovesey
- Eleemosynary, My Dear Watson – Barbara Paul
- The Greatest Gift – Loren D. Estleman

- The Rajah's Emerald – Carolyn Wheat
- The Christmas Conspiracy – Edward D. Hoch
- The Music of Christmas – L.B. Greenwood
- The Christmas Bear – Bill Crider
- The Naturalist's Stock Pin – Jon L. Breen
- The Second Violet – Daniel Stashower
- The Human Mystery – Tanith Lee

Sherlock Holmes: Adventures for the Twelve Days of Christmas – Roger Riccard (2015)
- The Seventh Swan
- The Eighth Milkmaid
- The Ninth Ladyship at the Dance
- The Tenth Lord Leaping
- The Eleven Pipe Problem
- The Twelfth Drumming

Sherlock Holmes: Further Adventures for the Twelve Days of Christmas – Roger Riccard (2016)
- The Partridge in a Pearl Tree
- The Two Turtledoves
- The Three French Henchmen
- The Four Calling Birds
- The Five Gold Rings
- Six Geese at a Gander

Sherlock Holmes: Adventures Beyond the Canon – Volume I (2018)
- "A Gentleman's Disagreement" – Narrelle Harris *(A sequel to "The Blue Carbuncle")*

The Confidential Casebook of Sherlock Holmes (1997)
- "A Ballad of the White Plague" – P.C. Hodgel

Curious Incidents 2 (2002)
- "Green and Red trappings" – Valerie J. Patterson

The Sherlock Holmes Stories of Edward D. Hoch (2008)
- "The Christmas Client"
- "The Christmas Conspiracy"

The Misadventures of Sherlock Holmes (1944)
- "Christmas Eve" – S.C. Roberts

The Chronicles of Sherlock Holmes – Volume Two – Denis O. Smith (1998)
- "The Christmas Visitor" (Originally published in 1985)

Sherlock Holmes and the Watson Pastiche – Karl Showler (2005)
- "Fulworth Christmas"

Sherlock Holmes: A Case at Christmas – N.M. Scott (2016)
- "A Case at Christmas"

Sherlock Holmes: To a Country House Darkly – N.M. Scott (2017)
- "Christmas on Dartmoor"

The Secret Files of Sherlock Holmes – Frank Thomas (2002)
- "Sherlock's Christmas Gift"

The Secret Adventures of Sherlock Holmes – Paul E. Heusinger (2006)
- "The Christmas Truce"

Watson's Sampler: The Lost Casebook of Sherlock Holmes – William F. Watson (2007)
- "The Matter of the Christmas Gift"

Tales from the Stranger's Room (2011)
- "The Adventure of the Christmas Smoke" – David Rowbotham

A Christmas Carol at 221b – Thomas Mann (2018 – Novella)

A Julian Symons Duet – Julian Symons (2000)
- "The Vanishing Diamonds"

The Chemical Adventures of Sherlock Holmes – Thomas G. Waddell and Thomas R. Rybolt (2009)
- "A Christmas Story"

The Singular Exploits of Sherlock Holmes – Alan Stockwell (2012)
- "A Christmas Interlude"

Magazine Adventures

- "The Christmas Poisonings" – Barrie Roberts, *The Strand Magazine* (Issue No. 7)
- "The Affair of the Christmas Jewel" – Barrie Roberts, *The Strand Magazine* (Issue No. 9)
- "The Ghost of Christmas Past" – David Stuart Davies, *The Strand Magazine* (Issue No. 23)
- "The Christmas Bauble" – John Hall, *Sherlock Holmes: The Detective Magazine* (Issue No. 28)
- "Watson's Christmas Trick" – Bob Byrne, *Sherlock Holmes: The Detective Magazine* (Issue No. 46)

Novels

- *Sherlock Holmes and the Yule-Tide Mystery* – Val Andrews (1996)
- *Justice Hall* – Laurie R. King (2002)
- *Sherlock Holmes's Christmas* – David Upton (2005)
- *A Christmas to Forget at 221b* – Hugh A. Mulligan (2002)
- *Sherlock Holmes: Have Yourself a Chaotic Little Christmas* – Gwendolyn Frame (2012)
- *Sherlock Holmes & The Christmas Demon* – James Lovegrove (2019)
- *Young Sherlock Holmes* – Film Novelization by Alan Arnold (1985)

Film, Television, and Radio Adventures

- *Young Sherlock Holmes* – Film screenplay by Chris Columbus (1985)
- "The Adventure of the Christmas Pudding" *Sherlock Holmes* – Screenplay by George Fass and Gertrude Fass (April 4th, 1955 – Television Series)
- "The Night Before Christmas" *The New Adventures of Sherlock Holmes* – Script by Denis Green and Anthony Boucher (December 24th, 1945 Radio Broadcast)
- "The Adventure of the Christmas Bride" – Script by Edith Meiser (December 21st, 1947 Radio Broadcast)

- "The Man Who Believed in Nothing" – Script by Jim French (December 23rd, 2001 Radio Broadcast – Also published in *The MX Book of New Sherlock Holmes Stories – Part V: Christmas Adventures*)
- "The Christmas Ogre" – Script by M.J. Elliott (December 20th, 2015 Radio Broadcast. Text version published as "The Handsome Ogre" in *The MX Book of New Sherlock Holmes Stories – Part V: Christmas Adventures*)

And what has appeared in print doesn't even begin to match the level of excellent writing about Holmes and Christmas that one can find at fanfiction sites on the web. In fact, for the last several years there has been a writing activity at *fanfiction.net* in which a group of authors compose and post something for the entire month of December, either a complete story, ranging from very short to full-length, to something serialized across the whole month. I've archived them in multiple binders and chronologicized them too, and it's amazing how it all fits together.

For more about the various Sherlockian Christmas stories, please see my essay "Compliments of the Season", an entry from my irregular blog, *A Seventeen Step Program*, at:

https://17stepprogram.blogspot.com/2018/12/the-compliments-of-season-sherlock.html

In the 2015 Foreword to the MX anthology volume *Part V: Christmas Adventures*, I wrote, "*. . . if there are already so many of them out there, why another book of Holmes Christmas adventures?*" As I explained then, for someone like me – and hopefully you too! – there can *never* be enough traditional tales about Holmes and Watson, two of the best and wisest men whom I have ever known. (And after reading and collecting literally thousands of stories about them for over forty-six years, I do feel like I know them.)

The other reason relates to the ever-increasing popularity of these MX Anthologies, and how it was time for *More Christmas Adventures*.

When I first had the idea for a new Holmes anthology in early 2015, the plan was to communicate with possibly a dozen or so "editors" of Watson's notes and see if they were interested in contributing. I had modest hopes that there might be enough new stories – maybe a dozen? – that could justify a new anthology. But the idea grew and grew until the first collection was three massive volumes of over sixty new adventures – really one big book spread out under three covers – and containing more new Holmes tales than had ever been assembled before in one place – at one time. (We've since surpassed that.)

A big part of what made the project so special was that the authors donated their royalties to the Stepping Stones School for special needs students, which was planning at that time to move into one of Sir Arthur Conan Doyle's former homes, Undershaw. By the time the first three books were released in October 2015, renovations were well under way at the school's future home, and it also quickly became apparent that the need for future volumes of *The MX Book of New Sherlock Holmes Stories* was very strong – many contributors reached out to me, wanting to contribute again, as did authors new to the party. The process for producing more anthology volumes was in place, a desire for more traditional Holmes stories is always there, and the school can always use more funding as provided by the sale of the books, so it was decided that what had initially been a one-time three-volume set would become an ongoing series.

Therefore, it was announced that there would be another anthology – but there was so much interest that it was quickly determined that *two* sets per year would be necessary, a general *Annual* in the spring, and another with themed stories in the fall. It turned out that the contributions for these spring and fall editions were so numerous that multiple volumes were required for each set. (Fortunately MX Publishing recognizes the value of these large collections, and doesn't try to limit their size as would some publishers – thus depriving the world of more great Holmes adventures. Rather, we add more and bigger books.)

With this set, we're now at 30 volumes, with more in preparation for Spring 2022, and I'm thinking ahead to a theme for Fall 2022. Right now we're nearing 700 stories from 200 contributors from around the world. We've raised over $85,000 for the school, with the very real possibility that it will go over $100,000 in early 2022.

At the time of publication, and as you will see mentioned in Acting Headteacher Emma West's foreword, it's been announced that the Stepping Stones School *at Undershaw* is changing its name *to Undershaw*, with the motto *"Eliminating the Impossible"*. With this action, the school further reaffirms its connection with the Sherlockian world, and I'm personally thrilled that these books can continue to assist in the great and important work that they do – while also bringing more and more traditional Canonical adventures about the True Mr. Sherlock Holmes to light, and into the hands of a world that is starving for them.

* * * * *

"Of course, I could only stammer out my thanks."
– The unhappy John Hector McFarlane, "The Norwood Builder"

As always when one of these sets is finished, I want to first thank with all my heart my incredible, patient, brilliant, kind, and beautiful wife of over thirty-three years, Rebecca, and our amazing, funny, brilliant, creative, and wonderful son, and my friend, Dan. I love you both, and you are everything to me!

During the editing of these particular volumes, I've been in the second half of my first year at my dream job – which has required a massive amount of figuring out new things in a hurry. (I've been dreaming about it every night, and – according to my wife – talking in my sleep for the first time in thirty-three years.) When the agency where I was a federal investigator closed in the 1990's, and I was figuring out what I wanted to do with my life, we lived near a beautiful park, and as I would walk there nearly every day with my son, seeing the trails and springs and streams and culverts big enough that kids were exploring them, and I realized that I was interested in infrastructure – and particularly working for that particular city. That led to my return to school to be a civil engineer. After a number of years working at various engineering companies, and getting my license along the way, and still wanting to work at the city, I was finally able to. Now I'm in an office just a few hundred feet from that same park. That has kept me extremely busy for the last few months, which kept me from replying to emails as fast as I would have wished, not to mention reading and editing stories as quickly as I did just a year ago, so I'm very grateful to everyone who patiently waited to hear back from me about their stories.

I can never express enough gratitude for all of the contributors who have donated their time and royalties to this ongoing project. I'm constantly amazed at the incredible stories that you send, and I'm so glad to have gotten to know so many of you through this process. It's an undeniable fact that Sherlock Holmes authors are the *best* people!

As mentioned, the contributors of these stories have donated their royalties for this project to support Undershaw, a school for special needs children located at one of Sir Arthur Conan Doyle's former homes. As of this writing, and as mentioned above, these MX anthologies have raised over $85,000 for the school, with no end in sight, and of even more importance, they have helped raise awareness about the school all over the world – which I'm told by the school is actually more important than the funds. These books are making a real difference to the school, and the participation of both contributors and purchasers is most appreciated.

Next is that group that exchanges emails with me when we have the time – and time is a valuable commodity for all of us these days! As mentioned, I don't get to write back and forth with these fine people as often as I'd like, but I really enjoy catching up when we do get the chance: Derrick Belanger, Brian Belanger, Mark Mower, Denis Smith, Tom Turley, Dan Victor, and Marcia Wilson.

There is a group of special people who have stepped up and supported this and a number of other projects over and over again with a lot of contributions. They are the best and I can't express how valued they are: Hugh Ashton, Derrick Belanger, Deanna Baran, Craig Stephen Copland, Matthew Elliott, Tim Gambrell, Jayantika Ganguly, Paul Gilbert, Dick Gillman, Arthur Hall, Steve Herczeg, Paul Hiscock, Craig Janacek, Mark Mower, Will Murray, Tracy Revels, Roger Riccard, Geri Schear, Brenda Seabrooke, Shane Simmons, Robert Stapleton, Kevin Thornton, I.A. Watson, and Marcy Wilson.

Next, I wish to send several huge *Thank You's* to the following:

- *Nancy Holder* – I first began corresponding with Nancy in 2019, and I've been pushing for her to write a pastiche for this collection ever since. (*Nancy: You're still invited!*) I was able to meet her in person at the Sherlock Holmes Birthday Celebration in New York City in January 2020, and found that she's just as nice as she'd been by way of email.

    In mid-2021, as this book was being prepared, she stepped up and agreed to write a wonderful foreword rather late in the game, showing what a truly consummate professional she is. Even though I haven't convinced her to write a Holmes adventure yet, I'm thrilled that she's part of these books. Huge thanks!

- *Steve Emecz* – Some people have a picture in their minds of a publishing company with several floors on some skyscraper, hundreds of employees running around like ants, with vast departments devoted to management, marketing, editing, production, shipping, etc. That is not always the case. Those old giant dinosaur publishers are still around, and they might squeeze out a Sherlockian title or two every year, but they don't represent the modern way of doing things. MX has become the premiere Sherlockian publisher by following a new paradigm. And they manage to get all of this done with a truly skeleton staff.

    Steve Emecz works a way-more-than-full-time job related to his career in e-finance. MX Publishing isn't his full-time job –

it's a labor of love. He, along with his wife Sharon Emecz and cousin, Timi Emecz, *are* MX Publishing. In addition to their very busy real every-day lives, these three sole employees take care of the management, marketing, editing, production, and shipping, and they absolutely cannot receive enough credit for what they accomplish.

From my first association with MX in 2013, I've seen that MX (under Steve's leadership) was *the* fast-rising superstar of the Sherlockian publishing world. Connecting with MX and Steve Emecz was personally an amazing life-changing event for me, as it has been for countless other Sherlockian authors. It has led me to write many more stories, and then to edit books, along with unexpected Holmes Pilgrimages to England – none of which might have happened otherwise. By way of my first email with Steve – *Only eight years ago!* – I've had the chance to make some incredible Sherlockian friends and play in the Holmesian Sandbox in ways that I would have never dreamed possible.

Through it all, Steve has been one of the most positive and supportive people that I've ever known.

Many who just buy books and have a vague idea of how the publishing industry works now might not realize that MX, a non-profit which supports several important charities, consists of simply these three people. Between them, they take care of running the entire business – all in their precious spare time, fitting it in and around their real lives.

With incredible hard work, they have made MX into a world-wide Sherlockian publishing phenomenon, providing opportunities for authors who would never have had them otherwise. There are some like me who return more than once to Watson's Tin Dispatch Box, and there are others who only find one or two stories there – but they also get the chance to publish their books, and then they can point with pride at this accomplishment, and how they too have added to The Great Holmes Tapestry.

From the beginning, Steve has let me explore various Sherlockian projects and open up my own personal possibilities in ways that otherwise would have never happened. Thank you, Steve, for every opportunity!

- *Brian Belanger* – Over the last few years, my amazement at Brian Belanger's ever-increasing talent has only grown. I initially became acquainted with him when he took over the duties of creating the covers for MX Books following the untimely death of their previous graphic artist. I found Brian to be a great collaborator, very easy-going and stress-free in his approach and willingness to work with authors, and wonderfully creative too.

Brian and his brother, Derrick Belanger, are two great friends, and five years ago they founded *Belanger Books*, which along with MX Publishing, has absolutely locked up the Sherlockian publishing field with a vast amount of amazing material. The dinosaurs must be trembling to see every new Sherlockian project, one after another after another. Luckily MX and Belanger Books work closely with one another, and I'm thrilled to be associated with both of them. Many thanks to Brian for all he does for both publishers, and for all he's done for me personally.

- *Roger Johnson* – I'm more grateful than I can say that I know Roger. I was aware of him for years before I timidly sent him a copy of my first book for review, and then on my first Holmes Pilgrimage to England and Scotland in 2013, I was able to meet both him and his wonderful wife, Jean Upton, in person. When I returned on Holmes Pilgrimage No. 2 in 2015, I was so fortunate that they graciously allowed me to stay with them for several days in their home, where we had many wonderful discussions, while occasionally venturing forth so that they could show me parts of England that I wouldn't have seen otherwise. It was an experience I wouldn't trade for anything.

  Roger's Sherlockian knowledge is exceptional, as is the work that he does to further the cause of The Master. But even more than that, both Roger and his wonderful wife, Jean, are simply the finest and best of people, and I'm very lucky to know both of them – even though I don't get to see them nearly as often as I'd like, and especially in these crazy days! In so many ways, Roger, I can't thank you enough, and I can't imagine these books without you.

And finally, last but certainly *not* least, thanks to **Sir Arthur Conan Doyle**: Author, doctor, adventurer, and the Founder of the Sherlockian Feast. Honored, and present in spirit.

As I always note when putting together an anthology of Holmes stories, the effort has been a labor of love. These adventures are just more tiny threads woven into the ongoing Great Holmes Tapestry, continuing to grow and grow, for there can *never* be enough stories about the man whom Watson described as *"the best and wisest . . . whom I have ever known."*

David Marcum
September 8th, 2021
A most important day,
for all kinds of reasons

Questions, comments, or story submissions
may be addressed to David Marcum at

thepapersofsherlockholmes@gmail.com

Foreword
by Nancy Holder

Sherlock Holmes and Christmas: Two fixed points in a changing world. The Great Detective, cracking the case with a dramatic flourish (and, often, a somewhat lengthy explanation). His faithful Boswell, marveling at the genius of Our Mutual Friend. Roasting chestnuts, glittering Christmas trees, carolers in hoop skirts and bonnets. A Victorian Christmas in all its holly-and-ivy splendor.

We who know and love The Canon – the fifty-six original stories and four novels written by John H. Watson (with an assist from Sir Arthur Conan Doyle) – wax nostalgic for the traditions of a time and place we will never see. At least I do, and I have spent the majority of my Christmases in Southern California, where guys in flip-flops spray artificial snow onto the windows of taco shops and sushi restaurants, and we watch *A Christmas Carol* with the air conditioning on – as do, I assume, my many friends in Australia, Hawaii, Florida, and so many other pleasant climes. Simply going by the cards I receive in December, Christmas as celebrated in late nineteenth century Britain and Ireland is the Ur of winter celebrations, and we perpetuate its hold on us with wholehearted devotion.

As a dedicated Sherlockian, I usually crack open "The Adventure of the Blue Carbuncle" to usher in Holmes at Christmas. This is the only story in The Canon that takes place at (or very near) Christmas. A review of the beloved tale is pretty much *de rigueur* at any December Sherlock Holmes cookie swap and/or Christmas jollification. How many of us have debated the various fine points of the story – (Why leave John Horner in the clink overnight? Does Peterson reap the reward for the gem?) – while sipping tea, brandy, or mulled wine and munching gingerbread? Nearly all of us – no matter if we celebrate Hanukkah, Diwali, Kwanzaa, or as is the case at my house, more than one winter holiday. For the duration of this one story, we happily transport ourselves to a Victorian Christmas.

But while "Blue Carbuncle" may be the only Christmas story in the Canon, it is, of course, not the only Christmas story featuring Holmes and Watson. MX Publishing, who published a lovely, hefty Christmas assortment in 2016, have done it again – a Santa sack brimming with Yuletide pastiches sure to please the traditionalists among us. Hewing close to the Canon, with no supernatural or fantastical elements, these are the kinds of stories sure to warm the heart (even if it's 98-degrees

Fahrenheit outside) and take us back to where we want to be for our winter holidays – with Holmes and Watson, wrapped in gas lamp frost, where it's always (or close to) 1895. Dozens of talented, clever, careful authors have penned wonderful stories tailored to this season of joy, wonder . . . and Sherlock. Whether it's Christmas in July where you are, or snowy with a chance of sugarplums, I urge you to unwrap and savor. What lovely gifts await you.

Nancy Holder, BSI
Near Seattle
July, 2021

"It is the Season of Forgiveness"
by Roger Johnson

In our minds, what do we associate with the stories of Sherlock Holmes? Crime, naturally, and mystery. Observation and deduction, leading to solutions, certainly. Gaslight and fog, yes. The mighty metropolis of London too.

But Christmas? There is, as we all surely know, only one Canonical investigation that takes place at Christmas time – it's "The Adventure of the Blue Carbuncle", and Dr. Watson's narrative famously begins: *"I had called upon my friend Sherlock Holmes upon the second morning after Christmas, with the intention of wishing him the Compliments of the Season."* Not Christmas Eve, then. Not Christmas Day itself, nor the one immediately following – Boxing Day – but *two days* after Christmas. One might be tempted the dismiss its credentials (I mean *two days*?) but of course the whole account is imbued with the spirit of the season, and that spirit casts its benign shadow over our mental image of the Detective and the Doctor.

Last year Belanger Books published an appealing little book called *Sherlock Holmes: A Three-Pipe Christmas*, edited by Dan Andriacco. At its heart are "The Adventure of the Blue Carbuncle" by Arthur Conan Doyle, "The Adventure of the Unique *Hamlet* " by Vincent Starrett, first published in 1920, and "The Adventure of the Unique Dickensians", an exploit of Holmes's disciple Solar Pons, written by August Derleth and first published in 1968. The stories are accompanied by essays, whose authors include the editor of this volume and the author of this foreword. How entertaining the essays are, you must judge for yourselves, but the stories are excellent and the book as a whole is delightful.

Starrett was one of the immortals of Holmesian scholarship. So was S.C. Roberts, whose charming one-act play "Christmas Eve" you'll find in his classic *Holmes and Watson: A Miscellany*, first published in 1953 and now available in a new edition from the British Library.

The combination of Christmas and Holmes continues to appeal, to authors and readers alike. A notable recent novel, for instance, is *Sherlock Holmes and the Christmas Demon* by James Lovegrove. And the association is strong on stage and screen as well. It's a rare Christmas in Britain when theatregoers don't have the choice of a new or old Holmesian comedy, or more rarely a drama, among the seasonal fare. In recent years we have enjoyed *Sherlock Holmes and the Warlock of Whitechapel*,

Tweedy and the Missing Company of Sherlock Holmes, Sherlock Holmes and the Hooded Lance, Potted Sherlock, Mrs. Hudson's Christmas Corker, Sherlock Holmes and the Case of the Christmas Carol, The Adventures of the Improvised Sherlock Holmes, and any number of riffs on *The Hound of the Baskervilles*.

Mention of that particular classic reminds me that one of the better aspects of the 2002 TV film *The Hound of the Baskervilles* was the decision to set the story around Christmas time, and make the legendary Hound a character in a seasonal Mummers' play. And the last of the classic Granada Television series with Jeremy Brett as Holmes, "The Cardboard Box" broadcast in 1994, also relocated its narrative to Christmas to good effect.

Young Sherlock Holmes and the Pyramid of Fear (1985) begins with a decidedly weird Christmas episode and ends with a sad but hopeful one. More than thirty years earlier, an entertaining episode of Sheldon Reynolds's television series *Sherlock Holmes* was "The Adventure of the Christmas Pudding". Like *Young Sherlock Holmes*, it can be enjoyed today. And we mustn't forget the outstanding TV dramatisations of "The Blue Carbuncle", in 1968 with Peter Cushing and Nigel Stock as Holmes and Watson, and in 1984 with Jeremy Brett and David Burke. Two different interpretations – compare Madge Ryan's performance as the Countess of Morcar with Rosalind Knight's, for instance – but both excellent.

Sherlock Holmes and Christmas – inseparable? The stories in this book suggest that they are. And, as always, editor and authors won't get a penny from it, because all proceeds will go towards the maintenance of Undershaw, Arthur Conan Doyle's former home in Surrey, which now houses the Stepping Stones School for youngsters with special educational needs.

Roger Johnson, BSI, ASH
Editor: *The Sherlock Holmes Journal*
August 2021

An Ongoing Legacy for Sherlock Holmes
by Steve Emecz

Undershaw
Circa 1900

The MX Book of New Sherlock Holmes Stories has now raised over $85,000 for Undershaw, a school for children with learning disabilities, and is by far the largest Sherlock Holmes collection in the world.

Undershaw is the former home of Sir Arthur Conan Doyle, where he wrote many of the Sherlock Holmes stories. The fundraising has supported many projects continuing the legacy of Conan Doyle and Sherlock Holmes in the amazing building, including The Doyle Room, the school's Zoom broadcasting capability (including Sherlock themed events), The Literacy Program, and more.

In addition to Undershaw, our main program that we support is the Happy Life Children's Home in Kenya. My wife Sharon and I have spent seven Christmas's with the children in Nairobi.

It's a wonderful project that has saved the lives of over 600 babies. You can read all about the project in the second edition of the book *The Happy Life Story*.

In 2021, we are working on *#bookstobooks* which sees us donating 10% of the revenues from *mxpublishing.com* to fund schoolbooks and library books at Happy Life.

Our support for our projects is possible through the publishing of Sherlock Holmes books, which we have now been doing for over a decade.

You can find out more information about the Undershaw at:

https://undershaw.education/

and Happy Life at:

www.happylifechildrenshomes.com

You can find out more about MX Publishing and reach out to us through our website at:

www.mxpublishing.com

Steve Emecz
September 2021
Twitter: *@mxpublishing*

The Doyle Room at Stepping Stones, Undershaw
*Partially funded through royalties from
The MX Book of New Sherlock Holmes Stories*

Undershaw:
Eliminating the Impossible
by Emma West

Undershaw
September 9, 2016
Grand Opening of the Stepping Stones School
(Photograph courtesy of Roger Johnson)

I am delighted to share the news that Stepping Stones School has a new name. From 1st September, 2021, we will bear the name *Undershaw*, inspired by the building that houses our school. Stepping Stones has such a strong legacy as a school full of life, dynamism, and hope for a more inclusive future for our children. Undershaw is that school. Our staff, students, and families are proud of our community and excited for what the next stage holds.

> We stand for aspirational education free of discrimination.
> We stand for specialists supporting each young person their way, at their pace.
> We stand for our students developing the life and work skills necessary to navigate their adulthood and secure fulfilling and lasting careers.

> We stand for breaking down barriers and creating a cultural shift in how workplaces of the future view diversity and inclusion so that they recognise the true talents and abilities of our learners.

These attributes run at the heart of everything we do, and I am thrilled that we are about to embark upon a new chapter in our story.

Sir Arthur Conan Doyle built Undershaw as a place of convalescence for his wife. It had an honourable purpose then, just as it has now. Together we have reignited the passion of Undershaw, firstly in 2016 by renovating the building as a state-of-the-art specialist centre for our students, and lately as an inspirational name for our school, as we take our philosophy forward and find our place in a wider societal conversation. Undershaw encapsulates our essence as we take the very best from the past and use it as the landscape for framing our future.

You have partnered with us for many years. Thank you for sharing our passion and ethos. Thank you for your benevolence. Above all, thank you for your good company. We could not do it without you. We have loved having you with us on the journey and hope you are excited to join in on our next chapter as we take Undershaw into 2022 and long into the future.

Emma West
Acting Headteacher
September 2021

Sherlock Holmes (1854-1957) was born in Yorkshire, England, on 6 January, 1854. In the mid-1870's, he moved to 24 Montague Street, London, where he established himself as the world's first Consulting Detective. After meeting Dr. John H. Watson in early 1881, he and Watson moved to rooms at 221b Baker Street, where his reputation as the world's greatest detective grew for several decades. He was presumed to have died battling noted criminal Professor James Moriarty on 4 May, 1891, but he returned to London on 5 April, 1894, resuming his consulting practice in Baker Street. Retiring to the Sussex coast near Beachy Head in October 1903, he continued to be associated in various private and government investigations while giving the impression of being a reclusive apiarist. He was very involved in the events encompassing World War I, and to a lesser degree those of World War II. He passed away peacefully upon the cliffs above his Sussex home on his 103rd birthday, 6 January, 1957.

Dr. John Hamish Watson (1852-1929) was born in Stranraer, Scotland on 7 August, 1852. In 1878, he took his Doctor of Medicine Degree from the University of London, and later joined the army as a surgeon. Wounded at the Battle of Maiwand in Afghanistan (27 July, 1880), he returned to London late that same year. On New Year's Day, 1881, he was introduced to Sherlock Holmes in the chemical laboratory at Barts. Agreeing to share rooms with Holmes in Baker Street, Watson became invaluable to Holmes's consulting detective practice. Watson was married and widowed three times, and from the late 1880's onward, in addition to his participation in Holmes's investigations and his medical practice, he chronicled Holmes's adventures, with the assistance of his literary agent, Sir Arthur Conan Doyle, in a series of popular narratives, most of which were first published in *The Strand* magazine. Watson's later years were spent preparing a vast number of his notes of Holmes's cases for future publication. Following a final important investigation with Holmes, Watson contracted pneumonia and passed away on 24 July, 1929.

Photos of Sherlock Holmes and Dr. John H. Watson courtesy of Roger Johnson

The MX Book of New Sherlock Holmes Stories

Part XXX
More Christmas Adventures
(1897-1928)

Baskerville Hall in Winter
by Christopher James

The sky has done its work.
Now the earth is the colour of pipe smoke.
Whole fields are swathed in white.
The trees offer little resistance,
reaching up, like escaped convicts
with their twisted limbs to the moon.
A star is balanced on an evergreen.
At Baskerville Hall, diamonds
are heaped on the ramparts;
windows are curtained with snow.
Ancestors sleep beneath the holly.
Beyond, the moor is untrodden,
except for the prints that lead
beyond the ridge, towards the mire.
A single red light pinpricks the horizon:
the glow of a pipe, as Holmes
trudges the empty land, exorcising
the ghosts of the past, the unsolved
cases that fill his shelves and
followed, like his own shadow,
by the black dog he cannot shake.

The Purloined Present
by DJ Tyrer

"Felicitations of the season, to you, Watson, my dear chap."

For those more familiar with the dour image my good friend, Sherlock Holmes, so often presents to the world, his joviality as I entered the rooms of 221b Baker Street might have seemed strange. The outside world most often sees him when his mind is focused with keen intensity upon a case, but when he first discovers one, the man can be as giddy as a schoolboy.

I didn't return his greeting immediately, but asked, "Who's this?"

There was a man seated opposite him and he did not look at all cheerful. Indeed, there was no doubt that he had come to see my friend with some misfortune, most likely relating to the beginnings of a bright shiner that was forming about his left eye.

"This is Mr. Stevens."

"My dear sir," said I, "are you all right?"

He nodded, but I leant towards him to check regardless. There were no signs of anything more serious than the bruise to his eye and a blow to his pride, so I stepped back and told him, "You'll live."

He managed a weak smile at my words, but said, "Not that it will assuage my mood."

The man was not, if my impressions were correct, a man of means, for his suit was somewhat worn, but one who maintained the proprieties of life in spite of his situation. Given the expression adorning his face, I felt an immediate swelling of sympathy for him.

"Oh, and, my felicitations to you, Holmes," I finally replied as he gestured me into a seat, "and my commiserations to you, sir."

"Commiserations, indeed," said my friend, "for a terrible fate has befallen Mr. Stevens here, and straight before Christmas, to add to his woes."

"Why, whatever happened?"

"Mr. Stevens was robbed in the street, not far from this area of town." He glanced towards him and said, "My friend, Watson, here, has my full confidence. Why don't you tell him what happened?"

The man nodded. "It wasn't more than an hour ago. I was on my way to visit my fiancée and bring her my gift, for I shall be working on Christmas Day – being unmarried, you see, it is my duty to allow those fellows with families a chance to spend the day with their loved ones."

He took a pause and then, added, in a ragged voice, "It was the gift that was stolen."

"How terrible," I said, feeling that the grin upon Holmes's face wasn't exactly appropriate in the circumstances.

"Begin at the beginning, man," interjected Holmes. "Tell him what the gift was and how you came to have it. Every detail – any little point could be relevant."

Mr. Stevens gave a sigh, from which I understood he must already have been pressed to give my friend the story several times, doubtless with many an impertinent-seeming question along the way, prior to my arrival.

I reached out to give him a gentle pat on the arm and told him, "In your own time. I understood how distressed you must be."

If you don't share my sympathy for the chap – well, you have never had a fiancée whom you wished to see happy more than anything.

"Thank you," he said, then, after taking a deep breath, he continued. "It all began in Scanlan's Pawnshop."

"Ah, yes, I know it." An associate of Sherlock Holmes was bound to know all such places where stolen and misplaced goods might turn up.

"I am not a man of money," he continued. "I have a steady job as a clerk, but it doesn't pay as well as I should like. It is my hope, of course, to work my way up through the firm, but it is a slow ladder climb. I explain this so that you might understand the reason why I sought a gift in a pawnshop and why its loss has hit me so hard."

I nodded. "I quite understand."

"I live within my means, something my fiancée, whose father is quite well off, doesn't seem to fully appreciate. In her mind, we should marry shortly and immediately take on a mortgage for a grand house. My needing to take my time to save up a deposit and ensure I'll have an income sufficient to our needs, without recourse to debt or the humiliation of relying upon her father to keep us, is a thorn in our relationship. That I cannot easily afford the kind of gifts she casts her eye upon also pains me.

"Thus, I avail myself of those places where better quality goods can be obtained at a fraction of their price. Yet . . . ."

He paused for a moment and Holmes supplied, "Yet, *there* is the mystery."

I looked at Holmes and shook my head. "I'm not sure there *is* a mystery. At least, I'm not hearing one yet. A man spends money he can ill afford upon a trinket for his fiancée and is robbed of it by some vagabond and finds himself unable to replace it. A misfortune, yes, and one for which he has my every sympathy, but not a mystery. He would do better speaking to a policeman."

"I did," said Stevens, "and, the man told me to come see Mr. Holmes. I half-suspect he was joking, but I took his advice, nonetheless, for I could see no other course out of my predicament."

Again, I looked at Holmes. "Well, what is it you have yet to explain?"

He laughed. "Go on, sir. Finish your description and allow Watson to be enlightened."

Stevens sniffed and continued. "I went to Scanlan's Pawnshop two days ago in search of something that might please my darling. Of course, perforce my lack of time and income, I had left it rather late, for many of the best items had already been purchased as gifts by others in similar situations to my own. But amongst the bric-a-brac, I spotted something that I knew was sure to catch my fiancée's eye: A brooch.

"The price upon its ticket was merely five shillings, yet the quality was good. I'm no expert, but I could see there was a definite fineness to it and that it would have cost much more brand new, and the look of it was as pristine as never matters. The brooch was of blue enamel with a sprig of juniper pictured upon it, set in hallmarked gold. I was lucky to have chanced upon it.

"Well, I bought it, naturally, and went home feeling most pleased with myself.

"The next day, I purchased a modest *papier-mâché* box in which to place it, and wrapped it gaily with some paper and a ribbon I had conserved from a previous Christmas. Then, today, I set out to present it to her, hoping that she would be delighted with it."

"But you were robbed?"

He nodded to me. "Yes, I was. I must admit that my mind was upon seeing my fiancée and I was paying but little attention to the street about me, so I didn't see the fellow approach. Instead, I was snapped out of my reverie as he barged into me and shoved me sideways into an alleyway, where a second man was waiting.

"I was punched to the ground," he gestured to his eye. "Then the one held me, whilst the other one riffled my pockets, taking out the parcel. He tore back the wrapping paper, flicked open its lid, and said, 'This is it,' then slipped it into his pocket, his accomplice trailing after him and leaving me in a heap upon the ground."

"'*This is it*'?" I echoed.

"Precisely, Watson, precisely. They purloined the present without a moment's hesitation and didn't pause to take anything else from him."

Mr. Stevens nodded. "I had a little money on me and my father's old fob watch. Nothing very valuable, but . . . .

"Anyway, I immediately found a policeman, but he wasn't very helpful. I didn't have a good description of the men, nor did he judge a pawn-shop brooch very valuable and worth his time. He promised to 'keep an eye out' and, when I pressed him, said, in a sarcastic tone of voice, 'Why don't you try Mr. Holmes of 221b Baker Street, for he is a consulting detective, and mysteries are more his thing than mine.' And, so I did."

"And very glad of it I am, too," said my friend, "for things have been awfully dull of late, as if people take a break from wily crime in the lead-up to the festive period."

He turned to look at me. "So you see that what, at first blush, might appear as no more than a mere street robbery clearly involves some deeper mystery, for these rogues wanted the brooch specifically."

"Indeed they did. But, why?"

"Well, that is the question, isn't it?" he said, archly. "And one I intend to answer in time to return the brooch to Mr. Stevens here before Christmas morning." He turned back to the man. "You may go now, and rest assured I shall find your missing property."

With a torrent of gratitude, the man rose and exited the room – I supposed to see his fiancée. I wished him all luck.

I could see we would be in need of some, too.

"Well, Holmes, you've set yourself a tight deadline, and I see no leads. A pair of nondescript criminals – London is full of them!"

"Seek not defeat, Watson, for we have a lead or two to follow. Come, let us pay a trip to Scanlan's Pawnshop, and see what we may learn."

We shook the light frosting of snow from our shoulders as we entered the pawnshop, which was very much typical of its ilk with everything from men's shirts to household items to books, both edifying and not, on display at enticingly-low prices. The bell jangled and its owner appeared as if by magic from amongst the shelves.

"Oh, it's you, Mr. Holmes," muttered Scanlan, a weaselly-looking fellow. "I thought it was a customer," The man almost seemed to cultivate the caricature of his trade. "Don't linger – you put the wind up my regulars, and this time of year is one of my busiest as people seek the means to purchase a little festive cheer."

He made as if to shoo us out, but my friend interrupted him.

"Ah, but I am a customer," said Holmes with a predatory gleam in his eye that caused the man to quail a little. But greed had its hooks in him and Scanlan leaned a little nearer my friend and asked him what he meant.

"Information, sir. I wish to purchase information."

"Information?" Scanlan repeated the word slowly, as if it were new to him, but gave a curt nod of understanding.

"Yes, about an item you sold."

"Oh, no, no, no, Mr. Holmes, and no. My customers require of me a sacred trust. Those who buy and sell here don't wish their business bandied about."

"You mean," I said, "half those from whom you purchase are crooked, and the other half are cheated by you."

"The impertinence!" he cried, but Holmes merely laughed and said, "Come now, Mr. Scanlan, we all know how so many of your kind operate, so allow Dr. Watson his little joke."

Scanlan harrumphed, but said nothing further.

"The buyer of this particular item was the victim of robbery and has engaged me to locate it and return it to him. Having taken me into his confidence, you can be open about the item's sale. As for the person who sold it to you . . . ." Holmes dug his hand into his pocket and jangled some coins. "I'm sure we can come to some arrangement to assuage any guilt that may gnaw at you . . . ."

Scanlan smiled, showing a mouthful of rotten teeth. "That we may, Mr. Holmes, that we may. What is it you wanted to know?"

Holmes described the brooch and Mr. Stevens, and gave the date of its purchase.

"Ah, yes, funny you should ask after that," said the pawnbroker. "I remember it well. A couple of fellows were in here just after I sold it, asking for it."

"And," I interjected, not a little heatedly, given the man's earlier protestations, "you promptly told them who had bought it."

Scanlan gave an inarticulate cry of anger at my contention.

"Calm yourself, Watson," Holmes said in mollifying tones. "Mr. Scanlan here isn't to blame. I can read him well enough. His annoyance is as much at his having failed to charge for what he revealed as your accusation."

"Too right, Mr. Holmes. Had I known they were so keen to know, I might have made a profit from them. Not, of course," his tone became unctuous, "that I would've wished the young fellow any harm, you understand, Mr. Watson."

I snorted, but let him continue.

"They asked after it. I didn't recognise them, but assumed they had been by earlier, seen it, and gone to fetch the money to pay for it, so I told them I was very sorry, but they were too late, as the fellow who'd left just before they entered had purchased it."

"And they immediately exited?" I asked, catching Holmes's reasoning.

Scanlan nodded. "Why stay?"

"Indeed," said Holmes. "So Stevens was right – they were specifically seeking the brooch."

"But why?" I queried.

"That may become a little clearer once our friend here has told about the person who sold it to him. Yes, yes," he added, seeing the expression on the man's face, "you'll be paid. The better your information, the more that – "

"Robert Powell," said Scanlan without waiting for Holmes to finish. "Robert Powell was the one. Said it belonged to his old dear mother. Of course, I knew that were a lie – he always gave forth about how he was a foundling. Still, I never questions my customers."

"Of course not," I murmured.

Scanlan shot me a look, but continued. "That's who you want to speak to. He came in a day or two before and pawned it to me. I gave him two shillings for it."

He sniffed and Holmes nodded.

Looking at me, Holmes said, "Pay the man, Watson," and strode for the door.

"This seems more than sufficient," I said, handing Scanlan thruppence and following after my friend and feeling less of the festive spirit than I had earlier.

"Pleasure doing business with you gents – call back anytime, anytime . . . ."

The snow had grown somewhat heavier in its descent as we stepped back out into the street, I pulled up my collar before turning to Holmes. "You seem familiar with this man, Powell."

"Indeed," he replied as he raised his hand to flag down a passing hansom. "As you are aware, I make it my habit to know everything related to criminality and the law, and Robert Powell is one of the multitude of petty thieves who infest our beloved city."

He gave the cabdriver an address and the hansom began to bounce its way along the cobbled street, carrying us in reasonable comfort in spite of the increasing chill.

"Powell," continued Holmes, "has been up before the magistrate more times than most. Nothing serious, merely incorrigible."

"So you don't believe he's involved in the assault upon Stevens's person?"

"No. Powell would happily pick a pocket or slide through an unlatched window, but the man has no spirit. Confrontation and violence aren't his way. No, the fool has blundered into something and our client has become innocently caught up in it for the price of a shilling."

"But why such a fuss over a brooch? I know that Stevens spoke of its quality, but it didn't sound anything particularly special – not to be worth all this fuss."

"Perhaps it has a sentimental value," mused Holmes, although I suspected by his tone that he was toying with me.

"You think there is more to this case, don't you?"

"Of course! If it were merely about sentimental value, or even monetary value, come to that, the erstwhile owners of the brooch would surely have approached Stevens and either offered him recompense above what he paid for it, or played upon his sentimentality in the hopes of regaining their lost item. Failing that, they could have availed themselves of the law. Yet, they didn't . . . ."

"Which means they didn't wish to involve the law, nor reveal themselves to him."

"Exactly. Although we cannot be certain yet, I believe there can be little doubt that the two men who attacked Stevens in that alleyway are no more the rightful owners of that brooch than Powell."

"A thief stole from a thief?" I said with a chuckle.

"It seems the most likely answer," said Holmes. Then, he added, "A-ha! I believe we are at our destination."

Our destination, I saw as Holmes paid the cabdriver, was a public house of a particularly mean sort. A sign in the form of a sheet daubed with cheap paint hung outside it, without a name, just a five-pointed star.

"You can guess what they call this place," Holmes said, as he led the way inside.

The place stank of cheap tobacco and cheaper beer, and I clutched my stick to myself protectively as the eyes of the dozen-or-so patrons turned to regarded us with appraising gazes.

"Barkeep," said Holmes in a loud and jovial tone, "no refreshments for us." He tossed a couple of coins onto the bar. "We're looking for Robert Powell."

"He hasn't been in for a couple of days," the barman replied as he scooped up the coins and dropped them into the pocket on the front of his grubby apron. "I heard there was some trouble." He looked at us. "You ain't trouble, are you?"

"No, not the sort that need worry you," said Holmes. "We need to see Powell on business."

"Oh, right." I guessed the barman assumed we were receivers expecting goods from the thief. "He's probably at the doss-house five doors down." He gestured the direction we should take.

"Thank you and good day to you, sir," said Holmes and we returned once more to the snow-dappled street and set along to the door indicated.

"I trust we can resolve this soon," I told Holmes. "The snow is settling and, should the fall grow any heavier, I intend to retire to the fireside with some mulled wine to warm me and not shift again until after the feast."

"No need to fear," he replied as we entered the dark and damp interior of the doss-house, "I believe we are nearing a conclusion."

We had no trouble finding Powell as the attendant pointed him out amongst those sleeping in return for a sixpence. He was laying on a palliasse, doubtless crawling with bedbugs.

Holmes gave him a kick that startled him awake and caused him to cringe like a mistreated hound.

"Robert Powell," said Holmes, fiercely, "we need to speak to you about the brooch."

"I already told you," the man moaned, curling up as if expecting a blow. He had, I realised, mistaken us for his earlier visitors and, as my eyes grew accustomed to the shadowy interior of the doss-house, I could see he had been gifted by them with cuts and bruises.

"I already told you," he whined, again.

Holmes hauled him to his feet and brandished his cane at him. I remembered what he had said in the hansom on the way over and realised the game he was playing, and I felt a twinge of sympathy for Powell, villain though he doubtless was.

"Not us," said Holmes. "We're looking for the men you stole it from – the ones who gave you those bruises. Now, tell us." He raised his cane just a little, as if for punctuation.

"Not them. Didn't steal it from them."

My friend and I exchanged a look. It seemed as if our conjecture had been off.

"Then why did they want it?" I demanded.

"Said they were friends of the lady."

"The lady?" Holmes asked, a little more gently now.

"Yeah, the lady. Stole it from a lady. Hadn't seem them before in my life."

"You'd better tell us from whom you stole it," I said.

"What are you? Police?"

"No," said Holmes. "Luckily for you, we're not. Tell us what we want to know and we'll not only see to it that the men who hurt you receive a payment in kind, but you can earn yourself a little money of an honest sort."

I could almost see his thoughts congealing as he considered what Holmes had said.

Finally, Powell gave us an address and a description of the building. It wasn't far away and certainly not the sort of place one would expect a lady to live who had good-quality jewellery.

Once again, I handed over a few coins and we stepped out into the snow.

"We're drawing near. We'll soon have the chance to play the part of Father Christmas and provide Stevens with his missing gift so that he might please his fiancée, and we'll have you warm in front of the fire with a fine cup of mulled wine in your hands."

"I hope so," said I, puffing on my hands to warm them. "I hope so. How do we do this?" I asked as we stopped outside the building. The address was a two-room annex with a door into the rear yard, which was reached by an alleyway.

"Just the one window and one door, according to Powell, and just the one way into the yard. If they are home, subtlety will avail us nothing. Better to approach directly and introduce ourselves, I think."

"As long as we don't need to pretend to be carolers," I said as we took the short alleyway into the yard.

"Stay back, just in case they attempt flight out of the window."

But there was no response to the raps he made upon the door with his cane and, when we peered through the window, it was quite plain nobody was there.

"In we go," said Holmes, leaning his full wait upon the door. There was a soggy splintering sound and it burst open, the damp-rotted boards having snapped away from the lock. I shuddered to think of anyone having to live within the dingy interior.

We began to search and, a mere moment later, I gave a cry of success.

"I have it. The brooch."

I held up the enamelled object in triumph. Even if we didn't bring the miscreants to justice, it seemed that we'd solved the case and saved Stevens's Christmas.

My friend gave a snort of dissatisfaction, but could hardly deny my discovery.

"Indeed, you do. Where was it?"

"Here on this bedside table. In plain sight as if they didn't have a care. And, look – there is the *papier-mâché* box, and the paper and ribbon, although I daresay he shall need to wrap it afresh." The men had been no more tender in their unwrapping of the gift than they had been with Stevens. "All present," I added, and chuckled.

Holmes didn't share my levity, but snorted again. "'As if they didn't have a care.' As if . . . Had they no care, they would hardly have gone to the trouble of retrieving it, yet here it is, as you say, abandoned in plain sight. Powell might not return – but any number of sneak-thieves could happen past and relieve them of it, and they might not be so lucky as to retrieve it again. No, it makes no sense, none at all."

"Does it matter?" I asked. "After all, we've achieved what we set out to do."

"I know that you yearn for your fire, Watson, but whilst we might have regained the brooch for Mr. Stevens, there is still a mystery here, and I cannot abide leaving a mystery unsolved. May I?"

I handed him the brooch and he examined it minutely, turning it over and over in his hands, looking at it from every angle.

As he did so, he murmured, "Perhaps they left it for the lady that Powell spoke of. But, why leave it lying about where it could be stolen again?"

Then he fell silent and peered at the rear of the brooch for a long moment.

"Here, Watson – what do you make of this?"

He passed it back to me and pointed to the rear in the vicinity of the pin. I looked at it.

"It seems discoloured here and here," I observed, "but less so in the centre."

"Precisely."

I shrugged. "Precisely what? It probably rubbed against the cloth of the woman's dress as she wore it, buffing it up a little."

"Perhaps, but perhaps not. Perhaps, instead, there was something else here. See? The shape of the shinier area is rectangular and the corners are where the pin is mounted."

I considered his words. "You're suggesting . . . what? That a piece of paper were held in place on the back of this brooch? Something like a poor-man's locket?"

"A piece of paper, yes, but not for any sentimental reason. Rather, I believe for concealment."

I gave a snap of my fingers. "I see! You believe that they concealed a note of some importance to themselves beneath the pin of the brooch and, after it was stolen, needed it back for whatever purpose. But why not just take the note and leave the brooch? And why did Stevens say nothing about it? Or was the note lost before the theft?"

Holmes pocketed the brooch and said, "I shall answer your questions in the reverse of their asking. The note was almost certainly not lost, for the thief looked at the brooch and was satisfied. Had the note been missing, he would have expressed some dismay, and likely questioned Stevens or Scanlan over it.

"No, the note was there and it was retrieved. As for why Stevens said nothing of it, I would guess he never noticed it. The hallmark was near the edge and he was doubtless more interest in the image upon its front than its reverse. Oh, he probably glanced at the pin, but I doubt he really observed the piece. In the normal course of daily life, most people are utterly unobservant.

"And as to your initial question, why did they not abandon the brooch? Well, most likely it was no more than habit, but it is possible they sought to distract attention from their real intentions by not offering the brooch up as a clue. Or it may have been as prosaic as them intending to return it to the woman who had worn it."

I nodded. It made sense. Then, I said, "Wait a minute – the note might still be here . . . ."

"I believe it is. As we have stood here talking, I have been casting my gaze about and I do believe that in the grate of the fire there is the remnant of a piece of paper, if you would be so good as to fetch it out."

I did so. The fire had been dead for some time and I accomplished the task with no more harm than some soot stains to my fingers. I looked at the paper: Half of it had been burnt away, but half remained with the words *Rowland and Sons* upon it, and the very top of some further ink markings.

"Clearly they wanted to destroy it," I said as I passed it to Holmes.

He nodded. "Doubtless whatever was written upon it was incriminatory."

"Well, it refers to a business, and I think those other markings might be the tops of numerals. Not an address, I think."

Holmes barked a laugh. "Well done. I do believe you've cracked it."

"I have?" I asked, a little startled.

"Yes, you have. I'll explain on the way."

"On the way?"

"Yes, we must return this box to Stevens, and then we must fetch Lestrade and lay a trap." Turning very serious, he said, "I'm sorry, but I do believe you shall not be having the convivial Christmas that you envisioned . . . ."

Stevens had been delighted to receive the brooch, but the scene I'd expected to form the conclusion of my tale was merely a prelude to its final act.

Instead, events reached an end with Holmes and me crouching behind a desk at Rowland and Sons, a reputable paper merchants, in the early hours of Christmas morning with our coats tightly pulled about us against the chill.

I caught the sound of a door being forced.

"Holmes," I whispered. "I don't think that was my teeth chattering."

I saw him nod in the faint glow of the snow-reflected moonlight.

An orange light began to bleed in about the edges of the office door – a lantern.

Once more, the sound of wood being forced, and the door swung open.

Two figures entered – doubtless the men who had assaulted Stevens and stolen the brooch.

The one holding the lantern directed the other to a large metal safe mounted in the wall at the far end of the room. He crossed to it and began to turn the tumbler.

Holmes and I rose as one, pistols in our hands.

"Stop right there," Holmes said.

The men spun about. The hand of one went for his pocket.

"Please, don't," said I. "I'll have no trouble hitting you from here. Draw it out very slowly and lay it on the desk over there."

He did as I commanded and laid a small derringer pistol down.

"Inspector!" Homes cried and, a moment later, Lestrade and his men entered the room and proceeded to take the villains into custody.

"You got her?" Holmes asked.

"Indeed," said Lestrade. "As you suspected, the business had taken on a young lady as a maid recently, only for her to give notice a few days before their closing for the Christmas break. We found her at the address you supplied, Mr. Holmes. Foolishly, she'd given the business her real name and answered to it when we arrested her. She'll sing, sure enough."

I couldn't help but laugh, but Holmes said, "She doubtless imagined that no one would ever consider a lowly maid of all work to be connected to such a cunning plan. Had it not been for Mr. Stevens reporting the theft of his brooch, probably nobody would have."

"Take them away," said Lestrade and his men hauled the two criminals off.

"So," I asked Holmes, "they sent the girl in to observe the office and discover the combination for the safe, which she wrote down and concealed upon her person beneath the pin of the brooch?"

"Correct."

He walked over to the safe and patted it, admiring its craftsmanship.

"No one could break into this without the use of dynamite – not unless they possessed the correct number."

He shook his head. "So it was assumed that money stored here could be left in safety for a few days without risk. Except the thieves' accomplice had procured for them the number. Had anyone become suspicious for any reason, they never would have found it. Who would think to look beneath a brooch pin? All they had to do was wait a few days for the business to shut over the Christmas feast and stroll in and rob it. An excellent plan."

"But, Powell stole the brooch, and their plan fell apart . . . ."

"Exactly – a fact for which the owners of Rowland and Sons will surely be most grateful."

"And what of that brooch?" Lestrade asked. "I cannot believe this girl came by it honestly."

"Who can say for certain?" said Holmes. "Most likely it was purchased from some pawnshop specifically for her allotted task. Perhaps it was stolen. Given that it has gone to a good home, I would suggest it might be best not to enquire too deeply into its history."

"Are you asking a servant of the law to turn a blind eye to a crime?"

Holmes slapped Lestrade on the shoulder. "I am asking you to show a little Yuletide spirit and absolve a decent man of any further difficulties concerning a gift to his fiancée. Having played the role of jolly old Father Christmas in returning it to him, I should hate to have to take it away again. Besides, haven't you sufficient crime to occupy you as it stands?"

Lestrade grunted. "True. Thwarting a major theft such as this *is* a coup, compared to which a potentially-pilfered brooch is small fry and easily overlooked. After all, it isn't as if it matches the description of any stolen property we have on file."

"Good man." Holmes turned to me. "Come, Watson, let us away and see if we can rouse Mrs. Hudson to provide us with a suitably-festive breakfast. I do believe we deserve it. Care to join us, Lestrade?"

The Case Of the Cursory Curse
by Andrew Bryant

It did not happen often in London. Some had never seen it happen in their lifetime. Others had missed it when it happened because it was so brief, or it melted before they even became aware of it. There would be no elephants walking on the Thames this time, but today, Christmas Eve, the cold had come and brought snow with it.

Every child was enthralled, as were a few adults, while most other adults cursed the inconvenience of it. But certainly, all children were enthralled – or so I believed. Word travelled through the city that children were sliding down Ludgate Hill on tea trays and pieces of wood, and that the slope in Greenwich Park beneath the Observatory was awash with youngsters sledding on all manner of conveyances, including the soles of their treadless worn-out shoes, as the Time Ball dropped unnoticed by them. These lively and enthusiastic children would soon enough be no more, replaced by the responsible adults they would hopefully become, but who, in the process, would lose the sheer joy of movement, the pleasure of falling, the energy generated by the cold and the companionship.

Snow can create feelings of both elation and melancholy. My mind had turned slightly to the latter as I looked out the window of our lodgings in Baker Street, so I turned to Sherlock Holmes for some conversation to alleviate the gloom, but the attempt was uncertain. He was definitely more on the melancholy side and appeared to want to remain there. Christmas with no family to visit, or having a family that cannot or will not be visited, saps the energy of the falling snow, and Holmes looked now like nothing more than a solitary man contemplating the passage of time that this weather anomaly emphasized. Nothing symbolizes the ongoing of years like an unexpected and random visit, whether it be natural or unnatural. This snowfall was like a long forgotten acquaintance showing up at one's door with past stories to tell, stories that one may not want told.

Holmes sat in his chair, concentrating on the window as if some meaning could be derived from the white swirling mass outside.

"This reminds me of Mr. Dickens," I said.

"Reality reminds you of fiction?" he replied.

I paused.

"Sometimes it can. When I stop and think about it, it happens quite often."

"Fiction should mirror reality. Not the other way around."

"So I have it backwards," I said.

"It appears so."

I smiled. Holmes didn't see it, but I smiled at his refusal to give in to sentimentality and all the fictions that sentiment engenders. I saw no harm in it, a small attentiveness to the imaginary. For some people, it was all that they had, especially at this time of year. But he would have none of it.

He was bored, not charmed, by the day. And when a knock came at the front door he leapt to his feet, ready for Mrs. Hudson's call. I turned back to the view while Holmes stepped to the landing. The front door opened.

"Is Mr. Holmes at home?" I heard a voice say.

It was a child, a girl or a young boy. Before Mrs. Hudson could answer, Holmes shouted down the stairs.

"Yes, yes. Mr. Holmes is at home. What is it, girl?"

"Someone has been found," the girl said.

"Was this someone lost?"

"I don't know."

"And yet he or she has been found."

"Seems so."

I joined Holmes at the top of the stairs.

"Send her up, Mrs. Hudson."

Mrs. Hudson showed the somewhat reluctant child up the stairs. The girl was about eight or nine years of age, her hair a warren of knots. Her toes, red from the cold, were sticking out from dilapidated shoes.

"What exactly is your message?" Holmes said.

"A man has been found dead. In Stepney."

"What man?"

"An . . . an ache-ologist."

"A man who studies aches?"

The girl laughed, her eyes bright for a moment. On the side of her head, pushing up through her hair, was a cyst the size of half a cricket ball. She saw me looking at it and tried unsuccessfully to cover it up with her hair. Her eyes deadened under my gaze.

"Why come to me?" Holmes asked.

"The Museum man put the word out."

"You mean Mr. Edward Thompson, Director of the British Museum?"

"Yes," she said, "and what else would you call a Museum that is in Britain?"

Holmes smiled slightly, and the girl brightened again.

"She has a cheek," Mrs. Hudson said.

"Yes," he replied. "And you know what that means, Mrs. Hudson?"

"Food and a stipend."

"Do you have an address for this archeologist?" Holmes said.

She gave one in Mile End Road in Stepney.

"There must be something of interest there for Mr. Thompson to be involved, and it will get us out of the house. Shall we be off?"

"If you don't mind, I'll catch up with you later. There's something I need to do here first."

"As you will," Holmes said, descending the stairs rapidly, putting on his hat and coat and going out into the winter world.

"Down to the kitchen, young lady, only you aren't one – a lady I mean," Mrs. Hudson said. They went down the stairs while I turned to fetch my medical bag.

When I entered the kitchen, the girl was already eating bread and cheese and sitting close to the hearth. Her damp clothes steamed in the warmth. The kettle was on the stove and Mrs. Hudson placed cups and saucers on the table.

I sat down next to the girl.

"My name is Doctor John Watson," I said.

She looked at me, not realizing that the normal protocol was for her to introduce herself to me.

"What's your name?" Mrs. Hudson said.

"Angelique."

"That's a beautiful name," I said.

"My mother gave it to me – or so I've been told."

"Where do you live?" I said.

She looked at me with eyes now years older than her age.

"Do you like the snow?" I asked.

"Too cold. There's no getting away from it."

I should have known better than to ask her either of those questions. Children such as her had no address, no home. They *lived* wherever there was an old mattress or a chair or a floor that was unoccupied by some other wastrel. Home was first-come first-served in whatever vacant space was available to them. And she hadn't been playing in the snow today.

"May I look at that?" I said, indicating the cyst.

She put her hand over it.

"Perhaps some cake?" Mrs. Hudson said.

The girl forgot about me when Mrs. Hudson cut a generous piece of sponge cake, jam oozing out the sides.

I took a scalpel from my bag, unnoticed by the girl.

"May I?" I said.

The girl nodded, mouth already full of cake, and I pulled the hair back from the cyst and cut an inch long incision along the bottom of it. There was a little blood, but she didn't feel it, and didn't flinch. I held a cloth up to the incision and applied pressure to the top of the bulge. The pus ran out onto the cloth. The girl didn't notice the pressure or the odour as I used my fingers to squeeze down the lump and empty it of all I could.

I wiped the incision with a clean damp cloth.

"There may still be some new accumulation of fluid, so I will need you to drain it with some force as I just did for the next few days."

She looked at me as if she didn't know what I was talking about.

"May I?" I said.

I took her hand and guided it down the cyst to show her how to drain it. She touched the side of her head, realizing now that something was missing.

"And you need to keep it clean. Do you have soap?"

She shook her head.

"Mrs. Hudson?"

"I'll cut a piece from a bar."

Angelique still had her hand on her head, feeling for the cyst.

Mrs. Hudson found a mirror and held it up in front of the girl, who turned her head this way and that. Then she started to softly cry.

"You are a very pretty girl," Mrs. Hudson said.

"Remember to drain it several times a day and wash it afterwards," I said. "And try to keep it as clean as possible. Come around here again in a few days and I'll examine it."

I got up then and put on my hat and coat to follow Holmes to Mile End Road. As I was leaving I looked into the kitchen. Angelique and Mrs. Hudson were drinking tea and chatting by the hearth, a piece of soap wrapped in a cloth on the table. Soon, Angelique's interlude would be over, her tears barely dried, and she would have to return to who and what she was. But for now, she could sit in the warmth with a china cup in her hand and be something other than what she had to be out there beyond our door.

I stepped outside, mindful of my footing, as leather-soled shoes weren't meant for this rare type of weather. I hailed a cab and we made our way through the ruts of churned-up snow already blackened in places by the ever-falling soot. Traffic was as bad as ever and, if it were possible, there seemed to be more people out than usual. Wagons laden, shoppers pushing carts, vendors with barrows, baskets overflowing with this and that. Nothing brought out the gathering instinct in mankind like a few inches of snow. Many of us citified people suddenly became country squirrels, finding every nook in which to hide our stores.

Sitting in the cab, I considered that Holmes usually found such journeys fascinating, as he was able to observe the city without actually being involved in it. He took a God's-eye view – that is, he was interested and curious but not involved. Myself, I preferred to get where I was going without a lot of spectating.

Finally we did get there. I paid the driver and went in through the front door. It was a rooming house – a shabby hotel – the flophouse home of poor bachelors and poorer spinsters and impermanent residents recently disembarked from ships flying any and all flags.

"Holmes?" I called from the bottom of the stairs.

"Top story," the shout came back down.

I made my way up through the various cooking smells of varied cultures, every floor a new culinary experience, and myself the object of curious and shy stares from doors ajar. At the top of the stairs the atmosphere changed abruptly. The aromas from below dissipated, and through the open door ahead of me came the unforgettable and unmistakable air of death.

Holmes was standing with Director Thompson near the open window, but other than that they didn't give any sign that the decomposing body on the floor beside them was in any way bothering them. At the window was a single empty chair facing out towards the city view.

"Ah, Watson," Holmes said. "Arrived at last."

"I had a surgery to perform."

"Nothing serious?"

"No, the surgery itself was very simple, but it may have profound results."

"You know Mr. Thompson, of course," Holmes said.

"A pleasure to see you again."

"And you, Doctor."

We shook hands.

"You're wondering why Mr. Thompson is here?"

"I'm sure there is an excellent reason."

"Yes, there is. Excellent, but also tragic. I'll let Mr. Thompson fill in the details."

Holmes left us and wandered about the room, minutely examining the door, floor, table-top, and chairs. He opened drawers and cupboards, occasionally saying something indecipherable to himself. The room was Spartan – bare wooden floors, plain furniture, no pictures hanging on the walls, and no other decoration of any kind.

Mr. Thompson began, "This man's name is Emlyn DeClawe – "

"The archaeologist?" I interrupted, looking at the body.

"Yes, you may have read his book on the excavations and discoveries in the Valley Of The Kings in Egypt."

"I have."

"He discovered several previously overlooked tombs and uncovered a trove of artifacts that he was in the process of shipping to us at the Museum. We are, as we speak, using the Rosetta Stone to decipher some of the hieroglyphs."

"All fascinating stuff."

"Indeed. But recently DeClawe's tone changed. His letters, which previously had been full of life and interest and almost boyish enthusiasm, became more like apologies for his actions."

"How so?"

"He began to question what he was doing and why he was doing it. He seemed to have taken on the opinion that we weren't so much excavating and researching as we were plundering and grave-robbing. He wrote to me that just because these goods end up in a museum instead of a private collection doesn't make the taking of them any less of a theft, which I thought an extraordinary statement from a man whose life was lived for nothing else than to scramble around in the desert with a pick and shovel digging these things up."

"A fit of conscience perhaps?" I said. "There are those who believe that the dead should be left undisturbed, even if they have been dead for three-thousand years in a foreign country."

"Interesting," Holmes said.

"Yes, some scholars and religious leaders do believe that it is a sacrilege – "

"Not that," he said, dragging the china chamber pot out from under the bed. He carried it over to us and held it up.

"What do you see?" he asked.

We looked inside.

"Mercifully, nothing," I said.

"Dust," he said, wiping his finger around the inside and showing us the smudge.

Holmes put the pot back where he found it, and Mr. Thompson continued.

"When he came back from Egypt this last time, he had the demeanor of a man ready to give up – to try and forget about the past, his own and that of all the subjects of his digs. He just didn't want to do it anymore. And he wouldn't stop talking about Ammit."

"Who is Ammit?"

"Who *was* Ammit? She was someone who died just before DeClawe's return home. She lived in Luxor and crossed the river every day with the men going to the dig, haranguing them all the while about the violation of their ancestors' bodies, souls, and memories. She called it an 'assault on the dead'. Some of the men believed that she was the reincarnation of the ancient Ammit – ".

"Who was?"

"The Eater of The Dead," Holmes interjected. "She devoured the souls of all sinners, thereby condemning them to eternal damnation."

"Quite right," Mr. Thompson went on. "Some of the men believed that her omens and exhortations had the ability to sicken and kill diggers at the site, and she had some success in keeping men away. Never more so than when one of them was injured or taken ill after being cursed by her. All coincidence of course."

"Or suggestion," I said. "Some of the worst maladies known to man have their genesis in a mere suggestion that is amplified in a superstitious and compliant mind until it becomes both a fantastic obsession and a seeming fact."

"You speak not just of physical ills," Holmes offered, while removing and stacking all the drawers from the chest of drawers.

"Empty," he added.

"So this Ammit's appeal to both the fears and the conscience of the diggers also affected DeClawe?"

"So it would seem. His letters and shipments became more erratic. Diggers were harder the find, the whole excavation slowed to a crawl until finally it ceased completely and there were no more letters and no more shipments. We requested DeClawe's return to London, and when he eventually came, he took up residence here."

"You spoke to him when he returned?" I asked.

"Yes, the very day that he docked. I asked him about the decline in artifacts and reports, and that was when he told me about Ammit's interference and harassment, although he called it her 'education and her illumination'."

"He had been influenced by her admonitions?"

"More than influenced. I would say somewhat controlled. He no longer believed in his right – *our* right – to pursue archaeological digs in foreign countries. He called them 'irreligious', even though the religion was pagan. He said that it was an attack on the past. He told me that he no longer believed in our mission and that we should all just let the past remain where it lies. I countered by reminding him that if we didn't recover these treasures, then private collectors would loot the entire country and no one would ever see or learn anything about the past. But he wasn't convinced, and remained adamant that he, and we, were morally and ethically in the wrong."

"These are Spartan conditions for a man of his achievements."

"He was used to sleeping in cots and in tents or on the ground in caves in all manner of weather and conditions. Personal and physical comfort were meaningless to him."

"What about books?" Holmes asked.

"Books?"

"Yes, books. Spartan attitudes aside, and understanding that stoicism and a degree of mania are necessities for his profession, what about the books?"

"There are no books," Mr. Thompson said.

"Why are there no books?"

"No one knows but him," Mr. Thompson replied, motioning to the body.

"Perhaps no one knows," Holmes replied, "but others can surmise."

"When he returned, his mental state was one of acute melancholy laced with regret?" I said.

"Yes, Doctor. Melancholy. Regret. And resignation, as if a long-held belief had been proven wrong and there was no way of ever again believing that it was right."

"Ammit's mission had been accomplished."

"So it would seem. DeClawe insisted to me that the Rosetta Stone be returned to Egypt, and that the Elgin Marbles be returned to Greece, and that the recent acquisition of Benin Bronzes be returned to Africa. Such was the extent of his conversion."

"Do you suspect that he might have been killed by those wanting the return of these artifacts to their homelands?" I asked.

"Not killed," Holmes said. "Died, as we all will one day. But our concern here today is to determine if the death was by criminal action, death by misadventure, death by accident, or death by personal intent."

"And which is it?" Mr. Thompson asked.

"Doctor Watson will have that answer shortly," Holmes replied, peering into the wardrobe.

"DeClawe also mentioned a curse," Mr. Thompson said.

"A curse?"

"Yes, and not just the usual curse that is directed at anyone who opens a tomb. This curse was directed solely at DeClawe, although it was inconclusive as he described it to me."

"In what way?"

"It seems that Ammit went to the dock on the day DeClawe sailed for home. She confronted him at the quayside and assailed him again for his desecration of her country. She concluded her verbal assault on him with the words 'May you rot in . . . .' And then she herself died, right there on the dock – collapsed, and was lifeless in a moment."

"Heart attack most likely," I said. "But it could also have been an aneurysm if it was that sudden."

"Repeat the curse if you would, Mr. Thompson," Holmes asked.

"'May you rot in – '"

"'In'?" I said.

"If you believe in such things, an unfinished curse is worse than a finished one. You would have no idea what to expect. I don't have even the slightest belief in the reality of curses, but as you gentlemen were discussing earlier, a susceptible mind may fall victim to such a superstitious influence."

"Usually it would be 'May you rot in Hell'," I said.

"Usually," Holmes replied, "but I believe from the ferocity of Ammit's battering as described by our friend here, that this curse would have been something far more infernal and soul destroying. A simple *Hell* doesn't seem enough for her."

"What then?" I asked.

"It may come to light later on, but at least now we know the how and the why of DeClawe's death."

"We do?" Mr. Thompson said.

"Yes, we do. But please carry on with your story."

"When I visited him here," Mr. Thompson continued, "his mind was racing. He talked about the digs and the artifacts, and went on about how would we like it if a group of Egyptian archaeologists arrived in England, smashed up the floor of the Chapel of St. Peter-ad-Vincula, and hauled away Anne Boleyn's bones to an Egyptian museum . . . ."

"A fair point," Holmes interjected.

"He raved about Ammit and whether or not she was a blood descendant of The Divine Bride of antiquity, and whether or not she had the gift of prophecy."

"To which you said – ?"

"I replied that the gift of prophecy is only acquired through the study and understanding of the past. That is, we always repeat our history and so need only to know the past in order to foretell the future."

"Agreed!" Holmes said, pulling all the covers from the bed and holding the pillowcase up to the window.

"And on what terms did you leave DeClawe?" I asked.

"Civil, if a little estranged due to our newly found differences of opinion on the reasons and justifications for archaeology. But I believe we parted with mutual respect, if not mutual understanding."

"And when was that?"

"About three weeks ago."

"And when did you last see him?"

"That was the last time. I sent him a few messages, but there was no response. I believed he wanted to be alone with his thoughts, so I didn't press myself upon him, although I wish now that I had. And then this morning I came around to visit and found him dead."

Holmes was on his knees beside the body, going through the pockets of DeClawe's jacket. He withdrew his fist from a side pocket and let a drizzle of sand slide out from his clenched fingers.

"Still wearing the clothes he had on when he left Egypt."

"My first thought was to call you, Holmes," Mr. Thompson said. "Even before the police. As he appeared in good health, other than his agitated mind when I saw him last, his death seemed mysterious to me."

"The reason for it has mystery at its heart, but the cause of it is very banal."

"I sent an urchin around to notify you."

"Angelique," I said.

"Angelique?"

"The urchin's name is Angelique."

"One of your *gang*?"

"I believe she is now, yes," replied Holmes.

"The police will need to be called," I said.

"Did he have any family?" Holmes asked.

"None that was ever mentioned. He seemed to appear fully formed as a man with only three aspects of purpose: To find, to dig, to discover. I don't believe he had any life other than that."

"He came home with nothing more than the clothes on his back."

"So it would seem."

"No, so it *is*, Mr. Thompson."

"Why would he come home with nothing?"

"Because he didn't need anything. When one comes home to die, one doesn't require anything."

"To die of what?" Mr. Thompson said.

"Would you mind examining the body, Watson?" Holmes said. "You're obviously the one most qualified among us to determine the cause of death."

I knelt down and felt the limbs through the clothes. They were thin, wasted. Knees and elbows distinct, seeming larger than they really were because of the lack of tissue surrounding them. I rolled up his sleeves and opened his shirt front. *Rigor mortis* had passed, and I determined that he had been dead only a day or so, but that he began to physically deteriorate much earlier. There was no blood loss, no signs of violence, no indication of murder.

"Poison?" Mr. Thompson offered. "Heart attack?"

"I can't rule those out, as there are no signs of trauma on the body."

"Not on the body," said Holmes, "but *in* the body."

"*In* the body?"
"More precisely, in the *mind*."
"He was killed by his own mind?"
"He chose to be killed by his own mind."
"Chose?"
"He died in this room of his own free will – or as free a will as a guilty man's conscience can muster."
"A guilty man?"
"DeClawe spent his life digging, excavating, removing artifacts and treasures, emptying graves. When Ammit made it clear to him, and he finally understood, that what he was doing was an affront to the old Gods and an affront to some present sensibilities, and that he was more plunderer – more grave robber – than he was anything else, he understood that what he was doing to someone else's ancestors was something that he, and us, wouldn't tolerate if we were on the receiving end of it. And after a lifetime of doing just that, he finally realized what had previously been unthinkable: He realized that desecration isn't an intellectual act, not a hobby or a pastime. He realized that the bones and relics of others history aren't ours to take and to display. Once the hypocrisy of his life's work had been revealed to him, he came home to end his life here."
"But how did he end it?" Mr. Thompson asked.
"His flesh is shrunken on the bones, Watson?"
"Yes, and although I never met the man in life and am not familiar with his natural build, I would say, from the bone structure and his ability to endure the hardship and labour of his profession, that he was most likely a robust man."
"Yes," Mr. Thompson said. "I would describe him as being of above-average build."
"Not much left in mind or body now," Holmes said.
"My conclusions as a doctor are that DeClawe died of both starvation and dehydration. The desiccated state of the body suggests that he didn't eat or drink for weeks, possibly not even on the voyage home."
"And my conclusions as a detective are that there is no cutlery or dishes in this room. No crumbs on the floor or on the table. The chamber pot hasn't been used. There are no glasses or cups. The drawers are all empty, and, there are no suitcases. No change of clothes. And, there are no books. Inquisitive minds are always surrounded by books. We are, are we not, Watson?"
"Of course."
"Mr. Thompson, are you not in constant danger of being the victim of an avalanche of books?"
"You have been in my office, Holmes. You know there are leaning

towers of them everywhere."

"And yet this man – " He pointed to the body. " – this man hadn't one book in his possession. The reason for his death is obvious on that one point alone."

"Suicide by self-neglect," I offered.

"DeClawe came home from Egypt suffering under the threatening delusion of an unfinished curse cast upon him by the supposed reincarnation of an avenging goddess. The curse, along with the guilt that Ammit had planted in his mind, suppurated to the point where he did not bathe, he did not change his clothes, did not eat, did not drink, did not read. He sat in the chair and slept in the chair, there was no dust on the seat. There are no hairs on the pillow and the bed was unused. He stayed in this room, waiting for the curse to be fulfilled, convinced as he was that he deserved whatever fate the venerable Deities had in store for him."

"A sad end for such a diligent and curious man," Mr. Thompson said.

"Indeed, but not inappropriate," I said. "Every time DeClawe opened a tomb, he violated ancient curses. Every artifact he shipped back here was a violation of the sanctity of the grave. Every shovel of sand he dug was a trespass on someone else's sacred ground."

"And here he ends up. A man once surrounded by treasures, lying here with nothing."

"All deaths are lonely," Holmes said. "But this one more so than most."

He and I moved towards the door.

"If you'll be so good as to send the police around," Mr. Thompson said, "I'll stay here with him until they arrive."

"Of course. And I will send them a report, at my convenience, with the resolution of the case."

"Thank you, Holmes. And you too, Doctor Watson."

"I wish Christmas greetings were in order," I responded, "but unfortunately they are not."

"Sometimes the season is grim."

We went down the stairs and out into the street. The snow falling heavier now, beautiful and aggravating at the same time.

"Do you want to walk?" I asked.

"Do you?"

"Yes. After being in that room with poor DeClawe, a breath of cold air would be a blessing."

"Then walk it is."

We bent our heads into the weather and trudged towards Baker Street.

"Holmes?"

"What is it?"

"We found the cause of death and the reason for it, but what of the curse?"

"What of it?"

"We'll never know what Ammit's eternal intentions were for DeClawe."

"We already know."

"We do?"

"'May you rot in . . . .'" Holmes said.

"'May you rot in . . . '?" I asked.

He gave me a sideways look.

"'May you rot in Stepney.'"

The St. Giles Child Murders
by Tim Gambrell

If there was any hope that the Queen's Diamond Jubilee year would end quietly for Sherlock Holmes and me, it was dashed on Thursday, December 23rd. I was carefully decorating the chimney breast in our rooms at 221b Baker Street when Inspector Lestrade arrived. Holmes greeted him with a brandy, while I applied the last few sprigs of holly in an attempt to bring some seasonal cheer to the place.

"A Merry Christmas, Inspector," I said, finally able to raise my glass in salute.

"I wish that it were, Doctor Watson," he replied.

Holmes spoke as I swallowed. "I take it the St. Giles situation is hanging heavy on you."

Lestrade nodded. "You've seen the newspapers?"

Holmes replied that he had. I was almost completely at a loss. I'd clearly missed something of the utmost importance. Holmes frowned at me.

"Did you not see the late edition, yesterday, bringing the total up to three?"

"Three? Three what?"

"Child murders in the parish of St. Giles," Holmes informed me. "All since Sunday last, the nineteenth."

I admitted I'd been too busy and hadn't seen a newspaper these last few days. "Three children murdered over four days?" I gasped. "'Pon the soul."

"Three days," Lestrade corrected. "Thankfully there haven't been any reported today."

We three then sat, forming a triangle around the fireplace. Holmes indicated that Lestrade should tell the tale. The inspector took a deep breath. His shoulder shuddered as he exhaled. I could see this was playing heavily upon his mind, despite his apparent stoicism.

"The children were of varying ages and from all kinds of backgrounds," he began. "They all died in a brutal and violent manner. All after dark, and not with any readily apparent motive that we've found."

"For some, simply the act of murder is reason enough," said Holmes, darkly, through steepled fingers.

"Families have been devastated."

Holmes leaned forward, his brow furrowed. "There has to be *something* connecting them all – other than them all living in the parish of St. Giles, that is."

"Having just visited the poor family of the last, I don't mind admitting it's left me somewhat at my wit's end," said Lestrade. "Some people have precious little joy in their lives. And when that's brutally taken away from them – and at Christmas, too – well, I had to stop one woman throwing herself on a kitchen knife. I know my good lady would have been of a similar mind should anything have happened to our lot when they were younger."

I was mightily moved by Lestrade's distress. It wasn't often one got to see how much the job affected him, and what hurts he carried inside.

Holmes stood and swiftly moved to the window. He gestured to someone at street level. It wasn't long before half-a-dozen pairs of feet came pummelling up the stairs, much to Mrs. Hudson's distress, and Holmes's Baker Street Irregulars lined up before us.

"I have a very particular task for you lot today," Holmes told them. "And there's half-a-crown each, if you're successful."

Their eyes glistened as Holmes held up a sample coin.

"Inspector Lestrade, do you recall the names of the victims?"

"I do indeed," he answered.

"Then, please, relate them to my Irregulars, here."

I poured the inspector another brandy. I knew he would be in need of it after such a gruelling task. He listed off the children's names and their ages. One was little more than a toddler, no doubt sent out by busy parents to cling to the hems and shirt tails of older children.

At the end of Lestrade's morbid list, I felt a tightening in my chest.

Holmes himself was predictably unaffected by any strong emotions. "I want you to uncover what you can about the children in question, and then report back to me as usual. Understood?"

"Yes, Mr. Holmes," said the tallest, whose name I could never remember. The Irregulars glanced amongst themselves. "Easiest half-a-crown each we've ever earned. We knew each one. We last saw them all on Sunday afternoon, at the Church of St. Giles in the Fields."

"Intriguing," said Holmes. "And what were you lot doing there?"

"We goes to church regular, Mr. Holmes. You knows that." The eldest pursed his lips. "Warm and dry in there."

"Yes, I'm sure," Holmes replied. "And was that why you were also there in the afternoon on Sunday?"

"We was all there for the same reason. We went to see someone who claimed he was Father Christmas."

I was curious at their cynicism, which belied their youth.

"All done up in green, he were, with a big bushy beard. Gave out fruit and sweet things to all the children. Said it was a special treat for the parish – for Christmas, like. We did all right, didn't us?"

There was a rumble of assent from the ranks.

"Course, there was two lots. One for the wealthy, and then the leftovers was given to us poorer folk."

Another spoke up. "We had to go up and speak to him, tell him what our lives was like, and what we wanted most in the world. Then we got given a gift."

"He didn't like us," said the first. "Cos we spends a lot of time roughing it."

"And you say all those other children were there, too?"

"That's right, Mr. Holmes. Two was poor like us. But that first lad, he must have had money, cos he was in with the first lot. Haven't seen any of them since. Reckon we now know why."

"Indeed. Thank you," said Holmes, who flipped a half-crown coin to each of the Irregulars in turn. "I am, after all, a man of my word. Here is your reward. And a merry Christmas to you, every one."

With a salute, they turned and left.

Holmes looked at Lestrade and me.

"I think, gentlemen, we have a place to start our investigation."

The day was cold and grey, but thankfully not wet. A short cab ride brought us to the rather splendid and historic Church of St. Giles in the Fields. Lestrade wasn't convinced this was a good idea. It was a church, after all. And Christmas. But Holmes would not be diverted. A church warden intercepted Holmes as the first of us to enter.

"Compliments of the Season to you, my good man," said Holmes.

"And to you three gentlemen, too. What can I do for you this day?"

"I was hoping to speak with the rector."

"Alas, gentlemen, the rector is out amongst the parish today. You may have heard of the tragedies which have recently befallen some of his flock. He has gone to offer solace to those most in need, and to remind them to take comfort in the Word of God."

"It was foolish of me to have expected anything else. I heard you had a very successful gathering with a Father Christmas for the local children at the weekend."

The warden brought his hands together in a clap of joy. "Indeed, sir, indeed! And, oh, how the children loved it, too! There were more than enough treats to go around, thanks to the munificence of some of our wealthier parishioners. This Jubilee year has been bountiful at times, indeed."

Holmes leaned in conspiratorially. "I had hoped to be able to see your Father Christmas myself."

"It is really for the children, sir," the warden replied, with a hint of admonishment.

Lestrade glanced at me and rolled his eyes.

"You mistake my meaning, sir," Holmes replied. "I wished to speak with him regarding another possible engagement."

The warden grinned. "Then, sir, you are in luck." He gestured to a printed poster on the shadowy wall to one side. "Father Christmas will be back here tomorrow, Christmas Eve, to help administer warmth and special aid to the poorer families of the parish, and also give comfort to our beggars. For sure, 'tis bitter cold on the streets this time of year."

"A noble endeavour, indeed. We shall return tomorrow," Holmes advised. He turned and led Lestrade and me away with a grand gesture towards Charing Cross Road. "I assume you have statements from all the next of kin regarding these child murders, Lestrade?" he asked, confidentially, when we were a suitable distance away from the church.

Lestrade gave a subtle nod. "Naturally, Mr. Holmes."

"I'd like to read them over, if I may."

Without waiting for a response, Holmes reached out and hailed a passing cab.

The statements made for particularly mournful reading. The same sentiments ran through all of them, no matter the upbringing: That of families torn apart by grief. Sweet children, full of life and hopes for the future – a future denied them by the actions of some devilish fiend.

Appended to each statement was a description of the corpse: How and where it was found, and in what condition. On these, Holmes sought my views. They were a mixture of slit throats and cranial haemorrhaging. The first of them occurred on Monday evening.

Lestrade returned to his office to check how we were doing.

"Any beggars, Inspector?" Holmes said. "Street-sleepers, drunkards? Any of those also reported dead in the St. Giles area at these times?"

"Probably," Lestrade replied with a shrug. "There's always something going on with that lot. Usually they do for each other."

"Can you check for me please?"

Lestrade turned to the constable who had followed him in and despatched him to investigate.

"You think there'll be further murders, linked to these?"

Holmes looked at him with hooded eyes. "I think it's worth checking, at least."

We continued to cross-reference the statements and the descriptions of the victims themselves. I found I could offer Holmes little in the way of insight, other than rather banal comments on how gruesomely violent each death appeared to have been.

The constable returned in due course with several sheets of paper. These were handed to Lestrade, who reviewed them first before passing them over to Holmes.

"It seems you may have been correct in your assumptions, Mr. Holmes," said Lestrade – a common enough sentiment between the two, it must be said.

Holmes took the papers and cast his eyes quickly over them. He cross-referenced with the papers on Lestrade's desk from time to time.

"I think we can discount the first two," he said after a brief consideration. "There is sufficient doubt cast by the relative times and locations, for a start. But the method of death is certainly more in line with the drunken in-fighting that categorises such occurrences. However, I believe there are serious grounds for considering the other two to be the work of the same hand – or hands – as the poor children."

Holmes passed the papers to me, and I took a look through them. I had to agree with his suggestion. One slit throat with no other obvious signs of struggle – aside from the usual physical attributions of a life on the streets. The other was the same, except he was stabbed through the heart. The empty bottles amongst which he was found suggested he'd been in a state of advanced inebriation when death came. Both male, possibly around middle age. Both were apparently alone at the time of the attack.

"As far as we can tell," said Lestrade, adding a qualifying statement to the end of the report. He shook his head. "Such indiscriminate death."

"Not indiscriminate, Inspector," Holmes corrected him. "That is what we're meant to think. My belief is that this is all very much pre-meditated. Our killer is selecting his victims very precisely. And they are all vulnerable in some way."

"Will he strike again, do you think?"

"Undoubtedly."

"But how are we going to catch him? We don't have the manpower to patrol every street all the time."

"Tomorrow, Inspector, will be key. We must all keep a close look out when we're at St. Giles in the Fields. If we are lucky, we may snare our man then and there."

"At the church? You want me to bring some constables along?"

"No, no. The three of us can operate perfectly effectively on our own. It is my fear that some disgraceful villain may be using the lure of Father

Christmas for his or her own wicked ends. I doubt that he or she will pass up on another chance tomorrow."

The following day was Christmas Eve. Holmes headed out early, telling me he had some gifts to purchase. He said he'd meet Lestrade and me at the church later. He'd never been one to enter wholeheartedly into the Christmas spirit while I'd known him. Small gifts, no more than thoughtful gestures, had passed between us in previous years, but I'd never known him to venture out specifically to purchase Christmas gifts before. However, if the mood had taken him, I wasn't going to stand in his way.

I met with Inspector Lestrade on the corner of Shaftesbury Avenue at the agreed-upon hour. The area was quite mad with traffic and shoppers, and I understood from some overheard comments that an additional Christmas matinee was being performed in most theatres. We waited for Holmes for some time, but he didn't show up. The day was less clement than our previous visit, with a persistent light rain that slowly soaked us. Aware that we had a task to perform, and eager to be somewhere more sheltered, we headed to the church hall. We were greeted at the doors by a man of whom I was aware but had never met until now: The rector, Doctor Henry Richards.

"Good afternoon, gentlemen," the rector said, rubbing his palms together against the cold. "Whom do I have the pleasure of addressing?"

"Doctor Watson at your service, sir."

"A notable name, indeed." He raised his brows as he looked at Inspector Lestrade. "But this is not Sherlock Holmes, surely?"

"We are due to meet with him," I advised, "but he has yet to arrive."

Lestrade cleared his throat and introduced himself. "Inspector Lestrade, Scotland Yard."

"Ah, yes." The rector gave a nod. "We met briefly before. You arrived to speak to the mother of poor Maisie Saunders as I was leaving. Have you found the devil behind these awful murders?"

"Not yet, Rector – " the inspector began.

"Well, I hope you haven't come to arrest anyone here. This is God's house, and we aren't harbouring any criminals."

Lestrade held up his palms in a placating manner. "The investigation is ongoing, Rector. That's all I can say."

The rector looked deeply troubled. "Gentlemen, please. It is Christmas, after all. The season of good will to all men. The deaths have hit our community hard. We are in mourning. This event today was conceived to offer some relief to the poor and needy, of which we have more than our fair share. I fear your presence here may cause more grief and concern than good."

"You mistake our purpose," I said on a whim. "We are here to offer something back to the community. To help."

I felt Lestrade's gaze, but I remained focussed on the rector, who was awash with relief. He took our hands in his.

"My dear sirs! Thank you! Thank you! Please, do come in. There is plenty to do – serving. Assisting."

He led us inside and we removed our sodden hats, although we found it prudent to keep our coats on, as the church hall wasn't overly warm.

I immediately looked around for Holmes, but it was obvious at a glance that he wasn't there. I hoped that he was all right.

There was a food stall with a large vat of wholesome-smelling stew, a pile of fresh loaves, and an area laden with assorted bowls, plates, cups, and spoons. There were also large pots of hot tea and coffee. Adjacent to the refreshments was a stall where miscellaneous items of old clothing and footwear were piled high. These had, presumably, been given by the parish for those in need. As far as I could see, they were all long past their best, and had probably been donated to such events several times already.

Then there was an area of seating, nearest to the somewhat ineffectual fireplace. Finally, on a single chair draped in green cloth, next to the decorated Christmas tree, sat Father Christmas himself. Clad in sumptuous green, with snowy-white trim and long black boots. He had a big bushy beard, as was the tradition, and several children were gathered around him, enjoying his laughter and attention.

Lestrade drew me to one side.

"Thank you for offering my services, Dr. Watson."

I smiled at his mild annoyance. "We are in, are we not?"

"Where's Mr. Holmes?"

"Never mind," I replied. "We have our own eyes and ears. Let's see what we can spot. Like that, for example."

There were three parishioners in the seating area, one gentleman and two ladies. I'd been endeavouring to discern if they were visitors, or there to help provide comfort to others. My answer came at that exact moment. They were joined by a beggarly-looking fellow, crooked and with a sallow complexion. The gentleman, in a good suit and with fine whiskers, immediately began to berate the poor man.

"Who are you?"

The beggar must have muttered a response because the gentleman continued.

"Speak up, fellow! A what? A beggar? Where do you live?"

"Out on St. Giles High Street, and please you, sir."

"No, it doesn't please me. Are you skilled?"

The beggar didn't answer, merely doubled over further with a hacking cough. The gentleman carried on regardless.

"How are you going to find employment with that attitude? Here you are, expecting handouts. I'll tell you what I expect: To see you still here at the end, offering to help clear up, that's what."

His lack of empathy was deeply unpleasant. I moved forward to intervene, but a hand restrained me. It was the rector. He shook his head at me.

"But – ?"

"Please, Dr. Watson. That is Horatio Williford-Smythe. He is a wealthy industrialist and a generous donor to our church. He is only trying to help."

"He goes about it in a most uncaring, uncharitable fashion, if you ask me."

"And these drains on society!" The industrialist gestured to a number of poor children, now crying nearby. "Better off in the workhouse than cluttering up the streets, but no doubt they're too lazy. Them and their gin-sodden parents." The lady parishioners nodded at the outburst but looked uncomfortable.

I would not see such sentiments go unchallenged, despite what the rector wished, but the situation was calmed by the intervention of the Father Christmas. He rose from his chair and gently offered treats and comforts to the children before checking on the beggar.

I looked at the rector, who nodded at me and smiled. He then guided me to the food stall, and soon I was dishing out stew for a long queue of poor people of all ages. It gave me a surprising sense of fulfilment, I must say. I cast occasional glances over to the heartless industrialist. After speaking with the beggar and the children, Father Christmas then took Williford-Smythe to one side and spoke with him, confidentially. Williford-Smythe *harrumphed* loudly a few times, then seated himself again.

Once the queue had died down, I took it upon myself to prepare a bowl of the stew and a hunk of bread which I carried across to the poor seated beggar. He gestured his appreciation by raising his hand, being unable to lift his neck owing to the crookedness of his spine.

I heard Williford-Smythe muttering about mollycoddling the fellow, and how he'd never better himself.

"Kindness doesn't cost anything, sir," I told him, keeping my tone low and calm.

"Oh, doesn't it, *sir*?" he tartly replied. "Well, it cost me a damn sight more than nothing to lay all this on." He gave an expansive gesture and I found myself immediately being shepherded away by the rector.

As the afternoon wore on, Lestrade and I continued with our efforts. I helped with the food, Lestrade with tea and coffee. I kept a close watch on Williford-Smythe. He spent the whole time scowling his disapproval of the poor and needy, while opposite him Father Christmas took the time to speak to all comers and offer them some seasonal comfort.

At three o'clock, the rector gave a sermon, which was followed by a carol service, accompanied by a piano. I was pleased to see that everyone stayed for the duration. The whole afternoon wound up by half-past-four. Holmes hadn't shown up at all, much to my disappointment. This was compounded by my subsequent realisation that I had focussed almost the entire time there on Horatio Williford-Smythe, rather than looking around for potential suspects as Holmes had asked us to do. I was almost beside myself with annoyance. Lestrade had done no better. The objectionable industrialist, with his forthright attitude, was surely too prominent a figure to be a suspect for such crimes.

As we began clearing away the remains of the food – of which there was little – the beggarly fellow who first attracted my attention came over and offered to help. I smiled at him genially and thanked him for his kindness. Then I sent him away. No doubt he had a hard enough few days ahead of him as it was, without the inconvenience of helping us clear the church hall. As he left, I met Williford-Smythe's steely gaze.

In due course, the rector came over to Lestrade and me. He thanked us profusely for our assistance and said the parishioners would finish what remained to be done. I was grateful for this, I'll admit. I caught Williford-Smythe's eye again as Lestrade as I left, and made sure the industrialist could hear as I said that Scotland Yard would be waiting for our report. It was perhaps a little uncharitable of me, but I took a great deal of pleasure in the aghast look on his face as we walked out.

"That was a waste of time," grumbled Lestrade as we hailed the first cab we saw.

"We may not have progressed the investigation," I told him, "but I should hope your heart feels a little warmer after bringing some joy and relief to those in need, Inspector."

"You shame me, Dr. Watson," he replied. "Now I'll bid you a Merry Christmas." And with that, he jumped into the cab and headed off to Scotland Yard.

The rain had stopped, but having been on my feet all afternoon, I didn't fancy the walk back to Baker Street, so I hailed a cab myself on Denmark Street. I arrived to find Sherlock Holmes waiting for me.

"My dear Watson," he gushed. "Please accept my sincerest apologies. I was unfortunately waylaid, although the diversion was worth it." He leaned in confidentially. "I have found Mrs. Hudson the *perfect* gift."

"Really?" I said, somewhat wrong-footed by this behaviour.

"Now, come, tell me of your excursion."

I took a seat and a large brandy to fend off any chill from the earlier rain. Then I told him of our strange afternoon. My observations of Horatio Williford-Smythe, the crooked beggar, and the Father Christmas. Further, I told him how disappointed I felt with myself for being distracted and not spreading my attentions across the whole congregation more thoroughly.

Holmes brushed aside my self-chastisement. "I think you and Lestrade have done a wonderful job. You have presented me with two potential leads."

"Two?" I was shocked.

"My suspicions have been aroused by both Horatio Williford-Smythe and the beggar."

"The beggar? Bless my soul! How you derive any wicked intent from him, I've no idea."

"Did you note whereabouts the beggar sleeps?"

I replayed the conversation with Horatio Williford-Smythe in my mind. "Out on St. Giles High Street was the best I could glean."

"Then that's our task for after dinner. I want you to head back to St. Giles High Street and spy on the beggar. I, meanwhile, shall be paying a visit to Horatio Williford-Smythe."

I wasn't entirely enamoured of this idea. I had been hoping for a warm, quiet Christmas Eve, not loitering around London's less-salubrious areas. I said as much.

"I shall join you immediately after speaking with Williford-Smythe," he replied. "And what could possibly be better for Christmas morning than to have this dreadful case all sewn up?"

I could hardly argue – the names of the murdered children echoing through my head saw to that. So we proceeded to dinner before once again heading our separate ways into the London night.

The thick night air of London in midwinter isn't conducive to loitering. I alighted from my cab on Charing Cross Road and proceeded to walk the length of St. Giles High Street through to Shaftesbury Avenue and then back, on each side of the street. The electric streetlamps struggled against the cloying, smoky evening fog, but really they offered no relief except to light their own poles. There were still a surprising number of people around, which made my task more difficult. Some were revellers who had enjoyed a little too much of the season that day. Some were workers on their way home. There was a general genial attitude, though, with the Christmas spirit showing through. I offered the Compliments of the Season to all who passed, and in every instance it was reciprocated.

I spotted a constable that I knew patrolling the streets. I made myself known to him and surreptitiously advised him as to my purpose. He tapped the side of his ruddy nose and walked on with a nod. His route took him some distance around, so I couldn't rely on his being on hand should I see anything. Although Holmes had said he would join me, we hadn't agreed on a time. I knew it was best to press on and, if he joined me, that would be a bonus. By around nine o'clock, I realised I would have to start peering into the dark alleys and doorways if I was to locate the beggar. If, indeed, he was there at all.

I leaned into the nearest alleyway, between two shop fronts, and struck a match. This was ostensibly to light a cigarette, but the brief glow allowed me to see enough to know the alleyway was empty, save for the scurrying of a few rats. I took a long draw and realised I would have to smoke myself sick if I was going to perform the same trick each time.

And suddenly, there he was: The crooked beggar. I'd know his gait anywhere. He was across the street, on the other side of the road. He passed under a streetlamp and became briefly lost to me until he was caught again by the lantern of a passing carriage full of celebrants. The beggar was looking my way and I quickly backed into a shaded shop doorway. I continued to watch him as he slowly progressed further along the road. At his speed, my eyes were able to follow him even through the darker patches of the street. But several times he paused and looked across to my place of concealment. He knew I was there, watching him. Through ill-fortune, I had managed to make my quarry suspicious. I was doubtful now that he would settle anywhere. Curse the air!

The beggar stopped almost directly opposite me and disappeared into an adjacent alleyway. I could no longer see him, but he would, no doubt, spot me if I stepped out from my doorway. Not only was he suspicious, but he had managed to trap me where I was. I berated myself for not simply walking up the street immediately upon sighting him and getting myself behind the fellow. Somehow, now, he had the upper hand!

I heard a group approaching. This was my opportunity. As they passed the doorway, I stepped out into their midst and walked with them some distance, hoping I hadn't been observed escaping by the beggar. They were too inebriated to notice or object to another suddenly joining their party. Just past the junction with Shaftesbury Avenue, I left them and crossed to the same side of the road where I had seen the beggar conceal himself. I had now convinced myself that I was being overly cautious, and the poor fellow was probably just bedding down for the night in his usual sheltered area, among the bins.

I didn't want to draw undue suspicion upon myself. I tried to walk naturally, but stealthily, to the point at which I'd seen the beggar hide. As I approached the opening, the beggar himself emerged in front of me, almost leading to a collision.

"Oh!" I ejaculated. "Good evening." I stepped out as if to move on, but the stooped figure clawed at my coat. I couldn't see his face.

"It's you, ain't it, sir? From the church do, earlier."

"Ah, yes. Well, a Merry Christmas." I tried again to extricate myself, to no avail. He held me fast.

"You aren't the one who did for them kiddies, are you, sir? Oh, sir. Please, I beg you, I'm a good man, honest. Don't kill me too."

"My dear fellow," I said, roughly removing his hands. "Have a care. I have no intention of murdering you, or anyone. You may rest assured of that."

"Gawd bless you, sir," the beggar fawned. "I thought you was a goodly toff when I saw you earlier."

"Yes, well. Is this your cot for the night?"

"Such as it is, sir, yes."

The man's breath was appalling, matched only by the stench of his clothes. I had to hold a handkerchief up to my face.

"You couldn't spare us a gasper, could you, gent? 'Tis Christmas an' all."

It seemed the easiest way to get past him. I opened the silver case and offered it to him. He selected a cigarette and flicked it expertly into his mouth. I swiftly provided a lighted match. He took a long, satisfied draw. Any smoke he exhaled mixed immediately with the thick night air.

"Thank you, sir," he growled, sounding happier than I had heard him yet.

"Yes, well, I must be off. Compliments of the Season to you. And if you see anything suspicious, there's a constable on patrol nearby."

I swiftly edged past the beggar and up the street. I looked back periodically. He remained on the pavement, enjoying the cigarette. I crossed to the opposite side again. The beggar still paid me no heed, so I slipped into another darkened alleyway where I could keep watch.

"You all right, there, sir?"

The voice took me so much by surprise that it was as much as I could do not to yell out and curse. I turned around and the constable, of whom I wasn't previously aware, unhooded his lantern and held it up. I quickly hushed him, and he closed it again.

"Sorry to startle you like that, sir," he said. "I wasn't sure if you'd seen me."

"What are you doing here, Constable?"

"Like I said earlier, sir. My patrol. I was watching you and the rough sleeper over there. Saw you help him out with a little seasonal comfort. Just like the other gentleman. I don't reckon you'll catch your murderer tonight, sir. Not Christmas Eve."

"Other gentleman?" I asked. "What other gentleman?"

"With the beard, sir. Out from the church, he was. Said he was delivering Christmas cheer to the needy."

"It is the night for such things, after all," I replied with a wry smile. "Did he remind you to hang a stocking out?"

"Ha! Not after a shift on these feet, he wouldn't," the constable replied chirpily. He flexed the polished toecaps of his hobnail boots in what little light there was.

"Well, I'll keep an eye out for the jolly gentleman and his noble endeavours, Constable, thank you. But for the time being, I need to remain at my post here. I have a duty to perform."

"As you wish, sir." He eased his way past me and out into the street with a jovial whistle, looking for all the world like he'd just had a pleasant tea break.

The stooped beggar, opposite, signalled a pleasant evening to the officer and stubbed out the end of his cigarette. He beat his hands on his arms to fend off the cold of the night before hobbling back to his shadowy bed.

A vague sort of calm then settled on St. Giles High Street. The sounds of traffic, revellers, and even some distant carols floated upon the air. But it was all coming from elsewhere. This continued for some time, broken only by the occasional passing carriage. No more pedestrians took this route. It was probably for that reason that I spotted the bearded gentleman as he approached. His footsteps were light, stealthy. He walked along the pavement opposite, on the same side as the beggar. I assumed this must be the church gentleman the constable had mentioned.

Occasionally the fellow would stop and listen. I could hear nothing except the distant echoes of traffic and fun, but he could obviously detect something. I watched him approach nearer to the alley where the beggar slept. I was gripped by the sudden likeness of his manner to a hunter in the wild. He looked about, surreptitiously, and then slipped into the darkness of the alley. Immediately I was alert. There was the sound of a struggle. I dashed across suddenly, only to find myself meeting the beggar, staggering out of the alley, a blanket about his shoulders, closely followed by the bearded gentleman, brandishing a large knife.

I drew my pistol, but the attacker was too quick. A swift boot sent the beggar cannoning into me and we both went sprawling into the road. I lost my firearm. As I tried to regain my feet, I found myself set upon from behind. An arm grabbed my head and yanked it back. I realised in a moment of panic that I was about to have my throat slit, as many others had that week before me.

It felt to me like the world had stopped. The moment lasted an eternity. But nothing happened. No pain, no blood. I was just as suddenly released. Spurred immediately into activity, I regained my feet and helped the beggar to his. I turned to find Inspector Lestrade with a gun – my gun – at our assailant's head. A number of officers surrounded us, including the chirpy constable I'd been speaking to earlier. The knife dropped harmlessly to the ground.

"Inspector," I said, relief rushing over me, "where on Earth did you spring from?"

"They've been positioned for hours," said a familiar voice, and I turned to find the erstwhile stooped beggar standing perfectly upright. He removed his false teeth, hairy brow, and wig to reveal himself as none other than Sherlock Holmes.

"It was you all along?" I was, yet again, flabbergasted at the man's ability with disguises.

"And I wonder, too, if you recognise this monster?"

Lestrade returned me my pistol and roughly dragged our bearded assailant under the nearest streetlamp. I felt the bile rise in my throat.

"I do," was as much as I could utter. It was plainly the man who had portrayed Father Christmas at the church, earlier. I called him out for the abominable fiend that he was, and then had to turn away. I heard the constables handcuff him and drag him into custody. No doubt they had a coach waiting nearby.

Holmes and I walked home to Baker Street in silence. I was somewhat shocked by what had occurred, and Holmes was doubtful that any cabby would allow him in, smelling as he did. It wasn't too far. The cold night air did me some good, I'm sure, but there were a number of things playing on my mind, and once we were both washed and changed I took it upon myself to challenge what I saw as pretty poor usage by my friend.

"I don't think we need attend Scotland Yard tonight, Watson," Holmes announced as I entered. "If we visit after Boxing Day, we can review any statements the fellow has made and possibly interview him ourselves."

"He nearly killed me, Holmes." I found the words problematic and the sentiment even more challenging.

"My dear friend," he said, approaching my chair with a generous brandy. "There was no danger. It was all planned. I trusted that Lestrade and his men would respond in good time."

"You did, did you? Well, I wonder how that would have played if I'd actually had my throat slit."

Holmes bowed his head and wandered over to the window. "You're right, of course, and the whole affair ran much closer to the wire than I intended. You feel ill-used. I can sense it in your demeanour. I am sorry for that, but you have to believe that my reasons were for the best."

I stood in anger. "This wasn't a mild deception. You *lied* to me. You said you were interviewing Horatio Williford-Smythe. Yet there you were, in actual fact our other suspect, bold as brass! Surely you could have told me what you'd been up to from the afternoon? Am I that untrustworthy?"

"Of course not," he countered. "And it's because of you – who you are and how you behave – that meant I couldn't reveal my plan until after the event. I'm just sorry it got so fraught, that's all."

I was angered and flattered in equal measure. I allowed him to continue, for I needed to understand his thinking.

"I needed you to remain steadfast and true throughout. The way you would react to the beggar, to the police constable – to anyone. I knew I could rely on you to do the right thing, but I thought that the easiest way to achieve that was by being economical with the truth. And it worked. You played your role splendidly."

I took my seat once again. I had been used like this before – and always for the best of reasons. But the situation had never become life-threatening until today. I could see that even he regretted this evening's turn of events. My anger began to soften. I suspected that it was as much due to exhaustion than anything.

"You always suspected Father Christmas, didn't you?" I said.

"I'm afraid I did. It was the first common link between the children. Alas, my suspicions were borne out when he assured me, this afternoon, that he would visit me later and provide comfort after the haranguing I received from the Williford-Smythe fellow."

"Some comfort, in cold steel."

"Indeed. But anyway, we have our men. And hopefully the parish of St. Giles can rest a little easier this evening."

"Men?" *Plural?* I hadn't expected this.

"Oh, yes. I had Lestrade take in that beastly industrialist earlier this evening as well."

"Horatio Williford-Smythe? For what reason?"

"As an accessory to murder."

"Good Lord! In what way?"

Holmes eyes gleamed with cunning. "I have an idea, but we shall have to wait until we interview Father Christmas to find out if I'm right or not."

I rubbed my fingers across my temples. There was much I didn't understand about the investigation, yet I knew that Holmes would only reveal details as his theories progressed from speculation to proven truth. I couldn't pursue the conversation further at that time.

He smiled. "It may seem uncharacteristic of me, but I shall take an early night after today's excesses. However, first allow me to place a little something on our expertly decorated chimney mantel for you, my dear friend, for the morning."

He stepped forward and set a small, wrapped parcel on the mantelpiece, next to the Ormolu clock.

I removed a similar-sized package from my smoking jacket pocket and placed it the other side of the clock.

"And for you, too. Merry Christmas."

"Merry Christmas,."

We shook hands and parted to our rooms on the best of terms. It felt like a resolution at the time, and more so the following day, when I unwrapped the engraved silver hip flask he'd given me. I was doubly elated that he appreciated my present, too – a monogrammed fountain pen. By some uncanny coincidence, we had each bought Mrs. Hudson a brooch. She, too, was thrilled. She prepared for us both the most wonderful Christmas lunch.

I was glad of such a pleasant and relaxing day, after the excesses of Christmas Eve. Boxing Day was similarly pleasant. We went to church in the morning, it being a Sunday, but by the evening Holmes was becoming restless through inactivity. I knew that, for him, the following morning couldn't come around quickly enough. He was desperate to tie up the threads of the St. Giles murders. I was less eager and slept fitfully that night.

A cab called for us shortly after breakfast on December 27th, with instructions to relay us to Scotland Yard. London was once again buzzing with activity and commerce. This was usual for a Monday morning, but doubly so after the two days of Christmas holiday. Holmes was like a hound, eager for the chase, urging the cab driver on.

Inspector Lestrade met us at the entrance and told us with evident satisfaction that no further murders had been reported in the parish of St. Giles since the twenty-second of the month. Holmes then went striding off as if his life depended on it, and it was as much as Lestrade and I could do to keep up. He managed to direct Holmes to the cell where Father Christmas was being held. I joined them at the cell door, having brought up the rear. "Why do you persist with calling him Father Christmas?"

"He won't reveal his real name," Lestrade replied. "He never even gave the rector a name. We checked."

"Then how was he engaged for the events?"

"He approached the rector directly and said he was available for the week leading up to Christmas."

"Have you told the rector what happened?" asked Holmes.

"Only as much as we can prove so far," Lestrade confirmed. "It was enough to shock the poor old man."

"Yes, I fear this is one Christmas he won't forget. And where is the Williford-Smythe fellow?"

"Next door," Lestrade indicated with a nod of his head.

"Right," Holmes barked. "Let's start with Father Christmas and see if we can't loosen his tongue."

Lestrade had the door unlocked, and ensured the constable remained on guard outside throughout.

The villain who called himself Father Christmas lay on his cot, looking serene. Immediately this made my temper flare.

There was little-enough room for all of us in the cell. Holmes squeezed past Lestrade, who had entered first, and affected to look out through the barred window. With a "Hmmph!" he then turned to the recumbent figure.

"Horatio Williford-Smythe, I presume?"

The man's reaction gave him away instantly, and he knew it.

Lestrade uttered a curse.

I was stunned. "The industrialist? Him?"

"The very same," Holmes confirmed.

"But then who is in the cell next door?"

"His younger brother, Sebastian."

"How do you know?" I asked.

"I recalled that Mr. Williford-Smythe wore a beard when I saw once before in Pall Mall, entering one of the clubs near the Diogenes. I know that a beard can easily be trimmed to whiskers. But I recalled that he shunned alcohol. The red eyes of the apparent Horatio Williford-Smythe on Christmas Eve were those of a regular drunkard, as were the constant refocussing of his eyeballs, whereas it was mentioned in an article about the family in *The Times*, only last year, how morally bankrupt Sebastian's lifestyle was, by comparison."

"Damn you, sir!" said the bearded figure, sitting upright. His demeanour was now nothing like the genial Saint Nicholas he had been previously.

"His brother was pretending to be him, just as I was pretending to be a beggar."

"But he was known to the rector," I argued. "You aren't suggesting Dr. Richards was in on this too?"

"Oh no, no. Nothing of the sort. But the rector confirmed to me, separately, that the industrialist was something of a silent presence in the parish, generally. The whole family was. He'd started to make donations in the run up to Christmas, sponsoring the special events on the nineteenth and then again on Christmas Eve. I suspect the rector had high hopes of further generosity, which was why he asked you to leave the man's behaviour unchallenged. Although you may have noted that after a quiet conversation with Father Christmas, here, the ranting industrialist did moderate his behaviour, somewhat, if not his attitude."

Holmes turned to the figure on the bed. "I assume you were concerned that your reputation might begin to suffer if your stand-in continued in the same vein all afternoon."

"Hang it all," grumbled the prisoner. "Who the devil do you think you are, sir?"

"If you'd had your way, I'd have been your next victim on Christmas Eve, as would Dr. Watson, here. Suffice to say, I am Sherlock Holmes."

There was a moment of silence, eventually broken when Williford-Smythe growled out a sullen, "Well?"

"The floor is yours, Mr. Williford-Smythe. I would like to know why you and your brother have perpetrated such crimes. What right did you have to bring so much pain and sadness to so many people?"

Williford-Smythe looked at the three of us standing patiently over him. "Sebastian wasn't anything to do with it, really. He's a drunken sot most of the time. Easily bought."

"He was drunk when we brought him in," confirmed Lestrade.

"He thought it was a game. Have you gentlemen ever worked in industry?"

We told him we hadn't.

"This world we live in – the society. The malaise. Something needs to be done."

"That's what politics is for," I said. "Not murder."

He scoffed. "This was just an experiment, a game. *From the mouths of babes*, or however the saying goes. I wanted to understand how the children viewed their lives and their prospects. What they wanted to achieve. What I learned sickened me. Indolence and entitlement from the wealthy children. A sense of baseless superiority bred into them. And a selfishness founded not on personal betterment but through expectation, greed, and avarice. Whereas acceptance of poverty and their lowly place in the social order seemed to flow through the veins of the working class and poor. Most were indolent and lazy. If any wanted to better themselves, it wasn't *for* themselves, but for their parents and siblings. Where was the energy, the drive, the lust for revolution?"

"And the beggars?" asked Holmes.

"They were the worst. Idle and self-obsessed. Not looking to drag themselves out of the gutter. Feeling hard done by and therefore expecting others to help them, rather than them helping themselves."

I swallowed uncomfortably. "Having learned these difficult truths, what led you to such a severe course of action?"

Williford-Smythe sat back against the wall and smiled. I felt sick.

"It was clear the wealthy children were never going to change, thinking only of themselves. So, I determined to visit them and teach them the value of . . . humility."

"Humility?" I could barely get the word out.

"And what was your justification for killing the poor children?" said Holmes.

"Like the beggars, they're a drain on society. Lazy and idle in the main. The more forward-thinking and industrious I allowed to live. Most were indolent. The burden on society needs to be eased. Otherwise we'll all be dragged down into the cesspit."

Lestrade had clearly heard enough. He grabbed Williford-Smythe by the lapels and sharply pulled him forward off the bunk. "It isn't your job to administer judgments!"

The villain seemed amused that he had pushed Lestrade so far. "Society is going soft, Inspector. I decided to take responsibility into my own hands. And at this time of the year, who would suspect good old Father Christmas, eh?"

We were all surprised when Holmes suddenly reached forward and grabbed Williford-Smythe from Lestrade, whirling him around and slamming his back against the cell wall behind us, winding him badly.

"You are a twisted, degraded villain," Holmes hissed in his face, with an anger I had seldom seen. "It is you who is the burden on society. You are already in the moral cesspit which you claim to protect. You have caused such grief to so many families and undermined the spiritual message of this time of year. You show no remorse or regret. How can those families affected *ever* look upon this time of year with any joy or charity again? And you claim to have done this as a *game*?"

"You would allow the situation to continue, Mr. Holmes? To see such negative attributes take a stronger hold in the approaching new century?"

I responded, instead. "For a start, I would sooner we found ways to help these people, rather than relieving them of their lives. How far did you intend your enterprise to go? Surely you didn't intend to travel all over, killing everyone who didn't share your vision of life?"

"From such are revolutions made," he replied, flippantly.

I must have looked like I was about to strike him, because Lestrade cleared his throat and spoke up.

"Mr. Holmes, Dr. Watson, I think our work here is done, for now. Thank you."

Holmes relinquished his hold and the two of us turned to leave.

"The only game left for you to play now is swinging," said Lestrade, without humour.

The door closed behind us with a clang of finality. I hoped it would never open again. We had no need to speak with Sebastian in the next cell. His guilt had already been proven by his brother. Instead, Lestrade led the way to his office. We would need to make a statement each, to confirm the details of our discussion. And I sincerely hoped that that would be the last we ever heard of the St. Giles child murders.

The Case of the Earnest Young Man
by Paula Hammond

It was a warm December day in 1898 when an earnest young man, barely old enough to shave, appeared at our lodgings in Baker Street. The tale that was to unfold was one of such delicacy that, although I record it now, while the memory is fresh, it may be many years before it ever reaches the public domain.

He was a lean whip of a man-boy, with keen eyes that were doing a very good imitation of staring lazily into the fire, while actually taking stock of everything in the room. It was done with such subtlety that few would have noticed. However, I pride myself in the fact that many years spent in the company of my singular friend, Sherlock Holmes, has taught me a thing or two.

Holmes himself made a fitting bookend to our visitor. He had the same spare, hungry look, eyes seemingly half-closed, but still making a keen inventory of our guest.

While the one leaned forwards to make the most of the modest fire, Holmes inclined his body towards the copper-headed youth, opposite, as though trying to absorb whatever truths he was imparting.

I could hear the boy speaking in clipped, sober tones as I entered the room. He stopped abruptly as I stepped over the threshold, and a flush stole across his face. Holmes's own expression was equally telling.

"Ah, my dear Watson!" my companion exclaimed, fairly leaping from his chair. "Why don't you pour us both a brandy-and-soda?" He waved airily in the direction of the spirit case and gasogene, nestled in the corner of the room. "Mr. Maybury, will you join us?"

"Thank you, I will," our visitor replied in a tone that suggested he wasn't at all sure that he should, and I wondered just how young he might be.

"Mr. Maybury, may I present my friend and associate, Doctor Watson, before whom you can speak as freely as you would before myself."

"Delighted," Maybury responded shyly, before glancing back toward Holmes. My companion gave a little nod, which Maybury took as a sign to continue with his tale.

"I am but newly arrived from India," he began. "Mamma and I went out four seasons ago to join my father, who had built a thriving import-export business. In September last, it became necessary to make a trip to Tirah." He paused, as though struggling to find the appropriate words. Then he continued in a heated rush. "Oh! They knew the trip was dangerous, but contracts had been signed. It was foolish, perhaps, but it was a matter of honor. They were at Saragarhi, Mr. Holmes! They were at Saragarhi!"

The defense of Saragarhi Fort by twenty-one Sikh Sepoys is an action that will surely be remembered by generations to come as one of the most valiant in military history. The families of those soldiers will someday take some comfort in that fact, but poor Maybury had no such recourse. His parent's deaths were to be but a footnote to another bloody chapter in the history of the Northwest Frontier.

His voice cracked and a look of anger flashed across his young features. It was the strength of that emotion, I think, that pushed him on. "All those brave men. My parents. Everyone. Butchered. But believe me when I say this, Mr. Holmes: I hold no hatred towards the Pashtuns. As the good doctor knows, the Northwestern Province is a powder-keg. Yet, the Afghans have no natural antagonism towards India. No! It has been those d--ned those Russians and their d--ned interference! People will continue dying as long as the Tsar continues to play his games – and that's the truth of it!"

For a moment a look of undiluted hate settled on his face. Then, he seemed to remember himself and became once again the reserved, measured schoolboy.

"I've old family ties here, and a not inconsiderable inheritance. So in short, I have come to London looking for a cause to task me. I've done little beyond joining some select clubs and making trips to the tailor's to buy a wardrobe more suited to this chilly climate, but I hope to do some good with what I have.

"Unfortunately, I fear my naïveté has singled me out as what one might call an 'easy mark'. Early last week, I was foolish enough to strike up a conversation with some chaps playing poker in the bar of my hotel. Needless to say, I ended up considerably out of pocket! Two evenings ago, to show that I bore them no hard feelings, I invited them up to my rooms for drinks. I awoke with a thumping head to find the place ransacked! Oh, I wasn't that foolish – most of my valuables were in the hotel safe, but they took some items personal to me that cannot be replaced.

"To be frank, Mr. Holmes, I feel as a fish out of water and much in need of assistance. I have spoken to the police and they, in turn, have spoken to the hotel staff, but I fear that nothing will come of their enquiries. Indeed, I've been told that I should consider myself lucky to have 'gotten off' so lightly. That may be so, but I should wish to have my personal effects returned, and the hotel manager mentioned you as the foremost consulting detective in London."

"The only unofficial consulting detective," Holmes interjected with a smile.

Maybury nodded eagerly. "Then surely you are my man!"

"I'm afraid," Holmes said slowly, "it's quite out of the question. You see, Mr. Maybury, your tale is such a thin veneer of half-truths that it's laughable in its transparency!"

Not for the first time in our acquaintance, I was shocked at Holmes's casual rudeness, and Maybury, too, seemed taken aback.

"Why!" he flushed, caught Holmes's eye, and then trailed off with a sort of short cough. For a while neither man spoke, but rather gave a very good impression of being a pair of feuding cats engaged in a silent stand-off.

"You said," Holmes began, with a look of deep irritation, "that you had spent time in India, and that is the only verifiable fact you have so far told me. Yet, I would suggest that, rather than a mere four years, you've spent most of your young life in that great country."

"How so?" Maybury asked, his tone subdued.

"Even on a mild day such as this, you shiver under your tweed like a native-born. I also noted, as you sat warming your hands, that your tan does not stop at your shirt sleeves. No, you've been in the Punjab at least since you were young enough to go about bare-chested. And curiously, given how dark that tan line is, it seems to be a habit you've continued into adulthood!!"

"Why the Punjab?" Maybury asked slowly, neither denying nor confirming Holmes's observations.

"There's a sing-song cadence that hangs on your words, which is peculiar to the region. Even when you speak English, it's there which, in itself, suggests that English is not the language you use every day."

"Go on."

"You claimed not to know either myself and, by extension, the doctor, yet you apparently knew Watson had been in Afghanistan." Holmes was smiling, now, clearly enjoying himself. "You've spent some few years mastering the accent and manners of an English gentleman, but that's not you. Forgive me if I'm blunt, but I speak as one who often has to adopt disguises. I recognize the study and the craft when I see it. The shyness, the red-faced embarrassment, the uncertainty about the drink, were nicely done. By-the-by, just how do you blush to order?"

"I have a nimbar thorn in my shoe," Maybury replied as simply as though he were offering up the recipe for egg salad. "Pain provides quite a flush."

"Quite so!" Holmes nodded appreciatively before continuing. "So the question remains who – or rather *what* – is Mr. Maybury? You see, the skills you exhibit are not easily obtained. Or at least not easily obtained by a military orphan, raised in straightened circumstances."

"Oh?" By now Maybury's face was the very echo of Holmes's – his features a picture of pleasure.

"Your small stature and lean physique tells of a childhood spent feral, but not destitute. No, I'd wager that you were left in the care of an overindulgent Indian *aya*, who gave you too much of your own way, and let you run hungry and wild. Then, it would appear that someone upped and dumped you at St. Xavier's in Partibus. It is the best school for Sahibs in the Punjab, after all," he added to Maybury's raised eyebrow. "Despite that seeming windfall, you're clearly used to a degree of freedom rarely enjoyed by regimental sons and heirs. That in itself is highly suggestive."

For a while no one spoke. "Can I be honest with you, Mr. Holmes? Maybury eventually asked.

"I do wish you would. And while we're about it, why don't you take off those shoes and make yourself comfortable?"

It was such a curious statement that I couldn't help but laugh. I laughed even louder when, with a delighted clap, Maybury did indeed throw off his patent leather pumps and settled into the armchair.

He sat in a curious half-crouch, legs drawn up so that his knees almost touched his chin. His hands were wrapped around his shins, while his toes wiggled gratefully at their newfound freedom.

"You are everything I'd hoped for, Mr. Holmes! And you, Doctor Watson – were you not taken in by my story even a little?"

"Why certainly, but I have the advantage of knowing Holmes very well. And I know the look Holmes has when he is balancing amusement with chagrin."

"Then I hope that you will forgive any irritation caused by Kimball O'Hara, Little Friend of all the World!" He chuckled. "I meant no disrespect but, in my world, men are seldom what they appear to be, and rarely what they pretend to be."

"And what world is that?" Holmes asked, his eyes glittering with delight.

"Why, that of The Great Game, Mr. Holmes. Although I am sure that you had already guessed as much."

"Mr. O'Hara, I never guess. As I'm sure my brother told you."

"Indeed he did! Well, then Mr. Holmes, we will work well together, I feel. And, Doctor Watson, if you would be kind enough to pour those drinks and take a seat, I believe the storyteller in you will find my tale an interesting one."

"Much of what Mr. Holmes has said is perfectly true," he began. "I am a stranger to these shores, having spent my early years as an orphan under the care of an Indian nursemaid. Until I was thirteen, the English tongue was as curious to me as the country that my parents called home. I raised myself on the streets – and was quite pleased about it. I did what I fancied and would, I think, have been happy for life to continue in that vein. Then, alas! My past finally caught up with me.

"By virtue of my father's old regiment and some Masonic papers of his that I foolishly neglected to burn, I found myself shipped off to school. I ran away, naturally, having mastered the skills of face-changing and mimicry from the beggars that ply their trade on the streets of Lucknow. The third time I bolted, it was decided that a young colt like myself should not be broken in a school of the Sahibs, but set to tasks more suited to his temperament. That day, I began another type of education, polishing those skills that, as you so knowingly pointed out, are not easily acquired.

"For many summers, I travelled along rutted and worn country roads. At my side was one who was all things to me: Father, teacher, brother, son. My companion was in search of legends and myths. I, too, chased the uncatchable. Prophesies and signs – a colonel and a red bull on a green field. Oh!" he beamed. "How those days together warm me still.

"*Ayee!* No matter. The wheel turns. The world changes and the rules of The Great Game are changing too, Mr. Holmes. We have new enemies and maybe new friends too."

As he spoke, it seemed to me that he became less and less the English gentlemen and more and more the Asiatic. Yet, I felt a great heaviness in his words. For there was a wistfulness and a longing for the past in his tone that I've only ever heard in very old men.

O'Hara shook his head sadly. "India is as spirited and as untamed its people. Oh, the Sahibs have tried to bend it to their will. For centuries, they have played their games and I have played my part. But I will give you the truth you crave, Mr. Holmes. As a child I did not question what others told me, but relished The Game for its own sake. As an adult, I have discovered that my heart and my mind are not always as one. So it comes to this: Until India can forge her own path, I will do what I must to protect her. But my loyalty is to India – not England, not the Crown, nor the Empire. India, always."

"Isn't that a dangerous line to take in your . . . *profession?*" Holmes asked.

"*Hai mai!*" O'Hara cried with a childlike grin. "The Little Friend of all the World has no illusions! The Sahibs will make use of me, and then try to – " He made a little whistle and mimed a cutthroat action that left me quite pale. "Oh, do not worry, Doctor!" he continued, blissfully unconcerned. "They will have to work quickly to catch me, make no mistake!"

"Well," Holmes replied. "Now – to the reason for your visit?"

"Another player has joined The Game, Mr. Holmes. Russia has long coveted Mother India, but a new faction has emerged who oppose such expansionism. They call themselves 'Marxists' but, given the nature of their beliefs, many feel they represent a much bigger threat to the British Empire than the Tsar and all his little apparatchiks. Who knows? What is known is that one of their most trusted agents is in London, seeking alliances with those sympathetic to their cause. Britain wishes to – what is the phrase – 'hedge her bets'? So, I am here to meet him. Sadly, he is proving frustratingly elusive."

"So you play the rich, earnest youth looking for a cause?"

O'Hara nodded.

"Why you?" I asked, glancing across at Holmes, who suddenly seemed oddly preoccupied by something – or some*one* – in the street, outside. Before O'Hara could answer, he turned abruptly and yelled, "Down!"

Seconds later, the window shattered into hundreds of razorlike splinters as a heavy engineering brick, with something tied along its length, was propelled into the room.

To this day, I have no idea how Holmes managed it. As I hit the ground, I saw him execute the most amazing feat of acrobatics and bravery I've ever witnessed. He practically flew across the room, spinning his long form in midair, hands outstretched. He caught the projectile and clasped it, full to his the chest, before rolling his body into a protective ball around it.

He landed with a thump and a curse, uncoiled, then leapt back upon his feet. As he did so, I finally got a glimpse of the projectile. Good Lord! *Dynamite!*

The whole escapade couldn't have taken more than five seconds, but with my nose pushed into Mrs. Hudson's rug, it seemed to me that time itself stood still. I saw Holmes's pursed lips, and his cool, piercing eyes, so focussed and intent. A blink, and there were his long, steady fingers, untangling the projectile from its delivery system. He worked with precision, delicacy, and with such speed that I could barely follow his motions.

Another blink, and I saw Holmes tugging at the blasting cap which – from my limited experience of such things – should have come away easily, allowing for the safe disposal of the explosive. Clearly, that was not to be!

I blinked once more and nearly missed it as Holmes – another curse on his lips – dashed to the shattered window, looked out, and then threw the dynamite towards the street.

The explosion that followed turned what was left of the window into kindling – but we had been lucky. The conflagration, still above street – did little damage. Holmes had been careful to verify that it was empty before releasing the bomb. I shudder to think what he might have been forced to do if there were innocent passersby beneath our window!

Or, so I thought. As Holmes vaulted over the armchair and raced towards the stairs, he shouted, "The chase is on, Watson! See to O'Hara!"

I glanced round. There was the young man, lying by the hearth, his face as pale as death.

I picked my way through the confusion of glass, wood, and shattered stone, towards my prone patient. A purpling bruise on O'Hara's temple told me all I needed to know, and smelling salts did the rest.

There was little time to contemplate events, however, for within seconds, Mrs. Hudson appeared. At first our redoubtable landlady was in a fury, assuming another of Holmes's experiments gone wrong. But when she saw poor O'Hara and myself bloodied and bruised, she set about putting things to rights as only a level-headed Scotswoman can do.

For the rest of the afternoon, Baker Street was a whirl of activity. The police arrived and, having established that, "No more hex-plosives were about to threwn about," were happy to give Holmes his head.

Glass swept, window shuttered, wounds dressed, and strong tea provided, I was just beginning to wonder what had become of my companion when I heard his tell-tale tread on the stairs.

Sherlock Holmes was always a man transformed when hot upon a scent such as this. The lust of the chase was upon him, and his features were consumed by that energy I knew of old.

"Any luck?" I asked.

"Lost him in Marylebone," was his surprisingly terse reply. Even more surprising was what happened next. Taking O'Hara by the elbow, he practically frog-marched the poor boy to the door.

"Feeling quite well? Good, good!" Holmes said, without waiting for a reply. "Quick about it now. I have a cab waiting outside with instructions to take you to an address known only to myself and one other. You'll be safe there. Stay put.

"Johnstone, here's your package," he called out, presumably to someone waiting downstairs in the hallway. "Make sure it reaches its destination. O'Hara, we'll reconvene in the morning. We will come to you. You understand?" Again he didn't wait for a response. Instead, he unceremoniously pushed our guest onto the landing. I followed, seeing a nondescript fellow standing down below.

Holmes descended and let them both out. He remained stood poised in the doorway until I heard the unmistakable noise of a two-wheeler rattling down the street. Then he turned on his heels and made a beeline back upstairs for the brandy.

"Well," he began, "what an interesting afternoon it's been."

"Interesting?" I exclaimed. "We could have been blown to smithereens!"

"Indeed, we could," Holmes said quietly. "Equally, our assailant could have placed a bullet in Mr. O'Hara's brain and avoided all the theatrics. As we know, Camden House across the street is well placed for such activity."

"But then . . . ?"

He refused to elaborate until he was safely ensconced in his armchair.

O'Hara's shoes still lay where he had left them, attesting to the speed at which our guest had been ejected from the premises. Noticing them, Holmes gave a short, dry bark of a laugh and stretched himself out upon the cushioned seat. "Now, shall I tell you what I've been doing these last three hours?"

"Please do."

"Let me begin by sketching out the events that occurred while you were out, before our guest's arrival.

"I received a telegram soon after you left and a cab arrived in short order. Rather, I should say *two* cabs, for no sooner had O'Hara placed those rather perfect pumps of his on the carriage step than a second cab pulled up across the road. The occupant made a show of consulting his pocket-watch, but I watched him watching O'Hara, and it seemed clear then that there was more to this appointment than a commonplace robbery."

"The man was in his thirties, with short, dark hair and neatly cropped moustaches. He was tall, with a muscular physique, hidden behind inexpensive but neat clothes. A pair of well-polished ammunition boots gave me the rest of his tale. Indeed, I would not be surprised to flick through the pages of Mr. Pryce-Jones' mail-order catalogue and find him there, filed under *M* for *Military*. Even when loitering, he positively stood to attention!"

"Mrs. Hudson opened the front door for O'Hara and, after seeming to note the house number, Military Man marched on. Or so it appeared, until I spied movement in Camden House opposite, and his very unmistakable silhouette."

"Well, you know how things played out from there. It was a remarkable throw, by-the-by. At least forty feet. Our man must be quite the weekend bowler!" He chuckled at the thought of it, reminding me how ghoulish Holmes's sense of humor could be.

"And then?" I asked, eagerly.

"Ha! It was quite the chase. I had the advantage at first, knowing the layout of the building and where the back door could be accessed. I nearly had him! I was as close to him as you are to me! If I'd only stopped to pick up my revolver!

"Curious character. He had a tremendously virile yet strangely vacant face. For a second he stood on the step, blinking at me, rather stupidly, I thought. One could practically see his thought processes as he debated this and that. In the end, he went with what he clearly knew: Action. He sprang forwards, hitting me with such force that I went down, winded. His momentum carried him towards the gate, which he leapt with enviable ease.

"His speed was incredible! Again, I had the advantage. I know these alleyways and darkened passages well, while he needed to pause and back-track. Nevertheless he quickly pulled ahead.

"Down Kennick, past Blandford, left into George Street, past the old Roman church, we raced. His was the larger, more muscular frame. Mine the lighter, but built for such bursts of speed. I could see him, just ahead, red-faced, head bobbing, all but spent. I dug into my reserves, thanking Providence for such long legs as, inch-by-inch, I began to gain on him.

"Then, disaster! Turning into Marylebone, we encountered a parcel coach leaving the post office. It was a three-horser, high-sided, and loaded up top with boxes and baskets. Military Man stepped right in front of it, intent on spooking the horses. The driver pulled on the brake, but the vehicle was sluggish, heavy, and slow to respond. The horses reared and I feared the whole charabanc would tip over.

"It was in the confusion that I lost him. Fortunately, the rest of my time was not wasted.

"I headed first to Holborn to hunt out an old acquaintance, Johnstone. Although you don't know him, he is a man to be relied on when things get hot. He will take care of O'Hara – or at least keep an eye on him, which I rather think is more to the point.

"As for Camden House, a half-penny candle shed enough light on matters to confirm what I had already deduced. The question is, is Military Man one of ours or one of theirs?

I trust that I am not more dense than my neighbors, but once again, I was oppressed with a sense of my own stupidity. "Why, whatever do you mean?" I exclaimed.

"I'm not at all certain. There are too many possibilities. Let us sleep on it and, tomorrow, we shall see what we shall see."

The next morning, I found Holmes in his dressing gown, smoking his before-breakfast pipe and perusing the papers with the look of one not-best pleased with their contents. "We seem to be quite the cause *célèbre*," he explained, throwing the paper down upon the table. I glanced at the headlines which not only mentioned the explosion but Holmes, myself, and "*an unknown* heir".

"Why!" I exclaimed. "How on earth? I've a mind to speak to the Editor!"

"Oh, my dear fellow, we will most certainly speak to the man responsible, but first, I suggest breakfast, and afterwards a jaunt to Bloomsbury to see what mischief Mr. O'Hara has managed in our absence."

The walk from Baker Street was a pleasant enough affair. The shops were already decorated for the festive season, which added cheery splashes of color, to their uniform black and gold frontages. The decorations seemed so curiously at odds with the mild weather.

We skirted Regent's Park, where the year-long heat-wave had left the grass scorched. Indeed, there was such a heavy dryness in the air that it felt more like mid-Summer than a week before Christmas. I was reminded of the cover of the latest *Illustrated London News*, which featured an ice-bound lady in pink, so laughably at odds with mild weather.

We turned towards the British Museum, where the crowds began to grow thick, milling about, going, it seemed to me, nowhere in particular. We turned into a tiny cobbled lane off Coptic Street and there discovered a narrow door, unnumbered, but emblazoned with the words "*Repent and Be Saved!*"

The door opened without us needing to knock and the head of a homely, ruddy-faced women appeared. She ushered us in and we followed her up a dark, narrow stairwell, barely wide enough to accommodate her not-inconsiderable girth. I noted that a chatelaine hung around her waist, and from it were three monumental keys which clanged together as her hips rolled.

"Johnstone found The Lord while awaiting Her Majesty's Pleasure in Pentonville," Holmes whispered as we ascended. "He has since determined to bring coercive salvation to any of London's young waifs and strays unlucky enough to cross his path."

At the top of the stairs were three heavy doors – left, right, and straight ahead – and it was to this middle door that the woman bent her attention.

The door swung open, and we entered to find Johnstone, sitting on a small wooden chair, arms folded, chin to his chest, regarding O'Hara with weary forbearance.

Our man-boy lay trussed on a collapsible camp bed, a look of fury on his face. "Son of a swine!" O'Hara spat. "Father of all the daughters of shame! Husband of ten-thousand virtueless ones! Why you, faithless – !"

His diatribe was cut short by our appearance. "Mr. Holmes!" he cried, switching from the tinny, sawcut English he had been employing to the authoritative tones of the English wellborn. "Tell this brute to unhand me."

Holmes nodded for Johnstone to do just that. "Give you much trouble?" he asked, eyes shining with humor.

"Tried to do a runner early this morning. Managed to snatch the wife's keys a few times too. Nimble little villain, ain't he? But don't you worry. It ain't nothing I ain't dealt with before!"

"Yes, well, double-negatives aside," Holmes chuckled, in that silent way he has, "I'm much obliged to you, Mr. Johnstone."

"Always a pleasure, Mr. Holmes. I'll leave you to it now. Knock on the door when you're ready to leave."

"This really wasn't necessary, you know?" O'Hara said, sulkily, gesturing around the bare little billet.

"It was for your own protection."

"Rot!" O'Hara scowled, but brightened up considerably when Holmes fished out a cold collation he'd assembled from the breakfast table.

O'Hara ate like boy who'd spent the last week starving – finishing off his meal with a rank cigarette pulled from a battered stash in his pocket.

"Now," Holmes commented, as our reluctant guest sat puffing at the filthy thing, "before we were so rudely interrupted yesterday, you were about to explain why you are needed to make contact with this Russian."

"Why, because I know the man, of course."

"And why do you need my help?"

O'Hara shrugged lazily. "I like to have the advantage, and would prefer that he didn't know me. I am indeed a fish out of water here. If I am to 'pass' in the role I must play, I need to be certain of my disguise. I have been tutored well, but there are few more uniquely qualified to test my abilities on than you, Mr. Holmes."

"And the explosives?"

"I would have thought that was obvious, Mr. Holmes!" O'Hara laughed. "Because I have rattled someone's cage!"

"You, or Maybury?"

"Oh! Who can say? One, both – it works well either way."

"So," my friend murmured, "you're a young heir, angry at Russia's interference in the Northwest Frontier, and willing to fund some anti-Czarist faction. Or a British agent – posing as such – who is having second thoughts about whose side they are on. Yes, that would do it."

"Precisely!"

"Wait!" I cut in, incredulous. "Are you saying O'Hara arranged the attack on Baker Street?"

"Certainly not," Holmes said.

"Well who did? And why are you so both damnably pleased about it?"

"Because, if I may paraphrase you, Mr. Holmes, 'The Great Game' is afoot!" As O'Hara spoke, his face took on a look of beatific joy. "That explosion has undoubtedly achieved what I've failed to do in a month of tedious hand shaking with all manner of anarchists, socialists, atheists, and vegetarians! If our Marxist friends don't notice me now, they never will." He nodded towards the morning newspapers, which lay at the foot of the bed. "*Hai mai!* I wish I had thought of it myself!"

Much amused, but not at all enlightened, we left Johnstone with instructions to escort O'Hara back to his hotel.

"Where next?" I enquired.

"If you're agreeable, I think we deserve a long lunch. Then, I'd say it's time we paid a visit to Brother Mycroft. Don't you agree?"

"Oh? I replied, hoping for clarity, but receiving none.

The City of Westminster is home to some of England's finest architecture. Here, in the City within a City, no expense has been spared.

All along The Mall, row after row of marble-fronted buildings lead the eye from Trafalgar Square to the sadly neglected East Wing of Buckingham Palace.

Lying one street north in Pall Mall is The Diogenes Club. The building could easily be mistaken for one of the many embassies, artistic institutions, and government offices that make their home in these rarified environs. With its Grecian columns, imposing steps, and mosaicked portico, its very grandeur ensures its anonymity. Some would say that is quite deliberate. For behind these doors, one can find the most unsociable, most unclubbable, most taciturn men in the England.

While Holmes is a dynamo of a man, his older brother, Mycroft, is of sedentary and singular habits. However, I knew that he often consulted Holmes on cases in which he did not care to exert himself.

The Diogenes Club is his home from home from a quarter to five-to-twenty to eight every evening, and it was there that we made our way after an engaging afternoon spent in the chop houses of High Holborn.

Green leather armchairs scattered around small, walnut tables, a dark red carpet, and heavy gold wallpaper gave the Stranger's Room a sedate, rather dated appearance, which I guessed suited its members well.

Mycroft was seated when we arrived but, on espying Holmes, he rose from his chair with more energy than I could have imagined him capable of.

"Good Lord, Sherlock!" his grey, watery eyes widened as he noted the cuts and abrasions that adorned our hands and faces. "Are you quite well?"

"Quite, though no thanks to you!"

Mycroft looked genuinely aggrieved at the accusation. "I can assure you, Sherlock, it was none of my doing! I may have suggested to O'Hara that a little *événements dramatiques* could move things along nicely, but I'd never do anything without giving you due warning!"

"Another department?"

"Possible, although it's unlikely that it would have slipped past me."

"What of that ex-military type?"

"Tall chap? Profoundly stupid? Enormously athletic?"

"Exactly so."

"I rather assumed he was some watchdog of yours."

Holmes shook his head. "The Okhrana then?"

"The Tsar's secret police? That's possible too. O'Hara has been rather a thorn in everyone's side over the years! 'Little Friend of all the World' indeed! It is a little showy for them, mind. Poisoned umbrella tips are much more their style."

"What of the story that was carried by *The Illustrated London News*? It contained details that couldn't possibly have been known by the press."

"*Non peccavimus!* Not guilty, I'm afraid."

This entire exchange was carried out at breakneck speed, with each brother seemingly privy to the thoughts of the other. Discussion concluded, Holmes threw himself into one of the armchairs with a look of deep dissatisfaction. Mycroft followed suit.

I stood listening to the heavy black clock on the mantelpiece tick away the minutes until finally I could stand it no longer. "Will someone please tell me what's going on?"

"My dear Doctor! I am so sorry. It is rather a puzzle. Sherlock here assumed, not unreasonably, that I had arranged the little escapade in Baker Street to – shall we say – 'sell' O'Hara to the Marxists as a person of interest. I assumed you had done the same. It appears we were both wrong. The only other concerned parties are either military intelligence or some Russian faction. Mr. O'Hara, as you may have noticed, has a way of getting under people's skin."

"Tell me, Brother" Holmes said thoughtfully, "how well do you trust O'Hara?"

"No more than anyone else in his line of work."

"And how much money did you give him?"

"The Great Game," Mycroft said airily, "has always been a *long* game. We set him up with enough to make his cover convincing and to finance whatever his new Marxist friends might have in mind. But we naturally keep types such as O'Hara on a very tight leash."

We returned to our digs in rather a funk.

I retired early and rose early to find Holmes still by the fire, curled up in his chair, with his black clay pipe thrust out through a fug of tobacco fumes. From the thickness of the air, he appeared to have been awake all evening.

I rang for breakfast, which arrived with the morning papers. I was just contemplating the day ahead when I lifted an unopened newspaper from the table and glanced my eye over it. It rested upon a heading which sent a chill to my heart.

"What is it?" Holmes asked, ever sensitive to my moods.

I tossed the paper across to him and watched as he read and re-read the report which had so alarmed me.

Fire Claims Young Heir
Tragedy Strikes in W1

At about twenty minutes past eleven o'clock last night,, a fire was discovered at the Hotel Alexandra, Great George Street, W1. Staff were alerted to smoke emanating from the topmost floor. A speedy evacuation was made of all guests. The porter, Mr. Duncan, succeeded in subduing some of the flames using a hydrant positioned on the floor for such emergencies. Messages were sent to W1 fire brigade stations, and three steamers quickly arrived. The conflagration was brought under control within the hour. The occupant of Number 24, Mr. James Maybury, was unhappily found, deceased, in the debris at two o'clock. Mr. Maybury was a young heir from India. Despite being in London for less than a month, he had become an active and popular member of several clubs in the locale. Due to the severe nature of the fire, it is believed that Mr. Maybury will be buried in a closed coffin, but friends and family may apply to view the body at the Coroner's Office.

He let the paper drop and for many minutes seemed lost in thought.

"I feared as much." He spoke with surprising calm. Such was his attitude, indeed, that I was left feeling quite low, knowing how Holmes's pride would be hurt by such a turn of events. I myself felt it deeply that we had failed one who had come to us for help.

I recalled O'Hara's curiously joyful tone as he contemplated his own death and wondered which secret group – maybe even part of the British establishment itself – had decided to end his young life.

"Shall we go to the Coroner's Office?"

"Certainly," my companion responded.

"You've no clues then? No idea who could have done this?"

"I've suspicions, but I fear, for now, that is all they must remain."

"My dear fellow, you mustn't blame yourself. You couldn't possibly have anticipated this."

"On the contrary, Watson" he sighed, in the same a tone of quiet resignation. "It is exactly what I should have expected."

Some days later, Holmes and I were sat by the fire, in silent companionship, as was often our habit of an evening.

The weather had finally taken up its winter mantle, but I found myself appreciating the flames more for their cheery glow than their heat. It would be Christmas Eve tomorrow, and my mind wandered back to O'Hara, who had so felt the cold. The sight of that poor boy's body – little more than bones and charred skin – seemed to haunt me. It wasn't his death. I'd seen plenty of that in my profession. It was the loss of such an untamed spirit. A flame too quickly snuffed out. I wondered, with some sadness, if he had ever experienced an English Christmas.

"About the O'Hara affair – " Holmes said, quite unexpectedly, seeming to read my thoughts.

"Oh! My dear chap!" I exclaimed. "You mustn't – "

"No, no, Watson, you misunderstand me!" Holmes said with a dismissive shake of his head. "In fact, I fear that you've been overly sensitive to my mood of late, mistaking my preoccupation with work for guilt over the fate of young O'Hara. In truth, I think his death was rather nicely done."

I put down my coffee cup, horrified, but before I could remonstrate, my companion raised a placating hand. "Please, Watson," he continued with a low chuckle. "I'm not quite the cold-hearted fiend you think. Here, take a look at this. The final pieces of the puzzle arrived this evening. I think you'll find the contents of this envelope most illuminating."

He turned up the lamp and threw a small manila envelope to me. I tipped its contents into my lap and, inside, found three pieces of paper.

One was a handwritten note from Limehouse Police Station. The officer began by apologizing for the slow response, explaining that, as no centralized system existed to collate the information Holmes had requested, the officer had been forced to make a personal inventory of every coroner's court, shelter, mortuary, and *post mortem* room within the timeframe and area specified. The note ended with the following comment: "*There was indeed one body stolen from a morgue on the evening of nineteenth – that of a young boy, likely a suicide, who had lain unclaimed for several days.*"

The second letter showed withdrawals from a bank account made in the name of "*James Maybury*". The bank manager regretted that he was not at liberty to release personal information about account holders, but could confirm that the account had been closed on the afternoon of the nineteenth.

The final paper was a clipping from a French newspaper. It appeared to be a report of a meeting of some socialist group that had taken place just the day before. Holmes bent his lean frame forwards to point out a well-done sketch of two figures. One was large, with a preposterously blank expression. The other was smaller and sporting an expression that made him appear considerably older.

"O'Hara!" I exclaimed.

"And I'd wager that our Military Man is the same Marxist character whom O'Hara had been tasked with meeting."

"When did you know?"

"O'Hara was the only one who could have spoken to the press. That was nothing in itself. A good agent would have used our little adventure to promote his cause. The fire, however, did seem rather convenient."

"So the dynamite . . . ?"

"Had nothing to do with the Tsar or the British. But it did lay the groundwork for his upcoming 'death'."

"A risky gamble!"

"His is a risky game."

"But why?"

"I think he told us why during our very first meeting." Holmes closed his eyes and repeated in O'Hara's oddly sing-song tone: "'As a child I did not question what others told me, but relished The Game for its own sake. As an adult, I have discovered that my heart and my mind are not always as one. So it comes to this: Until India can forge her own path, I will do what I must to protect her. But my loyalty is to India – not England, not the Crown, nor the Empire. India, always.'"

"He's fallen in with these Marxists then?"

Holmes nodded. "For now. And not only has he extricated himself from London's tight leash, but has gifted quite a sizable amount of money to the cause too."

"What will you tell Mycroft?"

"Oh, if I know this, then he surely does."

I thought once again of O'Hara's little whistle and mimed cutthroat action. "What will he do?"

"He will do what Mycroft always does. Watch and wait. As he remarked, 'The Great Game is a *long* game.'"

I looked once again at the news clipping. It was no pleasure to feel we had been bested, but I for one was more than happy to discover that the Little Friend of all the World had survived to vex us another day – and maybe even enjoy Christmas, after all.

The Adventure of the Dextrous Doctor
by Jayantika Ganguly

It is well known that my good friend, Mr. Sherlock Holmes, was not a man prone to making mistakes, nor was he a person who discriminated against different human races. To be honest, I sometimes found his ready acceptance of all manner of people a little strange. While my own travels across three continents had made me rather broad-minded myself, in my humble opinion, Holmes sometimes made fun of my "ardent and stolid British identity", as he put it. I merely considered myself a proud citizen of Great Britain. If anything, I would admit to a slight bias in favour of persons of my chosen profession.

Thus, I was quite surprised to wake up on Christmas morning in the year 1898 and find Holmes glaring at an odd young man in our sitting room. While Holmes was hardly a proponent of the cheerful Christmas spirit that pervaded London, it was unusual to see him so obviously angry. More often than not, his temperament was as cold as the snow currently drifting past our windows. I looked curiously at our guest and wondered what he could possibly have done to anger Holmes so. The man was caramel-skinned and long-haired, and although he was neatly dressed in a conservative fashion, the overall impression he gave was rather wild and free-spirited.

"You asked me to come, and so here I am, Mr. Holmes, although it doesn't appear that you invited me to celebrate Christmas with you." The young man said it mildly with a polite smile, in perfect English with a slightly discernible but distinct musical lilt typically found in southern parts of India. I was familiar enough with local affairs from my short (and largely unfortunate) time there to recognise the man's accent, as well as the sandalwood markings on his forehead which proclaimed him to be a high-born and devout Hindu.

"Do you know that it is a criminal offence to impersonate someone, Dr. Dexter – or, shall I say, Dr. *Daya*?" Holmes asked coldly.

The young man's smile grew wider and his dark eyes sparkled. "And pray tell me, Mr. Holmes," he asked innocently, "who is it that I am supposed to have impersonated?"

"The *real* Dr. Dexter, of course," Holmes snapped. "I have been engaged by a close friend of the original Dr. Dexter, who has been missing for at least half-a-year."

The young man laughed. "I don't suppose you would be willing to tell me who this 'close friend' is, would you?"

I was amazed at this man's ability to remain calm and amused when faced with the masterful aura of Sherlock Holmes.

"Oh, hello, Dr. Watson, and a very merry Christmas to you," the young man said, noticing my approach. "I am a great admirer of your writing, and also of your medical skills. You greatly helped a friend of mine suffering from a tropical fever a few months ago."

The only person with tropical fever I had treated in the recent months was a young American lady of considerable wealth and status who had recently married a British nobleman. Could this wild young man really be a friend of hers?

"Are you acquainted with Lady Bradley?" I asked curiously, immediately earning a glare from Holmes. I realised that I shouldn't have mentioned the lady's name.

However, the young man nodded happily. "Very much so," he replied. "Lily and I almost got engaged a few years ago. Unfortunately – or fortunately – her uncle disliked me very much and deemed me unsuitable for the niece he had raised like his own daughter, so we went our separate ways. I'm glad she found a much better and more suitable person. Edward truly cares for her."

His carefree manner of speaking and his familiarity with such affluent persons surprised me. However, I was certainly able to confirm that he did know Lady Bradley well.

The young man turned back to Holmes and smiled. "If that's all you wanted to see me for, Mr. Holmes, I shall take my leave now. I have a good number of patients waiting for me. The winter chill keeps us doctors rather busy – even on Christmas day."

Holmes seemed to restrain his anger with great effort. "We shall meet again soon," he said icily.

The man laughed, waved his hand merrily, and left.

Holmes stared after him for some time. Then he asked me, "What do you make of him?"

"Seems to be rather cheerful," I remarked, "and from your conversation, I gather that he's a medical doctor."

Holmes chuckled. "He is . . . possibly the most devious criminal I have ever met, with nerves of steel," he murmured. "Either that, or I may be making the biggest mistake of my career."

I was quite shocked by his words. "Who is he?"

Holmes sighed. "Have you ever heard of 'The Dextrous Doctor', who is also called Dr. Dexter?"

I nodded excitedly. "Of course. Most people in the medical community are aware of his exploits. He rendered great service in several war-ridden parts of the world, but no one seems to know much about his current whereabouts."

"The man you just met . . . he claims to be 'The Dextrous Doctor'," Holmes told me, "and he has been living under the assumed name of Dr. Dexter in London for several weeks now. Two days ago, I was approached by a former classmate and close friend of the original Dr. Dexter, who told me that the real name of this person masquerading as Dr. Dexter is actually Dr. Daya, and he has assumed Dr. Dexter's identity falsely. The real Dr. Dexter has been missing for over six months, and his friend fears that he may already be dead."

"I remember hearing some rumours about Dr. Dexter's disappearance in South Africa some time ago," I commented.

"You're right," Holmes said. "That was the last anyone had heard of him, until a few weeks ago, when this Dr. Daya turned up in London, claiming to be him."

"But. . . can you be absolutely certain that he is an imposter?" I asked. "He didn't particularly strike me as a criminal sort."

Holmes smiled slightly. "You are scintillating today, Watson. Would you care to accompany me to Cambridge after breakfast?"

"Cambridge?" I asked. "Why? And will it not be closed for the Christmas vacations at the moment?"

"My client tells me that Dr. Dexter was his classmate at Cambridge before he left England, and assures me that the retired professors I need to meet stay home for Christmas," Holmes informed me. "I would like to check if that is indeed the case."

I frowned, doubt niggling in the back of my mind. "I haven't heard before that Dr. Dexter studied at Cambridge. Surely a large number of people would be aware of his identity if he did?"

Holmes nodded. "I have also asked Mycroft to enquire."

Mrs. Hudson chose that moment to appear with breakfast. Holmes and I ate in silence. It was only after the dishes were cleared away that I asked the question that had been in my mind all morning.

"Who is your client?" I enquired. "It must be a doctor, if he is a former classmate of Dr. Dexter."

"It is someone with whom you are quite familiar. In fact," Holmes said dryly, nodding to a medical journal on the table by my chair, "you were quite impressed with his recent article on illnesses of the mind just a few days ago."

I was stunned. "Sir Percival Gordon!" I exclaimed.

Holmes nodded. "Indeed."

Sir Percival Gordon was one of the most respected (and most admired) doctors in London. His papers on the human brain and the human mind were acclaimed all over the world when he was still in his twenties. Although his published works had been rather sporadic in the two decades since – perhaps because he had concentrated more on developing his practice rather than research – his recent article was every bit as brilliant as the work of his earlier days which brought him much fame. If such a well-established person came to Holmes to request him to find his classmate and friend, it was no wonder Holmes was reluctant to doubt his words. I thought of the young man we had met just this morning. He appeared to be in his twenties . . . at most thirty. Sir Percival, on the other hand, was well over fifty – old enough to be the young man's father! Thus, Dr. Dexter would be as well.

We left early, but were fortunate enough to find a hansom cab quickly despite the festive cheer all around us. I was still ruminating over the issue when we boarded the train at King's Cross. Holmes was also brooding silently.

"It vexes me," he said finally, looking at the white-and-green countryside flashing past our train window. "From what I've been able to gather so far, 'The Dextrous Doctor' only appeared about fifteen years ago," he murmured.

"I was thinking along the same lines," I confessed. "If Dr. Dexter was indeed Sir Percival's contemporary . . . he should have been practising medicine far longer." I paused. "It could be that he was an ordinary medical doctor like myself for a number of years before he was inspired to take up the mantle of 'The Dextrous Doctor'."

"Oh, I wouldn't dare to call you ordinary, my dear Watson," Holmes said with a spark of amusement in his grey eyes.

I was embarrassed at his unusual comment, but felt pleased that he regarded me highly.

"Your conjecture is quite reasonable, however," Holmes continued. "I had a similar thought myself. However, several recent reports that I've read about the mysterious doctor mentioned him as a small, feisty, young man."

"Reports?" I asked curiously. "Have you already been working on this case for some time?"

"I was engaged yesterday afternoon," Holmes replied.

My confusion must have been apparent on my face, for Holmes leaned forward with a small chuckle.

"I was waylaid on en route to what promised to be an excellent choir performance on Christmas Eve, and instead taken to the Diogenes Club," he said. A corner of his thin mouth lifted upwards. "I was met there by Sir

Percival, treated to a very generous meal in the Stranger's Room, and then told about the matter. He had hired several investigators across various jurisdictions in the last few weeks – ever since the young 'Dr. Dexter' set up shop in London – and while he has been unable to find his friend, his investigators did manage to compile an impressive amount of information during this time. He handed me copies of all these reports, and I spent last evening looking through them while you were out for dinner with Captain Morgan."

"May I take a look at the reports later?" I asked.

"Certainly," the detective said. "I would appreciate it very much if you could. I'm carrying only two of them at the moment, and you're welcome to read them. Do tell me your opinion."

The two reports were only a few pages each, so it hardly took me any time to finish reading.

"Are these reliable?" I asked Holmes. "While both reports describe Dr. Dexter as small, feisty, and young – the first one calls him 'fair-skinned' while the latter calls him 'dark-skinned'. Isn't that contradictory?"

Holmes shook his head. "The first one talks about his work in Africa – in comparison with the natives there, most races of humans could be considered fair-skinned. The second one is from Scandinavia, where even some of our Continental friends could be considered dark-skinned."

That did make sense. The smiling face of the young Indian we had met earlier flashed in my mind.

"The one we met in the morning was certainly a small, feisty, young man," I murmured.

"Indeed. However, the person known by Sir Percival is a tall, blonde, and reserved elderly gentleman with a saturnine temperament," Holmes said. "Which matches the description of the companion that the young doctor was often seen with before he arrived in this country."

"I see that there is a passing reference to an elderly companion in the African report, but it lists no name. Is the name not mentioned in the other reports either?"

Holmes shook his head.

It appeared quite strange to me. "What do people call the older man?" I wondered out loud. "This report just contains half a sentence about him and nothing further."

"They simply called him 'Sir' – at least, that is what the young man called him, and in some of the reports I've received, the natives simply believed it to be his name," Holmes said wryly. "A good number of places in which our friend The Dextrous Doctor worked have no English

122

speakers, you see, and the elderly gentleman rarely interacted with anyone other than the young man with whom he traveled."

"And it's the companion that's missing."

Holmes nodded. "Indeed. The elderly gentleman was last seen in South Africa, which coincides with the reported disappearance of Dr. Dexter as well. The only difference is that the young man turned up in London, while the fate of the elderly man remains unknown."

A thought occurred to me. "And Sir Percival thinks the elderly gentleman is the real Dr. Dexter, and the young man we met has simply been stealing the credit for his work all these years."

"Perhaps," Holmes murmured. "I am unsure. Very unsure. How brilliant would a man have to be to be able to keep up such a farce for fifteen years? Hence, I wanted to meet him myself, and sent word to him last night."

"And what is your conclusion?" I asked immediately.

A self-deprecating expression, which I had rarely seen on Holmes, flashed across his sharp face. "I'm afraid I shall have to disappoint you, old friend. Beyond the fact that the man really is a doctor – and, in all probability, a really good one – he's fond of taking long walks around our London, has studied in New York, has travelled to more countries than I could name, speaks at least nine languages, is vegetarian and well versed in the culinary arts, was brought up in an affluent family, takes an ardent interest in several music and dance forms, is extremely difficult to intimidate despite a complete lack of any sort of combat training, possesses a charitable disposition towards marginalised segments of mankind, and has an intellect not inferior to my own. I could infer nothing else. However, it is absolutely certain that he is indeed the young man mentioned in these reports."

I had deduced some of these traits myself – such as the vegetarianism, which I knew from the sandalwood markings on his forehead, and that he had lived in New York, since it was Lady Bradley's hometown, and only an affluent Indian family could have sent their child to America to study. High-born Indians also tended to have an obsession for various art forms, so that wasn't too surprising either. His clothes, too, were well-made, so he couldn't have been struggling to make a living. I had witnessed myself that he had been completely unaffected by Holmes. The man had also been to India, America, South Africa and England, at the very least, and to many more places if even half of what the reports given to Holmes were true. Also, most Indians were at least bilingual . . . although nine languages was a bit too much.

I was somewhat befuddled by rest of Holmes's deductions, and I asked him outright.

"A man's hands can tell you volumes about his work," he said, leaning back in his seat. "All doctors have certain revealing calluses on their hands, and so do those who wield weapons of any kind. Our young man had all the calluses of a doctor, but none that signified any weaponry or fighting skills. On the contrary, there was a small burn mark on the back of his hand, the pattern of which is something that can only be caused in the kitchen if the cook becomes absent-minded for a moment – so he cooks for himself. Also, the man was quite nimble, you may have noticed, and his movements were smooth and fluid, like a dancer's. I also observed letters in several languages in his pocket, two of which were completely unfamiliar to me. A medical man with such extraordinary talents . . . I cannot imagine him to be any less intelligent than myself."

"And his charitable disposition?"

"I saw him stop and speak to some of the Baker Street Irregulars squatting by the roadside before he came up," Holmes replied. "He gave away his scarf and his gloves, and all the candies he had in his pockets."

"You almost seem to be rather admiring of him," I couldn't help but remark.

Holmes smiled bitterly. "I am, my dear doctor, I am."

I was confused. "If that is the case, then why were you so furious with him in the morning?"

"Because he is hiding something colossal! And I am unable to see his through his motives. He is either a formidable foe or an excellent ally, but I can confirm neither." His grey eyes glowed. "I've often said that a doctor is the worst of criminals . . . and if this one, too, falls into the criminal category, we shall have a very hard time ahead of us."

"And what about the elderly gentleman?"

"We should be able to confirm soon whether he is indeed Sir Percival's old friend and classmate," Holmes said as he straightened his hat, "or not. Get ready. We're about to arrive in Cambridge."

We soon found ourselves in the impressive university town. The usually bustling locale appeared rather empty, but no less picturesque, thanks to the light snow that enhanced the scenery. The river Cam, too, had a thin layer of ice. I was no stranger to Cambridge, and neither was Holmes, so it wasn't too long before we located the correct college and the alumni records office. In spite of the holiday, we managed to find a bored-looking fellow to let us in, once Holmes had handed over a letter from Sir Percival. Inside, we were immediately granted access to the relevant files. We quickly looked through the class list and found that there had been a student named Hugo Dexter in Sir Percival's class. However, no further information was available, and the person manning the office was only a temporary employee and couldn't tell us anything useful.

Sir Percival had also given Holmes the locations of three retired professors who had taught during the years when he and Dexter attended, so we visited them at their homes, one by one. What we heard from each was exactly the same – Hugo Dexter had been tall and blonde, clever but gloomy. He hadn't spoken with most of his classmates, and if it hadn't been for the persistence of cheerful young Percival Gordon, he wouldn't have had any friends at all. Despite his brooding nature, though, Hugo Dexter had been prodigiously brilliant. After graduating from Cambridge, he'd initially started working with Sir Percival, and then had suddenly gone off to India about twenty years ago. No one had heard from him since.

"How is that possible?" I asked as we walked to the final professor's home. I was confused. "Hasn't he been in touch with Sir Percival?"

Holmes tapped his chin thoughtfully. "Sir Percival allowed me to see three letters, which he had preserved with great effort," he said. "It appears that his friend wrote to him every few years, and their content was quite innocuous and friendly."

A few minutes later, we were in the sitting room of the third professor's cottage. "Would you happen to have any idea why Dr. Dexter suddenly left?" I asked the professor, who shook his head.

I had expected it – the other two professors didn't have any idea, either.

"Didn't he go because he had a falling out with Percival?" the professor's wife spoke up suddenly. "I remember Lucille's mother mentioning something of the sort back then."

Holmes leaned forward, his eyes glittering. "Lucille Adams?" he asked.

The elderly lady nodded. "Yes, Percival's first wife. She was Hugo's sweetheart, you know, until Percival swept her off her feet. It's a pity she died so young . . . ."

"Would it be possible to speak to her family?" Holmes asked.

"Lucille's parents have long since passed," the professor's wife told us, "but her brother still teaches at Pembroke. Just ask for Professor Lucas Adams and someone will take you to him. He's very popular, and he may even be the next Master."

Holmes thanked the old couple and we took our leave, making our way to Trumpington Street. A pair of enthusiastic foreign students, who had probably stayed back to experience an English Christmas, recognised Holmes and offered to assist us.

"Professor Adams is usually at the Old Court around this time," one student informed us. "He takes a walk, even when it rains or snows."

Sure enough, we found Professor Lucas Adams' near the Old Court. He seemed surprised to see us.

"How may I help you, Mr. Holmes?" he asked politely, waving away the students with whom he'd been conversing.

"We just heard that Hugo Dexter had a falling out with Percival Gordon over your late sister," Holmes said bluntly. "Would you happen to know anything about it?"

Professor Adams stared at Holmes in surprise for a moment and then burst out laughing.

"Is this the methodology that leads you to success, Mr. Holmes?" he asked curiously. "You shock the suspect into speaking the truth?"

"We don't suspect you of anything, Professor Adams," I said politely.

Professor Adams narrowed his eyes. "Are you telling me that Percival didn't send you here?" he demanded.

"He sent us to Cambridge," I replied, "but not specifically to you."

Professor Adams frowned. "But why would he send you here and *not* to me . . . ?" he murmured to himself. His eyes widened in horror. "Is he now trying to harm the child?" he cried angrily.

Holmes looked at the professor with an impassive face. "We're simply tasked with locating the real 'Dr. Dexter'," he said.

"'The real – '" Professor Adams rubbed his temples. "Mr. Holmes, I can tell you the truth about Hugo and Percival and Lucille. More importantly, I will do my utmost to help you save that child in Hugo's stead."

"What child?" I asked.

"The Indian boy – Hugo's protégé," Professor Adams said. "Although he's actually grown now."

"We saw him this morning," Holmes said. "He has been in London for several weeks, running a clinic under the name of 'Dr. Dexter' – and Sir Percival believes that he is fraudulently using his old friend Hugo Dexter's name."

"Utter rubbish!" Professor Adams cried angrily. "That reckless idiot of a child – making himself so obvious! I should have sent him a message before now – I shouldn't have delayed this long!"

Holmes and I remained silent, waiting for our host to explain. He looked around and then said, "Not here. I live nearby."

We walked with him in silence through several streets before stopping at a small cottage. The Professor noisily unlocked the front door, apologizing in a loud tone for the state of the house. "I live alone, you see, and have fallen into too many bad bachelor's habits."

He led us in the front parlour with windows facing the street and asked if we wanted any refreshments. We declined, but he excused himself, saying that he could use a brandy. He left the room and I started to ask a question, but Holmes held up a hand. The silence of the house was preserved, except for the sound of the older man in the other room as he went about his task. In a moment he returned with a small amount of brandy and sank into an overstuffed chair, facing us.

"Hugo and Percival didn't fight over Lucille at all," Professor Adams explained. "Hugo was sweet on my sister, but she had always liked Percival, so he never took any action. Hugo was gloomy, but brilliant – as you may have already heard. Percival took advantage of this quite often, and the two of them used to work together, publishing papers jointly, even though it was Hugo who did almost all the work. For the sake of keeping his only friend, however, Hugo never protested . . . until he found out that Percival had actually published several of Hugo's works as his own, and even won award nominations for two of them. Finally, Hugo could take it no longer and decided to leave. He came to visit me before he departed and told me the truth about their work, and also that Percival was seeing a wealthy foreign noblewoman behind my sister's back, and if I could, I should persuade Lucille to leave him. Then he left the country. I was unable to convince Lucille, and then she killed herself in despair three months into her marriage with Percival when she discovered his affair on her own. I haven't spoken to Percival since, not did my parents until their dying breath.

"The world may call it a suicide, but in our eyes, Percival as good as killed our Lucille with his own hands. In the years since, Percival has continued to release Hugo's work as his own, a bit at a time, but he's reached the point where there's none of it left, and his reputation has started to suffer.

"As for Hugo, I didn't see him again until ten years ago, when he and that young Indian doctor he'd taken in as his protégé briefly visited England – without Percival's knowledge! He was happy as a clam, and treated the boy as his own son. The young man, Daya, was equally respectful towards Hugo and behaved like a dutiful son, for in India, they regard their teachers with the same respect and loyalty as one's parents, you know. The two of them travelled across the world and built a name for themselves. Out of respect for Hugo, the boy adopted the name 'Dr. Dexter', and their work over the last fifteen years has been exemplary."

His tone darkened. "Six months ago, I learned that they had been taken hostage by a group of criminals that fled with them from South Africa to Madagascar, but somehow Hugo managed to escape. He couldn't locate where Daya was being held, and soon after he fell seriously ill. Thinking that he didn't have much time left, he returned to England, and not knowing where or how to look for his young ward, he wanted to see Cambridge for the last time. He stayed here for a while in secret and recovered – that's when he shared this story with me – and then he left for London about a month ago. I haven't heard from him since."

"Could he still be in London?" I wondered.

"It's possible," Professor Adams said tiredly. "But that foolish child has apparently come looking for his teacher and, failing to find him, opened a clinic, tossing around the names 'Dexter' and 'Dextrous'. That little idiot, putting himself in danger like that!"

I didn't understand why opening a clinic under Dr. Dexter's name would be dangerous, though I could understand its use as a beacon to draw Dr. Hugo Dexter to his pupil.

Holmes, however, had figured it out. "The abduction in Africa . . . It was upon instructions from England," he stated quietly.

I cast a horrified glance at Holmes. Could his words be referring to Sir Percival . . . ? But what could Sir Percival possibly gain from having his old classmate and Dr. Dexter's protégé abducted?

"Sir Percival needs something further from Dr. Dexter," Holmes stated. "More bits of knowledge or research that he can't obtain for himself, to maintain his reputation.

Professor Adams nodded his head. "Exactly. And now Sir Percival has you looking for Hugo. It's a wonder he didn't just snatch Daya instead and use him as a hostage to coerce Hugo into coming forward and helping him again – although if Percival doesn't know where Hugo is to let him know that he has Daya, then kidnapping wouldn't do him much good."

The Professor smiled slightly. "You are indeed as clever as they say, Mr. Holmes," he said. "Percival was certainly behind their captivity in South Africa, and now he's hired you to try things a different way." He stood up, his tone louder. "If you would care to accompany me to my study, I have a letter from Hugo which he left for me to be passed on to the child. I should have taken it to him sooner, but I so rarely stir myself these days."

We followed Professor Adams silently through the darkened house. I was lost in my own thoughts, while Holmes, as usual, observed everything around us. I considered the smiling face we'd seen that morning and felt a pang of dismay. The young man we'd perceived to be the villain was in fact a good person, while Sir Percival, whom I had admired greatly until now, turned out to be duplicitous.

In the cluttered study, Professor Adams handed us a sealed letter.

Holmes looked at the envelope and asked, "Professor, may I ask if this was written by Dr. Hugo Dexter himself?"

The professor nodded. "Of course! He wrote on the envelope right in front of my eyes." He fixed his deep eyes upon Holmes. "May I request that you return to London and deliver the letter as soon as possible, and then urge the boy to go into hiding?"

"I very much doubt he'll be willing to do so until he locates his master," Holmes replied.

Professor Adams sighed. "You may be right. I merely wish for him to be safe."

"Sending him away doesn't necessarily ensure his safety," I added quietly.

"Indeed, Dr. Watson," Professor Adams replied. "My apologies. It was a rather presumptuous request on my part."

I could see that Holmes seemed to be caught on the horns of a dilemma – seemingly wanting to discuss the matter further, while also eager to return to the capital. He chose the latter, and we quickly bade farewell to the professor and took a train. When we were in motion, I asked Holmes what he gleaned from the envelope. He pulled it from his pocket and examined it.

"The handwriting is an exact match to the letters shown to me by Sir Percival. I have no doubt that all were in fact written by Dr. Hugo Dexter himself."

"But why would Dexter have written to him in the past if they were enemies?"

"We're dealing with a very clever opponent," Holmes said enigmatically, not answering my question at all, "but it appears that Sir Percival has been a little too clever for his own good."

After that, Holmes bottled up and wouldn't tell me anything, no matter how much I asked.

Holmes had sent a telegram from Cambridge before we boarded our train back to London, so I wasn't too surprised to find the young Indian doctor waiting for us in Baker Street. Unlike the morning, however, he was no longer calm. As we entered the sitting room, he tossed aside a journal which he'd been reading and leapt up from his seat.

"Is it true, Mr. Holmes?" he asked, his dark eyes filled with emotion. "Have you really found my teacher? Where is he? When can I see him?"

"We have been to visit an old friend of his in Cambridge – Professor Adams." Holmes said. Dr. Daya nodded, perhaps remembering meeting his mentor's old friend a decade earlier. "Dr. Dexter stayed there with him several months ago, after his return to England. He left a letter for you." Holmes handed it to the young man, who tore it open. His expression hardened as he read it.

"May we know what it says?" asked Holmes.

Dr. Daya shook his head. "I understand now. Is was Sir Percival who has tormented us – he sought my teacher to make use of his gifts for himself – as he did when they were younger."

He pointed at the medical journal that he'd just cast aside – the same one that I'd been reading just a few days before. "That recent article on illnesses of the mind: Even though it was published under Sir Percival's name. I am certain that my teacher wrote it!"

"Then perhaps," came a dry voice at the open door, followed by the portly figure of Mycroft Holmes, "the time has come to pay Sir Percival a visit."

I was quite surprised to see him, and so was Holmes.

"Why are you here?" he asked curiously. "You have never showed any inclination to spend Christmas with family before, and this little matter can't be of national importance."

"*International* importance Sherlock," Mycroft said tiredly. "The South African Foreign Office has been buzzing around like an overturned hive of bees since this affair began."

"My apologies, Mr. Holmes," the young Dr. Dexter said, glancing at the newcomer, his cheeks flushed with embarrassment. "I will leave with my teacher as soon as we are reunited. We won't cause you any more trouble."

I introduced Mycroft Holmes, who said, "The trouble wasn't caused by you or Dr. Dexter lad. However, because of your initial abduction, other issues have come to light, and we were able to identify and get rid of several channels of private interference within our South African colonies."

"Would you like to accompany us?" Holmes asked his brother.

"No need to state the obvious, Sherlock," came the reply.

"To where?" I asked.

"Why, Sir Percival's home," was Sherlock Holmes's reply.

Thus, the four of us were soon on our way to Carlisle Place, even as I tried to understand what it was that the two Holmes brothers already knew.

A well-dressed footman greeted us when we arrived and we were shown to a luxurious sitting room. Holmes scribbled a note and handed it to the servant waiting with a tray.

In less than a minute, Sir Percival rushed into the room and froze abruptly as soon as he spotted the young Indian doctor with us.

"What is the meaning of this, Holmes?" he demanded. "I asked you to find the *real* Hugo Dexter for me, not this charlatan! I could have found *him* in his shabby clinic whenever I wanted."

Holmes arched an eyebrow. "I have an excellent memory, Sir Percival," he said coldly. "I was asked to find the real Dr. Dexter, also known as 'The Dextrous Doctor'. We now know that he was here, doing new work for you – the recent article in *The Lancet* is unquestionably his work – but the fish has since escaped your net."

"I don't understand what you mean," Sir Percival retorted, suddenly nervous.

"When did he flee?" Holmes continued. "Three days ago – just before you hired me? Ah, I see that I'm right. After you couldn't locate him yourself, you came to me. Very risky – After all, he was sure to tell me that he'd been kept captive if I spoke with him. What did you think – that I would report his whereabouts to you before I conversed with him, so that I never need know that he'd been abducted and held prisoner?"

Sir Percival's expression was now very ugly. "Where is he?"

"Safe. And now I shall bid you farewell, Sir Percival, on behalf of myself and my two doctor friends. I believe, however, that my brother still has some matters to discuss with you regarding what you were able to accomplish by way of your South African contacts. Mycroft, you may be interested in some supposedly preserved letters held by Sir Percival. I'm afraid I was deceived through my very brief examination of them into thinking that they were written over the last few years instead of just the last few weeks. I believe the technique used to age them bears a remarkable similarity to some counterfeit documents submitted to the British Museum a few months ago. Perhaps Sir Percival can help you locate the culprit who assisted him in the aging process – thus clearing up the Museum matter as well."

"I must leave now," said the young man asked as soon as we stepped out of Sir Percival's home. "My teacher is waiting."

"Yes," said Holmes. "In Cambridge. The letter must have told you how to find him. However, it's late – we can travel there together tomorrow."

Dr. Daya shook his head stubbornly.

Holmes chuckled. "All right, then. Watson – are you up for another train journey today? We should be able to catch the last train to Cambridge if we hurry."

How could I refuse?

Less than two hours later, after a silent train ride where nothing was explained, leaving me impatient and curious, the three of us were in Professor Adams's sitting room, finally face-to-face with Dr. Hugo Dexter, who had walked into Professor Adam's study from somewhere else in the house when he heard young Dr. Daya's voice. Their reunion, after being separated for so many months following their initial abduction and varied adventures, was quite touching.

"I told you it wasn't so easy to fool Mr. Holmes, Hugo," Professor Adams said ruefully. Then he looked at us. "Hugo was waiting in the other part of the house when you were here earlier," he explained. "We weren't sure then if you could be trusted – after all, you arrived here as Percival's agents."

"I knew that you were here, Doctor," explained Holmes. "As we were led through the house, we passed by the dining table, where two sets of used dishes remained uncollected – even though Professor Adams had explained that he lived alone. You had obviously shared a recent meal with someone, Professor. It was most likely that it was your old friend, hiding here until the letter could be sent to London to Dr. Daya, advising him where you were hiding."

Holmes glanced my way. "The ink on the envelope was quite fresh – written within the last day or so, and not six months ago, as Professor Adams asserted." He looked back toward Dr. Dexter. "I considered revealing what I knew then, but decided that there were still questions in London to be answered. Now, can you tell us how this all occurred?"

The elderly man ruefully shook his head. "I was foolish enough to fall for Percival's trap in Africa, when I learned that this young one was already in his agents' custody. When I managed to escape, I had no idea where you were, Daya. I didn't realize that you were already free, my boy, so I returned to Britain. I visited Lucas here and told him my story. We had no idea how to begin a search, and finally I became impatient and set off for London. I went to see Percival, to confront him, and he easily took me prisoner once again. He then compelled me to resume researching and writing for him, as I had when we were younger, and still friends.

"However, a few weeks ago, I managed to read a newspaper and saw that a 'Dextrous Doctor" matching Daya's description had set up a practice in London. I knew then that Daya wasn't a prisoner after all. I can only imagine that Percival left him alone because I was already being compliant and carrying out his research for him, and holding a second prisoner was more than he wanted to take on when it wasn't necessary."

"I bided my time and then, three days ago, I managed to escape. The household had become rather complacent, as I was always a model prisoner, so I simply walked away. Rather than remaining in London, however, or going straight to see Daya, who might be watched, I first came down to Cambridge, where I could hide, and Lucas and I could make plans." He looked at the young doctor. "We are rather old and helpless, I'm afraid. We never thought of seeking out someone like Mr. Holmes to help us, and we were quite intimidated by the resources Percival could bring to bear. I had written the letter, and we were deciding when Lucas could deliver it in person to your clinic when Mr. Holmes and Dr. Watson arrived today. During their conversation, Lucas was convinced of their sincerity and asked them to deliver the letter to you. But I still wasn't completely sure, and chose to remain hidden in another part of the house."

He looked at Holmes. "Thank you for taking the letter to young Daya here, and reuniting us. We'll leave England as soon as possible – and this time we'll both change our identities so that Percival can no longer find us."

"There is no need," said Holmes, raising a hand and explaining that Sir Percival's persecution of the two men was now at an end. After relating the details of our recent meeting in the man's Carlisle Place home, he added, "My brother, Mycroft, represents the Government, and this affair has served to uncover a great deal more than your abduction, Dr. Dexter. Sir Percival is about to withdraw from public life – and he certainly won't be needing your assistance any longer."

The elderly doctor nodded with gratification. "Percival was quite desperate, and it has led to his downfall. You may not know it, but his credibility has been declining in the research circles in the last several years – that's why he took such a risk and had me abducted in the first place, and went so far as to threaten me into writing papers for him again."

"How did you originally escape from your captors in Mozambique?" I asked curiously. "I doubt that they were as complacent as the staff at Carlisle Place three days ago."

"Before I was due to depart," Dr. Dexter explained, "I helped the bandit chief's gravely ill brother. After that, he told me that it was Percival who had hired him to abduct us and ship me to England. He never let on that Daya, kept in a different location, had already escaped. After his brother was healed, he chose to free me in gratitude, and thus I returned to Britain."

Then Dr. Dexter sighed. "But I think that now I'm ready to go back. We'll quickly wrap up your clinic in London, Daya, and depart within a few days."

The younger doctor smiled in agreement. And that was how the adventure of the Dextrous Doctor came to an end with a happy Christmas dinner in Cambridge.

The Mystery of Maple Tree Lodge
by Susan Knight

"It has stopped snowing," I said.

There was no reply. I turned from the window and regarded my friend. Holmes was sprawled in an armchair, intent on a paper he was reading. I repeated the remark.

"I heard you the first time," he said with a sigh. "However, I didn't consider it of sufficient moment to warrant an answer. So it has stopped snowing, has it? No doubt it will start again shortly if a thaw doesn't set in. But what is all that to me when I'm engrossed in a treatise on the cuneiform script of the ancient Sumerians?"

Well, perhaps it wasn't the Sumerians. It may have been the Babylonians, or even the Assyrians. In any case, I said no more but turned back to my contemplation of the scene outside. The urban ordinariness of Baker Street had been transformed into an Arctic wonderland. I should hardly have been surprised to see a polar bear or two wandering by. It had, indeed, stopped snowing for now, but the precipitation of the last few hours had left a pristine carpet of pure white on the road and pavements, unsullied for the moment by the churning trace of any wheel or the tread of any passer-by. The inclemency of the weather had, it seemed, kept everyone indoors.

If a crime were to be committed under such circumstances, I mused, how straightforward it would be to track the perpetrator. One would only have to mark his footsteps in the way that Good King Wenceslas had instructed his page.

I suppose the Good King was particularly on my mind because Christmas was only a week away. Not that we would be celebrating it overmuch here at Number 221b. Mrs. Hudson would do her best with a roast goose and plum pudding, but I'm afraid that, with regard to the festive season, my friend and colleague rather shared the *"Bah humbug!"* opinion of Ebenezer Scrooge – before the latter's epiphany, that is.

My musings on the subject were brought to an abrupt halt by a tapping on the door, followed by the entrance of our landlady herself.

"There's a 'gentleman' here to see you on a matter of grave urgency, Mr. Holmes," she said, with an arch smile quivering on her lips.

I could not forbear.

"It is impossible, Mrs. Hudson," I said. "I have been looking out of this window for the last quarter-hour and can attest that no one has come up the street in that time."

"Now," Holmes said, suddenly alert, "remember what I always say about eliminating the impossible. If Mrs. Hudson tells no lie – and she isn't a woman given to lying – then quite clearly there is another explanation. Our visitor must have used the tradesmen's entrance at the back of the house."

Our landlady laughed. "There's no foxing you, Mr. Holmes. Yes, indeed. And here's the 'gentleman' himself to prove the point." She turned and addressed someone standing behind her. "Come up, now. Don't be shy. Mr. Holmes may look as if he is going to bite you, but here is Dr. Watson to stop him."

Thereupon a most extraordinary apparition sidled into the room, skinny as a broomstick, with a mop of unruly ginger hair escaping from under a battered cap. A face so covered in freckles that the pink skin beneath was hardly visible, the big ears that flapped out from his skull calling to mind those of an African elephant. The lad looked to be all elbows and sharp corners, and there was a lop-sided twist to his mouth. He was aged about thirteen or fourteen and dressed in the rough-and-ready attire that I associate with the Baker Street Irregulars who often help Holmes out in his investigations. However, he was cleaner than they were, and wasn't anyone that I recognised.

"This is Billy Higgins," Mrs. Hudson said. "The baker's lad. Every day, he brings us the fresh rolls that you like so much with your breakfast, Doctor. He's a good young fellow, Mr. Holmes, and you can believe what he says."

Holmes stood eying the young man, who by now had removed his cap, turning it in his big red hands as if to wring the very life out of it.

"Well, Billy," Holmes asked. "What have you to say to me that is so very urgent?"

The lad twisted his features into horrible grimaces, mimicking the torture he was inflicting on his cap. Clearly he was suddenly tongue-tied at finding himself in the august presence of the famous detective.

"Go on, Billy," urged Mrs. Hudson. "Tell Mr. Holmes what you told me."

"It about the boy, sir," Billy said at last with a rush, in a high-pitched voice that hadn't yet broken. "I seen him, I did, honest. But then they says there wasn't no boy. But I seen him, so I did. I swear to God, I did. With my own two eyes."

Eyes that were bright and blue and honest.

"Now," Holmes went on, patiently enough. "This won't do, you know, Billy. You must start at the beginning and tell me everything as clearly as you can. Mrs. Hudson, perhaps you could bring up some of your most excellent Scottish shortbread and a hot drink for our friend. He looks as if he could do with it."

Indeed, Billy's trousers were soaked almost up to the knees from wading through the snowdrifts, and he was shivering.

"Sit you down here, near the fire, Billy," Holmes ordered, as Mrs. Hudson most willingly went to get the said refreshments.

"Thank you, sir."

For my part, I was no little astonished at the attentive way in which Holmes was treating the lad. I could only assume that the particulars of the cuneiform script of the Sumerians weren't proving as diverting as my friend might have wished, and that any distraction was thus to be welcomed.

Billy still needed coaxing to tell his tale in order, but here is what finally emerged.

Mr. McBean, the baker, being a man of pious bent, had, along with some of his fellow traders, organised their young employees and other youths into a band of carol singers, to go around the neighbourhood and collect offerings for the deserving poor of the parish.

I saw Holmes frown at this. Being musical himself, he was wont to rail against the abominations perpetrated in public at the present time of year on perfectly good melodies by those who couldn't sing a note.

"Do you enjoy that?" I asked Billy, before Holmes could make any disparaging remarks.

"Oh yes, sir," Billy replied, thoroughly relaxed by now and tucking in to the shortbread and other delicacies that Mrs. Hudson had promptly provided, along with a big mug of tea. "Yes, sir, I loves a good sing-song, me. And if I don't know the words, I just go '*La-la-la*'."

Holmes shuddered almost imperceptibly.

The little band, as Billy explained, had duly set off with Mr. McBean supervising – presumably, I suspected, to keep the lads in order and make sure no farthings or ha'pennies went anywhere but into the designated little velvet sack.

"Well, all was well and good," said Billy. "Till we comes to this here Maple Lodge place. McBean tells us to sing 'While Shepherds Watched their Flocks', if you know that one, sir. It's a real beauty. Well, when we come to the line about the shinin' frong – "

"The what?" asked Holmes, startled.

"The shinin' frong, sir. Of angels praisin' God."

"Ah yes, the *throng*. Go on."

"Well, I don't know why, but didn't I look up just then. I suppose mebbe I was hopin to see the frong meself. Don't know. Anyways, what did I see instead but a boy lookin' down at us out of an upstairs window. I waved at 'im and 'e waved back. Then he was gone, like as if someone pulled 'im away from the window."

Billy paused.

"And that's it?" Holmes asked, rather sharply.

"Oh no, sir. No. If that was all I wouldn't have thought no more about it. No, indeed."

He paused again. A master storyteller in the making if ever there was one.

"Well?"

"That was the night before last. Next mornin', McBean tells me to make a delivery to that very same Maple Lodge. So when I gets there, I asks the maid about the boy. See, I thought perhaps 'e'd like to come out singin' with us."

"Yes? What did she say?"

"What did she say, sir? 'There ain't no boy 'ere.' That's what she says to me, comin' on strong and cross, like. 'There ain't no boy 'ere, young feller, and don't you be goin' around tellin' folks there is.'"

"That is indeed strange, Billy. You are quite sure what you saw, I suppose?"

"Well, o' course I starts to wonder if I dreamed it. I asked the others if they'd seen a boy, but they adn't. Not McBean neither. I was goin to let it go, but then I starts thinkin' – I know I saw 'im. And if someone says I didn't, then they're lyin. And if they're lyin, well, I wonder why, see. It bothers me, so it does, sir. And then I thought o' you, and 'ow as you could get to the bottom of it all, if anyone could. And Mrs. 'Udson, she said there was no arm in askin."

After this great speech, during which Billy had leaned forward so far in his eagerness I feared he might fall into the fire, he slid back into the chair, helping himself on the way to yet another piece of shortbread.

"Hmm," Holmes said, frowning. "You pose a pertinent question, Billy."

"Do I, sir?" Evidently Billy wasn't sure if this was a good or bad thing.

"Yes, indeed. If you are one-hundred-per-cent sure you saw the boy, and someone tells you that you didn't, and that there is no boy to be seen, the question indeed arises, *Why?*" He turned to me, "What do you think, Watson? Some new puzzle to divert us in this dreary weather?"

Billy was delighted. "You'll look into it then, sir?"

"I will, but without making any promises as to the result."

The lad nodded wisely.

"Can you tell me anything more about this boy?" Holmes asked.

"Like what, sir?"

"What age he was? What he looked like? What he was wearing? That sort of thing."

Billy scrunched up his face again in a frown of thought. "It's a bit difficult, sir. See, there weren't no light."

"You mean the boy was looking out of an unlit room."

"Yes, sir. That's it. The room was dark. 'E was younger n' me by several years, I'd say. About the same as our Tommy. 'E's nine." He thought a bit more. "I couldn't see what 'e was wearin', sir, but 'e had dark hair and a pale face."

Holmes rubbed his hands together. "That's very good to be going on with, Billy. Thank you for being so observant. If you think of anything else, please don't hesitate to come and tell me."

"Thanks, sir. I'll be goin' along then." He stood up, looking reluctantly at the last of the shortbread.

"Take the biscuits," I said. "To share with Tommy."

Billy didn't need telling twice, but stuffed what remained into his pocket. "Thanks ever so much, sir. We can share with Betty and Peggy and Wally and Francie, and baby Jimbo, too."

"Of course you can. In fact, ask Mrs. Hudson to give you some more cakes and biscuits for them all. For Christmas. Say the Doctor said it was all right."

He nodded, his face almost splitting in half with a grin, his big ears flapping. "Very good o' you, sir. They'll like that, sir."

Out of the corner of my eye, I could see Holmes looking at me askance. However, the lad appeared undernourished, and I could only guess at the privations he and the rest of his big family undergone.

"Oh, one other thing before you go, Billy," Holmes said. "The address of this Maple Lodge."

"O' course." He gave us directions to a place near Primrose Hill.

That done, he left, and we looked at each other in silence for a moment.

"There's probably a perfectly simple explanation for it all," Holmes said at last, reaching for his pipe. "On the other hand, Billy may have stumbled on a true mystery. Yes, indeed." And with a satisfied sigh, he started to stuff his pipe with that noxious weed that he likes so much to smoke.

The next day, I found myself sitting at the bar of the Queen of Spain tavern in that genteel suburb of London that is Primrose Hill, partaking of a rather fine luncheon of roast beef and Yorkshire pudding. I was there under instruction from Holmes to make enquiries of the landlord about the residents of Maple Tree Lodge.

"And keep it subtle, for goodness sake," Holmes adjured. "We don't want to arouse any suspicions that might get back to the Lodge."

The pretext for my curiosity was an intention to purchase a property in the area. I trusted I led up to the subject in a way subtle enough for Holmes. Luckily, my interlocutor was a man of a garrulous disposition, particularly since the continuing bad weather had kept most of his regular customers away from the inn. No doubt they preferred, like the sensible people they were, to stay home by a roaring fire. Not that that the place where I was sitting was cold – there was a fine fire there too – but the journey thither had been rather less than salubrious – the snow, which had fallen again in the night, being of a considerable depth. Holmes and I had been obliged, moreover, to trudge around first in search of the Lodge. It would hardly do, as he had pointed out, for me to express an interest in a property without knowing what it looked like.

We found the place at last, little thanks to Billy's imprecise directions. Maple Tree Lodge proved to be a large, somewhat fortress-like building, set far back from the road behind a high wall. One could glimpse it well enough through the gates, but I myself ventured no further than that. As for Holmes, he had donned one of his many disguises, intending to call at the house to offer his services as an odd-job man.

So now here I sat in the tavern, endeavouring to elicit information from my genial host, while uncomfortably aware of soaked boots and socks.

"Yes indeed," the landlord was saying. He might have sprung fully formed from the pages of Mr. Dickens's *Pickwick Papers* – a jolly round ball of a man. "You could do worse than move to our neighbourhood, sir. You'll find very respectable class of person around here – very upright, if you know what I mean . . . ." He regarded me with interest. "What line of business would you be in yourself, if you don't mind me asking?"

"I am a doctor," I replied.

He nodded. "I thought as much."

I was amused and curious. Evidently my new friend possessed, or at least boasted, powers of divination akin to those of Sherlock Holmes himself.

"How ever could you tell?" I asked.

"Well now, sir, I couldn't actually say 'doctor' as opposed to 'lawyer' or . . . or . . . whatever. But I knows a professional man when I sees one."

"You are just the observant fellow I need," I said, jumping to the matter in hand. "There's a particular house I very much like the look of, and I was wondering if there is any chance of it being on the market."

"What house would that be then, sir?"

I made a show of consulting a notebook. "Here it is. Maple Tree Lodge on Stanhope Walk."

He scratched his head. "I know the street. Can't say I knows anything about the house, sir."

That was a blow. I had hit a brick wall. Where I was to go from here, I had no notion.

Then, "Hang on a moment, sir," the landlord said. "Hey, Andrew!" He called to a skinny old individual seated at the far end of the bar, nursing what looked to be a hot rum. "You know anything about Maple Tree Lodge? This gent is minded to make an offer on it."

Andrew was nothing loth to join us. If this was a neighbourhood of genteel folk, this fellow was definitely on the margins. His clothes were old and patched and grubby, and his skin was ingrained with dirt.

"Maple Tree Lodge . . . Yes, indeed. 'Appen I knows it well." He grinned at me, revealing a mouth lacking most of its teeth. "Seeing as how they have so many chimbleys up there, sir."

"Andrew is a sweep," the landlord explained. "I always have him clean my own chimney." He gestured at the fire. "You see how it ain't smoking. That's the sign of a good sweep, that is."

His occupation partly explained the man's appearance. That was soot ingrained in his face, not dirt.

I offered Andrew another drink.

"Thanking ye kindly, sir, and I will accept. A body needs a hot drink on a day like today."

The landlord hurried to provide two hots rums with alacrity, since I concurred with the wise words of my new acquaintance, and decided to join him in that warming beverage. The landlord then moved off to serve a couple of men who had just entered.

"You be asking about Maple Tree Lodge, sir." Andrew looked thoughtful. "Furriners they be. From furrin parts. Mind you, I didn't know they was plannin' to move out."

"No," I said. "I don't know that they are. I just hoped they might be open to an offer. The house is exactly what I want."

Andrew's expression reflected the saying, "There's no accounting for taste."

"An elderly couple are they?" I continued,

"I wouldn't say old," Andrew replied. "Not young neither, mind you. No. In between. Like you and me, sir."

I guessed Andrew to be quite a few years older than myself, but let the remark pass.

"Do they have any children?"

"Children? No. None that I've ever seen.. And you would see children, wouldn't you, sir? If they was there, like. If they was away, well, then you wouldn't see them. No." He paused and sipped his drink. "I wouldn't say they was plannin' to move out though, sir. No sign of that. Unless and all they wanted to go back where they come from."

"Where would that be, do you know?"

"Search me. All I knows is, they ain't British. See, I heared them one time, talkin' furrin."

"That's very helpful, Andrew. You wouldn't happen to know their name, by any chance?"

"I heared it but I couldn't tell you what it was. All spits by the sound of it."

"Spits?"

"You know, sir. All *esses* and *zeds* and that." He sniffed back a drop of water from his nose. "Furrin."

It seemed I had squeezed all the information I could out of Andrew. I ordered him another drink, paid my bill, and took my leave.

"You be back, I hope, sir, if you ever manage to close that deal," the landlord said, and I promised, readily enough, that I would.

My next destination was a nearby grocer's shop, where I made a few unnecessary purchases of tea and jam and anchovy paste and the like, and then repeated my question, in an offhand-enough manner, regarding the denizens of Maple Tree Lodge. It was to my advantage that the shopkeeper there was a woman, and one who proved only too ready to gossip. The trouble was that she had little to impart.

"I don't knows them to see," she told me, "but their maid, Edith Mott, comes here regular, like." She shook her head. "That Edith's a closed book, she is. All I know is what she buys for them." She paused.

"Yes?" I asked. It didn't sound promising.

"They must eat funny food there, sir, that's all I can say."

"Funny food?"

"That Edith, she asks for things I've never even heard of, and gets quite uppity when I says I don't have it. Like rye bread. Or sour cream. Well, my cream ain't never sour, as I told her." She sniffed. "And funny you should buy tea and jam." She pointed at my purchases. "Edith told me they puts jam in their tea instead of milk!"

She crossed her arms over her not inconsiderable chest and pursed her lips.

"Any nursery food? I heard somewhere they have a little boy."

She stared at me. "Where d'you hear that sir? Edith never said nothing about no boy. Mind you, now I'm thinking they get through a deal of porridge."

It seemed that was all the information I was likely to get, and, since I didn't feel like plodding about any more on a wild goose chase, I decided to return to Baker Street. No doubt Holmes would heartily disapprove of my lack of progress.

"Well done, Watson!" my friend said jovially, later that afternoon.

I could hardly believe my ears. "I didn't feel I achieved very much."

We were sitting in our room over warming cups of tea and some more of Mrs. Hudson's most excellent shortbread.

"You achieved more than I expected," Holmes continued. "Think about it. What do we know now about the family? That they are middle-aged, foreign, probably from Eastern Europe."

"How do you work that out, Holmes?"

"A surname full of explosive sounds. The nature of the grocery purchases. The habit of taking tea with jam – A specifically Eastern European practice."

I nodded – wisely I hope. I had never before heard of that particularly barbaric-sounding custom.

"In fact, you did better than I," he continued. "Except in one particular: The formidable maid that we now know as *Edith Mott* was certainly not inclined to let a disreputable-looking odd-job man over the threshold. Instead, she had me shovelling snow from the paths and driveway, and made sure I had done a decent job before giving me a miserable threepence for all my efforts. At least I was able to peer through the downstairs windows and ascertain there was no sign of a boy."

"There we are, then," I said. "No one I spoke to talked of the possibility of a boy either. Billy must have been mistaken."

Holmes smiled and tapped the fingers of his hands together. "Not at all. Billy is absolutely correct. There is a boy. Or, at least, a child."

"How do you know?"

"Footprints, my friend, footprints. As I was engaged in shovelling snow from the path at the back of the house, I espied two pairs of prints in the snow. One set belonging to an adult, a man I should think by the size and depth of them. The other undoubtedly those of a child. I imagine the prints were made very early this morning, after the snow had stopped falling in the night."

The significance of this led me to only one conclusion.

"A child! A boy!" I exclaimed in great excitement, "He is being held in that house against his will. A prisoner! Holmes, we must act at once to liberate him!"

He laughed. "Not quite so impetuous, please, my dear Watson. Fools rush in, and all that."

"But the secrecy, the denials – What are we to make of it all, then?"

"I agree that something most unusual is afoot in that house. It may be, indeed, that you are right, that a child is being held against his will. However, I saw no signs of that in the footprints."

I gazed at him uncomprehending. "Whatever can footprints tell you?"

"A great deal to those who look carefully. The child – we may justly I think call him a boy – walked without reluctance with his companion. There was no dragging, no pulling away. The prints were regular and neatly spaced. No, he was trotting along happily enough."

I shook my head. The matter was beyond me.

"Think about it," Holmes continued. "Early morning exercise was taken before anyone else was likely to catch sight of the boy. He is being concealed in the house for a reason. Who knows yet what it might be?"

"Maybe he is an imbecile and the family is ashamed of him."

"Hmm. That's possible but unlikely. He waved back at Billy and walks normally. No, we need to tread here as carefully as angels. I should like very much to discover what is going on. And yet . . . . You know, it may be that we should leave well alone – not to endanger the boy's safety."

"You think that a risk?"

"Well, let us say I'm beginning to formulate certain ideas which I'm reluctant to share even with you, dear friend, until I have established more concrete facts. For the time being, I doubt there is any great urgency in the matter. The boy is secure where he is."

With that, he reached for his pipe and I for another piece of shortbread, not too pleased with his reticence, but having, as ever, to put up with it.

The following day I had various business affairs to sort out, as well as a Christmas lunch at my club, and thus only returned home in mid-afternoon. I was somewhat surprised to find Holmes comfortably ensconced with a person of a decidedly working-man's appearance. They were poring together over an album of some sort.

"Ah, Watson. This is Mr. Wicks. He shares my deep interest in philately."

I shook the man's hand, somewhat puzzled. This was the first I had heard of any such interest on Holmes's part, though the man was such a fund of useless as well as useful knowledge that I supposed a stamp-collecting mania might possibly have passed me by.

"I am showing him my collection."

Now this was definitely something I had never clapped eyes on before, a handsome leather-bound album packed with neatly arranged stamps. As such, an object could surely not have remained hidden from me, its sudden manifestation causing me to suspect some ulterior motive.

"Mr. Wicks is a postman," Holmes continued, "and in his line of work naturally has occasion to come across many very interesting stamps."

"Yes indeed," the man said, a zealot's glint in his eye. "And if I may say so, Mr. 'Olmes, your collection is about the best as I've ever seen."

"You are too kind," Holmes replied. "Imagine how lucky I was to fall into conversation this morning with Mr. Wicks as he did his deliveries."

Light was beginning to dawn even in my poor benighted brain.

"Would that be in the Primrose Hill area?" I asked.

"Yes, indeed, sir," Mr. Wicks said. "And a very good area it is for the more unusual class of stamps, as I was just telling Mr. 'Olmes. 'Specially this time of year when people receive Christmas cards from all over. Some of the people I deliver to know of my little 'obby and very kindly give me the stamps off their envelopes. Others . . . well." He shook his head. "What good they're to them, I don't know."

"Mr. Wicks was indicating to me some of the stamps he recognised from his rounds. I think you said you had seen these before, didn't you?" Holmes turned a page to show a collection of large, brightly coloured squares. He laughed. "We agreed the smaller the country, the bigger the stamps."

I looked over his shoulder.

"*Bzdva*?" I said. "Good Lord! What a name! I confess I have never heard of the place."

"It is, I believe," Holmes replied, "a small principality in the Carpathian Mountains. And interestingly enough, as Mr. Wicks tells me, one household that he delivers to regularly receives missives from that very country."

"I wonder what house that could be," I said, scowling at Holmes.

"The people what live there must be from them parts," Mr. Wicks offered in his innocence. "Their name ain't English anyway."

"No," said Holmes. "Mr. Wicks has written it down for me. What do you make of that?" He shewed me the paper.

What I saw penned was *Strzhcic*, a name I couldn't even begin to pronounce.

"They aren't too keen on vowels, are they?" I remarked. "But the stamps are pretty."

"One time I asked for them, sir, but the girl near bit me head off and told me to mind me own business. Unnecessary rude, she was . . . But tell me, Mr. 'Olmes, sir – where did you get these 'ere splendid stamps, if you don't mind me asking?"

I was wondering the same thing myself.

Holmes airily dismissed the query with a wave of his hand, and a vague answer that he had people who acquired them for him. Then he removed one of the Bzdovan stamps and presented it to Mr. Wicks with some ceremony.

"For your collection, my friend."

And when the other began to demur, Holmes went on, "It's the least I can do. For Christmas, you know. And please," presenting the man with a guinea to send him on his way, "buy something nice for your good wife and all the little Wickses."

I gazed at my friend in astonishment. Suddenly he had turned into Scrooge redeemed.

"Very much obliged to you, I'm sure," the postman was saying, pocketing the coin and gazing at his prize. "It'll be the flower in my little collection, so to speak."

When he had gone, Holmes smiled at me, rubbing his hands together.

"Well, we are making great progress. Now we know their name and where they come from."

My private opinion was that there might have been easier ways to find out. However, I merely gestured at the album. "And that?"

"Yes, indeed. I'm not quite sure how I'll explain to Mycroft how one of his precious stamps comes to be missing. He will not be any too pleased."

"Oh, it's Mycroft's collection, is it?"

"Yes, I visited him this morning with the precise intention of borrowing it for the purposes of which you have been a witness. Dear Mycroft," Holmes went on. "My brother would no more consider visiting any of the places designated by these stamps as try to fly to the Moon. They are the nearest he will ever get to 'abroad'."

"I'm surprised," I said, "that he would entrust such a valuable collection to you at all, knowing as I do how pernickety he is about such things and how careless you can sometimes be."

Holmes leaned back in his chair and stretched out his long legs. "Well, as to that . . . ." He laughed. "He doesn't yet know that he has lent it to me."

"You stole it!" I exclaimed, horrified.

"Goodness, Watson, how you do exaggerate. But now," springing up and crossing to the bookshelf whereon lay an encyclopaedia, "let us find out all we can about Bzdva."

The answer was painfully little. We learnt where it was and a good deal about its troubled past history, and that the prevailing religion was Eastern Orthodox, but the encyclopaedia was sparse on anything to do with the present day. A subsequent visit to the British Museum Library the following afternoon, and a forage among the newspapers there, proved equally fruitless.

"There is nothing for it," Holmes remarked finally, "than to pick Mycroft's brains. If anyone knows anything about it, he will."

Holmes hadn't yet returned the stamp album, perhaps fearing the wrath of his brother, or else hoping for an opportune moment to slip it back without Mycroft noticing. As for the missing stamp, he had endeavoured to rearrange the page so that it wouldn't be noticed, but gave up. Mycroft had a precise system which couldn't be changed.

"I shall just have to acquire another Bzdovan stamp from somewhere," he said, "and hope my brother forgives me."

We duly made our way, album and all, to Mycroft's rooms in Pall Mall, hoping to catch him before he set off, as was his wont each evening, for the Diogenes Club. We were lucky. He was still at home, although he ostentatiously consulted his fob watch before permitting us to enter.

"I can give you ten minutes," he said.

Mycroft Holmes was taller and considerably stouter than his younger brother, his complexion florid, with tiny broken veins visible over his cheeks and nose, no doubt the result of an unhealthily sedentary life and a partiality for rich food and brandy. He was unlikely ever to consult me in my professional capacity, but if he did so, I should have prescribed regular exercise and a strict diet.

His abode always struck me as curiously impersonal. It might have been an office or an hotel room, with its utilitarian furniture and standard portrait of Queen Victoria over the mantelpiece. The one concession to individuality was a bookcase, and even that held only handsomely bound reference works. Not a novel, nor even less a volume of poetry in sight.

We sat ourselves down, and Holmes, conscious of the minutes ticking by and the knowledge that his brother would have no compunction in ejecting us at the end of the allotted time, asked straight away what Mycroft knew about Bzdva.

"A-ha!" the other replied. "How very interesting you should ask, Sherlock. That little place has been rattling around like billy-o the past while and causing all sorts of alarms."

"Really? In what way."

"As you have probably already discovered, it's a tin-pot principality in the wilds of the Carpathian mountains. A month ago there was a military coup – the ruling prince assassinated and his wife thrown into prison."

"Goodness!" I exclaimed. "I saw nothing about it in *The Times*, and they are usually prompt at providing news of that nature."

"I believe," Mycroft replied, "there was a very small notice in one of the papers. Who here, after all, would be interested in the fate of a country of which they have never heard? According to the editors of Fleet Street, not their readers, anyway. Our government, however, is become involved – and this is top secret – in that the son of the assassinated prince, his heir, was spirited away by a trusted servant of the family, and is at present somewhere in this very country. Indeed, the General now in charge, whose name I won't even try to pronounce, has sent a strongly-worded letter to our Prime Minister, demanding we hunt down the boy and return him, or, and I quote, 'Steps will be taken.'" Mycroft chuckled, his whole huge body heaving. "I'm not sure if the General intends to declare war on the British Empire, and if, therefore, we should be trembling in our boots."

"You don't know where the boy is at present, then?" Holmes asked.

Mycroft paused before answering, a faraway look in his watery grey eyes. "Despite the best efforts of our agents, they haven't been able to put a finger on him as yet."

"If you find him," I said, "will you send him back?"

"The General has assured us that the boy will come to no harm. Indeed, he has offered a large reward, albeit in Bzdovan crowns, for the return of the little Prince. Needless to say, we aren't about to publicise that fact right now. In any case, I think it most unlikely, *most unlikely*, Dr. Watson, that he will be found. Not by us, at least. So the question will never arise. Now, I think our conversation must end, for the ten minutes is up."

We rose to go.

"You may replace my stamp album where you found it, Sherlock," Mycroft said. "I shall hold you accountable if there is any damage to it. Or anything missing."

My friend had the grace to blush – a very rare occurrence for him, and something I had only ever seen before in the presence of his brother.

He babbled a confession regarding the missing stamp, and promised to replace it.

"I shall keep you to your word. In the meantime, please remember that there are persons looking for the boy, possibly to do him harm, so in the unlikely event that you receive news of him, please keep it to yourself and don't think to become involved in the matter."

We walked a little way up the road with Mycroft until our paths diverged. Holmes was thoughtful.

"I'm somewhat surprised," I said at length, "that your brother didn't ask what was our particular interest in Bzdva, and that you didn't tell him about the boy at Maple Tree Lodge, who must surely be the missing prince."

"My dear Watson," Holmes replied. "I didn't tell him because he knows it already."

"But he said – "

"You should be aware by now that there is often a sizeable distance between what Mycroft *says* he knows and what he actually knows. I imagine the authorities are fully aware that the boy is safely hidden away at Maple Tree Lodge. They also realise that once the General gets his hands on the little fellow, that will be the end of him."

"Good God! So what do we do?"

"I suppose we must stay out of it, as Mycroft instructed."

That however, wasn't to be. We returned to Baker Street to find a wide-eyed Mrs. Hudson in the hallway, informing us that a foreign lady wished very much to speak to us. This person was waiting at present, and impatiently, in our landlady's parlour, and in fact burst out of the room at the sound of our voices. We saw a woman not in her first youth but still attractively voluptuous, and of exotic appearance. She came accompanied by a strong and earthy scent of patchouli.

"Mr. Sherlock Holmes," she cried out in a thick foreign accent, looking from one of us to the other, "you must find him! He is in the gravest danger – if even it isn't already too late." At that point, she started howling and beating her breast, an action I had read about in novels but never before observed in practice.

Holmes gently urged the lady to come upstairs to our rooms. Once there he insisted she take a seat and begged her calm herself, to explain the matter fully.

Soon it emerged that this lady was none other than Madame Strzhcic, (approximately pronounced "*Strezh-chick*"), the same resident of Maple Tree Lodge of whom we had so recently made enquiries, and that the boy in her charge – "Dearest Mikel" – had been abducted that very afternoon.

"It is a catastrophe, Mr. Holmes."

"Yes, yes. But how did it happen, and how come you are here?"

"When I found they were gone, Little Mikel and that devil in women's clothes-es, I rushed into the street to look for them. But they were gone. Gone! I collapsed into the snow. It was there I was found by the kindness of a man – a man who delivers letters."

"Mr. Wicks?"

"Perhaps. I don't know. I told him what had happened and he advised me to come and see you."

"Not the police? I should have thought – "

"The police!" she almost shouted. "No, I will never speak to the police! Never! You cannot trust them. But Mr. Holmes . . . I hope I can trust you. I hope you can find our darling little Mikel."

She raised tearful brown eyes to look at him. Really, she was rather appealing, despite her melodramatic manner. My heart went out to her.

"You say it was a person known to you who took him."

"Yes. Mott. Edith Mott." She spat out the name. "I curse the day we brought that witch into the house."

"Let us proceed with all haste," Holmes said. "We have wasted too much time already."

The three of us travelled by cab back to Primrose Hill, Holmes enquiring for further details but allowing it to be thought, as the lady clearly intended, that we took little Mikel to be her own son.

The snow had stopped falling, but still lay thick on the ground. When we alighted from the cab, Holmes instructed me to accompany Madame Strzhcic into the house, while he conducted an examination outside.

"What is he doing?" she asked me.

"I presume he is looking for clues," I said. "For footprints."

"Ha!"

We waited in the comfortable parlour of the house – though just as with Mycroft's place, there was nothing much here of a personal nature – no photographs or knick-knacks to reveal the taste of the owners, if owners they be. Tenants more likely, I thought.

Soon we were joined by the lady's husband, a stiff stick of a man, his once-blond hair turning grey, his face haggard, and showing more wrinkles than one might expect in someone of middle years.

He said something to his wife in their language, and they continued speaking thus for a while in raised tones. Rather rudely, I thought, though under the circumstances, perhaps niceties go out the window.

"No news yet," she said finally.

The man clenched his fists. "By Satan and all the devils, if I ever get my hands on that woman, she is dead! Dead!"

Madame again spoke in their tongue in what seemed to me to be in warning tones.

To break the uncomfortable silence, and though it was hardly the time for small talk, I asked how long they had been living in London.

"A month or two," the man replied, offering nothing more.

"Do you like it here?"

They both stared at me, as if astonished at the question, and I gave up.

As the minutes on the handsome grandfather clock ticked into three-quarters of an hour, I could see Madame getting more and more angrily restless, though her grief seemed to have dissipated.

"Where is he? What is he doing?" She paced up and down the room, stopping occasionally to stare out the window at the driveway.

"Trust him. Mr. Holmes has his methods," I said, but my words washed off her. Indeed, I was wondering myself at the prolonged absence of my friend.

Mr. Strzhcic, meanwhile, was sitting drumming his foot on the wooden floor, on and on and on. I tried to curb my irritation, but it was Madame who finally cried, "Stop! For God's sake, Hedrik!"

At last, the familiar form of Holmes could be seen approaching the front door. He was alone.

Madame flew to meet him, almost dragging him into the parlour.

"You didn't find them, then."

"Not yet. I was able to follow their traces for a way but then lost them."

"Lost them!" Her voice was sharp. "So much for the great detective. I hope you know that the boy's very life depends on you."

"Yes," Holmes said quietly. "Yes, Madame. I'm fully aware of that." He looked at me. "Come, Watson. There is nothing more to be done here. I assure you, Madame, Sir, that as soon as I have any news, I will let you know."

"Everything must be done in the strictest secrecy," she insisted. "No police."

Holmes inclined his head in acknowledgement.

Mr. Strzhcic rose to his feet, clicked his heels in military manner, and shook our hands with a curt nod. Madame, by then sunk in a chair, merely made a vague gesture of dismissal.

"One last thing," Holmes said, as if the idea had just come to him. "A foolish request, indeed, but I wonder if you could give me any stamps from your country. For my collection, you know. Dr. Watson will tell you what an obsessive philatelist I'm."

The couple looked startled, as did I, though I soon gathered myself together and nodded agreement.

"Stamps?" said the man.

"Yes, I have none from your country and would love to add some to my album."

A rapid exchange followed in their guttural language, and finally Mr. Strzhcic crossed to a bureau and took out some envelopes. He was about to tear off the stamps but Holmes intervened.

"Oh no, please. Leave them in place. They need to be removed with care."

Mr. Strzhcic shrugged, and, after a moment's hesitation, passed three envelopes to Holmes, who thanked him warmly.

"How beautiful they are," he said. "Look."

I nodded, but stamps are stamps and of no particular interest to me.

Holmes was sunk in thought as we headed away. I supposed he must be very worried at the fate of the poor boy, but when I said as much, all he replied was, "There is great evil here, Watson. Very great evil."

"No one seems to have a good word to say of Edith Mott, anyway. What a hellcat she must be to abduct an innocent child. I suppose she did it for the reward money."

"The money is key, quite evidently."

He said no more, and I could tell he wanted quiet to order his ideas, and so we continued in silence, until of a sudden he turned to me, shaking his head.

"You go on home. There is something I must do."

I was about to protest, but he insisted.

"It's cold, my friend," he said. "Take yourself to Baker Street and get Mrs. Hudson to make you a hot punch." He laughed. "To put you back in the Christmas spirit."

I knew better than to argue further, though once more I was disappointed. His nose was twitching, a bloodhound keen to be off on the hunt, and he wanted rid of me.

Now the business is all over, I can look back and see clearly what he observed and I missed. At least, I could see it all clearly once he explained it. I only wish I had been there when he found the boy.

That fateful day, while I obediently sat by the fire, enjoying the hot punch so aptly provided by our landlady, and trying to concentrate on the newspaper, he was bringing the saga of the boy at the window to a conclusion.

As evening drew on and no still sign of my friend, I became ever more restless. Hearing carol singers in the street outside, I put on my greatcoat and wrapped a thick scarf around my neck to go out and join them, to try to muster up the joyful glow associated with the season.

The little group was clustered under a street light, flakes of snow starting to fall upon them, turning them into veritable snowmen. Nothing daunted, they next launched into "Hark the Herald Angels Sing" with more gusto than tunefulness, though it was impossible not to be moved. When the carol was done, I gladly contributed to the fund for the poor of the parish. Our friend Billy stood amid the "frong", for all the world like a ragamuffin angel. He waved at me, raising questioning eyebrows. What could I tell him? Nothing, without putting little Mikel in even more danger.

As the group started to move away, a hansom cab drew up to our door. It was with utter astonishment then that I descried the persons descending from it. Holmes of course, but accompanied by a small boy and a woman. He hurried them into the house.

I stood gaping for a second. Then Billy ran up to me.

"That's 'im, Dr. Watson. That's the boy what I seen. That's 'im."

He was calling too much attention to the matter.

"You'd better come up, Billy," I said.

He made his excuses to the man I took to be McBean and gladly followed me into the house.

Upstairs, we found Holmes standing by the table, and the boy and woman huddled round the fire, her arm round his shoulders.

"That's 'er," Billy exclaimed. "The 'orrible ol' devil from the 'ouse."

"Edith Mott?" I asked, looking at the stout, red-faced woman in front of me. Whatever was going on?

"Indeed," Holmes replied, "this is Mrs. Mott, and she is very far from being a horrible old devil, Billy. She may well have saved this little boy's life."

"You're my darling, aren't you, Mikel?" the same woman said, holding the boy even tighter. He smiled up at her, a beautiful child with black hair, olive skin, and long lashes over dark eyes.

"I knew I had to get him away," she said, "when I heard them talking. They didn't know, but I've picked up quite a bit of their language, minding the child. They were planning to sell him to the General. My little boy!"

She was deeply moved and started to cry, so now it was Mikel's turn to comfort her.

"I don't understand," I said.

Holmes started to explain. After becoming aware that the General was planning a coup, Mikel's mother, the Princess, had entrusted him to her maidservant, Adele Strzhcic.

"Take him to England," she had said. "He will be safe with my sister in Gloucestershire."

The Strzhcics, however, had other ideas. At first they had no fixed plan to enrich themselves at the expense of Mikel's welfare, but decided to keep him with them to see what transpired. Then, on learning that a large reward was being offered by the General for the boy's return, they had entered into correspondence with him.

"You noticed, of course, the official nature of the envelopes given me by Mr. Strzhcic, embossed with the palace insignia," said Holmes. (I had not. My eyes were on the colourful stamps). "The letters couldn't be from the Princess, because she is in prison. Therefore, they had to be from the rebels."

"Well spotted," I said, rather lamely.

"I was already suspicious of the couple before that," he went on. "Why had they not informed the British authorities of the young prince's whereabouts – surely the first thing blameless people would do?"

"But," I said, "the envelopes show that the General knew well where the boy was being kept. Could he not just send emissaries to pick him up and avoid paying the reward?"

"Excellent. You are thinking at last. However, it isn't so easy to abduct a child from the beacon of civilisation that is our fine country, especially with the authorities looking out for him. I imagine the idea was for the Strzhcics to travel back to the Continent with Mikel, hand him over there, and collect the blood money."

I shivered at the thought and looked across at the boy. Billy was now crouched beside him, chattering nineteen-to-the-dozen and clearly puzzled that Mikel had difficulty understanding him. However, Mrs. Mott translated and soon merry laughter could be heard, a most pleasing sound. More delights were to follow as our landlady entered with a laden tray.

"Mrs. 'Udson!" Billy exclaimed. "You're a right treasure, you are!"

On tracking down the runaways to Edith Mott's mother's house in Southwark – the safest place the good woman could think of to take the child – and having established from her the truth of his suspicions, Holmes had straightway sent word to Mycroft, along with the envelopes from the Strzhcics, as evidence, and also, of course, with their three fine stamps to replace the missing one. As we were to learn later, the treacherous pair were soon arrested, though not without some resistance. Strzhcic drew a pistol but was disarmed by a well-placed blow from a truncheon, while Madame inflicted deep scratches on the face of the unfortunate constable who was trying to restrain her. However, they were soon safely locked away in Newgate.

Our concerns just now, however, were for the safety of the boy. Where could he stay for the moment where he couldn't easily be found? It was Billy who came up with a plan.

"'E can come to ours for now, Mr. 'Olmes. No one'll notice one more among the lot o' us."

It was such an absurd solution that, as Holmes remarked, it might just work.

"Me ma and pa won't mind, honest. Better than shuttin' 'im away, like 'e was before."

The appropriate consultations were made forthwith, and indeed the Higginses proved happy to welcome Billy's little friend, an orphan as he was described, into their large and jolly family, without needing to know more about him.

"We'll make an 'appy Christmas for the pore little chap," said Mrs. Higgins.

Holmes, as I know, pressed a good few guineas into her hand, even though none was asked for, and what was offered only reluctantly accepted.

A few days after Christmas found us dining on cold roast goose and pickles. Holmes, reading the paper at the table – a most regrettable habit of his – gave a sudden start.

"Good heavens, Watson – Listen to this. An item dated December 25th:

> *Bzdva. Royalist colonels have engineered a counter-coup against the Republican generals who recently ousted and executed the ruling prince. Princess Denissa has been released from prison and will, it is hoped, soon be reunited with her son, Mikel, and have him recognised as ruler of the country. General –* (Some unpronounceable name, Watson) *– and his co-conspirators have been beheaded and their heads placed on spikes around the royal palace to warn off any others who might be tempted to rise up against the sovereign ruler.*

"My Lord! How very barbaric!" I said. "Of course, I'm delighted to hear that the General has been deposed, but I should not wish such a grisly fate on my worst enemies."

"Indeed. The Strzhcics are lucky to find themselves in the relative civilisation of Newgate."

"I must say, though, I don't like to think of that dear little boy returning to such a country. As ruler, indeed! Who knows when there might be yet another coup?"

"Nevertheless, go back I'm sure he must, and just in time for Christmas."

"Whatever do you mean? Christmas is well over."

"I presume that Mikel is of the Orthodox faith practiced by the rest of his countrymen. They celebrate the Nativity according to the Julian calendar, on 6 January. No, Watson, this year little Mikel will have *two* Christmases to put up with."

He shuddered at the thought, one season of goodwill being more than enough for Mr. Sherlock Holmes. *Bah, humbug!*

The Adventure of the Maligned Mineralogist
by Arthur Hall

According to the records stored in my dispatch box, Christmas was but a week away when my friend Mr. Sherlock Holmes finally put an end to a persistent situation which, had it ever been made public, would have caused a scandal and considerable embarrassment to our Royal Family. He had been jubilant since his recent success, and had informed me that he expected no further cases to present themselves until after the festive season, when he expected to bring to a conclusion several matters which had been slowly maturing.

As for me, I was glad to be able to spend time reading and regaining my strength. I was in a state of near-exhaustion, since the recent influenza epidemic had produced many more patients than I usually saw, and the physicians of the capital had barely sufficed to stem the tide of the afflicted.

My friend had mentioned his intention to spend the day bringing his index up to date and conducting a series of chemical experiments, so it was with some surprise that I looked up from my newspaper to see him staring fixedly out of the window.

"Clearly, something of importance is happening out there," I said, "to have captured your interest so completely."

He shook his head without averting his gaze. "No, I was merely observing a rather sparse religious procession, no doubt parading as a reminder of the meaning of the forthcoming holiday."

"So your absent expression was because you were contemplating affairs of the cloth?"

"Not at all. I was contemplating misunderstandings."

"What can you mean?"

He turned from the window and seated himself on the opposite side of the fireplace, holding up his hands to warm them near the flames.

"The procession was led by two men, carrying between them a sizeable banner portraying a cross."

I waited for him to elaborate, but he did not.

"I see nothing unusual in that." I concluded after a moment's consideration.

"Neither, apparently, do any of the faithful, anywhere in the world."

"Holmes, I confess to being totally confused."

"It is really quite simple. The cross is the recognized symbol of the device on which Jesus was crucified, even though that is not, in fact, the truth."

"That cannot be."

"But it is. You will recall that some research into the realms of religious history was necessary when I undertook that affair in which the Archbishop of Canterbury was remotely connected a few years ago."

"I remember that you forbade me to publish the details."

"Quite so."

"Be so kind then, to explain yourself regarding your remark about the cross."

"Certainly. During that enquiry I was obliged to peruse the Gospels, specifically the writings in the original Greek. I gained access to a copy by means of my slight acquaintance with a professor of antiquities at the British Museum. There I saw at once that the crucifixion instrument is described with the word *stauros,* which means a 'stake' or a 'tree', but never a cross. Since those accounts are those of witnesses to the actual event, I am forced to the conclusion that the symbol used ever since is not the correct one."

"But – " Not for the first time, I was astounded by the breadth of my friend's knowledge, and by his conclusion. " – this has always been taught in Christian churches all over the world."

"And long before those churches existed, in the ancient world. For example, in the Egypt of the Pharaohs, much the same symbol was called an *ankh.* That too had religious significance at the time."

I reflected that this wasn't the first of my friend's sudden revelations of this sort, and was about to present more arguments to what I considered to be a fantastical notion, when the loud ring of the doorbell intruded upon my thoughts. I rose and crossed the room to peer through the window, as he had done. Among the scant passers-by in Baker Street, an unfamiliar figure stood before our door.

"You may yet be presented with a further case before Christmas."

As I returned to my chair, I saw that his eyes glittered. His abhorrence of inactivity wasn't new to me, and I felt that our intended respite had already faded from his mind.

"The caller may be here on another errand – to see you perhaps. We will soon find out, for I hear Mrs. Hudson upon the stairs, leading a man with a heavy tread."

A moment later we rose as our landlady announced a middle-aged man of slightly above-average height, wearing a suit of the boldest tweed I have ever seen. Attempting to make use of Holmes's methods, I noticed at once the faint lines around his eyes and mouth that suggested humour and a warm nature. His smile embraced us both as his eyes travelled from me to my friend.

"Good morning, gentlemen," he beamed. "I trust that your breakfast is over, and that I haven't called too early. I have no desire to be an inconvenience."

"Not at all, dear sir." Holmes replied with a faint smile. "I am Sherlock Holmes, and this is my friend and associate, Doctor John Watson, whose assistance has often been of great value." He broke off, seeing that our landlady had remained at the door. "Yes, Mrs. Hudson. Tea, if you please."

Our visitor had removed his hat to reveal over-long grey hair that lent him a wild appearance. I guided him to the basket chair and we were soon all settled in our seats. The fellow didn't wait to be questioned as Holmes's clients often did, but launched at once into an informative tirade.

"Good sirs, I am Doctor Daniel De Witt Hall. You have doubtless already defined my accent as American, and indeed I am from West Virginia. I obtained my degree in the state of Ohio before setting off to work abroad. After my commission was completed, I decided to live in London for a while, and arrived two weeks ago to take rooms in Burlescombe Place near Charing Cross Station, in anticipation of the arrival of my dear wife in time for Christmas."

He paused as Mrs. Hudson knocked and entered the room bearing the tea-tray. Holmes, looking somewhat bemused in the face of our visitor's gushing introduction, waited until the door had closed behind her before making a quiet comment.

"And you are, I perceive, a mineralogist or geologist who has recently spent some little time in South Africa."

Mr. Hall adopted a look of disbelief. "How ever did you know that, sir?" He paused for a moment to reflect. "I surely didn't mention those things as yet. Why, this is fascinating! Are you a magician?"

I poured tea for us, noting Holmes's expression with amusement. This wasn't the first time he had been described thus.

"No, there is nothing magical about my work, Mr. Hall, but much of it consists of observation. When I see that your face is tanned, though not enough to have been exposed to the hot sun for a long period, and the badge pinned to your coat is that of the American Geological Society, I remember that I have recently read in several newspapers of much activity in the diamond mines a few miles from Pretoria. To connect you with this was no great feat."

"Nevertheless, I find it astonishing."

Holmes sipped from his teacup and replaced it in its saucer. "It is no more than elementary, as I have often stated. If you would care to explain your difficulty to us, Mr. Hall – but not of course until you have finished your tea – I will see what can be done to improve matters. Take a moment, if you wish, to put your thoughts in order and to ensure that you include even the smallest detail. There is no need to hurry."

We had all deposited our empty cups upon the tray before our client seemed ready to begin. I noted that his expression had become uncertain.

"Now that I consider things," he said, "such as the serious crimes that must have been presented to you gentlemen in this room, my own problem suddenly seems trivial. I refrained from consulting Scotland Yard for the same reason."

I knew that being thought of as a second choice after the official force must have irked Holmes, but he didn't show it. Instead, he encouraged our visitor to continue.

"Pray let me decide upon the importance of your situation, Mr. Hall. As Watson will affirm, the most mundane circumstances frequently have unexpected depths."

I nodded my assent, and our client shifted in his chair before beginning.

"Well, as I said, I arrived in your country two weeks ago. I was fortunate in finding accommodation almost immediately. It was as well that the rooms are furnished to an agreeable standard, since I had brought little more from Africa than my suitcase and the clothes I wore. I would have had more, but my house in Pretoria was burgled shortly before I departed. Although little appeared to have been stolen, the robbers left considerable destruction behind them. When the letters began, I had been here scarcely three days."

Holmes leaned forward in his chair. "Pray describe them to us."

"At first I thought that there had been a mistake, for although they were addressed to me, their content had no relevance. They were of a most scandalous and insulting nature, accusing me of acts that I would never contemplate. The first two I destroyed without a second thought, but when they continued to arrive, at irregular intervals and by both post and by hand, I retained them because it was by then clear to me that the sender was serious and that some action was required to set the matter right."

"I imagine that you have brought them with you?"

Mr. Hall reached inside his coat and produced a handful of crumpled sheets which he handed to my friend with a flourish. "There, sir. You will, I am sure, understand my concern at once."

Holmes read each sheet, slowly nodding, before handing them to me. Torn from a cheap notebook, each of the ten pages contained but one line. I noted that the ink also was of poor quality and that, although the spelling was correct, the style of handwriting suggested that the author didn't practice often. Also, the nib was worn sufficiently to cause the ink to spatter as the pen was returned from the inkwell. I perused each sheet in turn:

> *You are the lowest of men.*
>
> *Your scandalous conduct has not gone unnoticed.*
>
> *Have you no shame, sir?*
>
> *Your outrageous deeds must not continue.*
>
> *How many more poor women will you ruin before your conscience restrains you?*
>
> *You are no gentleman.*
>
> *Where is your honour, sir?*
>
> *If your true nature were revealed, your family would shun you.*
>
> *How can you hold your head up, sir, in the company of ladies?*
>
> *You can explain yourself, sir, in the reading room of the Charing Cross Hotel at 7:30 tomorrow evening.*

"I take it that this last message arrived this morning," Holmes said.
"Indeed, by the first post."
"And there is, of course, no truth whatsoever in these accusations?"
Mr. Hall bristled visibly. "I should say not! I haven't the slightest inkling of why I have been subjected to this persecution."
"Please don't take offence," I interjected. "It is necessary to establish the circumstances exactly before embarking on an investigation."
Our client nodded his understanding, his expression reverting to its former benevolence.
"And you are quite certain that you know of no one who could be responsible for this?" Holmes enquired.
"I haven't been in London long enough to make the acquaintance of anyone. It is a complete puzzle to me."
My friend adopted a thoughtful pose, his thin form tense in his chair. "Then it is almost certain that these events are connected to the time you

spent in South Africa. The burglary that you mentioned is highly significant."

"But how can that be?"

"From the information you have given us, certain things can be deduced at once. For example, your journey to London was anticipated by someone you knew in Pretoria or in your place of work." Holmes paused as if something more had occurred to him. "Kindly tell us of the nature of your activities there."

"I was hired to locate and determine the quality of recent discoveries. New diamond fields promised to rival those of Kimberley, those extensive undertakings near the Vaal and Orange rivers."

"I had surmised as much. I believe that we are dealing here with a well-organised smuggling gang. Someone familiar with the mine and with yourself probably telegraphed accomplices in London, for how else would it come about that you were followed and your place of residence established? Further indications of their presence here are the proposed meeting at the Charing Cross Hotel, and that some of the letters were delivered by hand."

Mr. Hall shook his head. "I taught minerology for years, in the state of Ohio, and I rode my students real hard, but I've yet to meet one who could analyse things as you do, Mr. Holmes, even after all my instruction. I can think of no one in South Africa who could be involved in this though – but then I met so many people."

"That is unimportant for the moment," Holmes picked his cherry-wood pipe from the rack but then, preoccupied with the matter in hand, laid it aside. "But at a later date I will suggest to Scotland Yard that they alert the South African authorities of possible smuggling operations in the area that you have described. It's clear that whomever began this sequence of events had some knowledge of you."

"How is that?" our client asked.

"I, also, am unable to follow your reasoning," I confessed.

"It is simplicity itself," my friend explained. "You saw our client's response when I enquired as to the truthfulness of the accusations put forward in these letters. He was outraged that there could be any doubt of his innocence, because he is a man of honour to whom such conduct is unthinkable. His accuser is aware of this, and knows that his victim will go to great lengths to set the record straight. Hence his confident assumption that the meeting at the Charing Cross Hotel will take place tomorrow night. A man of less principle would have simply shrugged the matter off and continued on his way. These conclusions must have been sent from South Africa, since Mr. Hall is unknown to the gang members in London, and it is therefore reasonable to assume that both the knowledge of his moral standards and the method of exploiting them originate there."

"You make it all sound so simple," our client remarked.

"It is merely an exercise in reasoning."

"Will you then consent to accompany me to this rendezvous? It may be that we can apprehend this scoundrel, together with any accomplices who he may bring along, and hand them over to the police."

"Neither I," Holmes replied, "nor Watson, for there is another aspect to this affair which must not be neglected. However, your encounter will be witnessed, and protection provided should it prove to be necessary. You may depend upon it, sir."

Mr. De Witt Hall was effusive in his thanks and enquired as to Holmes's fees. My friend explained that while the work is its own reward, his fees were on a fixed scale, and that his clients were also at liberty to defray any expenses that the investigation might produce. Appearing rather bemused at this our client left us, after receiving a repeated assurance that all would soon be well.

Looking down from our window, we watched as our visitor procured a hansom and was quickly lost to sight. At my friend's suggestion we stood at an odd angle, presumably because he wished to ascertain whether Mr. Hall was still attracting followers, without ourselves being observed while doing so.

"A peculiar business," I remarked when we had resumed our seats near the fire.

He laughed shortly. "Not so. Surely you remember that we have faced this situation before. It is obvious that the letters and the proposed meeting have a single purpose – that of ensuring that his residence is unoccupied for enough time to enable a search. You mark my words, Watson, Mr. Hall unknowingly brought something with him from South Africa, probably uncut diamonds, and the agents of the smuggling gang will go to any lengths to retrieve it."

"So you intend for us to observe his premises while he keeps his appointment?"

"Precisely. Are you with me?"

"As always," I smiled, feeling pleasure at his confidence in me. "But what of Mr. De Witt Hall? Is he not in danger at the Charing Cross Hotel?"

Holmes shook his head and lit his pipe. "We can, I think, avoid such a situation. When luncheon is over, we will venture out into this cold afternoon long enough to send a telegram to Barker, the private enquiry agent who has proved useful from time to time. I'll inform him as to the danger and, as he isn't a man to be overcome easily, he will provide adequate protection for our client. I imagine that the true purpose of the meeting is to ascertain whether Mr. Hall has already discovered the diamonds, if indeed that is what is involved here, and if so to force him to give them up. His tormenters seem to have covered the situation from every direction, which is what I would expect from a professional gang."

"When we set off Burlescombe Place then, I'll ensure that my service revolver is in my pocket."

"Capital!" Holmes said as, with the time for luncheon approaching, we heard Mrs. Hudson upon the stairs.

As I recall, there occurred but one more incident before Holmes and I departed the following evening.

We had just returned from the post office, the message to Barker despatched, and were about to resume our places around the fire.

"I see that the excessive chill has affected you, Watson," my friend observed. "Although dinner is some way off, I cannot think that a medicinal brandy would go amiss."

"That would be most welcome," I agreed.

Holmes picked up the decanter but froze as, once again, the doorbell rang unexpectedly.

"It seems that the Christmas season is to demand more activity from us than we had anticipated," he remarked as he abandoned the gesture.

I groaned inwardly. "Our respite has all but eluded us."

"Don't worry," he said pleasantly. "There will be time for everything."

Then the door swung open after a barely perceptible knock, and Mrs. Hudson showed in a striking young woman wearing a costume of powder blue.

"Miss Agnes Coldford, to see Mr. Holmes." Our landlady waited in expectation of instructions to bring refreshment, I thought. Receiving none, she withdrew.

Holmes rose, as did I, and we wished the young lady good afternoon. Holmes introduced us before inviting her to sit. Her bonnet covered much of her head, but the chestnut curls that had spilled out of the sides were of a good, rich colour. Had I been asked, I would have placed her age at more than twenty-five but not yet thirty and, I noted, she was tall and shapely. Her eyes, as I could make out when she drew nearer, were green, and seemed to possess an icy quality. This was belied by her facial appearance, which was that of an angel.

I made to offer her tea, coffee, or perhaps a brandy, although she showed no sign of exposure to the weather, but a glance from Holmes discontinued my intention. Surprised, I settled in my chair. For a moment our room was silent except for the whistling of the wind that had sprung up, and I waited in mild confusion for my friend to begin the interview.

"So, Miss Coldford," I saw his eyes glitter as he addressed her, but couldn't fathom the cause, "please be so good as to explain what has brought you here today. I perceive that you arrived by carriage, since your cheeks are not reddened by the cold, and that you are anxious to impart something which you regard as important, but nothing more. If you will kindly elaborate, Doctor Watson and myself will endeavour to assist you in any way that we can."

"Thank you, sirs," she answered in an unexpectedly submissive tone, "but my request is simple, and possibly the most unusual that has ever been put to you."

Both Holmes and I leaned forward in our chairs, our curiosity aroused by this unusual statement.

"I find myself intrigued," he said. "Pray continue."

"I ask that you do nothing."

My expression doubtless revealed my puzzlement, but Holmes's countenance was unaltered.

"Do you refer to something that has already been presented to us?"

"Indeed. Earlier today I followed my stepfather, and observed him as he entered this house. I assume he has consulted you?"

"You must appreciate that I cannot discuss the affairs of any other visitor. Every case is, of necessity, kept confidential."

"I do, Mr. Holmes, but there are hidden circumstances here. My stepfather, Mr. Daniel De Witt Hall, has no doubt spun a tale of robbery and persecution, in order to enlist your help?"

Holmes fixed her with a curious stare. "That isn't unusual, in my profession."

She held up her hands, as if exasperated. "But it is untrue, I tell you. This is far from the first such occurrence, for he imagines many strange things. I have seen him tell many wild stories to people he hardly knows, and he is believed because, although absent-minded, he has a convincing way of relating them. I imagine he told you of stolen jewels, or gold, or that he is the subject of threatening visits or communications. Believe none of it, sirs! His mind is unstable. There are days when he fails to recognise me, though I am obliged to listen to his ramblings. If I can compensate you for your wasted time I will do so but, I beg of you, spend no more of it on these imagined fantasies. That is all I have to say, gentlemen. I felt I couldn't let you remain under such misapprehensions as my step-father often leaves behind him."

Holmes and I looked at each other, and I saw that he now wore a look of great surprise. From outside the sounds of passers-by, some with a liberal dose of Christmas spirit, reached us. I heard at least two groups of carol-singers, possibly competing, engaged in shrill renderings until the harsh tones of a constable put an end to it. I concluded that they must have been over-enthusiastic, begging and causing annoyance. The voices hadn't faded when Holmes asked our visitor, "How did it come about that you know that Mr. Hall had been to Baker Street?"

"When I recognise that his mind is wandering, I often pursue him without his knowledge. I am forever afraid that her will step into the path of a carriage, or that he will lose his way."

"Has your step-father travelled abroad recently?" I enquired.

"Ah", she said, "you refer to the darkness of his skin. That came about from his falling asleep on a South Coast beach earlier this year. The resulting sunburn was quite painful for him, and he complained for several days after."

"You have told us much of which we were unaware, Miss Coldford," Holmes acknowledged. "I thank you. I see that we must now view the situation differently." He consulted his pocket-watch. "But now my next appointment is imminent, so I must bid you good-day. Doctor Watson will accompany you to procure a cab in Baker Street."

"Please don't trouble yourself, Doctor," she said pleasantly. "I have an errand which I must fulfil before returning to my home. Thank you, gentlemen, for your attention."

With that she rose abruptly and left us. Holmes sprang from his chair the moment we heard the front door close behind her. In an instant he was standing at the window, watching the street with satisfaction written on his face.

"As I thought," he said.

"You have seen something of significance?"

"Oh, certainly. Miss Coldford was delivered here by a private carriage, which waited for her throughout our interview. The driver, who has just met her to accompany her back to where their conveyance waits, is known to me."

"I, also, saw a falsehood in her revelations."

"Really, Watson? Pray elaborate."

"You will recall that I asked about her step-father's complexion," I began as he resumed his seat. "I enquired because Mr. Hall's sunburn was akin to that suffered by myself and most of my regiment during our time in Afghanistan. I cannot believe, taking into account the sunshine of an English summer and the little of it that we have been blessed with through the year, that he came by it within these shores. I consider that our client's explanation is by far the most likely."

Holmes clapped his hands delightedly. "Bravo! You improve constantly. Your observation was correct of course, but is far from all that can be discerned from Miss Coldford's visit. Tell me, did Mr. Daniel De Witt Hall strike you as at all absent-minded or in any way deficient of his senses?"

I shook my head. "Much to the contrary. The man seemed amiable, almost jovial at times, and related his difficulty in a most clear and concise manner."

"That was my impression precisely. Also, he presented the offending documents for our inspection, proving their existence. Had I mentioned this to Miss Coldford, she would doubtless have dismissed them as forgeries, or written by Mr. Hall himself."

"So her purpose here was to encourage us to abandon the case?"

"I suspected something of the sort from the moment she entered the room. You see, I am already acquainted with her, although she is apparently unaware of it. Her real name is Miss Rebekah Dornay, a twice-convicted swindler and pickpocket. I could show you, from my index, the history of her life of crime as depicted by the newspapers. No, the chestnut wig didn't deceive me and, of course, this clumsy attempt at distraction establishes a link with the criminal classes."

"You mentioned that you identified the man who met her after she left."

"Indeed I did. He is Seth Malter, a known burglar and jewel thief who is also suspected of a recent murder. He was arrested some time ago, but escaped as he was being transported to court. I'm sure that Lestrade will be delighted to see him."

The following evening we departed immediately after dinner. Darkness had long since fallen and the gas-lamps shone a ghostly sheen upon the pavements. As we passed, I noticed coloured streamers and other decorations in the windows of shops and houses alike. Clearly, all of London was preparing for the holiday. I imagined the aroma of a cooked goose filling Mrs. Hudson's kitchen while my friend and I waited in hungry anticipation. I brought my thoughts back to the present and shivered in the bitterly cold air while Holmes despatched a telegram to Scotland Yard. Clearly, he expected an altercation.

Holmes dismissed the hansom near Charing Cross Station and we walked the short distance to the enclave which lay back from the main road. Burlescombe Place, we observed, comprised four Georgian houses surrounding a frost-covered lawned area. Three of these appeared to be private residences while the fourth, according to the engraved plate upon the door, was divided into two separate accommodations.

At Holmes's gesture, we approached the darkened house quietly.

"They're already here," he whispered. "I saw a flicker of light in a room above."

We were about to enter when we heard heavy footfalls behind us. Three roughs rushed towards us brandishing cudgels, and my friend at once drew his swordstick that was sheathed within his walking-cane.

"Those three were lounging near the entrance from the main road," he said with a calm that I didn't share. "From the way we drew their attention, I suspected that they were lookouts. You are armed, Watson?"

"My service revolver is always with me."

"Excellent! Do not be afraid to use it, for I see that their weapons contain razor blades and nails."

Our assailants said nothing, but attacked immediately. The first, a huge man whose gold tooth glinted in the light of the nearby street-lamp, swung a vicious blow at Holmes's head. My friend barely avoided it and, as the man almost lost his balance from the expended force, lunged lightning-fast with his rapier. The cudgel fell to the ground, as its owner screamed and stared at his pierced wrist with disbelief. Blood flowed freely as he half-sank to his knees before an uppercut sent him sprawling backwards.

The remaining two thugs had concentrated on me, and the nearest received a bullet wound to his left thigh that caused him to fall in the path of his companion. The last attacker raised his weapon, but Holmes again thrust with his blade before I could get off a second shot, and his opponent held his hands against his bleeding ribcage as he fled.

"Some clearing up for Lestrade's men," Holmes indicated the two prone figures, "and there will be more to come. I fear, however, that we have lost the element of surprise."

He took out a police whistle, and the shrill sound pierced the night.

We were both rather breathless after our encounters, but thankfully uninjured. Holmes opened the door before us to be confronted by a deserted staircase.

"Keep your weapon handy," he instructed me, "for we don't know the extent of our adversaries, nor if they are armed."

We climbed slowly, but stealth was no longer necessary. At the top of the stairs we were faced with two doors, the nearest of which was ajar with a faint light spilling onto the landing. Holmes stood to one side and pushed it fully open. The first thing that took my notice was that the room was in a state of considerable disarray, doubtless as a result of a search that had been conducted with no intention of concealing the intrusion.

A gas lamp had been lit but turned low, and in the shadows two figures faced us with pistols aimed.

"Good evening, Miss Rebekah Dornay," my friend said calmly. "I trust that you realise that a revolver of such small calibre is unlikely to incapacitate at that distance." He turned his attention to her companion. "And here we have Mr. Seth Malter. No, Mr. Malter, I'm not surprised that you are involved in this affair, for you have included Miss Dornay in your misdeeds before, have you not? As soon as I realised that gems were the commodity in question, your name occurred to me immediately."

"Aren't you clever, Mr. Holmes?" he asked sarcastically.

"You recognised me when I came to your rooms?" Miss Dornay said with genuine surprise.

"Your picture has appeared in the newspapers, and your skill at disguise could perhaps be improved upon."

"If you want to live, Mr. Holmes, you will tell your friend to lower his weapon and allow us to leave. We have two firearms against your single revolver."

Holmes peered from the nearby window then moved aside, surprising me by his obedience.

"I recommend that you both review your position before leaving," he advised.

Miss Dornay crossed the room and looked out, as he had done.

"Seth," she cried, "half of Scotland Yard is out there."

"Watch them," Malter said, indicating Holmes and myself as he strode quickly to join her. I saw the blood drain from his face. "Lestrade is with them. If he catches me, I'm done for. It'll be the hangman." He glanced around him hopelessly, as if looking for other means to escape. "I'm sorry, Beck, but it's my life if I'm caught."

With that he ran from the room, his boots clattering on the stairs. I went to the window and saw him emerge into the night with his pistol raised, only to be seized by two burly constables before he could fire. Inspector Lestrade himself speedily secured him with police handcuffs.

Miss Rebekah Dornay let her weapon fall to the floor and dropped her head to her chest. She couldn't meet our eyes.

"It is all up with me, Mr. Holmes," she murmured as we left the house together and Lestrade's men closed in.

The following morning, Mrs. Hudson barely had time to clear away the breakfast things before the doorbell rang.

"That will be Barker," Holmes informed me as we heard her answer.

Moments later our landlady announced the Surrey enquiry agent, who appeared little changed from when I had encountered him previously.

His stern countenance was unaltered in its expression as greetings were exchanged, and I realized that the man was humourless. At Holmes's invitation he sat in the basket chair, placing his hat on a side-table. A ray of weak winter sunlight shone through the window, glinting for an instant on his grey-tinted spectacles and Masonic tie pin.

"It was as you suspected, Mr. Holmes," he began after refusing refreshment. "Jude Gorvin."

"I was almost certain of it, since he is known to be an accomplice of Seth Malter in at least six jewel thefts that have taken place over the past three years."

"This Gorvin was the man who met our client last night at the Charing Cross Hotel?" I enquired.

"Indeed," Barker confirmed. "I sat at a table near to them, in order to overhear the conversation. Mr. Hall I recognised from your description, and Gorvin was already known to me. He was quite charming at first, but grew steadily less so as Mr. Hall insisted that he knew nothing of diamonds from South Africa."

"He spoke the truth," said Holmes, "The gems were inserted in a suitcase identical to Mr. Hall's before they were exchanged under the guise of a burglary. Again, this suggests that someone close to him in South Africa is a member of the gang, for how would the appearance of his luggage be known to them otherwise?"

"You discovered the hiding-place, then?" Barker asked.

Muted sounds from outside reached us – a passing coach with seasonal Christmas bells attached to the reins, perhaps – in the moment that it took Holmes to answer. Then a horse galloped along Baker Street at an unusually fast pace, and someone shouted something that could have been "Merry Christmas!"

"Watson and I returned to Mr. Hall's premises after Lestrade's departure last night. Miss Dornay and Seth Malter's search was extensive but not thorough, and we found the diamonds, although in their uncut state they appeared less than attractive, concealed in the suitcase handle. On examining the stitching with my lens, its irregularity was apparent."

Barker nodded. "When your client continued to deny any knowledge of the jewels, the exchange became heated. Gorvin got to his feet and towered over Mr. Hall in a most threatening manner. He had apparently forgotten that they were in a public place, for his threats became loud and unrestrained. At that point it appeared that a fight would break out and I thought it prudent to intervene, but it proved to be unnecessary."

"A constable had been summoned," I suggested.

Barker's taciturn expression lightened slightly. "Not at all, Doctor, and I couldn't have been more surprised. Mr. Hall rose to face Gorvin and bristled like a bulldog in defiance. In quiet tones, he told the criminal how he had faced beasts and robbers while in South Africa, after which the threat he faced now was as nothing. I am convinced that your client would have given a quite adequate account of himself had the need arose, but Gorvin, seeing the attention he had drawn from the hotel staff and guests, thought it better for himself to withdraw. Needless to say, I followed him into the street and subdued him, before hauling him by the scruff of his neck to where I encountered a constable on his beat. I mentioned your name, Mr. Holmes, and the officer immediately took charge and carted his prisoner away."

"Excellent, Barker," Holmes acknowledged. "You have done well. That I think, concludes this affair, for Mr. Hall will be subjected to no more derogatory letters from an unknown source."

Barker rose at once, perhaps sensing that the interview was over. We all shook hands.

"As is usual," my friend continued, "you will receive my cheque by post in a few days. As for now, it remains only for Watson and myself to wish you the Compliments of the Season, together with a most contented and prosperous New Year."

Christmas Magic
by Kevin P. Thornton

I have mentioned in other writings that not all of my friend Sherlock Holmes's cases have been published. Some will never see the printer's ink in my time for varied reasons. Indeed, this narrative is part of the collection in my dispatch box, and if it has seen the light of day, then I am long gone. There are differing reasons as to why these stories were originally consigned to dusty history. There have been cases of some delicacy, and others that are classified under national interest. Some are both, moving from the backrooms of Whitehall to the boudoirs of Mayfair and back again with alacrity and distaste. The least said about such sordidness the better.

Then there are those about which the world is not ready to hear, matters of such fantastical and inexplicable occurrence as to seem to defy science. They will also remain locked away until a newer era is more properly able to understand what happened. By way of example, I would love to be at the point in history where someone can explain the Giant Rat of Sumatra.

I have also taken it upon myself to hold back those adventures where the spirit of the law has been honoured more than its letter. While Holmes cared naught for the frequent idiocies of the legal system and sometimes bent rules to serve justice, I chose to protect him from any possible legal ramifications. The world is not in a fine-enough shape for Sherlock Holmes to languish in jail on a technicality. He has always been needed at the forefront of criminal justice, and on a rare few occasions I chose moral lassitude over high dudgeon in judging his behaviour. While I have no regrets, the law has a long and unforgiving arm, so the embargo on those tales will be a lengthy one.

And there is one last category where I have made notes and not written stories. They are filed in my dispatch box under the word *Humdrum*.

It is a sad truth that, even if one is the world's greatest and only consulting detective, it is sometimes difficult to predict where a case might lead in terms of intrigue and suspicion. That is in some ways the *raison d'être* of a detective in the first place, helping the unknowing become more knowing, regardless of the potential mundanities. Despite his uncanny ability to refuse most of the vapid and monotonous puzzles that came his way, there were times where he was disappointed. A case that proved promising at the outset, looking like a miraculous murder mayhap, would peter away into a simple act of careless, callous calumny. A mysterious theft from a locked room would end when the senile grandparent remembered that he or she had used a valuable part of a Norman tapestry as kindling for the log fire.

For the most part, Holmes kept his senses and sense of humour intact, but over the years I had heard him cry out to the surrounding ethos in frustration at the boredom his career choice occasionally foisted upon him. He was addicted to mental stimulation and, while he would honour his commitment to a client, there were times when one addiction, unfed, could be replaced by another.

I would like to think my own sensibilities helped him change his ways. As his career progressed and he was able to choose his puzzlements more carefully, so too was he able to manage his periods of emptiness, and the slithering *ennui* that in the early years he defeated with cocaine gave way to more congenial habits. As his reputation increased, he was able to deal with his unoccupied times more ably, knowing that such were fleeting, and even the rare cases that failed to excite him were now no more the unfortunate vicissitudes of chance.

Such was the case during Christmas 1899. (I have been re-reading my dusty notebook about that time, after my mind was recently jogged by the obituary of a writer whom I never met, but whose contemporary Christmas story, first published less than five years earlier, had already become as much a part of the Yule tradition as Dickens's *A Christmas Carol*. Even though the story was originally mine for the taking, I harbour no regrets. Billy did a better job than I ever could, and its room in the pantheon of the festive season has been ever-growing and fully justified. I only wish I'd met him. Judging by his friend's tales, he was an American original.)

The matter itself was one of those I had determined to be insufficiently interesting to absorb my readers, so banal in its solution that filing it under "*Humdrum*" may very well have been the most exciting part. Holmes had received a message from Richard Moore Hall, an American businessman due in London at a point in the near future, asking if he could track down his brother, a man believed to be down on his luck.

"And that was all he told you?" I said.

"There is a description in his letter here," he said, passing it to me. "He is an older man, but clearly one of some vigour. He had recently served, and was quite badly wounded, in the American dispute in the Philippines. He was an officer with the Macabebe Scouts, a brevet captain, indicating a man of bravery. He has had a wide ranging career, having also been a marshal, a sheriff, sergeant-at-arms of the Texas Senate, and a military officer three differing times in three separate wars. He was also a Texas Ranger."

"Is that a special calling?" I asked.

"It seems to be," said Holmes. "They are detective adventurers on horseback, roaming across the vast unsettled swathes of Texas – a state that is more than six times the size of England by the way."

"It sounds like the kind of job for which you should apply."

"Nonsense, my friend. Who then would keep London's underworld at bay?" We were in our shared rooms at 221b, and Holmes stretched himself, rose from his angle of turpitude, and walked to the window.

"What kind of a wound?" I said.

"I believe it was a bayonet to the shoulder," said Holmes. I winced in sympathy, although my own long-gone injuries had been caused by A Jezail bullet from a large calibre rifle.

"And his brother thinks he is here in London?"

"He reached out to the U.S. Embassy when he first arrived, and my client, who is not without connections and resources, was informed of such. Subsequent to that, he hasn't left these shores.

"I presume you checked the docks first," I said.

"My dear Watson, sometimes your perspicacity astounds me." His gentle smile took the sting from his barb. "I have had my agents hunting the opium dens all along the docklands, and I expect to hear of his whereabouts soon."

"You have left the houses of ill-repute out of the search?" I asked.

"It appears that the missing man, Jesse Hall, chose to take the long way home from Aringay to Houston for a reason as yet unknown to us. His brother suspects he is suffering. This isn't his first battle wound, and he has disappeared before. I suspect when he left his ship here in London it is more likely he was looking for a means to overcome his physical discomforts as opposed to the delights of the flesh." Holmes paused, then said, "My experience in old war wounds come from watching you wince and suffer over the years. Not all are as strong as you in dealing with such hardship. Jesse Hall is running from his demons. We know this because his brother cares to try to find him, again. They have been down this road before. Whatever the state of his wound, he isn't over it. When I find him, he will need the keen eye of a good doctor. I hope you will accompany me."

"You know I will be at your side."

Holmes was right. Although there had been countless advances in medicine since the learnings of the Crimean War and the American internal conflict nearly forty years prior, pain management hadn't advanced apace and there was much self-medication, and much of that was addictive. Opiates and other drugs, along with alcohol, could numb the pain and the memories temporarily, but the cravings they created often caused the sufferers to jump ship to seek relief.

When the message came the next morning, carried by an urchin who looked as if his next bath would be his first, Holmes gave him a shilling and said, "We have found him Watson. There is no shortage of money in my client's purse, so rather than risk our own health among the blackguards of the drug world, I have arranged for a private carriage and some retired bare-knuckle men to take him from his opium den of iniquity into care at a sanatorium. Would you do me the honour of attending him with me?"

And so we did. Jesse Hall, while not on his last legs, might very well have been staggering towards his demise on his penultimate pair. He was alive despite his best efforts, though incoherent and nonsensical. The marks along his arms spoke of frequent drug use, and it was hard to reconcile his current state with the hero he had been in battle. There was a raw red wound on the left upper side of his chest where the bayonet had penetrated, and I suspected, given my knowledge of battlefield surgery, that much of his pain was caused by what was still *in situ* under the skin.

"There is nothing to be done for him now, save rest and healthy care," I said. "He will be fractious when he the drugs dissipate, but this is one of the best private hospitals in London and they are capable of handling his mood swings. As to his wound, it may heal by itself under good care and clean living. If it doesn't, it is a matter to be dealt with when he is stronger."

By the end of the week, Jesse Hall had been through the worst and the surgeon with whom I consulted was reluctant to put him under the scalpel again, a decision with which I concurred. "He has just been weaned of self-medication," he said. "I would watch him carefully and see if diet and exercise can cure the damage caused by the stabbing."

Holmes sent a telegram to his client, who promised to be on the next ship over.

I tended to Jesse Hall as much as time allowed. He was in good hands where he was, and I kept an eye on him more as a favour to my friend than to honour the Oath of Hippocrates which bound me. He was a sullen patient, unhappy with his saving. Although he didn't say it, he wasn't over the addictions he had found, and I suspected his brother would have his hands full.

When Richard Hall arrived on our shores some ten days later, he stopped in our rooms even before proceeding to his hotel. He was a healthy-weathered outdoorsman that a fine suit and good shoes couldn't hide. He had an honest, open look about him and the American frankness of a muscled handshake and a twinkled look right into one's eyes upon inspection. I suspected we were of similar age. Had we grown up together, I could imagine him as a fellow officer and professional man.

He listened carefully to my opinions and my thoughts on the treatment of his brother.

"I have the time and the wherewithal to stay with him until he is over his ailments," he told me, "although I have been down this road of addiction with him before and know it to be a rocky one. I cannot thank you both enough for your work. He is my older brother and, although he is headstrong enough to make a mule quake, I care for him and am glad my business dovetailed with you finding him. Obviously I shall be in London for a while. Perhaps I may take you and Mister Holmes out to dinner."

We agreed on a time and place. I remember the evening well as it was the first of many. He wined and dined us in an extravagant yet elegant manner. It was so enjoyable we agreed to do it again, and fell into the habit while Hall was in London.

He was a most agreeable man. Like his brother – indeed, like many Americans – he had lived a full and adventurous life. An engineer by profession, he had been a surveyor in Texas as the West opened up – 'A time of opportunity and adventure' he called it. Then he ranched for some years before holding elected office. He nearly ran for Governor of Texas before working as a lawyer. Now he was the President of a railroad company, the other reason for his visit to London.

"I say to one and all that I own a railroad company," he told us over port in the cigar room, "but I feel dishonest since we have no rolling stock as yet."

"So what do you run on your line?" I asked.

"Ah," he said, "we don't actually have a line either." He moved quickly to address my surprise. "There is no trickery, Watson. The company is a statement of intent, if you will. We wish to build a line that we believe will make money. To do so, we need to start a company. Unfortunately the distance between start-up and operation can take some years. It is much the same, I imagine, as your other career. One may call oneself a writer for a number of years, but in the end you have to write something. Is that not the case?"

"It is the wrong analogy," said Holmes, "because you have chosen to compare your own work to the strangest of careers. It has been my experience that quite the opposite happens. A man may be a writer yet still not call himself such, as if to do so would doom him. In almost all other instances of work, success breeds confidence. Watson, by way of example, is a good doctor who will only become better over the years. However as a writer with some degree of success – and on this occasion I shall refrain from my usual comments about his subject matter – he is still on occasion moribund and self-doubting. Why? Because he is a writer."

"You have little room to speak," I replied. "When it comes to the lethargy of boredom and self-doubt, you have no equal, Holmes. You are either frantic or in the doldrums. There is rarely a happy medium."

"And you will get no argument from me," Holmes replied. "But my unique personality and gifts are what make me as I am. The same doesn't go for all others in my field. Most detectives, even though their thinking is constrained by the bureaucratic policing forces they serve, rarely show an iota of originality or free thought. Thus their tedium never needs to be vanquished, as they live their lives quite thoroughly in quiet desperation. Writers, on the other hand, are all pessimists. It is if they are attracted to the profession because it is self-fulfilling."

Hall watched the two of us go back-and-forth argue with amusement.

The club we were in was new to me. My own was the Army and Navy. This was one of the newer places, created to capitalize on the *nouveau riche* of industry who weren't allowed into Whites or the Athenaeum. It had reciprocity with his own, the Houston Cattleman and Rancher's Club, and as I looked around and saw some of the dyspeptic members asleep in dark corners or hiding behind *The Times*, I pictured one of them riding up to a hitching post in Texas, dressed like a cowboy as described in the penny dreadfuls, possibly shouting, "Yeehaw!" I smiled, and when Hall asked why, Holmes answered in my place.

"He is imagining the occupants of this club and how out of place they would be in the west." Holmes was rewarded by the surprise on my face.

"Is that true?" said Hall.

"Yes," I said. "Seeing Holmes's parlour trickery up close like that will make you realize that, brilliant as he is, he can also be a difficult man to work with."

Holmes had the grace to try to look modest, though he mostly failed.

"Out with it then, Holmes," I said. "What of my behaviour or manner allowed you to read my mind?"

"It is the law of comparisons," said Holmes. "You rarely smile, Watson. It isn't because you are grumpy. Mrs. Hudson thinks you quite charming, and you have been a companionable chap to me for many years. No, it is because you are a gentleman of your time. Life is scarcely amusing in London. It is a place for diligent, honest, grown-up public schoolboys. Consequently, when I saw you smile as you sat back in your chair, I looked around to see what had amused you. It wasn't the meal, splendid as it was. Such approbation would have been displayed as the food was served. It isn't the surrounds either. You aren't a frequent club man, Watson, but, as is typical of your age and station in life, you have been inside such establishments enough for them not to be novel. But you have never been in a club in any other city, and even though Hall's place in Houston is no doubt similar to this – "

"Drearily so," said Hall. "Just with better weather."

"Quite," said Holmes. "Even though it is similar, it would be easy to imagine it as different, more in keeping with a saloon from one of those tawdry tales our friends across the Atlantic call 'Dime Novels'. And even as Hall is clearly as comfortable in our society, indicating that Houston is as modern and sophisticated as it is possible to be in a country barely more than a hundred years extant, your sudden smile was no doubt caused by the appearance of such a juxtaposition in your mind."

"You deduced what caused him to smile by eliminating everything that wouldn't," said Hall. "I'm sorry for the inelegant paraphrase, Doctor. I am an admirer."

"I am honoured, Hall, that you have read my stories. And yes, Holmes, you are correct, as you always seem to be. My apologies if I seem a little distracted. The fact of the matter is I have a quandary that I'm not sure how to solve. I have the most irksome writing task waiting for me, and I am stuck.

"You have never seemed at a loss for words before," said Holmes. "At least not written ones."

"Oh, do tell us what it is, Watson," said Hall. "It would be exciting to go back and tell everyone that the great Doctor Watson consulted me about a writing problem and that I was able to help. I have a friend, Billy Porter, who writes short stories, and his jealousy will know no bounds."

Holmes was fair twitching in barely disguised delight that the shoe was on the other foot, and for once I was the fawned upon. "Please, Doctor Watson," he said generously, "do let us help. At the very least, you will prove my postulation about writers and their fatalism."

"How so?" said Hall.

"If as a rancher you had a farming conundrum, you might seek advice from another rancher, but not from a detective. Similarly a doctor might consult another doctor, but he wouldn't seek a second opinion from an engineer. Yet a writer such as Watson has a writing problem, and believes he will get his best help and advice from two like us? It is a madness of thought only another writer would understand, yet that is the last person he will consult.

"What about a detective?" said Hall. "It is in your title after all. Consulting Detective. Who do you consult if you need help?"

"I don't know," said Holmes. "It has never happened."

Hall smiled as I shrugged before continuing with my problem.

"My late wife's cousin, Hortense," I said, "has become involved with a group of charitably minded ladies. They feel the need to help the poor of the East End, and to this end they are raising money for a soup kitchen by publishing a magazine of uplifting Yuletide tales. This they will have printed and sell to all their delightful friends and acquaintances this season, and presumably in all future Christmas seasons to come. They have asked several reputable writers to submit a tale to them. I can tell you that Retlaw Spring has accepted, as well as Richard André, C.J. Hamilton, and Clifford Merton." From Holmes I drew the expected blank look. I may have said Derby, Gladstone, Disraeli, or Salisbury – such was his lack of knowledge of the literary elite of the day.

Hall, however understood. "Those are prestigious names," he said. "To be ranked among them is a fine honour,"

"Thank you," I said. "You will therefore understand why I am reluctant to refuse, even though I feel I must."

"Oh," said Hall. "And why is that, pray tell?"

"Because he feels unworthy to be in the same company," said Holmes. "Stuff and nonsense. You are the equal of any of those you have mentioned."

"Well there you have it," said Hall. "I know my writer friend back in New York would be honoured to be in such company. So should you. Even Holmes thinks you are worthy. Did he not just say so?"

"Thank you, Hall, for your kind words, but I have known Sherlock Holmes for a long time and am aware of the directness of his opinion. When he said I was the equal of any of those I mentioned, it wasn't a ranking of greatness, merely a ranking. Holmes's opinion of popular writers is on a par with his thoughts about astronomy: Minimal and inconsequential."

"I'm sure you do yourself an injustice, Watson," said Hall, but a look at Holmes told the truth.

"What I said was the truth," said Holmes. "If those others you mentioned are up to the task, I see no reason why you will not be, Watson. You have already displayed a certain capacity for words. What is one more?"

Hall held his head in his hands in mock dismay. "You English accuse the Americans of being uncivilized and abrupt. We could take lessons from you, Holmes. Anyway, be that as it may, what is the real issue, Watson? Unlike your friend here, I have both read and admired your work.

You are easily the equal of these others. What could possibly be the problem that you need our help in solving?"

"I don't know how to start," I said.

"I beg your pardon?" said Hall.

"I said, I am stuck right at the beginning. Normally when I write one of the cases, I have a starting point: My notes, my memories, my thoughts formulated during the process of the adventure. I then start to write and I follow everything logically and even chronologically."

"Begin at the beginning," said Holmes, "and go on till you come to the end. Then stop." He was amused by the astonishment his comment made. "Dodgson said that. He was quite right too. He is an impressive mathematician."

The quote was Dodgson's, as by his alter ego *Lewis Carroll*. For a moment I wanted to find out how and why Holmes had found it useful to read *Alice's Adventures in Wonderland*, but to go down such a rabbit hole would be unhelpful to my current predicament.

"I don't understand," said Hall.

"Watson considers what he writes, as fanciful as they are, as reportage. He makes notes and tells a story. No matter how much I chide him for his fictional and fantastical alterations, nevertheless they are based on an actual event, one that anchors the story."

"And your putative Christmas story doesn't have that starting point," said Hall. "I see. Well, you have come to exactly the right people to help."

"Indeed?" said Holmes. "I have spent my entire life training myself to think rationally and logically. Watson will tell there isn't a notional figment to my make-up. None whatsoever. How then am I to be any use?"

"Because you are a *thinker*," said Hall. "By definition, you are given information and draw conclusions. In this instance, Watson and I will give you information, you will analyze it, and the end result will be the best storyline for a Christmas tale ever. Are we agreed, gentlemen?"

"I am," I said, intrigued by the possibilities.

"And you, Holmes?" said Hall. "You seem firmly settled into that armchair. If I continue to ply you with strong drink and good tobacco, will you stay and help your friend."

And Sherlock Homes, as relaxed and comfortable as I had ever seen him, relit his pipe and revolved his hand in the universal manner to proceed.

"Excellent," said Hall. "Then let's begin."

"I have done something similar with my friend back in Texas," said Hall. "He is one of the two greatest writers I have ever read, and present company doesn't permit me from naming the other to save his blushes." He smiled as he said this, and I hope I had the good grace to blush a little.

Holmes remained motionless, eyes closed, near horizontal, a latitude of lassitude. To Hall's querying look I answered, "He may appear somnolent, but he is alert in every manner save sight. He will hear all, know all, and comprehend all. Let us begin. Holmes will join in when he feels he has something to add."

"Very well, then. What we need to do is establish all the best parts of a Christmas story. For instance, unlike almost any other type of tale, almost every Christmas narrative ends on a happy note."

I stopped to think, "You're right," I said. "They are the only genre where that is almost guaranteed. It would be possible to write a sad one – it is possible to write anything – but for it to be successful it must fit the jollity of the season."

"It should also be redemptive," said Hill, "or at least well-meaning. The tweeness that is an inherent part of such fiction would become nauseatingly cloying were it part of any other type of writing, but it is necessary for a Christmas tale. Imagine if it was expected that you finished of all your stories about your friend Sherlock Holmes with a morally uplifting conclusion, as some of the dime novels tend to do."

He cleared his throat and leant forward in a conspiratorial way, exaggerating the drawl of his accent. "'And so my friends, as the great detective and his able chronicler stood by, the wagon from Scotland Yard took the failed miscreants away, showing once again that, as long as there are fair and decent men in the world willing to right wrongs, criminals will be caught, and *Crime will not pay!*'" He burst into laughter as he finished and I joined him. Even Holmes permitted himself the tiniest of smiles as he reached his hand across to the table for his snifter.

"Your points are valid, Hall," I said, "but they don't address the topic or starting point of the work I am to do."

"Patience, my dear Watson," said Hall. "We are establishing parameters. Like a good ranch, a man needs to know his limits. Once the boundaries are in place – well, then it's time to let the cows come home."

"This exercise will be more fruitful," said Holmes, "if you refrain from adding to Watson's collection of clichés."

"So noted," said Hall, imbibing thirstily before refilling all our brandy glasses. "In any event, there is another part of such stories that is important. It needs to tug at your heart. Almost all the great stories of Christmas have an emotional start. Someone is unhappy, or down on their luck. Dickens did it best. There were ghosts, sad employees, an irascible main character. All of that led to redemption we have already noted as he advanced his moral ideals. So too 'The Little Match Girl' which, while appearing to be sad, has a happy ending. And Tolstoy also had his story about Panov, writing directly to the Gospel quote, '*For I was hungry and you gave me food, I was thirsty and you gave me drink.*' What could be more emotional than that?"

"I don't know," I said. "What you say makes sense, but I'm not sure if it is something I am comfortable doing. I do enjoy fiction: Dickens, Clarke, Verne, Conan Doyle, Wilkie Collins, and the like. There's that young chap Hornung, who is writing delightful stuff. I'm just not sure if I can do it. There seems to be something deceptive about making things up, and while I can read other people's work, I'm not sure if I can do it myself."

"Of course you can," said Hall. "And you have accidentally touched on the last and best part of this formula: *The deception*. A twist in the tale is a wonderful thing and, while it isn't a requisite part of Christmas, it does add to the story. You will no doubt have noticed that the more popular stories you write of Holmes exploits are the more fantastical ones. Do you know why that is?"

I hadn't noticed, but Hall was quite enthusiastic and, while he had a little of the snake-oil salesman about him – in his real life he was after all trying to sell a railroad that didn't yet exist – I chose not to interrupt him while he was in full flow. He was entertaining and enthusiastic, a natural effervescent tonic to the more reticent Holmes.

"Err, no," I said.

"Readers love mystery and suspense. If you were to ask a question they cannot answer, even if you were to play fair and give them all the information they needed, the resolution to the question posed will make the ending of the story so much more satisfying. How does that all sound?"

"Umm," I said. Holmes rescued me.

"Intriguing," he said. "Instead of beginning with something concrete as he normally does, a story that at least ephemerally is based on fact, you want him to write a work of seasonal fiction that has a happy, slightly mawkish ending. It needs to be suspenseful, redemptive, Abrahamic yet morally upright, respectful of the season, emotionally resonant, and with a surprise ending that no one expects."

"Yes, that's exactly it," said Hall either missing or ignoring the impossibility of such a task. "Hmm," he said. "Start with two poor children."

"No," I said. "This idea of yours might work, but there are some things I cannot do, and writing about children is.one of them."

"Two adults, then," said Hall. "They're a couple, and they're poor. Not slightly poor – miserably poor. A combination of circumstances had held them back, but," he faltered for a second before rallying, "but at least they have each other."

"Maybe," I said, "they wish to celebrate Christmas, but they are unable to, as they have no money." That was where I stopped. "I don't know," I said. "If I were to write about two brothers who cared for each other so much that the one would travel half-way across the world to rescue the other, that would be a fine story and one I could write."

"Nonsense," said Hall. "There's no twist, no excitement, no redemption. It is a humdrum story, and I one I cannot see anyone either enjoying or even believing."

Holmes, who hadn't moved for five minutes, stirred himself. "You are a good man, Richard Hall, and I know this because in my line of work, I seldom come across good people, so it makes it easy to recognize you as such. Your brother is lucky to have you as family, and Watson and I have enjoyed your company. But you rank in the same pantheon of fictional storytellers as Watson."

"And you can do better?" I said.

"Here is what you need," said Holmes "You have it right not to trifle with children, and the young couple in love is a starting point. They are poor, as you say. The only thing of value in the house is his watch, which he keeps at home because the chain is damaged, he can't afford to replace it, and he is scared of losing it. It is valuable and has been in the family all the way back to when there was money.

"The woman however does have one captivating feature: Waist-length lustrous hair. She goes into town and has it cut off, selling it to a wigmaker and buying her husband the watch chain he wants and needs. And when he comes home, having sold his watch to buy her the ivory combs her hair needs, the irony of their situation is the end of the story."

There was a moment of silence. "Holmes," I said. "That is brilliant."

"It's better than brilliant," said Hall. "It is fiendishly clever. It has a twist no one will see coming. It has a happy ending. I do believe it checks all of our points. Now all you have to go and do is write it."

"I can't." I said. "I just can't."

"Why not?" said Hall.

I was at a loss for words. I knew I couldn't do it. I just couldn't explain why.

Holmes could.

"Watson is the most morally upright man I know," he said. "Even though I give him the story freely, he cannot write it because it is not his. To Watson, it would feel like stealing."

Hill looked puzzled. "Is this true?" he said to me. I nodded.

"Well, I never," he said. "So what will you do?"

"I will tell Cousin Hortense that I am unable to help her. She will be disappointed, but it is for the best."

"Well, then," said Hill, "if you are giving it away," he said to Holmes, "and you aren't taking it," he said to me, "do you mind if I share the bones of it with my writer friend Billy?"

"Do with it as you wish," said Holmes, and I concurred.

We left the club around midnight. As we were walking out I said to Hill, "You mentioned your friend's name, the writer, as Billy Porter. I looked for some of his stories and could find none. Maybe his tales haven't reached this far."

"They have," said Hill with an impish grin, "and you will have heard of him under his *nom-de-plume*. He's better known as *O. Henry*."

NOTE

William Sydney Porter, as O Henry, is one of the most famous short story writers of the Twentieth Century, and his story "The Gift of the Magi", first published in 1905, is one of the most loved Christmas tales ever written.

Sherlock Holmes never asked for any credit when the story came out.

The Adventure of the Christmas Threat
by Arthur Hall

In the years of my association with my friend, Mr. Sherlock Holmes, I was privileged to witness many demonstrations of his remarkable abilities. By means of his skill in deductive reasoning, he solved many an intriguing puzzle and brought villains to book who would otherwise have escaped justice. Murderers, blackmailers, and perpetrators of the vilest crimes found themselves in the hands of the official force as a result of my friend's investigations, far too few of which were ever accredited to him. There were also occasional cases laid before him which turned out in a most surprising manner, where Holmes's enquiries revealed that where wrongdoing was suspected there was none, and where it was thought that a criminal was at work was only circumstance.

As I reflect in particular upon these, the example which comes immediately to mind is that of Mr. Clarke Jefferson, who presented himself at our lodgings unexpectedly late on a Christmas Eve which had seen Holmes conclude no less than three cases without leaving our sitting room.

My friend stretched his thin body and sighed with satisfaction.

I lowered my newspaper, glancing towards the window and the thickening dusk. "I take it that everything has transpired as you predicted? Can we now allow some Christmas spirit to enter our lives before you embark upon another investigation? As your doctor, I advise rest and relaxation for the next few days at least. I have observed your recent behaviour, and your increasingly nervous demeanour hasn't escaped me."

"Don't concern yourself, old fellow." He sat up straight in his chair and folded his arms across his chest. "I have no work, other than four cases which I expect to see the end of early in the New Year, to occupy me. What else then can I do but spend my time idly, as you suggest? As for my behaviour, I admit that the Yardworth scandal has taken its toll of my resources, but I expect the effects to be much lessened before the month is out."

I gave him a critical glance before rising to pour us both a glass of port. We wished each other Compliments of the Season and reminisced for a while about his activities since this time last year. Presently Mrs. Hudson, our good landlady, brought us a fine dinner of roast pork, and I was glad to see Holmes attack it with unaccustomed relish.

When the remains of our food had been cleared away, we again repaired to our armchairs. I saw that my friend had paused to peer from the window, his attitude suddenly becoming wary.

"Has the snow ceased yet?" I asked.

"It has, and frozen hard. There isn't a cab to be seen, but my attention was drawn to a fellow slipping and sliding about the pavement in a comical fashion. It was only as I saw him scrutinize the doors as he passed that I realised that he is bound for here."

I put down my unlit pipe. "Oh no, Holmes. Not on Christmas Eve."

"It is possible that it's *your* assistance that he seeks."

"But unlikely. I have let it be known that I'm unavailable until after the holiday, except for extreme emergencies. Must you really undertake this now?"

"I have never stated that I consult only within certain hours." He smiled rather slyly, I thought. "But take heart, Watson. We don't yet know what this gentleman seeks. It may be something which I can settle here and now. At the very least, it will give me something to consider over Christmas."

I sighed and scowled as the doorbell rang, and after a short exchange, Mrs. Hudson announced a man of about thirty years and of average height. As she withdrew, looking rather surprised at the hour, he removed his hat and faced us cautiously.

His glance flitted from Holmes to me and back again. "Gentlemen, am I addressing Mr. Sherlock Holmes?"

"You are indeed, and this is my friend and colleague, Doctor John Watson. Tell me, Mr. Clarke Jefferson, what is it that brings you to us on a freezing Christmas Eve? But first, remove your muffler and greatcoat and come to sit near the fire, for I see that the cold has affected you."

Our guest complied, his face red from the icy wind. Before I took my seat, I poured a brandy from the decanter which he drank gratefully. Holmes leaned forward in his chair, with the air of a hound awaiting the signal to begin a pursuit.

"My first thought, sirs, was to take this matter to Scotland Yard, but then I realised that I have no actual crime to report. I confided in a passing constable who confirmed this, before I recalled seeing mention of you in the newspapers."

"That occurs more often than I would like. But please, begin your story at the beginning, leaving out not the smallest detail. You are far from the first to consult me while undecided as to whether there has been criminal activity. As for Doctor Watson, I assure you that you can trust him as you would me. He has been invaluable in many of my investigations, and is the soul of discretion."

Mr. Jefferson nodded. "Thank you, gentlemen. I will try to put my thoughts in order."

"Pray do so," said Holmes. "There is no need to hurry. All I know of you thus far is that you are of Scottish descent, that you work in a clerical capacity – possibly an accountant – and that you have at some time in your life barely escaped with your life from the ravages of a fire."

Our client's face went suddenly blank. "But how could you know those things, Mr. Holmes? Your landlady announced me by name, but I have revealed nothing more."

"Surely there is no mystery about it. Your accent betrays your birthplace, or where you have resided until recently. The ink stains upon your fingers and cuffs force me to an obvious conclusion regarding your employment, and the scars upon the back of your neck appear to be from burns, though not sustained recently. Is it these that begin your story?"

"Why no, sir." He shook his head slowly, looking confused. "I have no memory of anything of the kind. I always thought of the blemishes as birthmarks."

"Then perhaps they are. I have seen similar, before now."

"No, the matter that I'm here about has its beginnings five years ago, when I lived in Edinburgh. I received a letter on Christmas Eve bearing the message '*I am coming for you*', which I could make neither head nor tail of, so I discarded it. I thought nothing more of it, but it came to mind again the following year on the same day, that is to say Christmas Eve, when another message arrived containing exactly the same words. Since then, although I have moved to the capital, a similar such letter has arrived every year at the same time. Finally, I received another in this morning's post."

"But it was different on this occasion," Holmes ventured, "or there was something added."

"Why do you say that, sir?" Mr. Jefferson gave my friend a curious look.

"Why else would you choose to act upon this now, after the incident has been repeated for several years?"

"Of course. Yes, you are quite right, Mr. Holmes. The additional message was '*Today you will remember Miranda*'."

"Is that a name familiar to you?"

Our visitor shook his head. "Not at all. I should tell you that I have no memory of my past before the days when the first letter came to me. I can recollect only that a priest, Father Amos Wilton, and his good wife took care of me after I was found wandering the streets of Edinburgh by one of his parishioners. I have been told that I was raving like a madman and in some distress. The good fellow brought me to Father Wilton's home, where I was taken in. Apparently it was feared that I would end my days in an asylum, but the priest resolved to attempt to restore me to health."

"Evidently he was successful," Holmes observed. "You have said that you have no previous memory?"

"None whatsoever."

"Except your name?"

"Ah yes, only that."

"We have established that you occupy a clerical position. How then, in the circumstances that you describe, did that come about?"

"For that my gratitude to Father Wilton's wife is endless. Recognising that I would need to earn a living, she instructed me daily until I attained a level of proficiency. She herself had been taught by her father, years before. After two years, having fully recovered, I moved to London where I joined the firm of Cutler and Maybright. I have audited the books of many of their clients ever since."

"I know of them," Holmes murmured. "Near Westminster."

"These letters then," I interjected. "Could they not be some sort of jest, by someone from your unremembered past?"

"That is possible, I suppose, but as I have said, I have no recollection of either persons or events before Father Wilton appeared in my life. He often expressed hope that my memory would return one day, but that has yet to happen."

"You are certain that the words in the letters mean nothing to you?" Holmes asked then. "I perceive that they have caused you to fear, nevertheless."

Our visitor nodded. "I understood the message to be a threat, from an unknown source. As it has persisted for so long, it has begun to cause me anxiety. This the more so and – forgive me, I should have mentioned this: The first letter was posted in Edinburgh, as I have already stated, then Newcastle, Sheffield and Birmingham. But the arrival of this morning – suddenly much closer again"

He withdrew an envelope from his coat and handed it to my friend. "It was posted in Surrey."

"So it would seem," Holmes concluded, after examining the envelope and the single sheet that he withdrew from it. "The paper and envelope are quite ordinary and, apart from the fact that the writer uses cheap ink and holds his pen in a trembling hand, I can deduce nothing. It appears that the threat, whatever it may be, is now imminent."

"That, sir, is why I have consulted you at such a late hour. I have been going about my business cautiously until now, until there are but a few hours remaining. I know of no other place to turn."

"I take it that you live alone."

"That is so. My maid calls daily, but otherwise I'm rarely visited."

"You employ no cook?"

"None. I often eat in hotels or restaurants, save when I prepare a simple meal at home."

"Why, I wonder, has it taken the writer so long to arrive at a point to decide you are now within his reach," I mused. "He sent the first letters from Edinburgh while you still lived there, and clearly he has known of your whereabouts here for the following three years – else how could he have sent the additional letters?"

"Quite so, Watson." Holmes got to his feet and walked over to the curtained window. "Doubtless this will become clear as we progress."

He stood in silence for a few minutes, during which I knew his mind was racing. The crunching of a carriage along the snow-laden street reached us faintly and I saw our client shiver, although whether this was in anticipation of his forthcoming return to his residence in freezing conditions or of what might await him there, I couldn't tell.

"Could it be," Mr. Jefferson proposed, breaking the silence, "that I have been mistaken for another? Perhaps I'm being persecuted for deeds that I haven't committed."

Holmes glance settled upon him, and for an instant I thought that he was angered by the interruption of his thoughts, but his expression was one of mild concern as he spoke.

"Mr. Jefferson, I'm unable at the moment to form any definite conclusions. I advise you, therefore, to first furnish Doctor Watson with the address of your place of residence and that of Father Wilton, and then to return to your home. It won't be easy to procure a hansom, but there are bound to be several abroad despite the inclement weather. I suggest extreme care during the journey – ensure that you aren't followed – and that you examine the snow near your front door to ascertain whether your premises have been entered in your absence. Once inside, you must bolt your door and answer it to no one, save Doctor Watson and myself."

"I'm most grateful to you both," our visitor stammered, a little taken aback by my friend's instructions. "I cannot tell you the relief you have brought to me."

"Good evening to you then," Holmes said dismissively, and I took this as a signal to show our client out into the freezing darkness.

I returned to find Holmes leaning to peer through a gap in the curtains, remaining in that position for some little time.

"Mr. Jefferson has secured a cab," he informed me at last, letting the curtain fall back into place. "For where is he bound?"

I lowered myself into an armchair and consulted the notes I had made from our client's dictation. "He lives in Highgate, not far from Hampstead Heath."

Holmes nodded his head. "I regret I must leave you for a while, old fellow. With the poor weather aside, I cannot exclude the possibility that our client's mysterious correspondent might seek to do him some harm this night. I intend to prevent that, if I can." He reached for his ulster and ear-flapped travelling cap as I rose from my chair. "No, don't allow me to disturb you. I wouldn't presume upon your good nature, at such a time."

"Holmes, I insist."

He smiled warmly, handing me my greatcoat and hat. "I thought I knew my Watson."

We stood shivering outside our lodgings. I anticipated a long and possibly futile wait, but Holmes seemed little surprised when a hansom appeared after less than five minutes had passed. I watched as the cabby kept his horse at a slow pace, treading carefully upon the icy surface. He acknowledged my friend's instruction with a muffled sound from behind a thick scarf that he had wound around his face.

The journey to Highgate seemed interminable because of our necessarily slow rate of progression. Holmes said little, but looked out onto the icy scene from time to time with, I thought, some impatience. I could tell, from his frequent shiftings in his seat, that he was anxious for the welfare of our client, and I was glad that I had brought along my service revolver, although he hadn't requested me to do so.

Albermarle Street, and particularly Number Fourteen where Mr. Jefferson resided, was unremarkable. The heavy snow couldn't conceal the monotonous regularity of the dwellings, each with identical doors and darkened windows in a solid square structure. As the hansom driver, having received an extra half-sovereign, retreated slowly from our sight, we turned our attention to our surroundings.

"There are two sets of footprints approaching the house," I observed, "and one leaving."

"Indeed," Holmes replied. "As you see from their shape, those which both arrive and leave are of a woman, which will be the maid. There has been a fresh snowfall since early this morning, so our client's departure is obscured. Not so his recent return."

"We can be certain then, that no intruder awaited Mr. Jefferson tonight."

"Unless he gained entry elsewhere. This is unlikely, however, since the snow is undisturbed around the passage at the side of the house, and I can see no other means of ingress."

"If our adversary is to arrive tonight then, it must be soon."

Holmes smiled thinly. "And we shall be here to greet him. There is no need for us to seek a place of concealment for, as you see, our client's house has a deep doorway. If we stand within the alcove, we will be quite invisible, if uncomfortably cold."

Our vigil was indeed devoid of comfort, since we couldn't stamp our feet or otherwise move to maintain our circulations against the bitter cold for fear of alerting our unknown adversary. Yet we had stood, still and silent, for no more than ten minutes when a figure appeared from around a nearby corner, losing his balance frequently and barely recovering it while making his way towards us. As he approached, I saw in the light from a nearby street-lamp that his movements were that of a young man, but was able to discern little else, since his long coat almost touched the ice beneath him and his muffler effectively concealed his face. He carried, with some difficulty, a large square parcel which was covered in thick paper and secured with string.

"Good evening," Holmes said as the parcel was placed near the doorstep.

The effect on the young man was electrifying. For an instant he became absolutely still, before turning and retracing his steps at a run. Three times he fell headlong, and Holmes and I almost laid our hands upon him, but the treacherous surface defeated us and we were obliged to strive to remain upright. When he had disappeared around the corner from which he came, Holmes put his hand upon my arm.

"He may have fallen as he entered the next street. Come, Watson, we shall see."

We made our way carefully and almost disastrously to the other side of the street and around the corner. We were met by another deserted scene, with the only movement a cart diminishing unsteadily and already some distance off.

"He had his escape well planned," Holmes commented, "but I fear for the horse if he maintains such a speed."

We made our way back to our client's home and Holmes retrieved the parcel.

"I'm sure that Mr. Jefferson will soon display the contents for us," I anticipated. "Let us see if we can rouse him."

I raised my stick to beat upon his door, but Holmes at once prevented me.

"No, I think we will return to Baker Street with this. I don't propose to alarm our client further. If he remains inside with the entrances secured, as I advised, he should be safe enough for now."

It was fortunate that a passing police coach saw us and came to a halt as we trudged through Highgate. We had endured the appalling conditions as far as the High Street, when the familiar voice of Inspector Gregson offered to share the conveyance.

"We're much obliged to you, Gregson," Holmes said gratefully as we took our seats. I concurred and saw that the inspector glanced more than once at the parcel my friend carried, although he didn't refer to it. We arrived back at our lodgings with little conversation and without further incident, and wished our companion and his driver the Compliments of the Season before they left us.

I knew that Holmes would be eager to open the parcel before retiring, and my own curiosity compelled me to witness this, so it was with glasses of brandy in our hands that we sat with the flat object on the floor between us. After a single sip, he picked it up and ran his hands over its surface.

"About three-feet-by-eighteen-inches, wouldn't you say? No more than three inches in depth. The surrounding paper is firm at the edges but tightly stretched towards the centre, where the depth is approximately less by at least an inch."

He produced his pocket knife and severed the string, then carefully stripped away the paper to reveal a portrait of a strikingly beautiful woman.

"Mr. Jefferson's forgotten wife, perhaps," I ventured. "If there was one."

"Possibly, but in any event I think we have made the acquaintance of 'Miranda'."

He examined the frame which was new, as was the portrait.

"Is there any indication as to the artist?" I enquired.

"I should be very surprised if there weren't. Here, you see, is his signature, which appears to tell us that his name is J. Brunt, and this tiny metal plaque affixed to the back of the frame gives his address as 9, Mundell Court, Hammersmith, where we shall certainly call upon him in the morning."

Our Christmas breakfast was, not for the first time, more appreciated by me than by my friend. We then set out upon a walk until we eventually procured a hansom, which on Christmas Day wasn't without its difficulties. We arrived at Mundell Court to find the premises, between a saddler's and a maker of walking canes, locked and empty.

"He realised, perhaps, that we would be calling," I said as we stood before the tiny studio.

"Possibly, but it is more likely, I think, that he is at home celebrating. This address is clearly where he plies his trade, rather than his accommodation. Our adversary has made a serious error though, in neglecting to tell Mr. Brunt to refrain from leaving any indication of his name or whereabouts on his work. We shall see if he resumes his attendance here tomorrow, let us hope that he has sufficient commissions on hand to make that necessary."

Holmes had taken further steps to have our client and his residence watched. Then, the remainder of Christmas Day was spent contentedly in our lodgings. I have seldom tasted the equal of the superlative luncheon that Mrs. Hudson produced a little after mid-day, and was glad to see my friend in such fine spirits as to do justice to the roast goose and plum pudding. Holmes had put aside a fine wine to accompany our meal, and an excellent cognac which we shared with our good landlady when she appeared to remove our plates.

Afterwards, he stood staring from our window as I took my seat near the fireplace. The joyful strains of carol singers reached us faintly from the frozen street.

"Extraordinary, don't you think, Watson, how men suspend their grievances during the festive season. I have just seen no less than three examples of this, men who I know to be not on good terms now acknowledging each other cheerfully, though they are rivals or enemies."

I looked up from my copy of the latest edition of *The Standard*. "It is, after all, the season of goodwill."

"True, but can you imagine some of the vicious criminals that we have encountered on occasion changing their ways temporarily in acknowledgement of it?"

"I must confess – " But my response was cut short, for Holmes's posture had altered and I saw that something had arrested his attention.

"I wonder," he said after a moment, "if that young woman is connected with our present enquiry, or if she represents something new. She has evidently decided not to disturb us on Christmas Day, but I suspect she will return before long."

I put aside my reading. "What has happened out there?"

"A hansom discharged its passenger directly opposite, and the woman alighted. That she was enduring an agony of indecision was obvious from her movements, side to side and thrice starting to cross towards us. She looked up finally and saw that I was observing her, before returning to the waiting hansom and departing."

"If her need for your assistance is sufficient, then you may see her again."

"I consider that highly likely. But for now, Watson, let us enjoy an afternoon of pleasant conversation, and perhaps another glass of this cognac. In the morning we will once more seek out Mr. Brunt."

And so it transpired. As Holmes seemed in such a jovial mood, I seized the opportunity to secure his permission to send my accounts of more of our adventures to my publisher – specifically the affair of the

Dartmoor Hound. From the glitter in his grey eyes I knew that he had at once realised my use of the occasion, and felt a measure of relief when he agreed. Afternoon swiftly became evening, and I had little appetite for the cold meat and pickles that Mrs. Hudson served at our usual dinner-time, while he had none. We retired early, each pleasantly satisfied by a day spent, for the most part, in quiet companionship.

The following morning, the day after Christmas, saw us dispense with breakfast quickly. Holmes was anxious to return to Mundell Court early, so as to encounter Mr. Brunt on his arrival. The scene was unchanged until the artist arrived on foot, carefully avoiding the snowdrifts and patches of ice which hadn't yet begun to thaw.

From our concealment in an entry passage further along the street, we observed him remove the lock from the door and enter. Slowly, so as not to disregard the slippery surface, we crossed to the premises and stepped into a room piled with empty picture frames and smelling strongly of chemicals.

Mr. Brunt laid down the palette he was preparing, and I saw that he had recognised us.

"What do you want?" he asked rudely.

"Ah, I see that you remember us from our encounter of two nights ago Holmes replied. "My name is Sherlock Holmes, and my friend is Doctor John Watson. What I want, as you put it, is to understand your involvement in the continuing persecution of my client, Mr. Clarke Jefferson."

"Your client?" The young man wiped a grimy hand down the front of his well-worn shirt. "Then you aren't from Scotland Yard?"

"No, I am a consulting detective."

"Then I'm not obliged to tell you anything."

Holmes frowned. "That is of course your entitlement – as least until enough time has passed for me to summon an inspector to participate in our discussion. It is, I assure you, in your own interests to co-operate with us now."

"What do you want of me?" But I had seen the quick flicker of fear that had crossed his unshaven face, as he wondered how much he knew about this and heaven knew what other unlawful activities. Clearly, the suggestion that the Yard could be brought in hadn't been received well. "I painted a picture for him, that's all."

"How did that come to be?" Holmes saw the artist's reluctance, and I heard faint impatience in his voice as he continued. "Come, man, I'm concerned only with my client. Anything else you may be concealing is a matter for the official force, if they are sufficiently astute to have detected it. If you tell us all, they will learn nothing from us."

Mr. Brunt shrugged his shoulders, and a lock of unkempt hair fell across his brow. "I had a letter, a few months ago. It surprised me, because I don't get many letters. With the instructions was a cheque, for more than I usually charge, and a photograph to paint from. The subject was a woman, a lady by the look of her, and I was told to deliver the finished portrait on Christmas Eve to the address where you saw me last night. I should have known there was something strange about this."

"Did you, by any chance, retain the envelope?"

"I had no reason to."

"But you have never met the sender?" I enquired.

"Not that I can remember. I can't explain how he knew of me, either. The letter was unsigned."

"It is possible," Holmes stated, "that he is someone whose acquaintance you have made in the past, but cannot now identify. Were you given directions as to your acceptance of the commission?"

"I had to send a telegram to a post office, to be held as *poste restante*, without a name."

"Can you recall the destination?"

Mr. Brunt considered for a moment. "I think – no, I am *certain* – it was Birmingham."

I saw an expression of satisfaction cross my friend's face. "Excellent. I have but one more question. Why did you run? According to your account, you have committed no crime."

"I was instructed to make the delivery unobserved. This was written in bold capitals and underlined in the letter, but it wasn't explained. Also," he avoided our eyes, staring down at the stained floor, "I have other reasons."

"I have already stated that they are of no concern to us," Holmes reminded him.

"Then I will not be troubled by Scotland Yard?"

"If you are, for whatever reason, it won't be because of anything they have learned from us. My thanks to you. Good day, Mr. Brunt."

"I wonder why he fears the law," I mused as we searched the streets of Hammersmith for a cab.

"That is irrelevant now, I think." Holmes's gaze swept up and down the High Street. "Ah, but I see that the post office next to the church is open for business. Be so good as to look for a hansom, Watson, while I despatch a telegram. I do feel that the pieces of this puzzle are beginning to fall into place."

By the time he emerged, I was waiting in a conveyance nearby. As the horse broke into a trot, Holmes was about to enter into one of his silent reveries, but my curiosity was aroused and so I sought to prevent it.

"The telegram – was it to Lestrade?"

After adjusting his position in the hard seat he turned from the window, smiling faintly. "Why should I be seeking to communicate with the good inspector? He isn't concerned here. I have instead sent a message to Barker, the private enquiry agent whom I use from time to time. I've requested that he take tomorrow's morning train to Edinburgh. I must have confirmation of our client's version of the events in his life of five years ago."

"He is to enquire of Father Amos Wilton?"

"Precisely. As for us, I fear that another evening, or perhaps more, at Albermarle Street is indicated."

Both luncheon and dinner were hurried affairs that held little interest for Holmes that day. He had adopted that restless demeanour that I knew of old. It indicated with certainty that our enquiries had come to a temporary standstill while my friend's mind, racing engine that it was, refused to slow down.

Our landlady had scarcely cleared away the dinner things when he leapt from his chair eagerly.

"Our hours of enforced idleness are at an end. Let us retrieve our hats and coats and return to our client's home. It should be easier to procure transport now that the festivities are all but over, and I have a strong suspicion that our unknown letter writer will pay him an unwelcome visit soon."

Finding a hansom was indeed less of a problem for us. No sooner had we stepped out onto the icy surface of Baker Street than we were confronted with a conveyance delivering two jovial young fellows in evening dress a short distance ahead. We promptly boarded it and my friend gave the cabby our intended destination.

The horse had just reached its stride with my gaze flittering along the pavement, when something in the gas-lit scene arrested my attention.

"Holmes, I saw a young woman back there who I would swear was observing our lodgings. She turned away as we passed and vanished into the crowd."

"I hope she won't find the increasing cold too uncomfortable. You will recall that I noticed such a woman yesterday, almost certainly the same. I have no way of knowing her intentions, but it's become obvious that she waits for someone, or perhaps for some*thing* to happen, before approaching us. I believe that we'll make her acquaintance soon."

Albermarle Street was as deserted and dismal as before. A light shone in an upper room of Mr. Jefferson's house, and we concealed ourselves again in the deep doorway.

"Why are you so certain that our client's tormentor will appear tonight?" was my whispered question to my friend.

"You will recall that every letter was received on Christmas Eve," he replied in a voice so low that I could hardly hear, "and the latest one was different to the effect that it is the last and that the matter will somehow come to its fulfilment now. This time of year, therefore, holds some significance here, although our presence may be necessary on several more occasions if our adversary's actions aren't strictly accurate as to their timing. I've had the Irregulars watching, and so far they've nothing to report. A little patience, I think, is required, but I don't expect that it will be too long before we see some sort of development."

As always, Holmes was correct. My pocket watch showed the hour to be eleven o'clock precisely, which I discerned with difficulty in the meagre light, when a hansom appeared at the end of the street and moved slowly towards us. It came to a halt, the horse slipping but regaining its balance, directly outside our client's house. A thick-set man, no longer young by his movements, alighted carefully and picked his way across the snow.

"Holmes, he carries a picture, as Mr. Brunt did," I whispered.

"Quiet, Watson. Let him approach."

This man ventured nearer than his predecessor, laying down his burden against the door. Holmes's hand shot out and grasped his shoulder, startling him.

"Good heavens, sir. I didn't see you there."

"We are acting for the owner of this house. Kindly open the parcel."

"I was instructed to deliver it here, exactly at this time."

Holmes nodded and took out his dark lantern, which he lit with a vesper. "Pray enlighten us as to how this came to be. You are, I presume, an artist?"

"I am indeed," the man's grey head moved into the glow, "though I was for many years an engraver of tombstones, and after that a soldier. My name is James Pickman. To whom am I speaking, sir?"

"I am Sherlock Holmes, and this is my friend and colleague, Doctor John Watson."

Mr. Pickman's face brightened, as I stepped out of the shadows. "Why, I have read of you. Very exciting tales they are, too."

"I'm glad that you think so," I said, noting Holmes's glance of disapproval at my interruption.

Mr. Pickman's account had much in common with that of Mr. Brunt, given previously, except that he had actually met the man who commissioned the portrait."

"His face was hidden from me by a high collar and muffler, but I did see him again. I knew him by his walk. People rarely realise how significant that can be. We all move differently, but few know it."

"I have long been aware of it," Holmes said. "Such knowledge can be instrumental in my profession. But tell us, where did you see this man subsequently?"

"It was in the Four Keys, a tavern where I often spend my evenings, in Chelsea. I noticed that he sat alone, night after night, and that he seemed to be troubled with his breathing since he coughed a lot."

"But you didn't converse with him?"

"Not at all, sir. In fact, I began to feel sorry for him, sitting there with a sort of confused and despairing look about him. He showed no sign that he had recognised me. Once or twice I almost took it upon myself to approach him, but he looked as if such an intrusion wouldn't be welcome. If anyone sat near to him, he would suddenly rise to his feet and trudge up the stairs away from everyone."

"Did you gain the impression, then, that he had hired a room at the Four Keys?"

"That struck me as very likely, Mr. Holmes. At any rate, often after going upstairs he wouldn't return, for I've stayed there long after."

Holmes nodded. "You have been most helpful, Mr. Pickman, for which I thank you. Can we now see the picture? I assure you that its intended recipient, Mr. Clarke Jefferson, has allowed us full permission."

"Very well, sir." He proceeded to unwrap the parcel as a brougham appeared travelling at a fast pace. I had a glimpse of a single occupant wearing a top hat as it passed beneath a street lamp, before it vanished into the darkness. I saw from my watch that it was now exactly midnight.

Mr. Pickman held up the portrait proudly. "It was an unusual request, but I did my best to follow the gentleman's instructions. I hope this sufficiently resembles the photograph."

"I'm certain of it," Holmes confirmed.

Before us, in the light from my friend's dark lantern and the meagre glow from the street lamp, was a scene of a young woman surrounded by flames. Her arms were raised as if to protect herself, and her expression was one of absolute terror.

"I must confess," said Mr. Pickman, "that I have never received such a commission before now. I ventured to ask the customer the meaning of such a scene. He seemed reluctant to answer, but after a short silence he murmured '*In memoriam*' and left."

This seemed to have some significance for Holmes.

"My thanks to you, Mr. Pickman," he said again. "But now I see that your driver is getting cold, since he is beating his arms across his chest.

I'm sure that he will be driving his hansom home as soon as he has delivered you to yours. Good night to you, sir."

Holmes seemed in good spirits as we returned to Baker Street, despite the lengthy walk we were obliged to take before we discovered a hansom with its driver encased in a thick travelling rug, fast asleep. We retired soon after our arrival, but not before he had held the two pictures together and compared them.

"Both men are adept at their craft," he observed while noting the resemblance between the painted figures. "We will probably see the conclusion of this affair soon after tomorrow. As I suspected, our adversary had intended to call upon Mr. Clarke Jefferson at midnight, one hour after the delivery of the second picture and as close to Christmas as could be arranged. You didn't fail to observe the passing brougham, of course? We rather thwarted his intentions then, I think." He smiled as I stifled a yawn. "Well, I believe us both to be weary, and there is more to be done tomorrow. Good night to you, Watson."

Soon after breakfast, Holmes began to consult his index and add to it, though I'm uncertain as to whether this activity had any connection with our current case. I had a prior appointment which occupied me until almost mid-day, when an urgent call summoned me to an address near Charing Cross. Consequently, dusk was closing in as I entered our sitting room to find my friend brandishing a telegram which, judging by the torn envelope discarded upon the carpet, hadn't long been delivered.

"At last!" he cried. "I have been awaiting this for most of the day."

"The reply from Barker, I presume."

"Indeed, and it confirms much that I had suspected." He became silent abruptly, and I saw that he peered past me through our window, where he had neglected to draw the curtains. "The woman has returned, the one that both you and I have seen watching our lodgings before. Be so good as to go out and speak to her, and bring her in out of the cold."

I put down my bag and, remembering her hasty withdrawals of before, walked along Baker Street for a short distance. I then crossed to the other side and approached her unseen, noticing her apparent anxiety from some way off. I confronted her and raised my hat.

"Good evening to you. Forgive my forwardness, but I see that you are again watching our premises. Mr. Sherlock Holmes and I would be most pleased if you would consent to accompany me to our rooms, where whatever is troubling you may well be put to rest."

She was startled by my intrusion, her face full of alarm. But after a moment she seemed to collect herself, and spoke to me in a subdued voice:

"Yes, I suppose you are right, sir. There has to be an end to this. I will come with you."

Holmes had already called for tea as we settled ourselves around a blazing fire. The young woman clearly found the warming liquid most welcome, and she ceased to shiver after a short while.

I sat in my usual armchair across from Holmes as he filled his clay pipe from the Persian slipper and regarded our visitor with interest.

"Please begin your account when you are ready, Mrs. Sarah Hall. There is no need to hurry, and we'll do all that we can to assist you with your difficulty. We haven't yet made the acquaintance of your brother, but we will doubtless do so very soon."

Her expression was one of complete amazement. "How do you know these things, sir? I haven't yet disclosed either my name or that I'm searching for my brother."

"As a consulting detective, it is my business to know such things. Forgive me, but I found it unnecessary to introduce either Doctor Watson or myself, since you were evidently already aware of us."

"That is true," her eyes fell momentarily to the carpet, "for I followed Mr. Clarke Jefferson here on Christmas Eve, recognising your address and hoping that my brother would eventually arrive here also, since he is still seeking him."

"Does he intend to do him harm?"

"On my life, sir, I don't know. I haven't seen Gabriel for some years, although he has sometimes communicated by letter. I have prayed that he hasn't changed, for he was never a violent man."

"Let us hope that he hasn't become so. As far as I can tell, he has as yet committed no crime." Holmes blew a cloud of fragrant smoke into the air. "I must apologise again," he said hastily, "for I neglected to ascertain whether you have any objection to strong tobacco."

She shook her head. "None at all."

"Excellent. I take it that you knew of your brother's intentions from his letters, and when his travels took him so close to where Mr. Jefferson now lives, you perceived that a confrontation was imminent and resolved to travel here from Edinburgh in the hope of persuading him to abandon his quest."

"Indeed, sir. If I find him, I'm sure that I can convince him. I have lost my husband and my sister already, and cannot bear the thought of being deprived also of my only remaining kin. The law would surely find him and he would be hanged." I noted that her Scottish accent became more noticeable as her excitement grew and reflected, since Holmes was now aware of the situation, that Barker had done his work well.

"We will do our utmost to prevent this. If you would care to attend here at, say, three o'clock the day after tomorrow, I would expect to be able to set your mind at rest. Until then, Madam, I will bid you good evening. Doctor Watson will be pleased to show you out and procure for you a hansom."

When this was accomplished, I returned to our sitting room to find that Holmes had put on his hat and coat.

"I must send a telegram, if I can reach the post office before it closes."

"To Mr. Clarke Jefferson, no doubt?"

"You presume correctly, old fellow. I would recommend that he present himself here at the same time as Mrs. Hall."

He returned soon and Mrs. Hudson served a fine dinner of roast chicken and vegetables. After a dessert of apples and custard which he barely sampled, we repaired to our usual seats for brandy and cigars. We smoked and drank in companionable silence for a while, and I waited with enforced patience until our glasses were empty and the remains of our tobacco consigned to a crystal ash-tray.

"Holmes, I'm uncertain as to how this affair has developed. Do you intend to enlighten me?"

He leaned back in his chair, a look of contentment upon his face. "Providing our adversary, Mr. Gabriel Newman, is still in temporary residence at The Four Keys, I see no reason why the situation shouldn't be quickly cleared up to our client's satisfaction."

"Is Mr. Clarke Jefferson a criminal, since he is being sought so relentlessly by Mrs. Hall's brother?" I persisted.

"He is, in fact, completely innocent of any crime, as is his pursuer until now. We will attempt to cause Mr. Gabriel Newman to realise this before any regrettable action takes place, if we can find him at The Four Keys tomorrow evening. In my telegram to our client, I strongly advised him to remain at home until his attendance here."

"Barker seems to have been extraordinarily successful in his enquiries in Edinburgh."

"Very much so, although he discovered, regrettably, that Father Wilton has now passed away. His widow however, was most forthcoming, and has, since our client left them, pursued her own enquiries as to his previous life out of curiosity." He smiled as a thought occurred to him. "If there should ever be a requirement for female consulting detectives, she appears to be well qualified."

"Do we now know then *why* Mr. Jefferson is being so pursued?"

"We do. He is thought to be responsible for the death of Miranda, who was Mr. Newman's and Mrs. Sarah Hall's sister."

"But, as you implied, he is innocent?"

"Absolutely. Mr. Clarke Jefferson was engaged to be married to Miss Miranda Newman and they were dining in an Edinburgh restaurant. A fire broke out and spread quickly from the kitchen through the building, and in the panic that followed, Miss Newman lost her life. Mr. Clarke Jefferson was presumed dead, though his body was not found. In truth, he was injured, probably by a falling beam, resulting in a permanent loss of memory up until the time when he found himself in Father Wilton's care. In spite of Mr. Jefferson's name being known, the Wiltons apparently never established the association between their patient and the supposedly dead man."

"The scars upon his neck," I remembered. "Your original understanding was correct: They were the results of burns."

Holmes nodded. "Although he remembers nothing of the incident. It seems that he simply wandered away from the scene before anyone could tell him his name and somehow managed to stay undiscovered between the cracks, preventing him from learning his true identity. As I've stated, Mr. Gabriel Newman somehow learned of Mr. Jefferson's survival, and wants revenge."

"Why is he so convinced that our client was responsible for his sister's death?"

"According to Barker's investigation, Mr. Newman believes that Mr. Jefferson committed an act of great cowardice in abandoning his fiancée in order to save himself. He considers Mr. Jefferson's immediate disappearance to be proof of this – that it was effected to avoid facing his fiancée's family."

"But there is no substance to this?"

"None whatsoever. Both Barker and Mrs. Wilton were meticulous in discovering the truth."

"And since then Mr. Newman has been engaged upon a needless and mistaken quest."

"He has." Holmes took on a thoughtful expression. "But I cannot ascertain why he has waited so long to exact his revenge. Why this travelling from city to city? Why the letter on the anniversary of his sister's death every year until now? Why the different pictures? What are his intentions – bearing in mind that Mrs. Hall is adamant that he is not, or was not, a violent man? Doubtless we will discover the answers when we confront him."

The remainder of the evening passed quickly. The following morning brought Holmes a new client, Mr. Corey Whitehouse, who spent several hours with my friend while I ventured out for a much-needed walk. I was glad to see that the sun was shining and the thaw had begun. The pavements were wet, but the danger that the ice had brought to the streets had all but disappeared. Traffic had increased, with horses once again trotting confidently before hansoms or private carriages. I recalled that I had arranged an appointment which I kept and concluded within a short time.

I returned to our lodgings in time for luncheon. As we ate, I enquired of Holmes regarding his client of the morning, to which he responded dismissively.

"Pah! It was a simple matter. I could have resolved it in half the time, hadn't Mr. Whitehouse obscured the true problem beneath layers of irrelevant and unconnected facts."

I discerned that he was possessed of a reminiscent mood, as so we spent the afternoon in pleasant conversation concerning some of our past investigations. As the hour for dinner approached, however, I noticed a change in him that I concluded was brought about by the increasing nearness of our time for action. This was confirmed by the rapidity with which he dealt with his food. Refusing dessert, he drank two cups of strong coffee and stood up from the table.

"As soon as you have finished your cherry pie, we will set off. I've had someone watching Mr. Gabriel Newman's evening habits, and I would prefer to be at the Four Keys early."

I hurriedly ate the last of my food and gulped down the remaining coffee. I'd hardly regained my feet before Holmes handed me my hat and coat and was ushering me down the stairs. Baker Street twinkled with tiny patches of ice and snow, moreso as the temperature had once again plummeted. A hansom was easily found and we were quickly on our way to Chelsea through streets that were mostly deserted.

The Four Keys was an unimposing little tavern in an out-of-the-way backstreet that I hadn't previously known existed. Holmes, however, dismissed the hansom some distance from it and led us there unerringly. Not for the first time, my friend's seemingly unbounded knowledge of the capital was a source of some astonishment to me.

We entered the establishment to find it quite crowded, despite the evening being still young. The smoke-laden barroom had few vacant tables, but we settled upon a newly-vacated position in a corner from where it was possible to constantly keep both the entrance and the stairs leading to the upper floor in view.

"I cannot see our friend, Mr. Pickman." Holmes explored the room with his eyes, moving his head but a little. "He didn't claim to spend his every evening here, however."

I nodded. "If, as he surmised, Mr. Newman is resident here, he will enter by descending the stairs, rather than from the street."

"Quite so."

No waiter appeared, so Holmes approached the bar and prevailed upon the landlord for two pints of his best beer. We sat for about an hour, drinking and saying little as we observed the circus that surrounded us. A young man sitting at a table near the door blew enormous smoke rings and apparently accompanied these by humorous stories, since his companions erupted often into laughter. Several others, invariably the worse for drink, stood up to sing. The landlord had just left his post to eject a troublesome roughneck from the premises when someone proposed a toast to his friends and two obvious drunkards began to argue. My friend put a hand on my arm.

"There, I think, is the man we seek."

A tall, elderly fellow who, from his movements and frequent coughing fits, didn't appear to be in the best of health, had descended the stairs. His hair, rather long, was so grey to be almost white, and his skin seemed tightly stretched across his face. As we watched, he walked clumsily to where the landlord, in anticipation, held a whisky bottle at the ready.

"He has been here for some little time, or has consumed much drink regularly," I perceived.

"Excellent, Watson." Holmes smiled faintly. "But of course both alternatives could be valid. As Mr. Newman has found himself an unoccupied bench near the wall, I think we should now make his acquaintance. The necessity is unlikely, but keep your hand near your service revolver for the present."

We rose and made our way between the scattered tables, the noise becoming intolerable until we reached the other side of the room. We sat upon the bench beside Mr. Newman, earning ourselves a surprised and disapproving glare.

"Good evening, Mr. Gabriel Newman," Holmes began.

"Do I know you, sir?" The response was as unfriendly as I had expected, yet it surprised me to discover that the man had clear and kindly eyes.

"Only from last night. You will recall that you passed the house of Mr. Clarke Jefferson rather quickly in a brougham."

"You prevented me from visiting the scoundrel."

"Pray tell me," Holmes requested, "what your intentions were. It is futile to deny that you meant harm to Mr. Jefferson. All is known to us concerning this matter."

Mr. Newman appeared astounded. "How could you possibly be aware of the situation? Who are you, sir?"

"My name is Sherlock Holmes. I am a consulting detective. My companion is my friend, Doctor John Watson."

"And what have you to do with my business concerning Clarke Jefferson? Is he your client? Has he paid you to warn me off – or to kill me?"

Holmes smiled grimly. "We're not assassins, sir. Mr. Clarke Jefferson *is* my client, however, but my purpose is to ascertain the origin and reason for the letters you have sent to him over the past few Christmases. We mean you no harm, but we are bound to prevent any from befalling him. I perceive from the protuberance in the pocket of your evening coat, that you are armed."

Mr. Newman peered around us until he was satisfied that we were unobserved, then slowly drew a revolver from his coat. My hand tightened on my own weapon, but I saw that it was unnecessary.

"Take it," he said, handing it to Holmes, who quickly concealed it, "for I have discovered that I have no use for it. You will see that it is unloaded. If you know as much as you have stated, then you will be aware of the reason for my pursuit of the man who so nearly became my brother-in-law. Miranda was my younger sister, and no man ever loved a sibling more. I was happy beyond measure when she became engaged to a man whom I quickly befriended, and who seemed to me to be of a most sensible and reliable disposition." He paused to stifle a racking cough, and in that instant a possible reason for the different points of origin of the yearly letters came to me. "When that terrible blaze took Miranda from us, my heart was broken, yet anger such as I had never before known burned within me. There was much talk among the survivors of that blaze, and more than one of them told me with certainty that Clarke Jefferson had been seen leaving that smouldering wreck of the building without a backward glance."

"I must tell you," Holmes interrupted quietly, "that I have discovered that to be not quite the case."

Mr. Newman looked at us with a haunted expression. "But how can it be otherwise, sir? Why did he not come back to us and share our grief? Instead he fled, as I quickly discovered from paid agents whom I employed, to the capital after first hiding somewhere in Edinburgh. Why would anyone but a coward leave my sister, under his protection, in such danger, and then let people believe he had died, except to preserve himself? To this day, the memory of Miranda's funeral is clear in my mind, as is that of the many who enquired after her intended husband's absence."

"My sympathies are with you, sir." I said then, disregarding Holmes's sharp glance, "for I see that you suffer extensively from consumption to add to your difficulties. Is it not true that you despatched the letters to Mr. Jefferson from wherever you happened to be at Christmastime, from the cities containing the various medical institutions where you had continually sought a cure for your condition?"

"It is. Those places were chosen so as to bring me ever closer to where I believed him to be. Several times I was pronounced to be at death's door, but always I recovered. My hate for that man has, I'm sure, kept me alive."

Holmes frowned. "What is the significance of the pictures, pray?"

"My intention was to remind him, first of Miranda's beauty, and then of the appalling fate to which he abandoned her, and to cause him to understand that vengeance was at last at hand."

"Yet the weapon you carry was unloaded."

"In truth," Mr. Newman bowed his head, and succumbed to more coughing, "I have never been a cruel man. The weapon was purchased years ago as the instrument of my revenge but, as time has passed, my feelings have changed to wanting merely to confront Mr. Jefferson for an explanation. I carried the gun as a reminder of what I must not do – of what I almost became. I'm not long for this Earth, sirs, and I wouldn't like to leave it by means of the gallows. The letters, the pictures, became no more than a warning to him of a meeting that must inevitably take place."

"And take place it shall," my friend confirmed in a quiet and kindly voice. "If you would care to call on us at 221b Baker Street at three o'clock tomorrow afternoon, I have every expectation that this matter can be put to rest. I will say no more to you now, save to give you an assurance that all is not as you have believed, and that you will leave our premises without the hate and resentment that you have nurtured over the years." He rose and I did likewise. "For now, sir, we bid you good night."

We made our way through the smoke and the boisterous crowd to the street. As we reached the entrance, I looked back, to see Mr. Newman staring after us with a puzzled expression and trying in vain to restrain a coughing fit that shook him cruelly.

"That man hasn't long to live, Holmes," I remarked as we emerged from the shadows of the narrow streets into a main thoroughfare. "The treatment he has received has doubtlessly extended his life for a limited time, but I fear that time is near its end."

He raised his arm to attract a passing hansom. "I know it. All the more reason therefore, to settle his differences with our client. I have every hope that tomorrow afternoon will see the conclusion of this case and of their sad estrangement."

I confess to falling asleep during the journey back to our lodgings. Holmes woke me as we arrived and, by mutual agreement, we retired on regaining our sitting room.

He spent longer than usual over breakfast the following morning, alternating mouthfuls of food with opening his substantial post long after my coffee cup was emptied. I gathered from his expression that several letters contained items of interest to him.

"I have to attend my patients this morning, but I anticipate that I will have returned in time for luncheon."

"Kindly be here no later than two-thirty," he replied without looking up from his perusal of a crumpled sheet.

The day was unusual, inasmuch as my procession of patients all suffered from minor ailments which were easily dealt with, and so it was that I returned to Baker Street before two o'clock. We were served generous portions of steak pie, of which only I consumed all, with Holmes making no reference to either what lay before us or to anything that had arrived in the post.

"We will not have long to wait, I think, before the first of our visitors arrive," he said as we took to our armchairs.

"Mr. Gabriel Newman will be surprised by the proceedings."

Holmes placed a lump of coal on the fire. "He has been labouring under a misapprehension for a considerable time, so nothing but good can come of his enlightenment. Ah, but Mrs. Hudson has answered the doorbell, and I perceive from the footfalls upon the stairs that Mrs. Sarah Hall is here."

"I apologise, gentlemen, for arriving a little early," our visitor began when greetings had been exchanged and our landlady had withdrawn.

"That is of no consequence," Holmes said as he indicated that she should take the basket chair.

"Mr. Holmes, have you discovered my brother's whereabouts?" she asked anxiously.

"I have." He peered from the window. "He is in fact crossing Baker Street at this very moment, approaching our front door."

The doorbell rang for a second time, and Mrs. Hudson showed in Mr. Gabriel Newman.

"I don't fully understand the purpose of this meeting, gentlemen!" he exclaimed rather loudly as he entered, before coming to a sudden halt as he saw his sister.

"Sarah! What in the world are you doing here?"

Her expression was a mixture of relief and apprehension. "Do not be angry with me, Gabriel, I beg of you. I came to London because I knew you were searching for Clarke. I pray that you haven't found him."

"I had discovered where he is living," his glance took in Holmes and myself, "but these gentlemen prevented my approaching the scoundrel." He paused and his face became clouded by indecision. "Perhaps that is just as well."

"You are no murderer, despite what you have said before now."

"That is true, but I can never forgive his cowardice."

"You may not have to," my friend intervened, "if you can be convinced that there is none to forgive."

"Again you say this. You insisted as much when you approached me last night, but you have yet to explain."

"Be so good as to settle yourself in this chair, Mr. Newman, and I will elaborate with the assistance of Mr. Clarke Jefferson himself, for it is certainly he who is ringing our doorbell at this moment."

Anger reappeared on the elderly gentleman's face, and he stifled a harsh coughing fit. I was about to pour a glass of water to assist him when Mr. Jefferson was announced and the door closed behind him.

"Good afternoon, Mr. Holmes and Doctor Watson," our client began, before glancing without expression at the others.

"Clarke!" Mrs. Hall half-rose from her chair, looking somewhat relieved.

"I would much like words with you, sir!" Mr. Newman growled.

I vacated my own chair for Mr. Jefferson, who appeared to be in understandable confusion.

"Pray tell me, who are these people?" he asked Holmes after a few moments of confused silence.

"You don't recognise them?"

"How can I? I have never before laid my eyes upon them."

"Is this some manner of deceit, sir? A cheap party trick to escape your guilt?" Mr. Newsome's hands were white upon the walking-cane he held.

"Not at all," I answered on Mr. Jefferson's behalf. "Although I'm not fully conversant with illnesses of the mind, I'm very experienced in recognising the deceit of those who, for various reasons, seek to feign them. During our original meeting with Mr. Jefferson I observed him closely, from the moment he claimed to have no recollection of his past beyond those events subsequent to the tragedy of five years ago. I'm convinced he speaks the truth."

"What then, is his claim?"

Mr. Jefferson glanced at each of us in turn, looking increasingly puzzled. "I'm all at sea with this. I confess to being totally confused."

"You abandoned the girl you were to marry!" Newman said harshly. "You left my sister to the flames!"

The shock that filled our client's face was absolute. For the next few moments he was speechless.

"I assure you, sir," he said to Mr. Newman, "that I'm guilty of none of this. I can only assume that you have mistaken me for another."

"What then, can you recall of your life prior to your time with Father Wilton and his wife?" Holmes asked.

His outraged expression was replaced by one of horror, as he realised the implication. "Oh no! Oh, dear God!"

Mr. Newman then surprised us all for, after scrutinizing our client intently, his anger subsided. "Have you truly no recollection?" he asked in a calmer, almost-considerate tone.

"None." Mr. Jefferson raised his hands in despair, shaking his head. "Throughout the past five years, I have repeatedly attempted to recover what I have come to regard as my previous life, but to no avail. Before Father Wilton, I may as well haven't been born."

"You are either telling the truth, or are the most accomplished actor that ever was." Mr. Newman turned to me. "Do you swear, Doctor, that this is possible?"

I looked at him coldly. "I'm not accustomed to having my word doubted, sir. I have already said as much. It has long been known that a blow to the head can produce such an effect, either temporarily or, as is the unfortunate case here, permanently. I repeat: I'm convinced of this man's truthfulness, and our investigation has confirmed it."

The elderly gentleman turned his head away to submit to another fit of coughing. Afterwards, his gaze avoided our eyes. Silence settled upon the room for some moments, but from outside I could hear faintly the cries of barrow-boys and the thud of horses' hooves.

"For all of this time I have hated you," he said to Mr. Jefferson, "and now I find that I was in error." He paused, and I saw that his eyes glistened. "I suppose that some part of me never believed that you left Miranda because I knew you, but my grief at losing her consumed my reason. How can I begin to apologise, my boy? How can I make restitution?" He shook his head in an almost frantic manner. "How you must despise me!"

"I cannot despise you sir, because I don't know you," Mr. Jefferson replied. "Neither do I know this good lady. But I have never meant harm to anyone, nor have I ever lacked courage."

Mr. Newman nodded. "I can only apologise again, to you and to Doctor Watson. Is it possible that we can, on some future occasion, talk of things as they were before that tragic fire, and perhaps re-establish some of the friendship we once had? There is much that I can tell you of those times, if you wish it."

"I would welcome the chance to reclaim some parts of my earlier life," he said with some dismay, "for I have never expected to have the opportunity. As for friendship sir, it is my way to be, as much as is possible, at peace with all men."

For the first time, a faint smile stole across Mr. Newman's face. His expression was now one of concern. All three of our visitors showed some measure of relief.

"And now," said Sherlock Holmes, breaking the short silence, "that all is clear and we are all friends, I suggest we share a bottle of an excellent Spanish wine that I have been saving in anticipation of some special occasion. Watson, kindly be so good as to bring the tray from the table and fill the glasses."

Thus did this adventure come to its conclusion. There was no villain to be seen, no recourse to Scotland Yard, nor cause for urgent action. Yet, possibly because of the time of year, both Holmes and I felt a certain satisfaction at its end. It was true that Mr. Gabriel Newman had little time left to him to resume his friendship with our client, but doubtless they would heal the wound that had given rise to the letters and pictures that had been sent in anger and received in confusion.

Some hours later, when they had all departed and Holmes and I were again settled in our chairs contentedly, we reviewed the affair, and I added to my notes which might one day be extended to a story for future publication.

"It ended well," I said. "After a while, Mr. Newman took on the look of a man who has had a great burden lifted from his shoulders. Nevertheless, I confess to experiencing some surprise when he accepted that our client had no memory of his past. He didn't strike me as someone who is impressed easily."

"Nor I, old friend, but probably there were other factors. Mrs. Hall's apparent reluctance to believe badly of Mr. Jefferson, for example, that influenced her brother's change of heart. Or possibly, the spirit that is currently abroad had something to do with it. It is after all, as you were quick to remind me previously, the season of good will."

The Adventure of the Stolen Christmas Gift
by Michael Mallory

As I recount the events of a December long ago – 1901 to be precise – I remember a statement made to me by my friend and colleague, Mr. Sherlock Holmes, some years later: "Good old Watson, you are the one fixed point in a changing age," he told me. While I do not wholeheartedly concur with his assessment, I am forced to conclude that 1901 was indeed a year of many changes, both for me personally and for England, if not the world at large, for which I was not entirely prepared. On a personal level I was looking at my impending fiftieth birthday, which seemed to me as improbable as snow in August, given that my memories of being a young army surgeon in Afghanistan remained as fresh and vibrant as yesterday. I was also marking the twentieth year of my association with Holmes, much of which time was spent in these rooms in Baker Street. On a larger level, the year saw the loss of the Empire's Sovereign, the only one most of us had ever known in our lives, and her replacement on the throne by the former Prince of Wales.

Somewhere in between all of these in terms of portent was the Lyceum Theatre's promotion of Holmes's career, staged by the American actor William Gillette, and based upon several stories my literary agent had sold to him. I entreated Holmes to attend, which he finally did, albeit disguised with a wig and false beard so as not to be recognized, only to leave after the second act and speak no more about the play.

Then there was the matter of the missing fiancée.

It was Thursday, December 19th, less than a week before Christmas, and a time when I was still pondering what small token I might be able to give Holmes in order to celebrate the holiday. I had, in fact, asked him directly what sort of present he wished and his response was, "A case worthy of my time would be appreciated." It had been two months since the singular occurrence of prowling "mummified" cats in the British Museum had been brought to a satisfactory conclusion, and I had watched Holmes grow more and more restless by the day. That *ennui* was shattered, however, on that morning when our landlady brought to our rooms a compact, grey-haired man of middle-years, who was crushing a plain cloth cap in his hands as though attempting to wring the life from it. "Mr. Holmes, you must help me!" he said forcefully.

"What I must do, my good man, is thank Mrs. Hudson for showing you in," Holmes replied. "I must also entreat you to sit and compose yourself while I reflect upon the fact that you hail from the Isle of Portland, work as a stonemason, and have neither a wife, nor can you afford a manservant."

The man's mouth opened in surprise.

"Please do not gape," Holmes went on. "It is all quite obvious. Your hands are strong and calloused, indicating that you wield tools for a living. There is also slight coating of dust on your hat and shoes that is neither white nor grey, but rather of a bluish hue, the exact colour of Portland blue stone, which tells me that your profession consists of cutting and dressing such stone, carrying some of the resulting dust home with you."

"I see," the man said. "And I suppose you figured I'm not married because I don't wear a ring."

"That, and the fact that your waistcoat is misbuttoned, an eventuality no wife would permit were her husband to venture forth into public. Nor would a manservant, though your general dress bespeaks of your inability to retain a paid serving staff. Beyond that, however, I know nothing, and therefore must ask you to introduce yourself fully."

Taking a chair, the man said, "My name is Penniston, Edgar Penniston, and I am indeed from the Isle of Portland. It may surprise you, though, to learn that I am one of the wealthiest men in Dorset."

"It does, frankly," Holmes said, and I had to admit that I was also set back by the man's admission, given his appearance.

Penniston went on. "The reason I bear the dust of my trade is because I still enjoy working the stone myself, along with my employees, even though I own the quarry from whence it comes. But you are correct in that I am no longer married. My wife died twelve years ago."

"My condolences," I said, having experienced a similar tragedy slightly more recently.

"Thank you. As for my waistcoat – well . . . I was in a hurry to get here."

"And now that you are here, Mr. Penniston, what is your business with me?"

The man leaned forward in the chair. "My daughter's disappeared. She was expected on the 8:40 train yesterday evening, but did not arrive. She was coming home for Christmas, you see."

"Surely, sir, she cannot officially be listed as a missing person having only been absent for a matter of hours," I said. "Perhaps she missed her train."

"You are Dr. Watson, I presume?"

I acknowledged that I was.

"I've read your stories. That's why I'm here, in fact. As to your question, Doctor, no. Bethany – that's my girl, though I call her Beth – has never missed anything in her life. Punctual, she is. She wrote me when she'd be arriving, and she stated she could not wait to be home, so there was no reason for her not to have done so. Something must have happened to her."

"How old is Bethany, Mr. Penniston?" Holmes asked.

"Twenty."

"And is there a man in her life?"

"There is. In fact, she is betrothed."

"Indeed?"

"Rufus – that's the lad's name, Rufus Thourlby – was expecting her to arrive on time as well."

"Why was Bethany away from both her father and her fiancé?"

"She was spending time with her aunt in Salisbury to prepare her for her impending wedding."

"Prepare her?" I asked.

"Beth's my only chick, and I've done my best to take care of her. But I'm not her mum and never could be. I can't advise her about such things as being a wife, so I suggested her Aunt Adelia, my late wife's sister, advise her on womanly matters."

"Have you been in contact with the aunt?" Holmes asked.

"When Beth didn't arrive I made a telephone call to Adelia. She told me she had accompanied Beth to the station in Salisbury and then put her on the train right on schedule. So whatever happened to her happened between there and Weymouth, which was her final destination. Even though there's a small rail line going to the Isle, we travel by carriage."

"Have you spoken with anyone from the rail line?"

"Rufus sought out the station manager, but he knew nothing. The lad is beside himself over the disappearance, and there is nothing I can say to him." Penniston seemed to deflate in the chair as he added, "For the first time in my life, Holmes, I do not know what to do."

To my way of thinking there was no real mystery here: The girl had simply gotten off the train before it arrived at Weymouth, or perhaps had decided to take the connector train to Portland after all. Her father's presumption that she was as predictable as the sunrise I felt bespoke more of arrogance than the reality that her every thought and action could be predicted. I was, therefore, surprised when Holmes agreed to take on the case.

"Do you happen to have a photograph of your daughter?" he asked.

"I anticipated that you would request one," Penniston replied, pulling a small, framed image from his pocket. It showed a comely young woman with blonde hair and an engaging smile seated next to a dark-haired man with a full, dark beard and moustache, and an agreeable, rather than formal, countenance.

"I take it the man is her fiancé, Thourlby?"

"It is. This is their engagement picture. Rufus has promised to rid himself of that infernal bush on his face before the wedding, though I wish he had done so before this photograph was taken."

Holmes deftly removed the photograph from its metal frame and handing the latter back to Penniston. "Now if you would be so good as to provide Watson with information through which you can be reached, I will begin work."

"Thank you," the man said. "Any information you can provide will be appreciated." After dictating his personal information, Edgar Penniston left our rooms.

Once he was gone, I spoke up. "Really, Holmes, this case hardly seems like the one you were seeking that is worthy of your time. Surely it is an instance of the girl missing her train, or taking another one. Perhaps she decided not to get married after all and left the train before it arrived in Weymouth."

Holmes was studying the photograph of Bethany Penniston and Rufus Thourlby. "Did you and Mary sit for an engagement photograph, Watson?"

"Yes. Why do you ask?"

"Do you still have it?"

"In my bedroom."

"Bring it down, would you please?"

Retreating to my room, I opened the dresser drawer in which the cherished photograph remained, and even now felt a pang of sorrow as I gazed upon Mary's face. I took it down to Holmes, who held it up against the other picture. Then he laid them both on the table, and said, "Tell me what you see."

Looking at the photographs side-by-side, I simply saw two couples, separated by a number of years. "I see nothing unusual," I told him.

"Look at Mary's face, and Bethany's face. What do their expressions bespeak to you?"

"Happiness, I would say," I replied.

"As would I. Both are happy and their expressions betray the fact that they are looking forward to their betrothals. Neither is a picture of a woman having doubts. As soon as I saw that photograph, Watson, my suspicion that Bethany Penniston did not disappear of her own volition was confirmed."

"What do you propose to do then?"

"Commence investigating, of course," he said, walking to his small work desk and reaching for his *Bradshaw*. After thumbing through its pages, he announced, "We leave tomorrow on the 10:05 from Waterloo. You would do well to dress warmly, since the winds off of the Channel will be formidable this time of year."

After a pleasant railway journey through the snow-dusted landscapes of Berkshire and Wiltshire, we arrived in Salisbury shortly before one o'clock. Detraining, Holmes immediately sought out the station's ticket agent and presented him with the photograph of Bethany Penniston. "Oh, I remember her, all right," the man said. "A chatty one, she was, and she carried a package with her that she seemed inordinately proud of."

"Indeed?" Holmes inquired. "What was in it?"

"I've no idea. It was about this big – " The agent made a shape with his hands roughly resembling the size of a biscuit tin. " – and wrapped in paper. She said it was something that would change society, which unless it was a cure for Bright's Disease, seemed improbable to me."

"She gave no details regarding either the contents or her assertion?"

"Only that it was a Christmas gift for someone that was shipped across the pond from America. Now, if you please, sir, I have customers to attend to."

"Thank you, you have been most helpful," Holmes said, retrieving from him the photograph.

As we went on I commented, "I'm afraid I don't see what assistance the man gave us."

"It tells us, Watson, that she was even more eager to return home than we imagined, since she had in her possession a gift, presumably for her fiancé. That, in turn, tells us that she did not leave the train willfully."

"You think she encountered foul play?"

"I do not know, though something happened either to our missing fiancée personally, or that package she was carrying, or both. We must board the train to Weymouth and speak to someone in authority."

As soon as we were aboard, Holmes sought out the conductor, who was a small, white-haired man whose waistcoat bore a watch fob large enough to propel a bicycle. "Oh, yes sir, I remember this one," he said after glancing at the photograph. "She started yelling at one point that something had been stolen from her. She claimed it was something valuable, and then she said something I didn't understand. It sounded like a foreign word . . . *je let* . . . something like that."

"*Je let*," Holmes repeated. "If I am not mistaken, that is French for '*I read*'."

"If you say so, sir. All I know is the girl remained agitated until we pulled in to Dorchester, at which point she spotted a man jumping off the train from another car, and she ran after him. She claimed he had her package."

"Did she re-board?"

"No sir, not that I saw."

"Did you happen to see the thief?" Holmes asked.

"Through the window, briefly," the conductor replied. "All I can tell you is it was a man with a beard."

Holmes proffered the photograph again. "This man?"

"No, I don't believe so. The man the young lady was chasing after had a much longer beard than this. He was also heavier."

"Thank you," Holmes said, letting the conductor get back to his work.

As we sat back in the compartment I began to muse about the mysterious French words uttered by Bethany Penniston. "Do you suppose the package contained a book of some sort?"

"Possibly," Holmes replied, "though the size as described by the conductor argues against that. *Je let* must mean something else."

Holmes closed his eyes and retreated into his own thoughts after that, to the point where I wondered if he had fallen asleep. When we reached Dorchester, however, he became alert once more, though he remained seated as we pulled into station, staring out the compartment window.

"Are we not getting off the train?" I asked.

"What would disembarking here achieve?" he replied.

"We could follow the trail of Bethany Penniston."

"How? By knocking on every door in the city and ask if there is a rather distraught young woman there? While I daresay the chances of finding one would be would be reasonably high, the chances of finding the particular one we are seeking are miniscule."

"What are we to do, then?"

"Press on to Portland."

Upon arriving in Weymouth, we transferred to the smaller line that took us to the grey, windblown, foggy "Isle" of Portland, and then proceeded to the address Penniston had provided. His home was a large, stately stone edifice on grounds located just outside the village of Fortuneswell. A Christmas wreath made of holly sprigs adorned the front door, and inside we were greeted by a welcoming blaze in the main fireplace. Penniston himself, however, was not there.

"He will be at the quarry this time of day," his housekeeper told us.

"He still went into work even though his daughter has gone missing?" I asked her.

"Mr. Penniston says there is nothing he can do here except worry," the woman said, "and he can do that while still being productive. The master is a worker, sir. Always has been."

"Do you know how we can contact Mr. Thourlby?" Holmes asked.

A young man then strode into the foyer. "What is it you wish with him?" he demanded.

"Who are you?" Holmes inquired.

"I am Arthur Lunsford, Rufus's cousin. Might I ask who you are?"

"I am Sherlock Holmes, and this is my associate Dr. Watson."

"I should have guessed. Rufus told me that you were going to be called in. Have you discovered anything yet?"

"A few facts which, as of yet, do not add up to an answer. That's why I need to speak with your cousin as soon as possible."

"He is not well," Lunsford said. "This has been a terrible ordeal for him, and he has taken to his bed. I came down from Chippenham to offer what help I could. I arrived only this morning."

"So Thourlby is here?"

"Upstairs. He decided to move into the house until this crisis is over. He wants to be here when Bethany returns, you see. But as I have said, he has taken ill."

"I am a doctor," I said. "Perhaps I should look at him."

"That isn't necessary," the young man replied. "He took a sleeping draught. If his condition worsens, we will call for a local doctor, but I believe he is suffering from worry more than anything else."

"Are you acquainted with Miss Penniston?" Holmes asked.

"I met her once. Rufus invited me down to attend a celebration in honour of their engagement."

"Do you have any idea what might have happened to her?"

"Of course not."

"Very well," Holmes said, taking the photograph once more from his pocket and looking back and forth from it to Arthur Lunsford. "I can see that the two of you are related. You have the same ears."

The young man instinctively touched his ear. "We do?"

"Yes, it is really quite remarkable," Holmes went on, stepping toward the man to further examining the shape of his ear. "I pray you will humor me, Mr. Lunsford, but I find resemblance in families a fascinating subject, particularly since my own brother and I frankly look nothing alike. Well, enough of my personal interest. We shall be going now."

"Shall I relay anything to the master?" the housekeeper asked.

"Only that the good doctor and I are returning to London," Holmes replied. "I shall notify him if any new information presents itself."

With that we left the house. On our way to the village I asked, "Would it not be better for us to stay here and wait for Thourlby to recover instead of repairing to London?"

"We are not returning to Baker Street, Watson – not yet. I merely wanted them to think we were. I'm confident there is an inn somewhere in the village that will offer us accommodation for the night."

"And then what?"

"Then we see what Thourlby's cousin is up to . . . from a distance, of course."

It was all very puzzling, but I trusted that Holmes had already begun to formulate the disparate pieces of this puzzle into a cohesive picture. I did, however, ask what that business about Lunsford's ears was about, particularly since I couldn't agree with Holmes's assessment that he and his brother Mycroft were chalk and cheese. While it was true that one was corpulent and indolent and the other was thin and bristling with energy, their facial features were similar enough to easily mark them as brothers.

Holmes smiled. "It was a ruse, which allowed me the opportunity to take a closer look at Lunsford's hair, particularly the lock of hair behind his left ear, examination of which confirmed what I had detected a moment earlier. It was stuck to his head, as though with glue."

"A bit of pine sap, perhaps?"

"Have you observed any pine trees on the Peninsula? For that matter, any trees of consequence? There was not even a cut tree to celebrate the holiday inside Penniston's house."

While not a totally barren rock, it was true that the Isle of Portland was not a forest, either. As is often his wont, Holmes chose not to reveal to me the significance of the man's lock of hair.

We proceeded to the village where it took little time to locate a small inn called The Squire of Dorset. After taking our rooms and freshening up, I joined Holmes for an early dinner in the public house, which served a surprisingly good portion of mackerel in gooseberry sauce. He seemed to particularly enjoy the sauce as well, prompting me to think that I should perhaps buy a jar of it from the kitchen and present him with that on Christmas Day. Then, almost as though he was reading my mind, he asked, "What sort of things did Mary give you for Christmas?" After my initial startlement – Holmes rarely spoke of my late wife, yet this was his second reference to her in as many days – I realized he must have been thinking about the mysterious package Bethany Penniston had carried with her onto the train.

"Well, a new pipe one year," I told him, "even though she felt I was becoming too reliant on tobacco. A book I had wanted. A set of cufflinks, a shaving set – all quite conventional items, I suppose."

The edges of Holmes mouth pulled taut reflecting, while not quite a smile, an expression of satisfaction. "A shaving set," he uttered. "Something that a man who – what was Penniston's way of putting it? – had agreed to rid himself of the infernal bush on his face would have cause to use." Dashing up, his dinner only half-eaten, Holmes ran to the bar to consult with the publican, and then dashed back. "Stay here, Watson, and continue to enjoy your meal. I have a visit to make. Don't let the serving girl remove my plate, as I will not be long."

"Where are you going?"

"To the nearest barber shop, which the landlord says is only five buildings away."

True to his word, Holmes returned not ten minutes later, practically laughing out loud.

"What on earth did you discover?" I asked.

"A revelation that could be called positively *dramatic*," he replied, shaking out his napkin and replacing it on his lap before tucking back into his fish.

After a reasonably comfortable night (the mattress in my room being a bit too soft for my liking), we were up and breakfasted early, but instead of returning to Penniston's house, Holmes insisted we be at the train station by eight o'clock. "Have you changed your mind?" I asked him. "Are we returning to London without seeking out Thourlby?"

"We are not returning," he replied, "but there is a more immediate task at hand than questioning the would-be bridegroom. Look at everyone who comes through this station, Watson. In particular, look for a man with an unfashionably long beard."

The first train to Weymouth did not leave until 9:25, time spent examining each and every person who passed through the station, a task made easier by the fact that there were not that many people on the island. Finally I felt Holmes hand on my arm. "There, Watson – that man walking from the village." It was a fellow whose age could only be judged by the darkness of his long beard, the upper part of his face obscured by a wide-brimmed felt hat pulled low. He wore nondescript clothes and walked with a brisk, almost hurried pace. After buying his ticket, he approached the train, keeping his face down.

Holmes rushed to the ticket counter and said, "That man with the beard who was just here . . . Where is he headed?"

"The railroad prides itself in allowing privacy to our passengers, sir," the ticket agent said.

"I am Sherlock Holmes and I insist upon knowing where that man is going."

"Sherlock Holmes of London?" the fellow asked, appearing impressed. "Has the man done something wrong?"

"I plan to ask him when I see him. For now, time is of the essence! Where is he headed?"

"Dorchester."

"As I presumed. Two tickets to Dorchester."

"You'll have to change trains in Weymouth."

"I have confidence we can manage. The tickets, if you please."

After purchasing the tickets for us, Holmes hastened to board but kept distance from the bearded man so as not to be recognized. At least that was I what I surmised, until Holmes assured me that even if the man did recognize us, he would refuse to admit it. Instead, he wanted to keep a watch on him from a good vantage point.

At Weymouth, we followed the bearded man onto the next train. "Who is it we're following?" I asked Holmes.

"That, Watson, is the cousin, Arthur Lunsford."

"Lunsford? He didn't have a beard yesterday."

"No, but he had one on the day Bethany Penniston disappeared," Holmes said in hushed tones. "That spot behind his ear where his hair was stuck, which I noticed yesterday, was theatrical adhesive of the sort used to apply false facial hair – in his case rather unskillfully."

He said no more until we arrived at Dorchester, at which point the disguised Lunsford detrained and engaged a cab which was standing near the station. We followed suit, taking the next cab in line. "Stay behind the hansom in front of us," Holmes instructed the driver. "Never lose sight of it."

"Right, Guv," the cabbie responded.

Some fifteen minutes later the cab ahead of us pulled up in front of a plain-looking house and the bearded man got out. After paying for the ride, he walked to the front door but didn't open it, as it was padlocked. Looking around as though to make certain he wasn't being watched, he then went to the side of the house and opened a window, through which he climbed. Holmes likewise paid our cabbie and leapt out, but approached the house much more stealthily.

"Should I have brought my service revolver?" I asked.

"I'm hoping the situation is not that dire," he replied. "However, once we're inside, if you would place your hand in your coat pocket and leave it there, as though you are armed and ready, it might be of value."

The windows of the house, including the one through which Lunsford – if it was indeed he – had disappeared from view, were heavily curtained. Holmes examined the side window and found that our quarry hadn't bothered to fasten it securely behind him. "This bodes ill," Holmes said.

"If Miss Penniston is inside, as I surmise, leaving an open window must mean she is restrained and unable to escape."

As quietly as possible, he reopened the window and slid through, waiting for me to follow.

The house was dark and dusty, its meagre illumination provided solely by a lit candelabrum placed on a small table. The rest of the furniture was covered by drop cloths. Clearly it hadn't been inhabited for quite some time. Flickering light was also coming from another room, and voices could be heard emanating from the direction of the light as well: A man's voice, and a woman's. As we crept toward the illumination, Holmes whispered, "Hand in pocket, Watson." Then after another moment, he ran into the room shouting, "We are here, Mr. Lunsford, and I suggest you do nothing untoward! In fact, it is in the best interest of your health that you do nothing at all!"

That room contained a large dining table, which was now pushed against the wall, its chairs stacked on top save for one: That one, which was placed in the center of the room, held the terrified figure of Bethany Penniston, whose hands were tied behind it. A cloth sash secured her body to the back of the chair as well. Lunsford was standing next to her, his beard still intact, holding a lit candle. "How . . . ?" was all he was able to utter.

"We are armed, so do not react foolishly," Holmes called out, while I moved my hand in my pocket, reinforcing the untruth. "And do take care with that candle, Mr. Lunsford. Crepe hair and spirit gum are both highly flammable."

"How . . . ?" the man uttered again, but his voice was drowned out by that of Bethany Penniston, who was pleading with us to be released.

"Watson, escort this false-bearded blackguard outside and hold him there while I free the young woman," Holmes said. "If he attempts to use the candlestick as a weapon, you know what to do. The same applies if he endeavours to escape. You would be best not to attempt anything, Mr. Lunsford, as Dr. Watson is an excellent shot."

"Don't worry, I know when I'm beat," Lunsford said, blowing out the candle and dropping it on the floor.

When we were all outside, my hand still inside my pocket, feigning a grip on a firearm, Holmes asked if the young woman was well enough to fetch the nearest police officer, and the speed with which she departed proved that she was.

"What's going to happen to me?" Lunsford asked.

"Prison, I would imagine," Holmes replied, "for kidnapping, if nothing else."

"It wasn't my idea."

"Perhaps you should tell me whose idea it was, then?"

After stripping his face of the artificial hair, Arthur Lunsford quickly related the details of the entire scheme, including the identity of the person for whom he was acting as an accomplice. When he was finished, he sadly muttered, "I knew nothing good would come of this."

"Where is your partner at present?" Holmes asked, but before the man could answer, we caught sight of Bethany Penniston returning with two policemen in tow. "Watson, be so good as to take Miss Penniston back to her home. I shall return there once I've had the chance to speak with the local constabulary about this miserable fellow and his confederate."

Since I hadn't yet had the opportunity to introduce myself to the young woman, I made up for lost time and then hailed a cab to return us to the train station. Once inside the hansom, her previous resolve and defiance eroded as completely as a sand-castle when struck by a wave, and she collapsed into tears.

She managed to compose herself by the time we arrived at her father's estate on the Isle of Portland. When the housekeeper, whose name I learned was Greta, saw Bethany Penniston at the door she virtually threw herself at the girl, embracing her with such affection that one would be excused for mistaking the woman for the girl's own mother. "Oh, my dear, the master is going to be so happy!" she woman cried. "He is still at the quarry, but I shall send the Idwal to fetch him."

"Is Mr. Rufus Thourlby still incapacitated?" I asked.

"No, he is up and around, sir, but he is not here at the moment either. Idwal is the coachman, and he will bring the master back in two shakes of a lamb's tail." Then she walked Bethany Penniston into the sitting room and bade me to have a seat as well.

"I cannot believe it was Arthur," she said, hollowly. "It is inconceivable."

"Do you know why you were abducted?" I asked.

"I was being held for ransom. My father is quite well off. That is what I was told, at any rate."

"If you can," I suggested, "why not tell me everything you know about what happened to you?"

The young woman took a deep breath and began. "I was on my way back from Salisbury, and right before the train arrived in Dorchester, this man approached me. He had a full beard, which I didn't realize at the time was false. Neither did I recognize him as Arthur Lunsford. He attempted to strike up a conversation, which I endeavoured to ignore. Then he reached out and grabbed the package I was carrying, a Christmas present for Rufus, and ran into the adjoining car. I alerted the conductor, but he wasn't able to find the man. Once we came into station, I saw him dash off of the train and stand on the platform, holding my package up, taunting me with it. I left the train as well, wondering if this was some sort of joke. I followed him through the station and out into the town, and then . . . ."

"Yes?"

"There was another man working with him, one I didn't see at all, who came up from behind and placed a pistol to my neck. I was in instructed to keep my eyes straight ahead and not make a sound, and then to get into a cab, which took me to that horrible house."

"You never saw the second man's face or recognized his voice?"

"No. As I said, he told me not to look back, and spoke in a hushed, whispered voice. Neither did he get into the cab with Arthur and me. Once we were there, though, Arthur pulled out a small pistol of his own and pushed it against me to prevent me from making any appeal to the driver or attempt to escape. When we arrived at that place, I was shoved through a window and then tied up in that chair. Only then did Arthur remove his beard and admit who he was. When Rufus finds out what his own cousin has done, he will thrash him. He might even do worse."

As it turned out, we had the chance to discover his reaction not five minutes later, as Thourlby rushed into the house, laid eyes upon his fiancée, and stopped in his tracks, apparently stunned. Behind him was Edgar Penniston, every bit as dust-coated as when we saw him in Baker Street. "Sweets!" he cried, rushing toward his daughter, who rose to meet his embrace.

"Father! This was the most horrible thing that has ever happened to me."

Turning to me, Penniston uttered, "Where did you find her?"

I related the detail of the case, including the fact that it was her fiancé's cousin who was the behind the kidnapping.

"*Arthur*?" Rufus Thourlby cried. "That simply cannot be!"

"I'm afraid it is true," I replied. "Holmes and I caught him red-handed. He has been taken to the police."

"Where is Mr. Holmes?" Penniston asked.

"Here," my friend's voice cried from the foyer, as though responding to an entrance cue in a stage play. He walked into the room, holding a smallish box.

"My Christmas present for Rufus!" Bethany said. "But it has been unwrapped."

"It was that way when it was retrieved from Lunsford's coat pocket," Holmes stated. "He could not leave it within sight of you inside that empty house for fear you would somehow manage to reach it despite your being tied up and, knowing what the box contains, use it to cut through the ropes holding you."

"Tied up . . . cut through . . . What are you talking about, man?" Penniston demanded.

Opening the box, Holmes pulled out a strange, *T*-shaped metal object. "What in blazes is that?"

"It's the latest thing from the States," Bethany Penniston said. "They call it a 'safety razor'. There is a flat, thin blade inside the top positioned in such a way to minimize chafing or cutting. When I saw an advert for it in a magazine I knew it would be the perfect gift for Rufus, particularly since he has agreed to remove his beard."

"I fear, Miss Penniston, that you have wasted your money and put yourself to a great deal of trouble for nothing," Holmes said. "The man known to you as Rufus Thourlby has no intention of shaving."

"I don't understand."

At that moment Thourlby turned and dashed out of the room. He didn't make it far, however, and a moment later was marched back in by two uniformed constables.

"I took the liberty of asking members of your local force to accompany me here," Holmes said.

"I insist you let me go!" Thourlby declared, though the officers showed no intention of doing so.

"Good God in heaven, Holmes!" Penniston cried. "What is all this about?"

"There were two men involved in this abduction: Arthur Lunsford was one, and the other was Rufus Thourlby – better known to the Dorchester Police as Thomas Glendon."

"This cannot be!" the young woman uttered. "Rufus, tell him he is mistaken. Please!"

"I am sorry to inform you that Thourlby – or Glendon – had no intention of every marrying you. This was all about money from the start. You see, the Dorchester Constabulary is quite familiar with Thomas Glendon, since he has attempted this scheme once before. He found the daughter of another wealthy man, wooed her, made arrangements to marry her, and then with the help of his cousin kidnapped her and held her for ransom. The objective was to disappear completely once the money had been paid. Unfortunately, his last victim, one Sarah Rush, died in a desperate attempt to escape from that very house in which you, Miss Penniston, were held. She fell headfirst from an upstairs window. Since that house was Thomas Glendon's last-known address, he had to abandon it immediately, which is why it appears uninhabited. The police padlocked the doors so he could not return, yet he managed to force entry and exit through a side window and continue to secretly use the house."

"This is rubbish!" Thourlby shouted. "I should take you to court for this slander!"

"Oh, we shall both end up in the same court, have no fear of that," Holmes replied. "You shall be the defendant and I shall be a witness."

"Witness to what? You saw nothing!"

"I saw a photograph of you in police headquarters, one that had been distributed to all local constabularies after you disappeared. It was quite a good one. The only difference between it and the engagement picture you took with Miss Penniston was the beard, which, unlike Lunsford's, is real, but which you had no intention of shaving off. Had you, you would have been recognized as Thomas Glendon."

Edgar Penniston marched up to Thourlby, or Glendon, close enough to reach out and lay a hand on him. "Look me in the eye and tell me that man is lying," he challenged.

Instead, the bearded man smiled. "You stupid stonecutter," he sneered. "The ransom letter was set to arrive here tomorrow. By Christmas, Artie and I would have had £50,000, a somewhat finer gift than some absurd, colonial shaving implement."

"Remove this man, Officers," Holmes said. "I will come back to the station once everything here has been resolved."

Once Glendon had been taken away, Holmes said, "Miss Penniston, I am sorry."

"It's better we found out before something worse happened," the girl's father said. "In a sense, you saved my Beth." Taking her hand, he added, "Come on, sweets. Let's have Greta make us a pot of tea. Mr. Holmes, I am grateful to you."

"I only wish the resolution of this case were less hurtful to you and your daughter," my companion replied.

That evening we were on the train back to London, Holmes having finished his business with the police in both the Isle of Portland and Dorchester. "And all this time," I said, "I thought the key to this case was the gift itself, which Bethany Penniston seemed to equate with a treasure of some sort."

"It was an element, certainly, but not the centerpiece," Holmes replied. "No matter what the unfortunate woman had opted to gift her presumed fiancé, this would have remained a case of falsehood and treachery for money. Be content in knowing that it was your memory of Mary giving you a shaving razor that turned my thoughts to that being the mysterious gift, and led to my suspicion that Thourlby – or Glendon – was bearded for a more important reason."

"That is why you ran off to the barber shop?"

"It is. While I was there, I spotted this flier."

Reaching into the inner pocket of his coat, he pulled out a folded sheet of paper and handed it to me. It was an advertisement for the newly-invented safety razor, the image of which was identical to the real one I had seen at Penniston's house. "According to this, it has not yet been granted a patent."

"True, which means actually obtaining one of these items from America is not only a demonstration of devotion, but something of a leap of faith in its efficacy. Oh, and do please note the name of the manufacturer."

I studied the copy of the flier again, reading, "'*Patent pending, King G*' – Oh, good heavens!"

Holmes smiled broadly. "Pronouncing the name indeed sounds like *je let*, does it not? What is truly remarkable is that any time now that America wishes to export a questionable commodity to these shores, it bears the name *Gillette.*"

"You are enjoying this, aren't you?" I asked, unable to keep from laughing along with him.

"Almost as much, I am certain, as I shall enjoy that jar of gooseberry sauce that you have unsuccessfully endeavoured to hide in the pocket of your greatcoat, which I presume is the Christmas gift you have decided upon to present to me. The only question that now remains, Watson, is what *you* would like for Christmas in return?"

I leaned back in the compartment seat, knowing I had a long train journey in which to contemplate that.

The Colourful Skein of Life
by Julie McKuras

In looking back at the varied and interesting cases which I shared with Sherlock Holmes, I find a number which involved one of the greatest celebrations in the Christian calendar. "The Blue Carbuncle" hinged more on a goose than the day, but Christmas played a much larger role in another investigation. I hesitated for a number of years to put pen to paper about a story that combines the joys of Christmas with a criminal who preyed on the weaknesses of others. The time has come to record it, in hopes that it might alert those vulnerable souls who may cross with those who would betray them.

I arose one December morning, having slept in later than was my routine. Dressed and ready for the day, I entered the sitting room where I found Holmes standing by the cheery fire, staring at the plugs and dottles scattered on the mantelpiece. Leaving him to his thoughts, I crossed the room to the window. Silhouetted against the gray sky, the tree branches in the distant park were mostly bare, the last obstinate dead leaves hanging on until the cold winter winds came to take them.

Seating myself at the breakfast table, I examined the various dishes. "Holmes, you appear lost in thought this morning." He often neglected meals when engaged in an interesting case, but nothing had presented itself recently. The case I described as "The Adventure of the Priory School" was seven months past, and like the citizens of London I was focused on hopes for a peaceful Christmas and a happy 1902. After pouring my coffee, I dug into the ham and eggs while eying the orange marmalade.

Holmes approached the table, pipe in hand. "I received a communication from Mycroft early this morning. I thought it was a summons to his club, but he plans to visit us here. Rather soon, actually." When Holmes misses an opportunity to poke fun at my healthy appetite, it confirms that his attention is elsewhere. "He wrote that it is a matter of pressing importance requiring a private setting."

"More private than the Stranger's Room?" Mycroft generally preferred we meet at the Diogenes Club, which afforded solitude to those unsociable men who exhibited little or no interest in their fellow members. I finished my meal while unsuccessfully trying to recall any subjects which would cause Mycroft to interrupt his work day and – more remarkably – to alter his routine.

Shortly after Mrs. Hudson cleared the table and the fire was stirred, we heard heavy footsteps on the stairs. The door opened and Mycroft Holmes blew in, filling the doorway. Cheeks reddened by the cold, his coat and muffler trailing behind him, he went to the hearth without a word of greeting to warm his great hands. Accustomed to the two brothers attempting to outdo each other with their deductions, I waited for the usual exchange to start, but Mycroft immediately began to relate the reason for his visit.

He dropped into a chair and positioned himself. "As you know, bits of information and innuendo find their way to my office in Whitehall, and a most consequential situation has come to my attention. It involves the initial plans for a battleship with armaments so large and so advanced that it will revolutionize naval warfare. Robert Payne-Owen is in charge of the project and, recognizing the need for secrecy, only four men meet with him in his office. Yet despite precautions, we've had two unsolicited inquiries about supplying ammunition which could only be used with the new guns. When questioned, both companies responded that their proposals were made 'assuming' there would be a need in the future. There's never been a question of improper or illegal behaviour on either Payne-Owen's part or the others, and an after-hours search of their offices exposed nothing untoward. But if munitions manufacturers have information like this, we have to ask: What else might have left his office – or any other office in Whitehall for that matter?"

There was silence in the room as we considered the implications. Holmes spoke first. "And you need someone unconnected to Whitehall to look into this?"

"An appropriate observation, since we don't know where the leak or leaks originates. There are several other situations. For instance, one involves a cabinet member named Talman who had a change of heart about his earlier announcement that he wouldn't stand for re-election. He's only told two close allies about his decision, but within days, heinous, unfounded attacks about his moral character have been made in conversation and in the press." He held up a newspaper. "This is what appeared yesterday. *'Talman Feels Women Who Want the Vote Should be Beaten by Their Husbands.'* Last week, one issue carried a comment that Talman felt children of the poor were too ignorant to benefit from school and should seek physical labor instead. They're repeated *ad nauseum* with 'You all know about this' so it's almost impossible to refute such anonymous claims." Mycroft crumbled the newspaper and threw it into the fire where it quickly crumbled to ashes. "There's more, but no indication who started this character assassination. Suspicions point to who benefits from his downfall – in this case, a certain political adversary."

I found this appalling. "What kind of a gentleman would do that?"

"The type of gentleman who often runs for office, Watson." Holmes smirked, and began to pace, chin upon his chest.

"Payne-Owen's group and the cabinet member I mentioned are independent of each other. There are additional situations, yet the only commonality is that they've originated within the same time period. I fear there's more and consulted my sources, not all of them upstanding examples of our citizenry, but they're useful as they provide a window into your forte, the criminal world. Other matters outside of the government came to light which would never have been revealed if not for our inquiries. There are questions about a bank's instability, blackmail, substantial thefts on the docks, and a large department store. I've written down the names of those concerned for your review." He handed the list to his brother. "I have two requests for you two. One: I'd like you to consult your friends in low places to see if you can determine more about the origins of these crimes outside the sphere of Whitehall. Two: I've come up with a plan to begin to ascertain where the government leaks exist, and hope you'll agree to help."

Holmes rubbed his hands together. "What part do we play?"

Mycroft shifted uneasily in his chair, suddenly quiet as if at a loss for words. After a brief pause he answered. "We're going to begin by searching Payne-Owen's home."

"You want us to break into his house?" Holmes and I had some experience in this skill, as I've documented.

"Not exactly break in. Sir Thomas Ellington, the head of the department in question, has agreed we have to start somewhere with our investigation. Ellington asked Payne-Owen and his wife to stand in as hosts at the annual department Christmas party, claiming his wife is ill. Payne-Owen is ambitious, with hopes to assume Sir Thomas's position after he retires, and Ellington has hinted that this will indicate who will replace him. Mrs. Payne-Owen is anxious for the social opportunities such a post might provide, so they were quick to agree, knowing they will appear the gracious hosts without incurring personal expense or preparations, a perfect situation for anyone with ambition. The party for the department management and families is set at their home on December 13th."

I often thought myself intuitively slow compared to Holmes and this was one such instance.

"If we're not breaking in, will the party be a distraction for us to sneak into the house? We can't blend in as guests, or are we the hired help?"

"Not exactly. Sir Thomas is hiring entertainers and providing extra help, decorations, food, and gifts for the children. There will be about fifty guests in total, myself included. Sherlock, I know you've always had a flare for the dramatic, so you will be our thespian. Once the guests are settled, the program will begin with you performing a dramatic reading of a portion of *A Christmas Carol* and selected Christmas poems. Afterwards, using some excuse, you will retreat to the kitchen near the back stairway and, instead of returning to the party, you'll use those stairs to access and search their personal rooms. While you're doing that, a magician and then a musician will perform, followed by a break while the guests feast on cakes and puddings. Afterwards, Father Christmas will appear and greet each child and give them a gift. More carols and thanks to the hosts will conclude the festive afternoon, and hopefully your search. It should keep the hosts occupied."

"If our 'actor' is searching the premises, will I be assisting him?'

"No, Doctor. Until you're called upon for your official role, you will station yourself by the front stairways to observe if any members of the household wander in your direction. Should they use the stairs, you will cough loudly enough for Sherlock to hear you."

"What is my 'official' role besides watching for anyone going upstairs?"

"You will be Father Christmas's helper."

Holmes looked me up and down. "Watson an elf? I think he'd look rather smart with pointed ears." Needless to say, I found it less amusing, but knew if there was a question of a traitor, I would do whatever was asked. "And what will you be doing while this is happening? Dining with the guests?"

If Mycroft was a bit uneasy when he explained the plan, his reluctance to share more was plain to see. "I have a vital responsibility in this diversion. I'm sure you'll find this hilarious, but I shall be playing Father Christmas."

Holmes was rarely given to boisterous laughter, but today was an exception. He laughed until I thought he might weep. Finally catching his breath, he asked "And exactly how much experience do you have entertaining children?"

Jaw clenched, Mycroft looked at his brother for a moment before he spoke. "My work within the government has prepared me for working with children, if not in age then certainly in temperament."

Holmes's laughter tapered off as he assessed the grave expression on Mycroft's face. Walking to his brother he placed his hand on his shoulder. "If you're willing to act as Father Christmas, I'm sure I speak for both of us when I say we will do as you ask." He looked quite serious. "For King and Country."

He turned to me as I repeated it. "For King and Country."

The few days until the party passed both slowly and quickly. While decorations were hung in shops, families planned their holidays, and churches prepared for the holy season, Holmes rehearsed his story and poems and scoured the newspapers for reports of potentially related events. He spent the evenings in his old haunts with those who kept their ears to the ground for news of criminal doings. One night he returned to Baker Street just before midnight as I was preparing to retire.

"What news tonight?" I asked.

When he removed his coat I saw he was wearing workman's clothing. "It's a misspent evening when Shinwell Johnson can't put his finger on what's going on, other than talk among the lower elements of a new game in town. A plot to ruin a large banking firm with rumors about financial losses, a major department store with questions about selling stolen goods, blackmail, and unparalleled thefts on the docks have all arisen in the past few months. I don't trust coincidence, and if Moriarty and Milverton hadn't gone to their final rewards, I would have thought one or both of them might be connected to this. Tomorrow night we'll call at a spot Shinwell recommended. It's the type of place that might attract those who could cause troubles on the docks."

The next day I tried to focus on the book I was reading, but Holmes's repetitive recitation of Clement Moore's "The Night Before Christmas" distracted me. The day dragged on, but when darkness fell we prepared for our evening's work. Holmes had clothing to convince anyone we were dock workers, and added whiskers and grease smudges completed our disguise. Holmes stopped as were ready to exit. "Watson, we'll be visiting one of the most contemptable establishments in London. Violence isn't uncommon there. Perhaps it would be wise to bring your service revolver."

I patted my coat pocket. "Ready, should it be needed."

A hansom cab delivered us to a point within walking distance of the docks. The cold wind and effluence from the Thames assailed us, and within moments we came upon what I hoped might be the welcoming warmth of the tavern. I expected to see a blazing fire inside, but the accumulated dirt of years on the windows made that impossible. Once through the door, no boughs of holly or baubles greeted us, and the dim lighting barely penetrated the smoke that hung in the air. Holmes leaned over and said quietly "Welcome to the 3B's Pub. Watch your pocket and your back. The men here generally pose no danger, but it's hard to pick those who do from those who don't."

The floor was sticky and unwashed, which described everything else within the pub. With the door closed against the cold, the smell of the river still permeated the 3B's, but wasn't enough to mask the odors from so many hard-working, hollow-eyed men. Trying to forget the day as they huddled alone over glasses of cheap gin and ale, they drank, knowing the next day would be no easier. Making our way to the bar, we found two stools. I saw Holmes looking cautiously around the room, but his eyes stopped at one table with two men.

"Wouldn't be staring back there if I was you, mate." The man sitting next to Holmes spoke quietly and never looked up from his drink, which he held with cracked and reddened hands. He was a thin man with a long scar of the left cheek of his drawn face, a hat pulled low over his brow. "That's bad business going on." Holmes's brows rose slightly, surprised that he'd been noticed. Our seatmate rotated an inch in our direction and appraised us with a keen eye. "You ain't been here any time that I am, and I'm here 'most every night."

"We've no use for bad business, friend. We're just off the *Della May* and saw this spot." Holmes motioned to the barkeep that we'd like two glasses of ale. The glasses looked as unwashed as everything else in the tavern.

Our new acquaintance took a healthy drink of his gin. "Name's Rudy. So you're sailors, huh? Men with clean hands like you don't stumble on this place too often." He tilted his head imperceptibly toward the corner table. "That gent, the one with the dark hair and eyes, has soft, clean hands and nails. His clothes are clean too. Acts all friendly – finds someone and buys them a few drinks. That isn't something that happens here, at least until he started coming in this summer."

I looked past Holmes to Rudy. "So what's the problem if he wants to buy a man a drink?"

"Maybe nothing, maybe something. Whoever he's talking up gets tipsy, but he doesn't, not really. When his new chum is in his cups, that gent starts asking questions about ships and cargo coming and out, like he knows where they work but real casual like. Best to avoid him."

He finished his drink and looked us over. "Probably won't see you at the 3B's again." We left about ten minutes after his departure.

We retraced our route and found a cab willing to take us, only after seeing we had the funds to pay the fare. Holmes sat deep in thought for a moment, then roused himself. "I've always fancied myself a perceptive observer of others, but our friend Rudy turned the tables on us. He spotted us from the moment we sat down – probably from the minute we walked in. I knew that gentleman in the corner didn't belong there, but what hubris, what arrogance for me to think others don't note much from a person's appearance."

I was somewhat taken aback by this admission. "That may be, but are those incidences at the 3B's simply the common thefts which have always occurred, what with the value of the cargo shipped in and out?"

"Many a desperate man has found a day's work or ill-gotten goods on the docks. Yet Shinwell Johnson, whose own bad reputation allows him to know the workings of the criminal world, knew nothing beyond the rumor that something, or someone new was involved. The genial gentleman from the 3B's wants to know about shipping schedules and cargo which doesn't appear to have any commonalities with what Mycroft described. Questions remain if such disparate events have more than the common thread of timing and worse, if someone new has taken the vacated position at the centre of the criminal web. I can't put the pieces of this peculiar puzzle together."

Sinking into the silence that often marked his contemplative moods, he didn't speak as we exited the cab and, once upstairs, removed his coat. As he sank into a chair, I went up to my room and prepared myself for bed. Looking back as I departed the sitting room, I saw Holmes with his pipe in hand. I doubted he would rest that night and wondered if I would be able to sleep should he take up his violin.

I awoke the morning of Saturday, December 13th, huddled beneath the covers. No sunshine showed through the windows and a quick glimpse revealed a light snow was falling, perfect for the holiday revelries at the Payne-Owen household. I dressed and found Holmes settled at our dining table. He looked up. "So nice of you to join me this morning. Mrs. Hudson prepared a particularly pleasing breakfast."

I felt Mrs. Hudson always prepared a pleasing breakfast, while Holmes was rarely so complimentary. In between bites of his eggs, bacon, fish, and crumpets with the strawberry jam that Mrs. Hudson put up the past summer, he continued. "Mycroft sent a note early this morning along with our costumes for today. He's arriving at the Payne-Owen home about one o'clock, and we are to arrive no later than two, as the guests are expected at 2:30."

At the appointed time, we changed into our costumes. Mine was a simple red waistcoat, a green cravat, and a holly boutonniere. When he emerged from his bedchamber, I would have sworn I was looking at the author of *A Christmas Carol*. With his hair brushed forward in a strange style with curls at his temples, a neat goatee, and his suit and cravat, he could have been Charles Dickens himself. With a theatrical flourish, he carried a cane. Noticing my inspection of his outfit, he patted his waistcoat pocket. "It's in my pocket." I was glad his well-used burgling kit was close at hand, as it was sure to be used.

A quick carriage ride brought us to the Payne-Owens' lovely home in Eaton Square. The maid who answered the door quickly put us in our place, reminding us that the back door was used "by tradesmen and the like" before closing the door in our faces. Taking her direction, we rounded the houses and found the back door. Once admitted inside, we were shown to the first floor great room where the party was to be held. It was a hub of activity, with Mycroft directing the setting of the tables and chairs with a mere wave of his hand, making sure the chairs faced the stage and not the stairs. We approached him, weaving between those preparing the party needs.

Holmes appraised his brother, focusing on his midsection. "Mycroft, I see your padding is in place for your Jolly Old Elf costume."

"Ah yes, I see your wit and tongue are as sharp as ever. Are you both clear on what's to be done?" We agreed, and it wasn't long before we heard the guests entering.

The afternoon went off according to Mycroft's plan. The guests were led to the party room and Sir Thomas, with Payne-Owen and his wife at his side, welcomed them. After Sir Thomas gave a brief introduction, Holmes took the stage. As I noted early in my association with him, the stage lost a fine actor. When the applause subsided, he took his leave and, after accepting a few "Well done!" accolades, I saw him talk to one of the maids who gestured down a hallway. With a slight nod in my direction, he left the room.

The program continued. Mesmerized by the magician, the children could be heard whispering, "How did he do that?" with each trick. They sang along with the musicians and afterwards, there were delighted squeals as they filled their plates with the sweets and other treats laid on long tables. The families returned to their seats and, once their plates were empty, there was an announcement that a surprise was in store for them. All eyes widened when Father Christmas took the stage and I stood beside him. Mycroft cut a compelling figure, resplendent in his red robes, a convincing beard and locks, and a hearty laugh. The children were relatively patient as they waited to see the great man, anticipating how long it would be before it was their turn. Keeping an eye on the stairs, I led each child to Mycroft, who greeted them and asked their names. While I found the correctly tagged gift, he talked with them about their hopes for a Merry Christmas, and I wondered if the stage might have lost another fine actor as he put the boys and girls at ease. Their parents looked on, obviously proud of their children and their good manners. When each child had his or her moment, they took their seats. As the final carol was sung, I saw Holmes slip down the stairs and rejoin the group.

Sir Thomas took the stage and thanked the girls and boys for being so well behaved and his "dear friends", Mr. and Mrs. Payne-Owen, for their generosity and hospitality. It didn't take long after the guests bid their thanks that we were able to take our leave. Back in Baker Street, we waited until Mycroft arrived, and when we were seated Holmes began his narrative.

"There are two parts of this story regarding this afternoon. Let me start with my search of Payne-Owen's private rooms. As planned, I made my way upstairs where I searched the bedchamber and his office. It was all very tidy with nothing of consequence. No safe, no locked desk drawers, no loose incriminating papers, no cryptic messages or addresses, nothing. This doesn't exonerate Payne-Owen, of course, but I found no evidence of his involvement."

Mycroft nodded his head. "Frankly I couldn't imagine there would be, but it was a place to start."

"It was decidedly unproductive. But I can't say the same for what happened in the kitchen." Mycroft and I exchanged glances, wondering what Holmes found interesting. "After my performance, I went to the kitchen where I found the cook in her rocking chair, wrapped in a shawl with knitting in her lap. She agreed to my request for a cup of something soothing and, as she laid her knitting on the table to put the kettle on, I saw the scarf had a series of unevenly spaced knots in one row and some small holes in the next. She noticed I was looking at it, and moved her red yarn and needles under her chair just as Mrs. Payne-Owen swept into the kitchen."

Never missing the chance for a dramatic pause, Holmes walked to the window and looked at the darkened street below. "Apparently she frowns upon the help entertaining the hired entertainers in the kitchen, or so I gathered. 'Cook, the children need more fruit punch, and we need more lemons for the tea. You should have noticed, but it appears you're busy with this gentleman.' With that parting shot she left for the party room, but not before I saw the expression on the cook's face. It was pure hatred. I decided further conversation with her might prove productive."

"We're in the midst of questionable treason and other crimes, and you chose to question the help about the enmity she holds for the lady of the house?"

"Yes Mycroft, I did. In a home like the Payne-Owens', the help attend to the homeowner's every need, yet are often treated as if they're invisible unless there's a problem. With that invisibility and presumed loyalty, the conversation among family or with guests is often less than circumspect, so it's possible she heard something that shouldn't have been shared. Once Mrs. Payne-Owen was out of sight, I asked her, 'That one's got her nose up in the air. Is she always like that?'

"'No, she's usually worse. Not many a kind or thankful word from her, I can tell you.' She collected the punch and lemons and called a maid to take them up to the party room.

"'Sorry, I didn't introduce myself. I'm Edmund. And you're . . . ?'

"'It's not 'Cook'. I'm Beryl. I'm not sure Mrs. High-and-Mighty even knows my name. She only speaks to me to tell me what's wrong.'

"'Nice to meet you, Beryl. My nan used to knit quite a bit, so I feel right at home with you here in the kitchen.' I pointed to her yarn. 'Making that for someone? Thought I saw some knots and holes in it.'

"She became a bit flustered and was quick to make light of the mistakes, telling me she'd fix it later, but something was off with her. She was nervous, more interested in talking about Mrs. Payne-Owen and how she treats the servants, but is all too holy when others are around, always talking about her Christian charity. She said 'At least that means we get time off on Sunday morning to go to church services. Not her fancy church where she goes to be seen, mind you. I go to St. Anselm's and I'll be taking this scarf in tomorrow.' Apparently there's other parishioners who are in service like her, and join in donating knitted goods."

I'm not as intuitive as Holmes and failed to see where this was going. "So you know the lady of the house isn't as kind as she puts on and the cook takes her knitting to church, but what bearing does this have on the leaked information and crimes?"

"As our friend Rudy from the 3B's said: 'Maybe nothing, maybe something.' My instincts tell me an ignored older woman, destined to live out her life in someone else's kitchen, may have a story of her own. And something is nagging at me about that knitting. Tomorrow is Sunday, and a good day to observe the cook at her church."

After dining on a cold supper, Mycroft left us. Holmes pulled several books and a number of cards from his index, and then settled in for what I surmised was related to his question about knitting, although why this particular subject interested him escaped me. He was still reading when I began nodding off.

The next morning dawned with overcast skies and no sun to melt the previous day's snow. I could hear Holmes stirring in the sitting room.

"Watson! I was just about to rouse you for our Sunday services. Sabbath or not, the cook has to prepare breakfast for the Payne-Owens, so we'll attend the ten o'clock service. She didn't see you, so no need to alter your appearance, but it's a different situation for me. I'll join you shortly."

While he dressed, I had a light breakfast and looked at the newspaper. As familiar as I was with Holmes's disguises, when he entered the room I was taken aback by his ability to transform himself. He appeared much older with gray hair, poor posture which made him appear shorter, thick spectacles, a bulbous nose, and slightly bucked teeth. His waistline, normally so thin, had required a bit of extra padding in his costume of a middle-class clerk.

"How do I look? Do you think Beryl will recognize me as the distinguished actor from yesterday?"

I assured him that as I could barely discern his features, I doubted she would either, particularly as he'd worn a different disguise when they met. We were soon off to St. Anselm's. The light snow provided an appropriate holiday setting for the faithful who were entering the church to celebrate the third Sunday of Advent. The church embodied both beauty and simplicity, and while I admired the stained-glass windows, religious symbols, and statuary, Holmes scanned the assembled as we found a pew. It was a lovely service, and when it was over, the faithful filed out, thanking the priest who stood by the door to talk with the communicants. There were groups and individuals remaining inside, some in prayer and others in conversation with friends and family. In only a moment Holmes nudged me, and tilted his head toward a side aisle. "That's Beryl and it's certainly her knitted goods in that bag." The cook walked to an alcove where a small cluster of quiet churchwomen were sitting. Suddenly, Holmes sat forward and grabbed my arm.

"Take note of the new arrival. Do you see how the others are focused on her? I recognize her."

I found nothing familiar or outstanding in her appearance. Her features were rather plain, her clothing and hat what one might expect of a servant in her Sunday best. "Who is she?"

"She's *my* – or should I say *Escott the plumber's* – former fiancée, Agatha."

"Milverton's housemaid? It's been what, almost three years since you've seen her. Are you sure?" Having never seen the ill-used servant before, her entrance had no impact on me.

"Yes, it's her. I wonder if a piece of this puzzle may have fallen into place." His attention returned to the group as the women spoke quietly, placing a few items in an empty spot near Agatha, who appeared to soundlessly dominate the group.

"They're not here as a group of friends, but to see Agatha, aren't they?"

"My assumption as well. I'm fairly certain we're closer to discovering what's happening, but our time here is limited." Although they'd been together for only a short period, the ladies were already picking up their other belongings as if to leave. "I think we should follow Agatha."

As she left the church, we kept out of Agatha's sight. She carried a few small bags down the steps and dropped them next to a waiting landau. The coachman jumped down in haste and held the door for her, giving her his arm as she climbed inside, then placed the bags at her feet. He resumed his seat and, taking the reins, pulled into the street. We were able to hail a hansom to follow them at a distance and as we settled in, Holmes said, "One doesn't often see a maid met by a landau and such an attentive driver. It's going to prove rather interesting to see who Agatha is working for since the demise of Mr. Milverton."

With that, he removed his facial disguise and wig. Leaving the area with the church and surrounding small shops, we entered an area with fashionable homes. The landau turned into a mews and Holmes alerted the driver to stop. He paid him and jumped out, with me fast behind him. As we rounded the corner we saw Agatha, followed by the driver, enter the back of a large but not overly ostentatious house.

"We'll ask Mycroft to see who actually owns this house, which is presumably where she works. For now, a call at the Payne-Owens' home is in order." I reminded Holmes that Beryl could reasonably be expected to be preparing the midday meal. There was a brisk breeze but it was a short walk to Eaton Square, the snow covering some of the unpleasantness normally found in the streets. In hopes of avoiding Mr. or Mrs. Payne-Owen, we went to the back door where we were invited inside by a servant when Holmes told her it was vital we speak to Beryl. She showed us into the kitchen, a warm and comfortable room with the odor of cooking hanging in the air. There was a woman standing at the counter and she looked at both of us, especially at Holmes.

"Good day, Beryl. You might not remember me from the party yesterday." She looked unsure if she did. "I'm not an actor as I told you, and my name isn't Edmund. I'm Sherlock Holmes, and this is my associate Dr. John Watson." Her face paled and she put her hand on her chest. "I take it you've heard of us." I moved toward her, feeling it might be best for her to sit down.

"What is it you want with me?" Her question was a simple yet suspicious one. Holmes sat across from her, and leaned forward, elbows on his knees. In a calm voice he said "Beryl, let's not draw this out. When I was here yesterday, I noticed evident errors in your knitting and your nervousness when I mentioned them. Your reaction bothered me, and I think they weren't mistakes at all, but intentional. A woman at church taught you how to use a code to relay information, didn't she? Things you've overheard in this house about Mr. Payne-Owen's government work – particularly about a new ship."

Beryl's head was down and I could see the tears begin to roll down her cheeks. She spoke softly. "I've known this day would come."

Holmes was known for his gentleness toward women. "I believe things will go a bit easier for you if you cooperate. Please, tell us the whole story from the beginning."

It took her a minute to gather her thoughts. "I've gone over and over what happened, trying to understand how it got this far. I've always been a cook, and after my last family moved to Italy last year, it took a while before I found this position. I have no family nearby, just a sister in Dover, and I don't get a chance to meet people, so I joined St. Anselm's and their knitting group. I feel good helping with the charity work along with five or six women." She shifted uncomfortably, keeping her eyes cast downwards. "Sometime last spring, Charlotte joined our group. She was friendly and got everyone talking and laughing, and it didn't take long before we all looked forward to our brief time together after Sunday services. She was so interested in us, and complimentary. But it didn't last."

"She said her name is Charlotte?" Beryl nodded. "When did your time with Charlotte change?"

"Maybe mid-summer? She started complaining about how the family she served treated her. That's something we all have in common, one way or another, and it didn't take long before the short time we have after church turned into talking about our problems. You know, it felt good to share that, like I wasn't alone. We gabbed about the lady of the house, how the mister approached the pretty maids, all of the little things that happen every day. But some of it wasn't all that nice, and some of it should never have been repeated."

"Like what you overheard about the plans Mr. Payne-Owen is working on?" There was an edge in Holmes's voice.

"Mr. Holmes, much as I don't like the mistress, the mister isn't a bad sort. I heard him talking about a big new ship with the missus, but I didn't know it was such a secret. I guess I felt a bit special working for someone like him who's in charge of something so important."

Holmes was on his feet, hands on the back of his chair. "Go on with your story."

"One Sunday as we were leaving, I saw Charlotte pull one of our group, Margaret, aside and talk to her. The next week I asked her what it was about since she'd looked so unhappy, but she wouldn't say a word. Two weeks later it was the same thing, only with Ruth, and before long it was my turn. It turns out Charlotte listened to our gossip – not as a friend, but so she could use it against us."

"What did she threaten she was going to do with your gossip?"

"That's the bad part, Mr. Holmes. She'd already done it. Told me she'd sold that bit about the big guns to a company or two. Said she'd tell Payne-Owen that I was gossiping about him and his department secrets and if I wanted to keep my position, I'd tell her more of what I hear. I'm certain that's what's happened with Margaret, Ruth, Grace, Rose, and Winifred too. I'm so ashamed that I don't even want to attend church anymore, but Charlotte let me know if I stop, she'll tell Mr. Payne-Owen her story, and then what will happen to me?"

It was grim, and one could see the air of unhappiness and shame that hung over her. She resumed her tale. "I should have quit as soon as it happened. I went through what little money I'd saved before I found this situation, and if I left then for Dover and my sister's tea shop, I'd have gone with little to offer other than my baking. Staying here, I thought I could save some money to help with the shop – especially since Charlotte started giving us envelopes with a pound or two now and then. She acted like it was to help us, but that's not why she did it. We all took that dirty money and with the knitting, it tied us to her like a boat anchor. That fear of being found out has tortured me every day."

I'd been listening quietly, but there was a point that bothered me. "Beryl, you're together with these women on Sundays. Why don't you simply tell Charlotte your secrets instead of using some involved knitting code? That has to take a lot of time."

"It was just idle gossip when we talked in church, but by the time we were all tangled up with her, she wanted to make sure no one overheard whatever secrets we had to tell her. She didn't want notes because if one was lost or read over a shoulder she'd have a problem, and we don't have enough time away from work to go meet her. She showed us how to knit coded messages with names, numbers, and the like. The scarf you saw Mr. Holmes? Mine indicated exactly how many guns were on the ship. And you're right, Dr. Watson. I spend many evening hours knitting after a long day in the kitchen, but it isn't as if I have something to pass on every week."

Holmes was silent for a moment. "Beryl, before we leave you, one thing we do need to know for whom your fellow knitters work – and please note if you know what could be used against them. I hope you understand that I can't speak for what happens next, but I'm not going to say anything to Mr. Payne-Owen until we learn a bit more."

Beryl nodded and then spent some time writing down the names of her group with the information Holmes requested. "I know who they work for and what they said, but not where they live. And Mr. Holmes? I'm not going to try to run away, no matter how much I wish I could."

We left the unhappy cook of Eaton Square and went home to Baker Street. Holmes turned his attention to his index, comparing the names of the employers to his entries. It wasn't long before he looked me "Ah! Beryl's friend Ruth works for a leading officer of the bank that's been accused of financial problems. Margaret works for an actor who bribed a member of the press to write a terrible review of another actor's performance, thus limiting his competition for stage roles. Rose is a maid at a vicarage, one that a certain Lord visited to privately confess his problem of stealing small items from friends and shops. There's a few more notes here, but I think we can see how the information Agatha gathers is used by her employer."

Taking the list, I read the entries. "It also include Grace's employer, who doesn't seem to be engaged in anything criminal, but has responsibility for awarding a number of government contracts. That might be of interest to business concerns. But the other is something else. Winifred recently discovered that her employer embezzled money from elderly widows. But I see no mention of the other crimes Mycroft mentioned."

"You're right. He indicated there were two authors, a large department store, and a cabinet member who were experiencing difficulties, so one might presume Agatha and others in the same employ are insinuating themselves across the city in order to gain information. This may be more widespread than we know." He replaced his index file and took a chair. "There's nothing we can do this evening, Watson. Tomorrow, when Mycroft determines who owns the house where Agatha works, a visit to see who else lives there will be in order." Holmes leaned back into the chair cushion, Persian slipper in one hand and pipe in the other. "I think it will be advantageous for Mycroft and Inspector Morton to accompany us."

At first light, I awakened to the sound of Holmes's voice and found him at his desk having just completed a telephone conversation. "Mycroft has arranged for Inspector Morton to meet us at nine o'clock at the home where we saw Agatha. Hopefully her employer, Mr. Milton Charles according to Mycroft, will be there and we can find who else is working for him." Glancing at his watch, he suggested we leave within the hour. His nervous energy was evident as he paced around the room, and as I'd learned over the years, it was best not to interrupt him.

A few minutes before nine we met Mycroft on the corner we'd visited only the day before. Looking down the street, on the opposite corner we saw Inspector Morton and two members of the force. They walked toward us and we met not far from the house.

Mycroft looked at them. "It's just the three of you?"

The inspector shook his head. "No, I sent four others to the mews in case the rats decide to leave the sinking ship out the back way. Are we ready?" Nodding in agreement, we went up the front steps where Morton rang the bell. A lovely young maid answered the door and before she could say a word, we entered the house. Mycroft handed her his coat, much to her surprise.

Holmes smiled at her. "I believe you have a woman named Agatha working here? We need to talk to her."

She looked confused. "There's no one works here named Agatha. Do you mean Miss Agatha?"

That stopped Holmes in his tracks but he recovered quickly. "Yes. Please tell the lady of the house that an old friend has come to see her." She left us standing in the foyer as she went to announce us. He looked at me with an expression I seldom saw and said softly "I think it's possible that I underestimated my former fiancée."

Morton instructed the two police officers to remain near the front door as she returned. We were shown to an elegantly appointed morning room where Agatha and a man were seated comfortably in cushioned chairs. Well dressed, obviously at ease as they enjoyed their morning coffee, they turned slightly to look at their four visitors. A moment passed as Holmes and Agatha viewed each other. Having spent a great deal of time in the company of women, the quality and cost of her dress and jewelry was easy to identify, and out of place for the dowdy woman we'd seen at the church.

Agatha stood and was the first to speak. "You! I hoped I'd never see you again."

"Having followed you home from church yesterday, we decided to call to wish you the Compliments of the Season. Seeing you two so cozy, must I accept that it's too late to rekindle our romance?"

We'd been so intent on Agatha that it took a moment before I recognized her dark-haired, dark-eyed companion. "Different clothes and place, but you're the friendly gent from the 3B's who likes to get men drunk and find out what's coming into and out of the docks." He had no visible reaction other than the tightening of his hands on the arms of his chair.

Holmes turned his attention to the man. "So he is. Mycroft, Inspector Morton, may I introduce the gentleman behind the scene, Mr. Milton Charles. I'm sure we can depend on his good will to help us unravel and identify his web of criminals, Agatha included, who are engaged in theft, espionage, and blackmail. And please, don't insult us by denying it."

There was a brief pause and to everyone's surprise, Agatha began to laugh, quietly at first but then she laughed until she was bent over. "You prat, he's not Milton Charles. There is no Milton Charles."

It wasn't often that Holmes was caught flat-footed, but flat-footed he was. Every one of us stood in silence, waiting to see what would happen next. Collecting himself, a tight grin spread across his face. "Agatha, or Charlotte as you're known at St Anselm's, we came here thinking you were in this gentleman's employ. Then I wondered if you were partners with him. But he works for you, doesn't he?"

"The great Sherlock Holmes, or Escott if you prefer, thinks he's figured it out. Seems neither of us is always who we say we are, does it?" She paused, hands on her hips. "What is it you think you know?"

"I have five women from St. Anselm's who can provide proof of your blackmail, and I'm sure a thorough search of this house will provide even more evidence of the unfortunates you and your hirelings have preyed upon. Inspector Morton, please have your men look for notes about her accomplices and any knitted items as well." Morton left the room to instruct several of his officers currently in the mews to examine the house while others remained on guard. "By the way Agatha, now that your future is looking a bit bleak, perhaps you'll tell us how you came to be the spider in the centre of this extensive web"

I hastened to add, "And I think we'd like to know about this knitting code Holmes referred to."

Despite her current illegal vocation, she was a proud woman, torn between refuting the accusations and touting her ownership. "I can tell by the looks on your faces that you never considered a mere housemaid could do what I have." She pointed at Holmes. "You took advantage of me when I worked for Milverton. Both of you thought all I could do was keep his house tidy, but I watched him and knew what he was doing to make a pretty penny. I saw those letters that he locked up when people came to see him or when he left the house, but while he was home he sometimes left them out on his desk. Then he met his untimely end, which was timely for me. Most of what he had was destroyed, but I had a few odds and ends tucked away and thought if he could make a living blackmailing people, so could I. It's an easy thing to find people who work on the wrong side of the law, like Alvin here, to help, but it's taken two years to get where I am."

Holmes rarely expressed his anger. "And you did it by making those poor women think you were a household servant like them."

"That's all they expected of someone like me, so it wasn't difficult. That's what you thought when you saw me at church, so why wouldn't they? I know what their lives are like and how to talk to them. It was simple, actually."

I asked again. "But what about the knitting?"

"Milverton might have been a miserable old git, but he had a good library, and I used to sneak a book or two to read. Amazing what you can learn from Charles Dickens."

Holmes turned to us. "She's referring to the *tricoteuse* in *A Tale of Two Cities*. She knit the names of the guillotine's victims into her work."

"Very good, Holmes. Madame Defarge did teach me a thing or two. I made a fairly simple pattern for the alphabet and numbers and made sure those women learned it."

It was at that moment that one of Morton's men called to him. "Inspector, you should come look at this." Leaving the two officers to watch Agatha and her male companion, we followed Morton into the nearby study. The officer held up a sheaf of papers. "Sir, there's lists of names and some accounting that may be what you want." Mycroft took the bundle and examined several papers, and then said "This is exactly what we're looking for."

Our day was a long one which ended in the removal of Agatha, Alvin, and a number of the household staff to jail. Mycroft summoned a carriage and a few men from Whitehall to box up the papers, as well as several piles of knitted goods, all carefully labeled with the names of those who'd knitted them. Suffice it to say, this evidence was only the beginning of her downfall.

It was some days before we heard from Mycroft. He joined us in Baker Street on Christmas Eve, and after Mrs. Hudson's fine dinner we relaxed by the fire, each with a whisky-and-soda. Holmes spoke first. "Mycroft, I've been quite patient and promised myself I would wait to inquire about what official progress has been made regarding Agatha and her entourage."

"It isn't patience when it's only been a bit more than a week since arrests were made and her records seized. It's fair to say that Agatha's successful venture will collapse under the weight of her own tidy files. We know whom she hired to find those with information to pass on. The unfortunates they coerced are maids, cooks, secretaries, footmen, stableboys, and clerks. Most did Agatha's bidding because they knew if they failed to provide the information she wanted, their employers would be informed about their indiscretions and they'd be arrested – or in the very least, sacked without a reference, all because a loose piece of information or gossip fell on the wrong ears. Others did it because they were unhappy with their situations and saw a way out. Her dogsbody Alvin plied those on the docks with drink which loosened their tongues. It hasn't been decided what will happen to each of them."

"Why did Agatha go to St. Anselm's herself when she could have used one of her agents? If it wasn't for Holmes spotting her, do you think the case would have been settled so quickly?"

"Excellent question, Doctor." Taking a sip of his whisky, Mycroft continued. "She attended the church as a child and still had great fondness for it. Sadly it wasn't enough to redeem her. But I have a question for you, Sherlock. You told us that what focused your attention on Beryl and your question about knitting. I don't recall such domestic skills interested you, although it certainly led in the correct direction."

"It was the details which interested me. When I first met her, she had a lacy shawl over her shoulders, which would have required some skill to make. The simple scarf she was knitting had obvious flaws, and when I pointed them out, she tried to distract me with her comments about Mrs. Payne-Owen. She said she'd fix the holes and knots before she took it church the next day, but I couldn't see how she could do that in such a short time. Anyone who could knit such a shawl as hers wouldn't make those mistakes – and then it occurred to me it must be purposeful. Perhaps it was my appearance as Dickens that prompted a vague memory of a knitting code which I confirmed when I looked at my copy of *A Tale of Two Cities*."

We were all silent for a moment as we considered the toll that would be paid by so many because of one woman's greed. "A more charitable attitude from their employers would have made those in service far less susceptible to Agatha's plots," I said.

"You're right," agreed Mycroft. "If more respect was shown to them, it would have been a different story, and I hope when more of this is revealed there will be lessons learned. But that's the subject for another day. And speaking of charity, tonight it's fitting that we raise a glass to the spirit of the Holy Day we're celebrating. As Mr. Dickens wrote, this should be a reminder that we should honor Christmas in our hearts, and try to keep it all the year." We rose, and holding a glass, we toasted the spirit of Christmas.

Holmes raised his glass again, and added "And to the colourful skein of life."

The Adventure of the Chained Phantom
by J.S. Rowlinson
(Illustrations also by J.S. Rowlinson)

Chapter I

"Well, Watson, what have you resigned to keep from me?"

That was how I was greeted by my friend, Mr. Sherlock Holmes, upon my arrival. I was taken aback by his sharp challenge, as my visit to our old rooms at Baker Street had been quite unannounced. I had yet, even, to take my hand from the brass knob of the door.

"Good Lord!" I cried, "I haven't even wished you a good morning."

"Yes, well, good morning to you," he replied, in a dreamy, languid voice, quite superseding his initial outburst.

I have, on several occasions, seen my friend deduce the habits, character, and whereabouts of divers members of the public. However, I wasn't yet fully past the threshold, and the door was barely open, before Holmes's incredible supposition. He could see the perplexity upon my features and gave a little chuckle, sending up a string of small bluish puffs from his briar.

"My dear fellow," he continued, closing his eyes and folding his hands over his chest, making him look remarkably catlike. "You paused twice on the stairs, both intervals were quite audible from behind this door. Now, you have scaled that staircase many times, and Mrs. Hudson isn't renowned for her decorative variance, so there could have been nothing to catch your eye upon your ascent. I can observe by your insistence on wearing those plebeian Chelsea boots that neither were you tying up your shoelaces. Twin that with the heavy, muttering breath, which is most unlike you, and it doesn't take one of my talents to deduce you had some cerebral bone to chew on, if you'll pardon the expression. The first pause, I dare say, you were deciding whether or not to divulge your news. The second pause – and you were resolved against it, and that was confirmed by your pointed evasion of my eye when your head finally emerged. Content?"

The infernal peacock had hardly paused for breath, but he was quite right in every particular.

"So," intoned Holmes, "what has taken so much deliberation upon the carpet? Pray, brush the snow off of your overcoat and come sit down."

To continue the earlier feline metaphor, I felt entirely as would a mouse in the playful paws of a tomcat. Still mulling the thing over in my mind, I hung my coat, sat down in my usual chair on the opposite side of the fire, gave a knowing exhalation, and took the card (which I had picked up from the hallway table) from my waistcoat pocket. In an instant, Holmes had leapt up and snatched it from my fumbling hands, holding it delicately between thumb and forefinger.

In an instant, Holmes had leapt up and snatched it from my fumbling hands, holding it delicately between thumb and forefinger.

"Ha, just as I thought! I heard the bell ring this morning before I was up, though I presumed at the time it was the butcher's boy with the Christmas goose. The card is most ostentatious, and of quite spectacular quality – embossed and filigreed. My, my. Mrs. Hudson will have some keen words from me when she returns from delivering presents to that niece of hers. This should have been brought up with my soft boiled eggs."

He turned the card over and smiled.

"Well, Watson, I must say I'm surprised at your prejudice against such an honourable gentleman. Why should you not wish me to be consulted by a person of such lofty esteem?"

The card bore the name of Sir Cyril Oldfield, Earl of Stafford, and resident of the renowned Talbot Hall. On the reverse was a message of summons, of some considerable urgency. What I'd assumed Holmes was ignorant of were the incredible tales that had emanated from that ancient seat over the past few months. His next comment, then, surprised me greatly.

"I expect he wants to see me about his ghosts."

I was dumbstruck, as that was indeed my anticipated conclusion. I had brooked myself to replying on behalf of my friend, declining the Earl's kind offer, and so foregoing Holmes's stentorian mockery. He gave me another sidelong grin.

"I notice he doesn't deign to come to us, and I don't recall ever visiting that part of the country. Would your practice permit you to join me on this phantasmagorical sojourn?"

I said that indeed I could be spared for a day or two, should it be necessary, as I was closed for the festivities, but that I was most stupefied as to why he was taking the invitation seriously. Holmes clearly knew of the stories of ghostly apparitions at Talbot Hall, and soon showed me his recent clippings from the more sensational dailies. He continued on his earlier thread.

"He appears to be a man of quite inexhaustible means, as there was evidently no one waiting with the card, for Mrs. Hudson would certainly not have forgotten to present a message with the messenger still attached. Why go to the expense of such an act, when a wire would have been simpler, not to say cheaper? This Sir Cyril Oldfield certainly seems to do things his own way, regardless of cost or efficiency. I am quite intrigued, though I will reply by the less-florid form of the telegram.

"Watson, this noble gentleman wishes to see us today, and I fancy we have ample time to catch a train up-country. First, however, there are some details in this I need to explore before we depart. I'll meet you at St. Pancras in two hours."

And with that, his earlier languorous recline was transformed completely into a frantic dash about the room, sending papers flying in his wake. I stood, collected my hat, coat, and stick, and turned back for another glance at the card. It was garishly busy in ornamentation, but it was the accompanying message that made my blood run cold.

Written on the back, and an elegant flowing hand, bore the words:

Mr. Holmes,
For the love of God in Heaven,
come before darkness falls again.

Chapter II

I went back home, informed my wife of my intentions, and packed an overnight bag, as we wouldn't have sufficient time to return to London that same day. The chilling message on the card also seemed to hint at the very supernatural subject I had foreseen, so I also anticipated our being needed after dark. My wife was most put out, as it was very nearly Christmas, and she had made a cache of plans of intricate complexity that wouldn't do without me. I kissed her cheek and hurriedly departed for the station. I couldn't fathom Holmes's interest, so I sat with him in some considerable bemusement in our carriage as it pulled out of the city.

Holmes was as silent and self-absorbed as he habitually was when a case had interested him, so I assumed my own disquiet had gone unnoticed, when he spoke.

"This promises to be a most enlightening endeavour. Already several threads are glowing in my hand, and I feel only one or two more will be quite sufficient to shine a light on this little problem."

"I'm glad you're so illuminated. The whole matter is utterly oblique to me. Why on earth are we travelling all the way to the Midlands at this time of the year to hunt for ghosts? I must say, if this is only to stretch your legs in open country, we might just as easily have walked to Hampstead Heath."

"No, no," replied my friend, "I'm quite sure Sir Cyril's fear is genuine, even if I'm not anticipating a confrontation with unquiet spirits. He does seem quite an extraordinary fellow. You've been reading the papers, evidently. What do you make of him?"

I had indeed taken a great, if somewhat voyeuristic, interest in the stories of Talbot Hall that had appeared in the recent press. The Earl of Stafford was a renowned patron of boxing, and had been himself an amateur pugilist in his youth, much to the distaste of his father, the late Earl. He had been married, but had been a widower now for some considerable years, and had seemed to take no interest in remarrying. This was a surprise to some and a great concern to others, as his marriage had produced no heirs to the title or the estate, and Sir Cyril was by now not a young man. His reputation was good, so far as I could ascertain, and he still bore the imposing figure of his younger, more active days. I understood from inference that while he wasn't considered an overly bellicose man, he wasn't someone who would suffer fools gladly, and was accustomed to getting what he wanted – not that Holmes would be browbeaten by anyone, especially some gruff aristocrat.

The image of my companion unbending the iron poker twisted by Dr. Roylott, put a smile to my lips. However, that thought then turned to the dreaded serpent, and my mirth was soured entirely. "Ah. The speckled band," mused my friend, reading my thoughts for the second time that day. "I fancy Sir Cyril Oldfield is quite a different fish. For one thing, he has no relatives to murder. No, this case is quite unique. Consider: A noble of the realm, a man of enormous physical and social presence, frightened out of his wits by ghosts. If there were less heat in that blue blood of his, I would never have taken this case on. There is something in this, Watson – some force that, for all of my hypotheses, is still beyond my grasp."

The stories had been quite extraordinary. What was known about the Earl's character and history were in all the society papers, but it had been the more recent accounts of the supernatural that had brought the nation's attention back to Talbot Hall. While the reports had never been fully substantiated, it seemed that the once imposing Knight of the Realm was now convinced he was being visited by the ghost of a chained woman in his bedroom. He locked his door every night, but still was haunted by this encumbered spectre. It had seemed farcical, and that was certainly the general feeling in London, that the Earl had taken too many bashes to the brain in his youth and was beginning to lose his faculties. As a medical man, I could certainly understand the conclusion. Why then was Holmes so interested? What element had he understood, or uncovered, that had gone undetected by the rest of the reading public?

We changed at Birmingham, the pretty countryside mouldering into a labyrinth of black, slimy bricks, so that I was glad when our connection released us from the acrid gloom of industry. Our second train took us to Uttoxeter, where a dogcart was waiting for us, an urgent driver hurrying us along. The weather had turned, and a fine snow fell in whisps as we made our way out of town. I was surprised that we weren't escorted in something grander, or at least something less open to the elements, and said the same to Holmes, but he sat with his eyes closed in some deep state of concentration, so I pressed him no further. It was quite some miles to Talbot Hall, and being jolted along the track with our backs to the driver, staring at the receding road, I began to feel rather queasy, an unbalance rather like seasickness. It wasn't before time, then, when at last we reached the great estate.

The driver hurried along with our bags in his arms, for we had packed lightly, and urged us up to the house, leaving the cart and the single horse waiting on the gravel. He raced into the hall, putting our luggage down with careless haste, and presented us frantically to the butler, whom he called Langridge. The butler showed us, much more calmly, into the library. There awaited our host, and Holmes's newest client, the Earl of Stafford, Sir Cyril Oldfield. He was white as milk.

Chapter III

His greying whiskers and jowls showed a man that should naturally have been ruddy featured, but the Earl was completely drained of colour. He sat in a huge-backed chair, his hands rattling against the plush leather padding of the arms. As soon as we were announced by the butler he leaped out of his seat, as if burned by some unseen fire, and took my friend's slender hands in his thick, wet grasp.

He took my friend's slender hands in his thick, wet grasp.

"Thank God, thank God!" he stammered, "I received your telegram, but hadn't dared to hope. Another night and I think I would have gone mad, quite mad!"

He stared up into Holmes's grey eyes, a pleading expression upon his brow that seemed so alien to the reputation of the man, as well as to his physical bearing, for he was enormous. Not fat, but too old now to be truly muscular. He was large in the way a bear is large. Sweat trickled down the folds of his forehead in rivulets and dripped from the end of his nose. I could see his collar was soaked and he didn't smell freshly toileted. He let go of Holmes's hands and slapped his head.

"Oh God! Oh Christ! Save me, save me!"

It was unnerving, and had the Earl been a smaller or weaker man the display would have been quite pitiful to see, but the despair of such a person as he was grotesque. Holmes calmly and quietly offered the Earl his own chair. I called the butler for brandy, and we all sat down.

After a deep draught, the Earl seemed to regain something of his composure and was able to speak more clearly, and so answer some of our many questions.

"I have seen every medium, gypsy, and clairvoyant in the county, Mr. Holmes, and I'm at my wits end, sir, my very wits end!"

"So, why call for me, Sir Cyril? I have no pedigree amongst the conjurors and necromancers."

"I have exhausted that line of enquiry, you might say. You are the last man in England that can help me. It isn't a matter for the police, and those that purport to speak to the dead have been of no help, so it must be you, Mr. Holmes. You must help me!"

"Firstly, my Lord, if you would be so kind as to explain, in as much and as specific detail as you can, why you believe you are being haunted in this fashion?"

The story that he told us, which I now recount here, is the most incredible I ever heard in the company of Sherlock Holmes . . . .

"There is a legend attached to my family, gentlemen."

This was the first time he had addressed me as well, and I believe it was just then that he'd fully comprehended my presence in the room.

"A legend that goes back to the days of Charles II, the Merry Monarch, and my ancestor, the builder of this house, Sir Talbot Oldfield, First Earl of Stafford. He – well, that is to say – he had a mistress to whom he was unusually devoted. He had a secret room in the house built where he would meet her, the location of which only the two of them knew. One day, this mistress arrived at Talbot Hall with some priceless jewels, given to her as a gift from the king. The First Earl, understanding that the jewels were a token of affection and of familiarity with the king, flew into a blind rage. We have a reputation, we Oldfields, of being rather hot, as you gentlemen may be aware. Sir Talbot wrapped his mistress up in chains and locked her in their secret room, never to be seen again. Her ghost is said to haunt the line of the Earl of Stafford ever since."

"And you believe you are now being visited by the vengeful spirit of this lady?" mused Holmes quietly.

"I do sir, yes sir, and I don't *believe* it – I *know* it! I know it as I know you are sitting there now."

"When were you first visited by this phantom? I deduce it was in the last few months."

"Yes. How the devil? Ah, the reports in those infernal rags. You're quite right. The first time was three months ago."

"And why did these happenings only begin then, my Lord?"

At this the Earl blustered and told us it was none of our concern, and that the matter to be settled were the visitations, nothing more.

"In that case, Earl Stafford, I bid you a good afternoon and a happy Christmas. Come, Watson. If we hurry we may still catch the next train back to London."

Holmes stood and made straight for the door, a ploy I had seen succeed too many times to be surprised at its desired effect. The Earl wriggled in his chair before barking after my friend, who was purposefully still within the room.

"Yes, yes, you're right of course. You won't know – you couldn't have heard. It's one detail at least I've managed to keep out of the papers. You see, I found the jewels, gentlemen! I discovered the secret room, the treasure, the skeleton, the chains, and all of it. Now I shall not be telling you where, either of you, and that is final, but with any other matter or detail, and I'm completely at your service. Do you think that you can help me, Mr. Holmes?"

My friend looked away distantly, a finger pressed against his lips. At last, he turned to peer directly into the supplicant eyes of our host.

"And when does this spectral figure visit you. How often?"

"Every full moon, gentlemen – the three nights of the full moon, and last night was the first of three. She came for me, in the dead of night. She clangs her chains that are covered in a white slime, as is her face. And her eyes – Christ in Heaven, that stare! It freezes the marrow in my bones! She floats through my room, with her eyes wide and her black mouth open in a silent scream. She stares at me at the end of my bed, then disappears into the wall from whence she came. I cannot survive another night of it, Mr. Holmes. I dare not, and I'm not a man used to being frightened. That fiend is haunting me for the cruelty of my ancestor, and for my discovery of her final resting place."

"Where do you keep these jewels now, my Lord?"

"That is also a secret, but I keep them upon my person during the day, and in a hidden place in my room at night. And no, you may not see them, either of you. No one but me must know of their nature or value, for their safety."

Holmes looked completely unimpressed by this talk of secret treasure.

"If the ghost visited you last night, Sir Cyril, it is absolutely necessary that you let us into your room to investigate."

"I never let a living soul alone in there, Mr. Holmes, and that is why I'm so convinced this is no living soul. I dress and groom myself since my wife died, and keep the only key upon my person at all times. The only occasions when the staff are ever allowed in my room is under my close and constant supervision." He stood. "This way, gentlemen, though I need not tell you, I shall be keeping a surveilling eye on you also."

He led the way out of the library, through the hall, up the enormous staircase, and along a vast passage to his room. With his back to us, he took a unique key from his waistcoat pocket and slid it into the lock. He then asked us to wait for a moment, and after promising to touch nothing in the room which might be of evidence to Sherlock Holmes, he disappeared behind the door, shutting it behind him.

We stood on the other side, patiently, and I turned to my friend, trying to elicit some response from him about the newly discovered treasure – the jewels in the wall. His reply left me completely speechless.

"My dear fellow, he didn't find them anymore than you did."

Chapter IV

It was only moments before the Earl returned to us, still sweating, and ushered us into his room. I couldn't fathom the meaning of Holmes's last words, but I had no opportunity to consider them, for as soon as my friend was past the Earl, he threw himself about the room, stalking to-and-fro like a great black heron.

"And before you ask, Mr. Holmes, the room is just as I left it this morning. Aye, I've read about you in the press, just as you have read of me, though I must say, the illustrations do you no justice. No justice at all sir. Why, they look nothing like you! At any rate, I know of your methods, and it was the reported accounts of your doings and successes that led me to send for you."

Again, the Earl had the infuriating habit of speaking as if I wasn't there, but I swallowed my pride and walked over to where Holmes was bent, running a finger along a side table.

"That is all to the good, my Lord. Now, while I undertake my inspection, would you be so kind as to give us the fullest account possible of these . . . occurrences."

"Like I said before, I was first visited on the first night of the full moon, three months ago."

"And nothing out of the ordinary had happened before then?"

"Well, I'd heard bumps in the night before then."

"How long before then?"

"It is hard to say. Several months at least. It was always at night to begin with. I'm a very light sleeper, Mr. Holmes, I always have been, so I'm very sensitive to things, even when I'm asleep. I thought it odd. I woke to the sound of grinding and sliding about the room, very quietly. Then in the morning I found things out of order. Misplaced."

Holmes still made his way about the room, brushing the silken curtains of the four-poster, using his glass on the windowsill.

"You said 'to begin with'," he added. "What happens during the day?"

"The mediums call it 'poltergeist activity', which just sounds like damned German gibberish to me."

"It is German. 'Noisy spirit'. You have returned to your rooms at night to find that items have moved of their own accord?"

"Exactly. I knew it could only be unnatural then, as I keep this room locked, even when I'm inside it, and I have never once forgotten."

"You're quite sure there is no second key?"

"Very sure. The lock is no ordinary tinker's fix-me-up. It was custom made in Sheffield, and the key is as unique as the lock. Look here, gentlemen."

The Earl produced the key again from the long chain on his waistcoat, and it did indeed appear ingeniously complex.

"It unnerved me a great deal, what with the legend and all."

By this point in the interview, Holmes had climbed to look on top of the wardrobe, had put his pocket knife to the glass panes of the window frame, and was now on his hands and knees upon the floor.

"What is that?" he asked, pointing to a small white smear on the carpet.

"'Ectoplasm', they call it. It's some of that hellish slime from which the ghost is made. Or coated in, or God alone knows what. You see? I'm no madman – this thing is as real as anything under Heaven and Earth."

Holmes stuck his long nose down within a hair's breadth of the stuff before working what little of it there was between his fingers.

Holmes stuck his long nose down within a hair's breadth of the stuff. . . .

"Is that not the sickly stench of death, Mr. Holmes? Now, do you believe me?"

Holmes sniffed at it again, then wiped his hands with his handkerchief. He followed the tail of the smear and his eyes rested on the far wall, panelled high in ancient walnut. He moved over to it, put his hands to the wood, and sniffed again. Then he continued along the wall, from the back of the room to the front, stopping and sniffing at intervals. I was as clueless as our host, and my friend seemed unusually frustrated.

"She appears and disappears out of that very wall, Mr. Holmes. I've tried pushing and pulling it back, to reveal a secret door or somesuch, but to no avail."

"Well, my Lord, this is a pretty problem – though a challenge, I hope, of which I'm capable of overcoming. If you would be so kind as to retire with my dear friend, Dr. Watson, I have a few more itches I wish to scratch around your house, if I may?"

"By all means, Mr. Holmes – though I will be locking this room again as soon as you two gentlemen have left it. The rest of the house is quite open and at your disposal, if you think there's anything to gain in the matter."

"I wouldn't have suggested it otherwise. But please, let us all depart this room at once. Thank you, my Lord."

We walked out ahead of the Earl, and while he locked the room behind us, Holmes grabbed my arm with no uncertain force, and hissed into my ear.

"Keep him talking, Watson. Fill him up with port, laugh at his witticisms, and give me as much time as you can. I will be as quick as possible, but there is much to do. The game is afoot!"

Chapter V

We went back to the library, which was furnished to the same lavish excess as the calling card which had begun that perplexing day. There were printed paper decorations all over the walls and high ceiling, and an enormous spruce in the bay window, heavy laden with candles and baubles. The Earl to whom we had been introduced now seemed a distant dream, as Sir Cyril regaled me jovially with famous bouts of yesteryear. He seemed quite the expert on every fight, and rolled on in no uncertain detail about Heenan and Sayers, Tom Cribb and the like, though he held a particular place in his bosom for Trubshaw, that champion of his own county. He was most amiable, and the port needed no encouragement from me to flow freely. I had no inclination as to what Holmes was undertaking, or indeed what he was anticipating to uncover, though occasionally I was aware of a banging about the house which I could only presume to be my friend, charging to and fro on his errand.

As the libations continued apace, the conversation passed onto the subject of the Earl's late wife, whom he spoke of with an uncharacteristic tenderness.

"She was such a woman, Dr. Watson," said he, for the more drunk he became the more he seemed to notice and appreciate my company. Indeed, once the conversation moved to Holmes's exploits, as reported in *The Strand*, and the Earl had understood my part in the matter of writing them, he spoke to me as he would to a brother. It was both charmingly unreserved for such an illustrious man, while also becoming increasingly garish and unpalatable, for I don't make a habit of shining light upon myself.

The clock hadn't long struck seven when my friend reappeared, flushed of face and panting for breath.

"Ah, there you are. Watson. My Lord. I thank you for your hospitality, and the stimulation of such a mystery, but I'm afraid we must bid you *adieu*."

The Earl, in an instant, devolved into the broken, terrified man we had met upon our arrival. His hands shook and his jowls quivered as he fell out of his chair.

"Dear God, Mr. Holmes, you'll not leave me? How can you, with what you've heard and what you've seen? If you cannot solve my riddle – well man, say so, but for pity's sake stay the night. As my guests. Please, gentlemen."

We writhed on his knees, his hands held up in supplication.

"Please, Sir Cyril," snapped Holmes, "this is most unseemly. I wouldn't leave you alone for one second, were I to think any harm would come to you. Sit, my Lord, if it please you."

At the calming tone in my friend's voice, the Lord Stafford retreated to his great chair, a mixture of shame and entreaty upon his face.

"We will take the two bicycles I discovered in the stables back to town, as I wouldn't wish to inconvenience you of one of your carriages. You will be completely safe tonight, my Lord – of that you have my assurance. Watson, would you be so kind as to check the *Bradshaw* in my bag for our connecting train?"

As I rummaged through his bag, which he had brought with him into the room, Holmes stepped over to the Earl and spoke very gently to him, though I was still close enough to hear.

"Leave your bedroom door unlocked tonight, my Lord, and the front door as well, but tell no one you have done so. If you follow my instructions, to the letter, then all shall be well. If not – well then . . . ."

Leaving those consequences hanging in the air, we turned our backs on Sir Cyril Oldfield of Talbot Hall.

As we collected the rest of our bags from an antechamber, the butler passed us, going into the library, as Sir Cyril had just struck a bell for assistance.

"Langridge, isn't it?"

"Yes sir. Are you leaving us, sir?"

"We are indeed. Your master is quite beside himself, Langridge, and my good friend the doctor here prescribes port and brandy. If Lord Stafford is to sleep tonight, Lady Liquor must be his nursemaid."

"Very good sir," said the butler, and continued on to tend to his master.

I was slightly affronted at the commandeering of my professional opinion, but I did agree that Sir Cyril's nerves would need considerable numbing before he could attempt to rest. I was preparing to walk to the front doors when Holmes intimated with his head that we should go another way, back through the house and through the kitchen, with its sole cook, and into the scullery. Here Holmes stopped me again before I exited, and drew my attention to three enamelled pails on the tiled floor, sitting next to two old bullseye lanterns.

"Mark those three buckets, Watson. One soot, one ash, one lard. The whole case rests upon those three buckets."

He had evidently been that way before, and must also have visited the stables, as there were indeed two safety bicycles leant against a far wall. I couldn't help but notice that while Holmes had spoken of "not inconveniencing one of the Earl's carriages", there wasn't a single carriage in the block or yard. Barring the lone horse and open cart we had been driven in from town, there was no trace of wheel, tackle, or beast anywhere to be seen.

We rode our bicycles with little difficulty, though the light was beginning to fade, and I asked if we were to leave them against the railings of the station when we reached Uttoxeter again.

"We won't be going that far. There was an inn we passed on the drive up. I fancy it will suit our needs."

I was sat for some little time alone, with my pipe and my thoughts.

"Won't we miss our train?" I asked, incredulous. "The next service is the last to connect with London."

"Ah, but then, my dear friend, we aren't going back to London."

In a short time we came to a lively looking hostelry in the village nearest to the hall and warmed ourselves by the fire. Holmes returned from the bar with a quart-pot of ale and two mugs, and we supped some of the finest beer in the shire, for we weren't many miles from that brewing capital of Burton-upon-Trent. I eyed the locals warily, as they were a dirty sort, but Holmes seemed to be enjoying the conversation of the landlord greatly, and he of him, so that I was sat for some little time alone with my pipe and my thoughts.

What was at the heart of the mystery of Talbot Hall? Who was the spectral lady, and why had Lord Stafford only been tormented by her so recently? Was it truly vengeance against the discovery of the poor woman's final resting place? There were a hundred such enigmas fighting for supremacy in my mind, so that I was unable to concentrate on any one of them for many moments. The empty yard, the three pails, the locked room, the secrecy around the jewels – all was dark to me.

At a very great length, Holmes returned, an arched eyebrow and a glow in his cheeks.

"Well, Watson, I'm sorry for leaving you, but if you wish to dig for the root of a secret, take your trowel to the public house."

He sat down with a great thud and seemed to be extremely pleased with himself.

"So is all now clear to you?"

"Yes, it is. Quite clear. Is it not to you?"

"You know full well I haven't the slightest clue, and if you insist on suspending me in ignorance, I suggest you return to your conference with the landlord."

Holmes was enjoying my frustration, which did nothing to abate it.

"Ask yourself, Watson: *Why?*"

"That's all I have been doing. How and why? Neither make a bit of sense."

"Well then, allow me to introduce the correct chain of reasoning. How many staff did you observe at the hall?"

I thought for a moment.

"Why, three. The nervous driver, the collected butler, and the old cook in the kitchen."

"Excellent! There is also a maid, Alice. Talbot Hall operates on those four alone, for the driver is also the groom, and as Lord Stafford himself disclosed, since his wife died he toilets himself."

"Surely then, they are either in his confidence, or he can afford no others?"

I thought for a moment.

"But the Hall, the furnishings, and the extraordinary delivery of that card? Not to mention its lavish decoration. What's more, if he is short, well then, why not sell the jewels?"

"My dear fellow, you put the likes of Gregson and Lestrade to shame!"

"So what does that all mean?"

"Ah, on that score you shall see soon enough. For now, I fancy it is time to return to the hall. I hope you're safe to peddle the way in the dark?"

I informed my friend, in no uncertain terms, that while the Earl had been draining his glasses like a man drowning, I had but two small ports, plus the excellent pint while in the pub. Checking my watch, I found it had gone ten. The earlier snow had moved off to leave a clear sky, so that our way was lit by the heavens. It was no great distance, and while we were steady upon the white road, our tyres crunching, in half-an-hour we were back at the hall. There was still a light in the window of the library, so we waited in the bushes by the side of the great gates. One by one, the lights inside the hall dwindled – first the kitchens, then the library – and we watched the rest wink out one by one, till the only light visible was the one coming from Sir Cyril's room. The whole house was abed, for now it was well past eleven, but still Holmes kept us in the seclusion of the hedge.

At last, after another hour at least, my fingers frozen and my breath billowed out in front of me, lit by the stars, we made our move. We crept around the edge of the gravel at the front of the house and entered the front door, left unlocked as directed. Then we made our way back to the scullery, for Holmes had observed earlier that the latch was bent. He picked up one of the bullseye lanterns, lit it, and instructed me to take off my shoes, so as to make no sound upon our ascent to Lord Stafford's room.

There was a dead quiet in the house, and wherever the servants were sleeping, they were doing so silently. Inch by inch, we made our careful way up the stairs and along the hallway to the bedroom. Holmes picked something out of his pocket and ran his hand along the hinges of the door. Once this was completed, he attempted to push the door ajar, slowly and delicately. It opened, for the Earl had followed Holmes's instructions, leaving this unlocked as well, and my friend looked back at me with a wild excitement.

"Well, Watson," he whispered, "are you ready to see a ghost?"

Chapter VI

We made our way into the room, our unshod feet treading muted upon the carpet. All was complete darkness. I could hear the Earl in his bed, and the wall that had so interested Holmes was now opposite our position, crouched in the lee of the door. I hardly dared to breathe, and as the vigil wore on, a screaming cramp developed in my calves, and the ache from my Jezail bullet wound was painfully renewed by the cold. We must have been there for some time, yet another hour at least, before I heard something. In the abyss, with my senses tightened to breaking point, I became aware of a muffled, metallic sound, some way off. The Earl stirred in his bed, but was still asleep. It came a second time, a dragging, clinking, scraping noise that made my flesh crawl. It was getting nearer. With every moment that passed, the sound was closer and more distinct. They were chains, and they were coming from behind the far wall.

At that moment the Earl awoke in a gibbering panic, shouting and raving. I still couldn't see him, but I could hear him. We made no move to reveal ourselves, and I looked to my left where Holmes was crouched likewise, though even with him inches from my side he was only the merest impression of a dark shape against another, darker whole. The rattling came closer still. That dreadful cacophony was my only sense I had of what was occurring.

Then a white shape appeared from the far wall. It was partially obscured by the gossamer curtains of the Earl's four-poster, but as it detached itself, its hideous form became clear. In a death shroud, covered in chains that dripped a pallid, white radiance, was a woman. She had dark hair and dark eyes, but her face and hands were blanched, and she stared, unblinkingly, down at the Earl. I was reminded, horribly, of Mr. Dickens's festive novella, with its own chained phantom. She said nothing, just fixed him with her unnatural gaze, and I thanked God I wasn't the subject of her hexing. The whole world seemed to pause in disgust, and the only realisation I had that this wasn't some infernal nightmare was the high, whining scream that fell from the Earl's lips.

In an instant, Holmes opened the blinds of his bullseye lantern, spilling a shaft of yellow light upon the creature. She turned her wide eyes upon us, but her expression was one of astonishment, rather than malevolence.

"Quickly, Watson!" Holmes barked. "Over to the far wall, as quick as you can!"

*In a death shroud, covered in chains that dripped
a pallid, white radiance, was a woman.*

I raced from our hiding place, past the woman who I dared not countenance, and bounded towards the panelling that had so confounded

Holmes earlier. As I neared it, I fell into a large black shape, scuttling towards the wall, and landed in a heap upon it. To my astonishment, it cried out in a human voice. I felt for an arm and twisted the hand across the back to ensure whatever it was couldn't escape. The Earl's terror had bloomed into outrage, and he demanded to know the meaning of this extraordinary sequence of events. As Holmes turned on the electric light, I could see that I had indeed caught hold of a man, dressed entirely in black, with a thick black paste upon his face and hands. He cried out, but with my knee in his back, and his arm entrapped, he was completely at my command. The Earl was shouting and shaking, a mixture of tears and sweat spraying from his face like mist. The lady, who herself had frozen, blinking in shock, began to run towards me, and it was then that I noticed there was an aperture in the wall, to which she was heading.

"It's no use, my dear," spoke Holmes. "The game is up."

The command in his voice, which I had seen subdue rascals and ruffians by the score, was more than she could outrun. She stood, turning slowly towards him, and as she did so, I saw that she too had a thick slime upon her face, as white and luminescent as the smear we had discovered upon the carpet.

"My Lord," Holmes announced, "I believe you know these persons."

His teeth chattering still, the Earl stared at the two, darting his head from one to the other, sending more droplets flying from his face. His expression of incredulity turned to recognition, and then to apoplectic fury.

"Langridge! And Alice, by God! You shall swing for this, the pair of you!"

As I looked again at the blackened face of my prisoner, I saw with astonishment that it was indeed Langridge, the butler. He writhed and wriggled to no avail, until upon Holmes's instruction I relinquished my hold over him, positioning myself before the opening in the wall. He sat up, a look of baleful hatred directed at both the Earl and my friend. The woman, Alice, sat down next to him, her head in her hands. Sir Cyril started up his gibbering tirade, but Holmes held up a hand, a knowing smile upon his thin lips.

"Will you explain this all to me, Mr. Holmes?"

"I will trump that, my Lord. I believe the chained phantom herself can reveal all."

"Well, Alice?" demanded the Earl.

She looked up at him then, tears streaking the white paste on her head and hands.

"Damn you, sir!" spoke Langridge, putting his arm around the maid. With his other sleeve he smeared some of the black slime from his own face.

"You pay us next to nothing, treat us like dogs, while you still live in opulence. Why, if you gave us our dues, we would never have gone to such lengths to cater for our own needs."

"So, it is true," I added. "The Earl is no longer a rich man."

"Ah, no he ain't," sneered the butler. "It was the Countess who held the purse strings. Since she died, the whole fortune's gone to bouts and booze. Good money following bad till there wasn't a farthing left. He had to sell all the horses, all the carriages, the furniture, paintings and all. All quietly, mind. Everybody knew, but nobody spoke of it."

I looked to Holmes then, recalling his extended conversation with the landlord, and he gave me an affirmative tilt of the head.

"Kept up appearances, didn't you, my Lord?" continued Langridge. "All the rooms you take up would make a Caesar blush, but the others are bare or dust sheeted, and never a fair wage for us as live under you."

Again, I interjected.

"But if the treatment was so poor, why did you not leave his employment?"

"Most did, those he didn't sack. But he needs the four of us. Mind, old Sal the cook and that fool of a groom don't have any part in this matter. And Alice only followed my orders. He said we could reckon on no reference if we left, and what good's a servant with no prior reference? It'd speak volumes, wouldn't it? Closest thing to a death sentence to the likes of us."

Holmes spoke steadily and calmly.

"And then you heard of the Earl's discovery."

"Aye," spoke the butler, "and the promise of better pay, and back pay to boot. Kept us from grumbling for a month or two. But then the promise dried up, he still had the jewels but wouldn't part with them. Not for the sake of us. Wouldn't even let a man take a peep."

All the while the Earl said nothing. He just sat in his bed, grinding his teeth.

"I was dealing with woodworm, in the panelling of another room, when quite by chance I discovered that secret passage. It's only two feet wide, so as not to be noticeable, but once I found that, and where it led to, I was resolved to find the jewels and take back the earnings that were rightfully ours."

"The Earl noticed," spoke Holmes. "Only, luckily for you, he was already terrified of the legend."

"That's the truth of it, sir, exactly as you say. He came downstairs one day, white as a sheet. I marvelled he didn't suspect us, but then he was so sure there was no other way into the room. It was the simplest thing then. We searched for likely looking spots by day, then back to see if the treasure lay there by night. I got Alice all dressed up in a dust sheet and chains, which we kept hidden in the passage. We had all month to look, then we put on our little performances over the nights of the full moon."

"You remember I drew your attention to the three buckets, Watson? One ash, one soot, one lard. The Aborigines of Australia make face paint from white ash and pig fat, and it is simplicity itself to produce the same in any kitchen in England."

"My, but you're a rum one," spoke the butler. "I've heard of you, Mr. Sherlock Holmes, but it seems to me you're more of a magician than a copper. You're right enough. We knew the old man would wake at the slightest sound, so I decided to make sure he woke, and was so terrified by what he saw I could search, undiscovered. I crept about on my hands and knees, then as soon as I thought we were pushing our luck, I brushed my hand against Alice's leg, and we went back the way we came, silent and secret."

"The grease, Watson, the pig fat. That was what I could smell upon the carpet, and then on the wall. You recall I myself smeared the hinges of the door before we entered, to ensure there was no sound. The passageway, as you can see, is no hinged door, but slides on rollers, and can only be operated from inside the passage. There is no indication of it from this side whatsoever. A liberal smear of the same lard and the door would open silently. Quite apart from the intentional noise of the chains, from a darkened room you could have no possible comprehension it was ever there."

"Which begs the question how you found it?" retorted the butler.

"I looked for it, and when I observed that the next room is two feet narrower than this, and that the room after that isn't, it was obvious where the passage began and ended."

"But what is this passage?" I asked.

"I deduce, from its original relation to the house, that it was the secret passage the first Earl had made to sneak his mistress into his rooms."

"So why didn't they find the jewels in there when they discovered it, and why did Sir Cyril himself not know of that same passage, if he found the jewels first?"

"Because," spoke Holmes, "he never had found the jewels, and I don't believe truly that they ever existed.

The butler, the maid, and I all exclaimed our disbelief as one voice.

The butler, the maid, and I all exclaimed our disbelief as one voice.

"Consider it," continued my friend. "If he had found the jewels, could such a loud man keep the news of their discovery out of the papers, when he was unable to control the tales of his haunting? It would be much better to be considered a fortunate man than an unfortunate one. I wouldn't be at all surprised to learn that his staff weren't the only ones being kept on a long leash by his tale, and indeed I undertook some significant investigations into the Earl's finances before ever we left London."

"So what of the chained woman in the legend?" I enquired, trying to neaten off the frayed ends of this extraordinary episode.

"That was just it, Watson – a legend. All tall tales have an element of truth, and so the story of a mistress in the walls transmuted over the centuries into the lurid fable we have today."

"My God," spoke the butler, turning to the Earl, "is this true?"

The Earl said nothing, all his bile and bluster having cooled, leaving him a damp shell amongst the coverlets.

"All this for nothing? Damn you, Sir Cyril! Damn you to hell!" He turned to us. "Well, gentlemen, I am ready for the police. I have no stomach for more."

Holmes's mischievous eyes sparkled.

"I don't suppose the Earl is keen for any further revelations in the press, and while there never were any jewels, no crime has been committed, bar the unwarranted visitations into your master's room. No," reflected Holmes, "this is a house of lies and greed, and I do believe on that score, that you are all as one family. Goodnight, and a Merry Christmas to you."

Chapter VII

Several days later, when we were back in Baker Street, I read aloud to Holmes the announcement that Sir Cyril Oldfield, Earl of Stafford, was to have an auction of his remaining worldly goods in the New Year, to raise money for Talbot Hall. There was no mention of any jewels. My friend cackled in a most unseemly manner, making a snorting noise out of his nose, but then he settled and turned to me. There were still several details to which I was ignorant, and many of the facts I had didn't culminate into a single whole. I said the same to Holmes.

"Now, I believe I hold every card in the deck," said he, "and it's time to show my hand. To what are you still unclear, dear fellow?"

I could have said a great many things, but there were three key points to which I was at a loss. I told him so.

"Ah, well, all three are easy enough to explain," retorted my friend. "Why did I suspect the Earl of penury from the start? The card, Watson, the card. Such elaborate decoration speaks of a complete lack of taste and judgement. The man behind his card invariably resembles its qualities. Then there was no messenger with the message. The card was sent to impress, but a card alone is somewhat of an empty gesture. My suspicion of this was confirmed when talking to the landlord of that fine hostelry, who had seen the groom leave Talbot Hall first thing, and return late in the morning. The Earl had sent him on the first train to London, where he delivered the card unannounced, then raced back to Uttoxeter in time to meet us with the dogcart."

"But surely it would cost more for a train ticket to and from London than it would just to mail the card or send a wire?' I exclaimed. "And if he wanted to look wealthy enough to have the message delivered, why not have the messenger stay and be seen?"

'That, my friend, is the supposition of a reasoning mind, and Lord Talbot was in no such state. He couldn't leave his messenger here, as his remaining staff were so few in number that there would have been no one to meet us at our destination. Sir Cyril meant to deceive us as to his financial affairs, as he had done to so many others. The rumours were quite true. The late Countess was the manager of the Hall's successful economic functions, and the Earl is every bit as fiscally inadequate as we have heard.

"As to the second point, I can quite appreciate your incomprehension at Sir Cyril's willingness to believe in his ghostly apparition. The legend does indeed exist, even if the details wouldn't hold up in a court of law. That tale of vengeful spirits has dogged his family for centuries. What I can add to that is another enlightening scrap of gossip from the tavern: That Sir Cyril himself had a mistress upon a time, just like his ancestor Sir Talbot, and that he in some way blamed his own infidelity for his wife's untimely death. That was presumably why he never remarried, even without an heir to continue the family name. It seems that grief, guilt, ghosts. and insolvency don't result in the most analytical of dispositions.

"The third point is the most intriguing, and I shall here have to take you even closer into my confidence than you are accustomed to being. Why am I so convinced the jewels never existed? Well, as I told you, I made a thorough search of the house, while you were plying the Earl with port and your receptive ear. I discovered the secret passage between the rooms, with the chains and dust sheet hidden along the cavity, awaiting that night's haunting. Again, I told you how the room between the two sliding doors was two feet narrower than the others, and that on the next floor, which indeed was barren of furnishings, all the rooms were of equal dimensions. I'm afraid I wasn't entirely forthcoming. What I failed to divulge to the residents of Talbot Hall, and to you, dear fellow, was that I discovered another room, with another unaccountable narrowing of one wall."

"You don't mean!" cried I.

"I do mean, Watson, but I left them – the lady and the jewelry – where they were, to wait for a more deserving beneficiary at some point in the distant future."

Santa's Little Elves
by Kevin P. Thornton

Although there were many people who I felt should shoulder the blame for our Grand Family Christmas Party, my dear wife was surely first among equals. It was she who'd had the original idea to persuade her cousin Cholmondeley, recently back from making his fortune in Africa, that it would be a wonderful idea to air out the old mansion and invite the next generation of the family down for the Yuletide celebrations. It was she who, by dint of her enthusiasm, arranged who was to prepare what and bring whom, and it was she who set the tone of bonhomie and jollity which caused some of us to attempt tasks far beyond our capabilities.

So it was that by the time the women of the family had taken over, the party stretched from one event-filled night to an entire weekend.

It was *Anno Domini* 1902. The war with the Boers was finally over, a steam powered motor vehicle had driven at the ridiculous speed of nearly seventy-five miles-per-hour, and an Englishman, Ronald Ross, won the Nobel Prize for medicine. The Twentieth Century was well and truly upon us.

There were eight adults at first, later to become nine, and in typical tradition there seemed to be an entire gaggle of children. It was difficult to get a satisfactory headcount as they were forever on the move. The last I'd heard, there were thirteen of them under the roof, a most appropriate description, as the children were lodged in the nursery at the top of the house, out of sight if not quite out of mind. As is their wont, no sooner had they moved in when the demands came down for a bedtime story. The women of the house, because they could, decided it was up to their men to deal with this chore. I refer to the above comment, tasks beyond our capabilities, as a warning.

Cholmondeley, as the host, refused. "Five of the little brats are mine, and they have heard both of my stories a dozen times. Besides which, neither of them are Christmassy, and if truth be told both are more suited to the barroom than the nursery. John, you are the storyteller. Deal with it. Set up a roster, or dig out some of your tales. The longer and more boring the better. You're trying to put them to sleep, not give them the night terrors."

Sniffing a bit at the implication I was capable of inducing boredom, I went up that first night with no idea what I was about to face. I will say this: They were polite in their penetrating and accusatory examination of the tale. Still, I had only managed to get through about a third of my story before a combination of their punitive questions and their disbelieving stares had me fleeing down the stairs to the sanctuary of the library and the port.

The next night, second cousin by marriage, Algernon, fared no better. "I would rather face a charge by the Mahdi's followers at Khartoum again than try my hand at pacifying that lot in the nursery," – All this being babbled as he gulped a large snifter of brandy. "I was so miffed I nearly told them what happened to the prisoners' hands out there in the sands, just to give the little beasts nightmares."

"That won't work," said James. "Children thrive on horror. As Cholmondeley said, we need to bore them. Let me try tomorrow. I once had to sit through all four Sunday services of my cousin the Vicar of Derwent, a man known to induce somnolence in even the perkiest of curates. I don't know if I can recreate his drone, but I remember enough of the content to be able to retell it. If that doesn't put them all to sleep, nothing will."

He reported his failure the following evening. "Nothing doing," he said. "I skipped any parts remotely interesting and went straight to the blessed Vicarial analysis of the 'Begats'. It is pure tedium and I would have bet a bottle of your Chablis they would nod off. No such luck." He poured back his whisky like it was ambrosia before observing rather sombrely, "Speaking of begetting, begats – Whatever? – Are you sure we all begat those children? They seem far too evil to have come from such reasonable chaps as us. I shall be questioning my wife most assiduously later."

The next two nights were the same, and the men of the house were starting to cower when the question of who would be responsible for the last tale of Christmas, the most important one as the children had to be asleep before the festive secrets were unveiled, was left unanswered. The next afternoon I was about to admit my failure to my wife when the final visitor of the season arrived.

"I didn't even know you'd invited him," I said, "let alone that he had accepted."

"I didn't," she said. "If you remember, I left it to you."

I was sure I hadn't sent him an invitation. There was a long list in my head of things that he did not find acceptable, and a familial feast centred round a Christian festival that had overwritten a pagan one was near the top.

More surprising than his arrival was his behaviour. While he didn't jump gaily into the song-and-dance encouraged by the ladies – none of the men did – he was charming, urbane, and – dare I say it – even witty.

"Who are you, foul *doppelgänger*?" I muttered into my pre-cenal sherry, "and what have you done with my grumpy friend?"

"Don't be silly dear," said my wife. "I've always felt that you have over-exaggerated his personality quirks in your stories."

"If anything I have understated them," I said. "Still, watching him almost enjoy himself is enough of a Christmas present for me. Nothing could surprise me more."

As usual I was wrong. As the children came down after the evening meal to wish everyone good night, Cholmondeley's wife Maria surprised us all.

"If you are all tucked in and ready for bed in under five minutes, our new guest has promised to come and tell you a bedtime tale."

"Will it be a 'tecktive 'tory?" asked the youngest brat, she of the golden locks and endearing lisp. "Only Uncle John tried to tell one the other night, and it wasn't very good."

Amid the guffaws at this angelic critique of what I had come to see as my second career, my friend smiled at her and said, "Do you know, I've been telling him that for some time now. No, I won't be telling you a detective 'tory, I mean story. I have a proper Christmas story for you all."

As they scampered away like dainty hippopotamuses up the wooden stairs, he turned to me and said, "You told them the other Sumatra story, didn't you?"

"I don't – How could you? – Who told you that?" I looked at him with what I am sure must have been an expression of complete bafflement.

"Don't be so surprised," he said. "We have known each other for years, and whenever you are fortified with drink, as you no doubt were the night you faced the demons of the nursery, you have a tendency to fall back on old habits. There are two tales of our adventures concerning Sumatra. I know that one of them is so fantastical that you have sworn never to tell it, but it gnaws at you, gnaws at your soul. Perhaps that is why when you are in your cups you default to the other, lesser Sumatra tale."

"As usual," I said, "when you explain yourself, it all seems so logical."

"Indeed. Now is there any advice you wish to share before I go up to the nursery?"

"Oh no," I said, as innocently as possible. "I'm sure the little darlings will be as putty in your hands: Easily malleable and shaped by your brilliance and knowledge."

For once in his life there was a frisson of uncertainty in his manner, and I, evil acolyte that I was, delighted in it.

As he walked over to the ladies, James appeared behind me and muttered *sotto voce*, "Something else about putty," he said. "If it's mistreated, it becomes brittle and breaks easily."

"Oh, I do hope so," I said. "He is my friend, and I would happily jump in front of a bullet for him, but I suspect that this is the day he faces a foe he will not be able to best. He knows nothing of how vicious and mendacious a pack of children can be, and the ones bred within this family are viciouser and mendaciouser than most, if you'll excuse the ungrammatical turn of phrase."

"Happily excused," he said. Then, "You have spoken of this collection of offspring we have as a 'gaggle'," said James, "as if they were geese. I think the more apposite collective noun may very well be the one we apply to crows."

"A murder," I murmured. "Very good, James. Very good indeed."

I hurried to find my wife. "Do you remember telling me once of the spyhole one of your cousins drilled into the nursery from the closet in the room next door?"

"Yes," she said, "but you aren't to be so deceptive. If you wish to hear his story, go with him and sit next to him. He is your friend."

"A friend who will not thank me when I see him fail, as he surely must. He has many talents, my dear, but entertaining children isn't one of them. Please, if you love me at all, take me to this hidey-hole. I must hear his story."

She wavered, as I knew she would. I broke out my most genteel smile, the one she calls the slight grimace, and she took me up the back stairs against her better judgement.

The nursery stretched across the top and front of one side of the house. At the other end there was a store room that even in winter was warm and dry. It was used by the staff as an enormous airing area for the household laundry. As such it was rarely visited by family and guests, and it was also the room with the secret viewing spot. I didn't know why the hole had been drilled save as some childish prank, but when I looked through I had a clear view of the children on the floor surrounding the Nanny's chair in the corner, occupied by the man of the moment. He seemed relaxed – not what I expected . . . .

"Many peoples of the world," he began, "celebrate this time of the year with a personification of the spirit of the season."

> "How is he doing?" said James, suddenly so close next to me I near yelped in shock. "There is a second viewing hole," he whispered, by way of explanation. "I thought I would join the fun. Is he crucified yet?"
>
> "It's hardly the season for that form of torture," I replied. "He survives, for the moment, but he is already heading towards abstraction. His demise is imminent."

"What's a *pessonification*?" said the littlest one.

"It's when a person comes to represent the nature of the celebration, a good person normally. Some call him Saint Nicholas or Sinterklaas. He is also known as Father Christmas, the Christchild, Kristkind, or Kris Kringle, and in some places he is even called Santa Claus, or Santa for short. Which name would you prefer for the purposes of this story?"

Some of the older children mumbled, "Father Christmas," because they were polite and taught to answer when asked a question. Not the littlest one, sitting up front, legs crossed.

"Sandy Claws," she said. "I like Sandy Claws."

"Better let her get her way or we'll never hear the end of it," said her older sister.

"Very well then," said our intrepid story-teller. "Santa Claus it is. Now, do you know what Santa does on all the other days of the year when he isn't giving away presents?

"Nothing," said one of the older girls, as if such an idea was sinful.

"He works in the city," said one of the boys, who would no doubt grow up to be wealthy and dull.

The rest were silent.

"Well, I'll tell you. He makes the toys that he gives away. But he can't make them all himself, so he has helpers. Do you know who they are, and what they are known as?"

"Um, helpers?" said the dull one helplessly, in what he no doubt thought was a helpful manner. It wasn't, and the story continued.

"He turns to the little people of the woods and forests. Again, they have many names. In the north of Canada they are known variously as Mannegishi, Ishigaq, and even Canotila. In Africa they are Tokoloshe. In Scotland the Brownies, and in Ireland the Leprechauns. They are also known as Goblins, Fairies, and many other names, but for the purposes of this tale we shall refer to them as *Elves*, as broadly generic a name as it is possible to find."

> "If he keeps using phrases such as 'broadly generic,'" said James, "he won't last another minute."

> "I'm not so sure," I replied. "They're all still watching and listening."
> "They are toying with him. At the first sign of fear they will pounce, and he will be down the stairs, tail between his legs, revivifying himself with gulpings of claret."

"I like Elves," said the littlest. Before the story could continue any further however, she stood up and walked to the back of the nursery where she gathered a much loved doll.

"This is my doll," she said, unnecessarily.

"I see that," said my friend. "Does she have a name?"

"Yes. Feel her tummy. It's as if she is filled with little balls. I call her Miss Marbles." Then she plumped herself down, falling into the crossed leg position as she did so. "Please carry on," she said.

> James winced. "That's my wife's sister's girl. She is staying with us for a while. Her father died last year and her mother has had difficulty coping with the loss. She's very bright – quiet mostly – until she feels the need to be in charge. I can't wait to see who she'll pick as a husband one day, but he had better be adventurous."
> "Shh," I said as the story continued.

"Now then," continued the storyteller. "Every year, Santa always feels under pressure as December looms, and every year the elves come closer to revolt. Santa can be persnickety, and he is a perfectionist. He insists only that the best toys are good enough for the children of the world. His moods would test the patience of a saint, and trust me, elves aren't saints. Don't misunderstand – they love their job. There is no greater honour in the elf world than to be picked to work in the grand caverns of Santa's toy workshops. But they love to play as well, and when they finish work for the day, there is nothing an elf likes more than to settle into a snug with a glass of frothy elderberry beer and a meerschaum pipe, and tell stories.

"But relaxing after work takes time, and every year Santa goes to the elf leaders and says, 'We are behind. I must ask you to work longer and harder. We cannot disappoint the children of the world.' The elf leaders then go to their community and pass on the message. Most of the elves grumble and mutter, but none of them want to lose their jobs and go back to being troll guards – or even worse, pollen protectors or bear scarers. Every elf wants to work for Santa, so with a slightly louder grumble every year they work longer hours, drank less elderberry beer, and build enough toys for Christmas. They always manage to finish in time, although there are rumblings among the younger elves about Santa and his bad management. One elf in particular was seen by his peers as their spokesman, which meant the elder elves thought he was a troublemaker.

"The radical elf was called Tomidugless. Like all elves, his name had evolved over time. Tomi was his Mother's name for him because she was always calling him. Tomidug became his name when he was a fairy gardener, and the rest happened when he lost his magic spade and was demoted to the unicorn stables. Slowly he had worked his way back all the way to Santa's side, and every year he was the lone voice saying 'We know we're going to run out of time, so why don't we start earlier.'

"Nobody listened to Tomidugless until the year of the elderberry beer disaster. As usual, things had been going wrong, and as usual, Santa was getting grumpier and grumpier. That year, in addition to the tight deadlines, something had gone awry with the ordering and the elderberry beer was delayed. This meant that the elves' favourite tipple was going to run out, and Santa wasn't looking forward to breaking the news.

"Of course, he could have handled it better. He should have started with a discussion of how many toys were being produced, which the senior elves would have understood as being perilously low. Once they'd agreed on the extra work involved – well that would have been time to bring up the beer.

"Instead, Santa, tired and grumpy, faced the senior elves, also of a similar disposition. The bad news slipped out before he could stop himself. What he meant to say was 'There will be no beer supplies for two more weeks'. Instead he found himself stuck halfway. 'There will be no beer', he said, then he was stuck. 'What have I just said?' he thought to himself, followed by, 'I wish I'd brought Mrs. Claus with me.'

"The elves, as one, stood up and walked out of the Great Meeting Hall. At the door, Eddiebigears, He-who-reports-to-the-Elfqueen, paused and said, 'We have worked well together these many years, but you have wounded us today. There will be no more toy-making until you come to your senses. I bid you good day, Mister Claus.' And with that he swept his cape over his shoulder and left the room. It was a most impressive exit, and even though Santa knew he had made a mess of things, part of him wondered how he'd look in a cape.

"'Oh dear,' said Santa. 'What have I done, and how am I going to tell the Missus?'

"He didn't need to worry about that. Mrs. Claus could tell by the silence that something was wrong. She walked the special passages, past where Santa sat slumped in the Great Meeting Hall – there would be time for him later – and down to the elven quarters. There was no one about. It was as if they all had disappeared. She tried to find Eddiebigears or any of the senior elves, but they were hiding from her. In past years, Mrs. Claus had been the sensible link between the elves and Santa. This time it appeared he had gone too far.

"Mrs. Claus sighed and turned to go back. She could at least find out Santa's side of the story. There was a movement in the shadows, and she stopped, waiting.

"Tomidugless stepped out. 'Have you heard?' he said.

"'No. Tell me.' So he did. Halfway through, Mrs. Claus leant against a rock, as if her legs were wobbly. 'This is bad," she said. She repeated this twice more before Tomidugless was finished.

"Then she said, 'I need to see the senior elves. We must fix this. Think of all the little boys and girls who will be disappointed if we don't have enough presents.'

"'They don't want to see you,' said Tomidugless. 'This happens every year, and every year you calm Santa down and persuade the senior elves to carry on working. This year they feel he has gone too far and they are going to wait until he comes to his senses.'

"Mrs. Claus thought that if they wanted to wait until her grumpy husband came to his senses, it would be a very long wait. She loved her husband dearly, but he could try the temper of a well-fed puppy, and he wouldn't be reasonable now that he had backed himself into a corner.

"'And what do you think, Tomidugless?'

"'I think if we don't solve this quickly, it won't matter. We'll never catch up on the toy-making and Christmas will be ruined. We need to fix this, Mrs. Claus. I lost my magic spade once and it nearly killed my career. If the elves are part of breaking Christmas, I'll be sent back to the unicorn stables for a hundred years this time. That's a terrible job for an elf – especially one without a spade."

"'Can you get in to see the senior elves?' said Mrs. Claus.

"'I think so,' said Tomidugless.

"'Well then, here's what we do. We need to create a distraction.' And she proceeded to tell him her idea. When she had finished, Tomidugless said, 'It might work.'

"'It has to work,' said Mrs. Claus. 'You take the senior elves to the west end of the mighty passage, and I shall take Santa to the east, and this is how we shall proceed.' She told him of her plan

"'And what of the Great Meeting Hall in the middle?'

"'We'll need that for the negotiating.'

"Why is it?" said James, "that your friend can use words like 'negotiating' to the brats and they listen and understand him,

while they never seem to know what I mean when I say 'Clean your shoes'?"

"He is showing a side of himself I barely recognize," I said, but that was untrue. In the past he had connected with street urchins and the dispossessed with an ease that often belied his impatient manner, and that same connection was amply visible in the rapt attention of the children. He certainly could spin a tale, and I felt slightly guilty at anticipating his failure.

James stood up. "That's enough for me," he said. "Your friend is too smart for the children. Maybe I'll start to believe all those tales you tell about him."

He left, but I stayed. I wanted to enjoy the sight before me of his triumph in storytelling, and I also wanted to hear how it ended.

"Things proceeded forth-and-back."

"Don't you mean back-and-forth?" asked the littlest one. Her interruption disturbed the others children, who were caught up in the imagery of the story.

"It depends from which side one starts," said my friend.

"I 'speckt it does," she said seriously, hugging Miss Marbles ever tighter

East:
"Normally when Santa had to ask for extra work from the elves, or argued with the reindeer herders, he ended up with steam coming from his ears. This time, when Mrs. Claus entered the Great Meeting Hall, he looked despondent. Mrs. Claus patted Santa on the head as he groaned with frustration.

"'I don't know how to fix this,' he said.

"'Don't worry,' said his wife. 'I do.'

West:
"'We have to save Santa from himself,' Tomidugless said to the senior elves.

"'It's too much this time,' said Eddiebigears and the other elves all nodded in agreement.

"'Is that what you are going to tell the Elfqueen?' said Tomidugless. 'That you were willing to cancel Christmas over a few beers?'

"'It isn't just a few beers,' said one of the others. 'It's our way of life.'

"'And I'm sure that's the way the elven druids will remember it for all eternity as they record these events in the great book.'

"This troubled Eddiebigears. If he could see a way back, he would grab a firm hold of it, but he was not an imaginative elf. Fortunately Tomidugless rescued him. 'We need a negotiator,' he said. 'That way you can show you have tried your best."

"'Do you know one?" said Eddiebigears.

"'I do,' said Tomidugless. 'His name is Litigo Gerere. He's a pixie who specializes in agreeance counselling.'

East:

"'He's a concurrence conversion conversationalist,' said Mrs. Claus. 'His name is Pactus Negotium. I was lucky to get him. The elves have already hired one.'

"'A pixie?' said Santa. 'Aren't pixies too devilish to be trusted?'

"'Those are imps you are thinking of,' said Mrs. Claus. 'Pixies are notably trustworthy.'

West:

"'Santa must be feeling guilty if he's already hiring his own pixie,' said Eddiebigears. Tomidugless thought this wasn't the right time to point out they had done the same. Instead, he guided Eddiebigears, as per the plan Mrs. Claus had set out. 'We need a list of demands,' he said. 'About eight or nine.'

East:

"'Why so many?' said Santa. 'I only have two. Stop sulking and come back to work.'

West:

"'We have two,' said Eddiebigears. 'Santa must stop being in a bad mood, and bring back our beer.'

"'We need more,' said Tomidugless, 'so our pixie can negotiate with their pixie. That way when we insist that these two demands are non-negotiable they'll know we're serious.'

East:

"'That's a good idea,' said Santa. 'Er, I can't think of any others.'

"'Leave it to me,' said Mrs. Claus.

West:

"'These extra demands?' said Eddiebigears. 'Do we have a list?'

"'Leave it to me,' said Tomidugless.

"Litigo Gerere arrived in a cloud of dust. He was a fast-moving, vibrant pixie dressed in the forest green of his people. He looked down the list and pursed his lips. 'It's a long list,' he said. 'Let me get to work.' He left them in the west room and walk-skipped round the corner, down the cavern passage to the Great Meeting Hall. As he left, they could hear his wings beating faster than a humming bird's. Litigo Gerere was all get up and go.

"Pactus Negotium met the Clauses over on the east side. He too was in forest green. He had a measured way about his walk, like a slow march, and even his wings beat in a cadence so gentle they barely moved.

"'The Clauses,' he muttered to himself. 'Is that even grammatical?'

"'Never mind,' said Mrs. Claus. 'What did they say?'

"'They have a list,' he said, handing it over.

"'Ridiculous,' said Santa as he perused it. 'Dessert at every work table? That will never happen. They'll end up making sticky toys.'

"'Here's our list,' said Mrs. Claus. 'See what you can do.'

West:
"'Tiptoeing around Santa when he's hung over?' said Eddiebigears. 'We'd all have to be ballet dancers. Rejected.'

East:
"'Happy breaks for dancing? Rejected.'

West:
"'Honour "Santa Fridays"? Rejected.'

East:
"'Extra marshmallows for hot chocolate time? Rejected.'

West:
"'Santa grumble moments to be memorized? Rejected.'

East:
"'Five desserts for lunch instead of four? Rejected.'

"Every time Pactus came back, the list of demands had been negotiated down a bit more. Some were ridiculous. The reindeer were never going to share their candy supply. Others seemed to be flights of fancy. The elves wouldn't take over running the test gardens, no matter how much more the gnomes cost. Every time they heard Pactus Negotium's gentle shuffle down the passage from the Great Meeting Hall to the room on the east, Santa grew more frustrated and Mrs. Claus wondered if it would work. Then Pactus would go away again.

"Meanwhile, Tomidugless tried to keep up everyone's spirits, even as Eddiebigears and the others began to lose hope. Litigo Gerere would buzz back with a shorter list and they would pore over it. Finally it came down to two items on each side of the page.

"'Santa wants you to stop sulking and go back to work,' said Litigo. 'I think we can work with that.'

"'We're not sulking," said Eddidbigears, stamping his foot. 'We are angry because he stopped our beer. As to the other, we never wanted to stop working. He left us no choice.'

"'I'll see what I can do,' said Litigo as he flitted away.

"'The Elves ask that Santa must stop being in a bad mood, and to bring back beer,' said Pactus Negotium.

"'*I'm not in a bad mood!*' said Santa. Mrs. Claus placed her hand none too gently on his shoulder and sat him down.

"'My husband's mood is a result of not producing enough toys,' she said. 'Seeing as the elves are willing to come back to work, Santa's temper will be fine.'

"'The beer order won't be here for another two weeks,' Santa mumbled to his wife. 'That's what started all this blessed mess in the first place.'

"Mrs. Claus turned to stare Pactus Negotium down, or tried to. Pixies are notorious for not being easy to scare, and her very best withering look, the one she reserved for Santa on his exceptionally silly days, had no visible effect. 'Go back and tell them,' she said, 'that while the beer supplies have been disrupted for twenty-eight days because of this work stoppage, we will promise that they will have all the beer they can drink within fourteen.'

"'I can sell that,' said Pactus as he ambled back to the Great Meeting Hall.

"Santa watched him go. 'You lied to him,' he said. 'That is wrong.'

"Mrs. Claus had just about had enough. She was just about to remonstrate most forcefully with her husband when she saw how scared he was. She bit her tongue, patted his head encouragingly, and smiled at him. 'Yes, dear.'

"'Will it be all right?' he asked her. 'Do you think he can get their negotiator to agree?'

"'I'm sure of it,' said Mrs. Claus.

"And she was right, and they all lived happily ever after."

"That's a terrible ending," said one of the children.
"It is, isn't it?" said my friend, as he prepared to leave. "How would you like it to end?"
"With a happy ending. You just stopped."
"Then you can think of your own happy ending," he said with a smile.
"But they cheated," said the boring child. "They negotiated over nothing."
"You're right. Can anyone tell me why?"
"I can," said the littlest one. "It was because they were fighting over nothing."
"I see," said the boring one. "So they didn't cheat."
"They did," said James's niece who, in her enthusiasm, was strangleholding her doll so hard the marbles in her stuffing grated against each other. "They did cheat."
"Oh," said my friend. "And how did they do that?"
"There was only one negotiator."
The other children started to laugh, and her big sister said, "That's enough. It's bedtime."
"Wait," said my friend. "She's right. She's the only one who saw it. Tell me how," he said to her and he sat down again and placed her on his knee, centre stage in front of all the other children.
"Well," she said, "you made such a big thing about how the *negosheem . . . nego . . . negotee . . . .*"
"Negotiating?" he said helpfully.
"Yes. About how they couldn't fail. And then you told us about the pixies looking the same but walking and talking exactly the opposite, like two totally different people . . . or one pixie playing two pixies."
The other children were as quiet as a Monday congregation. The boring one said, "But," held up one finger, said "But" again, and then lowered the finger as the littlest one explained.
"That's how Mrs. Claus knew the pixies would agree – because there was only one of them. She arranged it so the elves would get back to work. She rescued Santa, and she rescued Christmas."
"That," said her big sister, "is a happy ending."

I left my hiding place and wandered as innocently as possible into the nursery.
"Next time you watch through a spyhole," he said to me, "be aware of your surrounds. The background lighting winked at me every time you moved, and one or two of your muffled harrumphs weren't as muffled as

you think." He was smiling as he said this, and the two of us started towards the stairs, only to be interrupted on the landing.

"That was a lovely story," said the littlest one, having evaded the bedtime herding for a moment. "I now know what I want to be when I grow up."

"And what is that?" he said. "A detective?"

"No, a 'toryteller. A 'tecktive 'toryteller. She smiled as she told us this, and then asked of my companion, "Is it all right to steal another person's story? We had a visitor last month from a man who said he was a writer, and he told us about a man who imitated another man by changing his walk, just like your pixie. I expect he told the story to you."

As she skipped her way back into the nursery, she turned back and said, "Watch for me. I'm going to be the best 'toryteller in the world.

And what name do I watch for?" he said.

"Agatha," she said. "It's Agatha Miller for now, but I 'spekt it will be different when I am old and married. Agatha someone. I'm going to be Agatha Someone."

"I'm sure you are."

As we walked down the stairs, I could barely contain my laughter. He allowed me my moment before he said, "He is young and precocious, but Mycroft thinks him one of the intellects of the next generation."

"I'm sorry. I don't follow," I said.

"The plagiarist who stole my plot, the one who told young Agatha my story. I didn't steal it from him. He stole it from me, although I wouldn't begrudge it of him." He smiled as he watched the apparent confusion on my face. "Two elves who were actually one person? Except when I told it in Mycroft's offices to a select gathering, I used it to compare how a waiter could be a gentleman and a gentleman a waiter. It was a test to see who could spot the deception. Agatha's young storyteller was the only one."

"It obviously impressed him enough that he used it in a children's bedtime story,"

"Yes," he said. "Just like Agatha, I expect we'll hear more from that young man. Chesterton, I believe his name was."

NOTE

G.K. Chesterton was never one to throw away a good idea, and he used it again in a Father Brown story called "The Queer Steps". As to the precocious young poppet? She did as her uncle imagined in her second marriage, wedding herself to an adventurous archaeologist named Max Mallowan and travelling all over the world, sharing in his adventures. She also became a writer and was better known under her first married name, publishing nearly a hundred books as *Agatha Christie*.

The Case of the Holly-Sprig Pudding
by Naching T. Kassa

The year 1902 had been a busy one for both Sherlock Holmes and myself, and as the Christmas holiday drew near, the need for my services as a doctor increased. The stuffy nose, sneeze, and occasional broken bone kept me busy from morning 'til night. I had time for little else.

One evening, a tall man with a great black beard entered my consulting room. He wore silver-rimmed pince-nez and his eyes twinkled behind the glass.

"Dr. Watson, I presume?" the fellow said in a pleasant tone. "The same Dr. Watson whose stories appear in *The Strand*?"

"I am Dr. Watson," said I. "But I'm afraid you have me at a disadvantage, sir. I do not know your name."

"My name is Wilshire Chetham. Is it familiar to you?"

"I cannot say that it is."

"Your friend, Sherlock Holmes, knows me. Has he spoken of me?"

"I haven't seen Holmes recently. Are you a client of his?"

"Your friend has been commissioned to find something which belongs to me. I stopped in at his lodgings in Baker Street, but he wasn't there, and I must reach him on an urgent matter connected to this problem. Would you happen to know where he may be?"

"As I said, I haven't seen him. Did you leave word at Baker Street?"

The man smiled. "I certainly did. However, if you happen to see him before I do, will you have him ring me? Here – You'll see my number below my address."

"I should be happy to," I said, taking his card.

"Thank you," said he. "I do hope he returns soon."

"I'm sure he will. Holmes is rarely gone for too long."

"Unless he is dead," Chetham said.

He must've seen the expression upon my face, for he broke into a booming laugh.

"Oh, I didn't mean it that way. I was speaking of your stories. When your friend failed to plummet into the falls. He disappeared from London for quite some time."

"Ah, yes."

"Thank you again, Doctor. I will take my leave. As I said, do ring when you see your friend."

After Chetham had departed, I decided I would pay a visit to Baker Street after my rounds and before returning home for the evening. It was my thought that I could succeed where Chetham had failed. I informed my wife of my plans, then charged my assistant with the closing of the office. When all had been accomplished, I grasped hold of my greatcoat and hurried out the door.

Queen Anne Street lay beneath a dusting of frost, the crystals gleaming beneath the streetlamps. A group of carolers stood at the corner, their sweet voices filling the air with tidings of the season. I passed a coin to the choirmaster before hailing a cab which would take me to Baker Street.

I stepped into the hansom and, before I could give the driver instructions, found myself moving. I fell against the seat as the cab rushed through the street.

Once I had recovered from my shock, I knocked upon the cab's roof and called out, but to my chagrin, the driver ignored my demands. We continued our mad dash through London, slowing only when we had reached Grosvenor Square. The driver stopped outside an alley between two fashionable homes.

I quickly stepped from the cab and faced the man who had abducted me.

"What is the meaning of this?" I cried. "Why have you brought me here?"

"To save your life," a familiar voice replied. Match-flame flared in the dark, revealing the face of Sherlock Holmes. He shrugged off the overcoat and tall hat usually reserved for cabbies.

"Holmes!"

"I trust I haven't ceased to surprise," Holmes said, taking a draw from his cigarette. "But when the most dangerous man in London enters the practice of my Boswell, drastic steps must be taken."

"Chetham? The most dangerous man?"

"With the death of Professor Moriarty and the incarceration of Colonel Sebastian Moran, he holds that dubious title."

Holmes climbed down from his perch. "He has been hunting me for three days. I returned to Baker Street this morning but a few minutes after he'd terrorized Mrs. Hudson and searched my rooms."

"He said he commissioned you to find his property."

"He isn't the one who commissioned me." Holmes pulled a carpetbag from his perch and rummaged among the contents. He pulled forth two masks and held one out to me.

"Burglary?" I asked.

"We have little time. If you will trust me, all will be made clear."

I took the mask from his hand.

"Good fellow!" Holmes said, tying his mask on. "Can you do without your coat? It will only hinder your movements."

I removed the coat and set it inside the hansom. Holmes walked the horse into the alley, and I followed him.

"Who are we to burgle?" I asked.

"713 Grosvenor Square."

"713?" I pulled a card from my breast pocket. "Why, that is Chetham's address!"

"It is, old fellow. And what better time to burgle? We know he isn't home. He is searching for us all over London. Ah! And here is our way in. The lock on this tradesman's entrance is a faulty one. I have seen to that."

"You have been in the house?"

"My alter ego has."

"I trust it is not Escott you speak of."

Holmes chuckled. "Do not worry, Watson. I haven't trifled with the affections of a young woman this time. No, I heard there was need of woodwork, so I answered as a carpenter called O'Hara."

He set the carpetbag on the doorstep and withdrew a short pry-bar. Within seconds he had pried the door open and granted us entry.

Holmes possesses the amazing power of seeing in the dark, one he has worked to refine for some time. He took my hand in his gloved one and led me through the gloom.

As we hurried through the house, my mind turned back to an adventure I have not recorded. (The world is not yet ready for the devilish doings of *C.A.M.*) We had run through a dark house then as well, our faces hidden behind silk masks.

Holmes led me through a corridor, toward the scent of mince pie and scones. We entered the kitchen, and then a windowless room which lay dark before us. A moment later, a light appeared, and I realized Holmes had produced a dark lantern. He lifted it and the glow flickered over the room.

A table, laden with scones, puddings, and mince pies, stood in the center.

"It is well Chetham detests dogs," Holmes said, his voice hushed. "Such an animal would put us at a great disadvantage. Still, we must be on guard. The staff quarters are above this room. Kindly stay near the stairway just there, Watson, and keep a sharp eye."

I did as he bade me and took my place at the base of the stairs.

Holmes turned his attention to the table, and one of the puddings set upon it. He removed the holly sprig from the top and, retrieving a knife from a rack nearby, cut the pudding in half. He carefully separated both parts.

Something gleamed in the glow of the dark lantern. Holmes pulled it out of the pudding and placed it on the palm of his hand. It appeared to be a brass key. He slipped it into his pocket and rearranged the halves of pudding before returning the holly sprig to the top.

Heavy footsteps sounded on the floor above. Holmes shuttered the lantern and rushed to my side. He pulled me back into the passage. We hurried down the corridor and out the tradesman's entrance.

Holmes and I sprinted to the hansom and I ducked inside as he climbed up. A man's voice cried out behind me. "You there! Stop!"

The cab lurched forward and gained speed as we hurtled out of the alleyway. The voice of our pursuer faded as we left Grosvenor Square.

We didn't stop for some time. Holmes wove his way through London as only he could and soon, we had left the more affluent confines of the West End and journeyed into the East. Holmes drew the cab to a halt behind a large warehouse and climbed down. I too alighted and removed my mask.

"We shall go on foot from here," Holmes said, placing the carpetbag in the hansom. "No, you needn't worry about the horse. Mycroft's man will be along soon enough. The cab belongs to him – one of my brother's fleet of vehicles. You will recall that it was he who drove you in the brougham those many years ago. I wouldn't doubt he has added a motor car by now."

Holmes led me through the slush-filled and lonely streets to Whitechapel's London Hospital. We entered, and I followed him through a maze of halls to a sick ward. Holmes approached the bedside of a man with wispy golden hair. He sat, propped against two pillows, rasping as he breathed. In the glow of the nearby electric lamp, his eye appeared swollen and purple. The right side of his face also showed marks of violence.

"At last," the man said, as Holmes seated himself in a chair beside the bed. "You have come, Mr. Holmes. Have you found them?"

"I have their location."

"Where is she then? Where is my wife?" The man lowered his gaze and shook his head. "It is as I feared. She wouldn't come."

"She cannot come," Holmes said, his tone gentle. "She passed from this earth three years ago. Her body lies in an Edinburgh cemetery."

The man covered his face with both hands and sobbed softly.

"All is not lost," Holmes said. "The child lives. I can bring her to you, but I must know everything."

"Everything?"

"I think some things should remain secret from your daughter, don't you?"

The man took a deep breath. His gaze fell on me for the first time.

"This man – is he trustworthy?"

"I trust him with my life."

"Very well, I will tell you everything."

He took a deep breath and began his story . . . .

> *My earliest memories are of the orphanage in Glasgow. My name was Billy Snow then. I was small, sickly, and my only friend was an older boy called Harry Mathews. We were mates, Harry and me, and when we grew older, we ran away. We headed for London, hoping to make our fortunes.*
>
> *What money we had vanished within a few days. We fell in with a bad crowd after that, and soon we were working the streets, picking pockets. Harry didn't last long in the job. He was too big, you see. But he was good at usin' a knife and his fists, so he moved up a bit quicker than me. It's what got him the attention of Sergeant Pickering and what got us into the Redbones Gang.*

"The Redbones Gang?" I asked. "I have never heard of them."

"And you had never heard of Professor James Moriarty either," Holmes said. "This gang was a secret one, marked by a crimson skull and crossbones tattooed upon each man's chest. They were at the beck-and-call of Moriarty until the end. They purloined, blackmailed, and killed for him. Several of their number were responsible for assassinations which affected political relations on an international level. Moriarty was the head of the snake and when he died, they died with him."

"And, I am ashamed to say, though I was never forced to raise my hand in violence against anyone, I obeyed every order the Redbones gave," Snow said. "We answered to one man, Sergeant Roger Pickering, and he answered to Colonel Sebastian Moran . . . ."

> *I didn't rise very far in the Redbones, but Harry did. He became Pickering's right-hand man and performed many a task for him. He possessed an extreme loyalty to him. And it was well known that anyone who betrayed or disrespected Pickering met Harry's wrath.*

"As well I know," Holmes said. "We had a disagreement over Sergeant Pickering's involvement with Moriarty and he knocked my left canine out in Charing Cross Station. But pray, continue."

All was well between Harry and me until I met my Rosie. She was a gentle girl, kind and church-going. She loved me, though she didn't love my life. I begged her to marry me, but she would have none of it. One day, she gave me a choice: I could quit the life and marry her, or continue with the Redbones and never see her again. I chose the former and left the gang.

We'd been married five years when Harry came after me. I'd left the old life behind and, having changed my name and moved to a new part of London, had obtained a good job as a rag-shop cove at a reputable bank. Rosie had given me a child, and a lovelier girl I have never known. It was a good life, and I didn't expect the gang to find me, though I should've known better.

One evening, in the spring of '91, I returned home to find Harry in my sitting room. He had my daughter, my Alice, on his lap, and Rosie seemed fair frightened out of her mind.

"Evenin' Billy," he said to me, smiling all friendly-like. I'd seen that smile before and knew what it meant. He'd broken many a head while smiling that way.

"Hello, Harry," I said. "What brings you here?"

"I heard you've become respectable and had to see for myself. The Sergeant was quite surprised when you left us."

"I married."

"And you did so without his permission. You know he must approve your leaving, and yet, you ran away like a thief in the night. I hope you're right well ashamed of yourself."

My Alice struggled against him then, and he held her back. I bit my lip, knowing any word I uttered might cause my girl harm.

"The Sergeant is a generous man, Billy. And he's giving you a chance to get into his good graces. If you do a job for him, a little job, he'll forgive you. And you'll be free."

"What's the job?" I asked.

Harry's grin grew wider. "I knew you'd come round. You always were the smart one. You have a key to the bank?"

My heart thundered in my chest. "No . . . but I can get it. It'll be missed if I keep it too long. I'll have to make an wax impression."

"An impression is all I need." *He released my Alice, and she ran to me. I scooped her up and held her close.*

"I'll be by for it next Tuesday," *Harry said, crossing toward my door. He paused on the threshold.* "I know you wouldn't think of betraying me, Billy, but I must give you the same warning I give everyone: You turn on me, you give me the wrong key, and you won't be the sorry one. But they will."

A chill ran through me, and I nodded. He stepped out the door.

Rosie tried to talk me out of it, but I knew what Harry would do to her and my Alice. I made the impression and on the Tuesday following, I sent them both off to Rosie's Mum. She didn't want to go, but I forced her. I didn't want her there when Harry arrived. After two hours of waiting, he came to my door.

"Good job, mate," *he said, taking the wax I handed him.* "I knew you'd come through. You've satisfied the Sergeant. But now, you must satisfy me."

My heart grew heavy in my chest. I'd known something like this would happen.

"What do you wish me to do?"

"Come with me to the bank tonight. Do this last job and you'll be out of the gang."

"Forever?"

"Forever."

I agreed, though in the back of my mind, I feared what he might do next and whether I would survive the night.

The job went like clockwork. Harry had brought McCall, the best safecracker in the Redbones with him, as well as two of his toughest lads. Harry opened the door with the key he'd made from my impression, then McCall opened the safe and the two toughs unloaded the gold. We slipped out, nice as you please.

The gold was split at the hideout, with McCall and the two toughs taking the larger share for The Sergeant. When they'd gone, Harry pulled out a small box and handed it to me. Inside were two small and perfect sapphires.

"Consider them a wedding present," says he, smiling in the dangerous way I know well. "And don't think the Redbones don't take care of their own."

"Are we square?" I asked.

His eyes twinkled. "For good and all. Goodbye, Billy."

I bade him goodbye and took my share of the gold and the sapphires with me.

Rosie was there when I got home, and she was less than pleased. She wanted me to take the gold back and turn the Redbones in, but I told her how dangerous they was. At last, I convinced her to take Alice and go. I would join them up north later. She and my girl left with the gold that night. It was to be the last time I saw them.

I kept the sapphires. I didn't know what Harry had planned for them. But I knew he'd want them more than he wanted the gold. I locked them away and gave the key to a trusted friend.

The next morning, I left the house as I always did. Failing to appear at the bank would be an admission of guilt. I forgot my umbrella and went back to get it. When I stepped out again, two men dragged me off the walk and into a brougham.

I learned later that all the Professor's people had been rounded up then. Word was, the Professor and the Colonel had fled England, leaving us all high and dry.

The worst was yet to come.

I'd been in Newgate five days when the fat man came to visit. He wanted to make a deal with me, said if I turned against the others, he could fix things for me.

There was one problem: I didn't know anything. I'd always been on the lower end. I didn't know about assassinations and such. Even if I did, many of the gang had been my mates and I wouldn't turn on them.

It was then he asked me about the gold from the bank and the sapphires. As soon as he mentioned them, I knew who'd given me away and I said nothing more. The fat man sent me back to my cell. And there I stayed.

A year later, there was an attempt made on my life. A fellow tried to kill me in the yard. The next week, another attempt followed, this one more serious than the last. I wound up in the hospital infirmary and the following day, I received a visitor. Only he didn't call himself Harry Mathews anymore.

"He'd become Wilshire Chetham," Holmes said.

"Aye. Now known as a man of charitable habits, disposed to the aid of prisoners and prison reform. He came to see me on these grounds, but I knew what he really wanted."

"So you slipped through the net," I said, once we were alone.

"It wasn't difficult. You of all people should know that," Harry replied.

"Two men have tried to kill me in two weeks. Can I thank you for that?"

"Why would I do that?"

"I'm a loose end. What did you tell them? That I'd turned? That I'd given evidence?"

"You always was the smart one, Billy," he said with a grin.

"I know what you want. I've hid them where you'll never find them."

"And I know exactly where they are. Glasgow isn't beyond my reach."

"It isn't my wife and daughter I speak of. It's the sapphires."

The grin faded from his face.

"Only I know where they are, Harry. I hid them the night you gave them to me. If I die, or if harm comes to my family, I will take the secret to my grave."

He scowled at me. "You've never kept a secret from me long, Billy."

"I can keep this secret forever, if need be."

"We'll see." He rose to his feet. "You'll have a long time to think of it."

The attempts on my life ended, but my time in Newgate did not. Every year, for ten years, he came to visit me. And every year, I refused to tell him.

The prison was to close, and I was to be set free. I thought I might see my family and, like a fool, I became too eager. As I've said, I'd locked the sapphires away and given the key to a trusted friend. I wrote a letter to this person, asking her to meet me at a pub once I was released.

Four days ago, I obtained my freedom. I made my way to the pub, watching to see I wasn't followed. Imagine my horror when I arrived and found Harry in my friend's place . . . .

"He had intercepted the letter," Holmes said. "And he had the key."

"Aye. He beat me to within an inch of my life, but still, he couldn't break me. He told me then he would fetch my wife and daughter – that they would suffer as I had."

"When they brought me here, all I could think of was you, Mr. Holmes. That is why I charged you with finding my family. I did not know . . . my Rosie . . . had already died."

Snow had grown weaker during his tale. He lay back against the pillow, his face pale. "That is my story, Mr. Holmes, the whole sad tale. You must protect my daughter."

"Your daughter is safe," Holmes said. "And I have a plan to keep her so."

He pulled the key from his coat pocket and held it before the man's face. Snow's eyes widened. "How?" he asked.

"I went to his home in the guise of a carpenter. Chetham is an arrogant fellow, forever congratulating himself on his intelligence, and disdainful of the average working man. It wasn't difficult to discover the whereabouts of the key once I had entered his household. I took it from the rather unimaginative hiding place his study desk drawer afforded, and would've absconded from the house if Chethem hadn't walked in on me. He recognized me, but an uppercut gave me time to run. I stopped in the kitchen and deposited the key in a Christmas pudding before fleeing the house. My friend and I recovered it this evening."

"He will not stop until he has it," Snow said.

"And I am counting on that," Holmes replied. "You say you have told me all, but you have not. Tell me the last thing, Mr. Snow, and I will end Chetham's hold on you for good."

Snow sighed. His gaze turned from Holmes to me and back again.

"The sapphires are in my former home at Merrick Square. This key opens the door to that house."

When we left Mr. Snow in his bed, Holmes advised me to call my wife and inform her of my situation. When I had finished, Holmes took a turn and made a brief call. I assumed it was to Mrs. Hudson, for he spoke of "putting the kettle on". When he'd rung off, we made our way to the outer doors of the hospital.

"Shall I call a cab?" I asked. "It's a long walk to Scotland Yard."

"And why should we go there?"

"Snow said we should find the sapphires at his former home in Merrick Square. If someone lives there now, we will need the aid of the police to enter."

"We won't find the sapphires there," Holmes said.

"Why?"

"Snow never lived in Merrick Square."

"How can you know that?"

"Mycroft had two men watching his house in Falmouth Street the day he was taken by the brougham. You will remember, he went back to fetch his umbrella? It was Mycroft's men who took him, and it was Mycroft who offered him leniency in return for information."

"The fat man!" I said. "Of course! Then Snow lied? Why would he do such a thing?"

Holmes took my arm and motioned to the windows set in the hospital doors. I watched as, beyond them, a carriage pulled up to the curb. Two men stepped from it. One, a short man with a thin face, pointed toward the hospital. The other, a tall man with a large black beard, nodded.

"It's Chethem," I whispered.

"We mustn't allow them entry to Snow's ward."

The two men climbed the steps toward the doors. Holmes and I stepped back.

"I wish I had my revolver," I said.

Holmes's face grew grim. "As do I."

Chethem entered first, followed by his underling. The bearded man blinked at us. A wide grin spread over his face.

"Well, if it isn't Holmes the Meddler and the gallant Dr. Watson!" He turned his gaze to me. "I must say I'm disappointed, Doctor. We had agreed you would call me when you found Mr. Holmes."

"It is fortunate I don't give my word to blackguards," I replied. "You are not Holmes's client."

"I never said I was. I simply said Holmes had been commissioned to find my property." He held out his hand. "Please, return what you have stolen."

"I'm afraid I cannot," Holmes said. "If you wish the key returned, you will have to take the matter up with the police."

Chethem raised two large fists in the air. "Now that won't do. That won't do at all. I think I'll just take it back."

"Queensbury Rules?" Holmes said, raising his own.

Chethem's grin grew wider and more devilish. "My rules."

As he and Holmes closed in on one another, I turned my attention to the underling. He'd somehow produced a knife from his person and now brandished it before me. I did what any unarmed gentleman in my position would do. I charged.

I'd been in many a scrum in my youth and, even at the ripe age of fifty, I hadn't forgotten my skills. When the fellow slashed at me, I ducked under his arm and collided with him, forcing him backward. I pinned him against the wall. The knife clattered against the floor.

A quick right dispatched the fellow. I turned back to Chethem and Holmes.

The villain towered a full head above Holmes and his fists, should they strike, were deadly. His speed, however, was slow and lumbering. Holmes, thin as a willow, easily avoided his blows.

They circled one another, each gauging the other for weakness. Holmes darted in and out, striking hard and fast. Chethem backed away.

Holmes's luck didn't last for long. Chethem struck him in the jaw, knocking him to his knees.

"It'll be more than your tooth I knock out this time," Chethem gloated. "You beat me once. You'll not do it again."

"How do you propose to stop me?" Holmes said, rising to his feet.

"This time, I won't let you live." He lashed out once more.

Holmes avoided the blow and responded in kind. Chethem dropped to his knees, blood streaming from between his lips. He spat something out upon the floor.

"I thank you for reminding me," Holmes said, nudging the tooth aside. He struck the villain across the chin with a thunderous right.

As Chethem fell to the floor unconscious, several uniformed men burst in through the hospital doors with a rodent-faced man in the lead. He halted before Holmes, his eyes wide.

"Ah, Lestrade," Holmes said. "Good of you to come. It appears you've missed all the excitement. If you will come with me, I shall introduce you to someone who can confirm the true identity of the gentleman lying on the floor – someone who is also prepared to swear out a complaint against him."

"But Mr. Holmes, this gentleman is Wilshire Chethem," Lestrade said.

"Also known as Harry Mathews," Holmes said smoothly. "And though he may enjoy immunity for past deeds, he has no immunity against those recently committed."

"Lestrade arrived just in time," I said, after Holmes had reemerged from Snow's ward and as Chethem and his underling were taken into custody. "Is that who you called at the hospital, Holmes?"

Holmes shrugged. "He has been waiting for my word all evening. I simply told him to put the kettle on." He led me to the door. "Come, Watson. Your wife must be expecting you. As for me, I must take this key to Falmouth Street. I believe there is a house there which bears my looking into."

The next day was Christmas Eve, and I received a call from Holmes asking me to join him at the London Hospital. I agreed and that afternoon, met him outside the hospital doors. He held a large parcel in his arms and, to my astonishment, I found he was not alone.

We made our way to the ward where Snow lay. He appeared much improved, but his face lit up when we brought the visitor to him.

"Alice!" he cried, as the girl rushed to the bed. He wrapped his arms about her and held her close. "Oh, my dear girl! You are so big! Can it really be you?"

"Yes, Father," the girl said, tears streaming down her cheeks. "It is I. Am I much changed?"

"Though you were but five when I left, I would know you anywhere. You look so much like your mother."

"She loved you until the end, Father. She told me every day."

"I apologize for interrupting," Holmes said, "but my time is not my own, even on this festive day. I have a present for the both of you and then my friend and I must go."

He set the parcel on the bed.

Snow glanced up at Holmes and then proceeded to unwrap it. He opened the large box and his eyes grew wide.

"It's a doll," Alice said. She turned to her father. "She looks like I did when I was little."

Snow looked up. "I have all I need, Mr. Holmes. We cannot accept this."

"Your daughter deserves this," Holmes replied. "As I said, it is a Christmas gift."

Without another word, he rose from the bed. He took me by the arm and together we left the ward.

"How did you find his daughter?" I asked as we stepped out into the street. The chill of the night air, which usually caused me pain, now invigorated.

"I have always known where the girl and her mother were," Holmes replied. "For over eleven years I have known."

"How?"

"Do you, by chance, remember a Mr. James Phillimore? The name should be familiar to you. The case was, at the time, unsolved."

"Phillimore? You mentioned him to me. His wife came to you with the problem of his disappearance. It seems his neighbor observed him leaving the house one morning. He stepped back into his house to retrieve his umbrella, and . . . dear Lord. Snow and Phillimore are the same man!"

"Precisely."

"And because his wife came to you, you knew where she and her daughter were. It's brilliant. I do have one more question, however: Did you find anything at the Falmouth house?"

"The house was deserted when I arrived and I found a way inside without much difficulty. There was a small door behind the umbrella stand, almost imperceptible behind the wallpaper. I unlocked it and found a box wrapped in brown paper inside."

"A box? Was there a doll inside?"

Holmes smiled. "There was."

"Was there anything inside the doll?"

"Unfortunately, no. The doll was empty."

"Ah, that is why you gave it to the girl."

"Did you notice the eyes, Watson?"

"Eyes?"

"The Doll's eyes. There were quite blue."

"The sapphires! But they must be worth thousands of pounds!"

"A man lost his wife and a great many years of his life for the theft of something he did not steal. I would say he and his daughter are most deserving, wouldn't you?"

"Yes. Yes, I believe I would."

The Canterbury Manifesto
by David Marcum

Part I

As a man with an experience of women which extends over many nations and three separate continents, and as a husband with experience of three separate wives, I can attest that there is special emphasis put on certain events – particularly firsts. Such was certainly the case throughout December 1902 as my new wife planned for our first Christmas together in our Queen Anne Street residence. Thus, when she insisted on changing those plans at the last minute, I was quite surprised – but probably no more than she was. Instead of supervising the preparation of the Christmas Day feast as intended, she was spending Christmas Eve in a first class compartment (*not* a smoker!) on a train bound for Canterbury, engaged in polite conversation with Sherlock Holmes.

They were pleasant enough to one another, but I expected the worst at any moment. My wife's plans had been spoiled after I had been summoned to the Diogenes Club on the previous evening, and Holmes had certainly never envisioned that she would accompany us to famed cathedral city.

Late the night before, on the evening of the twenty-third, I had voluntarily sequestered myself in my study, doing what any sensible man would in such a situation, the house being in a controlled uproar while the holiday celebration was being assembled. My wife, Priscilla, [1] had taken delivery of various items – chiefly comestibles – throughout the day, and on those rare occasions when I ventured forth to scavenge supplies and gather intelligence in order to get some sense of what was being organized, I couldn't believe the amount of food that was being assembled

By common agreement, we both ate a light dinner that evening, and I had only just returned to my study when the doorbell rang. In a moment, my wife appeared at the door, an envelope in her hand bearing a distinctive crest.

"I am afraid that you shall have to go," she said, handing it to me. I recognized its origin, as did she.

"Hmm?"

"To Pall Mall. To the Diogenes Club."

She said it in a flat tone, and I knew that she feared that I might be gone for longer than that evening, possibly even for several days. It was a fear that I shared.

Of course my wife knew Mycroft Holmes – in fact, his existence was much more common knowledge than either Holmes brother would have liked, due to my thoughtless indiscretion back in 1893. At that time, still grieving over what I believed was Holmes's death at the hands of Professor Moriarty atop the Reichenbach Falls, I was writing and publishing a series of narratives describing Holmes's past cases, so that his memory would remain green and his true gifts would be known and remembered.

I had written up quite a few of these accounts, and my literary agent, Conan Doyle, had been helping select which ones to place in *The Strand*. He liked the tale of the Greek prisoner and the interpreter who had been taken to communicate with him, and how I was introduced to Mycroft Holmes by way of the case. By that time, I was well aware of Mycroft Holmes's unique and valuable role within the government, but in the late summer of 1893, I was still grieving the death of my wife Mary, and my sensibilities were numb and blunted. Thus, I let Doyle talk me into publishing the story, not realizing the problems that it would cause for Mycroft when his existence was announced through the pages of a popular periodical. Fortunately I left the description of his duties rather vague, or it might have been much worse.

But I had withheld no such details from Priscilla, and she knew that a summons from Mycroft meant that the matter was serious – although she rather sarcastically asked if my opinion was needed to help in the selection of his brother Sherlock's Christmas gift. All I could do was laugh politely and get into my coat, hoping that whatever the problem was could be resolved quickly.

It hadn't taken long after I first met Mycroft to understand just how important he was in the functions of the British Government, and particularly in the secret intelligence services. In fact, it was soon clear that the Diogenes Club, while truly fulfilling its purpose as a place for unclubable men to spend their time, was also the location of much that occurred within the government to organize and manage those agents of Britain's secret intelligence services. And as such, I was almost certain that it was this connection that was behind my summons to the club that night.

I had received the message to attend the meeting at a little after nine p.m., and it wasn't much past the half-hour when the hansom deposited me at No. 78 Pall Mall, the modest building housing the Diogenes Club. I've written enough elsewhere about this unique establishment that a great deal doesn't need to be addressed here. Suffice it to say, the club was originally founded by Mycroft and several others as a retreat where they could go and avoid conversation for a time. No speaking was allowed within the club, save in the Stranger's Room on the first floor, overlooking the street. Over the years, I have been in that room, one way or another, more times than I can remember – with Holmes in order to confer with or receive information from Mycroft Holmes, or summoned there with the request that I assist in an investigation. At times, I've even been there on my own, to seek advice or guidance or help in various confidential matters that have sprung up on occasion.

Sherlock Holmes was already in the Stranger's Room when I arrived. He and I had recently been involved in some business that finished up at the London Hospital, and just the night before we'd been in a rough altercation, but he now looked rested and refreshed. He nodded as I entered. Mycroft waved in my direction, spoke a greeting, and indicated that I ought to pour something for myself from the sideboard. I did, taking a nice portion of the club's very memorable brandy.

While doing so, I noted with amusement the contrast to my own home. There, no open surface remained that didn't have some sort of holiday-themed greenery. Our door had a sizeable wreath upon it, and there were candles burning in every window. There was no such frippery here, and I wondered if any concession would be made, even on Christmas Day, by making the slightest changes to the otherwise rigid menu. I knew from encountering many of them that the Diogenes members maintained gruff exteriors – men who, like Mycroft, ran on fixed rails between work, the club, and home, with no time for what they considered foolishness. Yet was there some place deep within them that wished for a bit of holiday festivity, and a return, if just for a moment, to that sense of childlike wonder which unexpectedly makes itself known during the holiday season – even a solitary candle in the Diogenes window? Or were all sparks of sentimentality extinguished in their stony hearts? I knew that no answer could easily be found.

Before I drifted into a full reverie on the topic, I turned back toward my intended chair. When I was seated, Mycroft spoke.

"Have you seen the news?"

I frowned. I hadn't taken the time to read the late editions, and I recalled nothing of importance earlier in the day. I shook my head.

"The Archbishop of Canterbury died several hours ago."

"Frederick Temple?" I asked. "That's unfortunate," I added, but not certain yet what his death implied.

Sherlock Holmes spoke. "There is no indication of foul play – for now. The man had been ill for several weeks, after collapsing during a speech earlier this month."

"He was, after all, in his eighties, I believe," I said.

"Eighty-one," confirmed Mycroft.

"Then if there is nothing suspicious connected with his death, what is the interest of the . . . umm, Diogenes Club in the matter?"

The question held implied meaning. When I had first met Mycroft Holmes in September 1888, I'd believed that he held some small position within the government. It wasn't long after that, however, that I began to be aware of his much greater influence. In fact, he held a most unique position as something of a clearing house of information, able to see connections and hidden paths and links that others could not. Due to the value of his oversight, he often functioned *as* the government, his word deciding policy and guiding the country through some very rough waters that the average man might never perceive.

"One of the Archbishop's papers has been taken," explained Mycroft.

I raised an eyebrow, wondering what sort of paper belonging to a church leader could fall under Mycroft's purview. "I wouldn't have thought that would be a cause for concern – unless there was something in his past that might discredit him."

"Nothing of the sort. He was a man of the highest moral character. I assure you of that with all the authority of my position."

"Then did this paper hold information that might be used to embarrass someone else? Or to tarnish the Archbishop's reputation and legacy in some other way?"

"The latter," said Mycroft, "but his reputation is not our concern. The damage, should this paper be published, will be far worse to the nation as a whole – at a time when such things cannot be tolerated. What was taken was a previously unknown essay – a *manifesto* – that Temple was preparing which could rock the Established Church, and the rest of the nation along with it – apparently a fundamental shift in doctrine which he has apparently come to espouse in recent months, and which he had taken upon himself to aggressively announce, without reaching any sort of agreement to do so with others in the Church who should also have a say."

"Apparently," said Holmes with a smile and shake of his head, "the Crown is concerned as well.

"They are 'dismayed'," corrected Mycroft. "The King expressed distress that the man who so recently carried out his duties in the Coronation could take it upon himself to 'hijack the ship', as he put it.

"Temple was always something of a progressive type," Mycroft continued. "In some ways, I suppose it's a wonder that such a fellow espousing those views, good as he was, managed to be elevated to the position of Archbishop. Over forty years ago, he was promoting the values of science alongside faith, and seeing nothing within certain scientific theories of the time that were contrary to the teachings of religion. And more recently, he has preached at least one sermon espousing greater educational opportunities for women."

"Nothing so terrible in that," I said.

"Ah, but apparently he has been much more specific as part of this new overall proposal that he was working out on his own – a full-blown dash toward science as the new God, along with suggestions of radical Socialism. We should have seen it coming, I suppose. Even in the early 1860's, Temple welcomed the insights of Darwin's evolution theory, by way of a series of lectures. In recent months, from what we've been told by his secretary, one Stephen Smythe, Temple knew that his health was starting to fail, and he was hurrying to complete a document so shocking that it would leapfrog debate about various current issues and disagreements that he felt are hindering the Church so that the country will be ready, or so he believed, for whatever faces Britain in the new century."

"I'm puzzled," I said. "Are you referring to Germany and the Kaiser?"

"I am," confirmed Mycroft. "The Archbishop has been part of a committee assembled to examine the threat of rising German nationalism. Representatives from all areas of government and important industries have been meeting for several years in order to prepare for the eventual, inevitable German war which is bound to occur. Temple represented the Church."

I was well aware of the growing sense within a certain segment of the country's leadership that war with Germany would absolutely occur at some uncertain point in the future. The King's nephew, the Kaiser, had been ever-envious of Britain, and the aggressive expansions of Germany's military were ongoing and increasing. Mycroft had long been an advocate for being prepared, and he'd been pressing more and more for his younger brother to devote his energies in that direction, instead of wasting his time on those lesser cases that he viewed with disdain, once describing them as "the usual petty puzzles of the police-court". A sizeable number of Holmes's recent investigations had related to circumventing the Germans' activities, as I well knew from my own involvement.

"This missing paper," I asked. "Is there any sense that it was been obtained by foreign agents in order to cause disruption or embarrassment?"

"Not so far," answered Mycroft. "All we know for certain is that it is missing. We were caught unaware of Temple's intentions until earlier this afternoon when Smythe informed us that Temple planned to publish them on Christmas Day, against Smythe's advice. Apparently this young man was the only one included in Temple's secret plans, and only he knew the explosive nature of the Archbishop's proposed thesis. He was encouraging a delay, and to seek other opinions or approval before pulling the trigger, so to speak, but Temple must have sensed that his time was short, for according to Smythe, he'd spent much of the past week or so racing to finish the document. And Smythe confirms that as of just a few days ago, Temple *did* finish it."

"Can you be more specific?" asked Holmes. "Is it something really so dangerous?"

"Oh yes, very much so. It is a specific statement aligning the Church with a number of scientific theories – all correct, of course, or they are according to our current understanding, but still controversial to those of less-educated backgrounds. Smythe says that he has gone all in with the current thinking on evolution, for instance, and also investigations into atomic theory and universal astronomy – both of which have far more connections between them that one might think, despite the vast differences in scale between the two.

"And then there is his abrupt and unexpected push for reconciliation with the Catholic Church – which he felt was absolutely necessary to be in place as a unified guiding force when the great conflict breaks out. It seems that Temple has written that all of the various treaties between nations – secret and otherwise – which are looped 'round and 'round the necks of the various European countries, along with the ever-increasing need for raw materials from around the globe, and the competing and fractious colonization that goes with it, will eventually pull every great nation into a terrible world-spanning conflict, such has never been seen before."

"But you've predicted as much yourself," said Holmes. "Why is Temple's document any different? Why should it be so feared?"

"Because my opinions have been private – behind the scenes – with an eye toward preparation for something which cannot be avoided. To openly discuss it now – to incite the public to discussing it – might precipitate an acceleration toward the war. And Smythe says that the essay is written in just such a way, pushing British interests first so that it cannot help to offend others, and more likely throw us into war within a week – even with our allies. If such a thing were made public under the name of such a highly placed figure, it would only and immediately increase the nationalistic tensions and advance the pace of the coming war by decades – and England is nowhere near ready for that.

"For such a document to simply appear, with the Archbishop of Canterbury coming down on the side of legitimizing evolution and also suddenly proposing reunification with the Catholics in the same sweeping manifesto, and while doing so in such a highly offensive manner, will be perceived as the height of arrogance. Opinions will immediately inflame in all quarters, spinning into a nationalistic furor. The nation celebrates Christmas in two days. By New Year's day, the peace we enjoy would be finished."

"And this Smythe fellow was the one who sounded the alarm," I commented.

Mycroft nodded. "As soon as Temple passed, Smythe realized that something should be done to secure the man's papers. The absence of this new doctrine was immediately obvious. He had rushed to secure it and found that it was gone. He then notified me."

"Is he one of your agents then?" I asked. "You had a man watching the Archbishop of Canterbury?" I wasn't entirely comfortable with the idea."

"I have many agents – for without accurate and complete data, how else can I make good decisions? But in this case, the answer is no, Smythe is not working for me. However, the Archbishop and I have had some dealings with on another – there is more to his position, you understand, than just overseeing the Church and presenting the occasional important sermon – so it was no surprise that Smythe had heard of me as well, and when he perceived that the document was missing, he correctly sought me out."

I wasn't truly surprised, and to belabor the question would serve no purpose. "Who could have taken it?" I asked instead.

"That," answered Sherlock Holmes, "is what we have been tasked to discover."

I thought of my wife, and all the efforts that she'd made toward constructing our first Christmas as husband and wife. It was already late on the evening of the twenty-third – how many hours were left until Christmas Day? I glanced at the clock on the mantel. Almost ten p.m. So twenty-six hours until the 25th. Or something around thirty-four hours until that morning, when the day would actually begin for us when we awoke. It wasn't much time.

I suppose it was my look toward the clock that informed them both of my train of thought. "At least we don't have far to go," I said. "The Archbishop's residence is just across the river – a mile as the crow flies." I stood. Time was passing. "Should we make our way in that direction?"

Mycroft shook his head, and Holmes gave me a rueful smile.

"You're correct, Doctor," said Mycroft, "to think that starting at Lambeth Palace would be the proper place. Temple did pass away there. But for some reason he had gone out to Canterbury a few days ago, in spite of his failing healthy and that was where he completed work on the essay. He left it there when he returned to London, and that's where Smythe went in such a hurry – to secure it, only to find when he arrived that it was gone."

"So we must go to Canterbury," said Sherlock Holmes, looking my way and surely realizing what that meant to me and the chances of having a first successful Christmas in my new home and with my new wife.

If Holmes and I left immediately, I thought, we could be in Canterbury in the early hours of Christmas Eve – provided that we found a train running so late. Could we engage a special, much as Professor Moriarty had done over a decade earlier when we observed him from a hidden spot as he pursued us toward Canterbury after we'd decided to go a different way? Unlikely. And what could we accomplish in the middle of the night when we arrived? And even if we left immediately and didn't sleep when we got there, waking people up and working through until morning, could the matter be resolved in time to have me back in Queen Anne Street when my wife's Christmas plans were to be set into motion?

I looked back at Holmes, realizing that a bit of panic might be showing in my face. Of course he had read my thoughts as if I'd said them aloud. I never should have glanced at the mantel clock.

"We can but try," he said, with no indication that my staying behind was ever an option. "To be back as soon as possible. We can but try. I wouldn't want to add another grievance to that list with my name upon it that the good Mrs. Watson already maintains."

I started to protest that there was no such list, but in fact, she did have a few objections to my long-time friend – my being shot earlier in the year while assisting him being one of them. But before I could defend her, Mycroft interrupted.

"Nothing can be done tonight. Travel down first thing in the morning. I'll send word to the Archbishop's wife to be ready for your arrival. I trust that this will be resolved quickly."

"His wife?" I asked. "She's in Canterbury? Surely her place is here, with the body of her husband."

Mycroft shook his head. "Mrs. Temple is particularly strong-willed. When she learned of this essay and its explosive nature, and that it was now missing, she insisted on traveling to Canterbury, leaving the arrangements for her husband with others here that she trusts. She says that she knew Temple better than anyone – certainly true, I'm sure – and that she should be there in case her help is needed in any way."

Mycroft turned to his brother. "The woman is strong and capable. But her husband has died. Be . . . diplomatic, Sherlock." Then he forced himself to his feet from the heavy red leather chair that had likely been specially constructed for him long ago and placed there in the Stranger's Room. "And apparently, as it's Christmas, this makes his death even worse. Emotions will be on edge. Go carefully."

Then, with a nod our way, we were dismissed. Holmes and I walked out, passing through the silent building where no conversation was allowed. At that time of night, in rooms unseen to both sides of us, the place could have been mostly empty, or filled to capacity, and we wouldn't have known, as the members always took great pains to remain silent. Such a place definitely had its attractions.

Outside, in the brisk December air, I began. "Holmes, I – "

He raised a hand. "I understand, Watson. I was unaware until I arrived that Mycroft had involved you. If he'd asked beforehand, I would have convinced him to let you stay home for the holiday, but he rightly pointed out that your participation can only make the chances for success that much better."

I nodded at the compliment and didn't bother to correct him, for I had instead been about to try and convince him that my wife didn't have any great antipathy toward him, as he apparently believed. Yet now was not the time for that discussion, and we would have several hours the next day to hash it out on the train.

Holmes indicated that he had some research to do before our departure in the morning, and asked my opinion as to whether Lomax might still be found in the nearby London Library. I expected that he was, and offered to go along, but Holmes encouraged me to return home instead, and I didn't argue. We wished each other a good night, and then I had to walk to Waterloo Place before encountering a hansom. It wasn't a long journey from there, but the going was slow along Regent Street due to the upcoming Christmas holiday, even at that hour, and I had time to ponder my wife's general antipathy toward my best friend.

Just months before, in mid-1902, I had wed for the third time, at a period in my life when I had no expectations of entering such a state ever again. My first marriage in 1886 had lasted little more than a year before my wife, Constance, was taken far too early due to general poor health, greatly stressed at the end by an unexpected illness. My second bride, Mary, was also taken from me in 1893 after four years of marriage by a combination of maladies. When she passed, I assumed that I would remain a widower for the remainder of my life. However, that changed when I met Priscilla, and after a reasonable period of acquaintance, we both agreed that it was inevitable that we should join our destinies.

At that time, I had been living in again Baker Street for eight years, having moved back in the spring of 1894 following Holmes's return to London following the extended period when he was believed to be dead.

After Mary's death, I had maintained my practice, but with very little enthusiasm. Upon Holmes's invitation to return to my old digs, I sold out and resumed assisting him in a great many of his investigations. It was through the course of one of these that I met my future third bride, although neither of us initially knew then how our stories would join.

Priscilla was quite a different lady from Constance or Mary. I had met the former during a time in the mid-1880's when I traveled to San Francisco. Upon our marriage, we settled in London, but the intolerable fogs, so different from those of the northern California coast, had terribly afflicted Constance to the point that she was often forced to travel away with her mother, seeking restoration of her health while I remained in London, attempting to build my practice and our future – while still having time to assist Holmes as needed.

I had met Mary when she presented herself one morning in September 1888 as Holmes's client, and it was through that investigation that we quickly fell in love, being married the following spring. Due to this initial connection with Holmes, and having seen him in action, Mary had no objections when I joined him on his cases.

But Priscilla had a different perspective.

At the time of our marriage, I was about to turn fifty, and my bride-to-be was in her middle years as well. By then, each with several decades of accumulated adult experience, we approached our upcoming union with a certain practicality, and sensible plans were made in terms of purchasing the lease on the house at No. 9 Queen Anne Street, not very far from Harley Street, which would contain both my new practice and our residence. Arrangements were proceeding at a stately and comforting pace a few weeks before our wedding was scheduled when I was shot.

It occurred, as one might expect, in connection with one of Holmes's investigations. Perhaps I had become too complacent over the years, but I should have been more careful when dealing with a cornered criminal known by the sobriquet of "Killer" Evans. The bullet did no more than graze my thigh, although in such a way as to cause a burning sensation for quite some time afterwards while healing. I had received far worse wounds during my military service, and quite a few more after my return to England when associating myself with Holmes's investigations. (These included taking an unexpected Jezail bullet to the leg – and who expects to receive two of those in one lifetime, with the second wound occurring in England? – and also being stabbed in the upper chest with a red-hot poker. Both of these had occurred at different times in '88, and over the years there had also been numerous other cuts, breaks, punctures, gunshot wounds, and occasional poisonings.)

After being wounded by Evans, what I had thought would be an interesting story to tell Priscilla had turned into another of our firsts: Our first argument. The gist of her position was that as responsible husband, I should henceforth forego any activities which might put my life in danger, and instead settle meekly and for the rest of my days into my new role as a West End physician.

I disagreed.

The matter was gradually tabled without an absolute agreement acknowledged either way (although I held firm to my position), and we married as planned. Holmes, as he had been both times before, served as my best man, and he and Priscilla settled into a stiffly polite acquaintance with one another, while I walked the fine line between the two worlds of Baker Street and Queen Anne Street.

It had seemed to work rather well so far, as my practice was immediately successful (although I was fairly certain that a great number of patients initially crossed my threshold because of my association with the famed detective), and I also still found time to join Holmes on many of his cases. Most were rather benign, and in the instances where I encountered danger, I wasn't shot, so the question of being a responsible husband and avoiding such circumstances hadn't been reopened – but it was never entirely forgotten either.

And then came the Christmas season, and my wife's complex expectations for our first Yule holiday together, which I knew was at cross-purposes with the summons I'd received from Mycroft Holmes.

I'd had plenty of time to consider how to share my upcoming plans with her, as the journey from Pall Mall was quite slow. The second Boer War had ended half-a-year earlier, and while nothing about it gave the country any sense of pride or joy, there seemed to be some unspoken agreement that this season's celebrations should be especially festive. The shops and stores were highly decorated, and many had stayed open late with window displays that fought to outdo those of their neighbors – each successful enough to attract the great crowds who chose to stop and tarry for a while at each one instead of moving along. Those who did need to get from one place to another more quickly were often diverted out into the street in order to circle around the paused throngs, and that rippled into a general constriction of traffic.

I saw it all – the decorations and the crowds (with so many individuals awkwardly balancing their brightly colored purchases) and the unusual holiday smells, savory and sweet, that wafted above the typical horsy odors of the thoroughfare. For those of a mind to appreciate it with wide eyes, the journey would have been a treat. But I was headed home, with the premonition of my wife's reaction to my news.

And yet she surprised me. We turned from Regent Street into Mortimer Street, passing along Cavendish Square before traversing the short distance up Harley Street and so into Queen Anne Street. I had the cabbie release me several doors early and walked the remaining distance, pausing for a moment to look at the cozy building, with windows lit on all four stories by single candles, more powerful in their simplicity than the vast and ostentatious decorations that were to be found at other finer houses throughout the city. It was so different from the Christmases of my youth, growing up in Scotland where the holiday was nothing more than another religious day to be noted on the calendar – no gifts, no feasts, and certainly no Father Christmas.

My wife met me at the door. "Where are you off to, then?" she asked, trying to make her voice bright and interested, but the expression in her eyes revealing her true thoughts.

"Canterbury," I said as she stepped aside to allow my passage. "The Archbishop has died, and one of his most important papers has gone missing."

She stopped abruptly, turning around to fully face me. "The Archbishop? Oh, poor Beatrice!"

"I'm sorry?" I asked, nonplussed.

"Beatrice. His wife. I know her." She paused, not more than a pair of seconds, and then said, "I'm coming with you."

Over the remainder of the evening, I half-heartedly tried to talk her out of it – but I also remembered how useful Mary had been on a number of investigations. (Sadly, Constance's poor health had prevented her from providing any meaningful assistance.) Priscilla was practical and intelligent, and there was the added advantage that she knew the Archbishop's wife, a long-standing friendship that had begun long before Reverend Temple had been enthroned as the Bishop of London in 1885. They had maintained contact with one another ever since, although this was the first I'd known of it.

Priscilla set about pausing some of the Christmas preparations – but not those that would affect the staff, who would not be deprived of their holiday. And I wrote a short note to be delivered to Baker Street, explaining that Holmes and I would be accompanied to Canterbury in the morning. I expected no reply – frankly I hoped for none – and by the time we went to bed, there had been no response from that quarter.

Part II

Priscilla and I joined Holmes in the morning at Victoria, and there was no discussion as to Priscilla's presence. Holmes accepted the inevitable nature of the situation, and he seemed to flash a glance of approval at the very light amount of luggage brought by my wife – barely more than I carried myself.

I was relieved to find that Holmes and Priscilla got along well as we traveled, and he had no qualms at fully taking her into his confidence – or at least as much as he had me. He explained the circumstances to her, repeating much of what I'd related the previous evening after returning from the Diogenes Club, but also providing a bit more information that neither of us knew, concerning the names of a few rather concerned government officials who were monitoring the situation quite closely.

"Your friend Lomax was invaluable," Holmes explained. "It isn't just the forgotten dusty tomes that he can lay a hand on in an instant. He knows right where the information concerning current events might also be located. Within fifteen minutes, I had three other names – important men – and as I visited each in turn, they were able to tell more than even Mycroft had supplied." While the identities of those men isn't important, they did tend to confirm the concern that was felt by the Archbishop's sudden streak of independent thought when he sensed his time was short.

Holmes questioned Priscilla some about her friendship with the newly widowed Beatrice Temple, and I could see that her presence fit somehow with his plans, as he asked her to be especially certain to comfort the bereaved woman. Knowing him so well, I knew what he was really asking was for her to distract the new widow at those times when his investigations needed to be carried out without the woman's knowledge.

When asked to describe Beatrice Temple, Priscilla replied, "She is a strong woman – as much responsible for her husband's success and advancement as he was. She's originally from Kensington – she's several years older than I am, and she was originally a friend of my elder sister. We were thrown together much as I grew up, and eventually we became rather close.

"Her father died when she was young, and the entire family was forced to become stronger because of it. She and Frederick married more than a quarter-century ago, and they have been very happy together. I rather lost touch with her when her husband was enthroned as the Bishop of London in the mid-1880's, but she took time to reach out to me five years ago when he became the Archbishop. I've been down to the Archbishop's Palace quite a few times since then, but I see her much more often at their London residence in Lambeth Palace."

Holmes questioned her about Temple's sudden shift in belief, which had led to him writing the inflammatory document. Priscilla shook her head, puzzled. "He was always interested in everything, you see – science, nature. People and politics. Not what you'd think of as the titular leader of the Church at all. I suppose when I was younger, if asked, I would have imagined the Archbishop of Canterbury as a monastic type, given to gloom and grim pronouncements, dressed all in black and emanating final judgments wherever he turned. But Frederick was a laughing man – happy, intelligent, and a good leader. I can only think that his final illness had either given him some sense of urgency to accomplish a long-held secret agenda, or that his mind had been affected in ways no one realized, causing him to become so reckless at the very end."

As we each fell silent and into our own thoughts, I held my wife's hand while looking past her and out onto the winter-locked Kent countryside. The trip from London to Canterbury was only seventy miles or so, and accomplished in less than two hours, but in some ways it might have been a journey back in time. The little farms dotted here and there, decorated with their fascinating oast houses, probably looked the same as they had four-hundred years before. Living in the city, with every day being a headlong rush further into the Twentieth Century, sometimes made one careless in one's thinking, believing that everyone had the advantage of modern advances in electricity, transportation, and sanitation. Seeing this space between our departure and our destination made it clear that more of the country than not was still living within the constraints of the old ways, and would likely be doing so for quite some time to come.

I looked for some signs of Christmas along our journey, but it was rarely seen. A wreath here and there on a barely seen station, perhaps, but nothing on the distant lonely farms and houses. I could only hope that there would be seasonal happiness in all of them, and I silently wished them well.

We were quiet and pensive until our arrival at the newer eastern Canterbury Station – newer in the sense that it was constructed fourteen years after the western station, which was built over half-a-century before. Holmes and I followed Priscilla, who knew the way, out of the modest brick building to the cab rank, where she motioned for a growler. Holmes glanced toward me with a small grin, and I recalled his maxim, which he himself only honored on certain occasions, to take neither the first nor the second cab which might present itself. This was much more difficult when obtaining a cabbie's services in the ordered lines outside a station, and in any case, it seemed unlikely that any attempt would be made to abduct us here – although it wasn't entirely unknown in our combined experiences.

Once aboard, Priscilla surprised us both by giving instructions to set out for the Old Palace, as she called it. I had believed that we were bound for the Cathedral and the Archbishop's chambers there, and I could tell that Holmes had believed the same. Priscilla explained. "The Old Palace is within the limits of the Cathedral. When Frederick was installed as Archbishop, he set about restoring an Eleventh Century building on the grounds. He is – *was* – the first Archbishop to have lived there since the Seventeenth Century."

She barely had time to explain this as we reached our destination. If not for Priscilla's presence, I believe that Holmes and I could have walked, even carrying our light luggage, as it probably wasn't more than half-a-mile from the station.

I had been to the Cathedral before while joining Holmes in several different investigations, including the events which uncovered the true facts about the suicide of Thomas à Becket – a story for which the world is truly not prepared. I had never visited at Christmastime, and was surprised to see that very little had been done to decorate for the season. But upon reflection, I recalled that the typical festive decorations that we know so well, many having been adopted from various ancient pagan religions, probably had no place here.

The portion of the city through which we passed had embellished for Christmas, but the mood was notably muted, no doubt following the death of the Archbishop. Groups of men and women huddled in conversation, and as we approached the Cathedral, more and more of them seemed to be looking that way, as if speculating as to what might be occurring inside.

There was a large Christmas tree set up on a wide cleared spot, and nearby was a Nativity scene with nearly life-sized mannequins in familiar poses. But we only had a chance to see them for an instant before arriving at our destination.

The Old Palace was a lovely stone building, ranging intermittently between two and three stories. We turned into the circular drive off Palace Street and passed by a decorative fountain, stopping before a front door that opened from a small angled covered projection extending from the main building. There was a jarring mixture of traditional Christmas decorations (including colorful ribbons and secular holly and ivy) and black mourning drapery being installed across the front of the house by church workmen, as if both types of adornment were competing, and the winning theme had not yet been decided.

A stout woman in black had emerged as we drew to a halt, her hands clasped before her and holding a handkerchief. Beside her was a tall and painfully thin fellow in his early thirties, also dressed in mourning, his hands behind his back while he stooped forward, rather stork-like – apparently his natural posture.

Priscilla stepped down from our conveyance and went immediately to the woman. They embraced. Then, while still in that pose, the woman looked over my wife's shoulder toward Holmes. "We received your wire," she said, her voice steady and strong. "Thank you for coming. My husband's study is ready for your examination."

Clearly, in spite of her loss, she was a strong woman who had a clear idea of what needed to be done.

"Although it isn't necessary after all," said the man behind her. "The document has been recovered."

The woman – clearly Mrs. Temple – released Priscilla and stepped back. She glanced toward the tall man with a fleeting frown. "This is true. I suppose that Frederick thought he was being clever, but he hid his essay underneath a false bottom in a desk drawer. Stephen had forgotten about it, and I only thought to look there this morning, when we were straightening the mess in the office for your investigation, Mr. Holmes."

I didn't look at my friend, but I could imagine the reaction that he was struggling to suppress upon hearing that statement. If a Scotland Yard inspector had been so foolish as to utter such a thing about cleaning up and in the process destroying clues, Holmes would have had no hesitation at releasing a blistering rebuke. But this was the new widow of the Archbishop of Canterbury. Such a thing was not done – even by Sherlock Holmes, who typically had little regard for social mores.

"That is a relief," Holmes replied, his voice level. "Still, might Watson and I visit the study, and speak with Mr. Smythe, while you and Mrs. Watson reacquaint yourselves?"

Mrs. Temple nodded. She glanced again at Stephen Smythe. "Of course. I would like to gain some understanding why my husband have taken this course." She appeared to be on the verge of speaking further, but stopped herself, took Priscilla's hand, and turned to walk away toward the door, leaving us on the drive with the secretary.

"This way, gentlemen," he said after a few seconds, holding out a hand toward the door where the two women had just vanished, as if to prod us into motion.

"One moment," countered Holmes, seemingly oblivious to the cold December morning, or the fact that the tall thin man facing us had no winter coat. "As I understand it, you hurried down yesterday after the Archbishop's death to secure his papers."

The man nodded, folding his arms pointedly and tightly around himself in an obvious attempt to stay warm.

"You knew of this document. Was that specifically what you wanted to secure?"

"It was."

"If it was so important, why was it left here? Why didn't the Archbishop carry it back with him to London?"

"That I cannot say. I had been responsible for packing up most of the Archbishop's papers before our return to Lambeth Palace last week, but he himself took care of those he considered most important or confidential. It was only yesterday, before his passing, that he happened to mention that he'd left it here, in Canterbury. I assumed that he had a reason, but it didn't seem appropriate for me to question why. Not long after that, he died, and soon it occurred to me that this document needed to be secured. Explaining in generalities, but not specifically referencing the document in question, I excused myself to Mrs. Temple, came here as soon as I could, and found it to be missing."

"But then it was found this morning. Mrs. Temple recalled that it was hidden in the desk drawer."

He formed a small smile. "Actually, it was me who thought of the hidden cavity in the desk drawer, but Mrs. Temple was closer, and she opened it first. She now seems to remember that she thought of it." He shook his head, as if it were a charming memory.

"We found the original, but – " Here the smile slid from his face and he lowered his voice, although there was no one around to hear us. "I didn't inform Mrs. Temple, as I didn't want to disturb her fragile peace of mind, but there were *two* copies of the document – the original, and one made when it was typed, using carbonic copying paper. That copy, gentlemen, *is* still missing."

Holmes, who had seemed to be losing interest by the minute, straightened a bit, like a hound who hears a distant horn. "Then by all means," he said, " there is still work for us to do here. Please lead us to the study."

I could almost hear Smythe's thoughts expressed aloud: He had been attempting to show us in that direction when Holmes had paused, and he could have just as easily told us of the missing copy inside, where he would have been warm. The skeletal man didn't have much meat on him for such a cold day.

The transition from the chilly outside air to the front hall was abrupt, and I was glad to shed my overcoat. A servant took it and my hat, and collected Holmes's Inverness and fore-and-aft cap as well. I sniffed. The house was filled with a most enticing spicy smells suggesting the holidays – quite at odds with the recent death of the head of the house.

Smythe noticed my reaction. "Preparations for the Christmas celebration were already well under way when word came of the Archbishop's death. It was decided that the cooks should go ahead and carry on. If no celebrations occur here in the Palace, then the food can always be distributed to the poor rather than go to waste. Mrs. Temple is very forward thinking, you know, and quite practical. She has been a tower of strength so far, but I'm concerned that she will break at some point. They were married for over twenty-five years, you know. I'm glad that your wife accompanied you, Doctor. Mrs. Temple thinks the world of her."

He had shared this while leading us through the fine house, passing along corridors and through various parlors and sitting rooms before reaching a stairway up to the first floor. More turns brought us to a small room along the rear of the house. "This was the Archbishop's working study," he explained. "He has – *had* – more formal rooms elsewhere in the house for meeting with dignitaries and other important officials."

Smythe started to lead us inside, but Holmes held up a hand, preventing him. "It's too late to see the room entirely undisturbed," he said, "but I still may glean some obscure fact." Then he went ahead on his own, stepping carefully as he examined the space from different vantages before moving from the general to the specific.

"I apologize for Mrs. Temple clearing things up," explained the secretary, watching him curiously. "After the document was found, I didn't want to upset her by revealing that a copy was still missing. She seemed so relieved. Thinking that all was now well, she began to put things back in order that had been shuffled during the search. I'm aware that you might have learned a great deal from the scene if it had been left alone – who else might have been in here, and who might have taken the copy." He turned to me with a smile – quite ghastly on his cadaverous face. "I'm rather a student of Mr. Holmes's methods, Doctor, and an admirer of your published works. Your narrative of that Dartmoor devil dog earlier this year was rather fascinating, you know, and I was quite surprised at the conclusion. It never seems to be who you think, does it?"

I shook my head, paying more attention to Holmes than the words of the thin young man beside me. By now, Holmes was seated at the desk, looking half-heartedly through the stacks of documents on top before pulling out the drawers.

"Do you suspect," he asked Smythe, "that someone might have taken the copy?"

"I don't know. There have been no signs of break-ins, and the staff is completely trust-worthy. And there have been no visitors for the Archbishop in this office for months – long before he wrote his . . . his *manifesto*."

"We've been informed of the general nature of the thing, as you related to my brother," said Holmes. "Have you exaggerated?"

Smythe shook his head. "Not at all. In some ways, it might be worse than what I was able to convey. I know what it *said*, but there are those who will be able to pull it apart and twist it and imply things that are much worse." He looked from one to the other of us for a moment, to see if we understood. "There is much there for those who wish for an excuse to become angry. Very angry."

Holmes thought for a moment and then pulled some stacks of random files and pinned pages toward him across the desktop, turning them this way and that as he examined them. He then pivoted to look through the few sheets that were contained in the Archbishop's wastepaper basket beside the desk before shifting back to the desk, pulling at his ear for a moment before leaning forward and opening the deeper lower drawer on the bottom right. He looked inside and then leaned back to examine the outer dimensions. Then – apparently deciding that the inside was much indeed more shallow than the outside – he reached in, made a motion with his hand, and lifted the false bottom of which we'd been informed. I stepped forward and peered down. It was empty, which was no surprise at all. Still, I'd wanted to see it for myself.

"Was there anything else here besides the original document?" Holmes asked, leaning back in the dead man's chair.

"Nothing."

"And where is the original document that you recovered?"

"Here," said Smythe, pulling some folded sheets from inside his coat and handing them across the desk. "See for yourself – these are dangerous thoughts."

"Where is the typewriting machine?" I asked.

"Why, it's that one," said Smythe, gesturing behind me. There, along a wall near a window, was a much smaller *L*-shaped desk. The shorter leg of the *L* jutted into the room, holding an old Standard machine, manufactured in America by Remington. "We had it cleaned and refurbished earlier this year," the secretary continued. "It was becoming intolerable."

As I stepped over and leaned down to look at it, attempting to see the striking surfaces in the weak sunlight from the window, Holmes asked, "Did you type this, or the Archbishop?"

"Oh, he did," replied Smythe. "He copied it from his handwritten notes. I only knew of its existence when he was finished and asked me to read through it."

"When was that?"

"Less than a week ago. Let's see . . . It was on Saturday afternoon. The 20th."

Holmes took a moment more to read through the document, then looking at the edges and back of the pages before handing them to me.

"Strong stuff," he said. He gestured at the Archbishop's desk. "Where are the handwritten notes? I've only made a cursory search, but there isn't much here. I suppose he kept the bulk of his papers in London, and I see nothing related to this – no drafts, no supporting documents that might have been used for his research."

Smythe shook his head. "Last Saturday, when he let me read it, he said that he'd destroyed all the notes, as they might be too dangerous, and that there were now only two copies – 'Tossed them in the fire,' he explained about his notes, adding that no one had any business reading the unpolished version. I had the impression that it was more abrasive and offensive than what he eventually typed."

As he spoke, I myself looked through the four sheets and saw that this was indeed much more explosive than anything we had previously been led to believe. Not only did it contain the thoughts, ideas, and suggestions that Mycroft had described, but it was written in a highly nationalistic and insulting manner. For instance, it didn't simply suggest reunification between the Church of England and the Catholic Church – it advocated the complete absorption and subjugation of the latter by the former, with the removal of the Pope entirely, along with the recommendation that he be punished publicly for heresy.

It quoted scripture in twisted ways to affirm England's chosen status, while greatly diminishing – in extremely belittling terms – our Continental neighbors in a most jingoistic manner. And the xenophobic comments about immigrants were some of the most unchristian statements that I had ever seen, outside of disgusting letters to certain disreputable newspapers.

I was aware of how small turns of phrase and the most subtle of nuances could alter the meaning and outcome of diplomatic documents. There was no subtlety here. Should this be made public, as signed by the Archbishop of Canterbury, there would be fighting in our own streets within the week – and that wasn't even taking into account what footing England would find itself upon against other offended nations who only sought the slightest excuse to escalate toward violence.

"We will need to inform Mrs. Temple about the copy," said Holmes. "Can you go and fetch her?"

Smythe nodded and left the room. We heard him walk down the hallway, his footsteps fading until that side of the building was deadly quiet. Then Holmes jumped from the seat, where he had appeared to be slumped in some sort of middle-aged and defeated weariness. "Watch the door!" he hissed before seating himself at the secretary's desk.

I looked both ways down the hall, but we were alone. "The document – " I began, but Holmes interrupted me.

"No carbon," he said in a low voice. "There is no indication that a carbonic copy of the document was actually made – no smearing of the carbon ink at paper's edge, or where a finger might have touched the ink and then the original. And sometimes when a typewriter strikes a period or comma, it perforates the paper. When a carbon sheet is underneath, this carbon will show up on the back of the original sheet – on the perforated indentation. None of that exists. See for yourself."

I did and confirmed that the back of the sheets in hand were unmarked in the way he described. As I did so, Holmes was quickly opening and closing the drawers, pulling out various typewritten documents that were filed there. Then with a low whistle, he located a box of carbonic paper. He opened it and held some of the top sheets to the light. "New – not previously used." Then he replaced the box and began to go through the sizeable amount of litter in the wastepaper basket beside the secretary's desk.

"Some of these documents are more than three weeks old – clearly it hasn't been emptied in a while. Neither had the Archbishop's basket. There are no used carbon sheets in either place, so it's almost certain that none were thrown away. That's enough proof, I think. No carbon sheets were used, and the fact that the document you hold shows no signs of being copied in such a way is also enough."

"Enough for what?" I asked. "What does this mean?"

"You don't think that I came down here without doing my research?" he asked. "The only person who knew of the existence of this document was the secretary. It was he who took the trouble to notify Mycroft that it had been written and was missing. He has thrown us all – not just you and me and your good wife, but the entire grim machinery of the government – into a frantic scramble of attempted recovery and frantic preparation with his description of how destructive it might be.

"Now, having read it, we see that it's much worse. And how were we able to read the original? Because it was conveniently found for us. Smythe even let us know that it was he who thought of where it was hidden, although he noted that it was Mrs. Temple who recovered it. Now we don't have to take his word for how bad it is – we can read what it says for ourselves! But then he went on to inform us that there is a copy – and it's missing! A copy exists, and we only have only Smythe's word for that too, and as to how this extra document was produced in the first place – a story that's demonstrably false."

"Who is this Smythe?" I whispered. "It seems as if the has much to explain."

"Indeed. And yet, we can't show our hand too soon, before we understand his game. Clearly – "

But it was too late for him to explain further, as I gave a soft "Hist!" when I heard returning footsteps. Holmes slipped out of Smythe's chair, quietly replaced it under the desk, checked to make sure that the secretary's work area and wastebasket looked as they had before, and then settled back in the Archbishop's seat, slumping to the pose he'd held just moments before. He was that way when Smythe, Mrs. Temple, and Priscilla came in, but he pulled himself wearily to his feet and faced them.

"Mrs. Temple," he said, glancing at Smythe, who looked concerned, "it appears that things are not as resolved as we thought but few moments ago. We've just learned that there was a copy of the document, and it is still missing."

The widow held herself steady, only allowing her concern to be expressed by the appearance of a deep V between her brows. "I have read the sheets, Mr. Holmes," she said. "I understand what this could mean." Then Mrs. Temple's voice broke and Priscilla, her arm already holding her, squeezed tighter. "I . . . I don't know what could have happened. What could Frederick have been thinking? Do you think, Doctor," she asked, shifting her gaze from Holmes to me, "that he might have had some illness – a tumor perhaps – that would have made him take such an unexpected and dangerous path? This is so unlike . . . so unlike . . . the man who I was . . . ." With that, she began to weep – possibly for the first time since her husband's death – and pivoted to lay her head on my wife's shoulder.

I nodded toward Priscilla, and she led Mrs. Temple from the room.

"What now, Mr. Holmes?" asked Smythe. "What should we do? Where should we look next?"

"A very good question," responded Holmes. "Time is short, and the copy may already be in the enemy's hands."

I glanced from him to the secretary, my mind racing to catch up. Holmes had determined to his satisfaction that there was no copy, and yet he was going forward as if it actually existed, and allowing Smythe to agree with him. Further, he had proven that the secretary's story of the copied version was false, as well as pointing out that no one actually knew of the existence of this copy except for the secretary who reported it missing in the first place. What was Smythe's game?

The secretary nodded. "I attended the Archbishop's meetings, including those with members of Government. I understand what's going on in the wider world. By 'enemy', you mean Germany."

Holmes nodded. "Our relations with the Kaiser have never been easy, and have only deteriorated since the Queen's death." He paused, looking back and forth across the room as if to see if anywhere else needed examination. "It would make the most sense," he continued, "that, after hiding the original here, the Archbishop carried the copy with him upon his return to London. Are you sure that it isn't there? Did you search his office in Lambeth Palace before traveling here?"

"I did, but not as carefully as I might have. When I recalled that the document was here, I assumed that both copies would be together and hurried down to retrieve them. Then, when I found only the original, I kept the knowledge to myself, not wishing to upset Mrs. Temple further, and also because I knew that you were on your way."

Holmes nodded. "Then there's a good chance that it's still in London. Can you return there as soon as possible to examine the Archbishop's papers? In the meantime, if it truly is missing, I'll alert the Government to take the next steps toward mobilization."

"What do you mean?" asked Smythe.

"Simply this: If the copy of that document has fallen into our enemy's hands, war is imminent. Watson and I have been told that by my brother, Mycroft, whom you know and notified yesterday. If so, we will need every minute – nay, every *second* – to do what we can to prepare, ineffective though it might be."

Smythe swallowed and nodded. "The Germans – they are ready to fight now. That's what the Archbishop thought – that we should fear the Germans."

Holmes nodded. "I'm glad that you understand. Now hurry back to London – on the next train. Search anywhere in the Palace that the Archbishop might have left the copy and let my brother know what you find. In the meantime, I'll see what we can do here."

The secretary nodded and left the room. I followed quietly to the door and made sure that he was gone before turning back to face Holmes.

"Can you explain?" I whispered with some urgency.

"Not entirely," was his tense reply. "The idea of the copied document is an unexpected twist, and the fact that Smythe so clearly lied about it makes his other statements highly questionable as well."

"I see. For instance, we only have his word that Temple typed it."

"Exactly. I've established that Smythe typed it, not the Archbishop. This document – " And he tapped his finger on the four sheets that had been left lying on the desk. " – was executed by a skilled typist. Similar examples can be found in Smythe's desk drawer – samples that he clearly produced. But Temple was a very unskilled typist of the two-finger variety with a very uneven style. This can be verified from documents in his own desk that he clearly wrote himself. So that too is another one of Smythe's lies. The question is *Why*? What does he hope to accomplish, other than to throw the entire Government into a frenzied preparation of war?"

"So you believe, then, that just because there is no carbonic copy then there is no other actual copy at all? If he's such a good typist, he could have simply prepared another original."

"That is true, but he had access to the carbonic paper, and his story is that there was a copy, so why not go ahead and make a copy? For that matter, why 'find' the original and claim there was a copy, when he could just as easily give the original to whomever he wished and stir up as much trouble that way.

"No, he's playing a deeper game. Perhaps all he wishes is to have the country seen to be preparing for sudden war. Our enemies – and allies – can't help but notice it and become concerned, and they may then suddenly begin to escalate for war too. It might take longer for conflict to arise that way than if the letter were to simply be delivered to an embassy or published in the press, but the end result would be the same."

"But how does it benefit Germany to go to war with us now? From all that I've heard from Mycroft over the years, it's inevitable, but they aren't ready yet either."

"Not Germany, Watson. During my research last night, I asked questions regarding several of the players in this drama – some of whom you haven't met, and likely now won't need to. The staff at both the London residence and here, for example. A short *précis* of their various biographies contained a great deal of information, almost all of it quite useless. But I did see that Smythe is a Cambridge man, and that has certain implications."

"What?" I asked. "I don't understand."

"I'll explain later, when I've seen how things progress. In the meantime, I want you to stay here for a few minutes and help your wife comfort Mrs. Temple."

"A while?"

"Yes. Return to London on the next train – it leaves half-an-hour after the one that Smythe will catch – and I'll leave word for you at Victoria when you arrive. Your wife can remain here. In fact, it might be best."

"And where will you be?"

"I intend to be on the same train as Smythe – without his knowledge."

Holmes then instructed me to return downstairs, where he would join me in a few minutes. "Tell them I'm examining the house for signs of intruders."

I found the two women in a small parlor, and was relieved to see that once more Mrs. Temple was in control of her emotions. I explained the secretary's mission, leading them to believe that there was a possibility that the copy was still at Lambeth Palace, carried there a few days earlier when Temple had returned to London. Although I disliked withholding information from Priscilla, I didn't mention that in fact it was almost certain that such a copy as described did not exist, and that the secretary had apparently told us two demonstrable lies, thus undermining anything that he might profess.

Holmes had just rejoined us when Smythe presented himself to us before departing for the station, informing us that if he left then, he'd be in time to catch the next London train. As soon as he was out the front door, Holmes retrieved his case from one side of the room, where it had been left along with our bags since our arrival, and excused himself. Both Priscilla and Mrs. Temple looked at me in confusion, and I rather ineffectively explained that Holmes intended to travel back to London as well, after he made a few preparations.

"What preparations?" asked Priscilla with something that looked like amusement. I realized with a start that she might be enjoying this.

"I don't wish to be identified," replied Holmes, reentering the room almost as soon as he'd stepped out, and setting the case down where he'd removed it a few moments earlier. When stepping into the hall, he'd taken the opportunity to change his appearance into a familiar figure – at least to me – of the venerable old priest who had shared my train compartment as we fled the capital in April '91, just ahead of Professor Moriarty. Back then he'd used his skills to look older, but now, in his late forties, he had grown into the part. I recalled well the wide-brimmed hat and the black cassock. Clearly he'd expected to make use of them, having packed them ahead of time. But then, Sherlock Holmes wasn't anything if not prepared.

"Might I use your telephone?" he asked, and he was directed to a room at the rear of the house. "Any of the staff can show you," added Mrs. Temple.

After he had stepped out once again, I saw that both women had reached the end of their patience and wanted to know what was going on, but I was still evasive. Priscilla seemed to accept that, but the older woman was less tolerant.

"If there is something that you know – something else that is relevant – then I want to know it too." Her square face had a commanding expression, and any hint of the weeping woman from just a few minutes before was gone. Clearly she was able to set aside her grief when necessary.

I was uncertain how much Holmes wanted shared, and simply repeated what they had been told. "Holmes feels that as the original was left here, it only makes sense that the copy might be found London. Mr.

Smythe didn't look for it there before he came to Canterbury yesterday, and he's going back now to check."

Mrs. Temple shook her head. "Clearly Mr. Holmes intends to follow Stephen. I want to know why."

"I'm sorry, Mrs. Temple." I felt uncomfortable being evasive with the two women, one of them my own wife, and the other the widow of the Archbishop of Canterbury. "At times during an affair like this, it's best for knowledge to be held close to one's vest. Holmes likes to hold all the cards –"

"Nonsense! If there's some reason to suspect Stephen, then my opinion needs to be considered!"

"And that is?" asked Holmes, returning into our presence. His telephone call must have been quite brief.

"That I don't trust him. I haven't from the time that Frederick hired him a year ago."

"And why is that?" Holmes glanced at the mantel clock.

"Because he insinuated himself too earnestly, and too quickly. And Frederick was too – it was a weakness he had, especially over the last few years. He wasn't a proud man. He considered it a sin – and rightly too. But he did like it when someone listened to him, nodding and wide-eyed and encouraging him to express his thoughts wherever they might lead. Stephen did that, and I watched with amusement at first, and then with a bit of contempt, I supposed. Finally I quit paying attention to it at all, but I never lost the sense that Stephen cannot be trusted. He never seemed quite sincere, but he was always ambitious."

"I believe that you are correct to think so," said Holmes. He then looked to me. "As I've told Watson on many occasions, I have the greatest confidence in a woman's intuition. What I have strived to learn with such long effort and practice in the way of observation and inference often comes without thought to a woman who sees a dozen different little clues and behaviors and then senses – sometimes without even being consciously aware or able to put into words – that a certain person is exhibiting dishonest behaviors, or any of the objectionable aspects that mankind so often manifests."

I kept silent, remembering when he'd said the exact same thing a year or so after Mary and I had wed, when her opinion had been of especial value during an investigation into the activities of a highly respected minister who in truth was carrying out the most vile and dishonorable acts. Holmes had gathered the evidence, but it was Mary's intuition that had initially pointed the way for him to look.

"I believe that you are correct about Mr. Smythe," continued Holmes. "We'll know in a few hours – and we'll also have determined if the nation is truly at risk because of this dangerous document, or if this is all some sort of conjurer's misdirection. I wish that I had time to discuss it with you further, but now I must fly, for I have just enough time to walk to the station."

"Let me summon the carriage," said Mrs. Temple, rising to her feet and clearly pleased that her opinion had been respected, but Holmes held up a hand. "No need. I can be there shortly. I'm aware of several short-cuts." He turned to me. "Remember – the next train. I'll send word." And then he was gone.

Part III

The next ten minutes or so were rather awkward. The ladies had seen just a hint of Holmes in action, and both knew enough about him to understand that something exciting and important was happening. They also knew that I had knowledge that I wasn't sharing, and they continued to try – at least initially – to get me to tell more than I was willing. It was Priscilla who gave up first, physically throwing her hands in the air with a good-natured smile and telling Mrs. Temple that they would know soon enough. "They like their secrets," she said. "I've already learned that." Then she shook a playful finger in my direction. "But as soon as you can, John, we want the entire story."

I agreed, but saw that Mrs. Temple clearly wasn't prepared to stop querying me that easily. And yet, she too knew that I had told all that I could, and seemed to respect it. Eventually that time had passed and I rose, intending to walk to the station as well, explaining that I was looking forward to it before I too could be offered the use of a carriage.

And in truth I was. It wasn't far, and in spite of the Christmas Eve cold, I wanted to see the famed town decked out in its holiday best, even if I had to hurry through it. Kissing Priscilla and telling them both goodbye, I went to the front hall and retrieved my coat and hat. Then, letting myself out, I set off to the station.

The brisk walk was pleasant enough, but I soon forgot to pay attention as my mind wandered to the curious question of the Archbishop's secretary, and what he was up to. Clearly a document containing such dangerous rhetoric was of great concern, but how it might be used opened up too many pathways of speculation. Arriving at the station, I realized that it was useless to ponder "What If's" without further data. In hopes of mental diversion, I bought a newspaper which contained a great deal about the life of the deceased Archbishop, as well as additional articles about other men who had held the same office, and managed to stay distracted by it during the return trip to London –

– Or at least the portion of the trip wherein I remained awake. I'd discovered that as I aged, I tended to become more sleepy when I allowed myself to relax – and the rocking of a train on Christmas Eve easily contributed to my slumber. I awoke as we arrived at Victoria, and had barely stepped upon the platform while still gathering my senses when a ragged lad approached.

It was Derrick Britton, one of Holmes's current crop of Irregulars. He was a quiet and unsmiling lad, and I wondered if there wasn't some tragedy in his background. However, that was true to some degree with a great many of the Irregulars who had worked with Holmes over the previous decades, and I knew that in spite of their pasts, each was fortunate to be an Irregular, as my friend took them under his wing, making sure that they were fed and clothed and educated, and when they aged past their usefulness as his agents, he found them jobs or other opportunities.

Without a word, Derrick motioned for me to follow. I stepped lively to keep up with him as he nimbly danced through the crowd vacating the train, and soon we were in the street outside and at a cab driven by Abel Whitaker, a long-time acquaintance who frequently made himself available to Holmes when needed.

He nodded. "Step lively, Doctor. We must get you to Clerkenwell."

I turned to offer Derrick a few coins, but he had already vanished into the crowd. Looking back, I saw that Whitaker was favoring me with an impatient expression, so I quickly climbed into his hansom and had barely seated myself when we lurched into motion.

"Where in Clerkenwell?" I called up.

"37a Clerkenwell Green," was the reply. "Mr. Holmes said you'll remember it."

I sighed, recognizing the address,. It wasn't more than a couple of miles from Victoria on a straight line, but the separation between the two couldn't have been greater.

Traveling by the shortest route, we would cross the Thames and be almost within sight of the Palace before riding along some of the city's more prosperous and vital streets. But then north of Holborn, conditions would markedly and rapidly decline. I'd heard the story about how one of Charles Booth's assistants, when making his famous London poverty maps, had asked a constable to describe Clerkenwall. "It's a melting pot," was the reply – not in the sense that Americans use with pride when describing their own country and the strength which comes from the diversity of its many and varied immigrants. Rather, what he meant to tell Booth's man was that the area was "where all the stolen silver or jewels come to be melted or disassembled."

Holmes and I had been there just a few months earlier, when retrieving the specially made anointing oil, made from a secret and ancient recipe that was used on those rare occasions a Royal Coronation took place. It had been stolen in a poor attempt to delay or prevent the event from occurring. [2]

At the time the oil was stolen, we had followed a trail from the Palace to the chemist who prepared the oil, and so on to its recovery. Our way had taken us by 37a Clerkenwell Green and the shabby offices of *Iskra*, one of the many Russian revolutionary newspapers that one found all over London. Knowing that was our destination, I began to shift my perspective as to whether the responsibility for the current situation could be laid at Germany's feet after all.

We turned north along Red Lion Square and into Theobalds Road, winding through an ever-narrowing confluence of streets and dark-bricked buildings. However, instead of driving straight to No. 37a, I found that we were a couple of blocks away. No sooner had we pulled to a stop than Holmes appeared, stepping from a dark alley in our direction.

"I'll settle up later," he called up to Abel Whitaker.

"Right you are, Mr. Holmes," said the cabbie, touching a finger to his cap and turning the horse down a side-street. Rather than watch him depart, I followed as Holmes took my arm and led me into the alley from whence he had appeared.

"Things progress quickly," he said softly as we walked. I pulled out my service revolver. "While still at the residence in Canterbury, I was able to quickly question a few of the staff members. They have no liking for Smythe – 'A snake, that one! A cold snake!' said the cook – and they confirmed that he was often on the telephone when staying in Canterbury."

"But surely that would be part of his job," I said, striving to stay caught up as Holmes turned this way and that in the narrow lanes.

"Ah, but he had two behaviors when making telephone calls – those related to his honest profession were open and aboveboard. But there were others, late at night when it was thought he was alone, which seemed quiet and secretive. 'Sneaking!' affirmed the cook."

"Perhaps a romantic entanglement . . . ?" I asked.

"Perhaps. But while also still at the Canterbury palace, and before my departure, I telephoned Mycroft to set his Myrmidons in motion. As he'd already begun investigating Smythe last night, discovering whom the secretary was calling was no great difficulty. All of the calls were placed to our friend at 37a Clerkenwell Green."

"So it is the Russians who are behind this."

"So it seems."

"And that is where Smythe has gone now?"

"Where he was directed to go. By me."

"What? How did you accomplish that?"

"I contrived it on the journey back to London. The next train from Canterbury had several stops, and I was able to send a telegram to Mycroft during one of them with my plan. He set it into motion as Smythe and I completed the remainder of the journey. Your train was an express, so you've actually arrived at the perfect moment, being able to travel straight through, despite your later departure.

"When our train arrived at Victoria, Mycroft had Bert Deacon in place, ready to meet Smythe and offer him cryptic instructions that he should get to the *Iskra* office immediately – while of course taking all precautions. Thus, Bert was able to take an exceedingly tedious and roundabout way to Clerkenwall while the rest of the plan was put into place."

Bert Deacon was an old acquaintance of ours, a former rampsman-turned-cabbie who owed his life to Holmes after being falsely charged with a capital crime. He made himself available whenever necessary.

"In the meantime," Holmes continued, "Mycroft sent a note to our acquaintance Jacob Richter at *Iskra*, seemingly from Smythe, announcing that he was on his way, and that Sherlock Holmes and Dr. Watson were involved – nothing more than that. Bert should be dropping Smythe off in about five minutes – just enough time for us to get into position."

By that point we had navigated a thoroughly confusing series of alleys, passages, and near-tunnels, some of which we could barely squeeze through while turned sideways. At times the smell was atrocious, and occasionally we were watched by taciturn residents, standing and smoking with apparently nothing better to do. I had felt that we might go on like this for a while longer when Holmes stopped short and nodded toward a plain wooden door in a blackened brick wall. We had only been there for a moment when we heard a low whistle from around a nearby corner. Apparently it was a signal that Holmes recognized, for he nodded and crept forward. He had a lock-pick in hand, but there was no need. The door was on the latch, and he began to open it very slowly – enough so that any noise that it might have made was avoided. We might not have been heard even if the door had squeaked, for there were angry voices at the front of the ground floor.

"Why are you here?" snarled a man with a high-pitched Russian accent – clearly Richter, whom we had encountered the previous August when tracking the holy anointing oil. "I have nothing for you here! And this message – " There was a pause, and I could imagine him holding a paper out to Stephen Smythe. "'*Sherlock Holmes and Dr. Watson are involved.*' Can you imagine what this means? Involved in what? The

Archbishop's statement? What have you done, Smythe? You were told to lie low when the man died."

"It isn't the time to lie low!" was Smythe's hissed reply. "What better time to reveal this, when the Archbishop cannot deny that he wrote it?"

"You have set things into motion which you don't understand, you fool," countered Richter. "Yes, England and Germany will be pushed into war, but our own forces are not yet strong enough to take down the Tsar. We weren't ready for this yet."

"You are a coward, Richter," snarled Smythe. "You have been here since last April, and all you do is meet and plot, scurrying in the shadows like a rat, and you accomplish nothing! I have forced your hand. I've forced all of your hands!"

"You go too fast! The Committee does not agree with how you wrote this." We heard the rattle of paper. "We have been debating it, and choosing who will do the revisions. It wasn't time yet for the document to be released."

"Revisions! Who among you is worthy to revise it? You? Nadya? Georgy Martov?"

"If you're so proud of it," asked Richter, "and so confident that you've done the right thing, then why did you write that Holmes and Watson are involved? Why did you come here seeking my advice?"

"Write to you?" replied Smythe. "I didn't write to you. Who wrote that message?"

"You did. See here?"

There was a pause, and then Smythe answered, his voice suddenly more soft, as if he sensed danger. "I didn't write that. I'm here because of this message from *you*!" And there was another pause, as I imagined Smythe pulling a similar note from his own pocket and handing it to Richter.

The Russian groaned. "Ah, we are undone, you fool! You have walked us into a trap!"

I was surprised then by the sudden loud burst of a police whistle at my side. Without seeing Holmes repeat the action, and knowing what was coming next, I walked forward into the front part of the building, my friend at my side.

Iskra, or *The Spark* as it was known in English, was a shabby operation – nominally a newspaper, but nothing more than an outlet for revolutionary spew. The main office consisted of a number of tables piled with stacks of flyers and pamphlets, written in a number of languages besides English and Russian, and all espousing the same Socialistic claptrap demanding the overthrow of ordered society. Numerous places like this had sprung up all over London in recent years, some with much more influence that the one in which we now stood, facing the two men that had been speaking.

Even as Holmes and I stepped in front of them, their eyes drawn to my service revolver, the front door opened, allowing a number of burly constables and one smaller inspector to boil through.

"Nice to see you, gentlemen," said Inspector Lestrade. I assumed that he meant Holmes and me, and not the two figures standing between us.

Smythe had a wild look in his eyes, as if he might bolt or do something else equally foolish. Whatever might have happened was prevented as he was seized by two Bobbies before he could move. Richter, however, simply looked disgusted, and obviously there was no fight in him.

As when we'd met him in the summer, there was a strong stench about him, as if he'd never washed in his life. He was a very curious fellow to observe, with a high rounded forehead, and a prominent receding hairline that was so noticeable that it seemed to be made of wax. His eyes had a stretched and Mongol-like appearance, and his head was bulbous at the top, and narrowing toward a pointed chin, tipped with an asymmetrical and untidy goatee. As I had previously noted, his complexion was terribly marked by angry red patches of *Erysipelas*.

"You have no right to be here," Richter snarled. "Whatever this man has done has led to nothing. He typed a letter. Has it been published? No, it has not. There is nothing more terrible there than if you, Mr. Holmes, wrote an angry letter to the editor of *The Times* – a really vitriolic thing that would get you sued for all you were worth should it appear – but then you did nothing but file it away. Whatever this man has written has caused no damage at all."

"Wrong!" I cried. "He has impugned the reputation of a dead leader of high noble character whose only mistake was to trust a dishonest man." I flung the words at Smythe, but instead of shame, he simply smiled.

"Richter is correct," he said. "Nothing has been published yet. And in any case, I will swear that the Archbishop wrote that document. One way or another the truth will be told."

Holmes stepped forward, taking care to stay out of the path of my gun, and plucked a series of sheets from Richter's fingers. Looking at them, he nodded.

"He did make a copy after all – but it wasn't a carbonic copy. Rather, it's another original." He looked some more, and then pulled the sheets found in Canterbury from his pocket. Comparing them, he added, "There are some differences, but not enough to mention."

"There are other copies," said Smythe, trying to gain the upper hand, but there was something desperate about him. He would have made a poor card player, as his bluff was desperately obvious.

"I think not," said Holmes. "And even if there are, the government understands the nature of this threat now, and can act most expeditiously to counter it."

Smythe was crumbling, but Richter seemed to become more bold. "Where is your warrant, Inspector?" he asked, turning to Lestrade. "You have invaded my premises, and I see no evidence of a crime. I believe that my attorney will advise that I have grounds for a lawsuit."

"I think not," answered Holmes before the inspector could respond. "You see, Richter – or should I say Vladimir Ilyich Ulyanov, or Nikolai Lenin, or whatever name you're using this week – it's known that your return to London after last summer's ill-advised visit is illegal. The best you can hope for is to be deported back to Russia – although the Tsar's Government will be notified of your return, which might spoil your homecoming considerably. One can only hope. In any case, I would advise that you say away in the future."

He turned to Smythe. "And as for you? Once you tried to set this in motion – no doubt motivated by the death of the Archbishop – your background was immediately given the most thorough scrutiny. It wasn't difficult to see that you had been radicalized while at university." Holmes turned to me. "There is a certain group of Cambridge scholars who have an unhealthy admiration for revolutionary extremists like Mr. Richter here. We would be well advised to keep an eye on them in the future."

Looking back at Smythe, he asked, "The business about a copy – that was to panic the government into preparation for war, setting into motion mirrored activities amongst our friends and enemies, leaving the revolutionaries to carry out their own agenda amongst the chaos. But why not actually make additional copies? Why falsely claim to have done so?"

"I was adjusting my strategy as I went," was Smythe's reply. "When the Archbishop died, I decided to set things in motion, despite this coward's attempts to stop me." He sent a glare toward Richter. "I notified Mycroft Holmes, understanding that he could make the most occur quickly. But then he involved you, and you were coming to Canterbury, and I had no time to make more extensive plans."

"And you didn't notify Richter what you had done, preferring to let things grow on their own so that you could present him with a *fait accompli* before he could object."

"It doesn't matter!" snarled Smythe. "I'll tell the press what was in the document. I'll swear it. Some will believe it! And Richter here – he'll have no choice. He'll have to agree, because it serves his interests as well. He'll – "

"He'll do nothing," interjected Lestrade. "You'll be in an unmarked grave after an early morning firing squad at the Tower if you open your mouth, and Richter is too much of a weasel to say anything, knowing that he's being watched by the British Secret Service. And when he gets sent back to Russia . . . ."

I must have shown my surprise, because Lestrade said to me, "The Yard has been briefed on threats from people like these, Doctor. There's a war coming, all right, and we won't have our hands tied." He glanced back at Richter. "You can tell that to all of your vermin friends."

With that, the inspector jerked his head toward the door and the two revolutionaries were shuffled outside. Richter was deported, but he was back just a couple of years later after the events of Bloody Sunday in Russia in January 1905. He stayed for a while at 16 Percy Circus, this time under the name of Lenin, and with much more notoriety. As for Stephen Smythe: I never heard of him again, and have no idea as to his eventual fate. When I asked Holmes about it a few years later, he vaguely replied that it was a topic best left unexplored.

Within moments, the police had departed, leaving Holmes and me standing in the street in front of No. 37a. I realized that the door was left unlocked, but I made no move to do anything about it, or to ask if Holmes might use his lock-pick if no key was evident. We would do no favors for Richter.

There were a number of idlers watching us from different directions. All had faces ranging from expressionless to hostile, and the idea that this was Christmas Eve was clearly meaningless here. Surely there was no loyalty to a filthy specimen like Richter, so their attitude could only be something deeper. I realized that I still held my service revolver in my fist. Consciously and conspicuously, I slipped it back into my coat pocket.

Holmes, meanwhile, raised his fingers to his lips and blew a shrill whistle. In seconds, the sound of a cab lumbering into motion was heard, and then Bert Deacon drove around a nearby corner, sitting atop a hansom cab.

"Baker Street?" he asked.

"No," said Holmes. "Lambeth Palace."

The journey across London was mostly accomplished in silence, except for a few comments on my part as I thought of them.

"You thought it would be resolved more quickly to bring Smythe and Richter together."

Holmes nodded. "It was a unique opportunity, and by delaying Smythe's arrival, we were able to get the pieces in place to hear their conversation. Each thought the other had arranged the meeting, and fortunately, their previous disagreements gave them enough to discuss that they didn't immediately realize they'd been tricked. In any case, it was really unnecessary – Smythe's plan was already essentially understood at that point. It was just helpful to confirm with whom he was working, and just how many copies of the document we were dealing with."

Holmes pulled out both sets from his coat pocket, flipped through them once more as if to confirm that he had all the sheets, and then replaced them.

"I suppose those will disappear into Mycroft's files," I said.

"They will. He has a number of contingency plans squirreled away that aren't so different from these, but tailored to disrupt an enemy as this would have disrupted us. Perhaps there is some nuance here which will be of use to him – although I doubt it. Mycroft is already a master at these games." He frowned in distaste. "And he keeps trying to pull me in."

I started to reply, but he continued. "And the sad part is, I see no other option but to do so. War is coming Watson – if not with Germany, than with the revolutionaries, or combinations of the two, or even other possibilities that we haven't even imagined yet. It will be an ill wind, and those of us who can stand against it will have to do so, at whatever the cost . . . ."

His voice faded, and his gaze seemed to be focused far beyond the bit of passing street that we could see from the cab.

We arrived at Lambeth Palace some time later, and the door opened as we walked toward it. I was most surprised to see Priscilla coming toward me, her arms outstretched, as if I was a soldier returning home after a long war. She then held me closely for a moment without speaking, and I realized that to her, my participation in Holmes's cases would always seem to involve a certain amount of danger. That, and the death of her friend's husband, had made her especially sensitive on that day.

Inside, Holmes explained to me that he had sent a message to Canterbury at the same time he'd wired Mycroft, during his return to London, telling the ladies that they could return on the next train. They had done so, and had arrived at the Palace just before we showed up. He then spent the next quarter-hour describing our own adventures, thankfully downplaying any danger that we might have faced. (And in truth, when compared to so many other encounters that occurred during our investigations, this was not dangerous at all.)

Priscilla offered to stay with Mrs. Temple, but the older lady stoutly refused. "Be with our own husband on your first Christmas together," was her reply. "I shall be fine. Knowing that Frederick did not write that vile document, and that his faculties had not deserted him at the end, has comforted me more than you can know. Go, and make the best of your holidays."

And so we departed. Outside, Bert Deacon waited atop his hansom, and Holmes waved us toward it. "I'll walk," he advised. "I must brief Mycroft, and in turn learn if anything else is required to clean this mess up." He patted his coat. "And I have a couple of documents to deliver."

"I do hope that you'll join us tomorrow for Christmas Dinner," said Priscilla – not the first time she'd invited him.

He responded as usual. "Thank you, but no. I intend to conduct some chemical experiments – a rather quiet day – and then I'll wander over to see Mycroft at the Diogenes Club."

Having expected that response, Priscilla and I nodded and climbed into the hansom. But as we drove away and saw him following in the same direction on foot, I knew that there were other plans afoot to lure him to our house and our first Christmas together.

But that is another story entirely . . . .

Rev. Frederick Temple, The Archbishop of Canterbury,
and his wife, Mrs. Beatrice Temple

NOTES

1. There is a great deal of controversy over Watson's third wife, whom he married in 1902. Canonically, we know very little about her. As related in "The Illustrious Client", by September 1902 Watson had moved to Queen Anne Street, not so very far from Baker Street. This new residence was in the medical district surrounding Harley Street, and was certainly combined with his new medical practice. In *Hot on the Scent: A Visitor's Guide to the London of Sherlock Holmes* (Calabash Press, 1999, p.73), Arthur M. Alexander has identified Watson's residence and practice as No. 9 Queen Anne Street.

    In January 1903, we learn from Sherlock Holmes in "The Blanched Soldier" that *"The good Watson had at that time deserted me for a wife, the only selfish action which I can recall in our association."* This discreetly implies that Holmes didn't get along as well as he might have with the third Mrs. Watson – but as the many post-Canonical stories in which she appears show, their friendship and respect became a very real and tangible thing.

    In "Watson's Wives and A Question of Chronology", found on my irregular blog, *A Seventeen Step Program* (see link below), I provide some information about Watson's first two wives, and explain why this 1902 wife was Watson's third. I also list a number of stories involving her as pulled from Watson's Tin Dispatch Box by the likes of Michael Mallory, Michael Hardwick, Val Andrews (sometimes writing under his own name, and at others as John North), Stuart Palmer, Bert Coules, M.J. Elliott, Lorraine Daly, Daniel D. Victor, Stephen Kendrick, Donald W. Holmes, Philip Jose Farmer, and Nicholas Meyer, among others. They provide her with a variety of names: Amelia, Tilly, Coral, Emelia, Jean, Anna, Violet, Mary, and Julie – to name just a few.

    The name "Priscilla" as Watson's third wife is first introduced by my friend and excellent author, Tom Turley, in his story, "The Adventure of the Disgraced Captain", to be found in *The MX Book of New Sherlock Holmes Stories – Part XXVII: 2021 Annual (1898-1928)*. I'm very glad that that this current entry, "The Canterbury Manifesto", confirms what Tom introduced to us in that earlier volume.

    https://17stepprogram.blogspot.com/2019/11/watsons-wives-and-question-of-chronology.html

2. These events are described in "The Problem of the Holy Oil" in *The MX Book of New Sherlock Holmes Stories – Part VI: 2017 Annual*, as presented by David Marcum from Watson's original manuscript.

The Case of the Disappearing Beaune
by J. Lawrence Matthews

It was the forenoon of a chilly Christmas Day in the later years of my association with Sherlock Holmes, before he had left London for his retirement upon the Sussex Downs, and I called upon my old companion in his rooms at Baker Street with the gift of a bottle of Scotch whisky and the intention of inviting him to join my wife and me at our home for a traditional Christmas dinner.

I had prepared my words with some trepidation, for I knew Holmes preferred to spend Christmas Day at the chemical table working out some abstruse analysis or other – that is, if we had not been called out on a case that day! He quite welcomed the solitude the holiday season afforded him, especially when Mrs. Hudson took the occasion to visit her family, for it left him alone with his retorts and test-tubes. When darkness fell and his investigations were complete, he would make his way to the Diogenes Club for a quiet supper with brother Mycroft. I should hasten to point out that Holmes's Bohemian routine did not mean the significance of Christmas Day was lost upon him. Rather, he viewed society's embellishments upon it as unnecessary artifice.

"Why, I give thanks every time I enter a church," he would say. "I hardly need to leave my work behind today to be reminded of my blessings!"

And in all our years of companionship, he had never once accepted my invitation to dine.

But I was newly married, and my wife had determined that Holmes would, at last, accept it. The image of two grown men eating their Christmas meal in a hushed dining room surrounded by other silent, mirthless men without the accompaniment of friends, children, or other relations was "too sad to contemplate," she said, sending me out the door with a gift for Holmes and instructions to invite him and, of course, his brother, to a festive meal at our house.

It was her mission to accomplish the seemingly impossible feat of relieving Sherlock Holmes of at least this one of his habits, and I had spent the cab ride to Baker Street gathering my thoughts for the little speech I would make in that effort.

One way or another, she had assured me, Mr. Holmes would attend.

I let myself in at 221b Baker Street with my old latch-key and mounted the stairs while reciting my appeal one final time. Upon entering the familiar rooms, I found a warm fire in the grate and Holmes seated at the chemical table in his dressing-gown, holding a delicate glass tube to his nose and cautiously sniffing at the steam vapour escaping from the neck.

"Ah! Watson!" he exclaimed, turning briefly from his work. "Your Beaune is there upon the mantel, wrapped in some rather fanciful Christmas paper. I would hand it to you myself, but this particular experiment is coming to a head, and I must see it through."

"Thank you, Holmes, and Happy Christmas," said I, finding space for the whisky bottle next to the Beaune atop the mantel and summoning my most authoritative voice. "Mrs. Watson extends her compliments as well, and would be most pleased if you and your brother – "

"Thank you, Watson," Holmes interrupted brusquely. "And please give your dear wife my most gracious thanks. But as you can see, I am rather engaged at present."

I sighed and picked up the Beaune. Then I tried a different tack.

"My wife went to great trouble this year, Holmes. There are two ducks in the oven and the places are already set for you and your brother. It would be churlish indeed not to accept, especially when she has gone to such lengths to accommodate you."

"I thank you, Doctor, and please tell the good Mrs. Watson that although you employed every brand of persuasion in your limited arsenal, I remained unmoved."

My irritation at his firm refusal now gave way to curiosity, for the brightly wrapped bottle of Beaune I had picked up was quite a bit heavier than any wine bottle should be. I removed the wrapper, therefore, and took the bottle to the window, where I could see it was filled with a dark, coarse sand in place of the liquid contents. And the cork had been replaced by a lace handkerchief stuffed into the neck!

Holmes didn't notice my preoccupation. He was gazing intently at his glass tube, seemingly unaware that I hadn't left the room.

"Holmes?" said I, removing the handkerchief and peering down the neck of the bottle.

"Mmm?"

"Holmes!"

He glanced up with an absent expression. "Ah, Doctor, please excuse me for not seeing you out, but the re-agent hasn't had its intended effect, and I must – "

"No, Holmes, it's this bottle. Are you aware of what's inside?"

"Of course! It is an excellent pinot noir of the Gevrey-Chambertin region, made from the premier cru grapes – "

"The premier cru *sand*, you mean."

Holmes gave a start, then twisted around to face me. "I beg your pardon?"

I held out the bottle with one hand and tilted the neck until several small clumps of moist sand dropped into the handkerchief stretched across the palm of my other hand.

"I believe that is sand, Holmes."

He replaced the glass tube in its metal stand, carefully turned off the gas to his Bunsen lamp, and rose from his chair, gazing fixedly at the damp, dirty lumps scattered across the lace fabric.

"What the devil – ?"

He peered intently at my outstretched palm, bringing his nose almost in contact with the substance and vigorously sniffing at it. Then he took up a pinch between his fingers and studied it for some few moments. Finally, he pulled a lens out of the pocket of his dressing-gown and examined the particles on the tips of his fingers intently by the window light. A look of wonder came to his face, and now he put away his lens, rubbed his fingers clean upon his dressing-gown, and motioned for me to give him the bottle, which I did.

"What do you make of it?"

But Holmes did not respond.

He carried the bottle to his chemical table, trained a lamp upon it, once more whipped out his lens and now began studying every inch of the greenish-blue bottle as if it had been discovered at the location of a particularly ghastly crime.

"No finger-marks, I perceive," said he, finally. "Save yours, of course."

"Well, I couldn't have known it was a joke."

"Oh, this is no joke."

"Why do you say that?"

Holmes coaxed a tablespoon of sand out of the bottle and onto his scales, then carefully weighed it. "Hmm!" Now he scooped up a thimbleful and placed it in a glass beaker, into which he added a measure of water before turning on the gas and firing the Bunsen lamp. Then he set the beaker to the flame. When the water had steamed off, the remaining mixture within released a noxious smoke.

"I thought as much," said he.

"What is it, Holmes?"

"This sand is of a unique type," he pronounced. "And it is one with which I may be quite recently familiar."

There was something in his voice which suggested that this little experiment had filled him with a measure of the heightened expectancy that came when a case of particular interest had found its way to his attention.

"You evidently think there is something to this."

"I know there is." He rose and went to his cabinet, opened a drawer filled with small test-tubes containing soil samples from the various districts of greater London, and removed a tube half-full of grains that looked remarkably like those from the bottle of Beaune.

He sprinkled some of these onto a glass slide, set a pinch of the material from my bottle alongside, and sandwiched these two samples beneath a second slender plate of glass. Then he placed this assembly under his microscope, carefully trained light from the table lamp at it, and studied the samples through the lens for several minutes, muttering as he carefully manipulated the plates with one hand and adjusted the focus with the other.

"Hmm. Yes. Hmm! No doubt!"

When at last he looked up, his face was a mask of the gravest concern.

"Mrs. Hudson!" he shouted at the door. "*Mrs. Hudson!*"

"She is with her family. It's Christmas Day."

"Ah, so it is. Well, that explains one small mystery, anyway."

"And what mystery might that be?"

"Why, the mystery of the disappearing Beaune, of course! You don't believe Mrs. Hudson would let somebody enter my rooms while I was asleep to decant this bottle and replace its contents with sand, do you?"

"You mean to say there had been a genuine bottle of Beaune in that package?"

"Of course! I purchased it at Vamberry's, the wine merchant, in the company of brother Mycroft."

"And you didn't notice the change in the contents?"

"How could I? I set the package there upon the mantel that evening and thought no more of it."

"But why would somebody fill the bottle with this . . . *sand*?" I asked, shaking out the dirty handkerchief over the grate.

As I did so, the particles sparked and smoked in the heat!

"I said we had solved one mystery, Watson – how somebody managed to enter my rooms during the night without my knowledge – and I have now grasped the solution to a rather larger mystery on top of that."

"What is that?"

"The mystery of the sand itself. You saw how those particles flamed up in the fire?" He removed the glass slides from beneath the microscope lens and held them to the lamp at his elbow. "The sand evidently derives its bluish color and its flammability from the presence of anthracite coal that was spilled upon a roadway in north-central London and shoveled to the sidewalk awaiting disposal."

"You don't mean to say you can link the sand from this bottle to some dirt piled in the street!"

"Conclusively. The samples match."

"By why on earth would you have concerned yourself with that particular pile of sand in the first place?"

"Because it happens to reside outside the offices of a certain quiet bookseller, a mousy-looking gentleman I strongly suspect of inheriting the mantle of our old friend, the late Professor Moriarty. I was there only three days ago conducting an uninvited inspection of his premises, prior to my visit to the wine-store with brother Mycroft, although it wasn't very revealing. For a public dealer in black-letter editions, he is rather more secretive than the typical merchant. Upon departing, I naturally made certain that a quantity of the anthracite-laced soil outside his door found its way into my pant cuffs, to supplement my little collection of London sediment."

"And you think this bookseller has paid you a visit in return?"

"Most certainly!" Holmes turned off the burner and picked up the test-tube as he spoke in his most didactic manner. "Consider the facts: I retrieve this small measure of sand from a corner of London one afternoon, and three days later an entire bottle of the stuff appears in a wine bottle left upon my mantel. What else could it be but a message from one who sees himself as my adversary?"

"But why do you say the bookseller himself has done this, and not a hired hand?"

"An underling might just as well have slit my throat while I slept rather than go through the trouble of leaving me a bottle of sand. It would have eliminated the danger to his superior once and for all. But whoever did this had no intention of removing me from this mortal coil just yet. He wanted to leave a message from one intellect to the other. Inference: It was the man himself."

"You evidently think this fellow is quite an adversary."

"Indeed, he is. And one day you may learn more about him. But I lack sufficient evidence of my suspicions to even tell you his name."

"What do you propose to do now?"

"I propose to examine the dirty handkerchief which you absent-mindedly tucked into your pocket. It may provide us with other clues."

"Of course." I took it out and gave it to him. He spread it out upon his knee and began to inspect it with his lens.

Almost at once, however, he jerked his head up with a start.

"What do you see?"

"Good God, man!" He leaped to his feet, stuffed the lens in his pocket, and dashed to his bedroom, waving the handkerchief. "We leave at once!" he called over his shoulder. "And bring that wine bottle!"

"Where are we going?" I asked when he reemerged, now dressed for the cold weather.

"To the Diogenes Club – we must alert brother Mycroft!"

Holmes picked up his gloves and cap, then held the door open for me.

"You think that handkerchief signals some danger?"

"I know it does," said he, urging me through the door.

"But it's only a handkerchief that was used to plug a wine bottle!"

"I think it is rather more than that," he said, following me through the door and latching it behind us.

"What makes you say so?"

I have said before that my companion found it difficult at times to conceal his impatience with minds less keen than his own, and now was one of those times. He halted at the top of the stairs and held out the square of lace fabric when I turned to face him, his finger pointing to a tiny, delicately embroidered monogram in one corner.

"That is the mark of the former Prince of Wales," he said sharply. "Our newly crowned King of England. And why this article from his wardrobe was employed to stop up a wine bottle left in my rooms is something we need to determine with all due speed."

Then he dashed past me down the stairs.

As we descended to the front hallway we could hear a banging upon the outside door, and when Holmes opened it there stood before us an out-of-breath messenger, bent over and gasping for breath, an envelope in his outstretched hand. Holmes grabbed the envelope, ripped it open, and glanced at the message. Then he handed it to me without comment.

It read in this way:

Diogenes Club. Come at once.

M

Holmes pressed a coin into the hand of the still-bent-over-and-breathless young man and began searching for a cab, but traffic was light, and we didn't encounter any until reaching the Marylebone Road. There he flagged down the first hansom we saw and shouted the address as we climbed in.

"Fast as you can, driver!"

The cabby gave the horse its head, and so speedily did we rattle along the cobblestones that conversation was impossible. I merely hung on for dear life while Holmes stared out the window, grim-faced, and occasionally marked our progress in his quiet impatience to get there.

"Portman Square... Grosvenor Square... here we are. The Diogenes Club. Thank you, driver."

"Bless you, sir!" said the fellow as Holmes handed up a half-sovereign before dashing away. "Happy Christmas, sir!"

By the time I joined him, Holmes was already in discussion with the young doorman in front of the club.

Brother Mycroft, it seems, had been called away.

"But I just received a note from him!" Holmes said with some surprise.

"Well, sir, I'm afraid he went out, sir. And in a very big hurry he was."

"When was this?"

It took a moment for the doorman, who wore a heavy coat and muffler against the chill, to retrieve his watch.

"It was an hour ago, sir. Exactly one hour – "

"Impossible! The messenger only just brought us his note!"

"I can't speak to that, sir. I can only tell you Mr. Mycroft departed an hour ago."

Holmes appeared considerably agitated.

"And where did he go?"

"Don't know his destination, sir." The young man nodded up the street. "But he went that way – by cab." A queer look came to the doorman's eyes, and he seemed reluctant to say anything more.

"What is it?" said Holmes impatiently. "What are you hiding from me?"

"I'm sorry to tell you this, sir, but Mr. Mycroft was called away by a woman."

"A woman? Called for my brother? What sort of woman?"

"An attractive woman, sir, if that is your sort of thing. Very red hair. A bit on the rough side, but well-enough put together if I may say so. She called here in great agitation for Mr. Mycroft. Said she had information only he could understand."

Holmes put his gloved hand to his chin in wonder. "That sounds like Miss Kitty Winter, does it not, Watson?"

"It does indeed."

"By why would she come here for Mycroft?" Holmes asked himself. "And not to me?"

He glanced sharply at the doorman.

"Well? Did you hear nothing of her errand?"

"Not exactly, sir."

"'Not exactly'! What then? What did you overhear?"

The doorman appeared greatly disturbed. He glanced back at the door as if worried we were being observed.

"Well, what was it, man?" Holmes urged.

"I'm sorry, sir, but it is quite against club rules to repeat the conversation of a member to another person in the event that such person wasn't the intended recipient of that information," said the doorman, reciting the relevant by-law he had evidently learned by heart.

"You do know who I am?" said Holmes

"Yes, sir. Of course, sir."

"And you know that Mycroft Holmes is my brother."

"Of course, sir. But the rules – "

"Do those rules govern your conduct if the club member is involved in a matter of life or death?"

The doorman flushed. "I'm sorry, sir," said the chastened young man. "What I heard was, I heard them say something about a 'Lestrade.'"

"Lestrade!"

"Yes, sir. Mr. Mycroft said they must 'take it to Lestrade'."

"What then?"

"Well, this red-haired woman begins to pull away from him. Gets very excited, like. Says she can't go with him."

"And what did my brother do?"

"He says, 'If you don't come with me to Lestrade, my Lady, I'll have you in the dock on Boxing Day!' And off they went."

"Thank you, my good man."

But the fellow refused Holmes's offer of a tip. "Club rules, sir. I thank you all the same, sir."

Holmes shrugged and turned away.

"Mycroft and Miss Winter make for Scotland Yard. Come, Watson. Off we go."

No cab could be seen, however, and we began the short walk along Pall Mall in the direction of the Yard, Holmes sunk in the deepest thought.

It was I who called attention the mysterious driver.

His carriage – a rather fine-looking brougham – had been standing idle perhaps a hundred yards back up the road and opposite the Diogenes Club. It now started up and followed us slowly, pausing each time I glanced backward. When we eventually turned into the Strand, and the driver also made the turn, I nudged my companion.

"Holmes," said I, "we are being followed."

"And what of it?" Holmes continued his brisk pace, his mind evidently on the task at hand. "Ever since my return from the Continent eight years ago, I am watched wherever I go."

"Shouldn't we do something?"

Holmes chuckled grimly and shook his head.

"If he's like the others, he'll develop a thirst and stop at the pub soon enough. I think we owe it to His Majesty to get to Scotland Yard with all due speed."

"But this fellow is driving a gentleman's carriage."

Holmes started. "A carriage?"

"Yes. And he's been following us ever since we left the club."

"Excellent," said Holmes, without turning his head or pausing in his stride. "Can you describe the man?"

"No. He's wearing a cap pulled down almost to his eyes, and almost certainly a false beard."

"Does he know you have spotted him?"

"I think he does."

"Well, it cannot be helped." Holmes quickened his pace. "We're almost at the Yard. This is evidently a crisis of some national importance."

"Why do you say that?"

"You know that our new King was coronated less than four months ago?"

"Yes, I do live in England."

"And what better time to instigate a threat to the Crown when a new head of state wears it?"

"But why would this handkerchief signify a threat to the Crown?"

"You still don't see it?"

"No."

"A situation that demands the attention of both Mycroft Holmes of His Majesty's government and Inspector Lestrade of Scotland Yard cannot be a trivial matter to begin with. But when a handkerchief somehow makes its way from the King's new holiday retreat to my sitting room in London at this critical moment – why, it becomes positively momentous, don't you think?"

"But supposing it was found elsewhere by this bookseller or his agents and the timing is a coincidence? The King does have a reputation for indiscreet assignations, does he not?"

"He may have had a reputation, but he is undoubtedly our new head of state, and however the handkerchief was acquired, I think the message in that bottle is clear enough: There is danger to the King, and it stems from that nondescript bookseller."

"But why would this fellow leave you such a clue? Why not act first and take credit later?"

"Bravo, Watson! I have been wondering that myself. I rather think that is precisely what he intended, but thanks to the good Kitty Winter – if she is indeed the red-head who appeared at my brother's club this morning – I fancy his plans have been disarranged. She has brought some premature indication of the matter to Mycroft."

"Why would she go to him first, and not you?"

"That, also, I have been wondering, but I think I have worked it out." Holmes raised an eyebrow. "Miss Winter now inhabits a rather more refined circle of acquaintances than you might remember, and I have no doubt she is known to members of the Diogenes Club – not Mycroft, of course, but she would certainly know of his standing at Whitehall thanks to those other . . . friends. And if this plot involves our head of state, she has enough brains to realize it is Mycroft who must be informed at once, not his brother."

"Why, then, did she resist going with him to Lestrade?"

"The answer to that is rather more obvious, I think. You recall that Miss Winter spent some little time in prison for that vitriol-throwing incident involving the detestable Baron Gruner? Then you'll understand why she would have no desire to be reunited with the police."

"I suppose you're right"

Holmes glanced behind us as we crossed a street.

"But so have you been. We're being followed, and not by one of the dull fellows with whom I'm familiar. No, no – don't turn. Just keep walking. Whatever is planned for the King must be stopped, and we cannot be distracted from our task."

"Why should we go on to Scotland Yard, then? Why not make directly for Sandringham?"

"Because it may not be there that Mycroft and Lestrade are bound. You yourself indicated the King's appetites took him rather far afield. He could be anywhere, in town or country. Mycroft and Lestrade may not have had to leave town to find him."

"But how will we know where they went?"

"An inspector of Lestrade's rank is on call every hour of the day, even a holiday such as Christmas, and precisely for occasions like this. Once I've determined where he has signed himself out for the next few hours, we can make our next move."

The sergeant at the desk seemed not the least bit surprised at the appearance of Sherlock Holmes at Scotland Yard on Christmas Day, and he answered Holmes's questions promptly.

Yes, Inspector Lestrade had been called to the Yard – by a rather portly fellow in the company of a red-headed woman. The woman had told her story to the inspector, and then she was dismissed. Inspector Lestrade and the portly fellow left together by cab. No, the doorman didn't hear what was discussed. Yes, of course, Sherlock Holmes could inspect the time sheet.

He glanced at the book, thanked the sergeant, and turned on his heels.

"The 1:15 from St. Pancras, bound for Sandringham," Holmes said, searching for a cab.

"We have thirty minutes," said I. "Ought we get my service revolver on the way?"

He glanced at his watch and considered this for a moment.

"Your house is not so far out of our way that we would miss the train, provided the gun is a hand?"

"In my desk drawer, and newly cleaned."

"Excellent. Then we will make our way there at once."

"Certainly, if you think it is warranted."

"Oh, I do," he said gravely.

A cab had pulled alongside us, but Holmes waved him off.

"Why did you send him away?" I asked in some perplexity as the hansom drove away. "Surely you don't propose we walk to my house!"

"Surely not. But I rather think we must be more careful from here on. Our adversary plays a deep game. That cabby was waiting for us."

Holmes shook off the next cab as well. Then he crossed the street to an idle hansom. The driver had been adjusting a strap on his horse, but he nodded when Holmes asked if the cab was available, and soon we climbed in. I hadn't taken a seat when Holmes shouted my address and the cab abruptly lurched forward. Holmes sat back in the cushions and stared out the window, lost in thought.

On Regent Street we soon caught sight of a Salvation Army band with a white-bearded, costumed Santa singing Christmas tunes of various countries in a beautiful tenor. As we drew near them, something caught Holmes's ear. He sat bolt upright and stretched out his hand to me.

"Is your cap precious to you?"

"I beg your pardon?"

"Your cap. I perceive it is not your best."

"Well, no. My wife thought my old faithful was a bit ragged, so she took it to the shop for repairing. I used this ancient one instead." I handed it to him ruefully. "You're concerned I won't look presentable at Sandringham?"

"No. I'm concerned about what's inside that wine bottle." Holmes placed my cap upside down on the floor of the cab and stretched out his hand to me.

"Now, the bottle. May I have it?"

"Certainly."

I removed the bottle from my inner pocket and he took it. But instead of examining it with his lens as I had expected him to do, he turned the bottle upside down, pointing the neck at the floor of the cab. Then he began shaking it violently, spreading clumps of dirty sand into the cap at our feet.

"What on earth are you doing?" I cried.

He ignored my question and continued shaking out sand until a quantity had been released. Then he stopped his efforts, righted the bottle, and peered into the neck. "Hmm!"

Once more he turned over the bottle and resumed his baffling method of spilling out the contents, like a child without any regard as to the consequences.

"Holmes! May I ask what you're doing?"

"The sand, Watson. The sand!" he cried, once more righting the bottle and peering into the neck. Then he resumed his attack upon my poor cap. "What else is in this bottle besides sand?"

Holmes continued in this fashion, alternately emptying the bottle and peering inside it until only a few grains appeared to be left. Finally, giving the upside-down bottle a good thump with his free hand, a small, dirty, slender object plopped out of the neck and into the center of my cap.

Holmes picked it up in triumph, rubbed it clean and held it to his eyes. "I knew it!"

"Knew what?"

"The prize. I knew I'd find it!"

I shrugged my shoulders. "It looks like a dirty almond."

"It is an almond. *The* almond. From the Risalamande!"

"The riss-ala-*what*?"

"Risalamande. Rice pudding! The traditional Danish Christmas dessert. A single almond is mixed in with the pudding, and whoever finds the almond in their bowl gets an extra helping at Christmas dinner."

"And you thought you might find one in the sand?"

"I knew I would find it there. Once I heard that tenor singing the Danish tune, I remembered."

"Remembered what?"

Holmes fixed his eyes upon me.

"Alexandra, the Princess of Wales, is a Dane."

"Why, you're right. But what does it indicate?"

He placed the almond in his watch pocket and resumed his gaze out the window, his face now a mask of concern. Then he spoke slowly and gravely.

"It indicates, I fear, that the threat isn't reserved for the King only. It means an attack upon his entire family – perhaps the very line of succession!"

"How can we stop it?"

"By getting your revolver and making the 1:15 from St. Pancras."

Our cabman, however, evidently had other ideas.

We were flying up Tottenham Court Road and Holmes was silently mouthing the names of each street as we passed when I noticed him tense up. We hadn't yet reached the turn into the series of streets leading to my house, but the cab was already slowing down.

Holmes banged on the ceiling.

"Not here!" he shouted. "Don't turn here!"

But it was too late. The cab turned left down a narrow side-street.

"Goodge Street!" Holmes cried. "Why are you taking Goodge? It's a by-street! We'll never make it in time!"

The cabby ignored Holmes's shouts. Instead, he turned back onto Tottenham Court Road heading in the wrong direction!

"Brace yourself! This fellow isn't our friend. We'll have to jump for it at the next intersection." Holmes grabbed the door handle and pulled himself forward, crouching.

Sure enough, the cabby slowed suddenly, and at that instant Holmes threw open the door and leaped out. I followed him just as the cab suddenly started up again.

"Shall we pursue him?" I cried. "I have the bottle as a weapon!"

"No. That is precisely what he wants us to do."

"Then what?"

"We find another cab, but this time we use rather more discretion than the last." Holmes waved down the next hansom that came along, but instead of climbing in, he held the horse's reins and spoke to the young cabman.

"For whom do you drive?"

"McKenna's, Guv!" responded the somewhat startled cabby. "Why d'you want to know?"

"Where are the stables?" Holmes said sharply.

"Off Vincent Square!"

"Good. This cab should serve our purpose." Holmes gave him my address and climbed in. As we sped away, I asked about the cabby that had hijacked us.

"That fellow was in league with the bookseller, I suppose?"

"I have no doubt. The man plays a very deep game, arranging three cabs outside the Yard . . . I thought I was being careful enough rejecting the first two."

"You mean to say this entire journey – "

"Planned by my bookseller, yes. The same fellow who placed that bottle of sand upon my mantel with the King's handkerchief jammed into the neck and that fine touch of the almond in the 'pudding'. He evidently means to keep us from arriving at St. Pancras on time. But we will, Watson. By the Lord Harry, we will – and with your revolver!"

The cab turned into Queen Anne Street and Holmes ordered the driver to slow his pace while he instructed me on how to handle my brief visit home.

"Make it quick, Watson. And don't upset your wife. Pretend all is well. But don't remove your coat or hat – you'll need to make a hasty exit after you secure your revolver."

"But how should I explain my leaving her again?"

Holmes considered this for a moment, then nodded at my bare head.

""You have lost your cap thanks to my exertions with the wine bottle, but that works in our favour. You will enter the house and go immediately to your den to retrieve your revolver. When your wife asks what you did with your hat, act flustered. You have forgotten it and must fetch it. Do not tarry – "

Holmes had stopped speaking and was staring down the street towards my doorstep. As I followed his gaze, I let out a hoarse yell of shock and rage. The elegant brougham that had followed us to Scotland Yard was now standing outside my door! And a woman with flaming red hair was being pulled from the carriage by the man with the false beard who had followed us! The blackguard appeared to wrestle her to my front door, upon which he banged with his fist until it was opened. Then they disappeared inside, the girl giving a last wave of her arms in helpless agitation.

"Wait, Watson!" cried Holmes as I jumped from the cab, making a hard landing on the cobblestones. I was attempting to raise myself from my knees to dash to the house when I felt Holmes's strong hand gripping my shoulder.

"Watson! Stay yourself! This isn't the time to act in haste!"

"But the fiend has entered my house!" I cried, trying to break free of his powerful grip.

"Yes – but I am almost certain his aim isn't to bring harm to your wife."

"How can you know that? Let go of me!"

"Steady on! Think! That fellow entered by the front door with the unfortunate Miss Winter, in full view of us. Why? I rather think he wishes to draw us in. I told you my bookseller plays a very intelligent game, and this is all a part of it."

"Whether he wants me in the front or not, that's where I'm going! Leave go of my arm!"

"Please, this is no time for rashness."

"Time enough! My wife is in that house!"

"Yes, and so is a bruiser in the employ of one very dangerous bookseller. We must use our wits, not our fists."

I slackened my efforts at shaking off Holmes's grip.

"That's better. Yes, the more I think of it, the more I'm convinced that the scene upon your doorstep was designed to prompt a rash move on our part."

"But what, then?" I cried my voice filled with frustration. "What can we do?"

"First we summon the police." Holmes thrust a gold sovereign into the hands of the waiting cabman, who had been looking on in some consternation from beneath his cap. "Fly at once to the nearest police station! Tell the sergeant at the desk what you have seen here! Now!"

As the hansom clattered away, Holmes drew me into the shadow of a doorway from which he studied the scene several doors down, all the while keeping a grip of my sleeve.

"What are you doing?"

"What I should have been doing all along. Observing."

Holmes studied the passing traffic, which was light, then craned his neck at the houses nearby and the windows overlooking my doorstep.

"Well?" said I impatiently.

Holmes shook his head. For the first time in my many years by his side I perceived a state of perplexity emanating from his every word and gesture.

"I don't understand it. Why *your* house? Does this bookseller seek merely to cause us to miss the train? If so, surely any diversion would have done. And why Kitty Winter? If Mycroft and Lestrade have already heard her story, what need would there be to kidnap her? I should think all his efforts would have gone towards preventing Mycroft and Lestrade from taking that train. Unless . . . ."

"Unless what?"

"Unless his goal in this little chess match is to eliminate my powers of reasoning from whatever he is planning for the Royal Family."

"But you have yourself said that your brother's powers of deductive reasoning are far greater than your own."

"And they are." Holmes suddenly relaxed his grip, and a twinkle came to his eye. "But not by much!" he cried.

"You see a way?"

"There is a mews behind these houses, is there not?"

"Yes."

"And your kitchen opens into the mews?"

"Yes, but why? You suspect he will depart in that way?"

"No. His carriage is tied up out front, so I hardly think he will depart through the kitchen. Rather, I expect you will enter that way."

"But why the kitchen? He entered in the front!"

"Precisely. He wants you to follow him there. He knows your instinct for action. You believe your wife is in peril and you will naturally charge straight in after him. Therefore, you will do the opposite."

"To what end?"

"To this end: While you appear to be attempting to outfox the man by entering through the rear of the house, I will be making my way by stealth to the front door to take him unawares. You have your latch-key? Give it to me. Thank you."

Holmes stuffed the key in his pocket and glanced at his watch. Then he put his hand upon my shoulder and gazed at me with the piercing grey eyes that told me he had recovered his masterful self.

"It is five minutes to the hour. Make your way around by the mews to your kitchen, but not so quietly that your deception fools the ruffian! Rather, peer in through the barred window, bang into the dustbins, rattle the door-latch. Make yourself known! Then, exactly upon the hour, force the door open – with your shoulder if need be! That will be my chance to enter by the front, and we will have him!"

Holmes squeezed my arm and gave me a knowing smile.

"Mrs. Watson will be unharmed, Watson. It's me they want."

I could hardly disagree.

Several minutes later I was in the mews peering in at my kitchen window and bumping into the dustbins in accordance with Holmes's instructions. Then I tested the door. It was unlatched. I wouldn't need to use my shoulder to break it open, although, in truth, I had no intention of breaking into my own kitchen.

One minute before the hour I simply let myself in.

I pressed my finger to my lips when the cook looked up from her dishes to greet me, then made my way past the two large roast ducks and the plates piled high with boiled vegetables and roots of all kinds. Entering the dining room on tiptoe I found to my greatest satisfaction that it was filled with the friends and relations who had gathered to share Christmas dinner with Sherlock Holmes.

There were Kitty Winter of the flaming red hair and Shinwell Johnson, now stripped of the thick false beard of the brougham driver, enjoying their punch together and looking no worse for the little scene they had acted out upon my doorstep. And there were the five grown up Baker Street Irregulars, now shorn of the heavy mufflers, wigs and caps that had disguised them during their cab driving, doorman, and messaging duties, all with smiles upon their faces as they regaled Inspector Lestrade with the tale of how they had managed to pull one over on their esteemed old taskmaster, Mr. Sherlock Holmes.

And, of course, there was my wife, looking as happy as I had ever seen her in the knowledge that my friend and companion would finally be sharing our Christmas Day meal.

I caught the expectant eye of Mycroft Holmes, standing tall and portly beside the hall door on the opposite side of the room, and signaled that all was ready.

Exactly upon the hour a distinct metallic snick could be heard coming from the front latch. My wife held a finger to her lips to quiet our guests while Mycroft Holmes made certain the dining room door to the front hall was closed just enough to hide us from view.

Then a hush fell over the room.

Soon the faint creaking of a hallway floorboard could be heard, and everyone took in their breath when a slight vibration came to the door, signaling that Holmes's cautious hand had gripped the door-handle. And when the door was finally thrown open, we all beheld the astonished face of Mr. Sherlock Holmes.

There was confusion in his eyes, then what appeared to be a sudden realization of what had been done to bring him to our door, and, finally, embarrassment as a crimson flush overcame his pale, austere features.

In that instant, I felt regret, even shame for my actions.

How could I have been so wrong?

To embarrass my old companion in front of all these friends?

And on Christmas Day!

I berated myself in silence.

It was, of course, at my wife's instigation that the plot had been carried out, and I couldn't deny that Mycroft Holmes had enthusiastically approved of her notion, although he had doubted from the outset that his brother could be as thoroughly fooled as the expression upon Holmes's face indicated. Indeed, Mycroft had taken up his part with gusto, devising and staging the elaborate ruse that had roused his brother from the perfect contentment of the chemical table to this gathering of which it plainly appeared he wanted no part. Nor had any of the other participants expressed a reluctance to do their share. Quite the opposite! To a person they had been overjoyed at the prospect of being able to demonstrate in some small measure the esteem and affection in which they held this supremely rational man, whose efforts in the pursuit of observation and deduction had enriched the lives of everyone in that room.

But whether the ghastly expression upon my friend's face sprang from embarrassment – that he, the self-possessed master of observation and deduction, had been utterly fooled in that department – or mortification at the presence of so many individuals to whom he would be expected to exhibit the good graces and proper manners of the season, when in truth he would rather be alone, looking over some chemical compound or other, it was quite clear to me that his reaction to our scheming wasn't what I had anticipated.

Nor would it in any way suit the spirit of the season.

I was clearing my throat to bring the proceedings to a hasty end when Holmes somberly shook his head and motioned me to silence.

At that moment I felt my wife's hand curl around mine and squeeze it in the encouraging manner of the spouse who knows when a hard truth is to be revealed to her mate, and he needs to know he isn't alone to face it.

But then Holmes's startled round eyes gave way to a crinkled look of merriment, and a wide smile replaced the open-mouthed expression of shock upon his lips, and he began to laugh such a laugh as I had never heard from my friend and companion.

Then we all laughed, and tears of relief came to my eyes as one, by one, every person in that room greeted Mr. Sherlock Holmes with the Compliments of the Season using expressions of the utmost respect and deepest affection. And those affections were returned by Holmes, albeit in his own rather stiff and demure manner, to each in turn.

But his greatest warmth, I am pleased to say, was reserved for my wife.

It was when we were seated at the table and the meal had been placed before us that brother Mycroft began to explain how a visit to the Diogenes Club by Mrs. Watson one evening early in December – to the consternation of the club's membership, mind you – had resulted in the day's intricate staging. Mycroft said he had taken such delight in preparing the trap for his brother that he had inadvertently caused something of a scandal when his request for a disused handkerchief with the mark of the

King from his Highness's private secretary caused a stir at Downing Street, and a reprimand from the Prime Minister.

Mycroft was describing with relish the unconventional method by which Wiggins and the other Baker Street Irregulars whom he had been able to round up for the occasion had procured the sand from the sidewalk outside the mysterious bookseller whose affairs his brother had been monitoring, when I interrupted him.

"One moment, Mycroft. I imagine our esteemed guest by now has worked out all the details himself and wouldn't be averse to sharing with us the explanation of how your great feat was accomplished?"

"I daresay you know my brother as well as I do, Doctor," said Mycroft Holmes, turning his attention to the food on his plate. "Sherlock?"

"Why, thank you, Mycroft." Sherlock Holmes wore a satisfied grin. "I believe I do possess all the threads of the little adventure that led me here – 'The Case of the Disappearing Beaune,' eh Watson? – and if it pleases Mrs. Watson, I will do as the good doctor suggests and enumerate them while the rest of the company feast upon this most succulent-looking duck, knowing that my brother will not hesitate to point out where I go wrong."

Once more we all laughed together, and then the masterful and assured figure of Sherlock Holmes began to speak in his crisp, didactic fashion, describing the various methods by which the grown-up men, formerly of the Baker Street Irregulars, with the able assistance of Miss Kitty Winter and the estimable Shinwell Johnson, had enacted the elaborate stage-play crafted by Mycroft Holmes, with the assistance of Inspector Lestrade and my own small contributions.

"But it was the almond that was a stroke of genius, Mycroft," he concluded, with evident respect for his brother's talents. "I was certain we were facing a plot against the entire Royal Family."

Mycroft Holmes shrugged demurely. "Suggested by a Danish emissary whose brain I picked over lunch at the Club one day."

"Bravo, Mycroft. Bravo! There is, however, one thing upon which I am not clear," said Holmes. "Surely it was a coincidence that those Salvation Army musicians were playing Danish Christmas tunes on Regent Street as Watson and I drove past?"

"Not a bit, Sherlock. Every movement was choreographed, down to the old cap worn by Watson!" Mycroft then nodded at the young man across the table who, as a boy, had led the group of street urchins that were once the eyes and ears of Sherlock Holmes throughout the slums and by-ways of London. "Mr. Wiggins here has a most pleasing tenor, wouldn't you agree?"

"But what if I hadn't been looking out the window on that side of Regent Street?"

"Dr. Watson made certain you entered the hansom first!"

Holmes fingered his glass of the Beaune which had been rescued from the bottle in his own sitting room.

"My compliments, Doctor. Very well played. But as to Wiggins and the rest of you Baker Street Irregulars – " Here Holmes studied their faces with a stern countenance that caused me once more to hold my breath. "I'm sorry I trained you so well!" Then he broke into a smile and raised his glass.

"To the Irregulars!"

"The Irregulars!" we all toasted.

And once more we laughed, and none more so than Wiggins and his mates.

When the company were again subdued, Holmes made his final, and altogether softer and most sincere toast.

To my wife.

"Madam," said he, "I thank you for opening your home to Mycroft and me. I shall not refuse your kindness again."

And he wouldn't.

Such were the true circumstances behind the most satisfying Christmas Day I would spend with Holmes – indeed, one of the best days of the many of all our years of friendship.

And each year thereafter, even after he had left London for his cottage upon the Downs to tend his bees and write his memoirs, Sherlock Holmes attended our Christmas feast.

No invitation was necessary.

A Price Above Rubies
by Jane Rubino

Chapter I – The Singular Narrative of Miss Edith Woodley

In the more than two decades of my association with Sherlock Holmes, I can honestly say that the passage of time had not staled the infinite variety of his cases. There were the commonplace and the bizarre, the perilous and the comic, those which called upon his full mental and physical powers to bring about a resolution, and others where that resolution would likely have come about unaided, and where friend's only contribution was to hurry it along.

Such a case presented itself on a snowy morning, three days before the Christmas of '02. I had called at Baker Street to wish my friend the Compliments of the Season, and saw that the curtains at the ground floor window had been drawn back to reveal the bustling figure of Mrs. Hudson hanging, surveying, and then transposing the ornamentation on the large Christmas tree in her sitting room. From past experience, I knew that this exercise had begun immediately after the tree was carried into the house, and would occupy her every spare moment until, some time in early January, it was relieved of its embellishments and carried out again.

"Excellent work, Mrs. Hudson! It is perfection itself!" I greeted as I stepped into her sitting room to survey her handiwork, but she wasn't to be praised out of her conviction that the gilt angel had been placed too low, the blown glass orb too high, and that a few clove-studded oranges must be added to keep the ants from the gingerbread.

"Is he engaged?" I asked, and the landlady's reply was to wave me toward the stair as she scrutinized the tarnish upon her set of brass figurines.

I left her to her task and went up to our old rooms to find Holmes lounging on the sofa, wrapped in his worn purple dressing gown and puffing grimly upon his after-breakfast pipe.

"How does the tree get on?" Holmes greeted.

"As it always has," I replied. "When Mrs. Hudson is done with its transformation, it will look precisely as it did last year, and every year before that."

"Well, well, novelty and variety may add charm to one's profession, but they aren't always desirable qualities in our traditions. Some of those are better left unchanged."

"Then allow me to offer a traditional gesture," I said and handed him my gift, wrapped in red tissue paper.

He unwrapped it and chuckled when he saw that it was a copy of Johann Westphal's biography of Copernicus and then waved me toward his desk where I found a box of fine Havana cigars half-buried beneath a mound of envelopes.

"Your practice has the charm of variety, I see – or of volume, at least."

Holmes raised his eyebrows, quizzically.

"Most of these letters are unopened," I said with a nod toward the correspondence. "If you leave so many appeals unattended, then it follows that you have a great many others to occupy you."

"And yet, I am as you see me," he sighed, with a wave toward his worn dressing gown and the litter of newspapers on the carpet. "No, no, Watson, those aren't professional summonses. They are accursedly social. It is the bane of my success, and your determination to trumpet it, that my former clients will express their gratitude by encumbering the post with invitations to dine. They are especially persevering at this time of year. Here – " He frowned, and poked through the newspapers on the carpet with the stem of his pipe. " – is a sample of the professional appeal that the season of good will brings to my door."

He plucked a sheet of writing paper from the heap and tossed it to me.

My dear Mr. Sherlock Holmes, [I read aloud]

I have heard that you can see clearly into the workings of the mind and heart, and as there is no one I can rely upon to be impartial in the matter, I would be grateful to have your opinion regarding a proposal of marriage. If it will not inconvenience you, I will call at ten o'clock on Monday morning.

Edith Woodley

"I have sunk," he groaned, "to serving as our fair city's Beatrice Fairfax."

I couldn't help laughing at his downcast expression, and then the splash and clatter of hooves and the grate of carriage wheels drew me to the window, and I looked down to see a brougham-and-pair draw up to our door.

A young gentleman sprang to the pavement and, after a sharp glance up and down the street, he turned to hand down a lady whose features and figure were concealed by a long, hooded mantle. In her hands, she carried a metal chest of some sort which, from an exchange of gestures, I concluded the gentleman offered to carry for her, an offer which she refused. She paused before the lower window for a moment to admire our landlady's handiwork, and then stepped up to our door.

"Miss Woodley, I take it." Holmes rose from the settee, laid his pipe aside, and began sweeping the newspapers into a pile.

"It is a lady and gentleman. The lady carries a peculiar sort of metal box. Perhaps they are friends of Mrs. Hudson, come to deliver some token of the season."

"No, no. It is just ten o'clock now, and while the lady's note suggests an *affaire de coeur*, she writes with an economy that often goes in hand with punctuality."

Holmes was proved correct, for a moment later the page appeared bearing two cards upon the salver that identified the visitors as Alexander MacLeod, M.D., and Miss Edith Woodley.

"Stay, Watson," said Holmes as he dashed into the bedroom to exchange his dressing gown for a coat. "Romantic entanglements have always been more in your line. The name 'Woodley' – is it not familiar?"

"Jack Woodley," I reminded him. "The blackguard who abducted Miss Violet Smith."

"No, it isn't that. Well," he said, as we heard the footfall upon the stair, "we shall have our answer soon enough."

Miss Edith Woodley appeared to be thirty or thereabouts, her features unremarkable but for a pair of violet-blue eyes that were singularly sensitive and alert. Her gray mantle and black traveling costume were somber and unadorned, and from her attire and her air of quiet resignation, I concluded that she was a woman who has known what it is to make her own way in the world. In her gloved hands, she held a curious object, a metal chest no more than a foot long and four- or five-inches in height, with an intricate design worked into the body, clawed feet, a bronze escutcheon plate 'round the keyhole in front, and a large nacre disk in the center of the lid.

Doctor MacLeod was a tall, remarkably handsome gentleman dressed in a subdued, professional fashion, and wearing the same steadfast expression as the lady – that of one whose living had come by way of by industry rather than indulgence.

"I am Sherlock Holmes," greeted my friend, "and this is my friend and colleague, Doctor Watson. I trust that you have no objection to his presence."

"That is for Miss Woodley to decide," said Dr. MacLeod, "as she wishes to consult you on a matter too personal to be confided even to an acquaintance of long standing. I am only the humble guard-dog. Her employer wishes her to have an escort, and I am always at his service. And yours, Edith," he added. And then with a bow to us and to the lady, he said, "I'll wait in the carriage,"

"No, it is too cold," said she. "I won't have you or the driver loitering in the snow. Take yourselves to a coffee-house, and come for me in a half-hour."

"At your command," he said with a note of wry humor. With a bow to us all, he left the room, closing the door behind him.

"If it is a personal matter – " I began.

"No, don't leave, Doctor Watson," said Miss Woodley as she took the chair that Holmes held out for her and settled the metal coffer on her lap. "Your advice in the matter may be as helpful as your friend's."

"Miss Edith Woodley," said Holmes. "Your name is somewhat familiar to me, but I can't think why."

"My name may have been mentioned in passing at the time, Mr. Holmes, though I didn't figure in the case. But more than eight years have passed since that unhappy event, and I am not surprised that neither you nor Doctor Watson recall it."

"Miss Edith Woodley!" I cried. "You were engaged to Ronald Adair!" While it is true that Miss Woodley hadn't figured in the case, the case itself was one I could never forget, for it had been the murder of the younger son of the Earl of Maynooth, at the hands of the infamous Colonel Sebastian Moran, that had returned Holmes to London three years after he had been presumed dead.

Holmes's expression softened. "But it cannot be that matter which brings you here, Miss Woodley. As you say, it has been more than eight years since young Adair's death – and did you and he not end your engagement some months before?"

"Yes, Mr. Holmes. Two months before his murder, Ronald asked me to release him from his promise, and I did so."

"How long had you been engaged?"

"Four months."

"And if I may ask – What reason did he give for wishing to end the engagement?"

"We were from very different spheres, Mr. Holmes. I believe Ronald decided that his sister's governess, the daughter of a tradesman, wasn't the most suitable wife for the son of an Earl."

"But my dear Miss Woodley, when Adair made you an offer of marriage, was he not already the son of an Earl, and were you not a governess and a tradesman's daughter?"

"Yes. Perhaps if all of his youth had been spent among England's *beau monde*, he would never have made the offer at all. But when Ronald was barely twelve years of age, his father had been appointed governor of Victoria, and all the family was taken to Australia. Until Ronald returned to England to attend university, he lived in a society where matters of pedigree are less important than they are here. Ronald always spoke of that country's openness and informality with great admiration, and I must believe that his conduct had been influenced by that environment. He was certainly as unspoiled and unassuming a person as you would ever wish to meet. Never once did he make me feel that in making the offer of his hand, he was descending."

"Someone made *him* feel it, then."

The girl's pale cheeks flushed. "I cannot blame a fond mother for wishing her child to marry one who would bring something more than affection into the union."

"And he was particularly susceptible to his fond mother's influence, because at the time of your engagement, he resided with her in town."

"Yes."

"The Earl, I believe, remained in Australia. Had there been a separation?"

"Not a formal one, Mr. Holmes, but Lady Maynooth had never liked Australia. She had found both its climate and its society to be greatly inferior to what she had left behind. Had it not been for the birth of Lady Hilda, who suffered from childhood ailments that wouldn't stand up to the journey, I believe that Lady Maynooth would have left Australia much sooner than she did. At last, when an opportunity to return to England presented itself, she took advantage of it."

"Cataract surgery, was it not?" I said.

"Yes, Doctor. From something Ronald said, I believe her condition might have been managed in Victoria, but she insisted that only London surgeons would do."

"So Lady Maynooth and Lady Hilda return to England and take a house in town, where you became the daughter's governess and the younger son's fiancée. And what of the elder son? The present Lord Maynooth, is he not?"

"Yes. The Earl died two years ago. When the family moved to Australia, the estate at Doncaster had been left to the stewards, but it was the Earl's desire that after his elder son left university, he would take charge of the property and – " the lady hesitated for a moment.

"'And?'"

"'And see what could be made of it' I was going to say."

"A considerable responsibility for so young a man."

"Yes, particularly since it was said that the estate had gone down in the Earl's absence, and that its present income is scarcely enough to support it. Ronald once told me how glad he wasn't to be the firstborn since entailed properties, with all of their demands and expense, were often more burden than blessing."

"Did the father's will provide any material blessing that might lighten the burden?"

"I had heard from my present employer that the Earl had left a hundred-thousand pounds, but only half the sum was assigned to Lady Maynooth and her children. Half of *that* went to Lady Maynooth, herself, and the residue was unequally divided, with a greater share left to Lady Hilda to provide her with a dowry, I believe. Ronald and Lord Maynooth weren't left poor, certainly. Their parents were always quite liberal – "

"'Indulgent', you mean."

The lady conceded the point with a nod. "And on their twenty-first birthday, both Ronald and his brother were given a gift of ten-thousand pounds by their maternal uncle."

"Very handsome," I murmured.

"'Handsome' is relative," observed Holmes. "Ten-thousand would be a fortune to you, Watson, but membership in the *beau monde* is costly enough without the added expense of an estate in decline. Pray, Miss Woodley, how does your present employer come to have such intimate knowledge of the Earl's family?"

"He is the generous uncle: Lady Maynooth's elder brother – half-brother, to be precise, as he is the son of their mother's first marriage. Sir James Fitzwalter."

"Sir James Fitzwalter!" I cried.

The name was a legend to any soldier of fortune and to every lady of fashion. James Fitzwalter had taken a degree in geology and then embarked upon a life of adventure that had carried him around the globe. He had been called an alchemist for his uncanny genius at locating and extracting gems from rock and soil. Indeed, his exploits might have been dismissed as myth if the material evidence hadn't adorned so many aristocratic fingers, throats, and crowns. In the course of his career, James Fitzwalter had returned to England only once, to present our late monarch with a sapphire thought to be the largest in the world, and to be presented with a knighthood in return, whereupon he set off on a course of adventures once more.

"How did the gentleman come to be your employer?" Holmes asked.

"The morning after Ronald and I ended our engagement, Lady Maynooth summoned me and said that it would be awkward for all parties if I were to remain with the household. She promised to provide me with a good character, and then handed me a full year's salary, so that I might immediately find other lodgings."

"How very cold!" I cried. "Did Adair make no objection?"

"You mustn't think badly of Ronald," Miss Woodley replied. "When he heard of his mother's proposal, he offered to leave so that I might stay, but I couldn't allow Ronald to quit his home and family on my account, and so the day after my interview with Lady Maynooth, I found lodgings, gathered up my few belongings, and left her home. I immediately set about looking for another situation, but this proved more difficult than I had anticipated."

"Even with Lady Maynooth's good character to recommend you? Or perhaps," Holmes said, looking at her keenly, "her recommendation was withheld from households with eligible sons."

The lady gave a slight shrug of her shoulders. "A month passed, and then two, and still nothing at all turned up, and I began to wonder whether I ought to leave London and return to Carstairs. And then I heard of Ronald's death. I called at Park Lane to offer my condolences, but Lady Maynooth declined to see me. Perhaps she was afraid that I had come to ask for my old position back. At any rate, I was turned away and had just reached the pavement when I heard someone call out my name and saw a tall, gray-haired gentleman approach from the house. He was dressed in mourning and his features were drawn and haggard, his gait labored and slow. I thought at first he might be the Earl himself, for I had never met the gentleman, nor seen any photographs or portraits of him about when I lived at Park Lane. It wasn't Lady Maynooth's husband, however, but her brother, who introduced himself to me and said, 'I return to London only to be met with tragedy. I hope you will forgive Lady Maynooth. The poor boy's death has been a terrible blow.'

"'It is I who ought to be forgiven, sir," I replied, "for intruding upon a mother's grief.'

"'I have heard something of you, Miss Woodley, and I think I deduce the rest. Have you found a situation?'

"'Not yet, sir.'

"'Well, then,' he said, 'what is your opinion of a rough, undomesticated old adventurer who has spent his life bounding around the globe, and who may need some clever young person to re-educate him in the rules civilization? Would you like to work for such a fellow?'"

"I told him that I should like it very much, and he gave me his card with the address of the house he had taken in Grosvenor Place, and asked me to call the next day. We spoke then for no more than twenty minutes before we came to terms, and the day after that, I moved from my narrow room at a lodging house to a spacious sitting room and bedchamber at Grosvenor Place, and I have been there to this day."

"Not as a governess, surely."

"Oh, no. Sir James never married. Marriage would never have been worked into the life he had chosen. But years of bounding around the globe had taken a heavy toll and, even before Ronald's death, Sir James had decided he must settle where he might be near the best physicians and, of course, being in London would allow him to renew relations with his only family. My role was to oversee his household, and also to manage his appointments and correspondence."

"At what salary, may I ask?"

"One-hundred-twenty pounds a year."

Holmes raised his eyebrows. "For a housekeeper and secretary? A very generous wage, Madam."

"Those aren't my sole duties, Mr. Holmes. I provide Sir James with companionship, as well. Nothing romantic or improper," she hastened to add, with a blush and a smile. "Sir James is always a perfect gentleman. But the state of his health has made him something of an invalid, and he knows no one at all in England, save for his sister and her children. I accompany him when he goes for a stroll or a carriage ride, and in the evenings I read to him, or play the piano, or we sit down to cards or chess. Dr. MacLeod became Sir James's physician about a year after Sir James settled in town, and often stops in the evening to see how his patient gets on. Sir James insists that he join us in a game of Authors or Rhymes and stay for supper afterward."

"A great deal of time to be sacrificed to a single patient," I observed.

"I thought so, too, Doctor Watson, and once made some mention of it to him, but Doctor MacLeod has no wife or family to lay claim to his time. 'My evenings couldn't be better spent,' he told me. 'Loneliness can be more ruinous to health than disease, and a regular dose of society is its best remedy.'"

"Was he speaking about Sir James or himself?"

"Perhaps he spoke for all three of us," the lady replied. "And indeed, I don't think I can recall more enjoyable evenings. When we sit down to supper, Doctor MacLeod asks Sir James to recount one of his exploits, and then, at the most thrilling moment, he says, 'Why, look at the clock, Sir James! I ought to have taken leave an hour ago! I will have to wait until my next visit to know how the adventure ends.'"

"As with Scheherazade the tales prolonged the storyteller's life," said Holmes with a smile.

"You may be right, Mr. Holmes, for when Sir James first came to London, he was quite frail indeed. One physician advised him that he mustn't expect to live out the year."

"And that would be eight or so years ago, if it was around the time of Adair's death."

The lady nodded. "I must credit it to Doctor MacLeod's excellent care, and to the regular dose of society that he added to Sir James's regimen."

"And what of Sir James's relations? Did they also contribute a 'regular dose of society'?"

"Well, at first, his niece and nephew were eager to know their famous uncle, and called at Grosvenor Place quite often. But they have a great many friends, and I suppose it is natural to prefer the company of people their own age to that of an elderly relation. Every year they dine at Grosvenor Place on Christmas Night, and Sir James has always been invited to their family celebrations at Park Lane."

"Well, your narrative gives some shading to my original sketch of Adair's family," said Holmes. "But it is no more than the enterprise in which my good landlady is presently engaged it ornaments those branches of inquiry into Adair's murder with colorful, if irrelevant, detail. Your note suggested that there is a more particular reason for your visit: That you anticipate a proposal of marriage and want to know my opinion. It isn't a subject upon which I can claim any expertise, and my brief introduction to Doctor MacLeod, and your commendation of him, would seem to make him – "

"It isn't Doctor MacLeod, Mr. Holmes. I believe his affections lay elsewhere. It is Lord Maynooth."

"What! Adair's brother?" I ejaculated.

Holmes and I looked at one another in astonishment.

"I didn't understand that you were on familiar footing with that gentleman," said Holmes.

"I hadn't been. Oh, he and Lady Hilda were always civil enough when they visited Grosvenor Place, but his past conduct would never be taken for courtship."

"What of his *present* conduct, then?" asked Holmes.

The lady ran her hands over the box upon her lap once more. "Lately, I have seen a great deal of Lord Maynooth. You see, for years, Sir James's health has been very erratic. He would decline and then he would rally. But last month, he took a very grave turn. He is comfortable, and not yet confined to his bed, but Doctor MacLeod felt obliged to tell Sir James that he cannot expect to live more than another two or three months."

"Has the family been informed?"

"Yes, and they are very attentive. For the past month, Lord Maynooth has called every day, and Lady Hilda nearly as often."

"So," said Holmes, "when Sir James first settles in town, his relations fawn over the wealthy uncle who seems near his demise. But when the gentleman has the impudence to rally, their attentions subside, save for Christmas and birthday celebrations, those occasions when gifts are given or, to be more precise, received. Now that the gentleman's demise does indeed seem at hand, when he may be engaged in putting his affairs in order – drawing up his will if he hasn't already done so – his relations are all affection once more."

"You take a very cynical view of humanity, Mr. Holmes."

"I take what I am given, Miss Woodley."

"So do we all, but the business of living is less about what we are given than what we make of it."

"You will forgive my cynicism, but I know precisely what to make of the attentions paid by Lord Maynooth and Lady Hilda to their wealthy uncle. What I don't know is how far it will be rewarded. That, I presume, would depend upon the terms of the uncle's will, and how he means to dispose of his wealth. Do you know the particulars?"

"No, they're known only Mr. Milner – Mr. Godfrey Milner, the solicitor who drew up the will, and two of his clerks who were brought in to witness it."

"Milner. A friend of Adair's, was he not?"

"Of Lord Maynooth's. He and Mr. Milner have been members of the same clubs for many years, and even promoted Ronald's membership, but I don't believe there was any friendship between Ronald and Mr. Milner away from the card tables."

"Was it Lord Maynooth who recommended Milner to his uncle?"

"Yes, I believe so."

"Pray, continue."

"As I said, only Mr. Milner, the two witnesses, and Sir James know the terms of his will, or the extent of his fortune he leaves, but it is a fortune that has allowed him to make many substantial donations to the Geological Society of London, and to numerous charities which operate in the impoverished areas he had visited on his travels. He also made a generous donation to the British Museum with a gift of his large collection of rare minerals and gems. 'Those who might benefit from my good fortune should not be kept waiting because Doctor Alec keeps me in health,' he once said. 'It is better to have them pleased that I am living, rather than impatient for my demise.'"

"I should think those relations who stand to benefit from Sir James's demise might well be very impatient, if they imagine how they are to benefit from it."

"Or have been told by that fellow Milner," I said. "If he is a good friend of Lord Maynooth's, he may not have been as discreet as he ought."

Holmes nodded. "However, it would seem that Sir James's fortune, even allowing for his many charitable donations and what consideration he means to bequeath to his faithful retainers, will be substantial enough to atone for any impatience it had caused his two young relations. And that, Miss Woodley, suggests that if Lord Maynooth does mean to make an offer of marriage, it is a disinterested one. Unless," he added, "you haven't told me all."

"I haven't told you all."

"And is what you have withheld to be found in that box upon your lap?"

For her answer, Miss Woodley held out the object. Holmes took it and examined it with his naked eye and then with his lens. "I had taken it for an artifact of some sort some curio that Sir James picked up on his travels, but I see that it is fairly recent workmanship."

"Yes. It was made by my father."

"He was a metalsmith?"

"A watchmaker and engraver."

"Ah."

"Some weeks after Ronald and I were engaged, he sent this to me with a note. 'One day, it will contain something of great value.'"

"And does it?"

"Do you think you can open it?"

We heard the gauntlet in her words, and with a shrug of his shoulders, Holmes examined the object, probing the surface, studying it from all angles. "The escutcheon is a blind," he muttered. "It surrounds a sham keyhole. This, I think," he pressed the nacre disc upon the lid with his forefinger, "is the true one." He rotated the disc outward to reveal a small keyhole beneath.

Laying the object aside, Holmes retrieved from his bedroom a neat leather case that contained instruments essential to those occasions when justice had required him to skirt the law and, unrolling the case, he removed its set of adaptable keys. For twenty minutes, he worked diligently, trying one after another. With each failed attempt, he emitted a grunt of frustration, until at last, he abandoned the effort and handed the object back to the lady.

"Anyone would take this for a common jewel-box." As she spoke, the lady drew from beneath her collar a thin gold chain, upon which hung a small key with oddly configured bittings. She lifted this chain from around her neck, inserted the key into the keyhole, and gave it two full turns, which caused the four iron feet to pivot outward, revealing keyholes beneath each one. The same procedure was performed upon each of these locks, the rotation producing a slight click from within the chest.

"It is a version of an Armada chest," she explained as she set the box upright and opened the lid. "Other than my father, who fashioned it, only Sir James, and now you two gentlemen, have seen how it is unlocked."

Within lay a small satin pouch, but it was the underside of the lid that drew our attention, for covering its surface and extending to the inner sides of the box was an intricate arrangement of iron bolts and gears that was evidently some sort of complex locking mechanism.

"No skeleton key or file will work. Only the key designed for it, and then the locks must be turned in the correct sequence. Any effort to the contrary will engage the inner bolts and secure the lid even more firmly."

"A frustrated thief might take a bludgeon or a jemmy to it," I said.

"If he is certain it will not damage its contents in the process." She opened the satin pouch and poured into the palm of her hand six rubies: Three were cabochons, and three were exquisitely faceted.

Holmes emitted a low whistle and took one of the faceted gems between his thumb and index finger. He held it up, then reached for his lens and examined it. "It is a beauty," he murmured, and then laying it in her palm, examined the others. "Burmese, I'll swear. Pigeon's blood hue. Each of these faceted ones is superior to a ruby that hammered at seventy-thousand last year. How is it that you are riding around London with a cache of gems worth above-a-quarter-million pounds, Miss Woodley?"

"Sir James made an appointment with the appraiser for this morning. The last appraisal is several years old, and Sir James insisted that I must have a current one, since I cannot get an insurance policy without it. He wanted to accompany me himself, but Doctor MacLeod advised against it. Sir James's health will not stand up to the weather unless it is exceptionally mild."

"Miss Woodley, do you mean to say that these rubies are yours?"

"They are. Not long after Sir James was given his grave diagnosis, he sent for Mr. Milner and Doctor MacLeod, and when they arrived, he brought them up to his study and then asked me to 'unlock that pretty little trinket box your father sent and fetch it here.' I did as he asked and when we had all assembled, he opened a small safe below his desk. 'You, Doctor MacLeod, will attest that I am of sound mind, and you, Mr. Milner will be witness to the fact that I freely and without reservation make this gift to Miss Woodley – a very small return for the devotion she has shown me these many years.' He then took out this small pouch and laid out the gems upon his desk. I was quite shocked, and protested that Sir James had been more than generous to me, that I had never owned jewels, and that they would better suit his sister or his niece, but he only said, "They have trinkets enough – many which I've given them."

"And the gentlemen – what was their response to this extraordinary gesture?"

"Mr. Milner let slip some remark about the rubies' value, and that it exceeded the whole of what Sir James had disposed of in his will. He hinted that such a gift to one of his employees might stir up unpleasant gossip. Doctor MacLeod got very angry at that and said if anyone dared to slander Sir James or me, they should have him to deal with, and Sir James said, 'Surely, I have the right to give to anyone I please what I have taken from this earth before I am returned to it.' He then put the rubies back into the pouch and laid the pouch in the chest and closed the lid. "Your father was right about this little casket, you see. It does indeed contain something of great value. Let us keep it here for the present, until they are appraised and insured.' And with that, he locked this chest away in his safe, where it has been until this morning."

"So in the past month, Sir James has not only made his will, but has given you gems that his solicitor hints are worth far more than what the gentleman disposes of in that will. A quarter-million. It is no wonder that Lord Maynooth has taken to calling every day – and not only to visit his uncle, I daresay."

"No. After he takes leave of Sir James, he will stop at my sitting room to ask how I get on, or whether there is anything he can do for me. I took this for common civility at first, but now his attentions – or, perhaps, I should say his *intentions* – are unmistakable."

"How so?"

"Lately, he has said how odd he finds it that his uncle chose the bachelor life, and how he wouldn't like it for himself."

Holmes studied the flush that had crept over the girl's cheek. "What else?"

"That unless Lady Hilda is greatly deceived by Doctor MacLeod's attentions, he has become dissatisfied with the bachelor life as well."

"Indeed? And do you believe him?"

"Lady Hilda does seem to arrange to visit Grosvenor Place when she knows that Alec – Doctor MacLeod – will be there, and she often asks to speak with him privately."

"Not to discuss her uncle's state of health, I take it."

"I'm not a party to their conversations."

Holmes was silent for a moment. "You say that Lord Maynooth's intentions are unmistakable. Has he been more explicit than conveying his general dissatisfaction with the bachelor life?"

"On his last visit, he expressed regret for his mother's past conduct toward me, and for his poor brother's foolishness, and said that he would once have been pleased to have me for a sister, but lately he has come to think that there is a connection he would like even better, and that perhaps on Christmas Night, when all the family are together, he will make plain what that connection is, and that he trusts that it will please all his family and lessen the sorrow I must feel when Sir James is no longer with us."

"Well, that seems clear enough. What do you mean to do?"

"Given everything I have told you, Mr. Holmes, what would you advise me to do? What would you advise a sister of yours to do?"

"Well, you don't love him, so much is clear. But I understand that for a woman, there may be other motives for marrying: The protection of a husband, the security of a home, the domestic pleasures that defend against that loneliness which can be as ruinous to health as illness. But a man may also have motives that have nothing to do with affection, and if I had a sister, and she came into possession of such gems as these, I suppose I would ask her whether or not the gentleman knew about them."

"I don't believe that Sir James meant for it to be a secret, but I have never mentioned them to anyone. I don't think that Doctor MacLeod would, but of course – "

"Mr. Milner, who was present when the gift was made to you, may have dropped a hint to his good friend, Lord Maynooth. Well, Miss Woodley, my advice, then, is this: If you suspect that there is a mercenary object in Lord Maynooth's courtship, throw the rubies into the river. If he is still as smitten afterward as he had seemed before, that should settle the matter."

"Holmes!" I cried. "That is very cavalier advice!"

"No, Doctor, it is very practical advice." The lady gathered up the gems and dropped them back into the little satin pouch and laid the pouch in the metal chest. "Forgive the imposition on your time, Mr. Holmes," she said as she rose. "To a great mind, it must seem a trivial problem."

"It is no imposition, and 'trivial' is relative," Holmes assured her, kindly. "Sometimes a problem needs nothing more than to be talked through for the answer to reveal itself. If I may, Miss Woodley, one more question: Had Ronald Adair left a will?"

"I don't know."

"I ask because it was said that he had a considerable fortune for so young a man. The generosity of his parents and uncle, his own cleverness at the card table, and a natural turn for frugality may account for it. That, and the fact that his resources weren't drained by the burden and expense of an estate. I assume that what fortune he left behind went to his brother and sister."

"I imagine it did." Then, tucking the metal case under one arm, she extended her hand to Holmes and then to me. "I believe I hear the carriage. Doctor MacLeod is always punctual. I wish you both the very best of the season."

I went to the window and saw that the brougham had indeed stopped at our door once again. The young doctor alighted and after a several moments, Miss Woodley appeared and was helped into the coach.

"An extraordinary young woman!" I exclaimed. "What a fool Adair was! The poor fellow might be alive today if he had such a wife at home. Instead, he took to the card tables – "

"Was *taken* to the card tables," Holmes interrupted, as he reached for his pipe. "Remember, it was Lord Maynooth and his friend, Milner, who lured Adair to those card clubs. Perhaps they expected him to be as heedless at cards as he was in courtship, and his opponents would be the richer for it. But Adair had a turn for cards and rarely lost more than five pounds. Once, he and his partner – "

"Colonel Moran."

Holmes nodded. "They took more than four-hundred pounds from Milner and his partner. Sometime after Moran's arrest, I learned that it wasn't uncommon for Mr. Godfrey Milner to bring some well-heeled partner or other into a foursome with Adair and Moran."

"Do you say that Milner and Moran conspired?"

"Adair was murdered because he had discovered that Moran was a cheat, and threatened to expose him. Now, a partner's double-dealing may be more easy to spot than an opponent's, but it is possible that, had Adair not been murdered beforehand, he might have discovered that the two were in league with one another. If that was the case, then Adair's death worked to Milner's advantage."

"Holmes, that is monstrous!"

He shrugged his shoulders. "My cynical view of humanity might also observe that Lord Maynooth was probably none the poorer for his brother's murder. Who but Maynooth and his sister would have inherited Adair's fortune? They would also take Adair's portion of the Earl's estate, since Adair predeceased their father."

"And yet," I reminded Holmes, "fortune is relative. Miss Woodley said that the Earl left a hundred-thousand, but only half the sum was distributed to his wife and children. What could account for the other half?"

"Well, a principled gentleman might feel responsible for settling his son's debts of honor."

"Debts of honor! Fifty-thousand!"

"It is said that it was nothing for the notorious statesman Charles Fox to lose five, or even six figures, at cards, and that his father once settled a debt of over a hundred-thousand. At any rate, it is difficult to believe that Lord Maynooth's attachment to Miss Woodley, coming so soon upon her receiving a fortune in gems, is mere coincidence. And how shrewdly he courts her! He alludes to Sir James's death, which must deprive her of companionship and a home, and he persuades her that Doctor MacLeod has become attached to his sister, which must disappoint any hopes that Miss Woodley may have in that direction."

"If I am any judge, not only do her hopes lie in that direction, but her feelings are reciprocated. And yet, if MacLeod is fond of her, why did he not speak years ago?"

"Perhaps, years ago, he was too poor to provide for a wife, and now he is too principled to address an heiress."

I thought of my own feelings when I had believed that my dear Mary had come into a fortune.

"Well, well," said Holmes, "perhaps she will take my advice. She will toss the rubies into the Thames, which ought to reverse the attentions of Lord Maynooth and revive the hopes of the doctor, and all will be well."

Chapter II – The Dramatic Narrative of Doctor Alexander MacLeod

On the day after Christmas, sometime before dawn, I was awakened by an urgent knocking upon the bedroom door. I stumbled in the dark and opened the door to find our maid with an envelope in her hand. "Lad said it was most urgent, sir."

I thanked her and lit the lamp, supposing the summons to be from a patient, for it had been a bad season for bronchitis and my practice was especially active. The note, however was from Holmes, a terse *"Come at once."*

Such a note might mean that the game was afoot, or it might simply mean that after hours of solitary meditation upon a particularly vexing problem, he wished to talk through its details and perhaps elicit a remark or two, which might allow the answer to reveal itself.

It wasn't yet seven when I arrived at Baker Street, yet there were lights in the upper windows and when Mrs. Hudson admitted me, I saw a dark overcoat and black silk hat upon the peg.

"What is it?" I asked. "He isn't ill?"

"No, a visitor. The young man who stopped some days ago, all in a state and demanding to see Mr. Holmes. It wouldn't surprise me if the bell wire snapped in two. Mr. Holmes ordered coffee, but I don't know that something to steady the young man's nerves wouldn't do better."

I hurried up to the sitting room to find Holmes wrapped in his dressing gown, his long legs stretched toward the fire, his slippered feet on the hearth, his posture languid but for impatient manner in which his fingers drummed upon the arm of his chair as he surveyed young Doctor MacLeod, who was pacing back and forth across the room.

The gentleman was, indeed, "all in a state", for his formal attire, evidently donned the night before, was in disarray, the coat thrown open, his silk tie unknotted, and his collar askew. His hair was disheveled, and the pallor of sleeplessness was relieved only by two frenzied spots of color at his cheeks.

"Ah, Watson! You will beg Mrs. Watson's pardon, but I knew you wouldn't want to miss the affair. You remember Doctor MacLeod. I wouldn't have him begin his narrative before you arrived, but it seems that there has been a dramatic turn of events at Grosvenor Place last night."

"Is it Sir James?"

"No, no," said Doctor MacLeod. "He is in very good hands. The nurse I brought in last week to watch over him is a Tartar and will keep him from being troubled. I wouldn't want to distress him when there may be a perfectly rational explanation, but I will be d--ned if I know what it is! And then I recalled that Miss Woodley had come to you over some personal matter, Mr. Holmes, and I thought that there would be no harm in seeing what you could make of it before it becomes a police matter."

"A police matter?"

"It seems," said Holmes, "that Miss Woodley's rubies have vanished."

"What? Vanished! She hasn't really thrown them in the river!"

"Why the devil would she throw them in the river?" cried Doctor MacLeod. "With my own eyes, I saw them laid in her jewel-box at the appraiser's, and saw the jewel-box locked away in Sir James's safe. And yet when it was opened last night – It isn't possible! Oh, if you had seen the look upon Lord Maynooth's face!" He burst into a fit of agitated laughter.

"Calm yourself, Doctor!" Holmes ordered. "Stop wearing away the carpet, take a seat, and tell us what has happened."

The young man threw himself into a chair. "Forgive me, I haven't had a wink of sleep." He took a gulp of the whisky-and-soda that Holmes laid at his elbow. "Last night, I dined at the home of Sir James Fitzwalter. He has been my patient many years. We first met just after I had taken my degree. I worked as a *locum* because I could find nothing better and had no funds to set myself up. I had the good fortune to relieve an established practitioner at a time when Sir James had an appointment, and he took a liking to me and decided he would see no one else. He even offered to set me up in a suite on Harley Street, and when I refused, converted his offer to a loan so that I might take a modest office and surgery. I made payments to him regularly until the debt was satisfied earlier this year, but I will always be in his debt for more than his backing. He is a most remarkable man! What tales he has to tell! From me, you will hear nothing but praise for that gentleman."

"Last night it was a family dinner, I believe?"

The doctor nodded. "It has been Sir James's custom to have his family to dine on Christmas Night, and he has always been kind enough to include me, since I have few friends and no family of my own. Last night we were seven: Sir James, his sister Lady Maynooth, and her children, Lord Maynooth and Lady Hilda Adair, Mr. Godfrey Milner – he is Sir James's solicitor – Miss Woodley, and myself."

"Tell me, what do you make of Sir James's relations?"

"I have no opinion."

"'No opinion', or no opinion that does them credit?"

The doctor shrugged his shoulders. "Save for these Christmas dinners, I've seen little of them. Oh, they were often underfoot and thick with family feeling when Sir James first settled in London, but that soon fell off."

"When an improvement in his health suspended their expectations."

"You understand it exactly, Mr. Holmes."

"I understand that, quite lately, the family feeling has recommenced."

"It has."

"Well, nothing begets fondness so much as the prospect of a rich relation's demise. Now, as to last night, tell us what occurred and omit nothing."

"I believe that what occurred began a month ago."

"When Sir James called you into his study, together with his solicitor and Miss Woodley, who was asked to bring the jewel-case that her father had given her. When she brought it into the room, had she already opened it?"

"Yes."

"And was it empty?"

"Yes."

"Pray, continue."

"Sir James opened his safe, took out a small satin pouch, and laid its contents on his desk."

"Six rubies. Miss Woodley showed them to us."

"Sir James said that he had decided to give them to Miss Woodley, and had made up his mind to do so immediately, rather than bequeath them to her in his will, where they might be haggled over in the courts after he was gone."

"And what did you three make of that?"

"Well, they are Sir James's to give, and it is certainly not for me or anyone to dictate what a man may do with his property. Edith – Miss Woodley – was quite naturally taken aback and asked whether such a gift ought to go to his sister or niece, though I think she is a thousand times more deserving than either of them. Milner argued for delay and had the insolence to suggest that such a gift might impugn the reputations of Sir James and Miss Woodley! As if I should ever allow such a thing! Well, to his credit, Sir James stood firm, and then he placed the rubies back in their pouch, and laid it in the box, and then locked the box away it in his safe, where it remained until last Monday morning."

"When Sir James had arranged for Miss Woodley to have the gems appraised."

"Yes. He asked me to accompany her to the appraiser at Hatton Garden. When we arrived, Miss Woodley asked if she might step into a back room to open the jewel-box – "

"And what did you make of that?"

"At the time, I took it for modesty – that she kept the key to it on her person."

"So you have never seen her open it?"

"Not then. She joined us once more and took the pouch of gems from the box and laid them out for the appraiser. I could tell by his expression as he examined them that they were immensely valuable. He made several notes and promised to have his appraisal ready in a few days, and then he said to me, 'Keep a sharp watch over the young lady, sir, until those gems are locked away once more.' It wasn't until we were in the carriage that Miss Woodley told me she had an appointment with you that same morning. I urged her to stop at Grosvenor Place first, so that the gems might be put back in the safe, but she refused. I told her in that case, I meant to stay by her side until she was home again, but she said that the matter she wished to discuss with you was a personal one, and she wanted to speak to you alone."

"So neither Miss Woodley nor her jewel case were out of your sight from the time you left the appraiser until you left her here?"

"Not for a moment."

"And you were at the door when my interview with Miss Woodley had concluded."

"Waiting on the pavement when she stepped out – like the faithful dog that I am," he added, with a rueful smile.

"And you returned immediately to Grosvenor Place?"

"Yes. We went straight up to Sir James, who had spent the morning in the study which adjoins his bedchamber. He took the jewel-box from Miss Woodley and locked it away in the safe."

"Now, his study – is there any door that opens into a corridor or another room?"

"No, you must go through his bedroom. There is no other passage."

"And does anyone other than Sir James have the combination to his safe?"

"I don't believe so. When Sir James first showed us the rubies, Mr. Milner suggested that the combination be given to a trusted advisor or family member in the event – well, in the event of his death. Sir James promised to do it, but I don't believe he has done so yet."

"So last month, when Sir James announced that intended to give the rubies to Miss Woodley, you saw them placed in her jewel-box and saw the jewel-box locked in the safe. Earlier this week, you and Miss Woodley took the jewel-box to the appraisers, where the gems were removed, examined, and then placed back in the jewel-box. She had it in her possession when she stopped here, and when she left, you escorted her back to Grosvenor Place, where the jewel-box was locked away in the safe once more. To your knowledge, did the jewel-box remain in the safe for the entire time?"

"Until it was taken out last night, yes."

"Now, has Sir James had any visitors?"

"I understand that Lord Maynooth calls every day."

"Calls not only on his uncle, but on Miss Woodley as well, and has implied that he meant to make her an offer of marriage when all the family were together on Christmas Night."

"And he did so!" Again, the doctor burst into a fit of uncontrollable laughter. "I do beg your pardon," he gasped. "It is exhaustion, nothing more."

Holmes gestured for the doctor to continue.

"Lord Maynooth was at Miss Woodley's side from the moment he arrived. He took her as his partner and, all through dinner, dropped hints that he meant to ask for her hand."

"And did everyone seem pleased at the prospect of the union?"

"I certainly wouldn't begrudge Miss Woodley the title of 'Countess'," said MacLeod with some emotion. "Milner looked very conscious, as if he knew of Lord Maynooth's intentions. Lady Maynooth was all smiles – she who had once all but tossed Miss Woodley into the street when her engagement to Adair was broken off. And Lady Hilda made some remark about how much she would enjoy having a sister."

"It is my understanding that it wasn't only Miss Woodley they expected to bring into the family," said Holmes, pointedly. "And that Lady Hilda's conduct toward you couldn't be called 'sisterly'."

The doctor looked genuinely shocked. "What? You don't imagine that I have any interest in Lady Hilda. A silly nineteen-year-old girl! Good God! No one could think such a thing! Surely Edith – !"

Holmes raised his eyebrows. "If you say it isn't so, then I am mistaken," he murmured. "Pray, continue."

"I did think it may have been my imagination that Sir James was a bit troubled by the notion of his nephew's marrying Miss Woodley. After the ladies withdrew, I thought he looked pale and out of spirits, and so I insisted that he retire, and he agreed, but first he wanted to say good-night to the ladies. We went to the drawing room where we found Lady Maynooth and her daughter teasing Miss Woodley about rumors they had heard of a very special present Sir James had given her and how eager they were to see what it was."

"There was no mention of rubies?"

"I certainly had said nothing, but I suspect, from a look that passed between Milner and Lord Maynooth, that His Lordship was aware of them. Maynooth even made some vague remark that perhaps Sir James's gift was given because he anticipated a closer relationship to Miss Woodley. At last, Edith said, 'If it doesn't trouble Sir James to open his safe, it will not trouble me to open what is inside it.' Sir James said, 'See me to my room, Doctor, and I will give you Edith's trinket box.'

"As I walked him upstairs, I tried to argue him out of the scheme, insisting that it might only stir up envy in his sister and niece to see what an immensely valuable gift he had given to Miss Woodley. He replied that if they said anything amiss, I was to tell them that Sir James said the rubies are a small return for the many years of kindness and companionship Miss Woodley has given. He then took the jewel-box from his safe and as he handed it to me. 'There is something I believe Edith would value above these rubies and above hearing herself called "Countess",' he said to me, and then he sent me away and I returned to the drawing room.

"I saw Lord Maynooth sitting beside Edith, her hand in his, and everyone in a state of excitement, and when I entered Lady Hilda jumped up and cried, 'Doctor MacLeod, what do you think! Reginald has asked Edith to marry him!'"

"Indeed!" said Holmes.

The doctor nodded and then emitted a terse laugh. "He would soon wish he had put it off another half-hour. I handed Edith the jewel-box, and she gave me the oddest smile and then turned to Lord Maynooth, saying, 'You must not expect a princely dowry from a tradesman's daughter. I have nothing, after all, of value but this chest and what it contains, of course. It is yours if you like."

"She gave him the rubies!" I cried, astonished.

"Well, she gave him the jewel-box. He looked it over and at last said, 'But Edith, my dear, it is locked.' And then Miss Woodley drew a chain from around her neck, with an odd small key hanging from it and, taking back the case, she began to open a series of locks and then handed it back to him and he opened it. I couldn't see the inside, but his face went grey as ash and he leapt to his feet and cried, 'Why, what is this?' as the chest fell to the floor and out rolled – " The doctor's voice dropped to a hush. " – a large lump of coal!"

To be sure, it was a shocking turn of events: The gems gone, a lump of coal in their place – and yet there was something so absurdly comical in the scene as MacLeod had rendered it that Holmes and I burst into laughter.

"Mr. Holmes! Doctor Watson! I see nothing to laugh at!"

"You must forgive us. But a lump of coal! That which ought to generate heat cooled Lord Maynooth's ardor, I daresay. What happened next?"

"I scarcely remember. It was all commotion. Milner snatched up the box and began probing around the insides. There were all manner of gears and latches, and I suppose he thought that the rubies may have got caught up in them. 'I saw the rubies placed in here myself!' he declared, which prompted Lady Maynooth to cry out 'Rubies!' and then it seemed everyone had a theory of where they may have gone. Milner was of the opinion that they had somehow fallen out of the jewel-box when Sir James removed it from his safe, and that they were at the bottom of the safe or scattered around the carpet of the study. Lady Maynooth hoped aloud that none of the servants had picked them up and made off with them, and wondered whether their quarters ought to be searched. Lady Hilda spoke of burglars and wanted the police sent for at once, and Lord Maynooth wondered whether we had all fallen prey to some practical joke of his uncle's and would have gone upstairs to confront Sir James immediately, but there I put my foot down. 'I will not have Sir James disturbed. Milner is most likely right they must have fallen out when Sir James removed the box from his safe, and wherever they are now, they will be there when Sir James wakes in the morning.'"

"But, Doctor MacLeod, that theory has one obstacle: The gems couldn't have fallen out when the box was taken from the safe, for only Miss Woodley had the key."

The young doctor ran his hands through his disheveled hair. "I cannot explain it. And Edith – Miss Woodley – a fortune gone, and yet, she was as cool as snow. She only said that she agreed that Sir James shouldn't be disturbed, and that if the police were called in, they would first look to everyone in the house, not just the servants, and perhaps arrest someone on the spot, and how she would hate to see any of us spend Christmas Night in a cell. That sent both Lady Maynooth and Lady Hilda into hysterics. Lord Maynooth decided that they must be taken home, and begged Milner to assist him, and the four of them left."

"You ought to have detained them," I said. "Four people who would most certainly be regarded as suspects shouldn't have been allowed to leave the house. If one of them has made off with the rubies, they may be impossible to recover."

"The damnable rubies!" cried the doctor. "I wish I had never laid eyes on them! When everyone had gone, I told Miss Woodley that the loss must be reported to the police – that together we might manage it without disturbing Sir James. But she only said, 'The loss is mine, and so should the course of action be.' 'Well, what will you do?' I asked her, and she said, 'I'm going to sit for a while with Sir James so that Mrs. Peterson' – That is the nurse. ' – may have a bite of supper, and then I will go to bed myself, and I think you should go home and do the same.'"

"It is evident that you didn't take the lady's advice."

"We argued for some time over what ought to be done, but all Miss Woodley would say was that she agreed that wherever the rubies were tonight, they would be tomorrow, and she sent me away." He rose from his chair and began to pace once more. "I must have walked the streets for hours, and I confess I did have a laugh or two when I recalled Lord Maynooth's face! I daresay I was taken for a madman! It is a wonder I wasn't thrown into a cell! And yet, I saw those damnable rubies laid in the jewel-box and saw the jewel-box locked away, and when it was opened a lump of coal! The more I worked it over in my mind, the more I realized the business wanted more thinking than I could give it. And so I decided that it would do no harm to submit the problem to you, Mr. Holmes."

The young doctor stared as if he took Holmes to be a madman, for my friend had leapt from his chair, pulled the bell for the page, and then he stepped to his desk and dashed off a few lines, scribbled an address upon an envelope, and slipped his note inside.

"This is to be delivered immediately," he said, and then sent the lad off with the note and a few shillings.

"You've sent for Gregson or Lestrade?" I asked. "You do think it is a police matter, then?"

"Oh, no, I don't believe there is anything the police can do. Ah, Mrs. Hudson! You have deferred the redecoration of the tree long enough to bring our coffee! If it wouldn't trouble you, we will presently be four to breakfast."

The landlady was well accustomed to such requests, but I confess that my friend's conduct left both Doctor MacLeod and me baffled, for Holmes seemed to have lost all interest in the rubies, and instead busied himself with drawing the breakfast-table nearer the fire, arranging chairs around it, laying out the coffee cups, and waving off our attempts to return to the problem at hand.

Not twenty minutes later there was a ring at the bell, and shortly thereafter, Miss Woodley was ushered into the room.

"Edith!" cried the doctor, as he sprang from his chair and glancing over his disheveled appearance, he began tugging his attire into some semblance of order. "Why have you sent for Miss Woodley, Mr. Holmes? Is Sir James – "

"Sir James had a very good night," the lady assured him. "His color seems rather better this morning, and I left him enjoying an excellent breakfast in the care of Mrs. Peterson, who was telling him the most fantastic tale of the time she found a blue jewel in her Christmas goose. As for your summons, Mr. Holmes, I would have called upon you this morning in any case, for the question I put to you several days ago is no longer – "

"The question regarding an offer of marriage," Holmes interrupted. "I have given the matter some thought, Miss Woodley, and I have decided that you should accept it."

The lady gave a start. "That may be out of my power, Mr. Holmes. Last night, Lord Maynooth did make me an offer of marriage, but a slight disturbance took place before I could give my answer, and I have reason to believe that the offer will very soon be rescinded."

"I would hardly call the disappearance of six rubies a 'slight disturbance'. A sleight of hand, perhaps, for the rubies didn't simply vanish. They were replaced by a lump of coal. A lump of coal! A distinct touch!" Holmes chuckled. "I know that Sir James Fitzwater has been called an alchemist, but I think that converting gems to crude carbon, while they are locked away in an impenetrable chest, is beyond his powers of sorcery. At any rate," he continued, "the offer that I advise you to accept isn't Lord Maynooth's, but Doctor MacLeod's. Now that his debt to Sir James is paid, and he is well established in his profession, there is no obstacle to marriage."

"I believe Doctor MacLeod means to address Lady Hilda," she said softly.

"Lady Hilda!" cried the doctor. "Who put such nonsense into your head?"

"Lord Maynooth, I daresay," said Holmes. "He convinced Miss Woodley that you and Lady Hilda had come to an understanding."

"The devil we have!"

"Then why does she only call at Grosvenor Place when she knows you will be there?" Miss Woodley asked. "Why does she always ask to speak with you privately?"

"To inquire about her uncle's condition! At least, that was how it would begin, and then it sinks to a lot of nonsense. I can't recall a tenth of her rattle. Why on earth would Lady Hilda Adair set her cap for me?"

"I think *when* is more to the point than *why*," said Holmes. "Miss Woodley stated that Lord Maynooth's attentions to her began a month ago, and I gather, Doctor, that Lady Hilda had started to single you out at the same time."

"Yes, now that you mention it."

"And it is unlikely that Lady Hilda Adair would 'set her cap', as you express it, for a poor man."

"Entirely unlikely."

"It is equally unlikely that her standards have lowered in the past month. Therefore, your status must have elevated."

"But nothing has changed."

"Nothing that you are aware of, at present," replied Holmes. "And here," he continued, as he leaned back in his chair and pressed his fingertips together, "we find ourselves in the realm of probability. We may assume that it was Milner who told Lord Maynooth about the rubies, and it was that indiscretion which set off Maynooth's pursuit of Miss Woodley. Now, it has been my observation that a man who is indiscreet in one matter will be indiscreet in others, so it is likely that he also whispered something to Lady Hilda which made you a very eligible object – something that only came his way in the past month."

"Milner is Sir James's solicitor!" I cried. "It was he who set down that gentleman's will."

"Indeed he did," Holmes nodded. "None here in this room has seen that document, but I would venture to say that Sir James intends to leave his fortune – or a substantial portion of it at least – to the young physician who, for so many years, has shown him kindness and companionship."

"Why no, Mr. Holmes, you must be wrong!" the doctor gasped. "What would be said about such a gift? I could never allow it!"

"Is it for you, or anyone, to dictate what a man may do with his own property? You didn't object when Sir James gave a fortune in rubies to Miss Woodley, and as to what would be said, I am fairly certain that the lady wouldn't stand for it if anyone dared to impugn *your* character. So," said Holmes, clapping his hands together, "I see no further obstacle to your making an offer of marriage to Miss Woodley, and I am certain that Doctor Watson, whose expertise in such matters far exceeds my own, would agree."

MacLeod and the lady looked at one another. "Edith, would you?" said the doctor. "Would you forego 'Countess' for a simple 'Missus'?"

For her answer, the lady slipped her hand into his and smiled in a fashion that could only be taken for an affirmative reply.

"Well, an engagement certainly offers a novel experience to these humble rooms. And Mrs. Hudson, you have risen to the occasion!" he declared, as our landlady came in with the covers. "I don't think that our young guests can expect better at their wedding breakfast!"

"Sir James will be happy for us, I think," said Doctor MacLeod, when Mrs. Hudson had left us, "but I am afraid that the loss of the rubies will be a terrible blow."

"Well, well," Holmes observed, "I believe you will find somewhere in *Proverbs* that a capable wife is more precious than rubies. But, as to the rubies themselves, I have every expectation that you will see them again. In fact, I wouldn't be surprised to have them arrive at any minute."

MacLeod and I looked at one another in surprise, though I saw a flush creep across Miss Woodley's cheek.

My coffee cup was halfway to my lips when a shriek from below and a resounding "Merciful goodness!" caused me to splash brown liquid down the front of my shirt.

I heard the sound of our landlady's hurried step upon the stair and a moment later, our door was thrown open and Mrs. Hudson rushed into the room.

"Mr. Holmes!" she gasped, holding out her clenched fists, "See what I found hanging upon the tree!" She opened one hand to reveal the small satin pouch that had contained the rubies, and then slowly opened the other to reveal the rubies themselves.

"I am afraid we must deprive you of these ornaments," said Holmes, as he took the gems from the astonished woman. "They belong to this young lady, and must have somehow escaped from her jewel-box when she was here the other day. How extraordinary that they found their way onto your tree!"

Holmes gave the landlady a few more reassurances and sent her off to resume her rearrangement of the tree.

"How did you know?" Miss Woodley asked Holmes.

"Oh, once I heard Doctor MacLeod's tale, it was simplicity itself. The rubies were kept securely locked in your jewel-box – Doctor MacLeod,

Sir James, Milner, the appraiser, and lastly, Doctor Watson and I can all attest to the fact, and there is every reason to believe that Lord Maynooth and his family were also aware of it as well. When you sought my opinion regarding Lord Maynooth's courtship, I made a rather glib suggestion that you test His Lordship's sincerity by tossing the gems into the river, and sent you off imagining how that mercenary gentleman would react if he were to open the jewel-box and find it empty. And if it were opened just after His Lordship's proposal, so much the better. Indeed, I have no doubt that if Lady Maynooth and her daughter hadn't introduced the subject of Sir James's gift, you would have done so.

"Well, well, you had been treated quite shabbily by that tribe, and a modest reprisal was not unjustified. Of course, for such a practical joke to be stage-managed, the rubies must be taken from the jewel-box and hidden away. All that was wanted was a place where they might be safely concealed.

"And here is where coincidence set off inspiration, as it so often does. When you left this room, you hadn't re-locked the box. You happened to pass Mrs. Hudson's sitting room – the door had been left open when she had been called away by some task or other, I daresay – and saw her Christmas tree. That satin pouch of yours might easily camouflaged among the abundance of ornaments, and so you removed it from your jewel-box and concealed it upon the tree, where you had every reason to believe it would be secure for a few days until you called again at Baker Street to acquaint me with the epilogue to your dilemma.

"Of course, you could not know that it was Mrs. Hudson's practice to reposition the tree's finery and, frankly, I'm surprised that they were not discovered before this, but of course, there have been other holiday preparations to lay claim to my landlady's time. As for the lump of coal, it is probable that you meant for Lord Maynooth to behold an empty jewel-chest, but you saw my landlady's coal scuttle, you could not resist. The exchange was made, and when Doctor MacLeod saw you emerge with your jewel-box, he had no reason to think that it contained anything but the rubies he had seen placed there earlier that morning.

"Of course, now that the gems have been restored to Miss Woodley, she is once more an heiress, but your own excellent prospects, Doctor, should overcome your former reluctance to make her an offer of marriage. In any case, the offer has been made and accepted, so retract it at your peril."

"I have no intention of retracting it," the doctor laughed.

"Well, the matter is settled, then, and we may proceed with our breakfast, and then I would advise you to return to Grosvenor Place and deliver the happy news to Sir James."

When our guests had gone, Holmes reached for his after-breakfast pipe and said drolly, "A learned theologian once observed that the best rest is a change of occupation, and so, should I ever tire of my present profession, I think I may try my hand as our fair city's Beatrice Fairfax. I believe I have a decided talent for it."

NOTES

An Armada Box or Armada Chest dates from around the Sixteenth Century. It was an iron strong-box for protecting valuables. Characteristic of it was the complex locking system on the underside of the lid.

Holmes's remark about the best rest being a change of occupation echoes his line from *The Sign of Four*, that *"One of our greatest statesmen has said that a change of work is the best rest."* He likely quotes James Ormesbee Murray, DD who wrote: ". . . *the best rest one ever gets is by change of mental occupation."*

Beatrice Fairfax was the pen name of Marie Manning, novelist and freelance journalist, who launched the first U.S. newspaper advice column *Dear Beatrice Fairfax* in 1898.

As for Holmes's warning that Doctor MacLeod might retract an accepted marriage proposal at his peril, in Holmes's era, the withdrawal of an offer of marriage by a man was a breach of promise that was actionable. In 1886, barrister and Ripper suspect Montague Druitt represented a plaintiff in a suit for breach and won a judgement of fifty pounds. One does wonder what would have happened if Agatha, the maid to whom Holmes/Escott became engaged in the Milverton investigation, hauled him into court.

The Intrigue of the Red Christmas
by Shane Simmons

It will all be over by Christmas.

A popular refrain, repeated four years in a row, with less conviction each time. It seemed it might never prove true until, one day, it did. The war was over at last, with the next Christmas still a month and a half away. Time enough, perhaps, to wind things down at the front and send some of our boys home for the holiday.

Dismissing the troops over the subsequent weeks proved slow, however. Working as an attaché to Mycroft Holmes, I had been privy to a number of things being discussed within the corridors of power and behind closed doors. With Mr. Holmes ever in consult about affairs of the state and all matters related to wartime intelligence, I couldn't help but overhear things in his presence. So used to me being an appendage to the great man, many a major or minister, politician or pundit, had become quite candid in my company, regarding me as no more than a piece of décor in the room, incapable of speech, unable to hear or grasp what was being said. Their secrets were, of course, safe with me, but I had very much become the fly on the wall, gathering information well above my station.

I knew, for instance, that there was a division of opinion within government between those who wanted the men returned as soon as possible, and those who believed the real fight was yet to come. To them, the Boche had only been the first chapter. The deadlier enemy we faced were the Bolsheviks further east. Why draw down our forces now when we would inevitably be at war on the Continent again before long?

I knew where many of these powerful individuals fell on the issue. Close as I was to Mr. Holmes, however, his personal opinion on the matter remained shrouded behind a mask of stoicism that proved utterly impenetrable. His concern lay, as always, in maintaining our position of strength as an empire. To that end, as I entered Westminster to report for duty, I found Mycroft Holmes in heated debate with bureaucrats who were, once again, too thick to grasp his salient point. My arrival went ignored by all.

"Why are we still not issuing parachutes to our pilots?" asked Mr. Holmes pointedly, bringing up a point of irritation he had been trying to draw attention to for many months now. "Even the German high command, hardly known for the warmth of their human compassion, was still doing so throughout the final year of the war."

The stiff suit at the table opposite him repeated the same tired argument we had heard before.

"A pilot with a parachute on his back is more willing to abandon a damaged aircraft he might otherwise be able to nurse back to an airfield."

"The life of an experienced pilot is vastly more valuable than a piece of equipment," insisted Mr. Holmes.

"An *expensive* piece of equipment," pointed out another government penny pincher.

"Already factored into my calculations."

"Really, Mr. Holmes, given your reputation, I wouldn't have expected you to be a sentimentalist."

"I am a pragmatist," said Mr. Holmes. "Experienced pilots can only train inexperienced pilots if they remain alive. Inexperienced pilots cost us far more in lost lives and equipment than an occasional aircraft ditched because the man at the stick has decided there have been too many holes shot in his mount to see it safely home. What was the average life expectancy of a new pilot stationed to the front? Six weeks? Never much longer than that since the Germans first came at us with the synchronised forward-firing machine gun three years ago. We were quick to follow their example of how best to take a life in the sky. We should follow their example of how best of save one with equal vigour."

"Thankfully our pilots no longer face machine gun fire at ten-thousand feet."

"And yet the life expectancy of novice airmen has hardly improved."

"Powered flight is still in its infancy. I am certain improvements to the equipment will be made moving forward."

"You could start with the parachutes."

The silence that followed suggested Mr. Holmes's point may have finally been understood.

"We will take your recommendations under advisement, as always."

The room was cleared in short order, leaving only Mycroft Holmes and myself in the gigantic chamber that, despite its size and opulence, felt close and stuffy.

"They would do better to take my recommendations to heart! I could have ended this vulgar abattoir of a war a year or more sooner if they had listened to me more often."

"You asked to see me, sir," I reminded him.

"Indeed, Wiggins. Something has come up that requires your attention."

I wondered what that something might be. The war years had seen an aging Mycroft Holmes relying on me more than ever to be everything from his liaison, to his secretary, to his personal manservant. Sometimes the tasks he set me to were crucial to the war effort. Other times they were utterly mundane.

"A body has been discovered in France," he informed me.

"I imagine a great many have," I replied.

"A man has been murdered," he specified.

"Again," I began, "one would think – "

"Wiggins," he said, impatient with me, "do you really think I would summon you here concerning a lone casualty in a war that has killed so many?"

"I never know what you have in mind for me, so I try not to guess."

"Fair enough," he agreed. "You're heading to the village of Chemin-des-sangliers to look into it."

"I don't recall seeing that town on any of our tactical maps," I said.

"That is because it has been wiped off the map entirely. Destroyed in the first year of the war, abandoned since, and likely to never be rebuilt. The dead man was discovered a day ago by scouts policing the area for any die-hard Hun holdouts."

"You think this man was murdered by German soldiers after the cease-fire?"

"That is for you to discover. It is, I am assured, a murder most foul and unsettling. Our man in Arras will brief you when you arrive. Suffice to say the nature of this intrigue is such that it could have a demoralising effect. Already our troops abroad grow disheartened by the lack of movement in the weeks since Armistice. There have been outbreaks of disobedience, infighting, and vocal resentment. If word gets out about what happened to one of our own in the ruins of Chemin-des-sangliers, it could be the match that sets off a powder keg."

"I'll see about catching the first available ship out of Southampton."

"I need you on site immediately," Mr. Holmes informed me. "You'll fly."

"In an aeroplane?" I asked, my alarm instant.

"Unless you have sprouted wings I have failed to perceive."

I had, obviously, never flown before. Few men outside of our Flying Corps had at that time. It was a prospect that was, at once, thrilling and terrifying.

"Can I have a parachute?" I asked hopefully.

"Apparently they are in short supply on our end, so I suggest you remain onboard for the duration."

Our troops may have been slowly returning, but I, it seemed, was headed out. To the very front lines we had just spent so much blood and treasure defending.

The December air of the Channel was bitterly cold, especially at an altitude of several thousand feet above sea level. I was wrapped up in a flight jacket, helmet, goggles, and scarf, and I still felt like I was on an expedition to the North Pole rather than a quick hop over to France.

The pilot who had come to pick me up in Dover and chauffeur me through the sky was a veteran of The Great War, still stationed at one of our makeshift airfields. His name was Stanley Birkett, and so used to combat missions was he that ferrying me to France in the dead of winter was like going on leave to him. He hadn't seen home in years, so touching down on British shores, if only briefly, was a welcome errand.

"Is it safe?" I asked Birkett as I followed his lead and climbed into the rear cockpit of the two-seater aircraft.

"Safe as houses," he assured me. "Assuming the builders did dodgy work and those houses might come apart under you when you least expect it."

Mechanical failures were, I expected, a hazard of the job. Complete structural failure in mid-air was another thing entirely.

"They don't actually come to pieces during a flight, do they?" I asked, sure he was having me on.

"It's been known to occur," he said. "Even without the help of German bullets."

"What do you do if that happens?"

"Flap your arms as hard as you can."

"I hardly expect that to be any help."

"No," he agreed. "But it will give you something to do during the fall. It's a long way to the ground, and a good while to get there."

It occurred to me, once we were airborne, that Birkett had reason to be so flippant. He may have had many hours of flight experience under his belt, but he was also wearing a parachute, the lucky bastard. I didn't envy it so much for the security it provided in the event of equipment failure, but for the extra layer of insulation it offered against the piecing wind that whipped around inside the open cockpit of the biplane. I asked him where he got it, given that they weren't standard issue.

"Spoils of war," he shouted back at me over the drone of the engine. "The Boche had stacks of them when we seized their airfields, so we helped ourselves. Haven't gone up without one since."

It seemed the pilots well understood the benefits of being able to bail out of their aircraft, even if the generals on the ground hadn't figured it out yet.

"Have you ever had to jump?" I asked.

"Once," he said.

"What's it like?"

"It's like throwing yourself into the abyss, but with a final card to play to cheat the devil."

"I guess you played that card."

"I'm here, aren't I?"

As much could not be said for many of our flyers.

Our destination was the airfield at Filescamp Farm, once a station for some of our finest aces. Now there was but a skeleton crew of pilots and observers flying the occasional mission for post-war intelligence. The state of the silenced front still proved to be of interest to those who were planning to rebuild on land that had been levelled and spoiled.

I could see a lone man waiting at the edge of the field as we circled the farm and took an approach favourable to the wind. Once our wheels were down and the engine cut, we rolled to a stop not more than a dozen yards away from where this welcoming party of one stood vigil.

Dismounted, I pulled off my helmet and goggles and saw the familiar face of the man who approached. Mine was every bit as familiar to him.

"Wiggins," he said warmly, "welcome to France."

It was Sherlock Holmes who was my mysterious contact abroad. The famous detective had been a valued collector of actionable intelligence throughout the war. I had seen a number of written reports made to his brother, and the riddles he had been solving of late had much to do with the untangling of secret enemy plans.

"So you're our man in Arras!" I declared.

"For the last week, at any rate," said Mr. Holmes. "I have also been our man in Paris, Constantinople, Bern, Genoa, and Budapest, depending on the needs of the hour. Mycroft likes to keep me busy."

"Would you two care to join me in the mess hall for coffee?" asked Birkett. "The coffee is cold, but the stove is warm enough."

"I am afraid we have pressing business elsewhere," said Mr. Holmes. "Tell our driver to bring the car around at once."

Birkett left us alone. Only then was I able to bring up the sensitive nature of our inquiry.

"I hear we have a murder to solve."

"Quite so!" said Mr. Holmes. "And time is short. The demand for answers is most insistent."

"Does the murder of one man still matter after the world has spent four years murdering millions?" I wondered.

"It has to. Civility must return if we are to save civilisation, or we have fought and sacrificed for nothing."

"What's so special about this particular case?"

"You will know it when you see it."

"Your brother mentioned low spirits."

Mr. Holmes nodded solemnly.

"Demoralisation remains a critical factor for our armed forces, even with the war at an end. We have not been hurried in our efforts to demobilise, and there remain many tens of thousands of men still stationed at or near the front who are understandably eager to return to their lives. Their impatience builds each day, and there have been reports that mutiny is a very real possibility."

We were picked up by a burly sergeant at the wheel of a Wolseley and driven across new roads that had been cleared for the supply chain to-and-from the front lines. I could smell No Man's Land before I could see it – an acrid stench that reeked of burnt metal and chemicals and the decay of men and horses still lost in the mud. Wooden planks had been set out to allow passage across upturned soil and sections of bombarded land that were prone to pooling whenever it rained. The car made slow progress as the sergeant struggled to keep our wheels on the lumber rails that would see us across the former battlefield.

"My God," I said, as we passed through Hell itself.

"You have never seen the front," Mr. Holmes noted.

"Only in aerial reconnaissance photos. Pictures don't do it justice."

"We have spent years gouging a wound through the heart of Europe. It won't soon heal. I fear we might tear the scar asunder again if we aren't careful to make a lasting peace."

The village of Chemin-des-sangliers lay close to the German end. Though the frontline of the sector had been pushed back and forth over the course of the war – sometimes a mile or more, other times mere yards – Chemin-des-sangliers had always been in the crosshairs of one side or the other. A steady hail of artillery fire had levelled the area to such a degree, it was nearly impossible to picture what had so recently been a quaint countryside settlement.

Jagged stone walls stood broken and irregular atop exposed foundations. A few remained capable of supporting partial roofs, but all were so peppered with holes that the weather had had its way with the interiors, setting the wood to rot. Some homes and shops still sported spaces for windows and doors, but all were shattered or burned away entirely. Loose stones strewn about suggested at least one cobbled street, now left cratered and earthen by so many direct hits. Not a single living thing called this place home anymore. Even the rats had moved on to try their luck with the network of German bunkers nearby. The cold concrete of abandoned tunnels and fortifications promised a more welcoming abode than what had become of Chemin-des-sangliers.

"He's in there," said the sergeant, stopping the car outside one of the more recognisable structures left in the village. It was a modest house, once home to a family, now no more than an unstable wreck that looked like it might cave in upon itself in the next stiff breeze.

"Thank you, Sergeant," said Mr. Holmes. "We'll want a detail to remove the body once we have concluded our investigation. Discreetly, if you will."

"I'll leave the car for you and round up some men, sir," he said, exiting the vehicle and beginning his march back across the wasteland to the nearest outpost.

"Come along, Wiggins," encouraged Mr. Holmes. "Let us see what fresh horror this war has offered us so late in the game."

We let ourselves in and didn't have to search the premises long to find the fellow we had come looking for. The house was barren, deserted, with any personal possessions or furniture carted away by their owners or looted by thieves long ago.

The dead man was lying at the base of the fireplace. He was on his back with his head beaten in and his legs stuffed up the chimney. His red hood had come off, but he was still wearing the matching coat with white-fur lining. The straps holding his grand bushy beard in place had come loose from the violence that had killed him, and it remained hanging off the end of his chin. It would have peeled away entirely if the moustache hadn't caught on the lower teeth of a gaping mouth that was frozen in a terror-stricken grimace.

"Father Christmas doesn't look like he's having a happy holiday," I observed.

The resemblance wasn't casual. The seasonal attire was entirely intentional, and bizarre to find in the middle of such devastation.

Mr. Holmes was, at once, crouched next to the body and taking in details more subtle and obscure than any I was likely to find. I could hardly bring myself to see past the costume.

"How long has he been dead, do you think?" I asked.

"Difficult to ascertain. The layer of soot is nearly as thick as his red winter coat, and the temperature has been low enough to preserve him from decay. These walls certainly offer no insulation from the elements."

"How do we even know he's one of ours?"

"He is still sporting his uniform under the coat," said Mr. Holmes, pulling aside the collar and revealing the olive green of an RAF officer and a single-wing insignia.

"Why dress him up like that?" I wondered. "Is this meant as some sick Christmas present?"

"You see how wild rumours will spread if word of this gets out," said Mr. Holmes. "The symbology alone will give the tale legs, and it would not be the first time in this conflict."

I remembered the incident Mr. Holmes was referring to well. We all did.

"They say the Huns crucified a Canadian back in '15."

"Likely apocryphal," said Mr. Holmes. "Crimes and atrocities occur in every war, but some acts are so singularly foul, one must question if they happened at all, or are merely stories concocted to arouse the fighting spirit in men who wish to combat such evil."

"There were plenty of other accounts going around early on, all of them horrible."

"Propaganda meant to convince us it is not men we fight, but monsters. Such fictions crop up routinely, often coinciding with celebrations. It is as though they are invented specifically to bring such occasions low and drain the good will of men."

"This one looks real enough."

"You think it staged for our benefit?" asked Mr. Holmes. "What do you make of such a tableau, Wiggins?"

I walked around the bleak room so I could observe the body from different angles. None of them changed my opinion any, but it made me look like I was considering the scene carefully.

"I figure they dressed him up, smashed his head in, and stuffed him halfway up the chimney for good measure," I concluded.

"Why do you think the perpetrators would do such a thing – other than the fact that Father Christmas in a chimney suits the character?"

"They wanted to send a message?" I ventured.

"In a ruined and abandoned house? The body was only discovered by chance. It might not have been found for months. The entire building could have collapsed before anyone came upon it."

"I suppose you're right," I said to the man who was hardly ever wrong.

"More to the point, why would a British officer even come to this forsaken place, only to find himself dead and so ironically positioned?"

"Well, he certainly wasn't trying to deliver gifts to the good little girls and boys who don't live here anymore."

"No," agreed Mr. Holmes, tapping at his nose with the tip of his finger as he turned the improbable sequence of events over in his mind. "But there may have been gifts in the offing just the same."

Whatever else the scene might have told him remained obscure to me as Mr. Holmes led me back outside to survey the destroyed village.

"Let us make a tour of the area," he said. "I shall go on foot, you follow with the car."

"What do we need the car for?"

"To carry back any Christmas bounty we may find, of course."

As anyone who knew Sherlock Holmes understood all too well, there was no use trying to follow his train of thought. Not only would that train be several stops ahead of you, it could be steaming along a dozen different tracks at once.

Progress through the pock-marked terrain that used to be roads and squares was slow. I had my eye on the holes that I was trying to keep the car wheels out of, and was doing a poor job of scouting for whatever evidence Mr. Holmes was after. He led the way, stepping over deep puddles and rubble, until he confirmed the presence of something he'd anticipated back in the house.

"There!" he called out, pointing to spot ahead of us.

When I looked up to see what he had discovered, I didn't have to search for it long. I could hardly have missed it.

What I saw was a gift-wrapped present. The bright red paper and striking blue bow leapt out at me in a wilderness of scorched stone and blackened earth. It sat in the middle of the road like it was waiting for us.

Mr. Holmes marched over and retrieved it as I got out of the car and joined him.

"Merry Christmas, Wiggins," he said, passing me the colourful box.

"What is it?"

"Open it," he instructed. "I can't deduce everything myself."

"What if it's a trap?"

The thought occurred it might be some vile surprise left behind by a retreating enemy, lying in wait for any of our Tommies foolish enough to pick it up.

"It isn't a trap," he assured me. "That much I can tell without looking inside."

"If you say so," I said, and pulled the end of the bow until it became untied.

Nothing blew up in my face, so I proceeded, purely out of trust in Mr. Holmes's word. It had yet to steer me wrong in the many years of our acquaintance.

The box inside contained a single wrapped bar in a bed of tissue paper.

"Chocolate?" I asked, once I had a look at the label.

"Rations. From the Red Cross," said Mr. Holmes.

"Are there more?" I said, looking around.

"Most certainly," replied the detective. "We may collect them as we go, but it is their source we now seek."

We continued on foot and sure enough, there were other presents strewn about the village. Not all were as perfectly presented as the first we found. More than a few were badly dented or soiled by mud, but all contained some modest gift. Cigarettes, tobacco, and confections were most common, and I stopped checking their contents in time. One by one, we set them in the rear seat of the car as we circled back, often with armfuls of samples.

I didn't realise to what extent we were pushing our luck until I reached for yet another box and heard a loud click underfoot.

"What is it, Wiggins?" Mr. Holmes asked me when I froze in mid-stoop.

"This time it's a trap for sure," I announced, my voice suddenly hoarse.

"Nonsense," he said. "It is undoubtedly more rations."

"Not the present," I said. "The thing I've just stepped on."

Mr. Holmes set aside the boxes he carried and came to my side at once to see what had given me such a fright. He knelt down and turned his head until he could see precisely what my foot was resting upon.

"Hold quite still, Wiggins," he advised me. "You're standing on an unexploded shell."

I may have uttered something unfit for print at that moment. Of all the battle debris scattered about, that was the single worst thing I could have stumbled upon.

Mr. Holmes dug in his coat pocket and came up with a familiar tool of his trade. He positioned the magnifying glass next to the sole of my boot and struggled to get a better look at the device beneath it.

"One of ours, it seems," he observed. "Buried upon impact. It may well have lain here undisturbed for years."

"Well it's bloody disturbed now, isn't it?" I said, panic rising in my voice.

"Whatever it first struck upon landing failed to activate the percussion fuse, but it has sheared off a section of the nose cone, leaving the inner workings exposed. There is too much mud in the mechanism to see clearly, but your weight appears to be resting directly on the charge spring. I would not recommending stepping off it, or moving at all."

I took his advice and played at being a statue as Mr. Holmes spent an excruciating amount of time examining the wayward shell that had survived the war without fulfilling its lethal purpose.

"It is an explosive shell, not a gas shell," he announced at last.

"Ah well, there's a lucky break," I said. "When it kills us, it will be quick about it."

Mr. Holmes, still crouching in the mud, reversed his magnifying glass and slowly fed the handle under my foot. It was a delicate operation that took several long minutes until, at last, he had it where he wanted it.

"You may step off, Wiggins," he said.

"Are you sure?"

"No," he admitted. "But if I am wrong, we shall never know it."

Slowly, I raised my foot – not that doing it slowly would save us if the shell went off. Once I was clear, and we were still alive, I allowed myself to take my first normal breath since the moment I felt the metal casing under my boot.

Several steps away, still gasping for air, I noticed Mr. Holmes wasn't rising to join me. I understood, only then, that he hadn't defused the shell. He had only taken my place and was now in the same peril I had been spared.

"Get back to the car and fetch a bomb-disposal unit," Mr. Holmes instructed, pressing down on the exposed charge spring and keeping the thing from going off.

"You can't possibly hold that position for as long as it will take me to drive back to our lines and find someone qualified," I protested.

"Do as I say, Wiggins, and be quick about it," he said, keeping his eyes fixed on the simple but deadly apparatus only inches in front of him. One false move at this point would kill us both.

I knew better than to argue with Sherlock Holmes, but abandoning him in such a perilous position went against my every instinct. Already I was calculating how long it would take me to follow his orders. Likely hours – and with little sunlight left in the day. It seemed unlikely that even trained explosives engineers would be able to do much to save him in the dark.

It was with great reluctance that I hurried back to where we had left the car. No sooner had I passed the corner of a ruined church than I heard the single loudest sound I had ever experienced in my life. The church wall sheltered me from the explosion, but the concussion of the blast still swept me off my feet. I'm sure our shell-shocked soldiers, rattled and shaken for life, had become weary of the experience, but it was entirely new to me, and filled my soul with dread.

Picking myself up at once, I ran back to the place I had left Sherlock Holmes only moments earlier, already regretting ever leaving his side.

"Mr. Holmes! Mr. Holmes!" I shouted, as I rounded the bend and came within sight of the blast point.

A smoking crater was all that remained of the very spot where I had last seen the finest man I ever knew. I dared not look too closely, for if there was anything left of him to find, it was doubtless scattered all around the village rubble in pieces too small to identify. Better I should remember him as he was: Intact.

"Right then, Wiggins," said a voice behind me, "back in the car and off we go. We have dallied here long enough."

I nearly fainted when I saw Sherlock Holmes again, standing alive and well only a few feet away. Recovering my senses, I threw myself at him and wrapped my arms around his shoulders with a sense of relief greater than any I had ever felt in my life.

Letting me have a moment to recover, Mr. Holmes patted me on the back several times. It was meant to be reassuring, but it was also a clear signal that I might want to release him at last.

"Do I have to ask how?" I wondered, knowing full well that I was standing before a man known to perform miracles.

"You have doubtless seen the same reports I have about the efficacy of our bombardments," said Mr. Holmes. "Mycroft shares his data with me whenever I am in London, and I am certain you take in all you can read over his shoulder."

I remembered one such report I'd had a peek at only a couple of months earlier, when the war seemed like it would never end. Mycroft Holmes was doubtless aware of my snooping into his affairs, but clearly did not consider me security risk enough to put a stop to my curiosity.

"It said about one in three shells fired at the front were duds," I recalled.

"Amounting to roughly a thirty-three percent chance of surviving even a very near miss."

"So you just walked away and hoped it wouldn't go off?"

"I played the odds."

"The odds were against you!" I exclaimed.

"I have faced worse odds than that and survived. Fortune was with me once again."

"But it still went off," I noted.

"Yes," agreed Mr. Holmes. "Not such a dud after all. But enough for me to get clear, which was fortune enough. Doubtless such war detritus will poison the land for generations to come. Chemin-des-sangliers has been declared part of the *Zone Rouge*. Uninhabitable. One of many villages to have died for France."

"Well, there's no use us dying for France, too," I said.

"There has certainly been death enough already. Come," he encouraged, "let us depart before we add ourselves to the casualty figures."

We climbed back into the car and began to motor out of harm's way.

"Are we still looking for the source of all these presents?" I asked of our collection.

"Yes," confirmed Mr. Holmes. "And I believe I know where we might look."

I followed the sleuth's instructions as he navigated our vehicle out of the village and away from the poisonous landscape of No Man's Land. We soon found ourselves on what was once German-held territory, far enough back from the front to be unspoiled by war. Healthy trees and rolling waves of grassland greeted us, and it was easy to forget the years of destruction, provided we didn't look back over our shoulder.

"The gifts we found were part of a debris field," explained Mr. Holmes. "Where they had come to rest formed enough of a pattern for me to calculate the direction our hunt must turn next."

As the car bumped along dirt roads and open fields, Mr. Holmes opened the passenger door and positioned himself on the running board so he could stand up and better survey the landscape ahead.

"At our left!" he announced a quarter-of-a-mile later, referring me to a stand of trees at the edge of a stretch of tilled soil.

I turned the wheel sharply and set the car on a course across the frozen ruts that had been ploughed but never sown. It was a bone-jangling detour that threatened to shake the vehicle to pieces, but we managed to get to the spot Mr. Holmes had pointed out. There, at the base of a large oak, sat the crumpled remains of a two-seater biplane. It had been charred black by flames, and quite recently as far as I could make out. Some of the tree's branches had been stripped of their leaves by the blaze and hadn't had the time or weather to renew themselves.

"The prevailing west wind pushed most of the aerial encounters of the war over German-held territory," said Mr. Holmes, hopping off the side of the car. "Many of our downed aircraft crashed or landed out of our reach, which favoured the enemy enormously. The enemy may be gone, but the west wind persists, and stricken planes are still likely to fall on the same side of the former lines."

A roundel on the canvas indicated the aircraft was British, but it took time to find one that hadn't been obliterated by the flames.

"Crashed and burned," I said of the wreck before us.

"The reverse, I should think," said Mr. Holmes. "Likely an engine fire. Observe how the flames have seared lines across the fuselage. Most of the burning happened while the plane was still in motion."

"No sign of the crew," I said. "Do you suppose they survived the crash?"

"At least one did not."

It took me a moment to make the connection.

"You mean Saint Nick back there?" I asked.

"Our dead man was not placed in the chimney," Mr. Holmes told me. "He fell down it and came to rest at the base of the fireplace where we found him. His wounds were not inflicted by any weapon more sinister than gravity."

"Surely not!" I declared. "You mean to say a man dressed in a Father Christmas costume just happened to fall to his death, from untold hundreds of feet up, and put himself head first down a chimney?"

"I am saying that an airman bailed out of his burning plane as it passed over an abandoned French village. His motivation for being dressed as he was is incidental."

"But a chimney?" I reiterated, fixated on the improbability.

"He had to land somewhere," said Mr. Holmes. "The placement of his body might have seemed less remarkable if he had smashed through a roof, but he managed to strike a chimney instead."

"What are the chances?" I wondered.

"Not as unlikely as you might think. The village is dotted with chimneys, most still intact. He could just as well have found himself down any one of a dozen others."

Mr. Holmes was right. The stone fireplaces and their stacks had been, in many cases, the last thing standing in buildings otherwise razed. Landing on one was as likely as any other spot. It was his outfit that tipped the circumstances of his death into the uncanny.

"What about all these presents?" I said of our cargo.

"Shed from the distressed aircraft as it went down, just like the fallen observer. The single-wing insignia on his uniform tells us he was stationed in the rear seat. That leaves the pilot unaccounted for."

"No," I said, thunderstruck. "Not unaccounted for. I know just where to find him!"

"What great leap of deductive reasoning have you made that escapes me, Wiggins?" asked Mr. Holmes, amused I might have some insight that eluded him.

We found Birkett in the canteen once we returned the Wolseley to Filescamp. He was out of coffee by then, but the stove still held his attention. We were just as keen to warm ourselves after our excursion through the wastelands.

"Ah, hello gentlemen," he said when he saw us. "I hope you had a fruitful trip."

"Most enlightening," Mr. Holmes assured him.

"Found what you were looking for?"

"Not quite. There is one thing that remains for us to uncover."

"What's that then?" Birkett wondered.

"An explanation."

Birkett looked confused and I waited for Mr. Holmes to continue. But he remained silent, suggesting I be the one to carry on.

"He is your witness, after all," he said, gesturing at the aviator sitting across from us.

"A witness to what?" asked Birkett.

"You were the one who gave me a crash course in crashing this morning," I began. "You mentioned having to bail out of your plane once."

"Earlier this week, in fact. There was an engine fire and the whole thing started to burn."

"You weren't alone."

"No," he said, his eyes downcast. "My good mate, Quin, was in back. Quin Chapman. We'd flown many a mission together and came through it all without a scratch. Who knew it would be peacetime that would have it in for us?"

"What exactly was the nature of this final mission?" asked Mr. Holmes.

"It wasn't officially on the books as such," admitted Birkett. "It was more of an unauthorised side trip."

"Involving a Father Christmas costume?"

"How did you know that?" said the pilot, as though we had discovered a most terrible secret.

"Chapman's body has been discovered in No Man's Land," Mr. Holmes informed him.

"It was a foolish stunt, but well intentioned," Birkett said sadly. "We thought it might boost the squadron's spirits with the war over but home still out of reach."

"Where did you come up with the presents?" I asked.

"I suppose the whole lot came down with poor Quin. What a waste!" he said before explaining further. "The Red Cross has been checking on prisoners of war since this whole bother began. They could get letters and supplies through, and make sure families back home knew their boys were alive and well. Locked up for the duration, but otherwise safe. Come the holidays, they'd make an effort to deliver extra rations. This year, though, the war ended just short of Christmas, and there was nowhere for those goodies to go. All our POWs are being sent back to this side now and it seemed a pity to let such loot go unappreciated. Quin and I hatched an idea to pop over to a Red Cross camp in Belgium and see if they might put together a package for our squad. The nurses thought it was a fine idea and were even able to set us up with wrapping paper, a red coat, and a cotton beard. It would have been a grand time for our chaps to have Father Christmas himself hand out the trimmings when we returned."

"The second leg of the trip did not go as well," prompted Mr. Holmes, and I could see the memory of it pained Birkett greatly.

"I thought you told me there were plenty of parachutes to go around ever since you had your pick of German aerodrome supplies," I said.

"Quin would have had one on, but there was no room in the rear, what with him and that sack of presents. He figured he'd survived the whole war without a 'chute, what was one more flight? He left his pack behind in Belgium for the ladies of the Red Cross to use the silk as they wished."

"You made it back over the front but were pushed off course," said Mr. Holmes.

"The controls became fidgety," Birkett said. "I didn't know there was a fire onboard until it was too late. I tried to circle back to flatter land, but there wasn't enough time to set down. The whole thing was going up like a Roman candle."

"You still had the altitude to bail out," I said.

"Barely," Birkett recalled. "I didn't know what to do. Of course I had to jump. But how could I leave Quin behind? He must have known I couldn't bring myself to do it without him, so he made it easy for me. When I shouted to him over the dying engine, there was no response. I turned to look, but he was gone. There was only the open sack in the seat, and the wind sucking all the presents out of the cockpit as the plane banked. 'Flaming coffins' is what Quin called our deathtraps when a fire started and spread to the canvas. It was his biggest fear, and he always said he'd take the fall rather than burn alive."

The three of us sat quietly, contemplating the tragic end that Quin Chapman suffered, and those final seconds of terror he must have experienced as he plummeted, knowing his fate was sealed.

"We recovered some of the gifts you were planning to hand out," said Mr. Holmes. "They may yet make a merrier Christmas for your fellow airmen. You, however, will have to make a full report on the incident – not just the loss of a man and an aircraft as the record already states, but all the details related to this misadventure. You must do this before rumours of a dead man in a Father Christmas costume spread and imaginations run wild."

"I was already in hot water for taking a plane up off schedule. They'll ground me for sure when they find out the real reason Quin is dead."

"Be content that the next time you see England," advised Mr. Holmes, "even if it is by sea rather than sky, that you have survived to see England at all."

"I trust my brother will be content with the results," said Mr. Holmes outside.

"No murder and no mutiny should suit him well enough," I said.

"Then I will leave you to return to him as you may."

I considered my options, absent any orders from my employer.

"I think I'll take the long way. By ship. If my means of transportation goes down, I like my chances of jumping into water rather than a mile of open air."

"A prudent choice, I am sure."

"Will you be heading home now that the war is done, Mr. Holmes?" I asked.

"I expect a dispatch from Mycroft any moment now," he said. "There seems to always be one more matter of pressing state business he wants me to look into these days. With Kaisers and Czars alike being deposed, the world is changing rapidly."

"For the better, perhaps?"

"I wonder," said Sherlock Holmes.

In those tumultuous days, we all considered who we might turn to in order to make sense of it all. The War to End All Wars had done nothing of the sort, and long-established tradition seemed strange and abnormal now. All the rules had changed, and no one seemed to have any answers. For my part, at least, I placed my trust in the Brothers Holmes.

The Bitter Gravestones
by Chris Chan

Sherlock Holmes was not having a happy Christmas. He was tired, a little bitter, and would much rather have been back with his honeybees.

He hadn't wanted to spend the holiday at an isolated manor house in the countryside, but his brother Mycroft had requested that he make the visit and protect the nation's interests at a top-secret conference there. Although I cannot go into details as the event is still a state secret, by the morning of the twenty-fourth of December the matters being decided were satisfactorily resolved and the assorted diplomats had left hurriedly in order make their way home in time for the holiday. Holmes was under orders to remain at the manor house until Boxing Day to tie up loose ends and await the arrival of a government agent for further instructions.

Holmes had invited me along, privately warning me that my presence was necessary to preserve his sanity. He had previously met the Blurdells, the family who owned the manor, and they weren't the sort of people with whom Holmes would willingly spend time, given the option. Once Holmes had done his duty to King and Country and sent the last of the diplomats on his way, he retreated to his room and asked that his meals be delivered on a tray.

"Surely you don't intend to spend the entirety of Christmas in your room? I'm aware that you aren't feeling particularly warm towards the Blurdells – which, having gotten to know most of them over the last two days, I can rather understand. But Christmas is Christmas, and wouldn't you rather share your goose and pudding with other people?"

The glare on Holmes's face was far more chilling than the icy winds whipping around the mansion. "I can assure you, Watson, that having devoted all of my energies to maintaining peace on earth, I now no longer have the strength to muster any goodwill to all men. I have done my part to prevent the recurrence of those horrors that plagued our continent for four long and violent years. I don't deserve the torment of having to pull Christmas crackers with Lord Derek Blurdell or listen to Horace Blurdell's tired jokes as he drains a decanter of port. I have a quiet room, a couple of books, and enough paper and writing equipment to begin work on the monograph I've been planning for some time. Should for some reason I desire conversation, I can always speak to you, dear fellow. Otherwise, I shall be perfectly happy being left to my own devices."

I chose not to argue further, as in my heart I knew he was completely correct. For most people, any company is better than none at Christmas. Not so for Holmes.

We spoke little over the next few minutes, and I was about to return to my room and take a little nap before dinner when there was a knock at the door. Before Holmes could utter a response, a thirteen year-old boy hurried into the room and shut the door behind him. It was Duncan Blurdell, the only surviving son of Lord Derek Blurdell, his older brothers having perished in the war. "Mr. Holmes? Doctor Watson?"

"Yes, Duncan? What is it?" I asked.

"I need to talk to you about the gravestones."

"What's wrong with them?" Holmes asked, not bothering to hide the asperity in his voice.

"They're so *bitter*, sir. It doesn't make sense."

"How can a gravestone be bitter?"

"It's what's inscribed on them, Mr. Holmes. Six relatives I've never met or even heard of. They all died on Christmas, one a year for the past six years. And what's written on the gravestones is truly vile, sir. Not Christian at all. But if someone's died every Christmas for over half a decade – well, what if the pattern holds and someone else dies tomorrow? I don't know for sure, but it can't be a coincidence that six members of the family died on that date so regularly, sir. If we could find out what's going on, maybe we could prevent tomorrow's death, sir."

Holmes's facial expression and posture altered completely, and I noticed that familiar spark of interest that he gets whenever he decides that a problem is worthy of his skills. "Can you lead us to the gravestones?"

"Yes, sir. They aren't far from the house."

"Get your coat, Watson. I very much want to see these gravestones."

As I rummaged through the hall closet for my coat, I felt my eyes water from the abundance of pine. Multiple large trees had been installed in the entryway, and evergreen boughs festooned the archways. A few minutes later, we were walking along a lightly trampled pathway in the dead grass, wrapping our coats tightly around us to protect ourselves from the blustery wind. "How long have you been aware of these gravestones, Duncan?" Holmes asked.

"I just discovered them twenty minutes ago, sir. I don't like to visit the graveyard – it isn't a pleasant place. But I was playing with my dog, Rex. He's a spaniel. We were playing near the edge of the woods, about a quarter-mile south of the family cemetery, and suddenly he started running off. Well, I followed him, and when I got there, Rex was sniffing around these six gravestones in the corner. I tried to shoo him away, but he started howling, and he drew my attention to what was written on them, sir. Gave me the chills, it did. That's why I came to you, thinking you might be able to make sense of it all."

The wind grew steadily stronger as we made our way to the cemetery. It was a small square of land surrounded on three sides by the woods, and completely enclosed by an iron fence. Unlike every other portion of the estate, there were no Christmas decorations to be found around the graveyard. We pushed through the unlocked gate. There were about seventy gravestones scattered around the graveyard in no apparent order. Most of them were large, ornate slabs of shining marble. Duncan led us towards the back of the area, where six stones stood far apart from the nearest markers.

The first four in the line were small pieces of cheap tan rock, each about a foot tall. The first read:

Elspeth Blurdell Hill
June 3 1881 – December 25 1919
She Will Not Be Mourned

"Who would write that on a gravestone?" I asked.
"Wait until you see the others," Duncan informed me.
The words on the second stone were:

John Blurdell
3 March, 1884 – 25 December, 1920
Good riddance to Bad Rubbish

I was flabbergasted. Holmes looked fascinated. As we moved to the third we read the words:

Alicia Blurdell White
15 December, 1900 – 25 December, 1921
Liar
Adulteress
Murderess

"Murderess? Who is she supposed to have killed?"
"We shall have to look into that, Watson."
The fourth grave was no less malicious or baffling.

Gregory Blurdell
11 August, 1847 – 25 December, 1922
S.I.T.

Suffer In Torment

The fifth gravestone was a bit larger than the first four, and was made of much nicer material.

Thomas Blurdell
27 February, 1898 – 25 December, 1923
If only he had been stillborn,
the world would have been a happier place.

"What a heartless thing to write!"
"Possibly. Observe this sixth."
The sixth gravestone was by far the largest and most ornate. It was the only one to resemble the other prominent markers in the cemetery, and it actually had a poem inscribed on it:

Daniel Blurdell
2 January, 1897 – 25 December, 1924
Here rots the corpse of Dan Blurdell
The worst sinner since Adam fell
His breath gave off a loathsome smell
If he had virtues none could tell
Not once in life did he mean well
We hope the bastard roasts in hell

"How appalling!" I blurted out uncontrollably.
"Not appalling so much as intriguing. The odds of six people in the same family dying on Christmas over the course of six consecutive years defies the odds."
"Why would someone carve such sentiments on a gravestone, where anyone can see it?"
"Not anyone. Remember, this is a private graveyard in the middle of the countryside. The only people likely to ever see this are the Blurdell family and their servants."
"And not many of either group you mention, Mr. Holmes," Duncan chimed in, "Most of the family and servants don't much like to spend time in the graveyard. It's an unsettling place, sir. Every now and then someone comes in on an anniversary, but more often than not we never visit. There's a gardener who comes in once in a while to tidy up everything, but not many other people."
"Interesting. When was the last time you were in here before today, Duncan?"

"For my brothers' joint funeral back in 1919. They were all killed in the war, but we didn't get their bodies back until long after all the battles had ended. I've been at school when all of the other family members' funerals were held." Duncan pointed across the graveyard at four headstones, each with a stone bust on the top. "They all died during the last six months of fighting, sir. If the war had just ended a couple of months earlier, maybe a couple of my brothers could've made it home."

"I'm so sorry, Duncan."

"It isn't your fault, Mr. Holmes. I know I should come here more often, but, well, I just don't like it here. I'm away at school most of the time anyway. I didn't know them all that well because they were so much older than I was, but that didn't mean we weren't close, sir."

"You don't have to explain yourself." Holmes started walking around the other gravestones. "There seems to be a clear disparity in these monuments to the dead. The holders of the earldom, those who died in battle . . . most of them receive enormous headstones, often with some sort of tribute inscribed on it. Others, mainly women and those who died young, get smaller headstones, with much simpler inscriptions – just the names and dates. Still, the rest of these are made out of high-quality material, unlike those four stones there, which might crumble over a relatively short period of time when exposed to the elements. You can see the earliest bitter gravestone has already developed the first hints of a crack. It won't last another decade. So the point arises: Someone loathed these people enough that they were willing to carve their venom onto a slab of rock, but they didn't care enough to buy sufficiently durable material so that their rancor would last throughout the ages."

"And why are the last two headstones nicer than the others?" I wondered. "Do you think that whomever purchased them loathed the deceased, but thought that they deserved a lasting monument to their awfulness?"

"My father would have bought those headstones," Duncan noted. "As the head of the family, it's his job to handle all of the major purchases."

"Duncan, you understand that I have to ask these questions, even if they are rather personal," Holmes explained. "Are there financial reasons why your father might have been compelled to scrimp a lot on those headstones?"

"Not really, sir. He certainly spared no expense for my brothers' graves. He's complained about the cost of my school fees, but he's never been unable to pay them. The staff doesn't seem to be any smaller than it was in the past. I haven't noticed any paintings missing from the walls, and as far as I can tell my mother still has all of her jewels. Actually, my father's bought her an enormous diamond necklace for Christmas this year, but please don't tell her and spoil the surprise until tomorrow."

"I see. What do you know about the six people in the graves?"

"Nothing, Mr. Holmes."

"Surely you must have heard something about them?"

"Well, I can't be sure, because when my grandfather was alive before the war, he was always telling long and rambling stories about the family, but I never really listened, so it's certainly possible that he mentioned them at some point, but they didn't stay in my mind."

"Did you ever meet any of them?"

"No, sir, not as far as I can remember, but there are a great many family members that I've never seen. You see, a lot of my relatives have led rather . . . *scandalous* lives. Plenty of them have run off with lovers, some have wasted massive amounts of money on gambling. and there's no shortage of cousins who bear the family name, but whose parents were never married. There's probably dozens of relatives who are considered embarrassments. I suppose the official family policy is that if someone isn't considered sufficiently respectable, he or she is *persona non grata*. Their names are never mentioned, there are no pictures of them anywhere, and they're never invited to the manor house. Every now and then the family lawyers may send them some money, but I don't know why. Maybe they've been very good, or maybe they're in terrible trouble, or perhaps they're threatening to make an embarrassing scene and my father bribes them to mind their manners." Duncan shuddered. "We're a rather idiosyncratic family."

Holmes shrugged. "You're really not that different from other wealthy and prominent families."

"Do you know any others who write messages like this on gravestones?"

"No. Which makes this situation all the more intriguing." After a moment's pause, Holmes asked, "How many of your estranged relatives have been buried in the family plot?"

"As far as I can tell, none of them, at least since I was born. I've looked around, and I recognize the names of everyone who's died in my lifetime." Duncan gestured. "I see my grandparents and some great-aunts and uncles, and of course my brothers. I never met my great-aunt Cicely, who lived in Paris since she was twenty-one, but she was mentioned all the time before she died four years ago. Our cousin Gerald, who comes from the branch of the family with no money of their own, works in the family archives and traces the family genealogy. My parents often sit me next to him at family dinners, possibly because no one else wants to listen to him talking about our ancestors and distant relatives. Just last night at dinner, he was talking about someone rather high up on our family tree who fought at the Battle of Bosworth Field. I don't remember what side that person was on, though."

"Hmm. Let's take another look at the gravestones." Holmes walked back to the start of the line of markers. "Elspeth Blurdell Hill. Indicating that she was married, or possibly was the daughter of a Blurdell daughter who married a Hill and wanted to make sure the Blurdell name wasn't lost. A little under forty. Can you think of any other relatives named 'Ellie' or 'Ella', or any other potential derivatives?"

"No, sir. I have a distant cousin named Eleanor, but she's only six or so."

"Very well. Five words in the epitaph. '*She Will Not Be Mourned.*' Simple, terse, but vague. That is notable, especially when paired with some of the other headstones."

I was a bit confused. "What do you mean?"

"Simply put, writing an angry epitaph on a gravestone is the ultimate way of having the last word in an argument. It's a means of shaming the person you held a grudge against long after death. The deceased can't respond. So why not be more specific? *Why* won't she be mourned? *What* did she do wrong? We can't tell from this gravestone – only that no one is going to miss her. But that leads to other deductions. If she was married, then it assumes that her husband is either deceased or than they weren't on warm terms. If she had children, something so terrible must have happened that the maternal bond was absolutely severed. Surely what she did would have to be utterly horrific if it were to cut her connection with her own parents – unless of course they were already dead."

"That seems reasonable."

"But that ignores a major question: What is she doing here? Why is she buried here? Duncan, since you have no knowledge of her, can she really be that close of a relative? No matter how estranged she was from her family, they allowed her to be buried here. And if she wasn't that close to Duncan's father, Lord Derek, why would he have so much rancor towards her that he would carve those words on her stone?"

"Perhaps whatever the reasons for that estrangement, Lord Blurdell didn't want to expose the family to scandal."

"Then why put those words on the headstone at all? If he wanted to hush up the scandal, all he needed to do was put her name and the relevant dates. Nothing more. A comment like this is enough to raise eyebrows. If he had those words carved on the headstone, he must have wanted someone to see them. He clearly didn't think enough of Mrs. Elspeth to spend much money on a headstone, yet he willingly paid the engraver extra money to carve that vicious comment. Why pay for that, and use a low-quality stone that is likely to crumble within a decade? I repeat: If someone wanted to immortalize their bitterness in stone, why not spend a little extra money to make the anger last? It's contradictory."

"True." After listening to Holmes's reasoning, I was feeling a little dizzy.

"The same principle applies to the grave of John Blurdell. Once again, Duncan, you know nothing of him?"

"I don't believe so, Mr. Holmes. I know an uncle and a couple of cousins named John, but they're all alive and on good terms with the rest of the family."

"I see. The same questions from the first gravestone apply here. The inscription is cutting, cold, and completely devoid of context. The grave of Alicia Blurdell White is far more promising. Only twenty-one years old. A liar? That can be said for most of us. Adulteress? That implies that she was married to a Mr. White, but why would Mr. White want to advertise the fact that he was cuckolded? Why would anyone else want to advertise that fact in such a manner? And 'Murderess'? Whom did she kill?"

"Perhaps she killed her husband so she could marry her lover," Duncan theorized. "Or maybe she killed her lover to prevent a scandal,"

"Possibly, possibly. But why advertise this? In any event, I'm extremely well-informed as to the crime news in this country. I'm aware of every person who met a sticky end on the gallows over the past few decades, and I'm quite certain that Mrs. White's name is not on that list. Therefore, she wasn't hanged. Of course, she might have been tried and executed overseas, but would they have shipped the body back here? I suppose that could be true. Might she have committed suicide, or met a violent end at the hands of someone avenging the victim? Twenty-one is a young age to die of natural causes, though of course it happens all the time. And how are we to know that she was really guilty of murder? I know of no trial. It's possible that this woman was falsely accused."

"Not just of murder," I mused, "but of adultery as well."

"Very true. We have to bear in mind that these gravestones may not be telling us the absolute truth. It's quite possible that they're only telling one side of the story. Or rather, one side of six stories." Holmes cleared his throat. "And now, we need to address a critical issue: The dates on the tombstones. Not the birthdates, though there may be some points of importance there that might be unearthed through further study. It's the death dates."

Duncan nodded. "I was wondering that myself, sir. How come all of them died on Christmas? If this happened once, it's perfectly understandable, and twice is a coincidence, but it can happen. But six deaths, all on Christmas? It just seems to be beyond the realm of possibility."

"Left to pure chance, then I agree with you, Duncan. However, there's also the possibility of design, as well."

"You mean they were murdered? All on Christmas?"

"That is one of multiple possibilities. It is also perfectly conceivable that the death dates are a fabrication made out of convenience."

"What do you mean?" I asked.

"Sometimes when it isn't clear when people have died, a date is picked somewhat randomly. This happened a lot during the war. Often for various reasons, it could not be determined exactly when a person was killed. Perhaps it was in the middle of a late-night skirmish and no one knew whether the fatal bullet was fired before or after midnight. Maybe a solider was shot while travelling through the countryside and his body wasn't discovered by his comrades until a week later. Often, just to get the necessary paperwork out of the way, one date would be selected because it was just as good as another."

"That happened with two of my brothers," Duncan nodded. "They were in the Asian-Pacific theatre of the war, and one got captured and the other got separated from the others in an attack. When their bodies were found, no one knew when they'd died, so in both cases the authorities just went with the date the corpse was discovered. Luckily the legal question worked out without much confusion."

"What legal question?" I asked.

"Their wills, sir. My brother Timmy divided his possessions amongst his four brothers, and my brother Arthur said that his gold watch went to Timmy unless Timmy predeceased him, in which case the watch would go to his wife – Arthur's wife, I mean. Widow, now. Well, even though officially Arthur was supposed to have died a couple of days before Timmy, the bodies had clearly been dead long before they were found, so we just don't know for certain who died first. If Arthur died first, Timmy would get the watch, and since Timmy and my other brothers are dead, the watch would go to me. But if Timmy died first, Arthur's widow got the watch.

"It could've led to a big court battle if a lot of money had been involved, but Arthur's widow, she's a nice lady, and she told me she wanted me to have the watch." Duncan pulled a pocket-watch from his jacket. "I'd much rather have my brothers back, though. Arthur's widow got married again a couple years ago, and just had a baby girl. That's nice for her." He replaced the watch and turned away. I suspect a tear was forming in his eye and he didn't want us to see.

I believe that Holmes wanted to change the topic of conversation in order to provide young Duncan with some time to compose himself. "The remaining graves don't provide us with much additional information. '*Suffer in Torment*'?" A particularly piercing emotion, telling us exactly where whomever requested that epitaph believed Mr. Gregory's soul is now located. What did he do that led the person who ordered the gravestone to come to such a conclusion?"

"My father must have ordered those words," Duncan noted. "No one else would have done that or allowed such a thing to be inscribed without his approval."

"Yes. No point in trying to theorize what Gregory Blurdell might have done. Not enough evidence to draw any sort of conclusion. But what of your father, Duncan? Is he the sort of man to hold a powerful, burning grudge, so much so that he would flaunt the rules of decorum and the custom of never speaking ill of the dead?"

"No, sir, not at all. He's a most restrained man. He never has been much of one for showing emotion. That's why I can't explain this at all. It makes no sense whatsoever. He's a fierce believer in keeping family secrets away from outsiders. When his sister's daughter became – well, I mustn't say, sirs. You understand the need to keep things private." We did. "He'd never order grave markers like this. It's completely out of character."

"As you observed, this is a fairly private place," I noted. "It isn't like the standard church graveyard where any Tom, Dick, or Harry can walk in off the street and start scrutinizing the stones. And I don't think that most of your guests would ask to see this portion of the grounds."

"True enough," Holmes conceded, "but all it takes is one person to wander in here and start asking questions. In any event, there are plenty of options that could retain privacy. If one's malice towards a deceased person was so violent that he or she wanted to carve out a final parting shot upon a tombstone, why not have the body cremated and have the attacking words inscribed upon an urn? An urn could be hidden in a far more private place, even indoors, and since expenses were clearly spared in the first four cases, why not save even more money by choosing cremation over burial? If money was no object, why not build a crypt and keep the bitterness sagely locked inside solid walls?"

Neither I nor Duncan had any response to this, so Holmes continued. "Here is where the situation becomes even more perplexing. These last two headstones are far larger and of much better quality than the first four. The fifth is of a size usually dedicated to the maiden aunts of the family, whereas the sixth is almost the same size as one of your brother's markers, though without the bust atop it. Not cheap. An insult carved upon an obelisk like these will last for decades – perhaps centuries. One more point I forgot to mention about the four smaller stones: You can tell from the dead plant matter surrounding them that the grass has been allowed to cover them during the warmer months. So the groundskeeper has almost certainly been specifically ordered not to tend to those graves, which means for much of the year, the inscriptions would be unreadable. Why go through all the trouble of putting those comments upon the headstones, only to neglect the tending, meaning that the comments are only readable in the winter? Most perplexing."

Holmes coughed and adjusted his coat. "Moving on. The fifth stone's inscription is filled with loathing but is low on specifics. What did the deceased do to warrant such antipathy? It doesn't say. Perhaps the reference to his being '*stillborn*' means that he was a nasty piece of work ever since he was a child, but there is insufficient evidence to draw a solid conclusion. Hem! The final inscription is the longest and the most intriguing of all – a bit of doggerel devoted to telling the world what a rotter Dan Blurdell was. You know nothing of him either, Duncan?"

"Not a thing, Mr. Holmes."

"Interesting. If a man is referred to as a 'sinner', it's most probable that he was given to various forms of dissipation. Women? Alcohol? Gambling? All of the above? Prone to violence? Halitosis is unpleasant, but not necessarily an indicator of poor moral character. The previous headstone, '*Suffer in Torment*' also expressed a desire for the resident of this grave to reside in the depths of Hades. And to refer to him as the '*worst sinner*' is perplexing. Surely the worst sinners are the murderers, but if he had killed someone, why not mention it? Recall Alicia Blurdell White's gravestone. If she was identified as a killer, why not Daniel? Therefore, whatever his crimes, Daniel probably never took another human being's life, at least as far as the author of this inscription knew." Holmes paused. "Is your father of a poetic disposition, Duncan?"

"No, sir. He hates poetry. Mother loves it, though. She's always writing poems for our Christmas cards – " Duncan's drew in his breath so hard he whistled. "I just realized, sir. My father might not have been able to have bought the gravestone last year."

"Why not?"

"Family business, sir. He was called away to Canada in late November. He didn't get back until well after Twelfth Night."

"Then perhaps your mother ordered the stone and wrote the inscription herself. Possibly your parents share antipathy towards these people." Holmes took a step forward and slapped a hand against the sixth headstone. "No, it won't do. It won't do at all. It doesn't make sense." He stooped down, withdrew a folding knife from his pocket, and began digging in the dirt in front of the sixth gravestone. After carving out a little cone, he eased it out and studied it. "Just as I suspected. Observe, Watson. The ground's hard-packed and some layering is clear. I highly doubt that someone actually dug up the ground here a year ago in order to bury a coffin."

"But if no one's buried here – "

"Then perhaps the other five graves are empty as well." I didn't care for the gleam that appeared in Holmes's eyes as he spoke these words. "Duncan, do you know where we can find ourselves a shovel?"

"Holmes, you can't! It's indecent!" A memory flashed through my mind. "And probably illegal, too. Remember Mr. Frankland's comments during the Baskerville case? How it's against the law to disinter a corpse without the permission of the next of kin?"

"I'm a member of the family, aren't I?" Duncan observed. "If I say it's all right, that might take care of any legal issues, couldn't it?"

I was torn between feeling aghast and thwarted, and admiring Duncan for making a clever point.

Holmes allowed himself a little chuckle. "I dare say we should be able to make a compelling defense should the matter ever come into court, yet at this stage of my life I feel the desire to spend as little of it in a courtroom as possible. In any event, at my age I should avoid the heavy manual labor of digging a minimum of six feet into the ground. No, upon further reflection I shall not seek out the use of a shovel."

"I'm delighted to hear that," I responded.

"I am, however, in need of a bit of exercise. Would the two of you care to join me for a brisk stroll into town? I believe the village is just over half-a-mile down the road."

As we turned away from the graves, I asked Holmes, "What exactly is our destination?"

"The local monument mason – the person who designs and carves the gravestones. I noticed his shop next door to the undertaker's a few days ago, although I believe he self-styles as a 'memorialist'." Holmes froze and turned around. "Just a moment. There's one further point that I observed earlier but never got around to mentioning." He gestured toward the headstones. "Take a closer look at the lettering on the markers. Compare the first four to the most recent two. Pay particular attention to the letters 'J' and 'L', and some of the others."

Duncan's eyes were much younger and sharper than mine. "The lettering doesn't match, sir! The person who carved the first four tombstones, the ones on the poor-grade rock, was clearly a different person from the one who covered the other two stones. And . . . ." Duncan ran around the graveyard, peering at some of the more recent headstones.

"Whoever did the last two stones also did my brother's grave markers, as well as some other relatives who died over the past decade!"

"Indeed. I would very much like a word with your village memorialist."

Fifteen minutes later, we reached the village, and it looked as if everyone who lived there was filled with the Christmas spirit. Mistletoe dangled over many doorways, lit candles stood in most of the windows, and paper daisy chains were festooned everywhere. A quartet of carolers were strolling down the street singing "God Rest Ye Merry, Gentlemen", and a man on one corner was selling freshly roasted chestnuts from a little cart. I purchased a small bag and shared them with Duncan. Holmes declined my offer.

Eventually, we reached the memorialist's shop, one of the few stores in the village that was not decorated for the season – which made sense given the somber nature of the business. Holmes tapped on the door. Louder knocks produced no answer, but when Holmes tried the knob, the door swung open.

"Are you sure you should be entering?" I asked as we strode inside the shop.

"There is no '*Closed*' sign," Holmes replied, "and if he didn't want people walking in, he ought to have locked his door." A moment later the three of us were wandering around the shop. Holmes pushed through a second door inside the memorialist's workroom. "Well, well, well. Watson, Duncan – Come here and take a look at this fascinating discovery, please."

We followed him into the workroom, where a substantial obelisk stood in the center of the room. Traces of stone dust were strewn all over the floor. The room was rather dark, so Holmes struck a match and held it to the marker so we could read it.

Nancy Blurdell Jones
5 May, 1901 – 25 December, 1925

The epitaph was in huge letters that filled the rest of the stone.

THE WORLD IS A BETTER PLACE WITHOUT HER

Holmes chuckled, and I turned to him. "Do you find this kind of bitterness funny?"

"I'm in awe of this memorialists' powers, Watson. Not only is he a skilled craftsman who knows how to neatly carve words into stone, but he is also a psychic. How on earth does he know that Mrs. Jones will die tomorrow?"

I had a few seconds to reexamine the stone before Holmes's match burned down to his fingertips. "You're right! Even the best doctors wouldn't dare to predict when a terminally ill person will die more than a day or two before it happens. People have an amazing ability to linger longer than we'd expect– and sometimes they die much quicker then we think. Is she planning to commit suicide on Christmas? Or is someone planning to murder her?"

Though the light was dim, I could still see Holmes shaking his head. "No, I don't think that anyone can possibly kill Mrs. Jones. She can never be murdered, nor can she commit suicide."

"Why not?"

"Because she has never existed."

"I think you're right, Mr. Holmes," Duncan replied. "When I was little, all the young relatives came to the house several times a year. Even the children of relatives who were estranged from the family came, because the children weren't held responsible for what their parents did. But I never met a cousin named Nancy."

"And I'm quite willing to wager every bee in my hives that all six of the names on the other remarkable gravestones are similarly fictional."

"I believe you've got it"

I was utterly flummoxed. "But why? Why go through all of this absurd rigmarole? Why would anyone carve out such vile hatred onto six tombstones – ? "

"Seven, including this one."

"Seven tombstones, all for seven supposedly hated relatives who never existed? What could possibly be the point? Is this all some sort of dark practical joke?"

"I'm reluctant to cast aspersions upon Duncan's parents in front of him, but I believe that his father and mother are responsible."

"His parents?" I realized the truth of this observation as the words left my mouth. "Of course. His father bought all the headstones, except for last year's, when his mother had to handle the transaction."

"And the poem on the sixth one, sir. The meter. The rhyming. It's exactly the sort of thing Mother would write. It sounds exactly like one of her Christmas card poems, only with much more negative sentiments. I'm sure it's her work."

"I wouldn't be surprised if other members of the family were aware of what's going on here."

"But what is happening?" I wondered.

"Unfortunately," said Holmes, "I still don't have enough facts to draw a reasonable – "

He stopped at the sound of a door shutting. Wordlessly, he motioned us into a corner, and the three of us hid as best we could in the shadow of a tall shelf. A moment later a man and a woman entered the workroom.

"He's probably at the tavern drinking," the man grumbled. "He'll likely have to spend all of Christmas sleeping it off."

"Well, he can wait for his money," the woman replied. "While we're here, we might as well take a look at his work."

Holmes stepped forward. "Do you often come here on Christmas Eve, Lord and Lady Blurdell?"

Even in the weak light, the surprise and embarrassment on their faces was clear. Lady Blurdell was the first to regain her composure. "Mr. Holmes. Dr. Watson. Duncan. I'm rather surprised to see you here."

"That is understandable. Please accept my condolences on your relative's passing, which will apparently happen tomorrow. Very sad. I must say that I admire your efficiency on ordering the headstone. But please, if you will excuse my overwhelming curiosity, what exactly did Nancy do to make your believe that the world is better off without her?"

Lady Blurdell rallied, and responded to Holmes's question with frigid hauteur. "I consider that a most improper question."

"With all due respect, Lady Blurdell, you don't. In fact, you are anxious to know how I came to ask that question in the first place. A display of false indignation might work on many gentlemen, but quite frankly, putting on airs of being insulted has no effect on me whatsoever. You make cast whatever aspersions you like about me based on my words. I can assure you that I'm not moved one tiny bit."

Holmes's comments had a remarkable effect on Lady Blurdell. It was rather like watching a balloon deflate in a few short seconds. Lord Blurdell had the appearance of a schoolboy who had just gotten caught in a bit of mischief. "Perhaps we can work out some sort of deal," he murmured.

"Much wealthier men than you have tried to bribe me, sir, and far more powerful men have tried to threaten me. The thing you can give me now that I most desire is information. I want to know exactly what is going on with this little charade."

Lord Blurdell appeared to have no more strength left in him than his wife. "Please, not here. Anyway, how much do you know and how much have you guessed?"

"I shall recount the events of the last hour to you on the ride back to your estate. Once there, I expect you to answer all of my questions fully."

Lord and Lady Blurdell were both very quiet as Holmes informed them of everything that had happened since Duncan had come to us. Once we arrived at the manor house, the tension was cut a bit by the wonderful smell of roasting goose and cakes baking in the oven. The Blurdells led us into the library and locked the door securely.

"Would you care for a drink?" Lord Blurdell asked.

"No, just information." Holmes caught my eye and read my thoughts. "Watson will take something, though. A whisky?"

I agreed, and Lord Blurdell poured me a whisky-and-soda, and prepared a particularly strong one for himself. His glass was nearly filled to the top, and there couldn't have been more than a teaspoonful of soda-water mixed in with it. Lady Blurdell took a small tumbler of brandy, and Duncan had a glass of plain soda-water. Lord Blurdell swallowed his drink in two gulps and poured himself another of equal strength. Holmes took the glass from him and set it aside.

"I need you to be in a fit condition to answer my questions, sir. Now, you can start by confirming my suspicions. There are no bodies buried in those six graves, are there?"

Lord Blurdell shook his head. "No."

"And the names on the gravestones: Those people never existed, did they?"

This question caused Lord Blurdell to look up at us with a surprised expression. "Oh, no. They were all real. They just didn't live for very long. Over the years, there have been many Blurdells who died in infancy. The seven names we've used so far – they all passed away within a few days of being born. Most were born premature. It helped to have genuine birth certificates, though."

"I see. That makes a great deal of sense. The married names of the women were pure fictions, of course. Hill. White. Jones. You picked the most common names possible just to make it harder to track down their husbands if anyone was so inclined."

"Correct. We could have left them unmarried, I suppose, but . . . we thought that it might help to pair them up with wealthy husbands."

"In order to explain your inheritances, I suppose."

Lord Blurdell's face paled. "You know?"

"I do. Thank you for confirming my suspicions. At this time, many members of the landed aristocracy are pinching pennies. Many are suffering financially due to increased taxation, death duties, and all sorts of unwanted expenditures. You are doing quite well for yourselves. I see no spaces on the walls where priceless portraits have been sold off, no gaps on the shelves for missing antiques, no housing developments where large tracts of land have been put on the auction-block. Your staff is massive, your wines top-notch, and I have been informed by a reliable source that your Christmas present for your wife is absolutely extravagant. What does this mean? You are enjoying an impressive source of income, something that's allowing you to indulge in extravagances. I know that your home is used by the British government to entertain foreign dignitaries on a near-monthly basis. I believe you get some recompense for your hosting duties, but just enough to cover expenses. Unless, of course, you are finding ways to pad the bills?"

A very ugly smile passed over Lord Blurdell's face. "Blackmail, Mr. Holmes. It's been easy to stand aside and watch these powerful politicians lounge about our homes like they own the place. I've seen who they smuggle in at night. I know what substances they consume, and I hear them talk amongst themselves about how they've been skimming off the top of the various public funds at their disposal. Oh yes, Mr. Holmes. Our Parliament and Foreign Office are full of depraved and venal men. They don't govern our nation wisely. They simply live in the pursuit of pleasure, filling their pockets and living better than the King at the nation's expense."

"And you are particularly offended by this," Holmes replied. It was a statement, not a question.

"Those wretched degenerates killed nearly all of my sons!" Lady Blurdell finally broke her silence. She was a small woman, fragile in build, and the violence that coursed through her body gave the impression that the force of her rage would tear her to pieces. "My four eldest boys all died in the war, Mr. Holmes. And for what? Is the world any better than it was in 1913, before the conflict started? Are the nations of the world wiser and more humane? Did all those untold numbers of people make the ultimate sacrifice for the greater good? If they did, I can't see it! And who started the war? It was foolish, short-sighted, arrogant, pompous politicians like the ones who tell us they're commandeering our home at a moment's notice, and expect oysters and lobsters and thick steaks and the finest wines and liquor.

"We must find African violets for the Swedish ambassador's room – they're his favorite. It doesn't matter that it's January – we need to find some strawberries for the Spanish Consul. This mattress won't due for the Italian delegate's wife. Get another of the finest goose down right away. And speaking of the beds! They turn our home into a den of iniquity that Caligula himself would be ashamed to enter! These are the men who govern the nation, Mr. Holmes. These aren't statesmen – they're confidence tricksters who are addicted to power and dissipation. They ran us straight into four years of hell on earth, and at the end of it, when we were burying caskets full of our children and wondering if we'd ever be able to stop crying, these men made glorious speeches about how they were going to keep the world safe and secure, and while they bankrupted our friends with new taxes, they used those funds for their own endless revelry.

"Well, can you really blame us? We had the chance. We waited until they made their way back to their homes. I won't tell you who we recruited, but we managed to blackmail them in a way that they never suspected we were involved. We started several years ago, and soon we collected a small fortune from them. But then we were stuck with a problem."

As Lady Blurdell seemed reluctant to continue, Holmes prompted her. "How to explain the money? You needed to spend it. And so, like the American criminals who buy small legitimate businesses in order to turn their ill-gotten gains into income with which they could pay their debts and put in the bank, you needed a seemingly respectable avenue as a cover for your financial chicanery. It is a lot easier for a gangster from Chicago to buy a laundry and pretend to profit handsomely from it than it is for a British aristocrat to run a business. So how to account for the funds? You claimed to inherit them."

"I shan't give you the names of the people who helped us!" Lord Blurdell's voice showed defiance for the first time. "I won't get these decent people in trouble. They understood. They'd lost children of their own, they knew we were just getting our own back, and we paid them well to compensate them for the terrible suffering they endured. But you're right. At the end of the year, we totaled up all the money we'd collected over the past twelve months, and claimed that a long-estranged relative left us everything – to fund the maintenance of the family home. We explained that they might not have cared for us, but they had loyalty towards the house and grounds. The people who might have investigated were paid off, and after all of our expenses and dispensations, we were still enjoying a hefty profit."

"Yes, we paid a small fortune in death duties, but it was all going back to where it came from," Lady Blurdell explained. "The thieves in the government had less money, and much of it went back in, where hopefully some of it managed to find its way into actually helping the country. Of course, the bloodsuckers took some of the money right back, so we just had to take it from them again the next year."

"It was rather fun," Lord Blurdell mused. "But every now and then there was somebody– someone from the government who would ask us about what was going on. It happened immediately. That's when I realized. English 'gentlemen' hate to pry into people's personal scandals. Perhaps it's because they're afraid someone else will start asking about their own private affairs. And I do mean 'affairs'. So what better way to silence questions than to imply that these people who died were terrible people we couldn't bear to talk about?"

"Surely you didn't have to carve those words on their graves?" I wondered.

"Actually, that was the icing on the cake." Lord Blurdell smiled. "Whenever some official started inquiring, we'd show them to the headstones. When they saw those graves, they figured that something absolutely awful had happened in the deceased people's pasts, and being well-trained since birth to avoid other people's unpleasantness, they said their goodbyes pretty quickly. They figured that if I were to allow those words to be carved on a headstone, then the story must be too shocking for human ears. The looks on their faces! I've lost count of all the times I had to bite my tongue to keep from laughing! The first time a tax employee saw '*She will not be mourned*', his *pince-nez* fell off in shock and shattered on the stone!"

"But something went wrong two years ago," Holmes countered. "That's why you had to buy more expensive gravestones."

"The local memorialist was in the graveyard for an aunt's headstone being installed, and he saw the four cheap stones. 'Why didn't you come to me?' he asked. He knew something was wrong by our faces. So we bought a nice, big gravestone from him the next year to keep him quiet. The next year he dropped more hints, saying he got paid by the letter. So my wife wrote that little poem and bought that huge slab of rock, just to keep him happy. It cut into our profits a bit, but not too much. This year– you saw what we ordered. I don't mind. We're spreading the wealth around to people who need it. The memorialist lost two brothers and three of his seven children in the war. That's a reason why he drinks so much. I don't fault him."

"Why did you have all the 'relatives' die on Christmas?"

"We came up with a story about a Canadian branch of the families – ne'er-do-wells who married or gambled or otherwise connived their way into considerable fortunes, and after leaving England as expatriates, they wanted to be buried back home. We said they had interests in the Yukon gold fields, but the mail there only came out rarely, and as they'd died in cabins in the middle of nowhere, no one knew exactly when they'd died, but we just said Christmas for convenience, as that was about the time we'd receive a news update from our Canadian family members. We'd learn about their death on Christmas, so we'd say it just to have a date. People understood. Plus, we could claim that we'd held the memorial service when all the family was here for the holiday. No one else wants to come to a funeral at Christmastime. It was an easy way to keep the burials quiet."

"What do you intend to do now?" Holmes asked.

"Why, exactly what we've been doing!" Lord Blurdell explained. His demeanor had changed. The beaten, embarrassed man was gone. "We aren't going to stop. This is just compensation for the loss of our sons. And you won't tell anybody. Otherwise we'll provoke a scandal that will bring down the government. Given what we know, we'll never see a day in prison."

"We can't let this continue!" I blustered.

"You don't have a choice." Lord Blurdell had regained his backbone. "This is rough justice, and we aren't going to back down just because you have qualms about a little justified extortion."

"No, you won't!" Duncan yelled. "This is wrong, and you taught me to always do the right thing. I'm ashamed of you both!"

This started a huge argument. The three Blurdells all forgot that Holmes and I were there as they launched into a no-holds-barred shouting match. Father, mother, and son all screamed and fought, losing all sense of decorum and hearing none of what Holmes and I were saying.

After ten minutes, I can only explain what happened next as a true Christmas miracle. The butler pushed open the library doors, muttering, "Your Lordship. Your Ladyship. I can't believe it . . . ." Behind him limped a young man. He was gaunt, haggard, and looked as if every step caused him great pain. But the sight of him had an incredible effect on the Blurdells.

"Timmy!"

"Timmy?"

"My God! My son!"

The long-lost son gulped down a little brandy, and soon told his amazing story. He had been captured in the waning days of the war in Asia, and an enemy agent who resembled him superficially had been recruited to assume his identity. Apparently he had been killed soon after embarking on his mission, and his body had been mistaken as Timmy's due to the identification papers. Meanwhile, Timmy had languished in prison, not knowing what had happened or even that the war had ended. Due to all sorts of oversights and inefficiency, he hadn't been released for many years, and the government, thinking he was dead, hadn't made efforts to rescue him. When he was finally released a month ago without money or identification papers, he was compelled to beg until he had enough to buy a steerage ticket on a ship headed home. He would have sent a telegram, but he had no funds. He'd picked up some tropical disease in prison, and spent most of his days aboard the ship in a mild state of delirium. I examined him and, though he was in poor health, after proper treatment and plenty of rest, there was no reason why he shouldn't make a full recovery.

There is little more to say. Holmes spoke to Mycroft to apprise him of the situation. Over the coming months, there were a great many resignations from the government. I wasn't made privy to the details, but I assumed that the Blurdells went unpunished in exchange for their silence. Apparently, their thirst for vengeance faded with the knowledge that one of their lost sons had survived. The family wasn't whole, but it was happier.

Young Duncan was the happiest of all, and he wasn't the least bit upset that he was no longer the heir to the family fortune. His brother's survival was more than enough for him, and I was delighted for him and Timmy. Duncan had tried to give Timmy the watch he'd inherited from his other brother, but it was refused, and they eventually agreed to share it, though the details weren't clear. In a letter I received shortly after New Year's, Duncan told me how he and his family had celebrated the coming of 1926. That night, the Blurdells, with the help of some members of the staff, had taken eight gravestones and hurled them into a lake on the estate. Seven of the headstones were the ones with bitter epitaphs. The eighth was Timmy's. I'm told that the cheering was deafening as the stone bust on Timmy's grave marker sank beneath the water.

The Midnight Mass Murder
by Paul Hiscock

My dear Watson,

I trust that you have enjoyed a pleasant Christmas. As you are aware, I was expecting to spend the festive period alone. However, I unexpectedly found myself called upon to investigate a local murder, my account of which I hope might provide you with some brief entertainment.

My housekeeper departed on the morning of Christmas Eve to spend the week with her family, leaving enough food prepared to last me until her return. With her no longer present to object, I spent the afternoon setting up an experiment I have been hoping to conduct in the kitchen. Then, with little else to distract me, I enjoyed a light supper and retired to bed early.

My slumber was disturbed by someone banging at my door. Bleary-eyed, I examined the clock and established that it was just past one in the morning. I pulled on my dressing gown and slippers and went to investigate who was causing the disturbance.

When I opened the door, a woman was standing there. Although she was carrying an umbrella, it was doing little good against the driving rain, and I could see that she was shivering.

I ushered her inside, placed her umbrella in the stand by the door, and then helped her out of her sodden coat. Despite the time of the night, she was well-dressed, in a manner that suggested that she'd intended to attend a social engagement rather than take a walk on the Downs. She had very little with her, other than the umbrella – just a small purse, and a little book with a black leather cover, which she clutched tightly.

"Are you Mr. Sherlock Holmes?"

"I am indeed. How can I help you? It must be a matter of great urgency for you to have rushed here, straight from church, at such a late hour, and in such inclement weather. Your husband must be in a great deal of trouble."

"How did you know I had come from the church," she asked as I showed her into the parlour, "and that it is my husband who needs your help?"

"You're obviously dressed in your Sunday best, which would be curious at this time of night on any other day of the year. However, on Christmas Eve, it clearly indicates that you were attending the midnight service. Additionally, you are still carrying your Prayer Book, which tells me that you didn't return home, but came here directly. I doubt you would have made the journey to find me in these conditions unless someone very close to you needed my help. Your wedding ring tells me that it is your husband, for if he wasn't the one in trouble, he would certainly have accompanied you or come in your place."

"You are correct in every respect, Mr. Holmes. I was right to come to you. My husband is being held at his church, and they're accusing him of murder."

"At his church? Then he is the priest?"

"Yes, he is the rector of St. Simon and St. Jude – Reverend Horsley."

"And who is he supposed to have murdered?"

"The organist, Mr. Pemberton. He was found dead at the end of the service. Please – will you come with me, Mr. Holmes?"

"No," I replied, and observed an expression of panic cross her face. "At least, not immediately. Before we leave, I need you to tell me everything you know."

I steered her towards an armchair and made her sit down. Then I poured out a generous measure of brandy to calm her nerves before asking her to continue.

"We are new to the parish, Mr. Holmes. My husband was appointed just a few months ago, and this is our first Christmas here. I imagine you knew his predecessor."

I shook my head.

"I have very little to do with the church."

"Well, you will not have missed much. Reverend Locke was an elderly man, and I'm afraid he had let the church stagnate in the years leading up to his retirement. My husband, who is a much younger man, was determined to breathe new life into the place. However, he immediately met with opposition from some of the congregation."

"I assume that one of these objectors was the organist?"

"He was the worst of them. Under the previous incumbent, Mr. Pemberton had been allowed complete control over all music performed in the church, and he made it quite clear that he expected this arrangement to continue, and that my husband wouldn't even be allowed to suggest a hymn occasionally.

"Matters came to a head last Sunday. We had planned a carol service, hoping it would be a joyous celebration for the community. However, when Mr. Pemberton shared his musical selections, none of the familiar carols were included. Instead, there was a selection of dirge-like hymns, better suited for a funeral. My husband objected, but Mr. Pemberton wouldn't budge. He wouldn't play any carols celebrating Christmas during Advent."

"Who prevailed in this altercation?"

"I thought my husband had. Since he couldn't persuade Mr. Pemberton to compromise his overly strict liturgical stance, he asked a lady from the congregation to accompany the carols for just that service. She isn't very good, but he hoped that the congregation would sing enthusiastically enough to compensate. However, when the time came to prepare for the service, we discovered that the organ loft was locked. My husband went through all his keys, many of which he hasn't yet found a use for, but none of them would work. Eventually it was established that Mr. Pemberton held the only key. One of the churchwardens was dispatched to acquire it, but he returned empty handed. Eventually, we were forced to proceed without any accompaniment, to the disappointment of everyone who attended.

"In the days that followed, my husband tried to speak to Mr. Pemberton, but he wouldn't even come to the door. The first time we saw him again was this evening when he arrived to practise before the service. As is his habit, he headed straight for the organ loft where he hides for the duration of every service, not even coming down to share in the Eucharist. My husband pursued him to his lair and confronted him there. We could hear their raised voices from the nave below. It ended with my husband regretfully trying to give Mr. Pemberton his notice, only for that odious man to reply that he was friends with the Bishop, and that it was my husband who would come off worst. I am afraid my husband lost his temper at that, and everyone gathering for the service heard him shout, 'Tonight will be the last time you ever play the organ at this church!'"

"What happened after that?"

"The service went ahead, as planned. It was too late to find another organist then, even if Mr. Pemberton could have been removed. Everything seemed to be going smoothly until the time came for the last carol. We were all ready to sing 'Hark the Herald Angels Sing', but there was silence from the organ. My husband called up, to ask if there was a problem, but received no reply. We were all becoming concerned, so one of the churchwardens went to investigate, only to find the door to the organ loft locked from the inside. He was left with no choice but to break the door open, and found Mr. Pemberton lying dead on the floor."

"How did he die? Were there any signs of a struggle?"

"No, and we hadn't heard anything in the church below."

"Then why was murder suspected immediately? A natural cause of death would seem more likely."

"That is what we assumed at first. He wasn't a young man, although his wife maintained that he was in robust health. However, the local doctor was at the service and agreed to examine the body. We were all shocked when he announced that Mr. Pemberton had been poisoned. Of course, once he had told us that, the police were sent for immediately, and since Constable Anderson is out of town for the holiday, Constable Grout came straight over. We expected him to send everyone home, it being so very late at night, but he seemed determined to solve the murder immediately and insisted on starting to interview people there and then.

"It wasn't long before he heard about the argument before the service, and to establish that my husband had been the last person to visit the organ loft that night. He would have dragged my husband away to the jail in that instant, in front of the entire congregation, if I hadn't objected. I remembered, when we first arrived in the parish, being told that the famous detective Sherlock Holmes lived locally. At the time, it seemed to be an inconsequential piece of gossip, but at that moment I realised that it could be my best chance to save my husband. I asked the constable if I might ask you to review the case. I must admit that I might have suggested that we were already acquainted. I was surprised when he not only agreed to wait while I fetched you, but also seemed enthusiastic to have you involved."

I don't think I have mentioned Constable Grout to you in the past, Watson. He is a poor excuse for a local policeman, barely able to handle the occasional drunken brawl, and certainly incapable of investigating a murder. However, he suffers from the delusion that he is a great detective. He has, on more than one occasion, asked that I might recommend him to the detective branch at Scotland Yard, and I have no doubt that he is hoping to use this opportunity to demonstrate his feeble deductive skills to me.

A more competent officer would probably take the case over, eventually. However, it seemed likely that Reverend Horsley would spend Christmas in a cell, unless I intervened and conducted a proper investigation that night.

Armed with my hat, cape, and walking stick, I set out across the Downs with Mrs. Horsley. It was still raining, and the wind was blowing hard enough that it almost carried her umbrella away on more than one occasion. As a consequence, further conversation was nearly impossible as we travelled.

As we grew near, our destination became obvious. While everyone else slept, lights still blazed in the windows of the church. The sight seemed to enliven Mrs. Horsley. She surged ahead of me, and I had to increase my pace in order to catch up with her.

The hinges of the church door squealed as we entered, and everyone inside looked to see who had arrived. I counted thirty-seven people sitting in the pews. They all looked tired, and some were obviously angry at being held in there for so long.

As the door slammed, Constable Grout came over to welcome us.

"I'm glad you made it back safely, Mrs. Horsley. It is an unpleasant night. I see you managed to persuade Mr. Holmes to come."

"Indeed," she said. "I am pleased to have a professional handling this matter at last."

The constable held out his hand to me. I imagine he hoped I would shake it, but I handed him my stick and placed my sodden cape over his arm.

"It is good to be able to work with you again," he said, unperturbed by my obvious displeasure at having to deal with him. "It is a straightforward case, but I will be interested to hear your insights, which will hopefully put any doubts to rest."

"You plan to charge Reverend Horsley with murder? Did you even consider any other suspects?"

"Of course I did, Mr. Holmes. You will find my investigations were most thorough." Then his voice dropped to a whisper. "You wouldn't think it, but this church is a nest of vipers. It wasn't just the vicar and the organist who were fighting. They are all at each other's throats. The churchwardens cannot stand each other. The flower ladies fight over the Christmas display. The choir boys compete to sing the solos. And watch out for the caretaker – he'll be angry when he sees the muddy footprints you are leaving on the floor. He's already mopped the porch twice since I arrived."

"Where is the body? I need to examine it for myself."

"I knew you would. I left him up there, so you could see him as he was found. Isn't that right, Doctor?"

He beckoned to the local general practitioner, Dr. Frazer, who stood up and came to join us. I was pleased to see him in attendance. Although his knowledge of criminal matters is no match for yours, he is competent, and I knew he wouldn't have meddled with the body more than necessary.

"Good to see you, Holmes," he said. "This is a rum affair, and no mistake. Precious little Christmas spirit and goodwill to all men to be found here tonight. You'd better come with me, and I'll show you Mr. Pemberton."

He led me to a door. Behind it was a narrow set of stairs leading up to the organ loft. It was a small room suspended over the centre of the nave. It was just wide enough to contain the organ console, and was flanked on either side by banks of massive metal pipes which stretched to the edges of the building.

Mr. Pemberton had fallen backwards off the organ bench when he died, and was lying on the small area of floor just inside the door. Sheets of musical manuscript, which had obviously been knocked over when he fell, were scattered all around him.

I knelt down to examine the body. Dr. Frazer, who was standing in the doorway, started to explain his findings, but I gestured that he should remain silent, so that I could draw my own conclusions. I immediately noticed that the organist's face was bright red, and when I bent over, close to his face, I noted the distinctive fragrance of almonds.

"What did you make of the smell?" I asked Dr. Frazer.

"Of almonds? It's a common indicator of cyanide poisoning."

"Indeed. I have noticed it on more than one occasion in the past, but it is usually subtle enough that it is missed by most people. However, in this case it is surprisingly pronounced."

"He was obviously given a particularly large dose. It would have been a quick death."

"Possibly."

Resuming my examination of the dead organist, I noted a sticky residue on the thumb and forefinger of his right hand, and again I detected the smell of almonds. An examination of the organ console revealed corresponding sticky marks on some of the keys. He had been eating something during the service. I suspected what it was, but there should have been some evidence left behind.

I crawled under the organ bench to examine the pedals, but my hand slipped and depressed one of them. A loud note echoed around the church, and there were some screams and shouts of surprise from the members of the congregation below.

"What are you doing?" shouted Constable Grout, but I ignored him and continued my search.

It took a few more wrong notes, but eventually I found what I was looking for — a small blue-and-white striped paper bag that had slipped between the pedals. It was empty except for some granules of sugar and that same almond aroma.

Having learnt everything I could from the organ loft, I made my way back down the stairs and found the constable waiting for me by the door.

"It's quite ingenious, don't you agree? The rector found a way to poison a man in a locked room, while he was standing at the front of the church in front of everyone, giving him a perfect alibi. However, it must have been him. The victim was the only one with a key, and the rector was the only other person he let into the organ loft before the service."

"And how do you think he did it?" I asked. "Cyanide acts quickly. If it had been administered before the service, Mr. Pemberton would have been dead before the first carol."

"I'm not sure yet. It will be something ingenious – a needle concealed in an organ stop, or something like that. Don't feel bad that you couldn't find it. We'll probably have to take the whole instrument apart."

His suggestion was more preposterous than I could have imagined. I was unable to maintain a straight face, and burst out laughing. If you had been there, you would probably have reprimanded me for being cruel, but in your absence it was a woman from the congregation who spoke up.

"You vulture! How dare you come in here and treat our tragedy like entertainment? You should be ashamed of yourself."

"I am sorry, Mrs. Pemberton," said the constable. "I don't know what came over my colleague. I imagine he was just happy that we had solved your husband's murder."

I quickly composed myself.

"You are quite correct, Madam. I apologise. My behaviour was inappropriate."

"Well, is the policeman right? Have you worked out who killed my husband?"

"Not yet, but I promise I will have the answer very soon."

A young woman from the congregation came over to her.

"I'm sure the police will find Colin's killer, Agnes," she said.

Mrs. Pemberton pushed the woman away. She retreated to another part of the church, looking obviously upset.

Constable Grout whispered to me, "Mrs. Pemberton usually arranges the altar flowers at Christmas, but Mildred was chosen this year. I told you, everyone here is fighting with someone."

"Even if you find the murderer, it will be cold comfort for me," said the dead organist's wife. "I'll still be destitute. Out on the streets by the New Year, I imagine."

Mrs. Horsley now stepped in to comfort the widow, and her attention seemed more welcome.

"We won't let that happen to you."

"No home. No income. How am I going to survive? How could this have happened?"

Mrs. Pemberton rested her head on Mrs. Horsley's shoulder and started to cry.

"She is in a terrible position," explained the rector's wife. "Their house came with the organist's position – the church owns it, and she has no children or other family to take her in. I'm not sure what she'll do, but I know I will find myself in a similarly dire predicament if my husband is found guilty."

I was impressed by the fortitude of the woman, comforting others when her own position was so precarious.

"I don't think it will come to that," I said. "The constable has nothing but supposition, whereas I have evidence which I am confident will lead me straight to the real killer."

"Evidence, Mr. Holmes?" asked the constable. "What did you find? Did you find the concealed needle?"

"You have been reading too many lurid stories. While I admit that I have encountered some elaborate schemes over the years, the solutions to most crimes are far more mundane. If Mr. Pemberton was poisoned during the service, while he was alone, the obvious answer is that he administered it himself."

"Suicide?" said Mrs. Pemberton, angrily. "My husband would never do such a thing!"

"You mistake me, Madam. He didn't plan to poison himself. The fatal substance was concealed in something innocuous."

"Concealing enough cyanide to kill a man isn't easy," said the doctor, who had joined us at the bottom of the stairs. "Like its smell, the taste is quite distinctive."

"Indeed, but it is the strength of that smell in this case which points us to the solution. Where better to conceal the taste of almonds than in more almonds, or more specifically *marzipan*? During the service, Mr. Pemberton helped himself to confectionery from this bag, never suspecting that they had been laced with poison."

The constable took the bag and sniffed it.

"Ingenious," he said. "But I don't see why you believe this exonerates the rector. He was still the last person to speak with Mr. Pemberton, and not just speak but argue with him. He must be our primary suspect."

"Would you accept a bag of sweets from someone in the middle of an argument? I certainly wouldn't. No, I am quite sure that you have the wrong man, but perhaps he saw something that might help us find the real culprit. Where is he? I need to speak to him."

"The constable locked him in the vestry," said Mrs. Horsley.

"You can't be too careful with murderers. We wouldn't have wanted him to run off, or kill someone else, would we, Mr. Holmes?"

"Well, please fetch him now, and be quick about it. I am certain that I'm not the only one who wishes to make it home to bed before sunrise."

After a few minutes, the constable returned with Reverend Horsley, a clean-shaven young man wearing a black cassock and a dog collar. The rector took a moment to say a few words of comfort to Mrs. Pemberton, and then he hugged his wife before coming to speak to me.

"Thank you, Mr. Holmes. I dared not hope that you would come to the help of a complete stranger, especially in the middle of the night. I tell my congregation to have faith and the Lord will provide, but in this instance my wife's faith was stronger than mine. When he released me from my vestry, Constable Grout indicated that you have expressed some doubts about my guilt. Is there anything I can tell you which might help convince you that I'm innocent?"

"I'm more interested in what you saw or heard tonight that might help me uncover the real murderer."

"I don't know what I can tell you. Aside from my shameful outburst, nothing out of the ordinary happened, until we found the body."

"Shameful is right!" shouted Mrs. Pemberton. "My husband and I have devoted our lives to this church. You cannot come along and try to push us out!"

"I never meant for you to feel like that," said the rector.

"Of course he didn't," said Mrs. Horsley. "Neither of us did. We know this congregation is your family, and we will all be here to help you through this. Now why don't we let Mr. Holmes do his work so that we can find the killer and let all these people go home at last?"

Mrs. Pemberton reluctantly allowed herself to be led away to another part of the church, allowing me to resume my questioning of the rector.

"Unlike the congregation, you would have been facing the organ throughout the service. Are you certain that you didn't see anyone approach the stairs, or any sign that someone might have been up there with Mr. Pemberton?"

"Not that I can recall, but I'm not sure I would have noticed even if someone had. I have a lot on my mind during a service."

"What about before the service? Did you notice anything out of place while you were in the organ loft?"

"I really wouldn't know. I remember noticing it was quite messy. There were large piles of music all over the place, but I don't know if that was typical. I never usually go up there. That was Mr. Pemberton's domain, and he was fiercely protective of it."

"So you didn't notice this?"

I held up the paper bag that I had found between the organ pedals.

"What is in it?" he asked.

"Nothing now, but before the service it would have had marzipan sweets in it – sweets containing the poison that killed him."

"I'm not sure," he said hesitantly. "Maybe? Yes, I think it might have been next to the keyboard. Is that right?"

"It is consistent with the evidence, and confirms he wasn't given the sweets during the service. The people Constable Grout has detained here might all be innocent."

"I wonder if Miss Page might have seen something."

"Miss Page?"

"Yes, one of the younger members of our congregation. It's only that she and Mr. Pemberton arrived at the same time tonight. She wanted to be here early to check that none of the flowers needed to be refreshed – she is responsible for the lovely display around the altar tonight."

He was obviously referring to the young lady, Mildred, who had tried to comfort Mrs. Pemberton earlier. I sent the constable to bring her over.

"How did they seem to you?" I asked the rector. "Did you get the impression that they met at the door, or that they had been together for some time?"

"They were talking when they came in, and I did assume that they had been walking together. However, I'm not suggesting there was anything improper about it, whatever the rumour-mongers might be saying."

"Rumour-mongers?"

"Yes. Sadly, there seem to be some in every church, and the ones here seem particularly obsessed with Miss Page. I know that more than one young man in the village is interested in courting her. After all, she is single and attractive. However, it isn't the speculation about that which concerns me. More disturbingly, some people have been spreading scurrilous, and entirely unsubstantiated, rumours of relationships with married men, including Mr. Pemberton."

Seeing that the young lady in question was approaching, I decided not to pursue this line of questioning further with him yet, and instead turned my attention to her.

"Miss Page, thank you for coming to speak with me. I was hoping you might be able to shed some light on Mr. Pemberton's movements before the service. I gather from the rector that you arrived at church with him?"

"That's right. We met on the road, and he very kindly offered to share his umbrella with me."

"Did he say where he had come from, and did you meet anyone else?"

"I think he'd just come from his home. He was certainly coming from that direction. And we didn't see anyone. We were surprised to see each other, as neither of us had expected anyone else to be out just then on Christmas Eve in the rain."

"You must have been the last person, apart from me, to speak to him," said the rector.

Miss Page thought about this for a moment, and then she became frightened.

"You aren't suggesting that I murdered him, are you?"

"No, I didn't mean to suggest that," said the rector. "You don't think she killed him, do you, Mr. Holmes?"

I tried to keep the irritation at his interruption out of my voice as I asked Miss Page a final question.

"Did you see if he was carrying a bag of sweets? It would have looked like this."

I held up the paper bag, and she recognised it immediately.

"Yes, I gave that to him. It had little fruit shapes made out of marzipan in it."

Reverend Horsley gasped in horror at her admission.

"How could you do it? I know he wasn't a very likeable man, but to poison him?"

She looked confused for a moment, and then terrified.

"Oh my God!" she cried. "I *did* kill him!"

We saw that she was about to swoon, and Reverend Horsley quickly stepped in to catch her. He helped her to a seat in the nearest pew.

"You mean you didn't mean to kill him?" asked the rector, when she had recovered slightly.

"Of course not! How could you imagine such a thing?"

I immediately understood what must have happened. However, Reverend Horsley seemed confused by her seemingly contradictory response.

"Then why did you give the poison to him?"

"I didn't think nuts were poisonous. Most people seem to eat them quite happily, but they do make my face swell up and I get all these nasty red patches. That's why I didn't eat them myself. Even so, I didn't realise they could kill someone."

"Miss Page didn't put the cyanide in the marzipan," I said.

"Cyanide? Whatever are you talking about?"

"The sweets were poisoned," said the rector. "You really didn't know?"

"Of course I didn't. Poor Mr. Pemberton! Who would do such an awful thing to him?"

"Where did the marzipan sweets come from, Miss Page?" I asked.

"Why, they were left for me, along with a bunch of flowers. I'm not sure by whom."

"Didn't you find that suspicious?"

"Not really. I've received a number of Christmas gifts from admirers, and this wasn't the only one that was anonymous. I thought it was such a shame that I couldn't eat them myself, because of what happens to me when I eat nuts – I become violently ill – so I was more than happy to share them . . . ."

The poor young woman's words trailed off as she finally realised the implications of what she was saying, and she fainted.

Reverend Horsley called over the doctor, who set about reviving Miss Page with some smelling salts. I left them to tend to her, as I had learnt everything that I needed to know.

Looking around the church, it was clear that the congregation was becoming increasingly restless. Besides, there was little point in continuing to detain them, when the murder had been set in motion long before any of them had arrived for the service.

However, one small group seemed remarkably cheerful, despite the circumstances. The boys from the choir were chatting quite happily, and as I watched, I saw one of them take a round object from a paper bag and raise it towards his mouth.

We are getting older, Watson, and I at least am certainly less inclined to rush about than when we first met. Nevertheless, I'm not sure I have ever moved faster than I did that night. I ran across the church and slapped the sweet from the child's hand before he could eat it.

"My gobstopper!" the boy shouted and jumped down to crawl under the pews in search of his missing sweet.

I was about to stop him, but then I looked around and realised all the choristers were holding matching paper bags decorated with blue-and-white diagonal stripes, and that many of them already had sweets in their mouths.

I took the bag from the nearest boy and looked inside. As his compatriot had indicated, inside was a large gobstopper. I held the sweet up to my nose, inhaled deeply, and was relieved to discover that even I couldn't detect a hint of almond.

I put the gobstopper back in the bag and handed it back.

"Who gave these to you?" I asked.

"Why should we tell you anything?" one of them replied. "You're not the police!"

"That's right," said the boy who had been crawling under the pew, who was now emerging with his gobstopper and trying to wipe the dust off it. "Leave us alone or we'll call our parents."

Suddenly, they went quiet, and I turned to see Mrs. Horsley walking towards us.

"What is going on over here? You boys had better not be giving Mr. Holmes any cheek, after he has come out here in the middle of the night to work out what happened to your poor choir master!"

"No, ma'am," the boys said in unison.

"Very good. Now, what do you need, Mr. Holmes?"

"The bags – they match the one I found in the organ loft."

Mrs. Horsley looked at me in horror.

"Boys, spit out your sweets into the bags," she cried, "and put them down at once!"

Once they had all done as instructed, she turned to me.

"We should fetch Dr. Frazer. Maybe we acted fast enough, and there is still something that can be done."

"Fetch him, if you wish, but I don't believe these boys are in any danger. They have been eating gobstoppers, not marzipan fruit, and I couldn't detect any traces of cyanide on them. I believe that just the one bag, intended for Miss Page and consumed by Mr. Pemberton, was poisoned."

"Nevertheless, I would be happier if the doctor saw them," she said, and headed to the back of the church to fetch him.

Once she was gone, I turned my attention back to the boys.

"Who gave you these sweets?" I asked.

"Mrs. Pemberton," one of them replied. "She does it every Christmas. Two gobstoppers each to keep us quiet once we have finished singing."

"Can we have them back now?" another boy asked.

"I'm afraid not," said Mrs. Horsley, who had just returned, "but I will personally buy you replacements when the shop reopens after Christmas."

I looked around the church for Mrs. Pemberton. During my conversation with Miss Page, I had noticed her listening attentively. However, surprisingly she had remained silent, when anyone who had witnessed her earlier outbursts might well have expected a reaction to the suggestion that her rival flower arranger had murdered her husband. Now it was clear why.

Having spotted her, I went to fetch Constable Grout. He was sitting alone in a pew, looking dejected at having been so wrong in his assumptions. However, he cheered up considerably when I told him that I had solved the case and that he could make an arrest.

We walked over to Mrs. Pemberton and the constable smiled at her.

"I'm pleased to inform you that we have uncovered the identity of your husband's murderer."

"Why did you attempt to murder Miss Page?" I asked her.

The constable looked at me in obvious confusion.

"What are you talking about, Mr. Holmes?" he asked. "Miss Page is perfectly fine. She's sitting just over there. It was Mr. Pemberton that was murdered."

However, Mrs. Pemberton understood that there was no point in lying any longer.

"It was bad enough, her trying to usurp my place here with her fancy modern flower displays. I mean, look at that monstrosity! Have you ever seen anything so vulgar?"

I'm not sure how one measures the relative beauty of floral displays. The one at the altar seemed no better or worse than the others scattered around the church, just larger. However, it didn't matter, as Mrs. Pemberton didn't wait for a reply.

"She stole my place, and then she tried to steal my husband."

"So the rumours about an affair were true?"

"I am sure they were. It isn't like she's the first young hussy to turn his head. He was a lecherous old man, but he was mine, and I wasn't going to let anyone else have him. I don't know how she discovered the cyanide, but it was a cruel revenge to kill him, leaving me destitute and alone."

She started to cry, and Constable Grout went over to her, not to offer comfort this time, but to take her into custody.

"Miss Page knew nothing about your murderous intentions," I said. "I'm not even convinced that you are correct about the affair. No, Mrs. Pemberton, this tragedy is entirely of your own making, and we should just be thankful that no other innocent people were harmed by your jealousy."

I indicated to the constable that he should take her away. He still looked confused, but did as I instructed. I expect that he will appear on my doorstep after Christmas, and ask me to explain everything to him.

Seeing what was happening, the rector and his wife joined me. They were far more astute than the constable and quickly comprehended the truth of the situation.

Reverend Horsley climbed up into the pulpit, and the congregation hushed in expectation.

"Thank you for your patience. I know it has been a difficult night, and I am sorry you have been kept here so long, but now please go home and celebrate Christmas with each other." He paused, and then added, "Although you are all welcome to return for our Christmas morning service at eight o'clock."

There were some good-natured groans from the congregation. I guessed that very few people would take him up on that offer.

Reverend Horsley stood at the church door with his wife, speaking to each person as they left. Many tried to persuade him to tell them what had actually happened that night, but he assured them that everything would be explained later, once Christmas was over.

Finally, when just the three of us were left, I prepared to leave.

Reverend Horsley shook my hand warmly.

"Thank you for everything you have done, Mr. Holmes. I will celebrate Christmas Day more joyfully than ever before, knowing that if God hadn't sent you, I would have spent today, and possibly the rest of my life, in a prison cell."

"You should thank your wife. It was her, not God, who fetched me."

"Regardless," said Mrs. Horsley, "we are just thankful that you came. Can we express our gratitude properly by inviting you to join us for Christmas dinner? It seemed to me that you were alone when I visited your house earlier."

I thanked her, but politely declined, explaining that I had plans. Then I bade them good night and set off back to my cottage across the Downs.

When I got home, I went straight to the kitchen to check on my experiments. One flask was boiling a little too fast, and I turned down the burner. Then, satisfied that everything else could wait until after dawn, I retired to my bed.

It is now Christmas evening. My experiments are yielding positive results, and I hope to have the proof needed to close the Burton case by Boxing Day. I look forward to celebrating the festive season properly when you visit next week.

Until then, I remain sincerely yours,

Sherlock Holmes

About the Contributors

The following contributors appear in this volume:
The MX Book of New Sherlock Holmes Stories
Part XXX – More Christmas Adventures (1897-1928)

Brian Belanger is a publisher, editor, illustrator, author, and graphic designer. In 2015, he co-founded Belanger Books along with his brother, author Derrick Belanger. He designs the covers for every Belanger Books release, and his illustrations have appeared in the MacDougall Twins with Sherlock Holmes series, as well as *Dragonella*, *Scones and Bones on Baker Street*, and *Sherlock Holmes: A Three-Pipe Problem*. Brian has published a number of Sherlock Holmes anthologies, as well as new editions of August Derleth's classic Solar Pons mysteries. Since 2016, Brian has written and designed letters for the *Dear Holmes* series, and illustrated a comic book for indie band The Moonlight Initiative. In 2019, Brian received his investiture in the PSI as "Sir Ronald Duveen". Find him online at *www.belangerbooks.com*, *www.zhahadun.wixsite.com/221b*, and *www.redbubble.com/people/zhahadun*

Andrew Bryant was born in Bridgend, Wales, and now lives in Burlington, Ontario. His previous publications include *Poetry Toronto*, *Prism International*, *Existere*, *On Spec*, *The Dalhousie Review*, and *The Toronto Star*. His first Holmes story was published in *The MX Book of New Sherlock Holmes Stories - Part XIII*, with the second in *Part XVI*. The two stories in this collection are the third and fourth. Andrew's interest in Holmes stems from watching the Basil Rathbone and Nigel Bruce films as a child, followed by collecting The Canon, and a fascinating visit to 221B Baker Street.

Chris Chan is a writer, educator, and historian. He works as a researcher and "International Goodwill Ambassador" for Agatha Christie Ltd. His true crime articles, reviews, and short fiction have appeared (or will soon appear) in *The Strand*, *The Wisconsin Magazine of History*, *Mystery Weekly*, *Gilbert!*, *Nerd HQ*, Akashic Books' *Mondays are Murder* web series, *The Baker Street Journal*, and *Sherlock Holmes Mystery Magazine*. His latest book is *Sherlock and Irene: The Secret Truth Behind "A Scandal in Bohemia"*. He is also the author of *Murder Most Grotesque: The Comedic Crime Fiction of Joyce Porter*, published by Level Best Books. His first novel, *Sherlock's Secretary*, is published by MX Publishing.

Sir Arthur Conan Doyle (1859-1930) *Holmes Chronicler Emeritus*. If not for him, this anthology would not exist. Author, physician, patriot, sportsman, spiritualist, husband and father, and advocate for the oppressed. He is remembered and honored for the purposes of this collection by being the man who introduced Sherlock Holmes to the world. Through fifty-six Holmes short stories, four novels, and additional Apocryphal entries, Doyle revolutionized mystery stories and also greatly influenced and improved police forensic methods and techniques for the betterment of all. *Steel True Blade Straight.*

Steve Emecz's main field is technology, in which he has been working for about twenty-five years. Steve is a regular speaker at trade shows and his tech career has taken him to more than fifty countries – so he's no stranger to planes and airports. In 2008, MX published its first Sherlock Holmes book, and MX has gone on to become the largest specialist Holmes publisher in the world with over 500 books. MX is a social enterprise and supports three main causes. The first is Happy Life, a children's rescue project in

Nairobi, Kenya, where he and his wife, Sharon, spend every Christmas at the rescue centre in Kasarani. They have written two editions of a short book about the project, *The Happy Life Story*. The second is Undershaw, Sir Arthur Conan Doyle's former home, which is a school for children with learning disabilities for which Steve is a patron. Steve has been a mentor for the World Food Programme for several years, and was part of the Nobel Peace Prize winning team in 2020.

Mark A. Gagen BSI is co-founder of Wessex Press, sponsor of the popular *From Gillette to Brett* conferences, and publisher of *The Sherlock Holmes Reference Library* and many other fine Sherlockian titles. A life-long Holmes enthusiast, he is a member of *The Baker Street Irregulars* and *The Illustrious Clients of Indianapolis*. A graphic artist by profession, his work is often seen on the covers of *The Baker Street Journal* and various BSI books.

Tim Gambrell lives in Exeter, Devon, with his wife, two young sons, three cats and nine chickens. He has previously contributed to Parts XIII, XVI, XIX, XXIII, & XXVII of *The MX Book of New Sherlock Holmes Stories* from MX Publishing, as well as *Sherlock Holmes and Dr Watson: The Early Adventures*, *Sherlock Holmes and the Occult Detectives*, and *Sherlock Holmes: After the East Wind Blows*, all from Belanger Books. Outside of the world of Holmes, Tim has written extensively for *Doctor Who* spin-off ranges. He is the range editor of Candy Jar Books' *UNIT* series, and has written several novels and short stories for their *Lethbridge-Stewart* and *Lucy Wilson Mysteries* ranges. He has also written a novel, *The Way of The Bry'hunee*, for the *Erimem* range from Thebes Publishing. Tim has written audiobooks for Big Finish Productions, including *Blake's 7: The Palluma Project* (2021), *Signifiers of the Verphidiae* in *Bernice Summerfield: The Christmas Collection* (2020) and *Stockholm from Home* in *Bernice Summerfield: True Stories* (2017).

Jayantika Ganguly BSI is the General Secretary and Editor of the *Sherlock Holmes Society of India*, a member of the *Sherlock Holmes Society of London*, and the *Czech Sherlock Holmes Society*. She is the author of *The Holmes Sutra* (MX 2014). She is a corporate lawyer working with one of the Big Six law firms.

John Atkinson Grimshaw (1836-1893) was born in Leeds, England. His amazing paintings, usually featuring twilight or night scenes illuminated by gas-lamps or moonlight, are easily recognizable, and are often used on the covers of books about The Great Detective to set the mood, as shadowy figures move in the distance through misty mysterious settings and over rain-slicked streets.

Arthur Hall was born in Aston, Birmingham, UK, in 1944. He discovered his interest in writing during his schooldays, along with a love of fictional adventure and suspense. His first novel, *Sole Contact*, was an espionage story about an ultra-secret government department known as "Sector Three", and was followed, to date, by three sequels. Other works include six Sherlock Holmes novels, *The Demon of the Dusk*, *The One Hundred Percent Society*, *The Secret Assassin*, *The Phantom Killer*, *In Pursuit of the Dead*, and *The Justice Master*, as well as two collections of Holmes *Further Little-Known Cases of Sherlock* Holmes, and *Tales from the Annals of Sherlock Holmes*. He has also written other short stories and a modern detective novel. He lives in the West Midlands, United Kingdom.

Paula Hammond has written over sixty fiction and non-fiction books, as well as short stories, comics, poetry, and scripts for educational DVD's. When not glued to the keyboard, she can usually be found prowling round second-hand books shops or hunkered down in a hide, soaking up the joys of the natural world.

Nancy Holder, BSI, is a *New York Times* bestselling author who lives in Washington state. She has received 6 Bram Stoker Awards from the Horror Writers Association and the 2019 Grand Master "Faust" Award from the International Association of Media Tie-in Writers. She has written numerous Sherlockian pastiches and articles and is a member of several Sherlockian societies including *The Sound of the Baskervilles* and *The Sherlock Holmes Society of London*. She also writes and edits comic books and pulp fiction. Forthcoming works include two new comic book and graphic novel series with her writing partner, Alan Philipson.

Christopher James was born in 1975 in Paisley, Scotland. Educated at Newcastle and UEA, he was a winner of the UK's National Poetry Competition in 2008. He has written three full length Sherlock Holmes novels, *The Adventure of the Ruby* Elephant, *The Jeweller of Florence*, and *The Adventure of the Beer Barons*, all published by MX.

Roger Johnson BSI, ASH is a retired librarian, now working as a volunteer assistant at the Essex Police Museum. In his spare time, he is commissioning editor of *The Sherlock Holmes Journal*, an occasional lecturer, and a frequent contributor to *The Writings about the Writings*. His sole work of Holmesian pastiche was published in 1997 in Mike Ashley's anthology *The Mammoth Book of New Sherlock Holmes Adventures*, and he has the greatest respect for the many authors who have contributed new tales to the present mighty trilogy. Like his wife, Jean Upton, he is a member of both *The Baker Street Irregulars* and *The Adventuresses of Sherlock Holmes*.

Naching T. Kassa is a wife, mother, and writer. She's created short stories, novellas, poems, and co-created three children. She lives in Eastern Washington State with her husband, Dan Kassa. Naching is a member of the *Horror Writers Association*, Head of Publishing and Interviewer for *HorrorAddicts.net*, and an assistant and staff writer for Still Water Bay at Crystal Lake Publishing. She has been a Sherlockian since the age of ten and is a member of *The Sound of the Baskervilles*. You can find her work on Amazon. *https://www.amazon.com/Naching-T-Kassa/e/B005ZGHTI0*

Susan Knight's newest novel from MX publishing, *Mrs. Hudson Goes to Ireland*, is a follow-up to her well-received collection of stories, *Mrs. Hudson Investigates* of 2019. She is the author of two other non-Sherlockian story collections, as well as three novels, a book of non-fiction, and several plays, and has won several prizes for her writing. She lives in Dublin where she teaches Creative Writing. Her next Mrs. Hudson novel is already a gleam in her eye.

Michael Mallory is the Derringer-winning author of the "Amelia Watson" (The Second Mrs. Watson) series and "Dave Beauchamp" mystery series, and more than one-hundred-twenty-five short stories. An entertainment journalist by day, he has written eight nonfiction books on pop culture and more than six-hundred newspaper and magazine articles. Based in Los Angeles, Mike is also an occasional actor on television.

David Marcum plays *The Game* with deadly seriousness. He first discovered Sherlock Holmes in 1975 at the age of ten, and since that time, he has collected, read, and chronologicized literally thousands of traditional Holmes pastiches in the form of novels, short stories, radio and television episodes, movies and scripts, comics, fan-fiction, and unpublished manuscripts. He is the author of nearly ninety Sherlockian pastiches, some published in anthologies and magazines such as *The Strand*, and others collected in his own books, *The Papers of Sherlock Holmes*, *Sherlock Holmes and A Quantity of Debt*, *Sherlock Holmes – Tangled Skeins*, *Sherlock Holmes and The Eye of Heka*, and *The Complete Papers of Sherlock Holmes*. He has edited over sixty books, including several dozen traditional Sherlockian anthologies, such as the ongoing series *The MX Book of New Sherlock Holmes Stories*, which he created in 2015. This collection is now up to 30 volumes, with more in preparation. He was responsible for bringing back August Derleth's Solar Pons for a new generation, first with his collection of authorized Pons stories, *The Papers of Solar Pons*, and then by editing the reissued authorized versions of the original Pons books, and then volumes of new Pons adventures. He has done the same for the adventures of Dr. Thorndyke, and has plans for similar projects in the future. He has contributed numerous essays to various publications, and is a member of a number of Sherlockian groups and Scions. His irregular Sherlockian blog, *A Seventeen Step Program*, addresses various topics related to his favorite book friends (as his son used to call them when he was small), and can be found at *http://17stepprogram.blogspot.com/* He is a licensed Civil Engineer, living in Tennessee with his wife and son. Since the age of nineteen, he has worn a deerstalker as his regular-and-only hat. In 2013, he and his deerstalker were finally able make his first trip-of-a-lifetime Holmes Pilgrimage to England, with return Pilgrimages in 2015 and 2016, where you may have spotted him. If you ever run into him and his deerstalker out and about, feel free to say hello!

J. Lawrence Matthews has contributed fiction to the *New York Times* and *NPR's All Things Considered*, and is the author of three non-fiction books as Jeff Matthews. *One Must Tell the Bees: Abraham Lincoln and the Final Education of Sherlock Holmes*, his first novel, combines his passion for the original Sherlock Holmes stories of Sir Arthur Conan Doyle with his interest in American history as told on the battlefields of the Civil War. Matthews is now researching the sequel, which follows Sherlock Holmes a bit further afield – to Florence, Mecca and Tibet – but readers may contact him at *jlawrencematthews@gmail.com*. Those interested in the history behind *One Must Tell the Bees* will find it at *jlawrencematthews.com*.

Julie McKuras ASH, BSI discovered Sherlock Holmes at the age of eleven through the late night magic of the Basil Rathbone and Nigel Bruce films. It was a bonus to learn there were actually books written by Sir Arthur Conan Doyle. She served as the President of *The Norwegian Explorers of Minnesota* for nine years, and has been on the board of *The Friends of the Sherlock Holmes Collections* since 1997, editing their quarterly newsletter since 1999. Julie was the first editor of *The BSI Trust* newsletter as well. She is a frequent contributor to the *Friends* newsletter, and has had articles published in the *Baker Street Journal*, London's *Sherlock Holmes Journal*, *Through the Magic Door*, and *The Serpentine Muse*. Her essays have been included in *The Norwegian Explorers Christmas Annuals*, *Sir Arthur Conan Doyle and Sherlock Holmes: Essays and Art on The Doctor and The Detective*, "A Note on the Sherlock Holmes Collections" published in *The Horror of the Heights*, *Violets and Vitriol*, and *Sherlock Holmes in the Heartland: The Illustrious Clients Fifth Casebook*. She is a co-editor of *The Missing Misadventures of Sherlock Holmes*, and with Susan Vizoskie, she co-edited *Sherlockian Heresies*. Julie has been a speaker at a number of conferences and events, such as *The Sherlock Holmes Society of London*'s Statue Festival, Holmes Under the Arch, the Newberry Library, From Gillette to Brett, and the 2014 Reichenbach Irregulars Conference in Davos. She lives in Apple Valley, Minnesota with her husband, Mike, and with her children, their spouses, and her three grandchildren nearby.

Sidney Paget (1860-1908), a few of whose illustrations are used within this anthology, was born in London, and like his two older brothers, became a famed illustrator and painter. He completed over three-hundred-and-fifty drawings for the Sherlock Holmes stories that were first published in *The Strand* magazine, defining Holmes's image forever after in the public mind.

J.S. Rowlinson grew up on the Staffordshire/Derbyshire border, in the heart of England, near the market town of Uttoxeter where his story is set. He is now an art teacher in Plymouth, with the Mayflower steps to the south and Dartmoor to the north. Conan Doyle, for a short time, had a medical practice in the city, on Durnford Street. When not teaching or writing, he is a freelance illustrator, a singer of traditional English folk songs and ballads, and can often be found walking the desolate beauty of the moor with his dog, Jessie.

Jane Rubino is the author of *A Jersey Shore* mystery series, featuring a Jane Austen-loving amateur sleuth and a Sherlock Holmes-quoting detective, *Knight Errant*, *Lady Vernon and Her Daughter*, (a novel-length adaptation of Jane Austen's novella *Lady Susan*, co-authored with her daughter Caitlen Rubino-Bradway, *What Would Austen Do?*, also co-authored with her daughter, a short story in the anthology *Jane Austen Made Me Do It*, *The Rucastles' Pawn, The Copper Beeches from Violet Turner's POV*, and, of course, there's the Sherlockian novel in the drawer – who doesn't have one? Jane lives on a barrier island at the New Jersey shore.

Geri Schear is a novelist and short story writer. Her work has been published in literary journals in the U.S. and Ireland. Her first novel, *A Biased Judgement: The Diaries of Sherlock Holmes 1897* was released to critical acclaim in 2014. The sequel, *Sherlock Holmes and the Other Woman* was published in 2015, and *Return to Reichenbach* in 2016. She lives in Kells, Ireland.

Shane Simmons is the author of the occult detective novels *Necropolis* and *Epitaph*, and the crime collection *Raw and Other Stories*. An award-winning screenwriter and graphic novelist, his work has appeared in international film festivals, museums, and lectures about design and structure. He was born in Lachine, a suburb of Montreal best known for being massacred in 1689 and having a joke name. Visit Shane's homepage at *eyestrainproductions.com* for more.

Kevin Thornton is the author of more than a dozen Holmes short stories, as well as other crimonous fare. He has been short-listed quite a few times for awards. He has never won. He has written for *The New York Times* and has been in a top-selling anthology, but he is not an *NYT* best-selling writer. His singular achievement so far has been the locked room mystery he wrote where the door was not, in fact, locked. But that is not in this collection. He lives in Northern Canada. When asked, he will agree that it is quite cold.

DJ Tyrer is the person behind Atlantean Publishing, and has had fiction featuring Sherlock Holmes published in volumes from MX Publishing and Belanger Books, and an issue of *Awesome Tales*, and has a forthcoming story in *Sherlock Holmes Mystery Magazine*, as well as non-Sherlockian mysteries in anthologies such as *Mardi Gras Mysteries* (Mystery and Horror LLC) and *The Trench Coat Chronicles* (Celestial Echo Press).
DJ Tyrer's website is at *https://djtyrer.blogspot.co.uk/*
His Facebook page is at *https://www.facebook.com/DJTyrerwriter/*
The Atlantean Publishing website is at *https://atlanteanpublishing.wordpress.com/*

Emma West is the Acting Headteacher at Undershaw (formerly Stepping Stones), a school for special needs students located at Undershaw, one of Sir Arthur Conan Doyle's former homes in Hindhead, England.

*The following contributors appear
in the companion volumes:*
Part XXVIII – More Christmas Adventures (1869-1888)
Part XXIX – More Christmas Adventures (1889-1896)

Ian Ableson is an ecologist by training and a writer by choice. When not reading or writing, he can reliably be found scowling at a clipboard while ankle-deep in a marsh somewhere in Michigan. His love for the stories of Arthur Conan Doyle started when his grandfather gave him a copy of *The Original Illustrated Sherlock Holmes* when he was in high school, and he's proud to have been able to contribute to the continuation of the tales of Sherlock Holmes and Dr. Watson.

Wayne Anderson was born and raised in the beautiful Pacific Northwest, growing up in Alaska and Washington State. He discovered Sherlock Holmes around age ten and promptly devoured the Canon. When it was all gone, he tried to sate the addiction by writing his own Sherlock Holmes stories, which are mercifully lost forever. Sadly, he moved to California in his twenties and has lived there since. He has two grown sons who are both writers as well. He spends his time writing or working on the TV pilots and patents which will someday make him fabulously wealthy. When he's not doing these things, he is either reading to his young daughter from The Canon or trying to find space in his house for more bookshelves.

Deanna Baran lives in a remote part of Texas where cowboys may still be seen in their natural habitat. A librarian and former museum curator, she writes in between cups of tea, playing *Go*, and trading postcards with people around the world.

Derrick Belanger, PSI is an author and educator most noted for his books and lectures on Sherlock Holmes and Sir Arthur Conan Doyle, as well as his writing for the blogs *I Hear of Sherlock Everywhere* and *Belanger Books Sherlock Holmes and Other Readings Blog*. Both volumes of his two-volume anthology, *A Study in Terror: Sir Arthur Conan Doyle's Revolutionary Stories of Fear and the Supernatural* were #1 best sellers on the Amazon.com U.K. Sherlock Holmes book list, and his *MacDougall Twins with Sherlock Holmes* chapter book, *Attack of the Violet Vampire!* was also a #1 bestselling new release in the U.K. Through his press, Belanger Books, he has released a number of Sherlock Holmes anthologies as well as new editions of August Derleth's original Solar Pons series. In 2019, Mr. Belanger received his investiture in the PSI as "Albert, the Dove". In January 2020, Mr. Belanger was awarded the Susan Z. Diamond Award in recognition of outstanding efforts to introduce young people to Sherlock Holmes. Mr. Belanger dedicates "The Man of Miracles" to teacher extraordinaire Kimberly Kubsch, for introducing him to the wonderful world of Magical Realism.

Thomas A. Burns Jr. writes *The Natalie McMasters Mysteries* from the small town of Wendell, North Carolina, where he lives with his wife and son, four cats, and a Cardigan Welsh Corgi. He was born and grew up in New Jersey, attended Xavier High School in Manhattan, earned B.S degrees in Zoology and Microbiology at Michigan State University, and a M.S. in Microbiology at North Carolina State University. As a kid, Tom started reading mysteries with The Hardy Boys, Ken Holt, and Rick Brant, then graduated to the classic stories by authors such as A. Conan Doyle, Dorothy Sayers, John Dickson Carr, Erle Stanley Gardner, and Rex Stout, to name a few. Tom has written fiction as a hobby all of his life, starting with *The Man from U.N.C.L.E.* stories in marble-backed copybooks in grade school. He built a career as technical, science, and medical writer and editor for nearly thirty years in industry and government. Now that he's a full-time novelist, he's excited to publish his own mystery series, as well as to write stories about his second most favorite detective, Sherlock Holmes. His Holmes story, "The Camberwell Poisoner", recently appeared in the March-June issue of *The Strand Magazine*. Tom has also written a Lovecraftian horror novel, *The Legacy of the Unborn*, under the pen name of Silas K. Henderson – a sequel to H.P. Lovecraft's masterpiece *At the Mountains of Madness*.

Barry Clay is a graduate of Shippensburg University with a BA in English. He's dug ditches, stocked grocery shelves, tutored for room and board, cleaned restrooms, mopped floors, taught cartooning, worked in a bank, asked if you'd like fries with that (and cooked the fries to boot), ordered carpet for cars, and worked commission sales at Sears. Currently, he is a thirty-two year veteran of the Federal employee workforce. He has been writing all his life in different genres, and he has written thirteen books ranging from Christian theology, anthologies, speculative fiction, horror, science fiction, and humor. His Sherlockian volumes include *The Darkened Village* and *The Leveson-Gower Theft*. He volunteers as conductor of a local student orchestra and has been commissioned to write music. His first two musicals were locally produced. He is the husband of one wife, father of four children, and "Opa" to one granddaughter. He is honored to have been asked to contribute to this collection.

Craig Stephen Copland confesses that he discovered Sherlock Holmes when, sometime in the muddled early 1960's, he pinched his older brother's copy of the immortal stories and was forever afterward thoroughly hooked. He is very grateful to his high school English teachers in Toronto who inculcated in him a love of literature and writing, and even inspired him to be an English major at the University of Toronto. There he was blessed to sit at the feet of both Northrup Frye and Marshall McLuhan, and other great literary professors, who led him to believe that he was called to be a high school English teacher. It was his good fortune to come to his pecuniary senses, abandon that goal, and pursue a varied professional career that took him to over one-hundred countries and endless adventures. He considers himself to have been and to continue to be one of the luckiest men on God's good earth. A few years back he took a step in the direction of Sherlockian studies and joined the *Sherlock Holmes Society of Canada* – also known as *The Toronto Bootmakers*. In May of 2014, this esteemed group of scholars announced a contest for the writing of a new Sherlock Holmes mystery. Although he had never tried his hand at fiction before, Craig entered and was pleasantly surprised to be selected as one of the winners. Having enjoyed the experience, he decided to write more of the same, and is now on a mission to write a new Sherlock Holmes mystery that is related to and inspired by each of the sixty stories in the original Canon. He currently lives and writes in Toronto and Dubai, and looks forward to finally settling down when he turns ninety.

Martin Daley was born in Carlisle, Cumbria in 1964. He cites Doyle's Holmes and Watson as his favourite literary characters, who continue to inspire his own detective writing. His fiction and non-fiction books include a Holmes pastiche set predominantly in his home city in 1903. In the adventure, he introduced his own detective, Inspector Cornelius Armstrong, who has subsequently had some of his own cases published by MX Publishing. For more information visit *www.martindaley.co.uk*

Harry DeMaio is a *nom de plume* of Harry B. DeMaio, successful author of several books on Information Security and Business Networks, as well as the seventeen-volume *Casebooks of Octavius Bear*. He is also a published author of Solar Pons stories and stories included in the MX Sherlock Holmes series edited by David Marcum. His latest offering for Belanger Books is a seven-story collection: *The Adventures of Sherlock Holmes and the Glamorous Ghost.* A retired business executive, former consultant, information security specialist, elected official, private pilot, disk jockey and graduate school adjunct professor, he whiles away his time traveling and writing preposterous books, articles, and stories. He has appeared on many radio and TV shows and is an accomplished, frequent public speaker. Former New York City natives, he and his extremely patient and helpful wife, Virginia, live in Cincinnati (and several other parallel universes.) They have two sons, living in Scottsdale, Arizona and Cortlandt Manor, New York, both of whom are quite successful and quite normal, thus putting the lie to the theory that insanity is hereditary. His books are available on Amazon, Barnes and Noble, directly from Belanger Books and MX Publishing, and at other fine bookstores. His e-mail is *hdemaio@zoomtown.com* You can also find him on Facebook. His website is *www.octaviusbearslair.com*

Tim Gambrell *also has a story in Part XXVIII*

Paul D. Gilbert was born in 1954 and has lived in and around London all of his life. His wife Jackie is a Holmes expert who keeps him on the straight and narrow! He has two sons, one of whom now lives in Spain. His interests include literature, ancient history, all religions, most sports, and movies. He is currently employed full-time as a funeral director. His books so far include *The Lost Files of Sherlock Holmes* (2007), *The Chronicles of Sherlock Holmes* (2008), *Sherlock Holmes and the Giant Rat of Sumatra* (2010), *The Annals of Sherlock Holmes* (2012), *Sherlock Holmes and the Unholy Trinity* (2015), *Sherlock Holmes: The Four Handed Game* (2017), *The Illumination of Sherlock Holmes* (2019), and *The Treasure of the Poison King* (2021).

Dick Gillman is an English writer and acrylic artist living in Brittany, France with his wife Alex, Truffle, their Black Labrador, and Jean-Claude, their Breton cat. During his retirement from teaching, he has written over twenty Sherlock Holmes short stories which are published as both e-books and paperbacks. His initial contribution to the superb MX Sherlock Holmes collection, published in October 2015, was entitled "The Man on Westminster Bridge" and had the privilege of being chosen as the anchor story in *The MX Book of New Sherlock Holmes Stories – Part II (1890-1895).*

Arthur Hall *also has a story in part XXIX*

Liz Hedgecock grew up in London, England (a train and a tube ride away from Baker Street), did an English degree, and then took forever to start writing. Now Liz travels between the nineteenth and twenty-first centuries, murdering people. To be fair, she does usually clean up after herself. Liz's reimaginings of Sherlock Holmes, the Caster & Fleet, and Maisie Frobisher Victorian mystery series, and the Magical Bookshop and Pippa Parker contemporary mystery series are available in eBook and paperback. Liz lives in Cheshire with her husband and two sons, and when she's not writing you can usually find her reading, going for walks, or cooing over stuff in museums and art galleries. That's her story, anyway, and she's sticking to it.

Stephen Herczeg is an IT Geek, writer, actor, and film-maker based in Canberra Australia. He has been writing for over twenty years and has completed a couple of dodgy novels, sixteen feature-length screenplays, and numerous short stories and scripts. Stephen was very successful in 2017's International Horror Hotel screenplay competition, with his scripts *TITAN* winning the Sci-Fi category and *Dark are the Woods* placing second in the horror category. His three-volume short story collection, *The Curious Cases of Sherlock*

Holmes, will be published in 2021. His work has featured in *Sproutlings – A Compendium of Little Fictions* from Hunter Anthologies, the *Hells Bells* Christmas horror anthology published by the Australasian Horror Writers Association, and the *Below the Stairs, Trickster's Treats, Shades of Santa, Behind the Mask*, and *Beyond the Infinite* anthologies from *OzHorror.Con, The Body Horror Book, Anemone Enemy*, and *Petrified Punks* from Oscillate Wildly Press, and *Sherlock Holmes In the Realms of H.G. Wells* and *Sherlock Holmes: Adventures Beyond the Canon* from Belanger Books.

Paul Hiscock is an author of crime, fantasy, horror, and science fiction tales. His short stories have appeared in a variety of anthologies, and include a seventeenth century whodunnit, a science fiction western, a clockpunk fairytale, and numerous Sherlock Holmes pastiches. He lives with his family in Kent (England) and spends his days taking care of his two children. He mainly does his writing in coffee shops with members of the local NaNoWriMo group or in the middle of the night when his family has gone to sleep. Consequently, his stories tend to be fuelled by large amounts of black coffee. You can find out more about Paul's writing at *www.detectivesanddragons.uk*.

Mike Hogan writes mostly historical novels and short stories, many set in Victorian London and featuring Sherlock Holmes and Doctor Watson. He read the Conan Doyle stories at school with great enjoyment, but hadn't thought much about Sherlock Holmes until, having missed the Granada/Jeremy Brett TV series when it was originally shown in the eighties, he came across a box set of videos in a street market and was hooked on Holmes again. He started writing Sherlock Holmes pastiches several years ago, having great fun re-imagining situations for the Conan Doyle characters to act in. The relationship between Holmes and Watson fascinates him as one of the great literary friendships. (He's also a huge admirer of Patrick O'Brian's Aubrey-Maturin novels). Like Captain Aubrey and Doctor Maturin, Holmes and Watson are an odd couple, differing in almost every facet of their characters, but sharing a common sense of decency and a common humanity. Living with Sherlock Holmes can't have been easy, and Mike enjoys adding a stronger vein of "pawky humour" into the Conan Doyle mix, even letting Watson have the second-to-last word on occasions. His books include *Sherlock Holmes and the Scottish Question, The Gory Season – Sherlock Holmes, Jack the Ripper and the Thames Torso Murders*, and the *Sherlock Holmes & Young Winston 1887 Trilogy* (*The Deadwood Stage, The Jubilee Plot*, and *The Giant Moles*), He has also written the following short story collections: *Sherlock Holmes: Murder at the Savoy and Other Stories, Sherlock Holmes: The Skull of Kohada Koheiji and Other Stories*, and *Sherlock Holmes: Murder on the Brighton Line and Other Stories*, among others. *www.mikehoganbooks.com*

Christopher James *also has a poem in Part II*

John Lawrence served for thirty-eight years as a staff member in the U.S. House of Representatives, the last eight as Chief of Staff to Speaker Nancy Pelosi (2005-2013). He has been a Visiting Professor at the University of California's Washington Center since 2013. He is the author of *The Class of '74: Congress After Watergate and the Roots of Partisanship* (2018), and has a Ph.D. in history from the University of California (Berkeley).

Jeffrey Lockwood spent youthful afternoons darkly enchanted by feeding grasshoppers to black widows in his New Mexican backyard, which accounts for his scientific and literary affinities. He earned a doctorate in entomology and worked as an ecologist at the University of Wyoming before metamorphosing into a Professor of Natural Sciences & Humanities in the departments of philosophy and creative writing. He considers Sherlock Holmes a model of scientific prowess, integrating exquisite observational skills with incisive abductive (not deductive) reasoning.

Gordon Linzner is founder and former editor of *Space and Time Magazine*, and author of three published novels and dozens of short stories in *F&SF*, *Twilight Zone*, *Sherlock Holmes Mystery Magazine*, and numerous other magazines and anthologies, including *Baker Street Irregulars II*, *Across the Universe*, and *Strange Lands*. He is a member of *HWA* and a lifetime member of *SFWA*.

David Marcum *also has stories in Parts XXVIII and XXIX*

Mark Mower is a crime writer and historian whose passion for tales about Sherlock Holmes and Dr. Watson began at the age of twelve, when he watched an early black-and-white film featuring the unrivalled screen pairing of Basil Rathbone and Nigel Bruce. Hastily seeking out the original stories of Sir Arthur Conan Doyle, and continually searching for further film and television adaptations, his has been a lifelong obsession. Now a member of the Crime Writers' Association, The Sherlock Holmes Society of London, and The Solar Pons Society of London, he has written numerous crime books. Mark has contributed to over 20 Holmes anthologies, including 13 parts of *The MX Book of New Sherlock Holmes Stories*, *The Book of Extraordinary New Sherlock Holmes Stories* (Mango Publishing) and *Sherlock Holmes – Before Baker Street* (Belanger Books). His own books include *A Farewell to Baker Street*, *Sherlock Holmes: The Baker Street Case-Files*, and *Sherlock Holmes: The Baker Street Legacy*, and *Sherlock Holmes: The Baker Street Epilogue* (all with MX Publishing).

Will Murray has been writing about popular culture since 1973, principally on the subjects of comic books, pulp magazine heroes, and film. As a fiction writer, he's the author of over 70 novels featuring characters as diverse as Nick Fury and Remo Williams. With the late Steve Ditko, he created the Unbeatable Squirrel Girl for Marvel Comics. Murray has written numerous short stories, many on Lovecraftian themes. Currently, he writes The Wild Adventures of Doc Savage for Altus Press. His acclaimed Doc Savage novel, *Skull Island*, pits the pioneer superhero against the legendary King Kong. This was followed by *King Kong vs. Tarzan* and two Doc Savage novels guest-starring The Shadow, and *Tarzan, Conqueror of Mars*, a crossover with John Carter of Mars. He is the author of the short story collecdtion *The Wild Adventures of Sherlock Holmes*. www.adventuresinbronze.com is his website.

Tracy J. Revels, a Sherlockian from the age of eleven, is a professor of history at Wofford College in Spartanburg, South Carolina. She is a member of *The Survivors of the Gloria Scott* and *The Studious Scarlets Society*, and is a past recipient of the Beacon Society Award. Almost every semester, she teaches a class that covers The Canon, either to college students or to senior citizens. She is also the author of three supernatural Sherlockian pastiches with MX (*Shadowfall*, *Shadowblood*, and *Shadowwraith*), and a regular contributor to her scion's newsletter. She also has some notoriety as an author of very silly skits: For proof, see "The Adventure of the Adversarial Adventuress" and "Occupy Baker Street" on YouTube. When not studying Sherlock, she can be found researching the history of her native state, and has written books on Florida in the Civil War and on the development of Florida's tourism industry.

Roger Riccard's family history has Scottish roots, which trace his lineage back to Highland, Scotland. This British Isles ancestry encouraged his interest in the writings of Sir Arthur Conan Doyle at an early age. He has authored the novels *Sherlock Holmes & The Case of the Poisoned Lilly*, and *Sherlock Holmes & The Case of the Twain Papers.* In addition, he has produced several short stories in *Sherlock Holmes Adventures for the Twelve Days of Christmas*, and in November 2021 his fifth and final volume of *A Sherlock Holmes Alphabet of Cases* will be released. All of his books have been published by Baker Street Studios. Having earned Bachelor of Arts Degrees in both Journalism and History from California State University, Northridge, his career has progressed from teaching into business, where he has used his writing skills in various aspects of employee communications. He has also contributed to newspapers and magazines and has earned some awards for his efforts. He currently lives in a suburb of Los Angeles, California with his wife/editor/inspiration, Rosilyn.

Dan Rowley is a retired lawyer who practiced for over forty years in private practice and in house for a large international corporation. He lives in Erie, Pennsylvania, with his wife Judy. His father introduced him to the love of mysteries a long time ago. He inherited his creativity and writing ability from his children, Jim and Katy, now enhanced by Sherry and Prince.

Frank Schildiner is a martial arts instructor at Amorosi's Mixed Martial Arts in New Jersey. He is the writer of the novels, *The Quest of Frankenstein*, *The Triumph of Frankenstein*, *Napoleon's Vampire Hunters*, *The Devil Plague of Naples*, *The Klaus Protocol*, and *Irma Vep and The Great Brain of Mars*. Frank is a regular contributor to the fictional series *Tales of the Shadowmen* and has been published in *From Bayou to Abyss: Examining John Constantine, Hellblazer*, *The Joy of Joe*, *The New Adventures of Thunder Jim Wade*, *Secret Agent X* Volumes 3, 4, 5, and 6, *The Lone Ranger and Tonto: Frontier Justice*, and *The Avenger: The Justice Files.* He resides in New Jersey with his wife Gail, who is his top supporter, and two cats who are indifferent on the subject.

Brenda Seabrooke's stories have been published in a number of reviews, journals, and anthologies. She has received grants from the National Endowment for the Arts and Emerson College's Robbie Macauley Award. She is the author of twenty-three books for young readers including *Scones and Bones on Baker Street: Sherlock's (maybe!) Dog and the Dirt Dilemma*, and *The Rascal in the Castle: Sherlock's (possible!) Dog and the Queen's Revenge*. Brenda states: "*It was fun to write from Dr. Watson's point of view and not have to worry about fleas, smelly pits, ralphing, or scratching at inopportune times.*"

Joseph W. Svec III is retired from Oceanography, Satellite Test Engineering, and college teaching. He has lived on a forty-foot cruising sailboat, on a ranch in the Sierra Nevada Foothills, in a country rose-garden cottage, and currently lives in the shadow of a castle with his childhood sweetheart and several long coated German shepherds. He enjoys writing, gardening, creating dioramas, world travel, and enjoying time with his sweetheart.

Amy Thomas is a member of the *Baker Street Babes* Podcast, and the author of *The Detective and The Woman* mystery novels featuring Sherlock Holmes and Irene Adler. She blogs at *girlmeetssherlock.wordpress.com*, and she writes and edits professionally from her home in Fort Myers, Florida.

Thomas A. (Tom) Turley has been "hooked on Holmes" since finishing *The Hound of the Baskervilles* at about the age of twelve. However, his interest in Sherlockian pastiches didn't take off until he wrote one. *Sherlock Holmes and the Adventure of the Tainted Canister* (2014) is available as an e-book and an audiobook from MX Publishing. It also appeared in *The Art of Sherlock Holmes – USA Edition 1*. In 2017, two of Tom's stories, "A Scandal in Serbia" and "A Ghost from Christmas Past" were published in Parts VI and VII of this anthology. "Ghost" was also included in *The Art of Sherlock Holmes – West Palm Beach Edition*. Meanwhile, Tom is finishing a collection of historical pastiches entitled *Sherlock Holmes and the Crowned Heads of Europe*, to be published in 2021 The first story, "Sherlock Holmes and the Case of the Dying Emperor" (2018) is available from MX Publishing as a separate e-book. Set in the brief reign of Emperor Frederick III (1888), it inaugurates Sherlock Holmes's espionage campaign against the German Empire, which ended only in August 1914 with "His Last Bow". When completed, *Sherlock Holmes and the Crowned Heads of Europe* will also include "A Scandal in Serbia" and two additional historical tales. Although he has a Ph.D. in British history, Tom spent most of his professional career as an archivist with the State of Alabama. He and his wife Paula (an aspiring science fiction novelist) live in Montgomery, Alabama. Interested readers may contact Tom through MX Publishing or his Goodreads author's page.

Margaret Walsh was born Auckland, New Zealand and now lives in Melbourne, Australia. She is the author of *Sherlock Holmes and the Molly-Boy Murders*, *Sherlock Holmes and the Case of the Perplexed Politician*, and *Sherlock Holmes and the Case of the London Dock Deaths*, all published by MX Publishing. Margaret has been a devotee of Sherlock Holmes since childhood and has had several Holmesian related essays printed in anthologies, and is a member of the online society *Doyle's Rotary Coffin*. She has an ongoing love affair with the city of London. When she's not working or planning trips to London. Margaret can be found frequenting the many and varied bookshops of Melbourne.

I.A. Watson was shattered when he failed in his life's ambition to become a Christmas Elf, and turned for solace to writing stories of Sherlock Holmes (which are known to be Santa's favourites). In hopes of being allowed at least a turn as a reindeer, he has produced the books *Holmes and Houdini* and *The Incunabulum of Sherlock Holmes*, and over thirty short stories about the Great Detective, along with eight other novels and many novellas and short stories on less-Sherlockian subjects (most recently *The Death of Persephone*). Having to generate so many "About the Author" paragraphs requires additional eccentric author blurb – but heck, it's Christmas! An up-to-date list of I.A. Watson's work is online at: *http://www.chillwater.org.uk/writing/iawatsonhome.htm*

Matthew White is an up-and-coming author from Richmond, Virginia in the USA. A lifelong devotee of Sherlock Holmes, he maintains a Sherlockian blog, Baker Street Forever, at *https://bakerstreetforever.wordpress.com*. He can be reached at *matthewwhite.writer@gmail.com*.

Marcia Wilson is a freelance researcher and illustrator who likes to work in a style compatible for the color blind and visually impaired. She is Canon-centric, and her first MX offering, *You Buy Bones*, uses the point-of-view of Scotland Yard to show the unique talents of Dr. Watson. This continued with the publication of *Test of the Professionals: The Adventure of the Flying Blue Pidgeon* and *The Peaceful Night Poisonings*. She can be contacted at: *gravelgirty.deviantart.com*

The MX Book of New Sherlock Holmes Stories
Edited by David Marcum
(MX Publishing, 2015-   )

"This is the finest volume of Sherlockian fiction I have ever read, and I have read, literally, thousands." – Philip K. Jones

"Beyond Impressive . . . This is a splendid venture for a great cause!"
– Roger Johnson, Editor, *The Sherlock Holmes Journal,*
The Sherlock Holmes Society of London

Part I: 1881-1889
Part II: 1890-1895
Part III: 1896-1929
Part IV: 2016 Annual
Part V: Christmas Adventures
Part VI: 2017 Annual
Part VII: Eliminate the Impossible (1880-1891)
Part VIII – Eliminate the Impossible (1892-1905)
Part IX – 2018 Annual (1879-1895)
Part X – 2018 Annual (1896-1916)
Part XI – Some Untold Cases (1880-1891)
Part XII – Some Untold Cases (1894-1902)
Part XIII – 2019 Annual (1881-1890)
Part XIV – 2019 Annual (1891-1897)
Part XV – 2019 Annual (1898-1917)
Part XVI – Whatever Remains . . . Must be the Truth (1881-1890)
Part XVII – Whatever Remains . . . Must be the Truth (1891-1898)
Part XVIII – Whatever Remains . . . Must be the Truth (1898-1925)
Part XIX – 2020 Annual (1882-1890)
Part XX – 2020 Annual (1891-1897)
Part XXI – 2020 Annual (1898-1923)
Part XXII – Some More Untold Cases (1877-1887)
Part XXIII – Some More Untold Cases (1888-1894)
Part XXIV – Some More Untold Cases (1895-1903)
Part XXV – 2021 Annual (1881-1888)
Part XXVI – 2021 Annual (1889-1897)
Part XXVII – 2021 Annual (1898-1928)
Part XXVIII – More Christmas Adventures (1869-1888)
Part XXIX – More Christmas Adventures (1889-1896)
Part XXX – More Christmas Adventures (1897-1928)

In Preparation
Part XXXI (and XXXII and XXXIII???) – 2022 Annual

. . . and more to come!

The MX Book of New Sherlock Holmes Stories
Edited by David Marcum
(MX Publishing, 2015-)

<u>Publishers Weekly says:</u>

Part VI: *The traditional pastiche is alive and well . . . .*

Part VII: *Sherlockians eager for faithful-to-the-canon plots and characters will be delighted.*

Part VIII: *The imagination of the contributors in coming up with variations on the volume's theme is matched by their ingenious resolutions.*

Part IX: *The 18 stories . . . will satisfy fans of Conan Doyle's originals. Sherlockians will rejoice that more volumes are on the way.*

Part X: *. . . new Sherlock Holmes adventures of consistently high quality.*

Part XI: *. . . an essential volume for Sherlock Holmes fans.*

Part XII: *. . . continues to amaze with the number of high-quality pastiches.*

Part XIII: *. . . Amazingly, Marcum has found 22 superb pastiches . . . This is more catnip for fans of stories faithful to Conan Doyle's original*

Part XIV: *. . . this standout anthology of 21 short stories written in the spirit of Conan Doyle's originals.*

Part XV: *Stories pitting Sherlock Holmes against seemingly supernatural phenomena highlight Marcum's 15th anthology of superior short pastiches.*

Part XVI: *Marcum has once again done fans of Conan Doyle's originals a service.*

Part XVII: *This is yet another impressive array of new but traditional Holmes stories.*

Part XVIII: *Sherlockians will again be grateful to Marcum and MX for high-quality new Holmes tales.*

Part XIX: *Inventive plots and intriguing explorations of aspects of Dr. Watson's life and beliefs lift the 24 pastiches in Marcum's impressive 19th Sherlock Holmes anthology*

Part XX: *Marcum's reserve of high-quality new Holmes exploits seems endless.*

Part XXI: *This is another must-have for Sherlockians.*

Part XXII: *Marcum's superlative 22nd Sherlock Holmes pastiche anthology features 21 short stories that successfully emulate the spirit of Conan Doyle's originals while expanding on the canon's tantalizing references to mysteries Dr. Watson never got around to chronicling.*

Part XXIII: *Marcum's well of talented authors able to mimic the feel of The Canon seems bottomless.*

Part XXIV: *Marcum's expertise at selecting high-quality pastiches remains impressive.*

The MX Book of New Sherlock Holmes Stories
Edited by David Marcum
(MX Publishing, 2015-)

MX Publishing

MX Publishing is the world's largest specialist Sherlock Holmes publisher, with over five-hundred titles and over two-hundred authors creating the latest in Sherlock Holmes fiction and non-fiction

The catalogue includes several award winning books, and over two-hundred-and-fifty have been converted into audio.

MX Publishing also has one of the largest communities of Holmes fans on Facebook, with regular contributions from dozens of authors.

www.mxpublishing.com

@mxpublishing on Facebook, Twitter and Instagram

Lightning Source UK Ltd.
Milton Keynes UK
UKHW010340031221
394946UK00009B/458/J